news reporting, the aviation industry and the seamier sides of corporate and political manipulation. She keeps readers guessing until the stunning final surprises. Her debut is AS VIVID AND EXCITING AS A BOLT OF SUMMER LIGHTNING."

—*Publishers Weekly*

"DRAMATIC AND ENTERTAINING. MARVELOUS PACING AND TENSION-BUILDING. Heller throws the reader a couple of effective and climactic curve balls that should leave his or her head spinning."

—*The Flint Journal*

"A revealing tour of the world of investigative journalism. The obsessed reporter uses his experience, shoe leather and skepticism to break down a series of stonewalls erected by a band of chilling corporate criminals. Heller is a veteran journalist who has asked her share of tough questions in revealing the reality behind the smiling stewardess of airline industry television commercials."

—Patrick Sloyan
Pulitzer Prize-winning journalist, *Newsday*

"I recommend this COMPLETELY ABSORBING, scrupulously researched thriller to anyone who enjoys AN EDGE-OF-THE-SEAT READ. The conclusion is as shattering as the opening. This is ONE BANG-UP BOOK."

—*St. Petersburg Times*

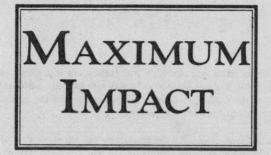

MAXIMUM IMPACT

Jean Heller

A TOM DOHERTY ASSOCIATES BOOK
NEW YORK

This is a work of fiction. All the characters and events portrayed in this book are fictitious, and any resemblance to real people or events is purely coincidental.

MAXIMUM IMPACT

Cover art by Tim O'Brien

A Forge Book
Published by Tom Doherty Associates, Inc.
175 Fifth Avenue
New York, NY 10010

Forge® is a registered trademark of Tom Doherty Associates, Inc.

ISBN: 0-812-51619-2
Library of Congress Catalog Card Number: 93-25417

First edition: September 1993
First mass market printing: June 1995

Printed in the United States of America

0 9 8 7 6 5 4 3 2 1

For Ray,
with love.

ACKNOWLEDGMENTS

I am a pilot. I have extensive experience in Washington, D.C. Yet even that combination proved inadequate to tell this story. I needed a lot of help.

Acknowledgments must begin with Win Blevins, a wonderful friend and author of Western historical novels that you should read if you haven't already. Over lunch at a Jackson Hole, Wyoming, restaurant one wintry afternoon in 1987, Win heard me spin this tale of intrigue and announced, "If you don't write that story, I will." I've come to doubt the sincerity of the threat, but I needed to hear it. Through the next year of false starts and self-doubt, he was always willing to serve as advisor, confidant, and gentle critic, amassing favors I will never be able to repay.

Nor could this have worked without the counsel of the late John Galipault, founder and president of the Aviation Safety Institute. Over a twenty-year friendship, John taught me aviation, convinced me to learn to fly, and, during the last months of his life, reviewed this manuscript for technical accuracy.

Dr. Ned Clarke, a veteran aviation accident investigator with a remarkable imagination, is solely responsible for the fact that this story has an ending. Ned, too, was kind enough to read the manuscript for accuracy and correct a few miscues. He also taught me to be careful where I eat peanuts—a reference you will understand in due course.

Mike Benson at the National Transportation Safety Board made sure I got the details right.

Dr. Martha Stearn taught me about the Circle of Willis and insulin.

Psychologist Andy Turner taught me about the horrors to which human beings can subject themselves when ravaged, rightly or wrongly, by guilt.

Book editor John Ordover helped me find and eliminate the flaws, and Melissa Ann Singer saw a difficult publication through to its happy ending.

Roz Targ never lost faith.

And, finally, I need to mention the NCAA basketball program. Only Ray will understand why, but that's all right.

To all, my thanks.

J.H.

PROLOGUE

Jimmy squeezed the trigger gently, just as he'd been taught, and saw dirt kick up a foot in front of the white-tailed rabbit sitting in an open spot in the cornfield, basking in the late-afternoon sunshine. The rabbit turned its head toward the small pock in the earth as if to see what had intruded on its moment of peace, and then, prudently, it ran to cover.

Shit!

The word flashed through Jimmy's mind. He wanted to say it aloud, but he wouldn't let himself do that in front of his parents, especially not his mother, who objected to this outing and was looking for an excuse to prove it a bad idea.

He felt his neck muscles tense to jerk his head. He fought it down, desperately. He recognized the first signs that the loathsome tremors were building inside him and soon would wrack his frail body if he let it happen. He clutched his .22 rifle tightly to his chest against the rising spasms, as if to gain strength from the firearm.

The ten-year-old turned his back on his parents, hoping they wouldn't see. He didn't want to worry her; she fussed over him too much anyway. But the stronger desire was not to disappoint his father, who was so proud of his performance this day. Two shots had hit their marks with only two misses, counting the latest one. He wanted more than anything to please the man whose gentle patience and encouragement were the only constants in his short and generally miserable life.

Jimmy feared that if his father noticed him losing control,

it would ruin what had been a glorious day of rabbit hunting in the sere cornfields of autumn. How he hated the monster in his brain. It overpowered his will and shook his body as the wind whips the trailings of a willow tree.

Jimmy's arms jerked once, sharply. The spasm sneaked up on him and burst out before he could will it away. He knew his father saw it.

"Jimmy, you've had a great day, son. Why don't you let me carry the rifle back to the car?" The man's big hand closed over the stock, but the boy yanked the gun away. "Please, Jimmy. You can have it back as soon as you take your medicine."

"No," the boy begged. "I-I-I'm all right."

Jimmy saw his parents exchange looks in the way married people communicate without words. He knew they were considering whether to press him and guessed they would relent. He'd heard his doctor tell them many times to avoid creating stress. The father shrugged slightly and nodded, muttering something about the situation not being critical; they were just a fifteen-minute walk from their car, where Jimmy's pills were tucked in the glove box.

The child's grip on the rifle tightened more as he felt muscle control slipping away.

Please, God, let me get to the car. Just to the car. I promise I'll make my bed every day for a month, and I won't leave my socks on the floor or my dirty shorts by the shower. I promise, promise, promise, promise. Just to the car. Ple-e-e-ease!

He walked deliberately, following his mother out of the field, his father tromping behind. One foot, then the other. Arms steady. Head rigid. Mind resolute. Dr. Wallace had said if Jimmy concentrated, he could stop the tremors. Not forever, but for a time. So Jimmy concentrated as hard as he could. But the monster in his brain would not be denied.

Even as their big Buick station wagon came into view, the jerking in Jimmy's arms became uncontrollable. "N-N-N-No!" He began to sob. He saw his mother turn and start toward him, and he thought he tried to drop his rifle. He thought he felt his hands loosen, and he thought the weapon started to slip from his grasp. Instead, in the grip of an intense spasm, his hands tightened again, and he pulled the trigger.

The sharp report startled him. *Did I do that?* He looked up at his mother. He saw first a look of disbelief on her face and then a moment of consummate sadness as she fell. She died immediately from the bullet that pierced her heart.

He felt his father push by him roughly and heard him calling, "Connie! Connie!" The big man knelt beside the still form that had been his wife, calling her name over and over, getting no response. He looked up at his son, and Jimmy saw the tears running down his face, his lips moving to say something that wouldn't form on his tongue.

Jimmy watched in wretched horror as his father lifted his mother's body and half-ran, half-stumbled to the station wagon for what would be a fruitless dash to the hospital. The boy dimly heard his father screaming for him to come along. "Run, Jimmy. Please! Hurry. Run!"

He dropped the rifle and followed. He climbed into the passenger side of the front seat, on his knees, facing the rear, and stared in mute disbelief at the still body lying across the backseat.

The rocking of the automobile as it dashed through traffic and the blaring of the horn under his father's clenched fist began to float out of Jimmy's stunned consciousness. He chewed on some dead skin beside the nail on his right forefinger, and he fixed his concentration on that. The rest of the scene, the ghastly rest of it, began to go out of focus.

Jimmy refused to let himself see the body with the blood spot on the front of the shirt. He refused to let himself think about his new rifle, now abandoned on the edge of the old cornfield. He refused to let his father enter his mind, or to imagine what his father would say to him later, or what he would answer. He chewed on his finger, and his mind began to drift away from the tragedy of the hunting trip and from the ordeal of life itself. It was so much easier not to have to deal with any of it.

By the time the Buick squealed to a stop at the emergency

entrance to the hospital, Jimmy had slipped from the real world entirely. For months to come, his father would hold him and stroke his head and tell him it wasn't his fault. His father would plead with him to speak, to cry, to scream. He would hug his son and cry himself, but there was never any response from the boy.

Jimmy was locked up tight someplace dark and deep within himself: a private place, a secret place, a place where brain monsters and dead mothers couldn't find him.

BOOK ONE

*Sixteen
years later*

1

For the third time in ten minutes, Captain Jackson Peck read the computer printout of weather conditions between Washington's Dulles International Airport and Los Angeles. The message hadn't changed. This would be a rough flight from takeoff to landing.

Peck passed the half-sheet of computer paper across the triple throttles of the Sexton 811 to First Officer Jeremy Dodds, who was finishing a stack of preflight paperwork. With the exception of a few spring storms along the Gulf and in the Midwest, the nation was dominated by fair weather. But the accompanying high-pressure domes sitting over Ohio and Nebraska were unusually steep, and the spring winds spilling off the invisible pressure peaks were brutal fuel eaters.

Almost all the way from the East Coast to the Rockies, winds above twenty-three thousand feet were tearing out of the west and southwest at speeds exceeding a hundred and thirty knots. Those headwinds, coupled with the inevitable traffic delays over Los Angeles, would mean significantly more time in the air than scheduled for Consolidated Pacific Flight 1117.

Dodds nodded to Peck and handed the weather update over his right shoulder to Flight Engineer Robert Carson.

"We need new fuel data, Bob," Peck ordered. "It's breezy up top today."

Carson glanced at the forecast, grunted in understanding, and bent to the task of determining to the nearest pound how much extra Jet-A it would take to move two hundred seventy-five tons of airliner, about fifty-three thousand pounds of passengers, and twenty-six thousand pounds of baggage and freight, plus the fuel itself, from Washington to Los Angeles against hundred-thirty-knot headwinds, to divert to Long Beach if something prevented a landing at LAX, and set down with forty-five minutes of fuel to spare, as Federal Aviation Administration regulations required.

There were reports of airlines offering bonuses to crews to fly with less than the FAA-mandated reserve—for economy reasons; it burns fuel to carry fuel. But Consolidated Pacific wasn't one of those airlines, and Jackson Peck was a rule-book pilot. As commander of Flight 1117, he had authority to load more fuel, and he ordered the ground crew to get to it. He had no choice, really. He'd filed a flight plan for thirty-nine thousand feet, and there was no alternative that would reduce headwinds and fuel consumption unless he went below twenty-three thousand feet, which wasn't practical. The fuel saved with lighter headwinds would be eaten up by denser atmosphere.

Chief cabin steward Frank Masselli materialized at the open cockpit door. "The SOBs are ready to board," he announced.

Peck shook his head. "Hold 'em up, Frank. We're not quite ready."

"Right," Masselli replied with practiced cheerfulness. "What, twenty minutes?"

"That should do it," Peck replied.

Masselli stepped through the aircraft's forward door into the mouth of the telescoped passageway that linked the 811 to Dulles's squat, gray mid-field terminal. Instead of using the telephone intercom, he walked quickly up the ramp to notify the unlucky agent at the gate that the three hundred twenty-one impatient SOBs in her charge were going to have to sit for a while because their flight was delayed.

He wondered what the customers would think if they knew the airlines referred to them as SOBs. It was shorthand for passenger counts; SOB stood for Souls On Board.

The term was not intended to offend, but it vaguely bothered Masselli, who thought counting souls related somehow to counting the dead. The thought made him queasy, and he pushed it away.

The pretty auburn-haired agent at the terminal door was plainly irritated. "We got the word to let 'em go," she said with a frown, glancing over her shoulder as the elderly and people with small children approached the ramp. "Here come the kids and crips."

"My fault. I thought we were ready," Masselli conceded.

Under the 811's left wing, the ground crew attached the yellow-and-black fuel line. In the cockpit, Peck, Dodds, and Carson could feel the gentle bumps of heavy baggage hitting the floor of the cargo hold, creating a subtle, almost subliminal, rocking of the airplane. Combined with the spring sunshine streaming in the cockpit windows, it threatened them all with drowsiness.

There would be enough of that to battle on the crosscountry flight, Peck thought as he slid open his side window. He glanced at Dodds with a silent request that he do the same.

Peck saw the ground crew move under the right wing to pump its fuel cells full.

Thus it was when ConPac 1117 taxied for takeoff on a warm and breezy spring morning in April, its fuel tanks were filled to capacity with one-hundred-five thousand pounds, or about seventeen-thousand five hundred gallons, of jet fuel.

It would make one hell of a fire.

Despite his usual heavy workload, Barry Raiford felt the effects of the warm spring day. He caught himself daydreaming about trout fishing. He shook the fantasy from his head but indulged in a few minutes of self-pity at having to work on the most perfect day of the year so far. It was one of those April spectaculars that caresses the mid-Atlantic seaboard each spring to reward the living things that survived the damp freezes of winter past and must endure the inevitable sauna of summer still to come.

The yellow haze that settles over the tumbling Virginia countryside with the strangling humidity of summer still was weeks away. On this day, Raiford could see to the horizon in all directions, and most of what he saw was greening land domed by deepening blue sky, broken only by a solitary line of scudding clouds to the west, toward the Blue Ridge. To the south, a pair of red-tailed hawks slid along the brisk air currents effortlessly, shifting the angles of their wingtips and tail feathers to steer themselves in search of prey, but otherwise expending no energy at all to stay aloft. It was little wonder humans yearned to fly. It was the epitome of freedom.

He glanced at the sea of aircraft hunkered around the busy airport. If you give determined men enough time, they'll not only copy nature, they'll convince themselves they've improved on it.

Raiford was a supervisor in the tower cab at Dulles, an airport nicknamed Dullest about two decades earlier, reportedly during a night shift when the under-used airfield logged fewer than two dozen takeoffs and landings in a seven-hour period. But times change. So many people now lived within easy driving distance of the sleek airport, and so many businesses had opened in—or relocated to—the surrounding areas, that Dulles had become one of the fastest-growing airports in the country.

Although young by airport standards, Dulles had a great aviation tradition. It was one of the first American ports for the Concorde SSTs. Then the behemoth jumbo jets appeared, and only six months ago the Sexton 811 that flew the daily ConPac flight nonstop to Los Angeles.

The 811 was the hottest jetliner in the sky. With a scheduled departure of 10 A.M., and gigantic engines that produced the speed to cut an hour off the transcontinental hop, the 811s that flew as ConPac Flight 1117 drew passengers who wanted to leave Washington at a civilized hour and get to the West Coast for lunch. It was little wonder bookings were almost always at capacity.

Raiford's tolerance for routine was at capacity, too. Traffic arrived and departed at a steady rate, and the unusually good spring weather coast to coast kept delays to a minimum. There were no backups to deal with, incoming or outgoing. It was the sort of day a controller worked by rote, the sort of day that dulled sharp edges of concentration, the sort of day mistakes were made.

At other stations in the tower cab, a ground controller found time to glance intermittently at one of the morning newspapers; another, who was waiting to come on duty, was reading an old John D. MacDonald mystery; and a third, who was on a break, was in the process of losing fifty-eight dollars to a co-worker at gin. The rest were conducting business in workmanlike fashion, talking quietly to pilots through their microphoned headsets and constantly updating their data on who was where and where they were going. An FM radio station was playing soft rock, stuff from the Bee Gees's old *Saturday Night Fever* sound track.

Raiford spent a few minutes absently watching people-movers roll like determined ants between the elegant main terminal and the gray, utilitarian mid-field terminal, where most of the jet flights arrived and departed. He hated the mid-field building and its boxy, lifeless lines, so totally unimaginative in the shadow of the grand and graceful original terminal building created by architect Eero Saarinen in the early nineteen sixties. Dulles was a showplace then. Now it was just another busy airport. Raiford considered the transformation a near tragedy.

As he glowered at the mid-field building, he saw a fuel truck move under the left wing of the ConPac 811. Given the winds aloft, Raiford understood why the captain wanted more fuel.

But he would never understand, thinking about it for days and weeks thereafter, why his attention was drawn abruptly back to the 811 about twenty minutes later. Maybe it was nothing more than a sense that the flight, already late, should be on its way. Or a premonition. Or neither. In any event, he was looking at Flight 1117 when the engine under the right wing coughed a cloud of smoke. Raiford considered calling the crew, but he decided against it. There was no recurrence, and if anything were seriously wrong, it would show up on the cockpit instruments.

He felt confident the ConPac crew could handle its job without him.

On the flight deck of the 811, the crew didn't see the smoke, but there was a bump when Number 3 engine started.

Dodds turned a questioning look at Peck, but the captain was busy watching the gauges and digital readouts monitoring the engine's performance. The instruments told him nothing.

"Damned if I know what it was," Peck confessed. He moved his headset mike to his lips and made voice contact with the ground-crew chief outside. "Ev, take a look at Number Three's intake and make sure it's clear, will you, please?"

"Yes, sir," the chief said. He backed up the full length of the cord tethering him to the 811 communications system and hopped up on a baggage trolley for a better view. "Looks fine, Captain," he reported. "But if she's off, the mechanics are two minutes away."

"None of the baggage carts bumped us about the same time we turned her over?"

"No, sir. Traffic was clear three, four minutes ago."

"Thanks, Ev." Peck turned to Dodds. "Might'uv been a compressor stall, but keep an eye on it."

Back in the passenger compartments, none of the nine cabin attendants and only two of the passengers noticed anything at all unusual about the start-up of Number 3 engine. Everyone else was too busy storing carry-on luggage and finding seat assignments to notice.

Harry Jacobs, an assistant counsel to the Senate Commerce Committee, came aboard with only a briefcase, which he tossed under the seat in front of him. He was settled in and buckled up when Number 3 turned over, and he felt the engine kick. It registered with him, but as a curiosity, not as an alarm, and he made a mental note to ask the head steward about it. But within minutes, Jacobs's attention was diverted by a stewardess who insisted on knowing if he wanted a complimentary soft drink or a three-dollar cocktail after takeoff. The jolt was quickly forgotten.

Eight rows back, Cloriss Colburn, a widow and a retired clerk from the Social Security Administration, settled into her window seat. She was headed for Laguna Beach to visit her son. Cloriss had traveled extensively in the early nineteen sixties with her husband, but he'd suffered a stroke at an appallingly young age, and she'd spent the next twenty-two years working and caring for her invalid spouse, until his death in nineteen ninety. This was her first trip on an airplane since nineteen sixty-five, her first ever on a jet.

If Cloriss felt the jolt when Number 3 started, it made no impression on her. But she saw the same black smoke Barry Raiford noticed from the tower cab. It curled under the trailing edge flaps and dissipated in the breeze. Cloriss had spent years of travel watching old piston engines belch smoke, and occasionally flame, and now the sight of the smoke brought back old memories.

She considered it perfectly normal.

Jackson Peck reached over the throttles and activated the second radio in his stack.

"Dulles Clearance, ConPac Eleven-seventeen Heavy is ready to copy," he told the controller who would give him his assigned altitudes and routing across the country. Although he had filed a flight plan with the standard routing for the trip, air traffic control could alter those plans for reasons of weather, traffic, or (sometimes, he thought) sheer perversity. No pilot ever was sure of the route approved for him until he got his formal clearance.

"ConPac Eleven-seventeen, you're cleared as filed. After departure, climb and maintain one-zero thousand; expect flight level three-niner-zero ten minutes after departure. Departure control is one-two-six-point-one. Squawk five-three-zero-five."

Peck finished jotting down the instructions. As he read them back, he set his ship's transponder on 5305. The codes assigned to the flight as it crossed the country would give traffic-control radar a constant readout on the jet's identity, speed, position, and altitude.

"Eleven-seventeen, readback is correct," the controller said. "Contact ground on twenty-one-point-niner when you're ready to roll, and have a good one."

Peck keyed his mike twice in acknowledgment as he turned to Dodds. "How about it, pardner? We ready to get this stage on the trail?"

Dodds gave him thumbs up, and Peck activated the radio set to 121.9. The ground controller offered the 811 captain his choice of Runway 30, a 10,001-foot strip close to his parking position, or Runway 19-right, an 11,501-foot strip an eight-minute taxi away. Either choice involved a stiff crosswind, but it was load factor, not winds, that dictated Peck's decision.

Another day, with a lighter load, he would have chosen Runway 30 to save the time and fuel he would eat up taxiing around to 19R. But with the passengers and freight he was hauling, the extra fifteen hundred feet of runway on 19R was a safety cushion too appealing to dismiss.

In the end, a different decision would have saved only one life, but that was not a subtle distinction to the man whose life it was.

For Howard Kisparich, that morning in April was the culmination of a commitment. Kisparich had passed his private-pilot checkride at nearby Manassas Municipal Airport two weeks earlier, and he was giving himself the week's vacation he considered his reward. It was a promise he'd made to himself after he took the hook.

The previous December, Kisparich had accepted the free, twenty-minute introductory ride Cessna offered would-be pilots, and he'd signed up for training, understanding finally as he wrote a check for thirty-eight hundred dollars, truly, there is no such thing as a free ride. He promised himself then if he got his license, he would take a week away from his law practice and do nothing but fly, logging maybe twenty hours or more to sharpen his skills. The first nice week after the license was it, and this was that week.

Kisparich had flown into Dulles before, although not often. It was too busy. Green general-aviation pilots and students who wanted to practice on the wide, long airstrips were invited politely to go elsewhere. Kisparich planned one landing and one takeoff in his rented Cessna 172, confident such an intrusion would not overload the field. He needed more radio experience at large, controlled airports, and the stiff breeze would give him a chance to practice a crosswind maneuver. He looked forward to that, but approaching the airport, he began thinking he'd wished too hard. The "breeze" was clocking nineteen to twenty-one knots, and he was grateful for the big Dulles runways that would forgive the mistakes of a novice pilot.

His first mistake that morning had been the coffee: three cups to read the *Washington Chronicle* by, and a fourth cup while shaving. Now his kidneys and bladder were in overdrive, and the anticipation of going into Dulles was supplanted by desperation for a bathroom. There were specialized plastic bottles to keep in the cockpit for these situations, but Kisparich never had been able to envision himself taking a leak into a bottle in the cockpit of an airplane. Missing the bottle and shorting out a radio, however improbable, was something he'd never be able to explain to his flying buddies at Manassas Municipal.

"What kind of a man are you, Kisparich, you can't piss and fly at the same time?" The sound of his own voice amused him. "Ladies and gentlemen of the jury, I ask you, would you soar on the wings of eagles with a pilot who can't relieve himself in midair? *Where is midair exactly? It's between high air and low air, stupid!* Would you trust your lives to a man who can't take a bladder break without parking his airplane? No Jimmy Doolittle here, ladies and gentlemen. This man is guilty of pansy piloting in the first degree.''

The summation died abruptly as Kisparich realized he was closer than he should be to Dulles without making radio contact. He dialed up 120.45 on his radio.

"Dulles Approach, Cessna niner-seven-four-seven-Papa is with you."

"Niner-seven-four-seven-Papa, this is Dulles Approach. Go ahead."

"Four-seven-Papa is ten miles west, near Middleburg, at three-thousand, three-hundred, squawking one-two-zero-zero, inbound for landing."

"Four-seven-Papa, roger. You're cleared to the pattern. Turn right heading one-two-zero for left downwind to runway three-zero. Winds are two-three-zero at one-eight, gusting to two-one. Altimeter three-zero-zero-one. Squawk two-niner-one-two and ident. Contact the tower on one-two-zero-point-one."

"Four-seven-Papa, roger."

He changed his transponder code and pushed the button that would send its signal to the radar station below.

"Niner-seven-four-seven-Papa, we have radar contact," the approach controller told him.

"Four-seven-Papa, roger," he replied.

Kisparich was elated. He wrote the information on his lap pad and performed as requested without having to ask for a repeat of the instructions. *Look out, United, here comes Air Howard!* He wondered if he sounded casual and confident on the radio. He wondered if the guys in the tower noticed that four-seven-Papa had a by-God good pilot. He wondered if they cared. He wondered if they'd be good enough to look the other way when he tried his twenty-one-knot crosswind landing.

Kisparich recalled with a twinge of resentment that at O'Hare Airport in Chicago, light aircraft whose pilots have the audacity to exercise their rights to land among the big boys are directed to a parking area marked with FLIB signs. Unless you asked, nobody would tell you that FLIB stands for Fucking Little Itinerant Bastards.

Half an hour later he rendered the verdict that it hadn't been such a horrible landing after all. Three bounces and no scratches wasn't a bad score. The third bounce was pretty damned small, as a matter of fact. Not even a bounce, really. He decided not to count it.

As he did a hundred-eighty-degree turn onto the taxiway, Kisparich stole a peek at the tower. He hoped they weren't laughing.

"Dulles Ground Control, this is Cessna niner-seven-four-seven-Papa, clear the active. Permission to taxi to Ludlum FBO."

"Cessna niner-seven-four-seven-Papa. Taxi to Ludlum via taxiway November One. Hold short of November Two until advised."

Kisparich could see the markings at the end of 1L off his port wing. Nearly three miles to the north, at the opposite end of the same ribbon of concrete, where 1L carried the designation 19R, a broad pod with wings and three huge engines poised for flight. Kisparich couldn't see it, of course, but he assumed there was something up there about to come roaring down the runway. Whatever it was, if it followed the centerline of 19R after takeoff, its course would intersect the taxiway he was using. Kisparich didn't want to wind up right under a big bird, so he stopped short of the intersection and pressed his legs together against the growing urgency in his bladder.

Forget the checklist and take off. We've got a boy with a problem down here.

If Howard Kisparich could have described it later, he would have marveled that he felt the vibrations of the 811's mammoth engines even before he could hear them throttled up for takeoff. He felt the vibrations in his feet against the brake pedals. He put his hand on the black throttle knob and felt them there, too, even at a distance of nearly three miles. He set his jaws together lightly, and he was certain he could feel them in his teeth. He tried to imagine himself in control of all that thrust, but the idea made his palms damp.

Although it was only ten forty-five, the spring sunshine

had baked the Dulles runways. As the jetliner came into view, Kisparich watched it through heat shimmers that gave it a quality of unreality. Gradually the airliner grew larger. At any moment the nose wheel would rise and the blue-and-silver bird would be airborne, any second . . . any second . . . any second!

Halfway down the runway, she was still earthbound. *She must be loaded to capacity. Come on, baby, get up.*

Inside the plane, in seat 33H, Harry Jacobs, the Senate aide and a veteran flier, looked up from the paperwork in his lap. He, too, had the sense the big Sexton was too long on the runway. He peered toward the front bulkhead, expecting to see it rise as the aircraft's nose pitched up. But it wasn't happening. He glanced at the passenger on his left, trying to gauge whether anyone shared his concern. But the young Asian in the center seat was wearing the headset of a Sony Walkman disc player and concentrated only on the heavy-metal sounds pounding his eardrums. Jacobs did catch the eye of the passenger in the aisle seat, an older Asian dressed as a tourist, who had been focused on the vista speeding by the window at Jacobs's right shoulder. The Senate aide thought he glimpsed a fleeting frown on the Asian's face before his own attention was captured by an unmistakable series of tremors vibrating through the Sexton.

He turned to his window and stared at the broad expanse of the right wing, its trailing edge flaps fully extended and down. He thought he saw the wing shudder, but not in a way that explained anything for him.

On the flight deck, the vibrations triggered simultaneous adrenaline rushes in Captain Jackson Peck and First Officer Jeremy Dodds. Peck's right hand and Dodds's left were overlapped on the triple throttles, a redundancy assuring that one man would retain control should the other die suddenly. The vibrations traveled through Peck's hand to Dodds's. Instinctively, their heads snapped to the engine monitors.

"EPR's nominal," Dodds reported after looking at the

engine-pressure ratios on all three power plants.

"It's Number Three," Peck said calmly. "Rejecting!" He keyed his mike. "Dulles tower, this is ConPac heavy—"

"No!" the first officer yelled. "Captain, I've already called v-one! We're past v-one! There's not enough runway left!"

"Stand by, we've got a problem," Peck told the tower.

"Shutting down Number Three," the captain said. "Full power to one and two!"

Dodds prayed the two remaining engines could get them safely off the ground. That was supposed to be possible. It had worked during his training in the simulator in Memphis. But this wasn't Memphis. And this was no simulator.

As they poured the power to the engines under the left wing and in the tail, the flight deck was jarred by what felt like an explosion.

"What was that?" Peck demanded.

"No clue," Dodds replied.

"Go . . . go . . . go!" Peck yelled as he and his first officer fought desperately to haul the jumbo jet's nose into the air. It was a losing battle.

Back in the aft cabin, Harry Jacobs was stunned by what he witnessed. The quaking in the right wing became more pronounced, and then a large wedge of dark metal sliced upward through the surface of the wing and disappeared above his line of vision. Jacobs thought he heard himself scream "No!" as he watched liquid—fuel, he knew—stream from the enormous vent torn through the center of the wing. A fissure began to snake from the rupture toward the trailing edge. More and more fuel sprayed from the growing breach.

Eight rows behind Jacobs, Cloriss Colburn uttered a desperate, high-pitched moan that was lost in the cacophony of screams from other passengers watching the destruction of the starboard wing, and from those who couldn't see what was happening but were no less terrified.

"Samuel, help me, please," she begged her long-dead husband. She squeezed her eyes shut and clenched her fists so tightly her fingernails clawed blood from her palms.

Outside the Sexton, in the rented Cessna, Kisparich lurched against his restraining harness when he saw a jagged piece of metal explode from the Number 3 engine pod and slice through the wing. The piece was flat, solid, and wedge-shaped. Like a misshapen Frisbee, it cartwheeled high into the air, then nosed over and tumbled to the infield grass below. By that time, Kisparich's attention was back on the big engine, which was vibrating hideously. It rocked in its mounting and began to yaw violently, as if trying to squirm free of some terrible agony. The huge pod ripped itself almost off its pylon, dangling by what appeared to be a single bolt connection. The force of its gyrations cracked the wing. Kisparich thought he could see jet fuel from ruptured fuel cells cascading over the broken airfoil and the mortally damaged engine. The aircraft was listing to the right and suddenly began turning in that direction. It headed straight for the puny Cessna, whose pilot had believed he'd stopped in a safe place.

The jetliner began to heel over, dragging the tip of the fractured wing along the concrete runway and creating a wake of sparks that set the leaking fuel ablaze within seconds. Before the flames obliterated his view, Kisparich saw the outboard two-thirds of the right wing tear away, taking the engine with it in a cascade of fire and smoke. The assembly catapulted into the air and bounced hard several times along the runway, shattering the wing structure and breaking the engine open. It finally came to rest, fully engulfed in flame, in the grass infield.

As the jetliner continued to roll, the stub of the right wing hit the runway so hard it was torn from the fuselage, ripping open the passenger compartment from seats 28H to 42H, the way the lid is ripped from a pop-top can. In seat 41H, Cloriss Colburn's heart stopped, ending her terror in harsh but brief pain. In 33H, Harry Jacobs was buckled into his seat next to the gaping tear in the airliner's skin, enduring wave after wave of fright mounting toward shock. He had a desperate urge to get up and run, although he hadn't the faintest notion of where. Even if he could have identified a haven, he couldn't have reached it. The tremendous wind created by the jetliner's race down the runway pinned him to his seat and grabbed at his breath.

Somehow, the young Asian beside Harry Jacobs tore free of his seatbelt. He snatched the seat in front and pulled himself to his feet. The older Asian on the aisle grabbed the young man and tried to force him back. The older man—the father, Jacobs thought—was screaming in a tongue that sounded like Korean. The boy kept shaking his head, fighting violently to escape. He was making some progress in getting past the older man, defying the floor's gradually increasing pitch to the right. Jacobs turned toward the boy and reached out for him. He hooked his left hand in the waistband of the boy's blue jeans and pulled him back toward his seat. Buckled in snugly, the youth had a chance. On his feet, he probably had none at all.

In that instant Jacobs realized the flight crew had no hope of righting the Sexton. Through a window across the cabin, he saw the left wing continue to rise, and he felt himself tipping ever backward, toward the hole in the fuselage. Afraid to look over his shoulder, he concentrated on the young Asian. The boy was still trying to claw his way past his father to the aisle. Only Jacobs's grip on his pants prevented it. The boy looked back to see who was holding him, and Jacobs saw the fear on his face turn to terror as his mind grasped that the aircraft was going over.

The youngster let go of the seat in front of him and put his hands to his head. His scream penetrated the roar of rushing air and chilled Jacobs's blood. The pitch of the fuselage grew greater, and the boy toppled into Jacobs's lap. He lay facedown over Jacobs's legs. The force of the wind threatened to snatch him, and Jacobs grabbed again for his clothing, clutching anything he could close a fist around. Suddenly the boy was trying to get through the hole, using a swimming action with his arms to push off from whatever he could touch. His shirt ripped out of Jacobs's hands.

"No!" the Senate aide shouted. "Don't!"

The boy flailed madly, seeking an escape that Jacobs

recognized as certain death. His head and shoulders were through the hole. Jacobs threw his arms around the youngster's legs, holding on desperately. The boy grabbed a jagged edge of the aircraft's skin and tried to boost himself through. Jacobs saw the sharp metal tear the boy's hands, and droplets, then rivulets, of blood whipped in the wind. The boy took his right hand from the metal. He looked back at Jacobs and threw his left elbow into Jacobs's face. The blow was true. It broke Jacobs's nose. Instinctively, the Senate aide reached for his face with his left hand. It was the chance the boy needed. He placed his palms against the outside of the airplane and pushed with the strength of madness. Feeling him start to slide through the hole, Jacobs grabbed for him again. But it was too late. The boy slipped away, the heavy material of his blue jeans tearing a fingernail from Jacobs's right hand.

Any additional pain Jacobs might have felt was masked by terror. The plane continued to keel over. Through windwhipped tears he could see grass beyond the runway's edge. But as the jet rolled, the grass moved up and out of view, and there was nothing but concrete rushing up to meet him. As the right main gear collapsed in an agony of sparks and screaming metal, the airliner crashed onto its side, rendering Jacobs and eighteen other passengers nothing more than grisly smears on the runway.

At the last second, Jacobs recalled the jolt when Number 3 engine started, and the last thought he ever had was overwhelming regret that he never mentioned it to anyone.

At almost the same instant, Howard Kisparich saw the aircraft explode in a fireball. *It looks like that space-shuttle accident, when there was a tiny spark on the side of the rocket booster and then everything blew all to hell. Oh, God, they're all going to die!* It took no more than a few seconds for the flames to engulf the 811, but it seemed to Kisparich it was happening in slow motion. The first orange-and-black balloon of flame and smoke gave birth to a second, and the second to a third, and they kept building on each other like a hideous cauliflower, expanding up and out from the dying airliner. *There can't be that much fuel in the whole world!* He could see blue paint blister and blacken; he could see chunks of burning metal rip away and tumble off the runway, trailing comet tails of black smoke. Thank God he couldn't see bodies, but they must be in there, strangling on the smoke or burning up. Then all he could see was the fireball, with the silver nose of the jetliner protruding, obscenely unscarred, from the front. And that was bad enough.

It occurred to Kisparich that he could see the last actions of the frantic crew on the flight deck, and with that realization came another, so terrifying it seemed to shrink the skin of his abdomen and threaten to crush him in his own panic. What remained of the jetliner was skidding directly toward him, already so close he could feel the heat. It blotted out his view of the terminals, took out a cluster of landing lights on the side of the runway, and plowed a fiery furrow through the grass as it bore down on him.

He felt warm wetness on the insides of his thighs and under his legs that signaled the end of the need for a bathroom, and he jammed the throttle of his idling 172 in full, trying to get beyond the horror that loomed beside and over him.

Had he acted thirty seconds sooner, Howard Kisparich could have pulled it off. But the little Cessna had just started to inch forward when the nose of Flight 1117 rolled over and crushed the airplane like a tin can. It pinned the Cessna and the remains of its pilot under two dozen tons of inferno and pushed the crumpled ruins off the taxiway and across Runway 30, until the entire mass came to rest in a grassy area still sodden from heavy spring rains.

If there were screams from within what remained of the jet, they could not be heard over the roar of the flames. If the fire trucks dispatched to the wreckage had been there already, neither man nor machinery could have closed in on the heat with any hope of saving even a single life. Under the warm sun of the most perfect spring day of the year, ConPac Flight 1117 and Cessna niner-seven-four-seven-Papa lay dead, burning and steaming like a nightmarish vision from hell.

2

The image would hang in Steve Pace's memory like a new picture on a living-room wall, so obvious at first, drawing the eye every time the owner enters the room. Over time, it becomes less apparent, but it hangs there, always ready to return to sharp focus when attention is called to it, or when something happens to renew the memory of the day it was purchased.

So, against his will, Pace bought and paid in pain for the picture before him. It laid an imprint so deep he thought he'd never forget it, and in truth, he never did, although months and years later it would become less a part of every day, less vivid, less sickening, but always there, a memory waiting to be recalled.

The Sexton 811 stopped burning after firefighters spent two hours smothering it in foam. The roiling waves of smoke that hid so much of the horror slid away on the cleansing breeze. Even from the vantage point where more than two hundred reporters, photographers, and television technicians were isolated behind police barricades, Pace, the aviation reporter for the *Washington Chronicle,* was awed by what he saw.

There was nothing of the 811 that remained undamaged. The tail assembly was barely recognizable. The vertical stabilizer was almost intact, although blackened and absent its rudder. The left horizontal stabilizer also was charred, the right horizontal stabilizer gone entirely, melted by the intensity of the fuel-fed flames. Blasted by the heat, the Converse engine mounted in the tail assembly shriveled gnarly and black. It no longer resembled an engine so much as a misshapen, rotten tumor. The left wing jutted toward the sky at an unnatural angle, looking like the remnants of an arm reaching up for help that wasn't there, an arm now frozen in death. The fuselage was torn or burned open in a dozen places Pace could see, and in several more he couldn't. It was blackened along its entire length. From where he stood, it looked as though the cockpit had ripped away from the rest of the aircraft and lay on its side like the battered head of a giant dead fish.

Through a pair of Nikon binoculars, Pace watched the frantic efforts to control the blaze, trading images with *Chronicle* photographer Tim Hogan, who was recording the scene with a tripod-mounted Nikon F4 and a gigantic one-thousand-millimeter reflex lens. Hogan, a blond, slight, soft-spoken picture wizard, inevitably nicknamed "Hulk" by his associates, was shooting roll after roll of film, but from what Pace could see through his binoculars, good taste likely would prevent the use of much of the photographer's material.

Through gaps in the aircraft's skin, Pace could see dead passengers hanging almost upside down, still strapped into their seats in the left and center sections of the airplane, their arms thrown above their heads like teenagers rocking at a Springsteen concert. All were damaged graphically by the heat and flames, but they could be recognized at least as human beings; indeed, in some cases, there was enough left intact that next of kin would be able to make identification.

He could barely imagine what had happened to the passengers on the right side. Most of those seats were hidden under debris and behind jagged curtains of metal, but those were the passengers who had taken the brunt of the impact when the 811 flipped onto its side. For their families, visual identification would be impossible, and that probably was for the best.

Around the perimeter of the wreckage, Pace spotted a few burned and blackened mounds. He dismissed them as

charred sacks of mail and baggage, until rescue workers
began covering them with plastic sheets.

But it was the ambulances that made the situation so final
and so hopeless. There were eighteen when Pace reached the
airport. More arrived, and eventually the fleet totaled
twenty-nine. Two hours after the crash, one ambulance left
with a sense of urgency, its lights flashing, sirens wailing.
Now the rest began to drift away, lights off, sirens quiet. It
was the final word, if any were needed, that no amount of
speed or urgency could help the passengers and crew of
Consolidated Pacific Flight 1117, who started their day
headed for Los Angeles but made fewer than three miles of
the journey before they died.

Behind the barricades, the press corps was getting edgy.
Airport police and officials of the National Transportation
Safety Board had arranged for them to watch the firefight-
ing efforts from about a quarter-mile away, close enough to
see the action but far enough removed for safety. Now the
fire was out, and there were increasing demands for permission to approach the wreckage.

Mitch Gabriel, the NTSB's chief of public information,
explained repeatedly that bits of the 811 were scattered over
nine acres of airport grounds, and no one but the agency's
investigators would be allowed within that area while the
debris was inventoried and recovered. Reporters and photographers had to be kept away to preserve the integrity of
the evidence.

"Mitch, is there anything you can tell us about survivors?" an Associated Press reporter yelled. "Was the ambulance that left first carrying survivors?"

"There was one survivor, a member of the crew," Gabriel
acknowledged for the first time. "Unfortunately, the individual went into cardiac arrest en route to the hospital, and
efforts at revival were unsuccessful."

"Who?" a chorus of voices asked.

"I'm sorry. I'm not at liberty to say until the individual's
family has been notified."

"Maybe somebody from the flight deck?" a WRC-TV

reporter asked. "The nose of the plane looks like it escaped the worst of the damage."

"I wouldn't speculate on that," Gabriel replied patiently.

"What were his injuries?"

"I don't know."

"Was it an experienced crew?" asked an NBC reporter.

"I don't know the identities of the crew members, but any airline's more experienced personnel generally get the jobs on the new-generation aircraft."

"What's the focus of the investigation right now?" Pace asked.

"Steve, I can't tell you that. I don't know."

Gabriel promised an NTSB board member would hold a press conference later to brief more fully on the investigation, but there would be nothing before that except what the journalists were able to witness on their own. That was standard procedure, but the press corps would get what it wanted or spend the rest of the day grousing about it. That, too, was standard procedure.

Pace was used to it. He'd experienced the same media reaction on his first air-crash assignment and on every accident he'd covered since. How many of them had there been, actually? Four? Five? He was a young reporter for the *San Diego Sun* in September, nineteen seventy-eight, when he covered his first, the in-flight collision over San Diego of a Boeing 727 and a Cessna 172 that killed a hundred and fifty people. Although a rival paper won a Pulitzer Prize for its coverage of the disaster, Pace's work was good enough to catch the attention of the editors of the *Washington Chronicle*, who offered him the open job of aviation writer.

The stage was set for his own Pulitzer just two months into the new job when an American Airlines DC-10 lost an improperly mounted engine and crashed on takeoff from O'Hare Airport in Chicago in nineteen seventy-nine. In the months that followed, Pace's investigative work produced exclusive after exclusive on problems with the DC-10 and airline maintenance procedures. His stories led to congressional investigations and a myriad of changes in

FAA regulations and earned him, at the age of twenty-five, journalism's highest award for national reporting.

And still aircraft kept crashing. He was on the scene five months after the American tragedy when a Western Airlines DC-10 crashed in Mexico City. And for the January, nineteen eighty-two, crash of an Air Florida 737 in the icy Potomac River in Washington. And a Delta crash in a storm at Dallas–Fort Worth in nineteen eighty-five. Another in-flight collision over San Diego in nineteen eighty-six. The nineteen eighty-eight Pan Am 747 shattered by a bomb an hour into its flight from London to New York, crashing in flaming pieces onto a quiet Scottish village in the midst of Christmas celebrations. United Flight 232 in Sioux City, Iowa, that DC-10 whose crew so deftly flew her for nearly an hour without hydraulic control, almost making the runway before it crashed and cartwheeled. The runway collision in Detroit. The ice-caused accident at LaGuardia in New York.

How many was that? Pace recalled each one, pressing the fingers of his left hand into his leg as he counted them off. Nine? No, with this one, it was ten! Jesus, how many deaths had he witnessed? Hundreds? Thousands, probably.

This disaster was the worst, and not because it had the highest individual death toll. The impact of the others had been mitigated somehow—the aircraft and its contents were smashed beyond recognition, or he'd arrived after the worst of the human devastation was cleaned up, or the plane wound up underwater, or he and other reporters were kept too far away to view the carnage.

But on this day, the carnage was everywhere, almost impossible not to see: dead bodies still buckled into seats, burned bodies on the concrete runway, a severed arm carried by a fireman, a crushed child cradled gently by a rescue worker.

The horror was cumulative, and Pace wasn't certain he could take much more of it. He berated himself that he wasn't hardened to this. But watching the aftermath of the ConPac disaster, he knew he never would be, and he was appalled suddenly at the idea of spending the rest of his career in a job where his biggest stories were of massive human tragedy.

It was time, perhaps, to think about another beat, possibly Congress, where the paper had an open slot, or the State Department, where a *Chronicle* staffer was retiring. But Pace cared little for the petty in-fighting on Capitol Hill. And he knew nothing more than any casual newspaper reader about the complex affairs of state. Hell, maybe it was time for a whole new career.

But where does a man who is thirty-nine go when he's spent eighteen years doing journalism, the last fifteen of them as an aviation specialist?

He felt trapped by who he was, where he was, and what he was doing. He was fast approaching middle age, was divorced and going nowhere, having been nowhere but a succession of airports, hayfields, and swamps, chasing answers to the ritual questions about why big metal birds fall out of the sky. He was good at the job. You don't win Pulitzer Prizes if you're not good. But he had reached that pinnacle at the age of twenty-five, and he since had the sense that there was little left for him to accomplish. The Pulitzer is the ultimate goal of every newspaper journalist, and he'd won his with forty years of his career still before him. How was he to motivate himself to fill all that time? To know you're good isn't enough. To tell yourself you're doing a public service isn't enough. Even the sharp-edged thrill that comes with the chase after a good story grows dull when all the stories begin to sound the same. Every year he watched colleagues walk away with major journalism awards, and he knew he'd already had his last, best shot and his own best moment. His time would not come again.

He was stuck in a one-way rut running down the middle of a dead-end street.

Pace turned away from the wreckage and mentally scolded himself for being so negative about a career most journalists would kill to match. He forced himself to breathe deeply and slowly. He concentrated on the NTSB people moving around in the grass, huddling over pieces of wreck-age large and small, charting what they found and where they found it. They were members of the go-team, a group of industry and government specialists in virtually all facets of aviation, who rotate on twenty-four-hours-a-day, seven-days-a-week alert to respond to major aviation disasters.

The men cataloging the wreckage were members of the structures group: engineers whose responsibility was to re-cover and examine the airframe and flight controls. They most likely would be the team that recovered the 811's two so-called black boxes; the cockpit voice recorder and the flight data recorder. They would be sent to the NTSB's Bureau of Technology downtown for analysis. There they would give up their records of cockpit conversation and aircraft-performance data that would help reconstruct the accident and the events that led up to it. Why they were called black boxes, Pace never knew, since actually they were bright orange.

At other places around the airport, go-team weather spe-cialists would be trying to determine if high winds were a factor. An air-traffic-control group would analyze all ATC services to the dead jetliner. Systems specialists would delve into the guts of the 811. There was a human-factors group to examine the actions of the cockpit and cabin crews, a power-plant group to tear down the engines, witness and maintenance-records groups, and other specialists, all com-ing from different directions in an effort to find as quickly as possible what error or breakdown had destroyed a jet-liner and all three hundred thirty-three people aboard. Within hours, the NTSB teams would be joined by engi-neers from the aircraft and engine manufacturers, who would lend their expertise to the investigation. The common goal was to find the quickest possible remedial measures to ensure that a similar error or breakdown did not happen again. Not ever.

Pace needed the roster of go-team members. Some of their investigative work would take weeks, but preliminary information would be making the rounds within hours. He knew a lot of people in the industry, and with any luck, there would be someone on the team who could be turned into a source. He felt a definite sense of urgency; he wasn't the only veteran reporter looking for the inside story.

As if on cue, he met the eyes of Justin Smith, chief aviation writer for *The New York Times* since before the invention of dirt.

Smith walked over to greet Pace. "This the damndest thing you ever saw?" he asked, a slight Georgia drawl rounding the edges of his words. "Wouldn't want to be the one to sort it out."

Pace held out his binoculars. "You want to get up close and personal?"

"Not 'specially." Nonetheless, Smith took the glasses and held them to his eyes for several minutes. "Jesus!" he whispered, handing the binoculars back to Pace. He jerked his head toward the main terminal. "Goin' back inside. Wanna tag along?"

Overhead, Pace counted no fewer than nine news choppers taking turns hovering over the wreckage for the video tape that would spice the five, six, and eleven o'clock news on five local stations and four networks. His black mood and the incessant clap of the chopper rotors had given him a headache.

He nodded at Smith, then bent beside Hogan, whose motor drive still whirred through frame after frame.

"There's nothing more I need out here," he whispered. "I'm going back to the main terminal to see what's up."

"Right," Hogan replied. "Call if you get work."

It hardly seemed possible, but the scene inside was worse than the mess outside. Outside, at least, the victims were dead.

Dulles was closed. Flights that couldn't be diverted to Washington National Airport or Baltimore-Washington International were canceled. Passengers left in private cars or in special buses for their new takeoff points, or they went home, some feeling too hassled and others too frightened to make another attempt at flying on this day.

Immediate relatives of the victims of Flight 1117, once identified by ConPac officials, were driven in people-movers from the main terminal to the mid-field terminal, where the doomed flight originated. In that now-isolated building, the stunned and grieving families were comforted by clergy and social workers trained to deal with sudden, unexpected tragedy. Yet, even cleared of family members and airline passengers, the main building was filled with people, wall to wall, end to end. Pace guessed most were airline and airport employees, friends and colleagues of the passengers . . . and the morbidly curious, those always willing to drive to a big fire or a fatal accident. Some let themselves consider what it must be like to die in an aviation disaster and were there out of a sense that it could have been themselves lying charred under black-plastic sheets on the runway. Everyone personalizes an airline accident, unconsciously quantifying it against his or her own experiences with aborted takeoffs, unscheduled landings, and near in-flight collisions.

When three hundred thirty-three people die, they leave a lot of living victims behind.

Adding to the terminal crowd were hundreds of journalists. Television crews zoomed in as ConPac representatives led the dazed and the weeping to privacy. Broadcast reporters shoved microphones into blank faces with glazed eyes. From discreet distances, print-photographers' strobes popped like halftime special effects at the Orange Bowl. This personal suffering was a part of aviation-disaster stories Pace loathed. He felt immense gratitude that those assignments fell to junior reporters; he didn't think he could handle all that agony.

"Pretty grim," Smith observed. "Sometimes I think this is the worst part of it, the way families stand around, building on each other's grief."

"I hate it," Pace agreed. "Why do we have to do this every time, feed on the emotionally crippled? Let them suffer in private." He ran a hand through the curly dark hair that framed his face and crept over his collar. "Christ, how in hell do you approach them, and how do you live with the questions later? 'So, Mrs. Jones, what's it feel like being a widow?' 'So you're little Tony. You know your daddy burned up in an airplane outside?' "

Somewhere in the crowd, Pace knew, *Chronicle* reporters and photographers, like the others, were gathering notebooks full of hesitant, probing questions and stunned, sobbing answers that would be given to a rewrite specialist at the office for a sensitive mood piece.

"It's all bullshit!"

"Can't quarrel with that," Smith agreed. "Can't change it, either, so probably not much sense worryin' over it."

For a moment Pace considered Smith with both amusement and irritation. The *Times* man was in his early sixties but had the unlined face of someone much younger and a body that looked quite fit in gray slacks and a blue blazer. Maybe those were the benefits of an easygoing attitude.

"You ever get hyper about anything, Justin?" Pace asked. "I don't recall ever seeing you really angry . . . or really jazzed, for that matter. If I run the gamut of emotions from A to Z, you sort of stay stuck between L and M."

Smith chuckled. "Naw," he said. "Got all the way up to B once."

"God, that must have been an incredible moment," Pace suggested.

"Was," Smith agreed. "Was in the spring of nineteen eighty-four. Discovered the best barbecue place on earth, a little shack outside Brunswick, Georgia. Worth fightin' through the pulp-mill stench to get to it, that's how good it was. Still is."

Pace shook his head and moved the conversation to the Sexton crash. "You got a great story on this?" he asked.

"Not yet," Smith replied. "Will have, though. Enough before deadline to beat you, Hoss."

"You wish," Pace said, chuckling.

They parted, and Pace circulated, carefully skirting the Consolidated Pacific offices, where more journalists stood the vigil of the passenger list, waiting for the airline to release the names of those on board Flight 1117, something that would come in small segments of five and ten names at a time as the airline confirmed that next of kin had been notified.

Notified! You think they don't already know? They're all here, milling around like fucking zombies while the bodies whose hands they shook or whose cheeks they kissed four hours ago are stuffed into body bags at the end of Nineteen-right. What are they going to be notified about? "We're sorry, Mrs. Johnson. We found all of Henry but his head."

Pace stuffed his notebook deep into the side pocket of his expensive Britches sport coat, where he hoped it would go unnoticed. Unconsciously, he lifted the press credentials hanging from a chain around his neck and slipped them into the breast pocket of his shirt. His black mood, forced aside briefly by Justin Smith's singular good humor, was back. Pace found himself wishing he could ditch the story and go somewhere—anywhere—else.

He leaned against an escalator handrail and scanned the throng, looking for nothing in particular. But one individual caught his eye.

She was standing with her back to him in a line of people—the families of the victims of Flight 1117—waiting to pass through the security checkpoints to ride out to the mid-field terminal. Pace thought he would have recognized the auburn hair anywhere.

Without planning it, he walked over and took the young woman's arm. She turned in surprise, her green eyes rimmed and reddened with tears. The sight took Pace's breath. All his memories of those eyes were of laughter and joy.

"Kathy?" He stared at her, open-mouthed. "What are you doing here?"

"Hello, Steve," she said, her voice cracking. "I should have expected to see you." She started to say something else but turned away suddenly and put a hand to her mouth. He saw her shoulders tremble.

He slipped into line beside her and took her arm again. The feel of her set off emotions he hadn't touched in the year since they'd drifted apart. He wondered how he'd ever let that happen. He put his arm around her shoulders and felt her press into him.

"Who was on the plane?" he asked as gently as a question like that could be asked.

"Jonathan," she replied. She closed her eyes, and he could see tears leaking onto her cheeks.

"Your brother? Oh, God, Kath, I'm so damned sorry." He thought he remembered that Jonathan McGovern was about five years older than Kathy. He was some big muckety-muck in the securities business in Chicago. Was he married? Yeah, and he had at least one child.

"Was his family with him?"

"No. Jonny was here for the day, for a meeting at the SEC, and he was going on to the West Coast for something, I don't know what." She was talking and sobbing softly at the same time. He squeezed her lightly. Their line had moved, and she was next to arrive at the security checkpoint. An agent looked at Kathy and waved both of them through.

Pace knew he shouldn't be there. The bus ride and the mid-field terminal were off limits to the press, but with his notebook in his jacket pocket and his credentials in his shirt, he passed for one more grieving family member. He wasn't trying to be devious. He was there at that moment for Kathy McGovern, not for a story.

"Have you called anyone?" Pace asked her.

She nodded. "Daddy's coming down on a flight tonight. I guess Betsy will be coming, too, from Chicago."

He guessed Betsy was Jonathan's widow.

"She's pregnant again," Kathy said, her fragile composure suddenly cracking. "Jonny won't ever get to see the baby."

He stopped and took her in his arms, letting her cry against his shoulder as he stroked her hair. He could think of nothing appropriate to say.

When she grew quiet, he tried to guide her to the gate where an airport bus waited to leave for the mid-field terminal. Although she'd intended at one time to go there, she resisted now.

"Why bother?" she asked in utter despair. "There's nothing out there for me."

"There are people out there who can help you and explain what happened."

"I don't need any help, dammit," she said with defiance. "I know what happened. The goddamned airplane crashed and killed my brother." She took a deep breath. "I had two brothers once. Now they're both gone. And my mother's gone. And none of it should have happened."

He steered her gently toward the bus. "Come on, Kath. I'll go with you."

This time she didn't resist.

Pace led her to a place where there were two seats together. She sat in silence, staring out the opposite window but seeing nothing. Many of the passengers had the same dazed and vacant stares. A few were crying openly.

The children broke his heart. There must have been fifteen of them on the bus, all too young to understand what was happening but recognizing in that way children have that whatever it was, it was horrible. Each was accompanied by at least one parent or grandparent stricken by tragedy and transmitting stifling signals of despair.

One towheaded little boy—Pace guessed he was three— was on his knees beside his mother, who was sobbing softly. He was wearing a western shirt and kids' Levi's rolled up at the cuffs over tiny cowboy boots. He threw his arms around her neck and buried his head in her shoulder. "Don't cry, Mommy," he repeated over and over. "Please, don't cry. Don't cry."

One old woman sat alone, her legs parted, the hem of her plain, lilac-colored cotton dress pulled demurely over her knees. She leaned on a cane, and tears rolled down her cheeks. Her expression was stoic, and as Pace watched, it never changed. But the tears dropped, one after another, onto her lilac skirt, leaving dark-stained dots where they landed.

He felt a hand on his left arm and turned to face a middle-aged man in such agony it hurt to look at him. "Who did you lose?" the man asked.

Pace drew a ragged breath. He cocked his head toward Kathy. "My friend lost her only living brother," he said quietly.

"We lost our children, our daughter and son-in-law," the man volunteered. "Just married yesterday. They were on their way to Hawaii for their honeymoon, and now they're dead." He groped for the hand of the woman beside him, his wife, who kept shaking her head and repeating, "No. No. No. No. No. No. No."

"She hasn't accepted it yet," the man said. "This soon, I guess that's to be expected, huh?"

"Probably," Pace agreed. "Where we're going, there'll be people who can help."

"They're alive. They're alive," the woman said. "I know they're alive. Jenny and Chris didn't get on that plane. They're waiting in the parking lot. Jenny and Chris need a ride home." She looked directly at Pace, and he felt his stomach curdle. "We're going to find Jenny and Chris and give them a ride home. They'll be fine now. We just have to find them and take them home."

The man took his wife's hands in his and looked at Pace in a silent plea for help.

"I'm sorry," the reporter said kindly. "I'm really sorry."

The bus reached the mid-field terminal and started its hydraulic rise to meet the gate. The passengers shuffled from the vehicle into the midst of the largest congregation of misery Pace could ever remember seeing under the same roof. Everywhere he looked, his brain recorded snapshots of anguish.

In ones and twos and small clutches, desperate people listened to the psychologists and clergy assembled by Consolidated Pacific to offer emotional and spiritual support. The faces bespoke disbelief. Kind words were flung aside, replaced by the rejection of reality, recrimination, and the single question: Why?

Within Pace's range of sight, three crews of emergency medical personnel tended to people who had collapsed. Two women were receiving oxygen. One elderly man sat at the gate of a canceled flight to St. Louis. He rocked back and forth and wailed. A young man in a priest's collar sat down beside him and spoke softly to him. The old man heard nothing; he continued rocking and wailing. Dozens of people sat and stared at nothing with the same vacant eyes Pace had seen on the bus.

A teenaged boy in a Kensington High School athletic jacket leaned over a gate partition and cried uncontrollably. Although two people stopped to check on him, their words of solace had no impact, and they were forced, reluctantly, to move on to those they could reach.

The young children cringed, holding tightly to the legs of adults. A raven-haired little girl jammed her thumb in her mouth and buried her head in her mother's skirt, clapping her free hand over one ear, doing the best she could to shut out the sights and sounds of suffering.

A woman approached Pace and Kathy McGovern. "I'm Rabbi Kirschner," she said. "Would you like to talk to me, or to another member of the clergy?"

Kathy shook her head. "Where are the airline officials?" she demanded.

"They're over there," Rabbi Kirschner said, indicating the United Air Lines Red Carpet Lounge. "They'll be there all day, and they'll answer any questions you have. It might help to talk about this with somebody else first."

Kathy set off for the lounge without replying.

"Thank you, anyway," Pace told the rabbi and hurried to catch up with Kathy.

Inside the lounge, Pace saw several dozen airline officials talking individually with grieving relatives, giving each very personal attention. He recognized two of the officials, and, unfortunately, one recognized him.

B.J. Houston, chief of operations for ConPac, excused himself from a middle-aged couple and strode toward Pace. "How did you get in here?" he demanded. He spoke in a

MAXIMUM IMPACT   39

whisper that was more like a hiss, but he took care not to
be overheard by those around him, who didn't need to
witness a confrontation at that moment. "This area is absolutely off-limits to the media."

"I'm not here as a reporter, Mr. Houston," Pace said
honestly. "I came with a friend."

"That's true," said Kathy, who appeared at Pace's side.
"My name is Kathleen McGovern. My brother, Jonathan,
was on Flight Eleven-seventeen."

"I am terribly sorry for your loss, Miss McGovern, but
I'm afraid I'm going to have to ask Mr. Pace to leave,"
Houston told her. "It's my experience that a reporter is
always working, and these people deserve privacy at a time
like this."

"I'm not going to interfere," Pace insisted.

"That's right, you're not," Houston replied. He waved in
the direction of a security agent.

"Please," Kathy pleaded. "He's my friend."

Houston looked at her apologetically. "I'm sorry, Miss
McGovern. We'll arrange transportation out here for anyone else you want, but we can't allow Mr. Pace to stay. I am
sorry, but that's an ironclad rule." Houston turned to the
security agent. "Escort this man back to the main terminal," he ordered. "And take pains to see he doesn't get out
here again."

Pace took Kathy in his arms. "I'll call you. I promise."

The agent took Pace by the arm and firmly guided him to
the door. Pace walked backwards, never taking his eyes
from Kathy's face.

"I'll call you," he repeated. She nodded. He wanted to
fight to stay with her. He felt like a jerk for allowing himself
to be rousted.

The agent hauled him through the door, and Pace's anger
overflowed. He jerked his arm from the man's grasp.
"Touch me again, and you're risking a lawsuit."

"I'm just doing my job, mister," the man said.

"You like pulling me away from a lady who lost her

brother out there?" the reporter snapped. "Some great, fucking job."

They rode together in strained silence back to the main terminal. The security man escorted Pace off the bus and pointed him out to the gate attendant. Pace was a marked man, and any attempt to get back to Kathy would be futile.

He found himself alone in the darkened rear half of the terminal and considered stopping for a drink at the bar at the far end of the passenger lounge. But the bar was closed, as was the Diplomat Restaurant to its right. The International Café, a mostly mediocre cafeteria, was open and doing a brisk business, but Pace didn't think it was worth the short walk to pay too much for substandard coffee. Instead, he found himself riding an escalator down to the ground-level commuter airline concourse, then walking past the fountains and the colorful posters hung as sirens to faraway lands. He stopped briefly at the bronze bust of John Foster Dulles, Secretary of State from nineteen fifty-three to nineteen fifty-nine and the man for whom the airport was named. A plaque above the bust noted the airport had been dedicated by President John F. Kennedy in nineteen sixty-two. It was such a long time ago.

Two solemn men in business suits with Federal Aviation Administration IDs hanging from the breast pockets brushed by Pace as he contemplated the bust. One inserted a key into the security slot above the call buttons for an elevator with dark-gray doors. Pace's apparently aimless wandering had delivered him to the base of the airport control tower. When the elevator doors opened, a passenger with a face the color of wet chalk emerged in front of the two officials waiting to get on. Without even glancing at Pace, the man who had come from the tower walked quickly up the corridor, past the siren posters, toward the escalator to the second level. He was halfway there when a light winked on in that portion of Pace's brain reserved for journalistic instinct.

It took a few seconds for him to catch up, and he fell into step with the man slightly behind and off his left shoulder.

"Excuse me," Pace opened.

There was no response. The two of them kept walking in a direction that had purpose to the ashen-faced man, but not to Pace.

"Excuse me, could I talk to you for a second?"

The man halted so abruptly Pace almost bumped into his back.

"What?" the man asked impatiently. Pace gauged him to be in his mid-thirties, although his pallor made him appear older.

"I'm sorry to bother you. My name is Steve Pace. I'm the aviation writer for the *Chronicle*. I saw you come out of the tower, and I'd like to ask a few questions." He tried to make the request sound like a simple one to fill.

The man shook his head. "I don't have anything to say to the press. No offense, but I . . ." His voice trailed off, and he held his hands up in front of his chest, palms out, as though trying to ward off an evil spirit. Then he shook his head again and walked off.

Pace followed and tried once more. "Look, I don't want to cause problems for you. I'm trying to get information on what happened to the Eight-eleven. I know you've probably told your story a dozen times already. I'd appreciate it if you'd tell it once more, to me."

The controller shook his head.

Pace pressed a little harder. "If you're worried about getting mucked up with the FAA or the NTSB, I'll protect you. I won't use your name."

The ashen-faced man stopped and confronted Pace at the bottom of the escalator, his feet spread, his body balanced like a fighter's. His eyes glinted in anger. "You don't know my name," he challenged. "And I can't get mucked up with anybody if I don't talk to you."

"Barry Raiford," Pace said flatly.

Raiford went a shade paler. Without taking his eyes off Pace's face, he slipped a hand inside his coat to a shirt pocket and came out with a pack of Marlboros containing two survivors. One was about to go.

"Do we know each other?" Raiford's belligerence was gone, replaced by concern. Pace thought his hand shook slightly as he lit the tobacco.

The reporter nodded toward Raiford's left chest, where an FAA identification card, complete with name and photograph, hung from the controller's jacket pocket. He saw Raiford wince. Pace knew from his own experience that after you wear plastic credentials for a while, you tend to forget they're there.

"So what now?" Raiford asked sarcastically. "I tell you everything I know or you make something up and put my name on it?"

"No blackmail. I'd like to hear what you saw. This city lost a lot of friends and relatives out there, and people want to know how it happened. Pilot error? Mechanical failure? An act of God? Are there other categories?"

Raiford's shoulders slumped. "Not here," he said. He ground the half-used Marlboro under a scuffed loafer and headed for a secluded space under the escalator, next to a set of locked double doors that led to a parking area for baggage and mail carts.

Pace followed without protest. He hadn't been in Washington long before he learned to accept the collective paranoia of its civil servants. Many liked talking to the media. They were willing, even eager, to discuss each other's mistakes, real or perceived—so long as their identities were protected. Pace came to accept the system as a fact of life, even to understand it. It gave each of them a sense of being more than a splinter in one of the planks on the vast ship of state.

Once Raiford assured himself they were hidden from others walking to or from the tower, he asked Pace, "What do you want to know?"

"Where you were and what you saw."

"And if I told you I wasn't there, and I didn't see anything?"

"The look on your face when you came out of the tower says that would be a lie."

Raiford shoved his hands deep into the pockets of his slacks and stared at his shoes. Long moments passed, and Pace knew the man was looking beyond the floor, into a nightmare, and was living it again.

"The fucker came apart," the controller began in a hoarse whisper.

Pace grabbed for his notepad and pen. "What came apart? The airplane?"

"The taxi was ordinary enough." Raiford hadn't heard the question. The story would come in its own way. "She stopped at the end of the runway, and the crew talked to ConPac dispatch. They said they were ready. It didn't sound like anything was wrong. We gave them takeoff clearance and the winds, and she started rolling. Routine."

Raiford paused. Pace forced himself to be patient.

After a minute, Raiford took a deep breath and started again. "She seemed to be having trouble rotating, uh, you know, getting airborne. I see so many airplanes take off and land, I get a feeling for timing, ya know? She was on the ground too long. I kept waiting for the nose wheel to come up. I kept thinking she would rotate or abort. Maybe they tried to abort. I couldn't tell. Maybe they reversed engines, and that's when it happened."

Raiford stopped again.

"What happened?" Pace urged softly.

The controller looked up from his shoes. There were tears in his eyes. "It disintegrated. The right engine started coming apart. It was on the far side of the plane from where I was, but I had glasses, ya know, and I was watching it, and I could see the pieces of metal flying all over the place. Then the plane veered off to the right and tipped over. A big section of the wing, I guess maybe most of it, snapped off and took the engine with it. The whole thing went flying through the air. Then the right main gear collapsed. It fell on its side and exploded." Raiford's voice started to shake. "Shit, I felt so helpless. I was standing up screaming for somebody to help them. Can you imagine anything so stupid? I was standing in the tower cab screaming at the airplane! I guess I was screaming at myself. I should have called them about that engine before."

Pace was confused momentarily. "Before what?" he asked.

The controller hesitated again. "I saw smoke when the engine started," he said reluctantly. "It wasn't much, nothing very dramatic, the kind of thing you get when an engine is flooded, and even the new C-Fans do that. I thought about telling the captain, but I saw a member of the ground crew take a look at it, and I figured they had it handled. I figured if there was anything wrong, the cockpit crew would be told. I didn't call them. Maybe it wouldn't have made a difference. But I wish I'd called."

Both men were silent for a few long moments. Pace was catching up his notes. Raiford waited quietly. When the reporter finished writing, he looked up, and the two men made eye contact. The sadness in Raiford's eyes was palpable.

"Did you hear anybody on the flight deck say anything?" the reporter asked.

"Not that I recall," the controller choked. "I was focused on that aircraft, and I don't remember anything else. The FAA is collecting the ATC tapes now, and I guess if there's anything on them, they'll release it all eventually. I didn't think to listen to the radio. I wasn't thinking about anything but that jet. I couldn't believe it was happening. All I could think was that somehow the crew would save the plane at the last minute, somebody would think of something to do . . ." Raiford looked away from Pace and asked the question he'd been avoiding all day. "How many were there?"

The query was oblique, but Pace knew what it meant. "On board, three hundred thirty-three," he replied softly. "It's the deadliest accident in U.S. aviation history."

"It's deadlier than you know," Raiford said.

This time Pace didn't understand.

"It keeps getting worse," Raiford sighed, almost overcome by emotion. He put out one hand to support his weight against the terminal wall and contemplated the floor again. "There was a small Cessna, a one-seventy-two I think, waiting near the end of Nineteen-right to taxi across. I think at the very last minute he tried to blast his way clear, but the jet rolled right over him. Poor bastard. He saw it coming and couldn't do anything about it. Whoever he was in there, he'll have to be scraped up with a putty knife."

Pace felt deeply for the controller. "It wasn't your fault," was all he could think to say.

"How can you be so damned sure?" Raiford demanded. His eyes were dry now, and a muscle jumped along his right jawline. The anger he felt over the events of the day exploded at Pace. "How do you know it wouldn't have made a difference if I'd called the crew about that engine? You bastard! You'll go back to your office and write your big story, then head out for a nice dinner, and maybe a roll in the sack, if you're lucky. You'll get a good night's sleep, and tomorrow this will be a dirty little memory for you. Meanwhile, I got to live with it for the next twenty, thirty years, 'cause I'm not so damned sure it wasn't at least part my fault. But then, I'm not a reporter. I'm not omniscient. Fuck you!"

Raiford spun on his heel and walked away, leaving the reporter standing alone in the shadow of the escalator.

For the second time that afternoon, Pace felt like a total schmuck.

3

The afternoon air over Washington was still and unseasonably heavy with humidity. But in the spongy glades of Theodore Roosevelt Island in the middle of the Potomac River channel, the air was cool on the skin and carried the earthy fragrance of generations of rotting oak and cottonwood leaves. The wild redbud were in bloom, the wild dogwood were trying to follow, and on the taller trees, the season's new leaves showed bright green.

Two men met in a clearing, by the statue erected to pay homage to the President whose name the island bore. If the two had cared to and listened hard, they would have heard the sounds of traffic zipping along Rock Creek Parkway past the Kennedy Center and the Watergate complex on the D.C. side of the river, or along the George Washington Memorial Parkway on the Virginia bank.

But history, scenery, and sensory effects were not the reasons they were there. Their principal interest was privacy. With the tourist season still two months away, and considering most residents of the area neither knew nor cared about the island memorial, they counted on sharing the place with nothing more than a few birds and the mountain of bronze sculpted to look like a dead President. They were forced to wait to discuss their business until two young couples vacated the clearing, laughing and talking about cleaning up and doing Georgetown on a Thursday night. The men were uncomfortable passing time and making small talk, and the young people eyed them with curiosity.

"They probably think we're gay," the younger and taller of the two men whispered. He was one of the most imposing figures the other had ever seen: black, six-foot-five, lean, muscular, and possessed of a pair of brown eyes that could sear a soul. His name was Chapman Davis. He was an ex-college basketball point guard, held an MBA in government affairs, and served as chief of the minority staff of the Senate Transportation Committee. That was his public persona. Those who knew him well—and few did—would have written the resumé differently.

"Digger" Davis: college basketball point shaver and bribe taker, small-time drug and numbers runner, loanshark collector, and self-satisfied killer of a sadistic pimp and a crack dealer who liked to distribute samples on school playgrounds. He had been arrested for killing the pimp, but the gun he used disappeared from a police evidence room, and the charges were dropped. No charges ever were brought in the death of the crack dealer.

All this transpired in the space of four years, a lifetime's worth of crime crammed between the ages of nineteen and twenty-three. He'd never been convicted of anything. He was kicked off Ohio State's basketball team under suspicion of playing to undercut bookmakers' spreads, and the assistant coach, who paid him two hundred and fifty dollars a week to do that, was fired. Charges were filed against the coach, but never against Davis. The only crime for which Davis ever was called to account was a minor drug possession in Youngstown, Ohio.

That was when he first met a local lawyer named Harold Marshall, who defended him against the drug charge. Davis never knew who paid Marshall to take his case, and on those occasions when he asked about it, Marshall told him not to worry. The lawyer got an acquittal.

Later, Marshall convinced Davis to return to Ohio State for his undergraduate degree and his MBA, and then talked him into joining his first campaign for the U.S. Senate. Marshall won, and rewarded Davis with a job on the Senate Transportation Committee, a position from which he rose quickly to Republican chief of staff.

Marshall occasionally alluded to Davis's dark past, but he never disclosed how he'd learned the full scope of the problems or, for that matter, whether he cared. The subject generally arose when Marshall proposed Davis undertake some political deed abhorred by the young man with the new respectability. Marshall applied the pressure directly. "Your previous experience as an enforcer uniquely qualifies you for this," he would say. Almost always the assignments were to the benefit of Marshall's most important constituent, the Converse Corporation.

One day Marshall confided to Davis that it was George Greenwood, then senior vice-president of Converse, who paid five hundred dollars a month for point shaving during Davis's abbreviated basketball career—the assistant coach was the conduit and kept half the cash for himself—and it was Greenwood who paid Davis's legal bill for the Youngstown drug defense.

"But why?" Davis had asked, dumbfounded.

Marshall shrugged. "He saw in you someone he could use to good advantage, I guess. You're not the only one. You're just the only one on my staff. He also paid for your education, MBA included, and influenced me to offer you a job on the Transportation Committee."

"Is there anything in my adult life I've decided for myself?" Davis demanded.

"Sure," Marshall said. "You decided to say yes when I offered you the job."

"And if I decide to say no now?"

"Well, my friend," Marshall had said, "there's no statue of limitations on murder. The evidence that would have convicted you of murder one for offing the pimp? George made it disappear, although it didn't disappear, exactly. I imagine it's still in his safety deposit box."

So, over his years on the Hill, Davis had undertaken a dozen missions ordered by Marshall on behalf of Converse. He wasn't proud of them, just as he wasn't proud of the assignment that brought him to Roosevelt Island. But, hell, he was good at intimidation.

The man he'd come to the island to meet was white and pale . . . and neither knew nor cared about the criminal credentials of his black companion. He knew only that he found Davis frightening and wanted to complete their business and be done with him. He nodded toward the two couples sharing the island with them. "I don't care what they think as long as they don't know us, don't remember us, and don't tell anyone they saw us here," he said. "Now let's get this done so I can get back to Dulles. They've probably missed me already."

Davis knew in situations like this, you always play to another man's weakness. In Elliott Parkhall's case, identifying weakness was easy; the dossier given to the Senate aide revealed a half dozen from which to choose. The engineer never closely held his anger over what he regarded as his dead-end career in government or his lack of the worldly goods that graced the lives of those he believed inferior technicians who happened to ply their trade in the private sector. Parkhall had been in the private sector once and had blown the opportunity through an utter lack of ability to get along with his co-workers. He wound up in a responsible job with the NTSB by dint of his engineering skills, not because anyone believed he would ever make a leader of men.

Parkhall commanded the power-plants group on the crash by the luck of the draw: It was his turn, nothing more. Davis recognized immediately that Parkhall could be manipulated if he were given an opportunity to lash back at those he blamed for abandoning him to a lower station in life than he was due. By according him the chance to get even, the money to live as he might have had his career taken a more favorable financial course, and the knowledge his life was forfeit if he failed, Davis calculated he could intimidate the engineer for as long as he needed him.

Watching Parkhall in the clearing, Davis could see he had succeeded in putting the engineer off balance. Parkhall fidgeted. He chewed on the fingernails of his left hand. He kept wiping beads of perspiration off his upper lip. He was frightened, and a frightened man could be controlled.

Finally alone, Davis described what he expected of Parkhall . . . and watched blood drain from the engineer's face. Davis told him what he would be paid, what he could earn in bonuses, and how the total sum would let him forget injustices inflicted in the past. Parkhall nodded but remained pale. He was willing to accept the gratuities of the job, but the risks concerned him deeply.

"Without risk, there is no gain," Davis warned. "You may elect to accept both, or neither. But be warned, if you elect to accept neither, this operation will proceed without you. If you raise objections, then life itself will proceed without you, if you get my meaning."

Parkhall swallowed hard. He felt his companion's eyes on his face, assessing every reaction. He looked up and saw in those eyes the reality that he was trapped. Then, in the span of a heartbeat, the black face around the dark eyes relaxed marginally.

"But if you choose to accept both the risk and the gain, you will have all the support you need to minimize the risk," Davis said. "And while the risk is assumed immediately, the gain begins immediately as well."

He took a thick manila envelope from the deep left pocket of the trench coat he wore despite the warm weather and slapped the package into Parkhall's chest. "This is the first payment," he continued. "The sum I mentioned is in here, plus a generous overage to cover expenses. If expenses run higher than expected, let me know."

He pushed the envelope deeper into Parkhall's chest, and the engineer grasped it with both hands, feeling what surely were bundles of bills inside.

"I don't have a choice, do I?" he asked softly.

"No, not really. You abdicated that choice by hearing my proposal on the telephone and agreeing to meet me. But if you follow instructions, you have no reason to be afraid."

"When do you want me to do this?"

"After dark, when you minimize the number of people likely to see you."

"The engine will have been examined already."

"Not closely. And not by very many people. There are no other members of your team scheduled in here until late tonight, and the Converse team won't even leave Ohio until tomorrow morning. That's been seen to. The engine is off by itself, isolated. Right now the focus is on recovering bodies from the fuselage. You shouldn't have any trouble at all."

Parkhall opened his mouth to say something, probably to voice another objection, Davis thought, but no words came. Davis acted to bring the meeting to an end.

"When you return to your car," he said, "two men will be waiting for you in a blue Ford van in the parking lot. They will follow you back to the airport and will, for the foreseeable future, act as your backup. They have my full trust, and they should have yours. They will take no action unless it is unavoidable, but by their presence, the serious nature of this business will be underscored. As you can imagine, they will be gauging your performance as well as assisting you. They have been told of your loyalty. I trust you will give them no reason to doubt it."

"Are they my bodyguards, or just guards?"

"That depends on you," Davis said. "They will be what they have to be."

"Who are they?"

"That's nothing you need to know."

Davis withdrew another envelope from the right pocket of his coat. It was larger than the first, and bulged slightly. Parkhall glanced down at it, knowing what it was and feeling revulsion.

"This is the material you must use tonight," Davis said. "We spoke of it earlier."

"I know," Parkhall said, recoiling from the package. "How about the equipment?"

"It's in the van. The men will transfer it to your car and instruct you in its use. As an engineer, I suspect you won't find it difficult."

Parkhall nodded, fear beating like a sledgehammer in his temples. He took the envelope gingerly.

Davis released his grip on it, making the transfer of ownership complete. "Perform well," he admonished. "By your actions, so go my interests and your future." Then he turned and crossed the bridge to the parking lot.

Parkhall could hear his footfalls for several seconds, and then he was alone. He sagged against the base of the statue and shivered once, deeply.

Shortly before 7:00 P.M., Vernon Lund convened the first NTSB news conference. He looked like a man who had succumbed to his responsibilities barely hours after assuming them.

His shoulders sagged perceptibly, his eyes were puffed and bloodshot. His blue suit looked slept in, the vest open and drooping from his crane-like neck. A red-and-blue-striped tie was drawn too tightly around a white shirt collar a size too large, so the collar points, rather than lying flat, stuck almost straight out. The suit coat was missing its center front button, leaving a space adorned by a small, unidentifiable, yellow-brown food stain. Lund's sandy hair was thin and going mouse-gray. Half-glasses slid down his thin nose and carried smudges etched into the lenses by days without the benefit of a cleaning. His chest, which could be described as hollow on its good days, was more concave than usual, sinking toward the backbone and then curving out to meet a belly slightly distended by a wall of muscle flaccid and puffy with disuse.

Lund was the NTSB board member who would oversee the operations of the go-team, without doing any of the hands-on investigative work. That would be under the supervision of the investigator-in-charge, James Padgett, who had gone to work for the NTSB as a professional accident investigator after retiring as director of safety for the North American operations of Lufthansa. Lund would expedite operations for the go-team, settle any disputes that arose between the NTSB investigators and other parties, including Sexton, Converse, the FAA, the pilots' union, even Dulles International Airport. And he would conduct the evening press briefings. Given the negative attitude Lund carried toward the media, Steve Pace held little hope the daily sessions would be easy.

"Ladies and gentlemen, I'll make this brief," Lund said, standing at the head of the conference table. "There was initially, as you know by now, one survivor from Flight Eleven-seventeen. Unfortunately, his injuries were so severe that he died on the way to the hospital. I've been given clearance to identify him as First Officer Jeremy Dodds, of Long Beach, California. He was taken to Fairfax Hospital, where he was pronounced dead on arrival. Doctors say he had massive internal injuries, a skull fracture, and two broken legs. With his death, the final toll is three hundred thirty-three. There were three hundred twenty-one passengers on board, including two unticketed children. The crew count was twelve. That total unfortunately makes this the worst airline disaster in U.S. history.

"We have no preliminary information on what caused the crash. Of course, as you would expect, our early investigative efforts will focus on the Number Three engine, which is lying separate from but proximate to the outboard two-thirds of the starboard wing, approximately a hundred and eighty yards from the main body of the wreckage. I cannot give you any sort of timetable for the release of a complete passenger list. That will depend on how quickly next of kin can be notified. I also cannot tell you with certainty when the job of recovering the remains of those on board will be completed, or when the wreckage will be removed from the runway area. The main fuselage section is lying in a somewhat precarious attitude, and it will have to be stabilized before we can permit anyone in there.

"Eventually, the entire aircraft will be removed to Con-Pac's Hangar Three here on the field. If any of you has questions, they should be directed first to Mitch Gabriel, our press officer, or to me. I will, until further notice, hold a briefing daily, right here, at six-thirty P.M. Now, if you have questions, I'll entertain them, although I assure you I have no further information available."

"What do you mean when you say the fuselage has to be stabilized?" asked Russell Ethrich, aviation writer for *The Washington Post*.

"The fuselage is rather delicately balanced, and if we start moving weight around inside, either by sending rescue teams in or by carrying remains out, it could shift or roll. With all the debris loose in there, we can't risk sending anybody in until we shore it up."

"How long will that take?"

"We'll be working on it through the night, and hopefully, we'll have it completed by sometime tomorrow morning."

"That will delay recovery of bodies. Will it also delay release of the passenger list?"

"I don't know. It could."

"What if somebody's alive in there? They could die before help comes."

"I assure you, no one is alive."

Justin Smith of *The New York Times* caught Lund's eye. "Can y'all tell us how First Officer Dodds was recovered? He get out himself, or did somebody have to go in after him?"

"He was recovered by two rescue crews," Lund said. "It is my information that one, maybe two, people entered the flight deck through a breach in the hull, cut First Officer Dodds loose from the debris, and brought him out. He was never conscious. That's all I know."

"And where were the rescue crews from, sir?"

"I believe there were elements from both Fairfax and Loudoun counties. I don't know their official designations."

"Mr. Lund," shouted a reporter from the *New York Post*, "can you characterize the condition of the bodies? Are they going to be difficult to identify?"

Lund looked positively repulsed. "I am not a forensic pathologist," he snapped. "I have no idea what the answer to that question is." He looked away before the *Post* reporter could follow up and recognized Pace. Although

Lund and Pace had had their differences over the years, Pace supposed Lund found even the *Chronicle* reporter preferable to the *New York Post*'s.

"It was Number Three engine that separated, was it not?" Pace asked, throwing an easy one.

"That's correct."

"Have you had a chance to look at that engine yet?"

"Well, we know where it is, as I said. It's in the grass infield west of runway Nineteen-right. I believe it's been given a preliminary inspection by one member of the power-plants group who is already on the scene. The rest, who are all aviation-industry people, will be coming in during the night or early tomorrow morning. I believe the Converse team will be here in the morning, as well."

"Why won't the Converse people be in tonight? For that matter, why won't all of your people be in tonight? Isn't that what a go-team's all about, a team ready to go instantly when there's a major accident?" Pace pressed. "The Sexton people are here already."

"Some of the Sexton people are here, not all of them," Lund corrected. "A few happened to be in Washington for a congressional hearing and came right out. The rest of the team will be here as soon as possible, I assure you. They're coming from all over the country."

The briefing droned on for twenty minutes, but the questions were redundant. Pace listened, not making further notes on subjects already covered. It was only then he realized that Lund had not mentioned the light airplane crushed by the Sexton. Had Lund avoided it because it wasn't true? Or had he simply forgotten? Pace started to ask, but thought better of it. None of the other reporters asked, which probably meant nobody else knew. It could be an exclusive angle.

Pace hung around until the conference room emptied after Lund finally called an end to the questions. Then he approached the NTSB official cautiously.

"Mr. Lund, I'm sorry about this, but I just remembered

something that didn't come up during the briefing," Pace opened.

Lund glanced at him and continued stuffing papers into his briefcase. "I'm certain a lot of things didn't come up during the briefing, Mr. Pace. The tension in the Middle East, for example."

Pace smiled, trying to make it look as though he appreciated the lame joke. "That's not exactly what I meant," he said, noticing Mitch Gabriel walking over to join them, or maybe he meant to referee. "I was told this afternoon there might have been a second aircraft involved in this accident—not in causing it, but in the aftermath. Is that true?"

Pace thought he saw a look of surprise pass fleetingly over Lund's face. "I'm not at liberty to discuss matters still under investigation," he replied curtly.

"I take that to mean you are investigating the possibility?" Pace said.

"You can take it as you please, but that's all I'm going to say."

Lund turned abruptly and left the room. Gabriel lingered behind. "Looks like you touched a nerve," he said.

"Protect me on this, will you, Mitch?" Pace asked.

"You're the only one who's brought it up, so I assume you're the only one who knows . . . assuming there's anything to know, of course."

"Of course," Pace replied. "Protect me."

"I'm not going to volunteer it to anybody, but if anybody asks, I'll have to give them the same answer Lund gave you."

"That's good enough," Pace said.

He headed for his car feeling better than he had all day. Sometimes an exclusive story could do that for you.

No one paid particular attention when the slight man walked into the circle of light created by the truck-borne stadium lamps ringing the perimeter of the area in which the Sexton's Number 3 engine and starboard wing had come to rest. It was after 10:00 P.M., and everyone at the scene was bone weary. The slight man was wearing proper identification; that was all anybody noticed. He carried by a handle in his left hand an awkward piece of equipment that must have been heavy, for his body listed. There was a package tucked under his right arm, a length of hose coiled over his right shoulder, and something narrowly cylindrical in his right hand.

The man's irrigation boots—the rubberized kind farmers and ranchers wear to work in muddy fields and pastures—made sucking sounds in the wet grass. Even after dark, there were plenty of people around, but most of them were involved nearly two hundred yards to the south with the ongoing job of shoring up the main section of the Sexton wreckage. Davis was right about the separated engine. It sat alone, awaiting the surgical team that would dismantle it to determine what horrific malady had befallen it. Tonight no one was paying it any particular attention.

Elliott Parkhall felt enormously conspicuous nonetheless, a sensation born of guilt, for he was about to do a deed so vile he had not yet come to terms with it. He felt himself trembling as he trudged deeper and deeper into the circle of light and finally stood by the enormous engine, which, even in its crumpled state, was nearly eight feet higher than he was tall. He moved to the back side of the metallic mass, where he was least likely to be seen, and unloaded his gear. When he was ready, he summoned a mighty force of will to push aside the conscious knowledge of what he was about to do, and set about the task of doing it.

What Parkhall didn't see were the eyes that watched him work, the eyes of a startled observer who had approached the engine from a different direction, eager to see it once more before going to bed.

The eyes belonged to Mark Antravanian, one of the aviation-industry members of the power-plants group. Antravanian, who immigrated to the United States from Eastern Europe while in his teens, was a brilliant aeronautical engineer and held an excellent position with McDonnell

Douglas in Los Angeles. He should not have arrived until later that night or early the following morning. But at the time of the Sexton crash, Antravanian was in New York City on business and was able to grab the shuttle to Washington. In fact, he was performing a preliminary examination of the separated Converse engine when Parkhall was meeting with Chapman Davis on Roosevelt Island at mid-afternoon. He had made some notes, dined alone, and returned late to recheck several details of his earlier observations.

Antravanian could not fathom what the man at the mouth of the engine was doing, and he would not know Parkhall's identity until the power-plants group met as a whole the next day.

By then, it would be too late.

4

Friday, April 18th, 8:30 A.M.

The room was awesome, precisely as Avery Schaeffer intended.

Maximum impact was Schaeffer's editorial style, and the editorial conference room just off the cavernous newsroom of the *Washington Chronicle* reflected the editor's philosophy.

The thirty-five-by-twenty-three-foot area was dominated by a cherrywood conference table. Around the table were twenty-four cherry-and-leather masters' chairs. Eighteen matching side chairs lined the room's west wall to accommodate the overflow when special events required more personnel than regular news meetings warranted. The long east wall was solid glass, fully exploiting the breathtaking view.

The new *Chronicle* plant was a ten-story glass-and-brick-building, almost a city block square, at Pennsylvania Avenue and 17th Street, a block west of the White House. It was one of Washington's more prestigious business addresses. Brilliantly tiled mosaic walls, depicting the history of American newspapers, dominated the lobby. An ancient Linotype hot-lead typesetting machine salvaged from the *Chronicle*'s original composing room stood vigil to the past on a display island at the lobby's west end. Beside it, on a similar island, was a unit from the newspaper's original press, cleaned up but not quite clean, its countenance oily and stained, its gears and rollers still breathing faint suggestions of ink and solvent. New printing plants were relegated to the suburbs: thirty-six acres of an industrial park near Rockville, Maryland, and thirty-one acres near Centreville, in Virginia. Proximity of the news and printing operations had been rendered obsolete long ago by the advent of computers and lasers.

City and suburban bureaus were scattered throughout the metropolitan area, but the big midtown building was the heart of the operation, particularly the top floors.

The ninth floor accommodated the business and features staffs, the photo department, the Metro, Virginia, and Maryland suburban sections, and the sports department. Sports, which always looked cyclone-swept, adjoined Virginia Suburban, despite Virginia Suburban's periodic mutinous efforts to have the "games people" moved to an outdoor or underground area as far away from journalistic civilization as possible.

The tenth floor was the apex of the newspaper, literally and figuratively. It housed the editorial department and the national staff, fully seventy-two reporters and editors who covered the White House, Congress, every cabinet department, every government agency, and every government-related subject in town.

Schaeffer believed in hands-on journalism, so departmental editors sat at desks in the newsroom with their reporters, although each had a small windowed office along the south wall to which he or she could retreat. Schaeffer allowed himself a private office, larger than those of the other editors, separated from the newsroom only by glass, lest he lose the karma of the place. He had drapes he could draw and a door he could close if a conference was private, and the door was closed on occasion, but no one could remember a single time when the drapes had been shut.

Schaeffer was slightly round, slightly bald, quick of wit, acid of tongue, and possessed of a world-class temper, which, to the everlasting gratitude of most of his staff, he was able to control most of the time. He had the reputation of being a reporter's editor.

On that rare occasion when there was an ebb in the electricity in the newsroom, Schaeffer never failed to sense it. He would heave his six feet out of his favorite chair and come bounding out of his office—invariably with tie askew and shirt-sleeves rolled to the elbows—to mingle with the troops, renew their vigor, and recharge their spirit. His unbridled enthusiasm nearly always proved infectious, and Avery Schaeffer was immodest about his ability. "It's a gift, and I intend to use it 'til I lose it," he said more frequently than he needed to.

But if Schaeffer was proud of his people skills, he was equally proud of his conference room. It was a paean to years of journalistic triumph; the walls were covered in a neutral, but very expensive, rice paper that served as backdrop for row after row of prestigious journalism awards. Plaques, scrolls, and certificates hung in meticulous order, and busts and statues—either the originals or, in cases where winners chose to take their honors home, fine replicas—rested on the cherry credenzas.

If that weren't enough to inspire all who entered, a wall of windows looked to the southeast, past the Old Executive Office Building to the White House, the Treasury Department and beyond, up Pennsylvania Avenue to the United States Capitol—a single vista sweeping the heart and soul of the most powerful nation on earth.

Occasionally, Schaeffer would go into the conference room, close the door, and sit in silence by himself. In thirty-one years with the *Chronicle,* he had seen the paper fight countless journalistic wars with the secretive federal establishment, with self-important politicians, with political appointees who invariably had overdeveloped senses of self-preservation, and with fellow big-league newspapers. This room was the quintessential symbol of the battles the *Chronicle* won.

Schaeffer believed journalism was a calling, like the priesthood, and represented the glue that held together the fabric of a great democracy. Newspapers were the last line of defense between the Constitution and those who would unintentionally—or willfully—erode the freedoms it guaranteed. In Schaeffer's mind, the newspaper's role was to protect the people from the excesses of government, regardless of the political extreme from which those excesses threatened.

Despite his idealism, he did love the hardware. There was nothing wrong with a fine priest being recognized as such by elevation to the papacy, and there was nothing wrong with tangible symbols of a newspaper's greatness, either. The prizes were Schaeffer's barometer of success, and rarely a day went by when he didn't remember that more of those prizes came during his eleven years as editor than in all the years of all the editors who preceded him. So he had designed the conference room and its display, and someone on the newspaper dubbed it the Glory Room. The name stuck long after the identity of the author was forgotten.

On this morning, the room was alive with activity a full four hours earlier than usual, and chairs from reporters' desks were shoehorned in to seat the overflow crowd. Everyone had a copy of the morning's final edition, and Schaeffer was in deep conversation with National Editor Paul Wister over one of the three pictures that dominated the front page. It was one Steve Pace had thought would never run, a telescopic shot of the interior of the dead Sexton 811, the passengers still hanging in their seats. The photograph had been altered during printing to leave the images of the bodies underexposed. Although the photo was taken from an angle behind the seats, concern remained that friends and relatives would recognize someone.

Wister had argued the previous afternoon against using the photo at all, in deference to public sensibilities. Schaeffer, who could have overruled his national editor, chose instead to call in Managing Editor Alec Stenofsky, Metro Editor Winston Henry, Virginia Suburban Editor Suzanne O'Connor, and Photo Editor Herman Golke and chair a half-hour free-for-all on the question. Schaeffer was not known to abdicate tough decisions, but this one could go either way. On one hand, the picture was too good to ignore, and on the other, it was of Washingtonians killed in a local accident, not of Nigerians or Chileans killed ten thousand miles away.

In the end, the consensus was to run the picture with parts of it underexposed. Golke, a huge Hungarian who professed to love photographs more than life itself, had thrown up his hands in exasperation. "You either run it or you don't, but you don't take a quality photograph and run it fucked up," he raged. But he lost, and the next morning Schaeffer and Wister were still debating the question, although both *The Washington Post* and *The New York Times* used similar shots. Unlike its competitors', however, the *Chronicle*'s photograph ran in color.

At 8:35 A.M., Schaeffer raised his hands to quiet the jammed room. His tie already was down to his second shirt button, and his sleeves were rolled to the elbows.

"I know most of you were here very late last night, and this is damned early in the morning for a meeting, but we have an entire weekend's work to plan," he commanded, and the room stilled. "Thank you. First of all, I commend each of you who had a hand in today's coverage. I think our package was head and shoulders above any other I've seen. The stories were first-rate. We got all the angles covered, and then some. The photos conveyed all the horror and grief as effectively as we could without gagging our readers.

"But the important thing is, we're ahead on this story, and I want to stay there. Better yet, I'd like to get even further ahead. I want interviews with the wife and kids of the pilot who almost made it. I want somebody with the ConPac people until we have the entire passenger list. I don't want to trust the wires on this one. There's too much lag time. When and if any important names show up, I want them phoned in so we can start follow-up immediately. I want the metro and suburban staffs on the families of the victims like glue: wakes, funerals, burials, memorial services, school tributes, the whole schmear. I want personal stories—people who are alive because they missed the flight, people who are dead because they took some special opportunity or had a special reason to be aboard. Winston, Suzy, you've got carte blanche to cancel days off, pay overtime, whatever it takes, and I want the photo department kept apprised hourly on what's going down. Understood?" Winston Henry and Suzanne O'Connor were nodding. "This is the human story. This is the drama. And I don't want to lose a drop of it, understood?" More nodding.

"All right. Paul—" he turned back to his national editor"—is Steve Pace here?"

Pace raised a hand off to Schaeffer's right, a gesture meant to catch the editor's eye, although it made him feel like a schoolboy asking for a bathroom pass.

Schaeffer nodded at him and grinned. "Yeah, Steve. You did one hell of a job yesterday. I didn't know one reporter could be in so many places at once. Your description of the mid-field terminal was heartrending. The other guys didn't have any of that. They also didn't have that eyewitness stuff from the controller, or the info on that poor bastard in the Cessna. You had a hell of a day. But the *Times* and the *Post* are after your ass now. What've you got to hold 'em off with?"

Pace felt himself grin and color slightly at the compliment, although he still didn't feel good about writing the story on the mood in the mid-field terminal. He had done it out of anger at B.J. Houston's decision to throw him out, but it made him feel as though he'd violated a confidence and invaded a lot of people's privacy. He hoped Kathy wouldn't object.

"I talked to Mitch Gabriel at the NTSB first thing this morning," Pace told Schaeffer. "He said the shoring operation on the fuselage would probably be done by noon. Then the investigators will go in, and the rescue teams will start bringing out bodies. The bodies will go into refrigerated tractor-trailer rigs until a morgue can be set up someplace."

Schaeffer turned to Golke to say something about getting photos, but the photo editor was already making a note of it. Silently, Schaeffer turned back to Pace and nodded for him to continue.

"The NTSB and Consolidated Pacific are still marking and photographing the wreckage. It will take some time, days probably, but they'll eventually move it all into Hangar Three, a big ConPac facility at the airport. It'll be sealed off during the investigation. The Sexton engineering team is on site, I'm told. If the Converse team isn't here already, it will be soon. The bodies of the victims, as you know, will be released to next of kin once positive identifications are made. A lot of them are going to be pretty tough, and it would make a good read to get one of our science writers to do a piece on how pathologists identify badly burned remains."

"Good idea," Schaeffer said. Wister was making a note of it.

Pace continued. "One of the things I need to do today is backcheck the Eight-eleven to see if this apparent engine failure is part of a pattern or just a fluke. I wrote today that the Sexton at Dulles had a clean history. But fleetwide, there have been some problems. The reports are on file at the FAA's records dump in Oklahoma City. They're public information, and I've asked for them. The fleet's been operational only six months or so, so the problems could be shakeout things. But we ought to be certain."

"Some shakeout, three hundred and thirty-four people

dead," Schaeffer said derisively. "What about the black boxes?"

"The NTSB recovered both of them yesterday," Pace replied. "They'll be on display for the media at eleven this morning, but it's more a photo op than anything else, so I didn't plan to go unless you think there's some reason for me to be there." Schaeffer and Wister were shaking their heads. Golke was taking more notes. "The FAA's air-traffic-control tapes will show if the crew said anything to the tower between the time the plane was cleared for takeoff and, uh, the end. The NTSB's taken control of the tapes, and they won't be releasing anything today or tomorrow, but generally you can expect transcripts within a week to ten days. The data from the black boxes could be kept under wraps for months."

"What exactly is in the black boxes?" Wister asked.

"The cockpit voice recorder is a thirty-minute tape loop that holds the last half hour of conversation and noises on the flight deck. The information on the flight-data recorder varies. The older models were fairly limited. But the new ones, including the one on the Eight-eleven, tell you almost anything you need to know about acceleration, engine performance, rate of climb, airspeed, flap and slat configuration—a whole checklist of information that can pinpoint the cause of an accident."

"Other leads?" Schaeffer asked.

"I'm taking a stab at getting a list of the members of the go-team, the people who will do the real nuts-and-bolts investigation. If there's anybody on the list I know, well—"

"Right," Schaeffer interrupted. "I don't want to hold you up. Get out there, and stay on this thing like a tick on a dog, and stay in touch with Paul. I don't want to put any pressure on you, so my only instructions are: Don't be wrong, and don't get beat."

Pace hesitated for an instant, but when the editor flashed him a what-are-you-waiting-for look, he began inching his way through legs and kneecaps, excusing himself all the way to the conference-room door.

When he emerged into the nearly deserted newsroom, Steve Pace realized he was sweating, and he could feel adrenaline pumping again. Blowing away the competition on a major story was all it took to relegate advancing age and career burnout to the emotional trash pile.

Pace walked quickly to his desk, Schaeffer's admonition on a tape loop in the very foremost part of his brain: "Don't be wrong, and don't get beat." He trusted himself to get the story right. The killer question, as always, was whether he could consistently beat the other papers to fresh angles every day.

He called Mitch Gabriel at the NTSB. Gabriel already was at Dulles. His assistant was in a meeting. Pace left a message.

Then he tried the Public Information Office at FAA headquarters. On the first three tries, the number was busy. On the fourth attempt, a secretary answered on the ninth ring, a lapse in efficiency doubtless caused by an unusually heavy call load. Conrad Phillips, the FAA's public-affairs chief, was on another line, already busy at an hour normally considered too early for the conduct of serious business in the nation's capital.

"Ask him to call me at the paper as soon as he can, would you?" Pace thanked the secretary and dropped the phone into its cradle. He looked up just as Jillian Hughes and Glenn Brennan trudged into the newsroom, both obviously done in after spending the last fourteen hours at Dulles.

Brennan was a black Irishman from South Boston who drank too much, smoked too much, and never could find clothes that fit him quite right or a hairstyle worthy of the name. His lifestyle was betrayed by a slight but growing bulge at his waist and a hint on his face of the jowls he would acquire later in life. Pace teased him that he was the model on which the Irish stereotype was built. Brennan always deferred modestly to Jimmy Breslin.

What Brennan lacked in appearance, he made up for in talent. He worked as a general assignment reporter and utility infielder on the *Chronicle*'s national desk, catching stories that fell into the cracks between beats and providing vacation relief for the beat reporters. He liked that role because it kept him from getting stale. He was a quick study who could slip into a complicated story and pick it up without missing a nuance. Pace admired Brennan's professional talents without qualification. The man's personal habits were something else again.

Jillian Hughes was arguably the best looking woman on the *Chronicle* staff, but she was cool, almost cold, in her relationships with her fellow journalists. She made it plain from the day she came on board that she didn't believe in dating at work because it could create conflicts in an atmosphere tense to begin with. The male population in the newsroom had to settle for friendship on her terms or no relationship at all. Some were put off by the ultimatum and opted out of her life, which suited her fine. Pace was one of those who was able to appreciate what Hughes added to the ambience of the newsroom and leave it at that.

Brennan, on the other hand, viewed Hughes as a personal challenge, and his efforts to bed her had become a good-natured sparring contest in which Hughes never failed to prevail. Pace was certain Glenn would faint dead away if Jillian ever accepted one of his invitations for "a couple of drinks and see how it goes."

Professionally, Hughes was considered one of the paper's rising stars. She was a full ten years younger than Pace but already held the Number 2 position on the *Chronicle* Senate staff.

Brennan and Hughes saw the overflow crowd in the conference room and chose to talk to Pace instead, pulling chairs up to his desk. Brennan nodded toward the meeting. "I gather that's a gang-bang on the crash," he said through a huge yawn.

"That's one way to put it." Pace laughed. "How goes the vigil of the passenger list?"

"We were up to forty-nine names when the relief troops showed up this morning," Brennan replied, sounding like a cheap imitation of John Kennedy. He lit a cigarette, holding it in his teeth with his head tilted back to keep the acrid smoke from curling into his eyes. He dropped the dead match on the carpet. Hughes leaned over, picked it up and deposited it in a wastebasket with a look of disgust. Brennan didn't notice, any more than he noticed the signs clearly proclaiming the newsroom a smoke-free environment.

Suddenly he sat forward in his chair, a broad grin splitting his face. "When our first edition hit the streets with your stories, it caused a hell of a stir out there, boyo. You should have seen it. The reporters were going absolutely apeshit. Apparently the NTSB found the Cessna, but none of the ConPac people knew about it, and the NTSB wasn't talking until this morning, I guess until they identified the pilot and notified his family. The guys from the *Post* were all over the airport people and ConPac about how you happened to get to the mid-field terminal. None of the people in charge admitted to knowing a thing about it. Jill and I were just sitting back loving it. By the by, I've got the Cessna pilot's name here if you want it."

Without waiting for an answer, Brennan started flipping through his top-bound spiral notebook, his illicit cigarette still clenched between his teeth, the ash growing precariously long. At the last moment, just before gravity would have taken it, Brennan cupped his hand under the ash, extracted what was left of the cigarette from his mouth with his thumb and forefinger, and dumped the whole mess into his nearly empty Styrofoam coffee cup. There was a brief but audible hiss. Pace could imagine what the muddy mixture of institutional coffee, powdered creamer, ash and dead cigarette must look like, but he didn't dwell on it.

Brennan found the notes he was looking for. "Howard Kisparich, that was the Cessna pilot's name," he said. "Virginia lawyer. The plane was out of Manassas, but nobody knows what it was doing at Dulles. He was alone."

Jill was rolling her head, trying to loosen up tight and tired neck muscles. "Alone. Only one more dead. That's about the only good news we've heard," she said absently.

"Not quite." Brennan smiled. "Among the passenger names released so far is the honorable representative from Orange County, California, Henry W. Whitlock, defender of truth, justice, and the American way, definitely not in that order. Another old Bircher gone to his great reward."

Hughes's head stopped rotating abruptly. "Glenn, that's terrible. You don't celebrate a man's death just because you don't like his politics."

"Ye do in my old neighborhood, Jillie, me sweet lass. Yes, indeedy, ye do."

Pace's phone rang. He whirled around and grabbed the receiver before the first tone died.

It was Con Phillips at the FAA. Pace asked him if there were any airworthiness directives on the 811 fleet—notices to aircraft operators when the FAA or the manufacturer believes something on a particular model needs to be modified or checked for trouble.

"I checked on it last thing yesterday afternoon," Phillips replied. "We have no record of any ADs on the Eight-eleven."

"How about accident or incident reports, or service-difficulty reports?" Pace pressed.

"I checked that out, too," Phillips said, his voice heavy with fatigue. "Fleet-wide, there've been twenty-nine service-difficulty reports, but Oke City tells me there isn't a serious problem in the lot. There are also eight incident reports, fleet-wide. That's not too bad for a new-generation aircraft. Apparently there's no pattern to the problems, or at least not enough that anybody here pulled them up for review. Specifically on the Sexton at Dulles, there's nothing. I think you had that in the paper this morning. I've ordered all the reports up, though, because I'm sure NTSB will ask. And, to answer your next question, they should be here late today or early tomorrow. But since they didn't arouse concern earlier, I doubt you'll find anything but routine problems."

"I need to find out for myself," Pace told the FAA flack.

"Hey, I know that," Phillips snapped defensively. "Call me late this afternoon, and if they're here, you'll come over.

I don't expect to be going home for a few days, so if it's late, it's okay. You have my after-hours number?"

Pace repeated it to him and got confirmation. Phillips started to hang up, but the reporter's voice drew him back to the phone. "Con, do you have a list of the members of the go-team?"

"Try the NTSB. It's their show."

"I tried, but nobody's available. So I'm asking you. Private question. Private favor."

"Jesus, Steve, what do you want from me? Yeah, I've got the names for liaison purposes only. And that doesn't mean liaison with the media."

"Come on," Pace urged. "That's not eyes-only information. I just want a look at it."

"Right, to see if there are any familiar arms you can twist. Media leaks are real sore spots with the pilot and controller unions. They're super-sensitive anyway, and they figure information leaked out of context amounts to a campaign to discredit their people. And I don't have to remind you how the NTSB hates speculation based on reports from 'informed sources.' It usually turns out to be wrong, but it puts them under enormous pressure for confirmation they don't have."

"What are you worried about? What I do isn't your responsibility."

"It's not in anybody's best interest to louse up relations on this thing."

"Let me look at the list, Con," Pace said again. "All I'm asking is a favor that will save me some time. You know *National Enquirer* isn't my style."

There was a pause on the other end. "You asshole," Phillips said. "I've got a meeting in forty minutes. Get here before then and maybe we can have a private conversation in my office."

"Hey, thanks, Con," Pace replied, but the FAA information chief had hung up.

The first thing Pace checked was the identities of the specialists assigned to the NTSB's power-plants group. The group

leader was Elliott Parkhall. His team was Howard Comchech, William Teller, and Mark Antravanian. None of the
names meant anything to the reporter, but there were two
other names in other groups that did.

The first was Captain Michael McGill, chief pilot for
TransAmerican Airlines and chief training pilot for Sexton
811 crews at TAA's facility outside Memphis. The NTSB
had assigned McGill to head the go-team's systems group,
and Pace couldn't think of anyone better qualified. They
had first met fifteen years earlier, when the pilot was assigned to the NTSB investigation of the collision over San
Diego. Their rapport was immediate. McGill's assignment
to the air-traffic-control group put him at the center of that
probe, and he gave Pace excellent guidance through the
story. After the American DC-10 accident in Chicago,
McGill suggested the series that copped the Pulitzer Prize,
a professional achievement for which Pace gave McGill
considerable credit. The two became fast friends, both personal and professional.

During subsequent years, McGill made himself available
when Pace needed technical advice on aviation stories.
Whenever Pace passed through Memphis, McGill met him
at the airport for a couple of drinks, or for dinner if there
was time, and they never failed to get together on those
more frequent occasions when McGill's business for Trans-
American brought him to Washington.

The pilot would be an excellent source inside the investigation, and if nothing else, he would be someone reliable off
whom Pace could bounce ideas and theories.

So, too, was Eddie Conklin, a computer specialist at the
NTSB's Bureau of Technology, whose name also appeared
on the go-team list. Ironically, Pace met Conklin at a party
on Capitol Hill the previous year, a party to which the
reporter had been invited by Kathy McGovern. Over loud
music and good Scotch, Pace and Conklin became friends,
and Pace made it his business a few weeks later to drop in
on Conklin and take the grand tour of the NTSB lab. Most

of the technology was over Pace's head, but he'd considered it time well spent.

Pace called Conklin before leaving the District of Columbia for Dulles and was told the technician was in a meeting. He started to leave a message, but decided it wasn't a good idea for anybody at the NTSB to be reminded that Conklin had a friend at the *Chronicle*. He had Eddie's home number; he'd get in touch with him later.

If Pace hadn't stopped to call Conklin and had arrived at Dulles a few minutes earlier, or if he had reached Conklin and been a few minutes later, he would have missed George Ridley in the airport parking lot. As it was, he spotted the chief of staff of the Senate Science and Transportation Committee emerging from the main terminal building and hailed him as he was getting into his car.

5

Friday, April 18th, 11:00 A.M.
George Ridley did not look happy.

He ducked out of his car when Pace called him and pushed himself to his feet. His face was deeply flushed. He was breathing heavily, and his ample stomach strained the buttons on the front of his blue shirt. The knot on his tie was almost hidden beneath his second chin and appeared to be trying to strangle him under a shirt collar a size too small. He had sweated dark circles through the underarms of his ancient seersucker suit coat, and the shock of brown hair that fell over his forehead was matted there, although the air temperature was barely seventy degrees.

Pace meant only to say hello and pass a few minutes

chatting about the Sexton accident; he was not prepared for the sight of a man who appeared to be a few heartbeats from a coronary.

"Hey, George, you okay?"

"Fine. What do you want?"

"Nothing special," Pace replied.

Ridley's breathing was fast and shallow, and Pace feared he would hyperventilate. He grabbed Ridley's shoulders and shook him slightly.

"What's the matter with you?"

Ridley's eyes flashed, and he threw his arms up roughly to loosen Pace's hands. "Get the fuck off me! I'm not in the mood for your glad tidings."

"Okay," Pace said, backing off a step. "We've established you're pissed as hell at me. Mind telling me why?"

Ridley inhaled once, deeply, and his breathing became more regular. "It isn't you specifically. It's the world, the whole fucking world, and the scumbags who inhabit it," he raged. "It's people who think God made them better than everybody else, so they don't have to be accountable like the rest of us slobs. It's one motherfucking senior senator from Ohio, if you want to be specific. One goddamn motherfucking senior senator from Ohio, who thinks I'm his goddamn go-fer. Thirty-one years I've got in on the Hill, and that prick still thinks he can use me for a goddamn go-fer. And all that's off the record."

Pace opened his mouth to reply, but the whole scene was so ludicrous he had no adequate response.

Ridley was pacing up and down beside his car, flapping his arms like an overweight mockingbird, scuffing at pebbles, real and imagined. Pace let him rant. That was George.

"What's Marshall got to do with you?" Pace asked when Ridley's tirade blew itself out. "He's a Republican. You're majority staff, unless I missed an election."

Ridley tossed his head in disgust. "Stop being naive. You know how things work."

"You're talking in riddles, George. I don't know the answers, because you haven't specified the questions."

"So I'll draw it out for you. But I mean this: off the record."

Pace nodded.

"That bastard insisted he needed a liaison with the investigators on the ConPac accident. The senior senator from Ohio is very solicitious of Converse. Converse makes its jet engines in Youngstown, Ohio—as you well know—and that makes the company a VFIC, one of Senator Harold Marshall's very fucking important constituents. So he wants to know everything the investigators find out about the accident."

Pace shrugged. "I don't like Marshall much, either, but that doesn't sound unreasonable, except he sent you instead of Chappy."

"That's the other thing pisses me off," Ridley snapped, beginning to pace again. "Chappy ain't anywhere around. All hell's breaking loose, and he goes off somewhere to contemplate his fucking muscles. So I tell Marshall, 'You can't get Chappy Davis, send somebody else from the minority side.' But he says he's got to have a high-ranking aide, that it's gotta be me or Chappy, and Chappy's busy. 'Make him unbusy,' I say. But the man says Chappy's doin' something really important, so I gotta do this. Then he puffs himself up and says, 'May I remind you that majority and minority staffs work for the whole committee, regardless of party.' He thinks I don't know that? He's lecturing me like I'm some snot-nosed intern, and he's so damned sanctimonious about it. I can't stand the bastard. Hell, my pension's vested. I could get some cushy industry job, build up another pension, and retire with big bucks and no ulcers. I have half a mind to go back and kick Marshall's ass so hard he'll shit through his collar for a week."

Pace couldn't help himself; he began laughing. Ridley's language was always colorful, but a good, righteous anger gave him supreme inspiration.

"It's not funny," Ridley protested. "The guy he sent me to see is Vernon Lund. You know Lund at all?" Pace nodded, but Ridley was too wound up to wait for a response and plunged ahead. "He a fucking-A asshole. Stuffed-shirt, self-righteous sonofabitch, just like Marshall. And you wanna know the message I had to deliver?"

Pace shook his head. "I hesitate even to hazard a guess."

"That the investigators better tread real light around Converse, and if they blame the engine for the accident, they better make damned sure they're right, or Marshall's gonna bring the full weight of the committee down on their heads. He said to tell Lund it would be better for everybody if problems with the engine were—and these are his words—downplayed as much as possible."

Now Pace wasn't laughing, either. "Marshall actually told you to say that?"

Ridley nodded emphatically. "You know what that is? It's called a Nixon, as in cover-up. At the very least, it would put the Transportation Committee in a hole full of shit if we had to conduct hearings on this mess. How are we gonna look unbiased if it comes out the ranking Republican's been threatening the NTSB?"

"Why didn't you tell Marshall to go to hell?"

Ridley shook his head and shrugged. "Because I didn't want the hassle. But I hate myself for it. Damn him to hell anyway—"

"Wait a second," Pace interrupted. "You sure you got the message right? You're not overblowing it a little because you hate the guy so much?"

"Absolutely not," Ridley insisted.

Pace frowned. "That's serious," he said. "Would Lund take Marshall at his word?"

Ridley had exhausted himself and leaned heavily on his car door, sweating again. "I don't think so," he said. "The NTSB doesn't cut deals; they're pretty self-righteous themselves about that. If it's your fault, they nail you. I just don't like working for Marshall. And I don't like being treated like a pockfaced sixteen-year-old page, for chrissake."

"I thought it was a snot-nosed intern," Pace recalled.

"Whatever . . ." Ridley waved off the joke, and Pace grew serious again.

"Still, if Marshall should carry through somehow, it would kind of fall to you to blow the whistle on him."

Ridley's head jerked up, his eyes narrow with suspicion. "I know my responsibilities, and they aren't to get you the good scoops."

"I'm not only talking stories here," Pace snapped. Ridley's accusation smarted because it was nearly on the mark. "I don't want to see *any* problem on a commercial jetliner covered up for *any* reason by *anybody.*"

Ridley nodded and scuffed at the ground some more. "Yeah, me too. The NTSB wouldn't let that happen, I'm pretty sure. That's not sayin' jerks wouldn't try." He waved his hand in a gesture of dismissal. "Hell, I should take it to my boss and let him deal with the bastard."

"Helmutsen never dealt with anything like this in his life," Pace said.

"But, of course, you'd be willing to take it on?" Ridley oozed sarcasm.

"Damned right," Pace replied.

Ridley put a hand over his heart. "I will sleep better tonight knowing you're out there willing to give your all for the integrity of the U.S. of A."

Pace laughed again. "I'm glad I'm not the one you're pissed at, George. You're tough."

"And don't you forget it."

Pace gave him a backhand slap on the shoulder and headed for the terminal building. "Not a chance. I'm outta here before you tear my face off."

Inside the terminal building, Pace leaned against a wall and scribbled three pages of notes on his conversation with Ridley. The subject might never come up again, but if it did, he would need a reliable record of Ridley's allegations. Pace wondered what had prompted Marshall to risk trying to influence an NTSB investigation. Ridley obviously thought Marshall's concern for Converse was sufficient motive. Pace didn't. If Marshall was trying to subvert the investigation, disclosure of that could ruin him politically. Hell, it could send him to prison. You don't take a risk like that in the name of constituent service. He made some further notes to cover those questions, snapped his notebook closed and rode an escalator to the main level.

The terminal was littered with the detritus of the thousands of participants in the tragedy of the day before. Empty maroon-and-white Marriott coffee cups, waxed-paper Coke cups, candy and sandwich wrappers, and crumpled cigarette packs were mounded in cylindrical receptacles that couldn't hold the volume.

The airport was operating again, albeit with only one of its three runways open, and the throaty roars of departures and arrivals came quickly, one atop another, as controllers sought to keep air traffic flowing under severely constrained conditions.

Pace couldn't see the crash site from the terminal, but he could make out the silhouette of the crane used to stabilize the fuselage. Glenn Brennan was down there reporting on the operation to recover bodies. Pace knew from experience the process of extracting victims and personal effects could take days, the removal of the wreckage even longer. In the meantime, for perhaps a week or more, passengers arriving and departing on Dulles flights would be able to look down and see huge pieces of the dead Sexton strewn around the grassland. After that, after all of the aircraft was removed, they still would be able to see the burned and blackened spots that would serve as Flight 1117's epitaph until spring growth next year covered the area in green.

Pace spotted two ambulances crossing the field under escort, their tragic cargoes undoubtedly bound for the refrigerated morgue trucks. There also were several baggage haulers pulling sections of black and twisted metal—small pieces that had been checked, inventoried, and cleared for removal—toward a gaping hangar that carried the ConPac logo. That would be Hangar 3, where the Sexton 811 would be reconstructed, and in all likelihood, where he would find McGill. Pace knew he couldn't get into the hangar. Somehow, he had to bring McGill out.

Behind him, he heard the alarm of a walk-through metal detector. Watching uniformed security people wait for the bewildered pass nger to empty his pockets, Pace devised his plan. It was slightly unethical, but hard times call for resourcefulness, and these times qualified as hard.

The airport police offices were located at the west end of the lower level. So Pace took the easternmost escalator down and ran the length of the terminal building. At the door marked "Dulles International Airport Police," he skated to a stop, achieving the effect he wanted. He was sweating lightly and breathing hard. Thirty-nine and out of shape, the typical American male. *Shit!* He pulled open the glass door, trying to look as though he were on urgent business. The officer behind the counter was young and smartly decked out in uniform.

"I'm Steven Pace from the *Chronicle*," he gasped. "Sorry to bother you, but I've got an emergency. I need to call my office right away. You have a phone I could borrow for a minute?"

"I'm not supposed to," the young police officer said hesitantly. "There are pay phones all over the terminal." His badge identified him as C. Arguilla. Pace fished for his wallet and pulled out his press cards, all widely recognized by police authorities around Washington.

"You're really Pace, huh? I read your stories about the crash this morning. They were very sad. Very good."

"Officer Arguilla, this is important." Pace's breath was coming easier. He sensed the young policeman would like to help and pressed his advantage. "Look, I've come up with some new information on the crash yesterday, and I've got to call my editors. It's an exclusive story. I don't want to have the conversation at a public phone."

That was too important a mission for Arguilla to send him away. He motioned Pace into the office and pointed to an empty cubicle at the back of the room. "You can go in there. You'll have privacy."

Pace thanked him and moved toward the cubicle fast enough to convey urgency. No sense lousing up a good show at the end of the first act.

He got the number for Dulles Operations out of his pocket address book and dialed it.

"Operations. Johnson."

"Yeah. This is Pace at Airport Police. You got the phone number for the NTSB over at Hangar Three?"

"Yeah, hang on."

Pace could hear papers shuffling and repressed an urge to hold his breath.

"Uh, yeah, here it is. Five-five-five-eight-seven-six-three."

"Thanks." Pace hung up quickly. Act Two had gone as planned, although he'd lied his way through it. Well, maybe lied wasn't the right word. After all, his name *was* Pace, and he *was* "at" Airport Police headquarters. He hadn't said he was "with" or "employed by" the police. The essence of truth made him feel better. Besides, he had a number where he could find Mike McGill, and that was what mattered.

On his way out of the office, Arguilla approached him. "What's your big story?" he asked with a grin. "When I see it in the paper tomorrow, I'll know I was there when you called it in."

Pace shook his head. "I work for an idiot," he said, feigning anger. "He isn't sure he wants to run it tomorrow. Maybe in a day or two. But I promise, you'll know it when you see it."

As he walked out the door, he saw Arguilla frowning. Either the police officer didn't understand, or he understood all too well. In either event, Act Three was not being well received by the critics.

Using the private number, this time from a pay phone, Pace reached McGill on the first try. Sometimes reporting was ridiculously easy.

TransAm's chief pilot sounded genuinely happy to hear from him, but he was in the middle of a briefing and couldn't get away. They agreed to meet for lunch in an hour at the airport's Marriott Hotel, headquarters of the go-team.

With time to kill, and remembering Schaeffer's order to
keep in touch, Pace called Paul Wister. He advised the
national editor he didn't have a lot yet for the next day but
was having lunch with McGill. He knew Wister would be
concerned about the slow-developing story; urgency was
Paul's style.

Wister was a tall, slim, studious sort who served as counterpoint to Avery Schaeffer. While Schaeffer worried about
the big picture, Wister worked the details. While Schaeffer
rolled up his sleeves and loosened his tie, Wister lectured on
the values of propriety, appearance, and duty. Wister never
loosened his tie or took off his suit coat at work, never
raised his voice anywhere, and only once in recorded history
had anyone caught him in a grammatical error. During a
staff softball game against *The Washington Post* in nineteen
eighty-five, after trying to stretch a triple to deep left into a
home run and being thrown out at the plate, it was alleged
he used a "he" where a "him" was proper during the ensuing argument with the umpire. Wister denied it to this day.
He also continued to claim he was safe. The incident was a
part of the *Chronicle*'s newsroom lore, and it was funny to
everyone but Paul Wister.

Pace could picture him leaning back in his chair and
considering the possibilities for Saturday copy, all the while
tapping his right temple with his fountain pen. Wister collected fine fountain pens. He worshiped at the altar of Wa-
terman and Mont Blanc.

"We need information on the probable cause," Wister
said. " 'Why' is still the biggest question. If it was the engine, why? If it wasn't, what was it? Keep after it hard. We'll
have a lot of good sidebar stuff, and Glenn's body-recovery
story, but the accident's still the lead. Sexton and Converse
issued the typical statements: There will be no statements
until the investigation is over. The desk is putting the wire
copy in your basket, but you ought to check with your
contacts to see if they'll go any farther, maybe on background."

On a whim, Pace told Wister about his conversation with

George Ridley. Wister reacted as Pace had, saying the information meant little unless Marshall actually interfered in the investigation.

"I'll mention it to Avery, though," Wister added with a chuckle. "It'll jump-start his heart."

"I could take some time and try to verify what George told me," Pace suggested.

"We can't spare you now," Wister said. "Besides, nothing improper's been done that we know of. Let it alone, and get after something for page one tomorrow."

Pace put in obligatory phone calls to Whitney Warner, vice-president for public affairs of the Sexton Aircraft Corporation in Los Angeles, and Cullen Ferguson, vice-president for corporate relations of the Converse Corporation in Youngstown. He'd talked with each the day before, after the accident, and they'd offered nothing of substance. Today neither was available. He left his office number with their secretaries.

There was nothing more to do at the airport, so Pace drove to the Marriott and found himself standing conspicuously idle in the lobby, with forty minutes to wait until McGill showed, assuming he was on time.

He bought a copy of *Time* with regret. The cover date said it was obsolete. "You have this week's edition?" he asked the counter girl.

"That's the only one," she replied indifferently. So he paid for it, sank into a comfortable lobby chair and began to read old news, the dullest material imaginable.

McGill arrived promptly at twelve-thirty and rescued Pace from a four-page takeout on the foreign-trade deficit. The pilot was dressed in Levi's, western boots, a Patagonia sport shirt, and had a cracked brown-leather flight jacket thrown casually over his right shoulder and held in place by a finger hooked through a chain loop inside the collar. He might have stepped from the pages of an Eddie Bauer catalogue. The outfit, so casually put together under a thick crop of salt-and-pepper hair and hazel eyes, served to show how well he cared for his body, even into his fifties. The effect was natural, not deliberate, but Pace could see by the hint of a self-satisfied smile on the pilot's face that McGill was well aware of the seven pairs of female eyes following every move he made through the lobby. Women, in infinite variety, were Mike McGill's top hobby.

Pace's pleasure at seeing McGill again was tempered only slightly by a news dealer's delivery man, who entered the lobby behind the pilot and threw a bundle of new *Time* magazines onto the floor five feet away.

"Easy come, easy go," Pace muttered and tossed his barely read edition into the white sand of an institutional ashtray.

Lunch began a little stiffly over prosciutto and melon. Pace asked about McGill's work, and McGill inquired about Pace's job and his love life. They talked about the weather in Tennessee and the weather in Washington. McGill needled Pace for what had to be the hundredth time about how he should get his pilot's license if he was going to be an aviation writer. Both skirted the reason they were having lunch together.

Pace was halfway through a nicely done bluefish fillet, feeling childish about his reluctance to broach the subject of the crash investigation, when he saw McGill grinning at him.

"This is the point at which you're supposed to put your napkin down, lean across the table, look to each side to make sure no one's eavesdropping, and say to me, 'Mike, small talk isn't the real reason I asked you here today.' " They both laughed, and Pace felt marginally better.

"I don't want you to think I'm abusing our friendship," the reporter said.

"I don't," McGill said. "I know what your job is, and I accept that. But right now I don't have anything to help you. We don't have the bodies out, let alone the wreckage in the hangar."

Pace frowned and nodded. "Any choice speculation?"

"Everybody's got a pet theory," McGill said. "Most involve the right engine, big surprise. Preliminary accounts from a few witnesses indicate there was an explosion in the engine, or a defect in the pod's attachment to the pylon. God, I hope it isn't another one of those.''

"Square One City, huh?"

McGill hedged. "Well, maybe not quite that bad. I picked up some scuttlebutt a couple of minutes ago that we might be looking at a bird strike.''

Pace looked surprised. He was almost disappointed that it should be anything so mundane. "A bird strike? Really?"

McGill held up his knife like a stop sign. "I said 'might be,' remember? Apparently there's something in the engine that looks like the remains of a bird. Nobody knows for sure. Lund will cover it at the press briefing tonight, I'm sure.''

McGill finished his sea bass, laid the knife and fork carefully across his plate, and sat back in the banquette. "I don't mind helping you on this, Steve," he said. "We've always worked well together, and I don't expect that to change. I don't mind telling you about the bird rumor, because a lot of people know, and it's going to come out later today anyhow. If and when it goes beyond that, I'll have to be circumspect about what I disclose, and I hope you understand. We're supposed to play things close to the vest, and there are good reasons. This is a system that's never been questioned, either in its effectiveness or its integrity. As much as I want to help you, I can't jeopardize that.''

Pace nodded. The mention of the integrity of the NTSB reminded him of his conversation earlier with George Ridley. He told McGill about it. The pilot's reaction was a little stronger than Paul Wister's had been.

"I don't like the idea of anybody trying to leverage us, but as you say, it may be nothing more than constituent concern. I've got things to worry about more important than a nosy senator.''

"But if you hear Marshall's pressing this, will you let me know?" Pace asked.

"You bet," McGill promised. "That's a whole new ball

game. I wouldn't hesitate to help you nail somebody trying to skewer our work."

Pace smiled. "I'll know I've pressed too hard when you quit returning my phone calls."

McGill laced his fingers together and leaned forward with his chin on his thumbs. He chose his words carefully. "I can't imagine a situation in which I wouldn't return your calls," he said. "Even though I'm going to be under constraints about what I can say, if you want to call to knock around some ideas, I'll try not to let you go to press with bad information. If you call me and tell me you've heard A and you've heard B, I'd be willing to tell you to lay off A. If you wish to infer that B's the right course, I can live with it, because I won't have violated my trust here. Am I making any sense to you?"

He was, Pace thought. Mike McGill always made sense.

"In the parlance of Washington, what you're saying is you'll give me guidance," Pace joked. "That's as opposed to going off-the-record, on deep background, plain background, and not-for-attribution."

"Ah, yes. The games we play in Washington, D.C."

"No games." Pace smiled. "Attribution is very serious business here. Not knowing the rules can lose you access to sources overnight. It's an art form. The best innovations are voted into a hall of fame and immortalized on a wall at The Grapevine, a press pub downtown."

McGill looked skeptical. "Okay," Pace said. "I'll test you. Name this official, and I pick up the check. He was best known as 'a senior official on the President's airplane.' "

"Come on, Steve. That's too easy."

"Okay, if it's so easy, who was it?"

"Henry Kissinger, during Nixon's second term, such as it was."

Pace's eyebrows arched. "How'd you know that?"

"The whole world knows it. The Russians, the Chinese, the Israelis, the Tierra del Fuegans. I think Kissinger probably told them himself: 'Watch for me. I'm the one who'll be identified as the senior official on the President's airplane.' "

They laughed, and then the waitress came and put the check on the table, a discreet equal distance between them. McGill picked it up and made a show of handing it to Pace.

"Let it be a lesson for you. You're not the only one who knows history. In fact, you weren't even in Washington during the Nixon administration. You only heard stories about the senior official on the President's plane. I was there."

"You were? I didn't know that."

"You knew I went to TransAm out of the Air Force?"

Pace nodded, and McGill grinned. "My last duty station was at Andrews Air Force Base. My assignment was pilot-in-command of Air Force One during the final months of Richard Nixon's first administration."

Pace's chin dropped. "Are you serious? As many years as we've known each other, and you never told me that?"

McGill eased out of the banquette and headed for the door. "Well, the crews never want to assume a very high profile. Part of the mystique, I guess. Besides, you never asked. First rule of a good reporter is always ask everything. I learned that on Air Force One, too." He put a toothpick in the corner of his mouth and waved. "Thanks for lunch. And call me anytime. I'll do what I can for you."

6

Friday, April 18th, 3:00 P.M.
After paying the lunch check, Pace walked out of the dark restaurant into the sunny lobby. He squinted in reflex and turned away from the windows. His gaze fell on McGill, who was performing his best manly act for the girl at the

hotel newsstand. It didn't look as though Mike was trying seriously to pick her up, just reassuring himself the act still worked.

Pace waited for him at the lobby door. "Aren't you a little long in years to be driven all the time by your glandular activity?" the reporter asked.

"Hormones 'R' Us," McGill responded, mirth dancing at the corners of his smile. "Actually, I was killing time waiting for you."

"I could see."

"No kidding. Thought you might like to come down to the field, breathe in a little of the color of the accident."

"Those bodies have been in the plane a long time. It's not color I'd be breathing."

"It's all part of the grim reality. But not to worry, I can't take you to the plane anyway. Just to the field."

"How? It's off limits."

"You can go with me."

"The IIC won't approve."

"Probably not. That's why I'm not asking him."

"Let's do it."

They went in McGill's official car. The guard at the gate by Hangar 3 looked closely at Pace's credentials and frowned.

"He's with me," McGill assured him. "Consider him under escort."

"Yes, sir," the guard said and waved them through.

They drove more than three-fourths of the way down Runway 19-right, stopping well short of the main wreckage, in an area filled with little red flags on wires stuck in the ground. Each flag marked a piece of debris. The concrete runway beside their car was deeply gouged.

"Let's see what we've found," McGill said as he stepped gingerly into the grass. Pace followed. The investigator crouched beside one flag and picked up a tangled mass of wires.

"A piece of the electrical harness," he said. "Might have come from the broken wing."

"How'd it get here?" Pace asked.

"Well, let's speculate," McGill suggested. "The main wreckage skidded to a stop in the grass off the end of Nineteen-right, down there." He nodded to Pace's left. "The tip of the right wing hit the runway about fifty yards back up that way." He pointed to the reporter's right. "You saw how messed up the concrete is by the car?"

"Yeah."

"That's where the engine and wing section were torn from the fuselage," McGill said. "They bounced once—that's the big gouge in the ground beside you—then cartwheeled and came to rest over there. They burned until the fuel in the wing cells was spent."

"So the runway right here is where she actually went over on her side," Pace said.

"This is it," McGill confirmed. "You just walked across it."

"God, that's eerie. You ever get used to it?" Pace asked, recalling his own discomfort as he watched the immediate aftermath of the accident.

"Never. And I never want to," McGill said.

Pace nodded at the wires in McGill's hand. "How did that get here?"

"Dunno. It probably fell out of the wing when it hit here."

"And all these flags mark other stuff that fell out?"

"That'd be my guess."

"Jesus, what a mess."

Across the grass, a man yelled, "Hey, Mike, can you take a look at something for me?"

McGill turned and waved. "Be right there." He turned back to Pace. "Wait for me. Soak up some atmosphere while I'm gone."

Pace strolled among the flags, careful not to step on anything. Most of the flags marked hunks of twisted metal. How anyone could identify what these scraps had been was beyond imagining.

Fifteen minutes passed, and McGill still was deeply involved in conversation with another investigator. Pace headed for the car to make notes on what he'd seen. It would make excellent descriptive material. Near the edge of the grass, he kicked something that felt like a stone. He glanced down and saw a metal ball rolling through the matted sod.

"Shit," he muttered, concerned that he'd disturbed a piece of evidence. But there were no little red flags in the area. He picked up the ball and saw a second one a foot away. He scuffed around in the grass, and within minutes he'd spotted three more, five in all.

He had no idea what they were, but since they weren't marked, they probably weren't important. He slipped the ball he'd picked up into the side pocket of his sport coat, intending to show it to Mike. But when McGill came running up to the car a few minutes later, Pace was deep into writing dramatic notes, and the metal ball was forgotten.

"I'm sorry I've got to cut this short, hotshot, but Vern Lund's looking for me, and he's all agitated about something."

"No problem," Pace replied. "This was very helpful."

After leaving McGill, Pace spent a useless hour prowling around Dulles, more for inspiration than information. He checked with his office, but neither the Sexton nor the Converse public-relations people had returned his calls. He felt frustrated about the bird-strike angle. It was his exclusive at the moment, but Pace hadn't the faintest hope it would survive the evening's NTSB briefing. It would be nice at a time like this to be a television journalist—to go on the air with a special report and give the world the big scoop that some off-course seagull had brought down a modern jetliner. *Now there's a defense system for you. Jonathan Livingston Starwars.* Then again, the bulletin would interrupt an afternoon soap, and viewers, instead of being grateful for the news, would be pissed at missing what Monica said to Kelly about Natalie. Hell, he'd stick with print.

Con Phillips at the FAA told Pace the accident-and-incident reports on the Sexton fleet would be available for all media in half an hour. Pace was stuck at Dulles at least until after the briefing. He asked Phillips to put a set of documents in an envelope and leave them for a *Chronicle* messenger, who would be sent to pick them up.

"No problem," Phillips said. "They aren't worth rushing back for."

"Well, so much for a great Saturday lead," Pace complained. "Anything else going on?"

"We've listened to the tapes of transmissions between Flight Eleven-seventeen and controllers," Phillips said. "There's not a lot there, either. The Sexton was cleared for takeoff, the captain rogered the clearance and said he was rolling. Thirty-eight seconds later he called back to the tower and started to say something, but he stopped, and that was the last we heard from him. If anything else was said in the cockpit, it was said without the pilots keying the radio mike."

"You releasing a transcript?"

"If you want it, I'll stick it in the packet with the A-and-I reports."

"What about the cockpit voice recorder? It's active even when the cockpit mikes aren't."

"The NTSB will sit on 'em for the usual sixty days. I've heard nothing to the contrary."

Pace called Wister. While waiting for the national editor to pick up, he considered the A-and-I reports. They must be duds. If there was anything in them, the FAA would drag its feet to prevent speculation about what happened to Flight 1117. Public documents are public documents, but some are more public than others.

He told Wister of the bird-strike speculation, including the expectation that Lund would make it public at his six-thirty briefing. He asked Wister to send a messenger to get the reports from the FAA, promising to be back in the office in time to go over them before the early deadline. The intriguing bits of information, he said, would be the FAA tape transcript and the investigative detail he'd picked up at the crash scene with Mike. Wister said he'd have the library research bird-strike problems nationally and locally and have the clips in Pace's computer when he returned.

The reporter bought a large cup of black coffee and carried it to the observation deck above the main terminal building. He was surprised to find himself in the company of Justin Smith.

"Mr. Smith comes from Washington," Pace cracked. "I liked that movie."

"What brings a nice boy like you to a lonely place like this?" Smith asked. "Spyin' on me?"

Pace chuckled. "Yeah," he said. "Hopin' to pick up some reporting tips from the master."

"Good thing you didn't say 'old master.' "

They leaned on the railing, gazing south toward the site where grim work continued on the wreckage. Pace sipped his coffee.

"I'm thinking about changing beats, Justin," he said.

Smith's eyebrows shot up. "God's name, why?" he asked. "Way you've been knockin' off exclusives, you should feel great about your work."

Pace shook his head and nodded to the south. "You've been down there," he said. "You've seen the carnage. Over the years, you've probably seen more of it than I have. I don't know how you deal with it."

"Don't think about it, mostly, I guess. Not like I caused it."

Pace smiled. "You mean it's nasty work, but somebody's gotta do it."

"Somethin' like that." Smith turned around and leaned his back against the deck wall, his weight on his elbows. "Somethin' I probably shouldn't be tellin' you, but it could have a bearin' on your decision to seek a new career," he said. "Be sixty-two in October. Already decided to retire early. *Times* management has talked to me about who'll fill my slot. Your name keeps comin' up."

"*My* name?" Pace was incredulous.

"Yep. Think you're probably the best available."

"Who thinks so, Justin? Management? You?"

"Both."

"That's nice, but it would be a hard jump to make."

"Still," Smith said, "even if you said no to the *Times*, management of your rag probably would offer you a hefty raise to stay put."

"I don't play those games," Pace told him. "That's coercion."

Smith looked at Pace and grinned. "Not so," he replied. "As they say in Texas, it's bidness."

"It's nice to know I'm well thought of," Pace said. "A lot can happen between now and October." He looked up at the bright, early evening sky. The sun hadn't yet set. "You know, I don't even want to think about October," he said. "The days start getting short. And they keep getting shorter until the end of December. It's depressing."

"What on God's green earth does that have to do with takin' a new job?"

Pace laughed. "Nothing, my friend. It's just that I'm a day person, and April is my favorite month. Daylight Savings begins, and the days seem to go on forever. It lifts my spirits, that's all."

"That mean you get all depressed on June twenty-first or twenty-second, or whenever the hell the summer solstice is, 'cause the days start gettin' shorter after that?"

Pace nodded. "Happens to me every June."

"You kiddin'?"

"Nope."

"Damn. I'm goin' back and tell my editors you're a good aviation writer, but you're fuckin' nuts."

They walked together down to the six-thirty briefing. The possibility of a job with the *Times* didn't come up again.

As expected, Lund was up front about the discovery of a "foreign material" in the Converse engine. He refused to say definitely it was a bird, although he came close.

"Why *can't* you say for certain it was a bird?" Jeffrey Hines of the *Los Angeles Times* demanded.

"Because it must be thoroughly examined and tested to determine that," Lund replied.

"Are there feathers?"

"A lot of the material was burned, but there appear to be feathers, yes."

"Are there any creatures on this earth except birds that have feathers?"

"I don't know of any."

"Then it must be a bird."

"That's your conclusion, Mr. Hines. We are only stating what we know, that there was a foreign substance found in the engine, and it appears to be the remains of a feathered creature."

"But you *are* ruling out possible sabotage by terrorists using feathered plastic explosives?"

"I'm not ruling out anything."

At that point the briefing fell apart. Hines told Pace later, as they left together, he hadn't intended to have that impact.

"What I was trying to show is how ludicrous the bureaucracy can be," he said. "He's not going to go out on a limb and say anything until he has seventy-two scientific reports to back him up, and the approval of his superiors to make a statement that means something. I'm going to try to get the paper to print the transcript of that exchange."

"I've got the headline," said Russell Ethrich of the *Post*. "NTSB gives *Times* the bird."

"That's not bad," said Hines. "I'll recommend it."

"One very good thing came out of that little sideshow," Pace offered. "I'm not going to be the only one in the room on Lund's shit list."

"Yeah," said Hines. "Between the *New York Post* yesterday and me today, we're making you look like one of the good guys." They parted at the front of the terminal building. "So what are you going to do, Steve?" Hines asked. "You going to say flatly it was a bird?"

Pace nodded. "I'm going to say flatly that Lund says flatly it might have been something with feathers. I'll let the readers draw their own conclusions."

"Going out on a limb again, huh?" Hines laughed.

"Have to," replied Pace. "That's where the birds are."

There was yet another editorial conference in progress when Pace got back to his desk shortly after eight that evening, and he was glad he'd have a few minutes to read the FAA reports closely before he had to give Paul Wister an assessment.

The first document was the transcript of the 811 crew's exchanges with air traffic control. Everything was normal until the tape picked up Captain Jackson Peck reporting, "Dulles tower, this is ConPac heavy— Stand by, we've got a problem." There was nothing else.

Pace sighed and went to the next documents. The twenty-nine service-difficulty reports were so ordinary as to be boring: burned-out light bulbs, cracked bolts, loose wires—not a thing to hang a story on. Pace knew there probably were more service difficulties with the 811 fleet than the FAA had on record; the reports were voluntary, and often airlines didn't bother to file them.

Pace tossed aside the SDs and turned to the incident reports. They covered more serious problems, and reporting was mandatory. There were eight reports, spanning the Sexton's six months of service. Two were obviously unrelated to the accident at Dulles. The first involved an emergency landing at Dallas-Fort Worth to get medical attention for a copilot with a burst appendix, and the second was an unscheduled stop in Philadelphia to get help for a runaway toilet.

Hot damn.

The remaining reports were only slightly more interesting. One was a landing-gear malfunction the crew corrected with an electrical release of the uplocks. There was one strange incident involving the simultaneous failure of all eight on-board radios, prompting the crew to make a forced landing in Indianapolis by encoding an emergency on the 811's transponder and following light gun instructions signaled from the tower.

Halfway through the reports and Pace had found nothing that linked up with the previous day.

A fifth incident involved the failure of the 811's main electrical bus, wiping out some of the electrical power to the cockpit. Like the bum radios, a partial electrical failure is a serious situation, but not unmanageable for experienced pilots; the aircraft involved got down in Atlanta without damage or injury. Then there was an aborted takeoff resulting in minor damage. The abort was triggered by what was described as a power failure. There were no details. The last two reports described a cabin-pressure problem, relieved by a fast descent to a lower altitude, and an in-flight fire emergency caused by a shorted wire. The small fire—if it even could be called that—was smothered by the flight engineer.

Zilch, zippo, zero, nada, nothing. The declension of the verb form "to be screwed."

The only incident that had even a remote chance of being tied to Dulles was the power failure. Pace remembered the controller, Raiford, told him ConPac 1117 seemed to have trouble gaining enough speed to rotate. Would that properly be termed a power failure? Pace thought not.

He looked back at that report. It was signed by Captain L.K. Junker. The aircraft was a TransAm 811–500, scheduled to fly from Seattle to Anchorage and then on to Japan. It was worth calling McGill. As TransAm's chief pilot, he should be familiar with the incident.

Pace reached him at Hangar 3. "You know a pilot named L.K. Junker?" he asked.

"Larry Junker, sure. He's one of our senior guys."

"Would he be willing to talk to a reporter about an incident a few months ago with an Eight-eleven?"

"You mean the one in Seattle? He shouldn't discuss it outside the company without proper authorization, and I doubt he'd violate that rule. Why do you want him?"

"I don't know. Maybe I'm reaching. His incident report talks about a power failure, and the controller I interviewed yesterday said the ConPac Eight-eleven seemed to be having trouble generating power. I don't know if there's a connection. I'm desperate."

"I doubt it's the same thing, but it's worth checking," McGill agreed. "I'll see if I can run him down. If he's flying, there won't be much I can do until he gets back, but if I find him, I'll authorize him to talk to you."

"Good enough. Thanks, Mike. I appreciate it."

It was 10:00 P.M. before McGill called back. Pace's story for the first edition was pegged to the foreign matter found in the wrecked engine. His next deadline was less than an hour away. The early story would stand if there was nothing to add.

"Sorry it took me so long to get back, Steve. Larry Junker's on a few days' leave, and it took a while to track him down. The bottom line is, he doesn't want to talk to you. Nothing personal. A lot of transport jocks don't like dealing with the media. But he gave me the details of the Seattle thing, and I don't have any problem talking about it. The incident report's public anyhow. You ready to take some notes?"

Pace already had a file open on his computer screen. "All set, Mike. Shoot."

"Let me say first, I'd put this in the realm of interesting, but not conclusive. The crew had initiated their takeoff roll when there was a, well, a bump is the way Larry described it. There was an immediate falloff in power in Number Three engine, and an abort was mandatory. Junker ordered Number Three shut down and taxied her back to the terminal without further problems . . ."

"Number Three!" Pace said in surprise. "That's the same one that failed here."

"Well, there are only three engines on the plane. You've got a one-in-three chance if one fails, it will be the same one that failed before. All the engines are identical. Even the one on the tail is the same as the ones under the wings. Anyhow, our maintenance crew tore down the engine in Seattle and found a crack in one of the turbine disks. We don't know why it cracked. Most likely it was a defect in the titanium alloy. It went back to Converse for testing and analysis. I checked with our ops people, and they say there's been no report yet from Converse on its findings. I presume the disk was simply replaced and the engine put back into service."

"The report said there was minor damage to the aircraft."

"Uh, yeah, I think that's right. Something bent in one of the wheel assemblies. Nothing serious."

"So what does that mean for yesterday?"

"I wish I could tell you it's significant, but I don't know," McGill apologized. "There's certainly the possibility of a connection, but it's far from definitive. There was no damage to our engine beyond the cracked turbine wheel. I'm going to give this to the guys in the power-plants group because I think they should know, but I'd be jumping the gun if I told you it was a key to the ConPac failure. That deed was done by a bird."

"Or something with feathers," Pace responded, telling McGill of Jeff Hines's confrontation with Lund earlier.

McGill laughed, but absently. He had other things on his mind. "Steve, there's something else Larry Junker told me that, frankly, I'd forgotten when we had lunch yesterday. But it's fascinating in the context of this accident."

"What?" Pace asked eagerly.

"In all the hoopla over the Sexton Eight-eleven, one of the things that got overlooked to a degree was the technology that went into the Converse Fan. You should remember. You wrote about it. The engine pod was designed specifically to be more efficient than older generations of engines at channeling ingested debris."

"That's right," Pace said. "There's supposed to be a ... what? A fifty-percent better chance that anything sucked through the fan blades would be routed around the engine instead of through it."

"That's what Converse claims," said McGill. "If you mention it in your story, it would help your readers to know the working part of this jet engine takes up only about half the space inside the pod. The rest is all open. If everything works right, what gets sucked into the front gets blown out the back through that open space around the engine. Every commercial jet engine has that design. The Converse Fan enlarged and improved on it. Seems to me the design should have mitigated the effects of a bird strike fairly easily."

"Unless the bird broke some of the fan blades, and they penetrated the engine."

"Could happen. Probably did happen. But the broken pieces of fan blade should have been routed around the engine works, too."

"What a hell of a story."

"Write it, then. Raise the question. You can quote me on the stuff about the Seattle incident, but raise the question about the engine design on your own. You have the expertise. Hell, it's in Converse's advertising. They made a huge deal of it. Ask how a damned bird could rip up an engine that was supposed to be impervious."

While the information wasn't conclusive, it was enough to allow the reporter to write a much tougher and more complete story, and Pace felt good about it. The competition might have some decent material tomorrow, but they wouldn't have the Seattle angle—thin as it was—and might not think to ask the more serious questions about the extent of the damage done by the bird strike.

He dumped the new story into Wister's computer along with a note saying he would call Converse on the chance of finding a spokesman working late. On a story like this, fairness dictated the company that built the engine be given the opportunity to defend it.

An answering-service operator told Pace that at ten-fifty on Friday night, all Converse employees and executives, including Cullen Ferguson, had left for the weekend and were not expected back until Monday morning.

"Isn't there anyone on call for emergencies?" Pace asked.

"Of course," the operator replied with a huffy edge to her voice. "But my order was to take messages from the media."

"Well, excuse me for disturbing your Friday evening," Pace snapped. "I don't want to interrupt anybody's bridge game, but if he has a free moment, maybe he could call me back."

Pace left his numbers at work and at home and slammed the phone down, already a little ashamed at venting his anger on an operator who was only following the orders of her employer. Wister caught his eye.

"Anything?"

"No," Pace grumbled. "They're only taking messages from the media. Can you feature that? Those idiots are treating this like a fender-bender on the Beltway."

"Did you try Ferguson's home?"

"Not yet. I just got done ripping them a new one at his office."

Pace called area code two-one-six Information and found what he was looking for.

There was no answer.

"You keep trying all weekend 'til you get him," Wister suggested.

"I'm going to. I've got a few niceties I'd like to exchange with Mr. Ferguson."

"You've got a long haul ahead of you on this story," Wister cautioned. "Don't waste your energy on useless confrontation. And don't alienate a source you're going to need later." It was good advice, but the way Wister said it made it sound like a lecture. Just once, Pace wished, Paul Wister would make a mistake he would have to admit.

His irritation showed. "Quit acting like a petulant little kid," Wister added.

Pace fiddled with a pen, running it back and forth between his thumb and forefinger. He felt stupid and childish. But the anger was dissipating. "Is it okay if I sit here and act morose and sullen for fifteen minutes?"

Wister smiled. "Make it ten. Then find a nice girl and take her out for a few drinks. We need you back in here tomorrow in a mood to work."

On an impulse, Pace tried to call Eddie Conklin at his apartment on the Hill. There was no answer. Pace found it hard to believe the NTSB technician could be working this late, so he made a mental note to try again in an hour or so.

For the most part, his day's work was done after a mere fourteen hours. Wister's comment about finding a nice girl reminded him he'd meant all day to call Kathy McGovern. It was nearly eleven o'clock. He hoped it wasn't too late, but he ached to talk to her. He looked up her number in his directory—there was a time when he'd had it memorized—and dialed her Georgetown house. She answered on the second ring.

"It's Steve Pace," he said. "I hope I didn't wake you. I just finished work."

"No, I'm up," she said. Her voice was heavy with sadness.

"I feel godawful about letting them run me off yesterday," he said. "How'd it go for you?"

"I appreciated you trying to help," she said. "They didn't really give you any choice. It wasn't the time or the place to make a scene."

"I guess not. Thanks for understanding."

"They couldn't tell me much. If I accomplished anything, it was letting them know Jonny was the son of Joseph McGovern. Maybe they worked a little harder to recover his body. The airline had a record of where he was sitting, on the left side of the first-class section." She began to cry softly.

"Do you want me to come over?" Pace asked. "I could be there in about ten minutes."

"You've already had a long day."

"Oh, I think I've got a few good hours left in me. Isn't that what friends are for?"

"We had more than that once."

"I know," he said. "I find myself wondering how we ever lost it . . . how I ever let it get away."

"I would like to see you, Steve. But I'm not sure you want to be here just now."

"Why?"

"Daddy's here," she said. "He's irritated with me because

I used his name as leverage to get them to look for Jonny right away."

"I remember you telling me how he never uses his name or his money as leverage," he said, a smile in his voice.

"But this is *different*," she insisted. "Isn't it?"

"It is," he agreed. "Why don't I come over and try to calm him down?"

"Thanks."

When Pace arrived at the O Street house, Joseph McGovern answered the door. The reporter had seen pictures of the patriarch of the McGovern household, but they hadn't prepared him for the reality. The man standing before him, well into his seventies, was robust, erect, and brimming with health. His thick white hair was combed straight back, and his handshake was firm.

"Mr. McGovern, I'm Steven Pace," the reporter said. "I can't tell you how sorry I am about your son."

"Come in, Steve," McGovern said. "Kathy has told me a great deal about you. I appreciate all you did for her at the airport yesterday."

"It wasn't all that much, sir. I was happy to do it."

"And it's nice of you to come out at this hour after the workday you must have put in."

Disarming and personable. I should be comforting him, and he's sympathizing with me. That's smooth.

"I wanted to make sure Kathy is all right," Pace said.

"Seems to me I recall she mentioned you a year or so ago," McGovern said as he steered Pace toward the living room. "The two of you were an item, as they say."

"Yes, sir."

"What happened?"

Pace was stunned by the question and felt himself smile in appreciation of the directness of the man. "I'm not certain," he replied. "We drifted apart. I'm sorry it ended that way."

"It's not like it has to stay ended," McGovern observed as they entered the living room. Kathy overheard the exchange.

"Dad, stop it!" she insisted. "This is hardly the time."

"It's as good a time as any," McGovern replied. "Life is for the living. Jonathan would not be offended by the topic of conversation."

She got up and hugged Pace. "I'm sorry," she said.

"No reason to be," he replied, stroking her hair.

She went back to her place on the sofa. Pace took a chair opposite her.

"How are you getting along?" he asked.

"We're trying to decide whether he should be buried in the family plot in Boston, or in Chicago," Kathy said haltingly. "Daddy wants to leave it up to Betsy."

"Have you talked with her?"

"Yes, of course," Joseph McGovern said. "I thought she was coming to Washington, but she was too upset to travel. She stayed home under a doctor's care. Her first instinct was to bury Jonny in Boston, with Joey and Mother. But I don't want to press her. She shouldn't make that decision while she's still in shock."

"That's very thoughtful of you," Pace said.

"Nonsense." McGovern snorted. "Just makes common sense."

Pace glanced at Kathy. He thought she seemed very uncomfortable with her father's matter-of-fact handling of the situation. Obviously, she wasn't faring nearly as well.

"I'm going home tomorrow to make arrangements with a mortuary to fly Jonny to Boston as soon as his body's released to us. They'll keep him until Betsy makes a decision," McGovern continued. "If she decides she wants interment in Chicago, I'll have the body flown there, and that's where the funeral will be, and we'll have a memorial service at home later."

"Are you going back to Boston with your father?" Pace asked Kathy.

"Not right away," she said. "I'll go to the funeral, wherever it is. If Jonny's buried in Chicago, I'll go there and then to Boston for the memorial service. For the moment, I'm going back to work. I've already taken two days off. Hugh needs me at the office."

"I'm certain Hugh wouldn't want you back in under these circumstances," Pace said.

"I think she should go back," McGovern demurred. "Keep her mind occupied."

"Whatever you decide to do, you shouldn't be alone," Pace told her.

"Well, my roommates are here, and Hugh's made it clear he and Gretchen are around if I need them. She even asked me to move in with them for a week or so."

"Will you?"

"No. I need to pick up my life and get on with it."

"You're being pretty hard on yourself."

"I'll be fine."

"I'd better be going, then," Pace said, and stood. He shook hands with Joseph McGovern.

"I'll walk you to the door," Kathy said.

On the long walk down the front hallway to the foyer, Kathy clung tightly to Pace. When they reached the door, she buried her head in his chest and began to sob.

"I'm sorry," she said. "I try, but I can't do it like Daddy. I miss Jonny so much."

He held her. "I wish there were something I could do," he said, lamely, he thought.

"You can," Kathy said, looking up at him. "You can find out why this happened. There must be a reason. Tragedies like this don't happen for no reason."

"That's what the federal investigators are doing," he replied.

"But what if they don't find out? What if they miss something?"

"That doesn't happen."

"But it *can* happen?"

"Yes, I suppose so."

"Then you find out," she insisted. "You find out for me why Jonny died."

The request wasn't entirely rational, or reasonable. But Pace took it seriously, for her sake.

"I'll be in touch," he promised.

"I'd like that," she replied.

At his apartment on New Hampshire Avenue, Pace chucked his sport coat over the back of the sofa, loosened his tie, and poured a stiff Jack Daniels. He sat down in his favorite chair and tried to remember everything about the year he and Kathy had dated. It had been pretty hot for a few months. They'd even talked about her moving in with him, but Kathy's strict Irish Catholic upbringing wouldn't quite let her do it. Pace argued that they often spent entire weekends together and she didn't get hives of guilt, so why not weeks, or months? Her reply was always the same: Having a place of her own somehow assuaged the spirit of Sister Mary Margaret, the sternest teacher at St. Martin's Academy for Girls, who had warned her charges daily that if they ever dared have sex out of wedlock or for any purpose other than procreation, she would come back to haunt them. Sister Mary Margaret didn't haunt Kathy in bed, only in her choice of a place to live.

He finished his whiskey and poured another, welcoming a soft Black Jack glow.

He thought of Kathy again. "Damn," he said quietly.

The answering-service operator in Youngstown had lied to Pace, just as she'd been ordered to. At precisely the moment the reporter called for Cullen Ferguson, the man was sitting with a stiff Cutty in his hand in a designer leather chair in the Converse office of the company's chief executive officer, George Thomas Greenwood. The sole topic of the meeting, which had been requested by Ferguson, was damage control.

After hashing through the possibilities, Ferguson concluded glumly that inevitably the Dulles accident would be hung on a failure of their engine, the mainstay of the Converse Corporation. The evidence was undeniable. All the reported eyewitness accounts spoke of nothing but an explosion in or a disintegration of that engine, and the four

personal phone calls during the day from Senator Harold
Marshall to Greenwood, relaying bits and pieces of intelligence from a variety of sources, only confirmed those accounts. That he could not sway Greenwood's unshakable
faith that the engine would be vindicated only served to
frustrate Ferguson more.

Both men had avoided alcohol during the evening in
order to keep clear heads, but the last call from Marshall,
thirty minutes earlier, brought the bottle of Cutty out from
Greenwood's cabinet. The call was a classic good-news,
bad-news update. On one hand, the NTSB had disclosed in
its daily briefing that what appeared to be the remains of a
bird had been found in the wreck of the Number 3 engine.
After all, Converse couldn't be held responsible for a bird
being in the wrong place at the wrong time. It was the rest
of it that hurt. Marshall didn't disclose the source of his
information, and the two Converse executives didn't ask.
Marshall said he'd received a late tip that the *Washington
Chronicle* would carry a story the next morning questioning
the ability of the Converse Fan to live up to advertising
claims for its capacity to withstand debris ingestion. The
story also would disclose the discovery of a cracked turbine
wheel in a Converse Fan engine on a TransAm 811 in
Seattle three months earlier. If the company had overstated
the engine's capabilities, or if it turned out the turbine disks
were brittle or flawed, the news would be devastating.

Converse, for the first time, was on the verge of gaining
a solid position among the leaders in the industry, but that
hold wasn't yet strong enough to withstand a severe backward shove.

Earlier in the evening, Greenwood and Ferguson, in a
conference call with Harold Marshall, devised a two-
pronged campaign—on the fronts of public relations and
finance—to mitigate the damage to the company. But the
campaign was predicated on having a few weeks to work
with. The *Chronicle*'s speculative story would deprive them
of any gear-up time at all.

Greenwood had heard about the incident in Seattle and

expressed concern at the time that the cause of the turbine-disk fracture be found as early as possible. Ferguson also was aware of it, and he knew the staff metallurgists studying the fracture were reasonably certain it had been caused by a defect in the titanium alloy, not in the engine design.

"Is it possible we have a subcontractor delivering faulty material?" Greenwood suggested. "That would shift some of the focus away from us."

"Are you asking me if that *is* possible or telling me it *should* be?" Ferguson challenged. "Ultimately, we have to take responsibility for what our subs do."

"Come off it, Cullen. You see what's been happening to our stock. This company can't afford that. If we can lay off any of the blame, by God, we're going to do it."

Ferguson shook his head. He didn't like the drift of the conversation. "The way the public and the industry react to us will be tied to how up front we are about this situation and how far we're willing to go to see it doesn't happen again."

"Like Exxon did in Alaska?" Greenwood challenged. "They stepped right up and took it, and they're going to be paying out the ass for the next century." Then Greenwood leaned forward in his chair to be certain he was heard and understood. "Look, Cullen, we'll go as far as we have to to prevent a recurrence," he said in a tone of deep conviction. "That was never in any doubt. We can't let this happen again. If it was our engine, we acknowledge the situation and correct the problem. That is a given, an absolute. But if there are mitigating circumstances, and we can bring them out, they can only work in our favor with the airlines and on Wall Street."

"I hate to be obstinate about this, G.T., but it isn't going to work very well if the press finds out we bought a United States senator who freaked out and tried to intimidate the NTSB, or that we didn't dispatch our engineering team to help the NTSB until the day after the crash." It was ground they'd covered already, but Ferguson felt deeply enough to pursue it further.

"As I said, it was my feeling that our team members should go to Washington together," Greenwood said. "Walt Havens was in Seattle, and he couldn't get back in time to go out last night. They all were on a company plane at seven this morning. It hasn't held up the investigation one little bit, and I seriously doubt the media would be interested, even if they knew, which they don't. As for Harold, he has become something of a loose cannon. But I can handle him. Now drop it."

Ferguson inhaled deeply and exhaled loudly through ballooned cheeks.

"You having second thoughts about signing on, Cullen?" Greenwood asked.

Ferguson shook his head. "Hell, any company in this business could have this happen," he said. "Most have." He paused, as if to add something, but he didn't. Greenwood finished for him.

"But Pratt and Whitney, GE, and Rolls Royce aren't in our financial shape, is that what you're thinking? Well, you're right. This engine is our great opportunity to break through, both personally and professionally, and don't you forget that. Boeing has been making inquiries about adapting it to their Eight-hundred series. To power the Sextons is a foot in the door. But if we could get in with Boeing, there's no telling how far this company could rise. And aside from corporate pride, do you have any idea what that would mean to incentives, bonuses, and stock options around here? We're in on the ground floor on an express elevator to the penthouse, Cullen, assuming nobody's stupid enough to push the stop button."

"I've thought of all that, G.T. Quite honestly, that was a major factor in my decision to come with Converse. But stock options are the up side of this job, and right now, for better or for worse, I have to deal with the down side, and I don't like the way it's going."

"What, specifically?"

"My posture with the media, for starters. I'm under orders not to go beyond our prepared statement, but it's the

standard pap about our corporate grief and our cooperation with the NTSB and that shit. It gets one day's play
buried somewhere in the news stories, then disappears. It's
not doing us any P.R. good at all."

"We're just following instructions from the insurance carriers."

"Well, fuck the insurance carriers. Maybe we should
show some human compassion."

"You do that, Cullen, and our liability losses will be in
the nine-figure range, maybe higher. Let's deal with the
future, my friend, and leave the past to the lawyers."

"That's fine. But the calls about the past keep coming to
me."

Greenwood took a deep drink from his glass and studied
Ferguson closely. The junior man was exceptional. He was
stylish, good-looking, possessed of a quick wit, and good on
his feet, the sort of combination that got excellent press
when the media came to visit. But he'd been hired out of a
news-magazine background, not out of industry, and the
CEO wondered if he could tough it out in a situation that
might require him to bend the truth for the good of the
organization.

"You lost a lot when you took this job, Cullen. Any
regrets?"

Ferguson started at the question, but the Scotch loosened
his tongue. "I guess. My wife didn't want to move from the
West Coast, especially to northeastern Ohio," he said,
laughing and a little embarrassed at having blurted that out.
"Taking this job ended my marriage, but, hey, it wasn't in
good shape, anyway. The move here was an excuse to cut it
off. It would have happened one way or another, one day or
another."

"But it still isn't easy?"

Ferguson took a last pull on his drink and took his glass
back to Greenwood's private bar. "No, it isn't easy," he
said. "I wish Anne were here, especially now. The last
twenty-four hours I've had a strong urge to pick up the
phone and call her. My problem is, I don't know whether I

miss *her* that much or I just need *somebody* right now. I can't bring myself to prowl the bars in this town to find, well, whatever you find in places like that." He splashed about an ounce of Scotch over his remaining ice, swirled it and drained it in one swallow.

"You need a little extemporaneous fun," Greenwood said. "I've got to be out of town tomorrow on a personal matter, but I'll be back on Sunday. Come on over about mid-afternoon. I'll get Pam to call some nonthreatening friends, and we'll swim in the heated pool, and barbecue, and generally raise the kind of hell that will make both of us feel better."

"I don't think anything's gonna make me feel better about the last two days, G.T. On the other hand, a swim in your pool would give me a chance to drown myself."

"Hey," Greenwood laughed, "every party needs a floor show."

It was nearly 1:00 A.M. when Steve Pace unwound enough to go to bed. He picked up his sport coat from where he'd tossed it on the sofa, doused the lights, and wandered into the bedroom.

When he hung up his jacket, he saw a small bulge in the side pocket. He reached in and found the scarred metal ball he'd picked up on the field at Dulles. In their rush to leave, he'd forgotten to ask Mike about it. *Damn.* If it was evidence, it should be back at Dulles, not in his bedroom.

Pace dropped the ball in an old souvenir ashtray on top of his bureau and told himself he'd figure out what to do with it in the morning.

7

"This is AP Network News. I'm Frank Greshhold—"

Pace hit the snooze alarm on the clock radio. He didn't want to sleep for another ten minutes, but it was the quickest way to turn off the noise and keep from waking Kathy.

Then he remembered . . . Kathy wasn't there. She hadn't been there in more than a year.

He only dreamed of her.

He toyed with the notion of turning on the radio again. He wanted to hear what the world was being told about the ConPac accident, but that would mean sacrificing the hazy remnants of his dream. And acknowledging the reality of her absence.

He smiled, remembering how she used to react to the alarm. She would say something that sounded like "humm-blebumpf" and turn over, away from the world's intrusion on her sleep. She had to be the hardest person on the planet to get out of bed in the morning.

He spent a few more minutes lying beside the memories of her, of his first solid union in the years since the divorce initiated by his wife, Joan.

The marriage had lasted six years and produced one child, Melissa, who'd had no full-time father since the day after her third birthday, when he'd walked away from their house in San Diego. He visited during the separation, and later, after the divorce, and they did the things fathers and daughters are supposed to do. But it was difficult for Melissa, who couldn't fathom why the father she adored had

left. And he couldn't tell her. Adult marital pressures, terms
like "growing apart" and "diverging interests," were things
a child couldn't understand. All Melissa knew was the pain
of separation, and it angered her. Because it hurt his daughter so deeply, it was agony for Pace.

For almost a decade, he left them pretty much alone,
conning himself with the notion he was doing it for his
daughter, but the truth was, he was doing it for himself, and
he knew it. He phoned on special occasions and listened to
his child become a young woman, but he didn't see Melissa
again until her thirteenth birthday two years earlier, when
he flew back to San Diego at Joan's suggestion. She told him
Melissa's anger was gone, replaced by a curiosity about a
father whose face she remembered only dimly.

He'd been nervous, but he went, and it was wonderful. He
and Melissa took long walks on the beach and sat on the
rocks, where the pounding surf sprayed them with briny
foam and cleansed their relationship. Pace was amazed at
the adult concepts his teenaged daughter grasped, and at
how Joan had done nothing to poison the girl's memory of
him. Indeed, Joan had given Melissa a sense her father was
a good man and the end of their marriage came not out of
a lack of love, but in the void of common interests. Except
for their daughter.

So exhilarated was Pace that when his ex-wife invited him
to stay the night, he had, and they talked the next morning
of starting over. That was impossible, but they shared positive emotions, and Melissa sensed it. She had come to visit
him the previous year, and was returning in a week, during
her spring break.

Pace worried that she still harbored hope of a reconciliation between her parents. He ached to renew his relationship with Kathy McGovern. He didn't know how his
daughter would react to that. When she came the year
before, she knew Kathy only as her father's friend. If she
saw Kathy with him again thirteen months later, she would
understand the relationship went beyond friendship.

Pace knew his feelings for Kathy went deeper than a

momentary obsession growing from his anxiety over her grief. But what would he answer if she asked why, if he loved her, he'd let a year go by without calling? He'd been busy, but that excuse didn't wash. The fact was, he'd been afraid of falling in love with Kathy, afraid she would put the job to which she was so dedicated ahead of him. And that would be cruel irony, since his dedication to his job was the sacrificial altar that had claimed his marriage and several relationships since. The odd hours, the weekends of work, the plans canceled at the last minute—all these had created too much pressure and tension.

Joan once accused him of loving his work more than his family, and he was unable to convince her otherwise. If it weren't true, Joan insisted, he could change. But his job was something he *couldn't* change. Neither Joan, nor the women who came later could or would accept that those demands came with him—his baggage—and as long as he remained a journalist, it would be so.

Kathy never complained about his odd hours or the sudden, unexpected demands on his time, as he never complained of hers. Yet those demands conspired to keep them apart, to load her down with Senate business on days he could get away early, or to toss a late-breaking story in his lap on evenings she was free. So they gave up.

They hadn't discussed it. There was no mutual conclusion that they didn't have enough hours in their days to share. He just stopped calling her, as she stopped calling him. What a waste.

Pace slid from beneath the covers and sat on the edge of the bed. He felt generally crummy. Too much booze and a restless night left him less than rested. He rolled his head around a few times to loosen up, but that only created a dull headache.

You're wonderful. A mere two days into one of the biggest stories of your life, and you start drinking like you're on a month's vacation. Five aspirin, a cold shower, and four cups of black coffee might bring you back to workable status.

Pace got off the bed and headed for the bathroom, then

detoured into the kitchen. He started the coffee and tried
Conklin again. Still no answer. Damn it, anyway. Either the
NTSB had its technicians on twenty-four-hour duty or
Eddie had turned off the ringer on his telephone.

Five aspirin, a cold shower, and black coffee did help, and
by the time Pace left his New Hampshire Avenue apartment, he was feeling halfway decent.

It was another gorgeous spring day, and he took his car
out of the underground garage reluctantly. He walked into
the newsroom shortly before nine-thirty and was surprised
to see Avery Schaeffer already there. A fresh copy of the
Saturday *Chronicle* was lying on Pace's desk. He'd scanned
it at home, but he opened it again. The banner headline
read:

  Bird strike eyed as cause of Dulles 811 crash

The deck below it read:

  Questions raised about
  design and strength
  of new Converse engine

It's provocative, Pace thought.

He sat down to reread the story. Given the jerky way it
had come together, his fondest hope was that it made sense.

He was well into it when he sensed someone sit down
beside him at the desk belonging to the environmental
writer, Jack Tarshis. It was Schaeffer. He leaned way back
in the chair, crossed his hands in his lap, and put his feet up
on Tarshis's desk. He nodded toward Pace's copy of the
Chronicle.

"Not bad for a beginner," he said. He was smiling
broadly.

"How'd the other guys do?" Pace dared ask.

"Not bad, but not great. All of them had the bird-strike
theory and those FAA reports, but you were alone with the
TransAm thing in Seattle."

"What about the engine-performance angle?"

"Justin Smith had a little of it, but I didn't think he was as thorough as you."

Pace was feeling good. "I wonder if Mike's caught any rockets from the home office," he said.

"He's a big boy. He knows, or should know, when he talks to a reporter, his name's gonna get in the paper. It's my impression McGill was talking on the record for Trans-Am."

"Yeah, on the Seattle deal, but somebody in Memphis might figure, since it's in the same story, he also had a hand in the questions about the Converse Fan. That wouldn't go down well in TransAm's glass tower."

"If he has any balls at all, and I think he probably has, he can take the heat."

"Balls he has," Pace said, smiling. "And he loves 'em too much to risk 'em for us."

They got coffee, passed some pleasantries, and wound up back at the adjoining desks.

"Tell me about your conversation yesterday with George Ridley," Schaeffer said abruptly.

Pace was surprised. He hadn't been at all sure Paul Wister actually would tell Schaeffer about the encounter with the Senate aide. When he finished, Schaeffer was quiet for a minute, mulling it over. "What do you think?" the editor asked.

"It's natural for Marshall to look after an important constituent." Pace shoved his hands in his pockets and turned to face Schaeffer so the two sat almost knees-to-knees. "But the message to go easy on Converse . . . that stinks. And he's taking such a huge risk. He must know Ridley detests him. Marshall has to know the story could get out, and if it does, it'll destroy him."

"Ridley's been on the Hill for a long time," Schaeffer said. "He didn't get to be chief of staff of a major committee without playing the game by its rules. Marshall's probably banking that Ridley won't change. In his place, I probably would, too."

"I don't much give a damn what happens to Marshall," Pace said. "But I'm concerned about the impact on the NTSB. If I could corroborate Ridley, I'd be pressing hard to write the story. Marshall's tampering with a federal investigation. That's a crime." Pace paused, seeing Schaeffer regard him closely. The editor said nothing, so he finished his thought. "What if somebody at the NTSB takes him seriously? What if they think he's a threat to their appropriations, or to their jobs? What if they follow his suggestion, and some serious flaw in the engine doesn't get reported? What if this thing happens again, and another three hundred people die?"

"Do you have that little faith in the NTSB?"

"No," Pace acknowledged. "And maybe," he added as an afterthought.

He leaned forward with his elbows on his thighs and stared at the carpet between his shoes. "I keep remembering a silly conversation I had with our family doctor when I was, oh, like in the fifth or sixth grade. His name was Angus Frankenhauser, but none of the kids could pronounce Frankenhauser, so we all called him Doctor Frank. He was talking to my mother one day about this big mess in town over the opening of an abortion clinic. Doctor Frank said he could never perform an abortion; he believed it was murder. I remember I butted in and asked him, 'Doctor Frank, if somebody offered you a million dollars, would you change your mind?'

"Mom was really pissed, but Doctor Frank sat back in his big leather chair—he wasn't upset at all—and he thought about it. Then he said, 'Stevie, I honestly don't know. What I do know is God didn't make any of us perfect. Every man's got his price. No matter how deep a man's convictions run, there's some price so high he won't be able to stand up to the temptation. Maybe it's money. Maybe it's fame. Maybe it's power. Maybe it's something else altogether. As much as I'd like it not to be so, I suspect I've got a price like everybody else. All I can hope is I never find out what it is.' "

Pace looked up from the floor. "It's one of those childhood things I've never forgotten. I can still hear him say it. It makes me wonder what Marshall's price is to save a big constituent. Or an NTSB investigator's price to protect his agency, or his job."

"I think Doctor Frank was probably a wise man," Schaeffer said. "What town was that in?"

"Big city," Pace said. "Litchfield, Indiana. It's on all the maps."

Schaeffer leaned forward in his own chair. "Steve, I think based on nothing more than the wisdom of Doctor Frank, you should watch Harold Marshall. But don't jump to the conclusion somebody's already found his moral shutoff button. I remember right after Watergate, kids were beating down doors to get into journalism schools. Every big-city paper, especially here, got applications out the ass from wanna-be Woodwards and Bernsteins. All these kids assumed there were Pulitzer Prizes waiting in the streets for them. They had all the enthusiasm with none of the tempering experience or judgment. Public officials aren't made to be broken. Most of them do the best jobs they can. A few work damned hard and turn out to be outstanding. You watch Marshall, but you assume his intentions are justifiable until you have absolute proof that isn't the case."

"The Sherlock Holmes test?"

"You got it. Report the story as far as you can, reject everything you can disprove, and what's left, no matter how strange, must be the truth."

Schaeffer heaved himself out of the chair and clapped Pace on the shoulder. "Don't let this little talk inhibit you too much. I still want you on the investigation like sweat on a whore."

"Sweat on a whore?" Pace asked with mock incredulity as Schaeffer walked away.

"Whatever," Schaeffer replied, waving his hand. "Just don't be wrong—"

"—and don't get beat, I know."

It was 11:00 A.M., 8:00 A.M. on the West Coast, early enough
that Pace thought he might catch Whitney Warner, Sexton's
vice-president for public affairs, in her office before she got
tied up in an endless series of meetings. Although the hon-
chos rarely worked on Saturdays, surely this Saturday
would be an exception. And if they were working, they
would be meeting. That's what corporate executives did on
the West Coast, Pace had decided once. They stayed in
meetings for eight or nine hours a day to avoid phone calls
from executives on the East Coast.

"Steve, well hello." Warner's voice purred along the fiber-
optic cable. She would be at her desk, Pace thought, her
blond hair loose at the shoulders, her makeup perfect. Because it was Saturday, she probably would be wearing blue
jeans tucked into high-heeled boots, and maybe a red silk
blouse with the perfect accents of gold jewelry. Whitney
Warner was one of those women who always looked just
right. Men fell in love with her despite no conscious effort
on her part to attract them. There was plenty of brain to go
along with the looks. She'd earned a masters degree from
CalPoly in molecular physics and a Ph.D. in aerodynamic
engineering from Cal Tech. She held an air-transport license, was rated to fly about every jet in the skies, and had
flown 737s for four years both as a first officer and as a
captain with Delta Airlines.

But her favorite toy was her Christen Eagle, a colorful
biplane that could stunt with the best. It was in that aircraft
that Pace first flew with her. "Mah instructah says it's verrah, verrah safe," she told him in soft, Southern tones. "Ah
just have to be careful not to let it spin." So of course, as
soon as they gained enough altitude, she stalled deliberately
and spiraled into a spin. In the front of the two tandem
seats, Pace grew dizzy and nauseous and found God.
Warner later swore he screamed, but Pace insisted he had no
recollection of any such thing, although he acknowledged
he might have whimpered once. He had not been her first
victim, but she said he was the best sport of the bunch.

"I'm sorry I didn't have time to chat with you yesterday,

Steve. It was more than a little bit mad around here. How have you been?"

"Probably better than you, Whit. I wasn't sure you'd be in today."

"I wasn't supposed to be, but there's too much to clean up. We've been getting fax copies of your stories. I see you've been busy, too."

"Keeps me out of worse trouble. Is there any speculation around you'd care to share with an old flying buddy?"

He heard the smile in her voice. "I didn't realize you were such a fan of my aerobatics. As to speculation, you seem to be doing most of that. After I saw your story today, I asked some of our people about the specs we required for the Converse engines. I also asked for any information they had on the cracked turbine disk in Seattle and on the probability a bird strike could cause the level of damage we saw at Dulles. They haven't gotten back to me yet. But if any choice tidbits cross my desk, unless they're for restricted distribution, I'll give you a call. The rest of my morning I've spent fielding calls from reporters and two members of our board about your story. All I get is questions, no answers."

"Who'd you send to work with the NTSB?"

"Dave Terrell. He's one of our best engineers."

"Well, I'll probably be calling again," Pace said. "By the way, how's Brig?"

"He's fine. NASA's flying him all over the place, showing off its astronaut hero, and he's about sick of it. He was coming home this weekend, but with the accident and all, well . . . he's going to work now and maybe get a whole week off later."

"Tough life," Pace commiserated.

"Well, it's hard to make babies long-distance. But we've waited this long, I guess another few months won't matter to the child."

"I didn't know you were thinking about it."

"Thinking and trying, finally." Warner's laugh carried twenty-five hundred miles and made Pace feel good. "AP did a story. Did you miss it?"

"I guess I did. I would have sent a card of encouragement, or something."

"I'll keep you posted. I'm sorry I couldn't be more help. I don't know any more than you do—maybe not as much."

"It was good talking to you, anyway, Whit," Pace said sincerely. "It's always good."

In Youngstown, the Converse operator was still in her "messages only" mode, but Pace caught Cullen Ferguson at home. Ferguson said he was sorry, but he couldn't go beyond the one press release the company had issued right after the crash.

"For God's sake, Cullen, that's two days old, and a lot's happened since then. What about the Seattle incident? What about the deflection capability of the engine design? What can you tell me about that?"

"Nothing right now. We're not going to speculate on what happened to the engine. We're checking to see if we can release any information about the cracked turbine disk, but our insurance carrier has basically told the CEO everybody's to keep his mouth shut, and those are the orders he issued to me."

"That makes it look like you're hiding something."

Ferguson exploded. "Well, we're not! Do you realize the position we're in? If we don't say anything, we look like we've walled ourselves in, but if we do, we could wind up screwed in court by our own words. We're damned sorry it happened. We said that two days ago. We have confidence in our new fan jet. We said that two days ago, too. And that's all we're going to say. Period. End of message."

"You have any people on the scene here?"

"Our whole team was in early yesterday."

"A day after the accident? Why didn't they come on Thursday?"

"For Christ's sake, Steve, be reasonable. We wanted to send our best, and that's Walt Havens. He was on business in Seattle, and it took time to get him back here, hook him up with the rest of the team and get them all out of town. They were on scene the next morning."

"Sorry, Cullen, but it's strange, with your engine at the center of the investigation, you'd wait until the day after the crash to get your people connected with the NTSB."

Ferguson reined himself in. He chose his words carefully and spoke slowly and deliberately. "We don't need you to tell us how to run this company. We do what we have to do, as quickly as we can do it. If that doesn't meet with your approval, that is too fucking bad."

The reporter had the name he wanted—Havens—and he had no other questions for which Ferguson would have answers, so the conversation terminated.

Pace was considering whom to irritate next when his phone rang. It was Con Phillips, at the FAA. Like everyone else, he was spending Saturday at the office.

"Welcome to the world of indentured slavery, Con. What's up?"

"You are indeed the wunderkind, the boy who can find magic in an innocuous FAA report," Phillips said sarcastically. "You sure got me in a barrel of hot oil. I've already had some hard questions from my colleagues, and three calls from other reporters who think I tipped you to the Seattle connection."

"You didn't. And we don't know for sure there is a connection."

"Tell me something I don't know. And while you're at it, maybe you'd like to tell me how you got onto that. The brass thinks maybe you should head the investigation. You're the only one in town with a working crystal ball."

"I can do without the sarcasm." Pace was irritated, but he thought he owed Phillips an explanation. "When I first read the reports, I figured your assessment was pretty good, there was nothing there. The Seattle incident was the only one even remotely interesting. I checked it out. Unless my Journalism one-oh-one instructor was wrong, that's what I get paid for."

"What rabbit are you going to pull out of your hat tomorrow? So I'm prepared."

"You'll know it when you read it in the morning."

"I'm tired, Steve. And I don't like surprises. I didn't mean to start a brawl. I really called to congratulate you. That was a nice scoop."

"Thanks. You want to help me find another one for tomorrow?"

"And bring down the wrath of even more of your colleagues? Not for a million dollars."

"Actually, I was thinking more of a million and a half."

"Still not enough. But, hell, you don't need me. I'm the one who told you there was no story in the SDs and incident reports."

"That's right. You're fired."

"Good. Maybe I can get tomorrow off."

"Hey, Con, before you go, you heard anything about what's in the black boxes?"

"Why would the NTSB tell me?"

"Gossip."

"Not a thing, really."

"Is that straight?"

"Would I lie to you? And if I did, couldn't you tell? You're the one with the crystal ball."

There still was no answer at Conklin's home at one-thirty. The after-hours number at the NTSB was answered by a man who said Conklin was at work but was not taking phone calls.

Pace vowed the sun wouldn't set on the day until he confronted Eddie and talked to him. Since the NTSB was transcribing the cockpit voice tapes, getting to him now was even more critical than in the immediate aftermath of the accident. Tape enhancement was Conklin's specialty.

Next, Pace called Glenn Brennan, who was at Dulles, and asked if Glenn could cover for him at the six-thirty NTSB briefing. He wouldn't make it if it took him all day to find Conklin.

"No problem, Kemo Sabe," Brennan answered.

"I once heard from somebody that Kemo Sabe means horse's ass," Pace said.

"I heard that, too," Brennan replied with a laugh.

Pace first went to the bookstore across the street from the office and bought a couple of magazines. Then he stopped at his favorite deli on G Street, where he got a gigantic ham-and-Swiss on rye, side of slaw, and Coke to go. With his lunch and his reading in hand, he took a cab to the L'Enfant Plaza East offices of the NTSB. He found a comfortable spot in the sun and prepared to stake out the place for the rest of the day, if necessary.

It was a gamble. If Conklin had driven his car, he could get to the garage and leave without Pace seeing him. But it was another nice spring day, and the technician lived only about a mile away, on Capitol Hill. Pace guessed he had walked to work and would leave by the front door to walk home.

It was a good guess, but a long wait.

It was nearly four o'clock when Conklin emerged, scanning the street for a taxi. So intently was he engrossed in his own thoughts that he walked within three feet of Pace without seeing him. For his part, Pace had become involved in an article in *Omni,* and if he hadn't heard someone walk past, he would have missed his friend.

"Hey, Eddie, wait up."

Pace gathered his trash and belongings, and caught up with the technician. Conklin looked tired.

"Didn't mean to startle you, buddy," Pace apologized, putting his lunch trash down while he struggled into his coat. He handed the magazines to Conklin. "Hold these a minute. Let me put myself back together."

Conklin looked dumbfounded. "How long've you been out here?"

"Oh, I don't know. Two hours, I guess."

"Waiting for me?"

"Yeah. I've been calling your place at all hours without reaching you. I figure you've been working your butt off. I knew I couldn't get close to you inside without an appointment. So I thought I'd wait 'til you were off and buy you a beer."

"You don't buy me a beer, and I don't buy your story," Conklin said with a hint of a grin turning up the left side of his mouth. "You haven't reached me because I didn't want you to, or any of the other media, either. I've been staying with a friend up near Dupont Circle."

"Lady?"

"Is that your business?"

"Okay, if you don't want me to buy you a beer, you buy me a beer, or we'll go Dutch—no favors given or expected. Eddie, give me a break. I need to talk to you about the Sexton."

"I'm not supposed to talk about it. That's why I'm not staying at home. I didn't want to have to go through this every fifteen minutes. There's not much I can tell you anyhow. The material from the flight data recorder is still being analyzed. We're pulling transcripts from the cockpit voice recorder, but I don't know when that process will be completed."

"Shit. I need to get a better handle on what's on those tapes. There must have been some pretty dramatic stuff. A lot of confusion. Does that jibe with what you know?"

"Yeah, generally, although there's much more."

"Like what?"

"You leech." Conklin strode off down the sidewalk, then turned around to face Pace, who had followed him. "You can hear them dying, for chrissake! I'm not going into details. The tapes are horrible. They're terrible. It's enough to make you sick. A couple of guys who heard them did puke, as a matter of fact. You want something for a story. There, use that. It's all true. But that's it. No more. I know we're friends, but no more. If you value our friendship, you won't ask."

"I'm sorry, Eddie. I have to ask. It's my job, damn it. Why do I have to explain that to everybody today?"

Conklin nodded in reluctant acceptance of that explanation.

He caught the eye of a cabbie on the other side of the street, and the two sprinted through traffic as the driver pulled to the curb. "You going back to the paper?" Conklin asked Pace, who nodded. Conklin gave the driver his temporary Dupont Circle address and asked him to go there by way of the *Chronicle* Building. As the cab pulled out into traffic, Conklin sat back heavily in the seat.

"I'm sorry I took your head off, Steve. The last three days seem like forever, and I'm tired. I also had an old friend from college on that plane. This would be hard enough work anyhow, but it's being personal and all makes it that much tougher."

"Christ, I'm sorry, Eddie. There's a lot of that going around."

"What do you mean?"

Pace told him about Jonathan McGovern.

"Good Lord." Conklin shook his head sadly. "Hey, I know Kathy McGovern, don't I?"

"Yeah," Pace said. "I was dating her when you and I first met."

"And you're still together? That sounds serious."

"Getting back together is a better way to put it. Maybe. It's my idea. I don't know how she feels about it yet."

Conklin sighed heavily. "Listen," he said, "you can call me in a few days, maybe a week, when the heat's off. Maybe I'll be able to tell you more. You can use the stuff I told you back at the office, but if you do, no names, huh?"

Pace nodded. The rest of the ride passed in silence.

By the time Pace got back to the office, he was running right up against his first deadline, but he was able to base a story on the material from Conklin, quoting him only as an informed NTSB source. Glenn, as promised, had covered the Lund briefing and filed a memo to Pace's basket. Steve read it with a sense of relief. There was nothing new, but he pumped a few quotes from the NTSB official into his story to flesh it out and gave Glenn a credit line at the end.

Schaeffer, who had returned to the office about the time Pace found Conklin, kept his distance from the production process most of the evening, leaving the editorial decisions to the men and women paid to make them.

But on his way home, shortly before eight, he stopped at Pace's desk to watch the new information take shape on the computer terminal. He grinned broadly. "So, you finally tracked down your friend, huh?"

"I staked out the building this afternoon," Pace said, continuing to type. "Actually, I don't know if it was worth the time. The quotes are good, but they don't tell us much."

"Well, you're chipping away at it. That's the way these things go. You only get lucky in detective and spy novels. In real life, it takes time and a lot of trips down blind alleys."

Pace wished he felt that confident.

Julia Hershowitz, the Sunday national editor, finished with Pace's copy shortly before nine-thirty and gave him a thumbs-up sign.

"Another winner, Steve," she said confidently.

"They get thinner every day," Pace complained. "I wish I could get my hands on some substance."

"It'll come. As long as you're out on the streets twenty hours a day, seven days a week, looking for it."

"Gee, thanks," he replied.

He was shutting down his computer when Bobby Clack, a young news intern, hailed him. "Hey, Steve. The call on line four's for you."

He punched the button and picked up the receiver. "Pace."

"Steve, we've got to talk."

Pace recognized the voice immediately. But the cryptic greeting was unlike Mike McGill. "Sure, Mike. Go ahead."

"Not over the phone. Someplace I can get to pretty quick from Dulles, but someplace where no one will know us."

Pace's concern grew. This was squirrelly as hell. "How about a place called the Toodle Inn? It's on Route Fifty about ten miles east of where you are. Do you know that area at all?"

"I know Route Fifty. I never heard of the place. Are you

serious? The Toodle Inn?"

Pace gave him directions.

"Okay. An hour. Be there. Something lousy's coming down."

8

Saturday, April 19th, 9:25 P.M.

Harold Marshall was more than fashionably late, and Evelyn Bracken was furious.

Evelyn's annual spring bash, a society-calendar highlight in the nation's capital, was well into its third hour. Marshall had promised to get there early to help with final preparations, but he'd called at seven, as the first guests arrived, to say he was detained unavoidably on Capitol Hill by events relating to the Dulles accident.

Angry though she was, Evelyn put on her party face and explained to her guests that Marshall's tardiness was due to the *incredibly* important responsibilities of his Senate position. By touting her longtime lover's status, she elevated her own, and that alone made her feel marginally better about spending the first critical hours of her party—including the dinner—unescorted. So convincing was she that when Marshall finally made an appearance in the elegant, lantern-lit gardens behind Evelyn's Potomac, Maryland, manse, it was an entrance of sorts.

It was attention he received too rarely since the Republicans lost control of the Senate in nineteen eighty-six and he was forced to hand the gavel of the Transportation Committee back to the Democrat, Garrison Helmutsen, whom Marshall regarded as a singularly retarded Minnesota farm boy.

The senator was enjoying the moment, saying brief hellos on the three brick steps at the end of a corridor running from the main front foyer through the house to the backyard. Evelyn swept the conversation away by embracing Marshall, kissing the air beside his right ear and crooning, "Darling, I was certain you'd *never* be able to come because of that *simply awful* mess at Dulles. I'm *so* delighted to see you. Come, let's find someone who can fetch you a drink. You must be dying." She drew out the last word as if she were playing a scene, as indeed she was.

When they reached a spot on the trimmed lawn somewhere between the magnolias and the dogwood, dimly lit by two Polynesian flame lanterns, Evelyn stopped abruptly and withdrew her right hand from the crook of Marshall's left arm. Amid the lanterns, Evelyn Bracken was on a burn of her own.

"There's nothing about that damned accident that couldn't have waited until Monday morning. Do you do these things on purpose, to humiliate me?"

Marshall, who had drawn a deep breath in anticipation of this sort of confrontation, exhaled slowly. He looked down on Evelyn from a height of six-feet-two and put his hands on her shoulders.

"Darling, don't you think, instead of railing at me, you should be singing the praises of whatever deity gave you this magnificent evening for your little gathering? No? Well, since you insist on railing at me, I must tell you this isn't your average Senate business, and no, it could not wait until Monday morning. I do not crash large aircraft with more than three hundred people aboard on purpose, especially if they are powered by engines built in my state. And you are not humiliated. You are the consort of United States Senator Harold Kingsley Marshall, who would appreciate it if you would act the part . . . and your age, while you're at it."

"Harold, stop it. I hate it when you lecture. This is my big occasion. It only happens once a year. It's all so difficult to manage properly in the best of circumstances, and it's particularly difficult without an escort. Is it any wonder I'm miffed?"

"Miffed?" Marshall repeated with mock alarm. "You're miffed? Does that go hand in hand with beautiful, rich, and bitchy?"

Evelyn smiled and dropped her eyes. "I'm sorry. How would a double martini suit?"

"Fine, in a minute," Marshall said in clipped words, his voice suddenly cold. He held her by the upper part of her left arm, his grip tighter than it needed to be. "Don't *ever* question me, or my office, or my business again. I will do what my duties—and my peculiar personal interests—require, and then, as time permits, I will get to you." Evelyn was trying to pull free. Marshall continued, holding fast to her arm, his cold blue eyes intent and angry on her face. "We've had this conversation before," he said. "I do not wish to have it again."

He released her. "Now I'll have that drink," he said.

She spun to the task of his martini, catching the eye of a cocktail waitress working the crowd. "Be a dear and fetch me a double Absolut martini, on the rocks with a twist, very, very dry. On second thought, make it two. I could use one myself."

Evelyn turned back to Marshall, but he had been cornered by Charles Lauder, the Republican congressman from Los Angeles and the ranking minority member of both the House Public Works Committee and its aviation subcommittee. As important as it was to Marshall to have Converse in his state, it was equally important to Lauder to have Sexton in his district.

Evelyn feared the men would remain locked in conversation on the fringes of her party for the rest of the evening, although by their presence they added to the desired prestige of the get-together in her garden. And their conversation, carried on at a voice level that would not reach nearby ears, added an aura of intrigue that would spice reports on the party in Monday's newspapers. The old adage about politics in Washington was proved again: There is more business conducted over drinks after 6:00 P.M. than in all of the regular working hours combined.

Evelyn's thoughts were interrupted by the cocktail waitress bringing the two drinks.

"Thank you," the hostess said, turning toward the earnest conversation behind her. "Pardon me for interrupting, gentlemen. Your drink, darling," she said, handing one large martini to Marshall. "Charlie, you look wonderful, handsome, and oh, so sexy. If it weren't for the presence of this buckeye from the other body, I might try to bed you."

Lauder laughed, allowing himself to be pulled into the game. "Evelyn, that's a splendid offer, but whatever would we do with my wife?"

"Jeannine?" Evelyn leaned in very close to Lauder's face, letting her left breast rest against his arm. "But, Charlie," she said in a loud stage whisper, "Jeannie and I are best friends. Surely she'd understand. I'm harmless."

Lauder raised a hand to Evelyn's shoulder, copping a feel of his own on the way up. "I think that's what the asp said to Cleopatra, my dear."

Marshall took two long sips from his martini as the scene played out before him. At that point, he'd seen quite enough.

"Evelyn, be a darling and circulate without me for a few more minutes," he said. "Charlie and I have some business to finish. We won't be much longer, I promise." His mouth smiled, but his eyes didn't, and Evelyn left the two men as quickly as she could without appearing to follow an order.

Both men watched her move away, appreciating the care she'd taken of her body over fifty-plus years. Lauder was still watching when Marshall interrupted his appreciation period.

"When was the last time you talked to the Sexton brass?"

"What?" Lauder pulled his concentration back to the conversation at hand. "Oh, not since, I guess, about six o'clock yesterday. There's nothing to talk about, Harold. So far as we can see, the aircraft itself wasn't at fault. I'm sorry for your people, but it looks like the engine will take the rap on this. And the seagull population, I suppose, which lost a valued comrade." His eyes carried an expression of complete sympathy, but he was smiling.

"Look," he continued earnestly, "a one-time malfunction can happen. Everybody's all bent out of shape because so many people died, and I understand that, but it was one problem with one engine. I don't see any reason to sit shiva for Converse."

"To what?"

"Sit shiva. It's Yiddish. It means to wear sackcloth and ashes, and to mourn, I think. You never heard that?"

"What makes you call this an engine malfunction?" Marshall asked, dismissing the ethnic lesson. "Bird strikes aren't engine malfunctions."

"They are if you've bragged to the world that your engine can withstand that sort of thing," Lauder insisted. "You haven't thought this thing through, Harold. That *Chronicle* story this morning's got everybody wondering about the Converse Fan. By raising the Seattle incident, the paper's raised the possibility of a defect in the engine. And by questioning its fail-safe value, they've raised doubts about the design. Maybe there's no relationship, but that's not how it reads."

"True," Marshall said. "But don't toss it off like it doesn't have implications for Sexton. If the Converse Fan goes down the toilet, it will take the Eight-eleven with it."

Lauder frowned. "That's crazy. One accident—even two incidents—isn't going to take down the Fan or the Eight-eleven."

"Don't bet on it," Marshall insisted. "It could happen if the *Chronicle* keeps hammering at this thing, which is exactly what that rag plans to do."

"How would you know?"

"Actually, I feel pretty smug about that," Marshall said. "One of my legislative aides is dating a *Chronicle* photographer. She gets a bonus for information about what the paper's up to. Would that I had such feedback from a couple other newsrooms."

Lauder looked horrified. "You're running a whore?"

"I'd say it's more like a mole in the promised land, Charlie. She's not whoring. She really cares for this newsie. She can use the dough, and Converse can afford it. I'm just the conduit. I've also sent word to the NTSB that they'd better not mess with Converse, or they're going to be messing with me. You always want to take action before action takes you, Charlie."

Lauder wasn't convinced. "I'm sorry, but those sound like arrangements you wouldn't want leaked to the press. I wouldn't brag about them if I were you."

Marshall snorted. "You're weak, Charlie." His voice was thick with contempt. "You worry too much about the things you think you can't control instead of taking control. The public won't differentiate between an aircraft and the engine that powers it. What the masses understand is that a Sexton snuffed itself and three hundred thirty-four died. People start losing confidence in the Sexton Eight-eleven, the way they lost confidence in the DC-Ten—deserved or not. Ticket sales go into the toilet, and not too long afterward, aircraft sales get flushed right along with them."

Lauder called time-out long enough to order another drink. Marshall drained what remained in his glass and did the same. The congressman took two steps deeper into the shadows and gazed up at the moon, a day away from being full. It was surrounded by a soft halo of light. He shivered.

"You ever hear about a halo around the moon meaning somebody's going to die?" he asked. "Is it an old sailors' superstition?"

"Hell, I don't know. What does that have to do with our problem?"

"Nothing," Lauder acknowledged, taking his fresh drink from the waitress, who had found the two men in the shadows. When she was out of earshot, Lauder continued. "Except it would be certain political suicide if you're caught meddling with an NTSB investigation."

"Meddling is your word, Charlie. From my point of view,

I'm simply doing the job my constituents sent me to Wash ington to do."

"One constituent, anyway," Lauder replied derisively. "Take care, Harold. These things have a way of coming back to haunt."

Marshall was infuriated. "Don't lecture me, you sonofabitch. I don't give a shit what happens to Sexton. I'll take care of my people, any way I have to, and yours can go straight to hell." He whirled around on the damp grass, the first double martini making his head spin for a moment, and stormed off to look for Evelyn, or at least for a new conversation.

Later, well after two o'clock, when the last of the guests and the hired help were gone, Marshall took Evelyn Bracken to bed. But there was no love in their lovemaking. Evelyn was still smarting from the abuse she'd endured earlier. There was no desire left in her. Marshall was distracted and angry and more than a little drunk, and he drove to his own climax with a fury, neither trying to bring Evelyn along, nor caring that he didn't.

At about the same moment Harold Marshall made his entrance at Evelyn Bracken's soiree, TransAmerican Flight 14 was preparing for departure from San Francisco. Its destination was New York's John F. Kennedy Airport, with an intermediate stop and a layover of a few hours at Chicago O'Hare. Although it was 10:00 P.M. in Washington, it was just 7:00 P.M. on the West Coast, and the setting sun reflected boldly from the silver-and-blue skin of the new Sexton 811. On its tail, the Sexton carried the registration number: N464TA.

TransAmerican flight service personnel had swept and polished and dusted the inside of the aircraft until it looked as though it rolled from the finishing terminal at the Sexton plant in Los Angeles that very day. In fact, it had rolled out less than a month earlier and performed flawlessly in almost continuous service since. The maintenance chief noticed that when he checked the aircraft's logs several hours earlier.

"Hasn't even needed a light bulb," he told a member of his crew. "Don't see that often."

Still, they went over her by the book, leaving nothing to chance.

When the maintenance crew finished, the baggage handlers appeared, feeding aluminum containers filled with mail and baggage, one coffin, two dog porters, and one cat carrier into the maw of the cargo compartments via conveyor belts.

The flight crew showed up about forty-five minutes before the scheduled departure. The cabin attendants busied themselves with food-service deliveries: full-sized bottles of liquor and fine Mondavi wines for first class, shot bottles and Sebastiani for business class and coach. They checked the first-class appetizers of Brie and pâté. They peeked at the greens to be certain they were fresh. And they stowed the first-class entrées, including filets mignon, lobster fettuccini, and salmon steaks. Baked Alaska desserts were set in the galley freezers. The process went much faster in the center and aft sections, where the main courses—baked chicken with almonds and haddock—were simpler and the courses fewer.

On the flight deck, the captain checked his flight plan against his high-altitude charts, and the engineer recalculated fuel requirements, then took a flashlight and left the plane, walking around it slowly, checking tires, wheel wells, the appearance of flaps and slats, ailerons and rudders, even the nuts and bolts that held everything together. Some of the two hundred seventy-one passengers waiting to board Flight 14 watched the inspection from the windows of their gate. To those laymen, it appeared the first officer was being meticulous. And to the extent that a flashlight and human eyes can see problems, he was meticulous.

It would have taken an electron microscope to see the fracture developing in one of the turbine disks in Number 1 engine. The weak spot that generated the fracture should have been—and normally would have been—discovered on final inspection by the manufacturer before the disk was shipped to Converse. It didn't take long for the vibrations of the fan jet to pound the flaw into a microscopic crack. Now the crack was spreading in tiny increments, and would continue to do so until it weakened the structure of the titanium alloy and the disk disintegrated. It could happen this night, or the next, or the next. No one could foretell the schedule. But if it happened in flight, the result could be the total destruction of the airliner and the death of everyone on board.

It was Saturday night, about ten forty-five, when Pace walked into the Toodle Inn. The bar was half full, but the smoke was thick and the music loud, and none of the patrons evidenced the slightest interest in each other. Pace found an isolated booth and ordered a beer to sip while he waited for McGill. He was surprised that he'd beaten the pilot there; he'd had to drive twice as far.

McGill arrived just as Pace's drink did. He ordered black coffee.

"You giving up sex, too?" Pace asked. McGill ignored the line.

"I hope I didn't call you out here for nothing, but you said you wanted to get involved."

Pace frowned. "What's up?"

McGill pulled a single sheet of computer paper from his pocket. It was the kind accountants use, with alternating green and white bars. Nobody bothered to tear off the perforated feed-strips.

"This was in my mailbox at the hotel when I got back after dinner," he said, handing the page across to Pace.

The reporter unfolded it and moved it around, trying to find enough light to read by. He gave up and pulled a yellow glass bowl containing a lighted candle from between the table's salt and pepper shakers and held it beside the paper. It was adequate, if not comfortable.

"This place obviously doesn't double as a library," he

commented as he strained over the note. "And the printer could use a new ribbon." But he fell silent as he read the message.

> To Capt. McGill:
>
> I am leaving this for you because I don't know who else I can trust, and I hope I can trust you. I believe I have information of a conspiracy to cover up the real cause of the ConPac crash. I have known about it since the night of the accident, but I have been afraid to confront anyone. I am desperate. I don't know where to turn. Please help me prove something is wrong. I will call your room at midnight, and I hope that by then you will have received this note and have some advice for me. I hope you'll forgive me for not signing my name, but I am frightened.

Pace looked up from the page. Then, without a word, he bent and read it again.

"Hoax or real?" he asked when he finished it a second time.

"I have to work on the assumption it's real," McGill said in a voice so low Pace almost couldn't hear him over the noise of the band.

"Why come to me?" the reporter asked. "If you think this has any basis in fact, why not go to the IIC with it?"

"My first instinct," McGill nodded. "Then I remembered the conversation you had with the guy from the Hill yesterday. If what's in that note is true, maybe the IIC's been reached and—"

"Padgett?"

"Yeah, and if he's been reached, maybe Lund's been reached. If Lund's been reached, how much higher could it go? I don't normally believe in conspiracies, but Jesus, who'da thought a burglary at Watergate would leave a trail to the President of the United States?"

"Whoa, Mike. I think you're reaching."

"Yeah, maybe. Maybe not."

The waitress came with a pot to refill McGill's coffee cup

and nodded toward Pace's empty beer glass. The reporter shook his head, and the waitress looked irritated.

"Big spenders, you guys, huh? I hope you tip good."

Pace waited until she flounced off, then leaned over the table. "You still haven't answered my question, Mike. Why me?"

"Who else would you suggest? I know you. I trust you. I need help. And you asked me to call you if anything like this came up. I can't go public with it. Can you imagine me calling a press conference to expose an alleged conspiracy on the basis of an anonymous note? And if this is true," he nodded toward the message lying on the table, "the people responsible for the cover-up would burrow so far underground you couldn't nuke 'em out."

"You can't judge this until you know who wrote it," Pace said. "When he calls at midnight, assuming he calls, why don't you ask him to meet you somewhere?"

"How about *us* meeting him somewhere?"

"Sounds good."

"This cloak-and-dagger stuff is more up your alley than mine."

"I'm in."

"Fine, so what do you suggest we do?"

Pace cupped his right fist inside his left hand and rested his chin on his thumbs. He fought to remain calm, but the excitement of the mystery had pumped him up.

"When this guy calls you, try to arrange a meeting someplace private. Tell him you've brought me in on this, and we're both eager to talk to him."

"Not a good idea," McGill objected. "If this guy is legit, he's scared, and I think if he knows the press is involved, it'll spook him. It would be better if I arrange a meeting for him and me but set it up for someplace where you can listen without being seen."

"Okay. You going to set it up for tonight?"

"The sooner, the better."

"I haven't pulled an all-nighter since college. I don't know if I can do it anymore."

"Think of the stakes. They'll scare you awake." McGill caught the waitress's eye and signaled for the check. She placed it between them. McGill picked it up.

"You bought yesterday when you were asking for help." He smiled.

"I'm a hell of a lot cheaper date than you were," Pace replied.

"I keep telling you, I'm older and wiser. By the way, you got any idea where we should meet our friend?"

"Let him choose," Pace suggested. "He'll be more relaxed in a place he knows."

"I knew there was a good reason to bring you along."

McGill threw a ten-dollar bill on the table, figuring that would cover the check and the angst of the waitress, and the two men walked into the parking lot together.

"We might be hoping for different outcomes on this, you and me," the pilot said. "I hope this is a crock of shit, that there's nobody out there with any proof of any kind of conspiracy. I don't want there to be a midnight phone call. I think you're wishing for the big story. I would be if I were you. But if there's no midnight call, if this is a hoax, it stops right there. I won't help you blow a hoax into a big story, and I hope that doesn't put us at odds."

Pace couldn't help it. Professional recognition is addictive and once tasted, not easily forsworn. He *would* be disappointed if Mike didn't get the midnight phone call; he couldn't help that. He *would* be disappointed if this didn't turn into a very big story. But what the hell. He'd been disappointed before and survived. He'd survive again.

McGill misread Pace's silence. "Man, I don't believe you!"

Pace shook his head. "It's cool, Mike. I was just having a couple of personal thoughts and private doubts. Nothing to do with this. If the bastards are out there, let's bring them to ground. If not, we'll forget it and catch up on our sleep."

They shook hands on it.

As midnight approached, McGill paced his room and Pace sat quietly in a straight-backed chair, contemplating the carpet beneath his feet. The closer it came to the appointed hour, the more certain McGill was that the phone would not ring. Which was why he jumped when the oversized telephone bell shattered the silence in his room at eleven fifty-eight, a full two minutes earlier than scheduled.

"McGill." He held the phone away from his ear so Pace could listen.

"I gather you received my message." McGill thought he heard a hint of an accent in the voice, something vaguely familiar.

"I got your message, but for all I know, you're some crank who crawled out from behind the woodwork with a novel idea for a practical joke that isn't very funny." The insult elicited no rise from the caller.

"I understand. But I'm no crank. I'm a desperate man living a nightmare and looking for help. The investigation is rigged." Pace thought he detected tightness, almost pain, in the voice.

"If that's true," McGill said, "I'm ready and willing to help. But I don't have any way to judge your integrity or your ability to distinguish a conspiracy because I don't know who you are."

"How do you suggest we resolve this dilemma?"

"I suggest we meet somewhere, in a private place you may choose, and you tell me who you are, what you know, what you suspect, and how you got involved."

"When?"

"Tonight."

The caller thought for a minute. "You know where Georgetown Pike is? It's Route One ninety-three."

"No, but I can find it."

"Be careful," the caller said. "It's a narrow, hilly, winding road."

"Right," McGill replied.

The caller gave the pilot very specific directions to a small bridge near Great Falls, where, he said, there was a secluded pullout that would afford them privacy while they talked.

"Can you be there in an hour?" the caller asked.

"No problem," McGill replied. "You're certain you'll be there?"

"Sir, this is neither a practical joke nor a joking matter. I'll be there."

The line went dead.

The telephone replaced in its cradle at the other end of McGill's connection was in Hangar 3. The hand that held the receiver belonged to Mark Antravanian, who had spent his entire professional career dealing through channels, not anonymously over the telephone in the middle of the night. He hated what he was doing, and he was frightened. But he had no choice.

Thursday night he'd witnessed a man wearing an NTSB identification badge tampering with the crumpled starboard engine of the doomed ConPac flight. When the saboteur finished his task and left the scene, Antravanian took a quick look at the engine and recognized immediately what had been done to it. At that moment he had been too stunned to believe what he saw, let alone to act on it. It wasn't until the power-plants group met early the next morning that Antravanian recognized the stranger at the engine to be the very man who would head the investigation of its performance.

The engineer flirted with the idea of confronting Parkhall at the breakfast table in the dining room of the Marriott Hotel in front of the two other members of the power-plants team. But his Eastern European civility wouldn't allow him to make an accusation publicly before confronting Parkhall privately. His decision to wait was sealed by the approach of three men. Antravanian recognized the squat, barrel-chested, balding man in the lead as Walt Havens, and he reckoned correctly that the other two also were representatives of the Converse Corporation, who would have come both to aid in the investigation and to oversee the interests of the engine manufacturer.

So Antravanian waited until after breakfast, when the group broke up to reconvene at the site where the Converse engine rested. He carefully moved into a position at Parkhall's elbow as they walked out of the hotel into the parking lot.

Antravanian considered a diplomatic opening, but in the end, when the two were isolated from the others, he blurted it out. "What were you doing to the engine last night?"

Parkhall's head snapped around as though he'd been struck from the other side. Antravanian saw the color drain from the man's face. Nonetheless, he managed a benign expression.

"What are you talking about . . . Mark, is it? I wasn't out at the engine last night."

"Yes, you were," Antravanian insisted. "I saw you there. And after you left, I looked at the engine. I had seen it for the first time during the late afternoon, and I saw immediately the difference. I didn't know who you were until this morning, and now I demand an explanation, or I will go to higher authority."

"All right," Parkhall relented. "Ride out to Hangar Three with me, and I'll show you. It's nothing to get all lathered up about."

Inside a maroon Dodge sedan, Parkhall used his car telephone. "The warehouse. Five minutes," was all he said. They rode across the airport grounds and through the guarded gates in silence. Antravanian once tried to press his questions, but Parkhall waved him silent. They parked beside the hangar. Antravanian started walking toward the entry door, but Parkhall called him in the opposite direction, toward a small warehouse behind the facility.

Inside, they were met by two men who looked out of place, more like retired pro football tackles or soldiers of fortune than aviation engineers. Parkhall sat down behind a small desk. Antravanian stood in front of him, his back to the door and the hired help. Antravanian thought Parkhall looked more comfortable since they'd entered the warehouse. He surmised correctly the men standing behind him were hired muscle and the diminutive NTSB engineer felt less threatened—and more threatening—with them acting as back-up.

Without hesitation, Parkhall told Antravanian he'd been given a great deal of money to pay for an investigative conclusion that exonerated the Converse engines from blame in the Dulles accident. He said he was willing to share the money in return for Antravanian's silence about what he saw Thursday night.

Even before Parkhall got into the details, Antravanian's reaction was explosive, an accusation that Parkhall had gone mad. Parkhall remained calm, explaining that if Antravanian did not intend to accept the money, or meant in any way to cast doubts on the contrived engine report, there was more cash available to take him out of the picture.

"What does 'take me out of the picture' mean, exactly?" Antravanian demanded.

"Well, let's see," Parkhall thought aloud. He was wearing the smug look of a bully when his gang of friends is nearby. "You could be discredited, your life and career ruined. Or, as our friends at Langley would say, you could be terminated with extreme prejudice."

"That's bullshit," Antravanian screamed. "That is total bullshit. I don't know why I'm even standing here talking to you. You can't do those things. I don't know how you could ever condone the suggestion of a false report. That's ludicrous! That's insane!"

"Mark, hear me out. If we do this thing, we get rich, and I've been assured the Converse people won't rest until they find the cause of the engine failure and fix it on their own. Nobody gets hurt unless somebody screws up."

"I don't believe what I'm hearing," Antravanian breathed. "I will not be a party to this. I won't even stand here and listen to anymore of it."

Parkhall came out from behind the desk and put a hand on his arm as Antravanian took a step to leave. "Mark, I've agreed to go along with this. I can't back out. And I can't let you out, either."

"And I'm saying, no way." Parkhall glanced over Antravanian's left shoulder, but the gesture made no impression on the angry engineer. "I'm going to Padgett, and if I have to, I'll go to Lund. If I get no satisfaction from either of them, I'll go higher. *Somebody* will stop you."

"It won't do any good, Mark. Everyone's been reached."

"Everyone?" Antravanian blanched, then regained his outrage. "Then I'll go to Congress, to the White House!" he screamed. As he tried to turn, determined to leave, he was grabbed from behind by four hands, two on each arm. He attempted to twist away, but the hands on his left jerked his arm up to shoulder height and slammed it down at the wrist across a steel bar on a baggage trolley.

The sickening sound of his own bones breaking was accompanied by a shock wave of nausea and blinding pain that buckled Antravanian at the knees. He opened his mouth to scream, but one of the hands on his right stuffed a balled-up rag in his mouth, stoppering both the sound coming up from his lungs and the bile surging up from his belly. He blacked out for a few seconds and was lying flat on his back on the concrete floor when he opened his eyes. Parkhall was standing over him, straddling him at the knees.

"That was stupid, Mark. But you know now this isn't a game. There are people who can do exactly what I told you they can. They not only can, they are very willing. I hope there's no need to call them back to break your other wrist? Or something more critical to your survival?"

Antravanian managed to shake his head weakly.

"Good. There are plenty of security people around who can get you to a place where that arm can be looked after. After that, you go back to your room and take the rest of the day off, and tomorrow, if you need it. I'll tell everyone you've had an accident. When you feel well enough, you can rejoin the group, and you and I can come to an understanding."

Parkhall departed, leaving Antravanian on the floor. The engineer stayed there for several minutes, trying to will away the pain and terror. He pulled the rag from his mouth with his right hand and attempted to call for help, but no useful sound crossed his dry tongue. Gingerly holding his crippled left arm against his stomach, he worked his way to his feet, closing his eyes and gulping air to put down the persistent nausea. Eventually he was able to stagger to the door of the warehouse and out onto the asphalt apron, where he got the attention of a security guard. Antravanian lied to the guard, saying he was injured when he tripped over something and fell.

At a hospital, the wrist was checked by an orthopedic surgeon, who said the break was clean and the healing should be complete. Antravanian was put in a cast, given some pills for the pain, and advised to watch where he walked. He went back to his room to lie down.

Through that night and most of Saturday, he stayed in his room, taking medication for pain, calling room service when he got hungry, struggling to decide how to handle the very real nightmare into which he had fallen, unbidden. At one point he almost decided it would be best to go along, but he knew that was a conclusion born more of fear than common sense. So late Saturday afternoon, instead of calling Parkhall and bowing to his demands, Mark Antravanian went to the small desk where he had set up a personal computer and with his one good hand, typed the note McGill would find in his mailbox several hours later.

But when Antravanian went to the lobby to deliver his envelope to the front desk, he was seen by one of the two men Parkhall had stationed there. He was seen again at eleven-fifteen, when he left the hotel and drove away. The watcher reported to Parkhall that Antravanian appeared to be heading for the airfield, possibly for the hangar.

So it was when Antravanian made his midnight call to McGill from Hangar 3, believing the phone there was more secure than the phone in his room, Parkhall was standing in the shadows, listening to every word. When the conversation ended, he allowed Antravanian to leave alone, then made a call of his own to the two who had muscled the engineer the day before and kept him under surveillance since. Parkhall didn't want any more killing. To know it was going on was bad enough. To order it himself was to sink to a depth he'd never believed possible. He would have preferred to pay off Antravanian and bring him into the fold. But now that was out of the question.

Parkhall's orders were clear and predictable. All the choices but one were gone.

Pace hunkered down in the backseat of Mike McGill's rental car, up against the wide metal post separating the side from the rear window. In the dark, he wouldn't be seen, and he could run the side window down enough to hear the conversation.

The two headed east on nearly deserted Georgetown Pike, McGill behind the wheel negotiating the treacherous curves. A few moments later Antravanian swung his little Chevy onto the same road, driving carefully with his right hand. His plaster-encased left arm was lying softly in his lap, the constant throbbing in his wrist elevating to real pain over every bump in the asphalt. He nudged the injured arm up against the steering wheel to steady the vehicle as he took his right hand away for a second to flip the rearview mirror to its night-vision setting. Some idiot was driving a van so close it was almost in the Chevy's trunk, and he was using his high-beam headlights.

Antravanian was driving skillfully, but his mind was less on the road and more on the upcoming meeting at the bridge. In the last hours, his terror had turned to fury. He was determined to bring down everyone who would take money to fake an accident investigation.

As he passed through the chic little town of Great Falls and entered the darkness of the oak-and-cottonwood canopy that enclosed the road for the next few miles, he was rehearsing what he would say to McGill. When he hit the hilly, curving part of the Pike, he was barely aware of the light-blue Ford van pulling out to pass him. A fleeting question crossed his thoughts about why the stupid driver had waited for a double solid-yellow line when there had been plenty of opportunity to pass on the straightaways behind them.

So certain was he that the driver was drunk, it was almost no surprise when the van slammed broadside into his Chevy. He struggled with his one good arm to keep his damaged car on the road. He stepped on the brakes, thinking if he slowed down, the van would go by. But the van slowed, too, and body-slammed the compact car again. This time Antravanian had more trouble controlling the weaving. Pain stabbed through his useless arm, and the certainty hit him just then that he had met the occupants of that van before.

Antravanian's anger washed over the lines of reason. His only motivation was revenge as he turned the little Chevy's steering wheel sharply to the left and slammed into the van.

"You bastards!" he hissed. "Now it's coming at you, how do you like it?"

He whipped the wheel over and hit the Ford again, but this time a misshapen piece of the Chevy's front bumper got caught in the undercarriage of the van. The little car was dragged, out of control, about three hundred yards down the road. Antravanian fought the drag by turning his steering wheel hard right, away from the truck. When the bumper let go with a bang, the Chevy veered to the right, leaped a low crash barrier and fell into the creek gully bordering the road. It bounced through the thick trees clustered along the creek's bank, thrown around like a bearing in a pinball machine, and finally came to rest upside down with all four wheels spinning and steam rising from the shattered radiator.

The battered van stopped about twenty yards beyond the point where the Chevy left the road, then backed up until it was directly above the crumpled compact.

The van's passenger, dressed in a dark jumpsuit, lowered himself to the road gingerly, nursing his own bruises, and picked his way down the embankment toward the Chevy. In his left hand he carried a pencil flashlight, in his right a .357 Magnum. He saw no evidence of life in the car, and when he knelt down and directed his flash through the splintered windshield, he saw Antravanian, dead or unconscious, pinned between the steering wheel and the seat. He worked his way around to the rear of the car and played the narrow beam of light over the exposed fuel tank. He allowed himself a smile when he found a spot at which the tank had ruptured, allowing a thin stream of gasoline to trickle down the hillside. This was almost too easy.

From a pocket in the jumpsuit, he took a butane wand—the kind sold for use in fireplaces and charcoal grills—and thumbed on a shaft of flame that he touched to the gasoline rivulet snaking toward the creek below. There would be no incriminating matches left behind.

The gas went up with a *whoosh,* and the jumpsuited figure scrambled back up the embankment.

The van pulled away as the flame reached the Chevy's gas tank, which exploded in a fireball. The van was well away from the scene, hidden in a dark, tree-lined driveway a mile to the east, when the first police car flashed by, siren screaming.

"Suppose that's about that poor fellow back there?" the driver of the van asked. His name was Sylvester Bonaro, and although his name and his swarthy, olive complexion suggested Italian ancestry, Bonaro actually was the product of a Greek-Turkish liaison, a bloodline in conflict, to which he always attributed his mean streak.

"I hope not," replied the passenger, a burly man named Wade Stock. "I hope they don't find that motherfucker until he's nothing more than cinders. He like to tore my arm off."

"Yeah, well, the night's not over. Get the camera ready, and tomorrow you can whine all the way to the bank."

McGill paced beside the Toyota. It was one-fifteen, and there wasn't a sign of anybody who wanted to have a meeting at that hour. The anonymous caller was fifteen minutes late.

"This is your town, Steve. Are we at the right place?"

"According to the directions, this is it," the reporter replied quietly from the backseat.

"Goddamn, I was almost ready to believe this guy was for real," McGill cursed. "There was something about his voice." He shook his head. "I can't place it."

"You think you know him?"

"I think I should. It was the accent. Nothing I can identify, but it was familiar."

A screaming police car raced up the highway past their turnout, and the TransAm pilot instinctively turned away from the road. "Christ, I'm acting like a criminal," he said with a short laugh. "Whadda you think, hotshot? Have we been had?"

Pace had a sickening hunch. "Mike, get in and follow that cop," he suggested.

Ten minutes later they witnessed the last of the firefight on the Chevy. They had pulled off the road as if they were casual passersby come to watch the action. At least, Pace thought, it wasn't as ghoulish as the two guys from the blue van who pulled off ahead of their rental car and ran across the road to shoot video tape. Pace and McGill stayed with their car, away from the action. They saw all they needed to half an hour later, when four medics labored up the hill with a stretcher containing a black, zippered body bag.

"You don't suppose that's him, do you?" Pace asked.

"If the fear I heard in his voice was well-founded, I'd say it very likely *is* him, or whatever's left of him," McGill answered. "Jesus, what in hell have we fallen into?"

"This is no proof of anything, Mike. It could be nothing more than a Saturday-night drunk who couldn't manage the road. Maybe we should go back to the bridge for another hour or so. Maybe your guy was held up."

"Tell me the truth, hero. If you had to make a guess, would you say our chances are better of meeting my tipster at the bridge or saying good-bye to him right here?"

The question was met with silence.

9

The battered blue Ford van pulled into the parking lot at the Dulles Marriott, squealing as it turned into a parking space, because somewhere under the newly caved-in right front side, metal was scraping metal.

Bonaro and Stock got out, stripped off their jumpsuits and threw them into the back of the van. Stock reached in and pulled out two cases, one containing his video camera, the other a VCR with an assortment of cables. He was a bulky man with a beer gut, but a lot of what looked like flab was steroid-enhanced muscle. He'd gotten hooked on the stuff while playing high-school football in Jersey City, and he'd stuck with the drugs when he entered his present line of work. They let him maintain maximum strength with minimum effort. Stock didn't think of himself as lazy or as a junkie; it was more a conservation of his time.

Under the discarded work clothes, both men were dressed in jackets and ties and looked wholly respectable, perhaps two businessmen returning after a long sales session. The disinterested fellow pulling the graveyard shift at the front desk looked up briefly, but he had his nose back in an old Louis L'Amour western before they disappeared down the corridor that housed rooms 101 to 148.

Bonaro knocked twice on the door to 122. They could hear the sound of a television set. When the door opened, Elliott Parkhall stood there in his bare feet, dressed in an old pair of blue jeans and a yellow T-shirt. Parkhall motioned them in and closed and locked the door.

Stock went directly to the television and unplugged it reluctantly. Parkhall had been watching an adult movie on one of the hotel's cable channels. Stock set up the VCR. Bonaro scanned the hotel room. If he was looking for anything special, there was no sign he found it.

"Went off without a hitch," he said when he saw his partner reconnect the television to the wall outlet. "We blew him off the road, and Wade torched the car. They're gonna be a while coming up with an ID. Fuckin' gas tank must have been full. Looked like the Fourth of July."

"Witnesses?" Parkhall asked.

"Not another soul on the road. We saw one car go by us when we were headed east after we did the job. That musta been the guy turned in the alarm. We waited for a cop to show before we went back. That way, cops were there before we showed up again. We shot the thing like tourists. Another car with two guys came by and stopped to watch. Got 'em on tape, too."

Stock popped the video-tape cartridge from his camera, slid it into the VCR and clicked the play bar. There was the usual brief delay while blank leader wound through the heads.

What Parkhall saw over the next half hour was riveting. His assassins had shot vivid action footage of the fire and the efforts to put it out. But his biggest reaction came when the video camera panned to a silver Toyota that pulled up behind the blue Ford van. Two men got out. One of them Parkhall knew on sight.

"McGill," Parkhall whispered. "So you're the one."

"The one what?" Bonaro asked.

"He's the one Antravanian called, was going to have the little meeting with. I don't know the other guy. Either of you recognize him?"

Bonaro and Stock each shook his head, neither moving his eyes from the television screen. When the fire was out, rescue workers extricated what was left of the driver from the burned ruins of his car. When the victim was carried in a black body bag up the hillside, the police could be seen ordering spectators to leave. And the tape ended.

Parkhall realized his hands were sweating and wiped them up the thighs of his jeans. He was an engineer by trade, and he had little appetite for the work done that night. But his distaste was overcome by his greed. His pot at the end of this rainbow held both gold and revenge.

He'd spent twenty-four years of his career at Warner Woolcott, a small, innovative company doing remarkable work on aviation and space programs. He'd quit abruptly seven years earlier after being passed over for promotion. WW executives told him he wouldn't be promoted until he learned, assuming he could learn, to get along with his peers and supervisors. He was frequently arrogant and often preposterous, and other engineers went out of their way *not* to work with him.

Parkhall had walked out with nothing but his vested pension and an expression of interest from the NTSB. Although agency officials were aware of Parkhall's reputation, they'd lost so many people to the glamour, prestige, and salaries of the private sector that the temptation to take a little back was great. Parkhall accepted the government job at a significant cut in pay in the belief another private company would snatch him up as soon as his departure from WW became known. He even fancied a bidding war for his services. But he was shunned as a problem not worth the return.

He languished, growing more bitter and more certain when his time came to strike back at the industry that rejected him, his would be a monumental blow. This was his opportunity, his distaste for violence notwithstanding. There was a million dollars in this for him, and there was no act of violence, no deed of sabotage, no threat to public safety he was unable to rationalize for that sum.

"You did well," he said, crossing the room to a nightstand. He pulled a hotel envelope from the drawer and handed it to Bonaro. "This is payment in full. I know where I can reach you if we need you again. Take the equipment. Leave the tape."

Bonaro and Stock nodded and dismantled and packed their VCR. They left without a word.

Parkhall wandered over to the window, which looked out over Dulles. The noise-proofing and the distance from the terminal prevented any sound from penetrating. He whispered to the night that couldn't hear him, "Stay out of this, McGill, or you're dead, too."

If Parkhall had been in New York at John F. Kennedy Airport instead of at Washington Dulles, he could have seen a big silver-and-blue Sexton 811, owned by TransAmerican Airlines, glide in for a perfect landing on Runway 13R.

As they taxied toward their assigned gate, the captain and first officer grinned at each other.

"This is a dream ship," the first officer gushed.

"No less," the captain agreed. "She feels so damned solid, like she could fly on forever."

But the aircraft they had come to love carried the registration, TA2464N.

And flying forever was one thing she would not be able to do.

Pace picked up the *Chronicle* lying in front of his apartment door and shuffled in wearily as daylight began to brighten the eastern sky. He was still a little bit drunk.

He and McGill had remained at the scene of the accident until the Virginia cops ordered them and the two who'd arrived in the beat-up blue van to leave. They'd gone back to the Dulles Marriott to have a drink and talk things over. The bar was closed, but McGill had a bottle of Black Jack in his room. So they got a bucket of ice, set the ice and the bottle between them on the round, phony wood-grain motel-room table and tried to make sense of the night.

They'd had little success in coming to any supportable conclusions, although they'd had a great deal of success depleting the supply of Jack Daniels. Pace thought he wasn't being affected by the liquor, until he got up to leave several hours later and felt the room tilt.

McGill suggested he spend what was left of the night in the unused second double bed right there, but Pace said he had to be at work early and insisted on going home. McGill let him go after extracting a promise that Pace would stay off roads like Georgetown Pike and stick to highways that were wider and straighter.

They'd walked to Pace's car still debating whether the death they witnessed earlier had any connection to their investigation.

"I guess we'll know when you find out who the poor sap was," McGill said. "I keep thinking about the voice of the man who called. It sounded sincere and frightened. I'm not imagining it. I wouldn't have called you out in the middle of the night if I hadn't been convinced it was legit."

"That's the fourth time you've said that, Mike. It's beginning to sound like an apology."

"That's not the way I mean it."

They reached Pace's Honda sedan. "Let's do as we agreed and go on with our jobs and see where this leads us, if anywhere," the reporter summed up. "You watch goings-on at the hangar, and I'll check on the body's ID first thing in the morning."

"It *is* morning," McGill said, checking his watch.

"Oh, fuck," Pace responded, giggling drunkenly. "I'll do it first thing *later* this morning."

He got into the car, keyed the engine, and thumbed the electric buttons that lowered the front windows on both the driver and passenger sides. He would leave them open, and perhaps the fresh air would clear his head.

"Put your seatbelt on, hotshot," McGill ordered. "And drive carefully. I'll call you later."

Pace made it home with a minimum of weaving, although he did draw a long look from a Virginia highway patrolman who passed him on the Beltway. Pace nodded and apparently was sufficiently convincing. By the time he turned the key in his door, he felt ready for the junk heap.

The red light on his answering machine was flashing. Pace hit the playback button.

It was Kathy. She'd called late the night before.

"Hi, Steve. It's just before eleven, and I thought you'd be home. You sure are working hard." Pace heard her take a deep breath. "Daddy called this afternoon. The airline released Jonny's body to us." Her voice cracked. God, how he wanted to be with her. "I'm flying to Boston early tomorrow for the funeral on Monday—Betsy decided Jonny should be buried in the family plot—but I'm not going to stay in Boston very long. You know Daddy. Get over the grief and get on with life. He told me he wants me to come back to Washington right after the funeral. So I'll be home Monday night. Before I left, I wanted to say thanks for everything you've done, and I wanted, well, I'd like to see you when I get back. Good luck with your stories. 'Bye."

He also had a message to call Glenn Brennan if he got home before midnight, but he was many hours late for that.

Pace fixed coffee and breakfast—if a single English muffin is breakfast—and sat down to read the Sunday *Chronicle*. The big headline said:

Last seconds of Flight 1117; crew terrified, confused

Underneath was a subhead.

Sources say voice tapes reveal agony

It carried his byline. He hoped the story wasn't as flimsy in the reading as he'd thought it in the writing the evening before. He didn't have the stamina to find out. He left the table and went to his bedroom to shower, but he couldn't hold his eyes open. He flopped on the bed with the thought that if he could rest for a few minutes, he'd be fine.

Thirty seconds later, still fully clothed, he was sound asleep.

10

Several colleagues stared as Pace eased himself down at his desk. If he looked as lousy as he felt, he could have been taken for a vagrant. Glenn Brennan wandered over.

"It was either an all-night binge or a wild and crazy sex orgy to which I was not invited," Brennan said as he dropped into Jack Tarshis's chair. "You didn't have an orgy and forget about your old buddy Glenn, now did ye?"

"None of the above," Pace replied weakly. He needed a lift, but Brennan's needling wasn't the ticket. It would have to be something more profound, something like Kathy keeping her promise and asking to see him when she returned to Washington.

"Ah, denial," said Brennan, waving a forefinger in the air. " 'Twould lead me to believe 'twas the orgy, then, ye no-account scoundrel. I want details, man. Details!"

"Glenn, I don't need this today. What are you doing here anyway? It's Sunday."

"There's a memorial thing on the Hill today—not that he deserves it—for the fascist congressman from California, and they called me in to cover it. But don't be changin' the subject. I want details of this affair."

"There was no all-night party. No sex orgy. I was working."

Brennan stared at him, scowling. " 'Tis scum ye was born, and 'tis scum ye will die," he continued. "Glory, but yer a dog-faced asshole."

Pace raised an eyebrow. "I didn't know asshole was an Irish word."

" 'Tis, since the Irish met you."

Brennan laughed aloud, delighting himself with his joke. Pace rubbed his eyes and tried to stifle a yawn. He drained one cup of coffee from the office cafeteria and started on another, anticipating a third, except the acid was beginning to wear away the lining of his stomach, which hadn't been offered solid food, save for one English muffin, since lunch in front of the NTSB offices the day before. It seemed like a month.

He heard Brennan get up and felt a hand on his shoulder. "Somethin's worn you down. If I can help, I've got the time." Brennan reverted to his normal brogue, which was thick enough.

"Thanks, Glenn," Pace said.

"Is it professional or personal?" Brennan asked.

"Professional," replied Pace.

"Something wrong?"

Pace shook his head. "I wish I knew." He glanced up at Brennan. "You really want to help? You'll have to listen to a story that could conservatively be called bizarre."

"Absolutely. I love bizarre."

"What time is the memorial thing for Whitlock?"

"Not 'til two this afternoon. They're givin' time for the faithful to get to church and eat first."

"Speaking of eating, I've got to get some food in me. Is the G Street deli open on Sundays?"

"Yep. I doubt the Sunday staff would survive without it."

"Come with me while I devour an entire cow."

"Wouldn't miss it."

Pace got up from his desk and snapped his fingers. Through the twin veils of exhaustion and hangover, the night before looked very fuzzy. But he remembered clearly his promise to check out the identity of the victim of the car wreck on 193.

"I've got to do one thing first," he told Brennan. "It'll just take a second down in Suburban."

Brennan sat down. "Think of me as your faithful dog, Patrick. You call, I'll be there."

Pace snorted. "Patrick was a saint, not a dog."

"Well, I'll be a saint of a dog," Brennan promised.

"If you try to lick my face, I'll deck you."

Pace headed for the stairway down to Suzy O'Connor's floor, but a signal from Wister detoured him. The look on the national editor's face could have soured a quart of milk. Pace guessed it was due to something more than having to work on Sunday.

"I didn't like the idea of Glenn covering the NTSB briefing last night," Wister scolded without so much as saying good morning. "He doesn't have your expertise. On top of that, I expected you in earlier today, ready to do some serious business, rather than obviously hung over and playing to Glenn's ill-conceived notions of hilarity. There is a certain amount of responsibility that goes with the privilege of working for the *Chronicle,* you know."

Pace hadn't intended to charge overtime for his work the night before. But so furious was he at Wister's officious lecture that he decided to put in for every minute of it, including the time spent drinking Black Jack with Mike McGill.

"I was *not* out partying last night, Paul," he lashed back. "I worked on a lead on the Sexton story until dawn. I got home after six. You can believe it or not. I don't give a shit. But I'm not going to stand here taking abuse from you when you don't know what you're talking about."

"Don't be insubordinate," Wister cautioned. He looked at Pace skeptically. "You were working all night on a lead?"

"Yes."

"Did it come to anything?"

"No. Ah, not yet. The truth is, I'm not sure. There's something I have to check with the Virginia suburban desk."

"I think we'd better talk to the Old Man first. He's in the Glory Room going over the Sunday papers. He's been waiting for you."

The man Pace found in the conference room was dressed in well-worn Dockers, a faded, kelly-green Polo knit shirt, and Topsiders without socks. His face was ruddy and his hair windblown. He could have stepped off a yacht on the Chesapeake Bay. Pace had seen Schaeffer casual before, but never at the office. Paul Wister, of course, was in a three-piece suit, this being a weekend notwithstanding.

Schaeffer noticed them standing at the door and grinned broadly. "Steve, come in and see what you did to the opposition, or have you seen it already?"

"No," Pace replied. "I saw page one of ours this morning, but I didn't get up until after ten, and I haven't had a chance to look at the *Post* or the *Times*."

"You sleeping in on the job?" Schaeffer grinned. "We're paying you handsomely, and all we ask in return is you work a solid eighty or ninety hours a week."

"I didn't go to bed until dawn, Avery."

"He says he was working on a lead all night," Wister said, "but he hasn't told me anything about it except it didn't pan out."

"You didn't give me a chance to tell you," Pace responded.

Schaeffer looked from one to the other, the expression on his face growing serious. He motioned for them to sit down.

"If you two have a problem, take care of it," he ordered. "I don't want it in the newsroom interfering with business. I don't want it anywhere interfering with the biggest story of the year. I want it handled. Today."

He sat back in the chair at the head of the table, and his face brightened as though the mere act of dismissing discord had ended it. "Now let's talk about tomorrow." He nodded toward Pace. "What's this great lead of yours?"

Pace retold the story, including most of the details. But as he heard himself telling it, it sounded trite, as though he'd been out all night playing cowboys and Indians, like a six-year-old. He didn't have any evidence to support the theory of a conspiracy. There was a mysterious voice on the telephone and a coincidental fatal automobile accident on Georgetown Pike. Nothing more.

When he finished, Pace stared through the plate glass at

the ornate grayness of the Old Executive Office Building. It was the best alternative he had to the scorn he thought he'd see if he looked at the two faces across the table.

He was right about Wister's. "So you went gallivanting all over the Virginia countryside in the middle of the night with an ex-jet jock on some wild-goose chase precipitated by a crank phone call," the national editor summed up. "Jesus, Pace, when are you going to grow up?"

Pace had had enough. "Damn it, Paul, you don't know it was a crank call," he insisted. "It sounded straight to me. Mike couldn't dismiss it, either. We trusted his instincts before. There's no reason to stop trusting him now."

"Except he's suddenly become your editor, telling you where to go and what to do. That's not his job or his privilege."

"He did not—"

"Stop it, both of you!" Schaeffer was sitting forward in his chair, a deep scowl furrowing his face. "I told you to end this. This sparring between you two is over. Now! Is that clear?"

Both Pace and Wister nodded.

Schaeffer nodded in return. "So when do you plan on checking out the dead body?" he asked Pace.

"I was on my way to ask Suzy if her people had anything from the Fairfax County Police when Paul said you wanted to see us."

"Avery, I don't think this is getting us anywhere," Wister protested. "Steve's going to be all over the place looking for conspiracies under every rock while the *Post* and the *Times* clean up on the central story. We'd be better off staying in the main channel with this thing."

"I don't want to stray far from the main channel, either," Schaeffer concurred. "But I think we can spare a little time to explore this side channel. We have two reasons to do so. The first is Mike McGill's reliability. The second is Pace's conversation on Friday with, ah, that guy from the Senate Transportation Committee." He was making circles in the air with his left forefinger pointed at Pace, asking for help with the name he couldn't pull from his memory.

"George Ridley," Pace said.

"Ridley, right." Schaeffer plunged on. "He doesn't call the Harold Marshall thing a conspiracy, but that's what he's talking about. Maybe it's nothing. Maybe it's something. We don't know. Now one of the insiders on the investigation gets a couple of oddball messages that a conspiracy exists. We don't know who the caller was. It might have been Ridley. It might not. Probably not, because McGill wouldn't be the logical person for Ridley to call. But if it wasn't Ridley, then we've got suspicion originating from a second source. And where there's smoke—"

"—more often than not, somebody's blowing it," Wister interrupted.

"Maybe," Schaeffer conceded. "But if that's the case, that's a story, too, some creep running around inventing dark plots. I want the story, either way." He turned to the reporter. "But Paul's concerns are valid. There are still lots of questions about the crash to be answered. You know that; you raised most of them. Unless and until something harder develops on the conspiracy theory, the central story is your priority."

"I understand," Pace said.

Wister nodded glumly, and Schaeffer turned back to the Sunday papers in a silent gesture of dismissal.

Leaving the conference room, Pace was eager to stay out of any further conversation with Wister. It was one thing to get up on the wrong side of the bed; it was quite another to bring the bed to work with you. So he made a sharp turn toward the door leading to the back stairwell and took the steps, two at a time, to the Suburban department.

Suzy O'Connor was everybody's mother. She was in her late forties, slightly rotund, and had a broad face highlighted by brown eyes that twinkled most of the time. She wore her graying hair pulled back severely, trying to counter the elfin expression that dominated her face even when she was angry. Her wardrobe ran to suits—her power clothes, some called them—and her collection of shoes was of the variety most commonly known as sensible. O'Connor had been the matron of the Suburban desk for twelve years, taking promising green reporters and either turning them into national-desk material or turning them onto the street. Now and then a successful one would opt to stay with a suburban beat rather than move up and away from Sister Suze.

Pace and a few others on the national side had avoided her whips and chains because they had been hired as experienced reporters from other papers for specific national beats. Pace sometimes thought that by skipping Suzy O'Connor's finishing school, he had somehow missed one of the great professional experiences extant. On the other hand, he wasn't sure he would have survived it.

Suzy was hunched over her computer terminal, her back to him, cursing some hapless reporter whose copy she was finding it necessary to rework. He stopped behind her and watched over her shoulder for a minute as she moved the cursor over the copy, cutting, pasting, moving, deleting and replacing words, phrases and paragraphs like an army general moves battalions during war. When she sensed his presence, Suzy turned in her chair and uttered a small shriek.

"All rise, the national staff is here," she announced, coming to attention. A few reporters raised their heads to look at Pace and smiled, but none joined O'Connor's ritual. It was her show. "And to what do we owe this great honor, my liege?" she asked.

In every newsroom, some reporters are singled out as the elite, the corps given the opportunity to handle major stories. It's a system that creates hard feelings among reporters given fewer opportunities. In Washington, the elite are the national reporters, and the idea of elitism on the *Chronicle* was passed like tribal scripture from one generation of suburban reporters to the next with the help, even the encouragement, of Suzy O'Connor. She tried to create in her staff the conviction that they were the underdogs against the big guys, always striving to make page one despite the handicap of covering the less newsworthy subjects. She instilled a camaraderie and competitiveness worth more journalistically than good spelling and grammar. After all, any old computer could check spelling, and as far as grammar was concerned, that's what God made editors for.

"I need a favor, Suzy," Pace said, ignoring her theatrics.

"A boon, my lord? 'Twould be an honor."

"It's a good thing you're a good journalist, Suze, cause you're a lousy actress."

She shrugged. "I do better with Shakespeare and Neil Simon. The material is everything. Whatcha got?"

"Car wreck on Georgetown Pike early this morning. The car and the driver were toasted. I need an ID on the driver."

"So call the cops."

"I thought maybe your people picked it up."

"I haven't seen a story, and I've got a new gal out there, Sally Incaveria. She's still feeling her way around the beat, and I don't expect to hear from her until one or a little later. I'll have her check. Involve a friend of yours?"

"I don't know. I haven't the faintest idea who it was. But it might be important."

"I'll let you know," Suzy promised.

"Thanks," Pace said. "I owe you."

"I won't forget."

Finally it was time to take care of his stomach.

"Come on, Patrick, let's go, boy," he said to Brennan. When Glenn got up from his desk, Pace laid it on. "There's a good boy. Heel."

"Shut up," Brennan replied.

They went to the G Street deli and sat at a chipped formica table well away from other Sunday diners. Brennan ordered a cheeseburger and fries. Pace ordered a large grapefruit juice, cantaloupe, three scrambled eggs with lox and onions, hash browns, two bagels with cream cheese, and coffee with cream.

"Do you want any blueberry muffins?" the waitress asked. "They're today's special."

"No, thanks," Pace replied. "Moderation is everything."

It took the better part of forty-five minutes for Pace to relate the events of the night before and to finish eating. At that, he left half the hash browns. It came down to eating the rest of the potatoes or the remaining half bagel. Since there still was cream cheese on his plate, it was no contest.

"If you'd go to the bathroom and stick a finger down your throat, you could finish your potatoes," Brennan suggested. "You can't be an official glutton if you leave stuff on your plate."

"My eating habits are not today's topic of conversation," Pace said.

"They will be when I get back to the office and describe this. It's unbelievable. However do you keep your boyish figger?"

"I'm like a snake," Pace told him. "I eat one meal a week, but it's huge, and you can watch the bulge pass through my body."

"Spare me," Brennan said with a look of disgust. "Tell me more about last night."

"You heard the story. What do you think?"

Brennan shrugged. "You know Mike McGill; I don't. Has he ever acted depraved or shown any sign he's given to fantasies?"

"No. He's one of the sanest, most pragmatic people I know."

"Then what's the problem?"

"When I was talking to Avery and Paul, I felt like a damned idiot, like I was out playing children's games instead of doing honest work."

"Sounds to me like a case of hives around the brass."

"It was."

"Wister can do that to you."

Pace nodded thoughtfully. "What about our mystery? Does the story ring true to you?"

"I believe somebody wrote Mike that note, probably the same person who called him. But whether it's a hoax or a real conspiracy, that's for you to prove. Finding out who died in that car wreck is a logical first step."

"That's why I went down to talk to Suzy. She says she's got somebody new covering out there. I don't know how well she knows her way around the Fairfax County Police Department."

Brennan smiled lecherously. "I think the new reporter's name is Sally Incaveria."

Pace nodded. "It was Sally something."

"Then you want to get your skinny little ass out to Virginia and help her," Brennan said. "She's hot. You could use a little love in your life."

Pace smiled. "Yes, I could," he acknowledged. "And I'm hoping that situation looks up, maybe in the next few days."

"Anybody I know?"

"I think you've probably met her."

"Who?"

"I'd rather see what develops before I start talking about it."

Brennan pushed himself back from the table. "Shit," he said. "You never tell me any of the good stuff. All I get to hear are the cockamamy stories about running around in the woods with a middle-aged flyboy."

"That's a pretty good story, you'll have to admit."

"It is. And if you need any help on it, don't look any farther than me. I'd love to have a piece of it." He started for the cash register, then stopped and turned back to Pace. "You know, if you turn this story, you're a cinch to bag your second Pulitzer. Anybody ever won two?"

"Oh, sure," Pace said. "But that's a bit premature."

"Just planning, boyo. Just planning."

Back at his desk, Pace immediately began making his round of regular calls: to Whitney Warner, Cullen Ferguson, the NTSB, and the FAA. He was reaching nobody who could help with a Monday lead when Suzy showed up.

"You hear from your rookie?" Pace asked.

"Yeah," Suzy said, "and if I hadn't red-flagged the story, I wouldn't have known to send her back with more questions. Then we wouldn't have known there's something curious here."

Pace spun in his chair and motioned for Suzy to sit at Tarshis's desk, which was getting more work than when the environmental writer was in the office.

"What?" Pace asked.

"On the surface, it looks like a typical one-car fatality," Suzy said. She looked down at her notes. "Fairfax County Police say the car left the road, turned over several times, bounced around and went *whoosh*. Coroner will do an autopsy tomorrow to determine cause of death. There's no ID, at least none of any use. Police found the remnants of a wallet, but everything in it was too badly burned. Apparently labs can bring info up off burned paper and plastic, and I guess they're going to try, and also go for an ID off dental records."

Suzy looked up to see if Pace had any questions so far, and he did.

"How can they ID him off dental records if they don't know he was local?"

"Don't know," Suzy acknowledged. "They look at everything, I guess, including the car."

"They don't know the car was local, either," Pace pointed out.

"Right. But there's an identification number on the engine that should help trace it to its owner. The number's smudged, but it's stamped into the engine block, so it wasn't destroyed by the fire. They'll be able to bring it up, and that could help ID the driver. There's a kicker." She looked at Pace expectantly.

"So? What?" he asked. "What, for God's sake?"

"This came to us off the record, and I mean that, 'cause the cops don't know what to make of it," Suzy said. He nodded. She continued. "According to a police captain named Clayton Helm—that's C-l-a-y-t-o-n H-e-l-m—there are some very strange skid marks associated with the accident that haven't been explained yet."

"Skid marks?"

"Skid marks. Before the car left the road, it left skid marks for nearly two hundred yards."

"So what?" Pace shrugged. "The guy was going too fast, tried to brake, and skidded before he went off the road. That's no mystery."

"Not for two hundred yards—that's two football fields, boy—and not with this kind of skid mark. The cops say— and this makes sense—that a guy trying to regain control of a runaway car would leave skid marks showing tread patterns. The tires might be weaving, but they would stay pointed more or less down the road. This accident wasn't like that. The victim's tires were turned sideways, hard to the right, like he was trying to make a right turn. He left rubber smudges, no tread lines."

"So?"

"So, he had the tires turned toward the ravine on the right, yet the car went two hundred yards down the highway in more or less a straight line. If you're in a skid and you turn the wheels sharply, you ain't gonna continue in a straight track unless you're being dragged."

"What?"

"Dragged, son. As in something is pulling you down the road against your will. If you don't believe it, go out on a highway, turn the steering wheel sharply to the right, and try to keep the car going straight for two hundred yards."

"Be nice, Suzy. Look how interesting I've made your day."

"I'm all gratitude. So what have you given me besides interesting? What's the story here?"

Pace ran his hands through his hair. He had no answers for those questions.

"If he was dragged, what does that tell the cops?" he asked.

"They're not saying. I suspect they don't know what to make of it."

"Would you or your reporter . . . what did you say her name is?"

"Sally Incaveria."

Pace grinned. "Yeah, that's the one. Would you or Sally have any problem with me talking to this Clayton Helm?"

"Not if you take her along for the interview."

"Suze, this is serious business," Pace protested. "She doesn't need to get involved. She wouldn't understand—"

"That's bullshit," she snapped. "If there's some sort of special story here, it happened on Sally's turf, and the story's hers. At the very least, she gets a piece of it, or I go to Wister."

"Okay, joint venture," he conceded with a smile. "Have Sally set it up. She knows the guy. I've got to come up with a crash story for tomorrow, so the later the appointment, the better."

"You wanna tell me what you suspect?"

"Not really," Pace said. "The story's pretty farfetched, and if there's anything to it, it's so sensitive I can't risk having it get around. Except for Glenn Brennan's sexist observations, I don't know anything about Sally Incaveria."

"Okay, suppose you tell *me*. I'll tell Sally only what she absolutely has to know."

Pace inhaled deeply and exhaled slowly. O'Connor had a legitimate right to know the background on a sensitive story involving a member of her staff.

So he told it a third time, in abbreviated form, and without naming names. It didn't feel as good as the telling to Brennan, but he didn't feel as foolish as when he'd told Schaeffer and Wister. And when he finished, O'Connor didn't scoff.

"I can see why you're spooked about it," she said. "I don't think Sally needs to know any of it. But in return, I'd like a favor from you. If anything comes of the work you two do together, how about giving the kid a break and putting a double byline on the story?"

"No problem," Pace promised.

"I'll have her set up the interview."

Shortly before three o'clock, Pace heard from McGill. Mike said he would have called sooner, but he was late getting to

Hangar 3 and had been tied up with his systems group for hours.

"Your team found anything?" Pace asked.

"No," McGill replied. "We're just getting into the guts of the plane."

"Where are you calling from?" Pace asked.

"A pay phone in the lobby of the main Dulles terminal. I picked it at random, and there's nobody within twenty yards of me."

Pace brought him up to date on his morning.

"You've got the big boss interested, though," McGill pointed out.

"This is true, but I can't afford to alienate Paul. As much as I sometimes wish it weren't so, I have to work for him every day."

"So don't push him, but get to that police captain, even if you have to do it on your own time. This stuff is fascinating. I'm beginning to feel like someone picked me up and set me down in a Ken Follett novel."

"Just so it isn't 'The Twilight Zone,' " Pace said.

"I'll call you later tonight," McGill told him. "Don't try to reach me unless it's an emergency. You know the old line, the walls have ears."

"Christ," Pace said. "It *is* 'The Twilight Zone.' "

By six-thirty, Pace was back at Dulles, sitting in the NTSB's conference room. He hated leaving his side investigation, but he didn't dare miss another briefing, not after Paul's fit. He hoped the session would be short, and vowed not to ask any questions of Lund that might prolong things. The bird evidence had taken the mystery out of the crash, and answers about the Converse engines probably were months away.

Lund announced the last of the bodies had been recovered from the fuselage, and the next morning the main section of aircraft would be hoisted by a crane onto a motorized dolly that would carry it into Hangar 3. An area near the hangar had been roped off for media wishing to film or photograph the event.

The session deteriorated rapidly into redundancy. There were fewer reporters present, a sign the story was receding for lack of developments. Those who came had few questions, and the briefing lapsed into a debate on the apparent inability of the C-Fan to survive a bird strike.

"You think we can reach a consensus here, but that isn't going to happen," Lund said by way of ending the session. "The answer will come through painstaking investigative work, and the evidence probably will not be made public until we go to the public-hearing phase." He paused, and there were no further questions or comments.

"Now," he continued, "that brings me to the announcement that we are suspending these daily briefings. We don't expect any major new developments, and it seems unnecessary to tie everyone to this fixed schedule. I will continue to be available as needed, as will Mitch Gabriel, to answer questions on a one-to-one basis. However, if something should develop and we feel the need to get to all of you, a briefing announcement will be placed on the wire service daybooks. In that event, we would endeavor to give you at least several hours' notice. Thank you."

As the reporters shuffled out of the room, Justin Smith of *The New York Times* wound up at Pace's side.

"So what are you going to hit us with tomorrow, Steve?" Smith asked.

"I don't want to hit anything but a bed," Pace replied. And he meant it.

Shortly after 9:00 P.M., Pace transmitted his story into the storage file for the national-desk editors. As he listened to the ticks and purrs of the computer complying with his commands, he wondered if Suzy O'Connor was around this late. He'd been antsy all afternoon about talking to the Fairfax County Police captain, and it occurred to him it would be most productive to talk when Helm was off duty and more relaxed about discussing an ongoing investigation. He took the stairs and found O'Connor at her desk, on the phone.

"You are *not* working for the women's section of the *Catfish Falls Gazette,* although you *might be* if you send me another piece of shit like this," she was saying. Actually, hissing would have been a better way to describe the manner of her speech. "This is the *worst* kind of shoddy reporting. The story doesn't tell me enough about *why* Loudoun County housing prices are soaring, and it doesn't have a goddamn single example of the average family, driven *out* of Fairfax County by exorbitant costs and taxes, now having to go *beyond* Loudoun County to find a home they can afford. In short, it doesn't tell me *shit!*"

There was a pause. Pace hurt for the green reporter who must have been struggling for composure on the other end of the line.

"You're damned right you're going back to redo it, Sally," O'Connor answered what must have been an apology on the other end. She listened for a moment, then nodded and hung up.

Pace was suddenly wary.

Sally? That's the kid she wants me to work with. Wonderful. I'm supposed to share an investigation of a possible complex conspiracy with a rookie who can't get a housing story right. Suze, I'm gonna kill you.

O'Connor turned around, and Pace saw her smile at the uneasiness that must have been obvious on his face.

"Hey, just because she can't report a housing story doesn't mean she can't handle a mysterious traffic accident," O'Connor said, reading his mind and grinning. "Actually," she continued, "Sally has set up something for you and her and Clayton Helm at seven tomorrow night in the Heritage House Restaurant in Reston. Can you make that?"

"I can make it. The NTSB called off any more scheduled briefings. They figure they've got the cause of the crash. The Heritage House?"

"Yeah," O'Connor replied. "Know it?"

"No, but I'll find it. It's a good idea to catch the guy off duty."

"That was Sally's first instinct. She ain't bad."

"That's not the message I just heard."

"Oh, this?" O'Connor said, waving toward her terminal. "It's part of the series about how the high cost of living is spreading. Sally didn't do a bad job, actually. Just a few things missing."

"From the way you were chewing on her, it sounded like more than a few things."

"That's the way I wanted it to sound." O'Connor smiled. "If you tell them they're great all the time, there's no pressure to get better."

"Suze, do you *ever* tell them they're great?"

"Yeah. When they leave me to join you. I tell 'em not to let you assholes intimidate them, 'cause they're good as any of you, or I wouldn't let 'em go."

11

Monday, April 21st, 9:10 A.M.

"All things considered, George, I'd say you are relatively unscathed. A mea culpa here and a little contriteness there, you'll come through with no permanent damage. You just have to take a little care your explanations are plausible and cover all the bases." Senator Harold Marshall was holding what had become his daily morning telephone meeting with George Thomas Greenwood, chief executive officer of the Converse Corporation, in Youngstown, Ohio. Marshall sat with his back to his massive desk, gazing through his Hart Senate Office Building window at gray storm clouds blowing in over Washington from the west. "You can imagine I'm still somewhat concerned about my role in this coming to light," he added.

"Harold, none of us has it entirely the way he wants it," Greenwood replied. His voice was raspy, as though he'd been up too late the night before, drinking too much and smoking too many of his precious Cuban cigars. "I don't like having to send notices to our customers to do disk inspections, but what the hell . . . if it restores airline and public confidence in the C-Fan, it's a small price to pay. If we find any more like Seattle, we'll make a public show of replacing them under warranty and announcing a change in subcontractors. It'll put all the onus on the old sub and make us look earnest and forthright."

"If you don't find more? You still have to explain why the Fan didn't contain the failure."

"Harold, you worry too much. Some problems even the NTSB can never explain. This will go down as an inexplicable case of a bird hitting the fan blades and starting a chain reaction of catastrophic proportions. Nobody will ever be able to determine why. It's a done deal."

"I know it," Marshall said quickly. "I wish it were over."

"Be reasonable, Harold. These episodes aren't ever over for years. Slowly, methodically—with appropriate public-relations hype—we'll take care of inspections, replacements, whatever the C-Fan needs. Life, and profits, will go on. Your investments are safe."

"It's not my investments I'm concerned about right this precious minute. It's my political and personal neck."

"You're insulated. Christ, you're better insulated than my house. Chappy Davis is the one whose neck is exposed."

"This was a dirty deed, my old friend," Marshall said sadly.

"Well, life ain't always fair."

N464TA sliced into the midday sky, outbound from Dulles en route to Denver's Stapleton International Airport. The gathering clouds Harold Marshall watched from his office window had bloomed into full-fledged thunderstorms, with tops to fifty thousand feet. There was a solid line stretching in an arc from Louisiana north and east all the way to upstate New York. TransAm Captain Eric Bijoren and First Officer Fred Cooper fought to keep the swirling winds from blowing them off course as they climbed out under full power, noise-abatement procedures be damned.

Earlier, when the storms closed in on Dulles, all westbound traffic was held on the ground; lightning, high winds and hail were too great a threat, even to a mighty Sexton 811. N464TA sat on the apron of Runway 19L for half an hour, waiting for weather radar to find a break in the storm line. At one thirty-four, the break came. A Delta 727 bound for Dallas-Fort Worth was first off. The flight crew reported severe, but manageable, turbulence. A United 767 bound for Seattle was next out. Its flight crew reported similar conditions.

"TransAmerican seven-sixty-two heavy, the storm line is closing again," a controller radioed to Bijoren.

The captain checked his radar. It was painting a barricade of red and yellow storm cells thirty-five miles to the west, running along the east side of the Blue Ridge Mountains. But there was a break in the line near the Linden VORTAC, the radio navigation station near Warrenton.

The first officer saw the same thing. "Heading two-seven-zero will get us there," he said.

"Dulles control, this is TransAm seven-sixty-two heavy. If you can clear us with an immediate turn out to two-seven-zero, we'll be able to make it through."

Since decisions involving aircraft safety always rest with the captain, and because the controller could make out a light spot in the dark wall of clouds to the west where Bijoren planned to fly the 811, he gave clearance for immediate takeoff.

"TransAm seven-sixty-two heavy, cleared for takeoff. Turn right after takeoff to two-seven-zero. Climb and maintain three thousand feet."

"TransAm seven-sixty-two heavy, roger. We're rolling,"

Bijoren acknowledged, even as he shoved the triple throttles forward.

N464TA hit the cloud ceiling seconds after wheels-up, and the buffeting became intense. Two passengers seated near the tail became ill. Others looked out their windows apprehensively, their faces drained of color, although there was nothing to see but gray wetness engulfing them.

On the flight deck, the crew saw lightning flashing in storm cells embedded in the clouds.

"One minute, twenty seconds to breakthrough," Cooper called out.

Bijoren glanced again at the radar. The "gate" was still there, but it appeared to be shrinking. If it closed any more, he would have to return to Dulles. He would not subject the aircraft or its passengers and crew to the danger of flying with violent storms off each wingtip. He asked for and got from Departure Control permission to climb through three-thousand feet.

"One minute," Cooper reported.

The turbulence moderated slightly, and the 811 continued to climb, still punching through slashing rain.

"Thirty seconds."

"Good deal," Bijoren responded.

Then suddenly they were through. The 811 burst clear of the roiling clouds into sunshine so bright that the three pilots squinted and grabbed for sunglasses. All around them, mountainous thunderheads soared upward, but the buffeting abated.

Cooper laughed nervously. "I wouldn't want to do that again today."

"Call departure control and advise them of conditions," Bijoren ordered. "I don't think anybody else should do that, either."

N464TA leveled off at thirty-seven thousand feet. The air was smooth. The passengers were placated with a round of free drinks.

But deep inside the cowling of Number 1 engine, the condition of the flawed turbine disk had become serious.

The hammering of the full-throttle takeoff and climb-out had enlarged the microscopic crack and divided it, so the disk was splitting now in two directions.

Its time was running out.

Pace was ten minutes late for his seven-o'clock dinner at Heritage House, a two-year-old building constructed to look like a colonial inn of two hundred years earlier. It had a flat weathered-wood front, small double-hung windows with leaded-glass panes, a front porch with wooden rocking chairs, electric lights that looked like old oil lamps, horse tie-ups, and a livery boy who doubled as a doorman. The place might have been from the Revolutionary War era but for the asphalt parking lot filled with late-twentieth-century cars.

One can carry authenticity only so far.

The period look carried through the interior, with exposed beams, dim lighting and dark wood, but it bypassed the maître d', who fancied the traditional black tux and led Pace to his party with a practiced smile. The menu was two slabs of wood held with a leather thong. The host laid it on the pewter serving plate at Pace's place and pulled out the chair. Pace didn't know if he should tip him or kiss him, so he opted for a nod of gratitude. Apparently that was sufficient.

If he'd had to pick Sally Incaveria and the police captain from among all the diners, Pace probably would have guessed incorrectly. He'd pictured Sally as a very young, very shy Mexican or Puerto Rican, just out of college and feeling her way, alone in the world for the first time. The woman across the table from him was young, all right, and appeared to be Hispanic, although Pace was ready to bet she also was part Indian. But she was neither shy nor apparently feeling alone in the world. Sally was stunning and slim, with very dark eyes, very dark hair, very high cheekbones, and a smile that nearly took Pace's breath away. She appeared to have been dressed by a fashion house in Paris, and she took charge of the introductions immediately.

"Steve, it's a pleasure to meet you," Sally said, extending a hand with long fingers and immaculately done nails at the end of a slim wrist encircled by several expensive-looking gold bracelets. "I was telling Captain Helm that despite the fact we work for the same newspaper, I'm rarely in the downtown office, and you're rarely in Virginia, so we could have gone years without meeting face-to-face."

"It would have been a pity," Pace replied.

Sally nodded toward the other man at the table. "Steven Pace, Captain Clay Helm of the Fairfax County Police."

Helm was not your stereotypical Southern cop, either. Even seated, he appeared to be about six-feet-four. He had very broad shoulders above a well-developed chest, obvious even beneath his light-wool suit coat. His face was narrow but not thin, his features chiseled, his hair sandy and stylishly long, and his eyes were the clearest blue Pace thought he had ever seen. And if he was a day over thirty-two or thirty-three, Pace was ready to eat the wooden menu.

"You're *Captain* Helm?" Pace asked.

Helm smiled broadly, and even before Pace saw them, he guessed the teeth would be perfect. They were.

"I started young, right out of high school," Helm said, standing and extending his right hand. "Got my B.A. from George Mason by going to school days and working nights. It's tough, but it can be done."

"I suppose you've got your Ph.D. by now," Pace said with a smile.

"Only a masters in criminal investigation from Georgetown."

"Maybe I should go sit at another table," Pace suggested, and they laughed.

Pace felt good about his dinner companions. He'd fretted all the way to Reston about why he and Sally were having dinner with a dumb cop when they could have interviewed him over a beer somewhere in half an hour. But now he thought he was going to enjoy himself. They had drinks and made small talk, ordered dinner and got to know each other. Slipping into the mood of the place, Pace let himself be talked into a traditional colonial peanut soup and Virginia ham with redeye gravy. Helm had something done with pork tenderloin, and Sally had blackened red snapper that would have to be classified as Cajun Colonial to qualify for the theme of the restaurant. But all the food was excellent. It wasn't until the dishes were cleared for coffee that they got down to the business that brought them together.

"We need to set some ground rules first," Helm suggested. "I don't mind talking to you about the accident, but we'll have to go off the record for most of the conversation. On the surface, this looks like a routine one-car fatality. But some of the evidence associated with the accident is very strange. When I put those items together with an invitation to dinner at a very nice restaurant with two reporters from the *Chronicle,* including one of the top guns who would normally never cover a mere traffic fatality, it sets my perverse mind atwitter with wonderment. In short, if I'm going to tell you what I know, I want to know what you know."

"Perverse?" Pace asked. "I don't think I ever knew a cop who used words like perverse."

"It's a word I learned to describe reporters," Helm said. "It fits you all." He fiddled with his unused butter knife, making railroad tracks in the white tablecloth. "I should have told you before dinner what my ground rules are," he said. "I'm not trying to job you for a meal. If you don't want to share information, we'll have coffee, I'll pay my third of the bill, we'll tell each other we were happy to have met, then go on our way."

He looked at Sally. "I'm along for the ride," she said with a shrug. "This is Steve's gig. My editor conned him into sharing the action since the story happened on my turf. In return, I called you for dinner and made the reservation."

Helm turned to Pace. "I'll consider the information proprietary," he said. "Nobody else from the media is interested in this accident, but if that changes, what you tell me stays with me."

Pace nodded reluctantly. He didn't want to say he trusted the cop, that it was Sally he wasn't sure of. But there was a kind of half-smile on her face indicating she knew what was in his mind, and a sincerity in her eyes that promised trust.

And so he told the story again. He told it without names, but in intricate detail, and he enjoyed watching Sally's big eyes grow wider in wonder. Helm's expression didn't change; the captain was too experienced to be surprised by anything. But a small twitch along his left jawline betrayed his intense concentration.

"I don't know what I was expecting, but that wasn't it," Helm said when Pace finished. "On the state level, you're talking murder-one and conspiracy to commit murder. On a federal level, you're talking tampering with a federal investigation. That's a fistful of felonies."

"But we've got nothing concrete," Pace said. "Maybe the calls *were* hoaxes. One of my editors thinks my source is making this up and I'm nuts to spend time chasing it. I don't think so, but until we know who was in the car, we haven't got enough to justify putting the cost of this dinner on expense account."

"Getting the ID's a matter of time," Helm said. "Meanwhile, have you been briefed about the skid marks we found?"

"Sally's editor passed it on to me," Pace nodded. "You think the car was dragged."

"That's the only theory we could come up with," Helm said. "And the evidence keeps growing. This afternoon, about twenty yards uproad from where the vehicle went off, we found a front bumper that would fit a car of the general size of the one that burned."

"Uproad from the accident?"

"Yeah. Let's say the car was being dragged by the front bumper. The driver was trying to get away, so he turned the wheels to the right, putting pressure on the drag line. When the pressure got too great for the bumper to hold, it ripped loose and was thrown off the road a little farther on. The driver was free of the tow, but with his front wheels turned hard to the right, he couldn't regain control of his car before he left the road."

Pace rubbed a salt shaker back and forth between his palms, staring at it but not seeing it.

"That doesn't make sense," he said. "Why would anybody tow a car by the bumper? And if the driver was under tow willingly, why would he try to get away?"

"Maybe he didn't want to be under tow, but somebody snared him," Helm suggested.

"Oh, come on. You're talking about snagging a car like you rope a bull, but in the middle of the night, on a dark, twisting, hilly road, with both cars moving at thirty-five miles an hour? No way."

Sally, who had been quiet through the conversation, looking from Pace to Helm and back again, sighed deeply. "So how would a car get its bumper torn off in the middle of a highway?" she posed. "Maybe our victim fell asleep at the wheel, crept up on the guy in front of him, hit him and locked bumpers. When he tried to pull free, he ripped his bumper off. Or maybe he ripped the back bumper off the front car, and that's what you found."

"Won't fly," Helm said. "Think it through. First off, I'm certain the bumper we found belonged to the victim's car. It looks a lot more like a front bumper than a rear bumper, it's about the right size for the burned car, and the wreck was missing its front bumper. That all adds up. Second . . ." he paused, his brow lined in thought ". . . if you fell asleep at the wheel and hit a car in front of you, you'd wake up."

"Yeah," Sally said, "and you'd brake hard to get loose, maybe get dragged two hundred yards, and maybe rip your bumper off."

"And your skid marks would be in a straight line, not turned off to the right," Helm followed. "Besides, the driver of the front car wouldn't drag you that far before he stopped to see what hit him."

"You're assuming the guy in the rear car was the victim," Sally said, getting into the mystery. "Suppose it was the other way around. Suppose the victim was in the lead car, and the guy who came up behind him was trying to force the lead car off the road. Maybe it was the attacker who lost his front bumper, went off the road and died."

"You'd have to be a pretty stupid assassin to try to force a car off the road by hitting it square in the rear," Helm said.

They were quiet for a moment, and then Helm looked up, his expression saying *Eureka!*

"But I'll tell you what *will* work. We're operating here on a theory that maybe the driver was killed on purpose, forced off the road, right?" The reporters nodded in unison. "If you were going to force somebody off the road, how would you do it?"

"Like they do in the movies," Sally said. "I'd slam him from the side." She blinked and did a double take as she realized exactly where Helm was taking them.

"So maybe that's what happened," he continued. "What if another vehicle rammed the victim's car from the side, and the car's front bumper got caught up in the frame of the other vehicle somehow? The victim would have tried to get away by turning his wheels to the right."

"That would explain the skid marks," Sally said jubilantly. "That would explain the bumper your people found." Her face grew sad. "That would explain murder."

"It explains something else, too," Pace said. "It explains why, somehow, we've got to convince the FAA to ground the entire Sexton fleet."

"Why?" Sally asked.

"Because one crashed at Dulles, and we don't know why. The NTSB says a bird strike. But somebody committed murder to cover up something, and that might mean there's more wrong with the Eight-eleven than birds it can't digest."

"You know," Sally said to Pace, "it's possible—even if our theory is correct—that it didn't bear any relationship to the crash at Dulles. Maybe it was coincidental that you and your friend were expecting to meet somebody out there at the same time the bumper-car incident was going down."

Pace and Helm looked at Sally for a long moment.

"On the other hand," the young reporter said, "I guess I wouldn't want to bet another three hundred lives on that."

"Bright girl." Helm smiled.

"You can't have her," Pace said. "She belongs to the *Chronicle*."

"But I'm taking her home," Helm replied.

The phone was ringing when Pace let himself into his apartment. It was Mike, eager to hear about the reporter's dinner with the cop. The pilot listened without interruption to Pace's account.

"That's fascinating," he said when Pace had finished. "So the cops are ready to call this a murder case."

"Not cops, Mike. Cop. Singular. And not ready to do it, exactly, but ready to consider the possibility. All of which means nothing until we know who the victim is."

"Any timetable?"

"Helm says you never know. But I'd bet next week's salary he'll be on the medical examiner's back until he gets that report."

When Pace hung up, he checked his recorder for messages. There was one.

"Hi, Steve, I'm home. I got in about eight and thought you might like to have a brandy, or a cup of coffee. You're working incredibly long hours, aren't you?" Kathy paused, but only briefly, so the recorder didn't cut her off. "The funeral was okay, as those things go. Mercifully short. Daddy said no High Mass because he knew Jonny wouldn't have wanted it, and, of course, Betsy isn't Catholic. She held up pretty well, but she said she felt sick. I hope she doesn't lose the baby. I'm rambling. Call when you can."

She sounded anguished. His watch said it was ten forty-five, and he took a chance she'd be up at that hour, despite her difficult day.

Kathy answered on the second ring.

"Hi," he said. "I hope I didn't wake you."

"No, I'm up," she said, an edge of exhaustion in her voice. "Even if I went to bed, I couldn't sleep."

"How are you holding up?"

He heard her begin to cry softly. "I don't feel like I'll ever get over this," she said. "The funeral was gut-wrenching, especially for Betsy, with the baby coming and all." Kathy sighed heavily. "I wanted so much to do something for her, but I can't even hold myself together. I wanted to stay, at least the night, but Daddy wouldn't hear of it. I wanted to because they put Betsy under a doctor's care, mainly to protect the baby. But Jennifer said she would take care of everything and I should come home. She's just like Daddy."

Jennifer Wheaton was Joseph McGovern's second wife, and from all accounts, Pace thought she must be one hell of a woman.

"Is there anything I can do for you?" he asked.

"What I want most is an explanation," she said, again. He desperately wanted to give her one; the bird-strike theory seemed so mundane and inadequate.

"I know," he said. "We're all doing our best. Do you want me to come over?"

"Oh, it's probably too late now."

"How about tomorrow, if you feel up to it?"

"I'd like that."

"I'll catch up with you late tomorrow afternoon, when I see how the day's going."

"Fine. I'll be at the office."

Pace shook his head. "Don't you think you deserve another day to yourself?" he asked.

"And do what? Sit around here crying? That won't help anybody."

"As Daddy would put it?"

"And as I would put it."

"Oh, shit!"

Pace cursed himself as he emptied the pockets of his slacks onto the top of the bureau in his bedroom. Sitting there in the old souvenir ashtray where he normally kept his change, staring at him like an accusatory eyeball, was the metal ball he'd found at Dulles when he was on the field with Mike.

He picked it up and inspected it closely. Deep scratches

marred the surface, and it was chipped in two places. Maybe the balls weren't from the Sexton after all. A fairly new aircraft shouldn't have any parts that badly worn. It probably was a discard from some old aircraft, or from another type of vehicle entirely. Pace tossed it back into the ashtray and headed for a shower.

Later, dressed only in a pair of denim shorts, he went to the kitchen and poured himself a stiff Black Jack on the rocks. Comfortably settled in his favorite chair, he let his head fall onto the top of the backrest and allowed his mind to wander to Kathleen McGovern, the mysterious metal ball forgotten completely.

When he opened his eyes again, it was two-thirty. Half his drink stood untouched, diluted by melted ice.

He set it in the kitchen sink, turned off the lights, and went to bed.

12

Tuesday, April 22nd, 7:00 A.M.

"This is AP Network News. I'm Frank Greshhold."

Pace was at the dawn of consciousness, the half-sleeping, half-waking time when reality and dreams intermingle and the mind is at peace. He was aware he was in danger of losing the thread of a pleasant dream about Kathy and himself and a child he didn't know playing with the wind on a catamaran in the middle of a body of water that could have been an ocean, or the Gulf of Mexico, perhaps. He fought to shut out the voice threatening to sever the fantasy.

He was lying on his left side, his head on one pillow and his right arm thrown over another, the covers creating the right degree of soft warmth in the air-conditioned bedroom. The effect was a sense of well-being he would not willingly relinquish. He thought he had fifteen minutes to listen absently to the world and national news. But the opening story smashed his reverie and left his dream as splintered as if the imagined catamaran had shipwrecked on a rocky shore.

"*The New York Times* reports today the crew of ConPac Flight Eleven-seventeen, the one that crashed and burned at Dulles International Airport last Thursday, apparently tried to take off on two engines after the engine under the right wing suffered catastrophic failure. The effort to get the crippled Sexton Eight-eleven into the air was doomed, because whatever destroyed the right engine set off a chain reaction that also destroyed the right wing, something the crew could not have known in time, according to the *Times*. Although officials of the National Transportation Safety Board unofficially attributed the accident to a bird strike, the *Times*' report raises new questions about the structural strength of commercial aviation's newest aircraft. The Sexton Corporation had no immediate comment on the story, nor did the NTSB. The accident outside Washington, D.C., killed three hundred thirty-four people, making it the worst in U.S. aviation history. More after this . . ."

Pace's fist hit the off button as the first notes of a familiar jingle for a popular headache remedy drifted from the speaker. He stared at the radio in disbelief, his body shocked by a rush of adrenaline and awash in perspiration. He could feel disappointment knotted high in his stomach.

Justin Smith had passed him on a straightway and taken the lead, with sources someplace deep inside the NTSB. He'd lost his advantage without even feeling anyone brush by him. How could that information be around the agency without Eddie Conklin knowing about it, and if he knew, why hadn't Eddie alerted him, especially if he knew the *Times* had the story? Or was Eddie the *Times*' source? Had he pushed Conklin so hard that he pushed him right into the *Times*' arms? Or did the *Times* have a source inside the go-team? Elliott Parkhall, head of the power-plants group, or Vernon Lund? Pace had a dozen questions. He lacked even a single answer.

He sank back on his pillow. What had he missed? He hadn't spent enough time talking to sources at Sexton or Converse. He'd alienated Cullen Ferguson when he should have been stroking him. He hadn't cultivated enough sources on the go-team. Mike McGill couldn't be everywhere. Eddie Conklin invited him to call when things quieted down, and he hadn't done it. It was one of the things he'd planned to do today. If he'd done it last night instead of going to dinner, instead of chasing some wild theory about a conspiracy, he might have been able to match the *Times*' story. While a tie wasn't as good as a win, it was a damned sight better than an outright loss.

"I blew it," he said softly. "I totally fucking blew it."

Pace could read his colleagues' reactions in their body language when he walked into the newsroom at nine-fifteen. He could feel them watch as he walked to his desk; he could see them glance up from their newspapers and look away as quickly. A few made eye contact, their expressions running the gamut from sympathy to accusation. Paul Wister's back was turned. He believed Paul knew of his presence but deigned not to turn around.

Pace sat down and saw that someone had put a copy of the *Times* on his desk, the same edition he had bought on the way to work. Now he had redundant reminders of his failure. He tossed one of the papers into a wastebasket and started reading the other. Justin Smith's story was centered on the front page under a subdued two-column headline. Typical of the *Times*. It never shouted. The headline in the *Chronicle* would have been six columns, bold and black.

The intercom on Pace's telephone beeped softly, but still he jumped.

"Pace."

"Come in the office, and we'll talk." Schaeffer's voice was soft and calm; Pace wondered at the editor's control. He expected outrage, and he was prepared to accept it. A pound of flesh for an unforgivable error. It wouldn't even the score, but it would close the gap.

As Pace passed Wister's desk, the national editor rose to follow. Double-teamed. Double trouble. *Double displeasure, double your fun.*

Pace stopped inside Schaeffer's office door and allowed Wister to duck past him and sit down in an occasional chair on the right-hand side of the editor's desk. The reporter took the sofa.

Schaeffer looked up from the newspapers on his desk. He had the *Chronicle,* the *Post,* and the *Times.* Pace wondered what the *Post* had written.

"What happened?" Schaeffer asked. Nice. Clean. No preliminaries. No trying to hide the reason for the meeting.

Pace cleared his throat and looked straight into his editor's eyes. "I honestly don't know, Avery. I talked to my source in Hangar Three as late as last night, and he didn't say anything about this."

"Would he, if he had known?" Schaeffer asked.

Pace was honest. "I don't know."

"Maybe he didn't know," Wister suggested. "The NTSB probably got onto this from data in the black boxes, and Smith's source probably is inside the NTSB." He turned to Pace. "I thought you knew somebody at the lab."

"I do," Pace acknowledged. "He was first on my list to talk to today."

"A day late and a dollar short," Wister snorted. His voice became hard. "The *Times* didn't have this story in the first edition. That means one of two things: Either Smith didn't get it until later, or they held it for later editions to prevent anyone else from catching up. I suspect the first and doubt the latter. You don't hold an exclusive for a tactical advantage. That means the story developed late, and Smith was around to sweep it up. Where were you last night?"

Pace felt a hollow spot develop in his stomach.

How's this sound, huh? I was out with a rookie suburban reporter and a cop, chasing rainbows.

He answered the question, and he pressed his story even

as Wister tried to interrupt, determined to make them understand there was a police captain out there who was getting ominous vibrations about the car accident, too. During the telling, he saw Schaeffer listening intently. Wister kept shaking his head.

"Damn it, Pace, we told you to follow up on dead time," Wister exploded. "Obviously, last night was *not* dead time!"

"I had no way of knowing that, Paul," Pace insisted.

"Then you haven't got the right sources," Wister snapped.

Schaeffer finally stepped in. "Okay, we're not going to get anywhere chewing each other to pieces. It's plain that I'm not happy about being so far ahead and then losing the lead, especially to an out-of-town newspaper."

Involuntarily, Pace glanced at the *Post* on Schaeffer's desk.

"The *Post* was beaten, too," Schaeffer said, picking up on Pace's glance.

"But since the *Post* wasn't in the lead, it didn't have as far to fall," Wister pointed out. "You not only got beaten, Pace, you got stomped. Around here, that's unacceptable."

Pace was tired of the abuse, tired of the pressure, tired of Wister, even tired of the consuming good heart of Avery Schaeffer.

"Do you want my resignation?" he asked.

Schaeffer sat forward in his chair so abruptly it rocked on its pedestal.

"God, no," he said. "We're disappointed. I'm sure you're disappointed. But those guys get paid, too. They weren't going to roll over and play dead for you. I'm concerned because we lost sight of our objective, as Paul feared. I'm not sure I know how to prevent it. You thought you had a hot lead on what would have been an incredible story. I don't like to put too close a rein on a reporter with a good idea. Obviously, we didn't have the right mix of priorities."

"So what now?" Pace asked. "Where do you want me to go from here?"

"We have to catch up," Schaeffer said with distaste.

"Find out if the *Times* is right or wrong, although I doubt Justin Smith is wrong. We'll have to do something for tomorrow. Call your friend at the NTSB lab. Maybe he can give you additional details. Do the best you can."

There were a few moments of awkward silence.

"Look Steve, nobody goes through a career without getting beat now and then. It's never pleasant, but it's not the end of the world. The sun will still rise tomorrow, and there will be a new edition of the *Chronicle*. Go back to work."

Pace nodded and rose to leave. He noticed that Wister remained seated, apparently waiting to say something to Schaeffer privately. The reporter figured he was to be the subject of the further discussion. Schaeffer might accept the defeat and live with it; Wister never would. He expected perfection from himself and from everyone else and was loathe to accept less. Pace knew for a certainty his relationship with the national editor had deteriorated, perhaps beyond salvage.

When Pace returned to his desk, he found a message from McGill. It asked that the reporter call Hangar 3. It wasn't a call Pace was in a mood to make.

"I was as surprised as anyone by the *Times* story this morning," the pilot said. "I wanted you to know I wasn't holding out on you."

"I know. Thanks."

"You weren't the only one unhappily surprised, by the way. I had breakfast with Lund, and the story was news to him, too."

"What?" Pace's reaction was more a bellow of disbelief than a question.

"I'm not kidding. And boy, is he pissed about the leak."

"I wouldn't necessarily believe him. He's not above leaking it himself and lying about it."

"Lund's okay. He's a good bureaucrat."

"That's an oxymoron."

"That's your prejudice."

"Acknowledged."

"You're in an even lousier mood than I expected."

"I don't like getting beat."

"We still have our own mystery to solve."

"Hell, Mike, there's no mystery. The call was a hoax. The wreck was a coincidence."

"That doesn't sound like the reporter I used to know, the one who wouldn't rest until the questions all had answers."

"That's my problem. I kept after those answers when I should have been asking the questions Justin Smith was asking."

"Now you're feeling sorry for yourself."

"Bullshit. I'm pissed, that's all."

"I gather you haven't heard any more about the ID on the driver?"

"No. And I don't know if I can get it today. Schaeffer wants me to stay on the main story, and I think I'll do what he wants. I'm in such deep shit now, I might never shovel out."

"You ever hear the story about the two brothers, optimist and pessimist?"

"I don't know. Is this Aesop redux?"

"One kid is the happiest child in the world. The other, the saddest. Parents are desperate. Want little optimist to understand reality and little pessimist to lighten up. A psychiatrist suggests putting each in his own room, little pessimist with all the toys he ever wanted, and little optimist with ten tons of horse manure. Teach each of them that things are never as bad, or as good, as they think. Parents do it. Five hours later, they check on the kids. Little pessimist is crying. Parents ask him why. He says he's played with all the toys and he's bored. In the other room, little optimist is singing at the top of his lungs, digging in the manure as fast as he can. Parents ask the kid what he's so happy about. Kid replies, 'With all this shit, there must be a pony in here somewhere.'"

"Hold the thought."

George Thomas Greenwood hadn't been surprised to find two messages from Harold Marshall waiting on his desk that morning. He was getting tired of nursemaiding the guy, but Marshall was taking some tough chances for Converse. Nobody could question his loyalty, so Greenwood would hold his hand as long as necessary. From the moment Cullen Ferguson called at 6:00 A.M. to tell Greenwood about *The New York Times* piece, the CEO had expected the next ring of his phone would be Marshall. So he'd turned the ringer off and enjoyed his breakfast.

"Harold, I can't guess why you're calling," Greenwood said jovially when Marshall's secretary put him through to the senator's private office.

"I want to hear how your scenario stands up now," Marshall said.

"It stands up fine. I've told you all along, no problem. I don't know why you're making so much of the *Times* story. So the crew tried to ram the plane into the air and the wing shattered. That's Sexton's problem, not ours. If their airfoil wasn't tough enough, then the crash is in their laps, and they're welcome to it. We're off the hook."

"That's a huge stretch," Marshall said.

"We're on very solid ground here, Harold. Don't flare out on me."

"Oh, for chrissake, I'm not flaring out," Marshall protested. "I wanted to talk it through."

"Okay, it's talked through. Feel better?"

"About Converse? Yes. About Senator Harold Marshall? I think he sold his soul."

"Perhaps," said Greenwood. "But the price was right."

N464TA flew a grueling round trip this day from New York to San Francisco and back. The flights were uneventful.

But inside the cowling of Number 1 engine, the twin hairline fractures in a titanium turbine disk continued to spread.

Pace struggled against the instinct to cancel his plans with Kathy. The possibility of a renewal of their relationship was a prospect too wonderful to risk by succumbing to a bad day at the office. He'd been beaten on stories before; he'd be beaten again. This one was especially painful because his editors attributed it more to his recalcitrance than to Justin Smith's reporting skills. He wondered if they weren't right.

His decision to go out anyway was the correct one. Kathy was a sympathetic ear.

"Did you have to try to match the *Times* story?" she asked.

"Yes, and that's a humiliating thing to do," Pace told her. "Everybody you talk to knows you got beat and you're playing catch-up."

"Maybe you're attributing feelings to them they don't really have," she suggested.

"Some of them do. Con Phillips has been kidding me about having a crystal ball, seeing things other reporters don't. Today he said he heard the crystal ball had been stolen. Offered to give me a tip on where I might find it. He thought it was pretty funny. Bureaucrats love to see reporters take headers in the dirt."

"Maybe because reporters take so much delight in pointing it out when bureaucrats do," Kathy suggested.

He smiled and tipped his glass of sangria in her direction.

They were having a late dinner at Diablo, a restaurant at 20th and K streets that billed itself as gourmet Mexican.

"So did you get what you needed?" she asked.

He swallowed a sip of wine and nodded. "I got most of it. It's still pretty speculative. The NTSB won't release stuff from the flight data recorder, but Justin Smith must have gotten some access, because the recorder is the only place there would be information on engine thrust."

"But you got enough to write it?"

"I got enough to mention it. My story's pegged to whether the FAA is thinking about grounding the Eight-eleven fleet."

"Is it?"

"Apparently so. Nobody will come right out and say it, and it might not happen, but I got enough positive feedback to be able to write that it *is* under consideration."

Kathy looked puzzled. "The chances of another Eight-eleven hitting another bird must be pretty slim," she said.

"It doesn't have to be a bird," Pace replied. "A bird triggered this accident, but the engine should have been able to take the bird strike and contain it. Something else is wrong."

He reached across the table and took her hand. "All we've done is babble on about my problems," he said. "How was your day? How are you getting along?"

"It's easier when I don't talk about it, at least not in terms of how I feel," she said. "I'm still pretty shaky. Everyone at the office was very solicitous. I talked to Daddy this morning, and he sounded strong. They've still got Betsy in bed, but I guess she's talking about going back to Chicago tomorrow or the next day. I told Daddy to make sure she didn't fly on a Sexton Eight-eleven, and from what you've told me tonight, I'm glad I did."

Pace felt the hairs bristle on his neck. Kathy saw a look of concern cross his face.

"What is it?" she asked.

He shook his head. "I completely forgot to check Melissa's flight Sunday. I don't want her on an Eight-eleven, either."

"You can switch her to another flight," Kathy said. "But if you've got a discount ticket, it'll cost you some money."

"A cost we can bear," he said. She knew exactly what he meant.

"I remember when Sissy visited last year," Kathy said. "I really liked her. I'd love to see her again, if you have time to fit me into your busy schedule."

"I think Sissy would like that, too," Pace agreed. "I'm going to see about taking next Monday off. I thought we'd go up to the Blue Ridge for a picnic. It would be great to have you go along."

"On a work day? I don't think so."

"Why not? The Senate's not back from its spring break until Wednesday. Take a day's vacation, or personal leave."

She cocked her head and smiled. It was the first time he'd

seen her smile in over a year. "Maybe I'll consider it," she said. Then she grew pensive. "Do you think there's something really wrong with the Eight-elevens?"

"I don't know," he replied. "But I think we have to look at that possibility."

"Find out the truth," she said. "I have to know."

"My word on it," he promised.

He drove Kathy home to Georgetown after dinner. She asked him to come in. He declined. He knew where that could lead, and somehow it didn't feel right so soon after her brother's death.

But as they stood in the doorway and kissed deeply, the kiss of two people rediscovering something each had thought lost, Pace almost changed his mind.

13

Wednesday, April 23rd, 10:00 A.M.

The last twenty-four hours left Pace spent, physically and emotionally, by a crazy-quilt pattern of highs and lows. The professional side was low. He hadn't been beaten this day, but he hadn't scored any major victories, either. Both Justin Smith at the *Times* and Russell Ethrich at the *Post* had the angle that the FAA was considering grounding the Sexton 811 fleet as a precautionary measure. The personal side was high. He would rather have dwelt on that, on Kathy, but business intruded.

He had to follow up the Virginia accident. Although he'd dismissed the idea of a conspiracy yesterday when he talked to Mike, he hadn't been able to let it go. Mike had him pegged right: He would stay with it somehow until all the mysterious questions had answers.

He stopped by his mailbox and found two pink tele-phone-message slips, one from Sally Incaveria, the other from Clay Helm. Maybe, finally, there was an end to the car-accident investigation. He returned Helm's call first. The message slip said he'd called at 8:30 A.M.

The captain was in, but he was on another line. Pace left word.

Then he called Sally at the paper's office in McLean, Virginia. She'd called shortly before nine and was waiting to hear from him. "Have you talked to Clay?" she asked immediately.

"I had a message, but he was on the phone when I called back. Did he turn up something?"

"The ID of the driver. I wrote the name down, but it doesn't mean anything to me."

"Who was it?"

"Mark Antravanian. I don't know anything about him. I didn't try to find out where he lived, because I didn't want to call his family."

"I know. Those calls are tough."

"I keep thinking, maybe they don't know yet. I'd hate to be the one to break the news. Does the name mean anything to you?"

It was vaguely familiar, but Pace couldn't place it. "Spell it," he said.

"A-n-t-r-a-v-a-n-i-a-n."

"Mark?"

"Right, with a 'K.' "

"Damn, I've heard it before. Did Helm tell you anything else?"

"A couple of things, but I think you should—"

Pace's phone beeped.

"—hear it from him."

"Sally, I've got another call. Maybe it's Clay. I'll give you a call-back later."

"Right."

"And, thanks."

It was Helm. "You talk to Sally this morning?" the police officer asked.

"Just now. She gave me the name. Said there was more I should hear from you."

"I asked her not to give you the details until I had a chance to talk to you."

"Why?"

"This is your story. I'm not going to ask you to give way to the police and not pursue it. But I think we should work it together. The car that burned was a rental. The driver was a man named Mark Antravanian. He was a specialist on turbine-engine performance from McDonnell Douglas. He was a member of the team investigating the Sexton crash."

Pace started to say something, but his throat closed. Every nerve in his body was trilling. His mouth went dry, and his heart raced. He tried to get saliva across his tongue, but he couldn't generate any. He squeezed the telephone receiver in a death grip.

"Pace?"

"Yeah." His voice was barely audible.

"This could be bigger than you ever imagined."

"I know."

"What are you going to do?"

"I have to talk to someone."

"Don't do anything on your own."

"I'll get back to you."

"Wait. There's something else."

"What?"

"I checked around. This guy was never reported missing. If I was on that investigative team and one of my people suddenly disappeared, I'd say something to someone."

"What does that mean?"

"I don't know. But if I were you, I'd ask the question."

"You mean all this time and his family didn't call anybody?"

"He didn't have a family that we can find. But he had co-workers. None of them called."

"That poor bastard."

"I want you to do two things for me, and you can consider this a formal police order. First, don't go anywhere to see anybody without telling someone where and how long you'll be. And if you attack anything head-on, don't go alone. Clear?"

"I'll try. Things happen fast sometimes. You can't always make those arrangements."

"Yeah, well, you try. Real hard. Cause if you fail, I'm going to be waiting for you when you get back, *if* you get back, and I'm gonna kick your butt."

Leaving the receiver between his head and his left shoulder, Pace thumbed the telephone peg clearing his line, then dialed the number at Hangar 3.

"Is Mike McGill around?"

"Yeah, but he's in a meeting."

"With who?"

"Who's calling?"

"That's not important. But it's urgent I speak to Captain McGill."

"I don't think they want to be disturbed. I won't even ask unless you tell me who you are."

"Could I leave a message?"

"Sure."

"Remind Captain McGill that he was out late with somebody a few nights ago and ask him to call that person as soon as he can."

"What is this, some kind of riddle?"

"No, it's important."

"I'll see he gets it."

"Thanks."

He called Glenn Brennan at the Pentagon.

"Howdy-doody," the Irishman said. "What's up?"

Pace told him about Mark Antravanian.

"Holy shit!" Brennan exploded when Pace finished. "That changes everything."

"Now we've got the mysterious phone calls to Mike, the meeting he set up, the guy who didn't show—"

"I know the scenario," Brennan interrupted. "What does that Fairfax cop think of this?"

"He thinks there's something to it. He's treating it as a homicide." Pace didn't tell his friend of Clay Helm's warning. He considered it a cop's overreaction.

"Damn you, anyway!" Brennan groused. "Why do you get onto these things on a day I'm stuck over here in the fudge factory?"

Pace laughed. "I'll keep you posted," he promised. "And if I need help, I'll ask for you. Meanwhile, you should consider yourself fortunate."

"Why?"

"You're only playing war games over there. I'm about to beard Paul Wister, and that's a lot more dangerous."

Avery Schaeffer was saying good-bye to a visitor to his office, and Pace waited at a discreet distance until the two men parted and the editor returned to his desk. Then he knocked softly on the doorjamb. Schaeffer looked up and smiled.

"Yes, Steve?"

"I'm sorry to bother you, but something's happened you and Paul need to know about."

"Did you talk to Paul?"

Pace was taken aback. Business at the *Chronicle* was never run strictly through channels.

"Well, no," he replied. "I was hoping to tell you both at the same time."

"Okay. Ask Paul to come in."

"You got another hot tip?" Wister asked. He was smiling, but the words had an edge.

"Yes," Pace replied tightly.

"Got any facts to back them up this time?"

Pace held his tongue and allowed Wister to lead him back into Schaeffer's office.

"You want the door closed, Steve?" Schaeffer's question was a surprise. His office door almost never was closed.

"I don't think that's necessary."

"Go ahead, then. What've you got?"

"Let me go right to the bottom line. The person killed in the car wreck on One-ninety-three Saturday night was Mark Antravanian. He was a turbine-engine specialist from McDonnell Douglas, and he was a member of the go-team's power-plants group."

Schaeffer and Wister exchanged looks, and the national editor blew a low whistle.

"Close the door," Schaeffer ordered. Then he told Pace to proceed from the beginning.

"Well, when I got in this morning, I found a couple of messages—"

"No, I mean from the very beginning. I want to hear the whole story from the start."

"Back to Saturday?"

"All of it, from wherever it started."

And so Pace told it all again, finishing with his failed attempt to reach Mike McGill.

"Does the switchboard know you're in here?"

"No."

Schaeffer lifted the receiver and punched the 0. "This is Schaeffer. Does Steve Pace have any recent messages, like in the last thirty minutes? Fine. If he gets any calls now, transfer them to this extension. He'll let you know when he's back at his desk."

He put the receiver down and turned back to Pace. "Is it remotely possible, from all you know of the NTSB, past investigations, the FAA—the whole schmear—that these investigators can be reached?"

"You mean bribed?" Pace asked.

"Bribed, intimidated, threatened, anything."

"In my heart, I'd like to believe not."

"What does your head tell you?"

"Everybody's got his price."

"*Could* it be done?" Wister insisted. The straight arrow was finally interested.

"I don't know. The airline-regulation apparatus is riddled with potential conflicts that wrongheaded people could use to good advantage."

"Like what?" Wister asked.

"The FAA's congressional mandate for one. It's supposed to promote commercial aviation and regulate it, too. A lot of people wonder whether the agency can serve two masters, and a lot of people have concluded it can't. For another, the FAA's use of designated engineering reps."

"Of what?" Schaeffer asked.

"Designated engineering representatives. DERs. They're the people who oversee design, construction, and modification of airplanes. The FAA would have to hire a cast of thousands to do all that work itself, so it designates representatives from aerospace companies to do it instead. The DERs know the projects, because they work on them."

Schaeffer's mouth was open. "You mean the FAA is relying on the judgment of individuals whose first loyalties are to the companies building the aircraft?"

"That's about the way it goes." Pace sat up straighter to emphasize the point. "And it works most of the time. As much of a conflict of interest as it is, the system doesn't break down often."

"What about the NTSB?" Wister asked. "Same thing?"

"No," Pace said. "There's been an accident or two when the NTSB blamed pilot error and I thought the evidence pointed to something else. But I never thought there were any dark motives involved. The NTSB's biggest problems are short staffing and overwork. You get out in the field, you find yourself working five accidents at once, having to consult your files all the time to make sure you don't attribute findings to the wrong investigation. You see guys at your pay grade working for the FAA or the Defense Department making twenty percent more money for fifty percent less effort, so you get out. The turnover's very high."

"That doesn't answer the question of whether a cover-up is possible," Wister reiterated.

"I don't know, Paul," Pace said. "I honestly don't."

"Who would know? Who could you ask that you would trust?"

"Mike might know, and if he didn't, he'd know how to find out."

"Go out to Dulles and find him," Schaeffer ordered. "You're off everything else. Find Mike McGill and get me a scenario. I have to know if we're dealing with something plausible or a goose too wild to chase."

"When I called earlier, he was in a meeting in Hangar Three," Pace repeated. "I can't get anywhere near that place. I'm willing to go, but I could miss his call if I leave the office."

"Take my car," Schaeffer said. "It's got one of those cellular phones in it. I hate it. Only damn time it rings is when something's gone wrong here or when Cornelia needs me to pick up a bunch of parsley for dinner. I'll call the garage and tell them to bring it up. Leave word with the switchboard if anybody calls you, they're to be referred to the phone in the car." He scribbled the number down on a piece of paper and started to hand it across the desk when his phone buzzed.

"Schaeffer . . . yes, he is." He handed the phone across to Pace. "It's your man."

"Pace. Hey, Mike, our Fairfax police friend called and—"

"I know," McGill interrupted. "The word got around here this morning."

"You knew him?"

"Not well, but I've been involved with him off and on for a number of years. He was a good guy. Remember I told you there was something familiar about the voice, the slight accent? I don't know why I didn't recognize it. If he was our mysterious caller, and he was the one who believed there was a cover-up in progress, I think we have to take it seriously."

"I'm with you. Where do we start?"

"I've already started. I just finished a profane exchange with Lund."

"Over what?"

"Over the fact that a key investigator disappeared and

nobody reported him missing."

"You braced Lund with that?"

"You bet I did."

"What did he say?"

"He was defensive about it at first. But he said he'd take it up with Elliott Parkhall."

"Did you just alert the chief suspects?"

"I don't give a damn. Mark was too good a man to let his death pass without an explanation. Besides, if he was my caller, I owe him."

"We need to talk."

"Why don't you meet me in two hours at the Marriott?"

"Can you get away?"

"Absolutely. So far as I'm concerned, this is now a legitimate part of my investigation."

"I'll be there. Meanwhile, keep a low profile."

"What's that supposed to mean?"

"Clay Helm thinks this could get dangerous."

"I'm sure it could."

Schaeffer, Wister, and Pace spent another forty-five minutes going over options for the *Chronicle*. If other papers tied Mark Antravanian to the Sexton crash, his role in the investigation would be the second paragraph in a six-paragraph story about a car wreck. They were confident they alone knew of the possibility Antravanian was on a special mission on the night of his death. There was no need to rush into anything. They could take all the time and care they needed.

But for what?

What were they getting into, getting the *Chronicle* into?

It was Wister who put their concerns to words.

"We have to find evidence that supports a cover-up theory," he said. "We have to see the evidence and get expert analysis of it. But whom do we trust? What's left of the power-plants group is suspect. Vernon Lund is suspect. So we go higher. But how high? How far do we have to climb to get out of the conspiracy, assuming there is one?" He looked to Pace.

"I suspect it's limited to people at Dulles," the reporter said.

"I'll tell you what we do, we start pushing," said Schaeffer. "We ask questions. We press for answers. We play it like a boxer looking for an opening in the opponent. We jab and step back, jab and step back. We press and irritate, and sooner or later someone will take a wild punch and give us the opening we need."

"No," Wister said emphatically. "If this thing is happening, it cost one man his life already. Sometimes a wild punch has a way of hitting the mark. We'd be risking too much."

"There are three hundred thirty-five people dead now," Schaeffer said emphatically. "Doing *nothing* is risking too much."

"Let me ask Mike," Pace suggested. "He knows the players. He'll know the right moves."

"I don't want you out of touch at any time," Schaeffer reminded him.

Pace got up to leave. Wister put a hand on his arm. "Steve, I owe you an apology." He extended his hand.

Pace accepted it gratefully. The pieces of his life were falling back into the right places. "Thanks."

Wister smiled. "Sometimes when we tilt at windmills, there's really something out there."

"If it's out there," Pace replied, "we'll find it."

Pace and McGill sat and talked in Schaeffer's Mercedes in the far corner of the hotel parking lot, away from potential eavesdroppers.

The spring breeze was chilly, but it carried overtones of the humidity that would spread a summer-long blanket over the region. The weather was the last thing on their minds.

"A cover-up would be horribly risky," McGill was saying. "And I'm not sure how you'd prove it. All things being equal, it looks like the NTSB came up with a competent and plausible explanation for the crash. I don't see any holes in it. If you and I weren't sitting here talking about it, there'd be nobody around asking questions, because there wouldn't be any reason to."

"Then why do you say it's so risky?"

"The number of people you'd have to involve. Let's say you're the villain, and the problem you're trying to cover up is in the engine. That's the logical target, since it's central to the accident. All the members of the power-plants group would have to be involved, as well as anyone else who poked around the engine. It would be a massive conspiracy. I don't think it could be done."

"Why?"

"Why what?"

"Why would you have to involve everybody concerned with the engine?"

"Because they're all going to examine the sucker. You can't get an engineer to say the accident was caused by X when his own eyeballs tell him it was caused by Y."

"So how many people are we talking about here?"

"The four we talked about before. Parkhall, Antravanian, Comchech, and Teller."

"Anyone else likely to look at the engine?"

"Well, certainly the Converse engineers on the scene. They'd be all over it."

Pace nodded.

"Padgett and Lund would see it, of course. The Sexton people would nose around it, too. How many is that?"

"Too many," Pace said glumly. "It won't wash."

"It won't," McGill agreed.

"So what have we got?" Pace asked.

McGill shook his head, a pained expression masking his face. "A very nice and able man who lost his life trying to bring me a message of warning. And now that I've got it, I can't make sense of it." He shook his head and pounded the window frame with his fist. "And there's another element, maybe the toughest of all. Let's say you could involve everybody you needed to pull off a cover-up. That's a ridiculous assumption, but let's make it. Since members of the go-team rotate weekly, and since our villain wouldn't have any idea when or where the next major accident would be, how would he know who to bribe, or muscle, or hypnotize, or whatever he did?"

"Unless he had exhaustive computer files on all the people in the country qualified for go-team duty. But to have that . . ." Pace paused ". . . he'd almost have to be inside the NTSB."

"Jesus." McGill sighed. "I don't even like to think about that."

"You got any better place to start?"

McGill was forced to make a silent admission that Pace had logic on his side.

Pace, who'd slumped in the driver's seat, pushed himself erect. "Mike, we need help from somebody inside the agency. We're going nowhere on our own. We could come up with a thousand different scenarios, and we could miss the one that's right. We need somebody high up."

"High up where?"

"High enough in the bureaucracy to be above suspicion, if there is anybody that high," Pace explained.

"Normally, I'd say Lund."

"He's on the list. Besides, he hates my guts. He'd never help if I'm involved."

"I can't believe Lund could be turned, or that he'd reject his responsibilities because of a personality clash. But if we rule him out, I guess I'd recommend going right to Ken Sachs."

"The NTSB chairman."

"Ken's solid."

"What makes you think he's not involved?"

"He's not working this accident. Why would he be?"

"Okay," Pace said with a little reluctance. "I think we should see him together. The story will be more credible if he hears this from two people, especially if one of them's you. Do you have the time to talk to him?"

"I can arrange to be away for a few more hours."

"Let's call from your room."

"Why not from the car phone?"

"Car phones can be intercepted," Pace said and grinned. "That paranoid enough for you?"

"Appropriately so, I'm afraid," McGill replied.

They locked the Mercedes and walked toward the motel entrance, unaware that thirty feet away, in a battered blue Ford van they might have recognized from Saturday night had they noticed it, two men watched their every move.

In McGill's room, Pace called Sachs and learned he was in a meeting. The reporter left a message and the number and said McGill would wait in his room for the chairman to return the call. He stressed it was urgent that the two speak as soon as possible.

"I think Mr. Sachs will be able to return Captain McGill's call in about an hour," the secretary said.

Pace then checked in with Wister and told him where he was and what was in the works. Wister told him not to worry about a story for the next day, that Schaeffer wanted him relieved of all other duties until the Sexton matter was resolved.

Then there was nothing to do but wait.

"We're making a terrible mistake if you're wrong about Sachs," Pace said to the pilot.

"I'd stake our lives on Ken Sachs being clean," McGill said.

Involuntarily, Pace grimaced. We might be doing just that, he thought.

An hour and ten minutes later, the phone rang. McGill picked it up. It was Sachs.

"Sorry to bother you, Ken, but something real important has come up at Hangar Three, and if what I suspect is true, Steve Pace and I have to talk to you as soon as possible, today if you can manage it . . . We're out at Dulles, but we could be at your office in an hour or so . . . Yes, it does . . . I can't go to him. There's a possibility he's involved, and what we're talking about is serious business . . . Screw channels, Ken. We're talking about conspiracy, murder, and God knows what other felonies. If Lund's involved, talking to him is the last thing I want to do . . . Yes, I'm damned serious . . . Because Pace is as much a part of this as I am. Ken, please! Hear us out, and then if you want to throw us out of your office, you can pitch us all the way across town."

McGill looked at Pace and rolled his eyes.

"Well, cancel the damned meeting. The budget's not going anywhere. And frankly, if what we believe is true, and if it isn't stopped right here, there might not be any NTSB to budget for . . . You're goddamned right, I'm serious . . . One hour, right. Thanks."

McGill slammed the receiver down. "Goddamned bureaucrats," he swore. "Let's go, hotshot."

At four o'clock that afternoon, Pace and McGill arrived at the secretary's desk outside Sachs's office. The wait for Sachs to call back and a late-afternoon traffic snarl downtown had McGill out of patience. He snapped at the receptionist, "Captain McGill to see the administrator. He's expecting us."

The secretary, who recognized Pace immediately since his beat brought him to her desk often, was quite taken aback by McGill's tone. But she reckoned him not a man to challenge.

"Mr. Sachs, a Captain McGill and Steven Pace to see you," she said into the intercom on her telephone console. "Yes, sir." She replaced the receiver and looked, pointedly Pace thought, at him alone. "Mr. Sachs says he'll be with you shortly."

And shortly it was. She no sooner finished the sentence than his office door opened and the NTSB chairman stood there, obviously uncertain of what he was getting into, regarding the two visitors with a mixture of curiosity and apprehension.

"Come in," he said finally.

Sachs was a man who wouldn't draw a second glance in

a crowd of two. He was Jewish, as his name hinted and his face couldn't deny. He looked distinctly Mediterranean, with the olive complexion, dark-brown eyes and prominent nose, yet his name indicated Germanic ancestry. In fact, he had a mixed heritage, with the European side of the family dominating the lineage and the Mediterranean side ruling the genes. Sachs was relatively young, in his mid-forties, but his thick, dark-brown hair was receding. One day he would wind up with no more than a fringe.

Pace liked the NTSB chairman and accepted Mike's assessment that Sachs was a man to be trusted. But he came out of an airline background—as a vice-president of something for United—and Pace wasn't certain how that would affect his attitude about the story he was about to hear.

They hadn't started off on the right foot, that was certain. Sachs wasn't pleased by McGill's push for the late-afternoon appointment, and he said so.

"I have a lot of respect for you, but I don't like being bullied, and I don't like pulling end-arounds on the other board members," he said. "Vernon Lund is absolutely trustworthy, and he's the board's rep. If something's wrong, he's the man you should be talking to. I'm also very annoyed Steve is here, although it's nothing personal, Steve, believe me. But the press has no place in an NTSB investigation until we're ready to announce our findings."

"Steve isn't here because he pushed his way in, Ken. He's here because circumstances dragged him into a situation no one could possibly have foreseen. Before you make judgments about what this is or isn't about, you should hear him out."

Sachs turned to the reporter, his face flushed. "What's the bottom line?" he demanded.

Pace wished again he felt more certain about Sachs's loyalties.

"That somebody's trying to cover up the real reason for the ConPac crash, and members of your highly respected go-team are up to their armpits in the conspiracy," the reporter said bluntly.

The chairman blinked in disbelief. "That's absolutely preposterous," he said. "I've never heard such drivel in my life. A conspiracy? Cover-up? Jesus, what have you guys been smoking?"

"Maybe you'd better hear the whole story, Ken," McGill suggested.

"It'd better be a damn-sight more substantial than what you've given me so far."

They started with Pace's chance meeting with George Ridley. Each told the part of the story with which he was most familiar. Sachs's expression alternated between disbelief and horror. He didn't interrupt, but he never lost interest. His eyes shifted from one to the other as they took turns speaking. When Pace came to the end, to the identification of Antravanian, Sachs fell back in his leather chair as though he'd been hit in the face. He hadn't heard earlier of the engineer's death. Pace thought he saw a hint of glistening in the chairman's eyes.

"I knew Mark well," Sachs said, barely above a whisper. "My God, this is unbelievable." He swallowed hard. "I wonder why Vern, or somebody, didn't call . . ." His voice trailed off.

"Even though his death appears as a cause-unknown accident on police records, off the record, the Virginia cops are treating the case as a possible homicide," Pace said.

"And you suspect Lund's involved?"

"That's no more than a concern at the moment," McGill said. "I braced him this morning about how a key member of the key group on this investigation could disappear on a Saturday night and on the next Wednesday morning still not be reported missing. He was more defensive than concerned, and that bothered me. Call it a hunch. I didn't want to take this to him."

Sachs drew some meaningless lines on a memo pad and sat in silence for nearly a minute, shaking his head.

"This is very hard for me, very hard," he said. "Elliott Parkhall can be a bit of a jerk—a lot of a jerk, actually—but he's a solid scientist. I know the other members of this go-team by reputation. Everything I know is acceptable. They wouldn't have been appointed otherwise." He glanced from McGill to Pace and back again, his face a mask of incalculable pain. "To think so many of them, and maybe Vern Lund, could be . . . tell me again why you suspect Lund."

"It's totally circumstantial," Pace repeated, "based solely on the fact that Harold Marshall sent somebody to meet with him early in the investigation. The message carried an implied threat."

"But your source told you Lund was angry about the message," Sachs added.

"Yes, but a conspiracy theorist would suggest that was for show."

Sachs shook his head again. "And you think somebody sabotaged the Sexton, and that's the reason for the cover-up?"

"That's only one possibility," said McGill.

There was silence for a long moment. Sachs gazed at a blank spot on his desk blotter. "How can I deal with something like this?" he asked dismally.

"By letting somebody independent of this go-team look at the evidence," McGill suggested.

"What?"

"The conspiracy, if it exists, lives or dies on the assumption that a lot of people are overlooking, ignoring, or altering evidence," the pilot explained. "Get the evidence in the hands of somebody you trust implicitly and start at square one. Hell, Ken, you're the administrator. You can do anything you want."

"Not really. But I'll take the night to think out the best way to approach this," Sachs said. "In fact, I'll probably have to take several days. I'm on a very early military flight tomorrow to mend some political fences in Illinois for the President. I'll keep in touch with one or both of you while I'm out of town, and when I get back next Monday, we'll meet again and decide how to proceed. I don't think the delay will hurt. Nothing will be set in cement between now and then."

"NTSB people always say they have to get to an accident in a hurry, because so much of the evidence is so fragile," Pace reminded him.

"If this conspiracy exists, we've already lost evidence to tampering, but that deed's done," Sachs said. "The NTSB has full control of the remaining evidence, and a few days won't exacerbate the damage. In the meantime, I'll have Susan expunge any record of this meeting so there's no chance of anyone finding out you brought this to me."

He regarded his visitors for a moment. "I don't know whether to hate you or thank you," he said. "I want to get to the bottom of this accident. That's part of my job. And if somebody's standing in my way, I want him, too. The integrity of the Safety Board has never been questioned before. But this conspiracy, if it exists, could destroy us."

"It isn't the integrity of the Safety Board in question, it's the integrity of a few people working for the Safety Board," Pace reassured him. "Even if our worst suspicions are true, a prompt and complete reaction from you would go a long way toward mitigating the damage. Hell, the NTSB has been around for more than twenty years. Maybe something like this was inevitable."

"But why?" the administrator demanded.

Pace shrugged. "It could be anything. Money. Power. Both. Who knows?"

"Well, some Godfuckingdamnbody knows," Sachs suddenly thundered. "And when I find him, he'd better give his soul to God, because his ass belongs to me!"

14

At the *Chronicle* office, Pace turned over his desk and telephone to McGill, who needed to check in with his systems analysts at Dulles. Pace was chatting with Paul Wister when the pilot finished, and the three of them went to Schaeffer's office. After exchanging introductions, Pace and McGill took opposite ends of Schaeffer's sofa.

"Okay, you two cowboys, suppose you bring the foremen up to date," the editor said.

They took turns in the telling, and when they finished, Schaeffer regarded them gravely. His question sounded bizarre in the context. "Why," he asked, "should we do this? Why shouldn't we drop it right here?"

Pace was stunned. "Drop it? Why?"

McGill frowned, and even Wister looked puzzled.

Schaeffer explained. "We have an intriguing mystery before us. We have a high-level Senate aide who's furious about carrying water for a member he despises. We have a couple of anonymous phone calls alleging some sort of cover-up, and a horrible death that appears to be related. But does it mean anything? The aide's allegations are far from definitive. He might have read something into the situation Marshall didn't intend. We have nothing to corroborate the allegations of Captain McGill's tipster except, unfortunately, his death, and that isn't proof of anything, really. It could have been a coincidental accident. He—"

Pace, deeply frustrated, interrupted. "But the Fairfax police—"

Schaeffer held up a hand. "Let me finish, Steve." He picked up the thread of his argument. "We have no hard evidence to argue for continuing. We have a series of interesting events that lead nowhere. And we know nothing about the NTSB that would suggest the agency or anyone in it would ever be party to a cover-up. In short, we've got nothing."

"And what do we tell Ken Sachs?" Pace asked with a harder edge in his voice than he wanted his supervisors to hear.

Schaeffer shrugged. "I'd tell him the truth . . . we went over the evidence and came up short."

Pace was desperate. "You were so excited this morning. What happened?"

"Nothing happened. I'm not saying I want out. I'm asking why we should stay in. I don't want to treat this project any differently than I'd treat an item on the AP daybook. You look at the potential for a good story, evaluate it in terms of the needs and interests of your readers, plus the time and resources it will take to cover it, and then you make a decision to go or to pass. That's all I'm trying to do here, make a cold decision whether we go or pass."

"Leaving George Ridley and Harold Marshall out of it for the moment, don't we have sufficient reason to try to explain what happened to Mark Antravanian?" Pace asked.

McGill had a thought. "I'm probably out of line in suggesting what you should do, but Mark was a man who in the normal course of things, you would be predisposed to believe," he said. "Since we don't know anything that would cast doubt on his credibility, you have to assume he stumbled onto something worthy of concern."

"I'd have to agree, Avery," said Wister.

"*If* he was your mysterious caller," said Schaeffer. "We don't know that, do we?"

"I think I do," McGill said. "I told Steve at the time there was something about his accent I recognized. When I heard the crash victim was Mark Antravanian, the voice and the identity matched perfectly."

"That's the key, then," the editor said, nodding. He smacked his open right hand down on the desktop. "We go."

"You had me worried there for a second," Pace said with a smile.

"Good," said Schaeffer. "I'm probably going to worry you a few more times as this investigation goes along. We're going to take careful stock of where we are and where we're going each step of the way. And I have to warn you, there could come the day when I tell you it's time to pass. If that day comes, you're going to have to accept it and walk away."

Pace nodded. He and McGill stood to leave.

"What do you say we have dinner?" Schaeffer suggested suddenly. "Who's got anything better to do, and I could use the night out. I'm batching it these days." He smacked his palms together in the manner of a man with a bang-up idea and heaved himself from his chair. "Every so often my wife gets some bee in her bonnet about going off to Great Britain for two or three months to do castles and drive through the heather. When the urge strikes, I send her up to her sister's in Philadelphia, and that cures her traveling itch for a year or so. I sent her away for the cure again last week, so whatta you say? Paul, you can get away for an hour or two, can't you?"

"I don't think so tonight, Avery," the national editor replied. "We've got the Central American aid bill snarled up in filibuster, and there's a major hostage situation going down in Baltimore. We have four people on the way. I need to hang tight."

Schaeffer turned to the sofa. "What about you two? Steve?"

"I need to make a couple of calls first."

"Sure. Mike?"

"I don't see any reason why not."

It was settled. Three for dinner at Maison Rouge, one of the best French restaurants in the city and, handily, a half block from the *Chronicle*'s front door. It was Schaeffer's favorite place.

Pace placed a call to his ex-wife.

Melissa answered the phone. "Hi, Dad," she said cheerily. "I hope you're not calling to cancel next week."

"Not a chance, kiddo. I'm looking forward to it. Is your mom around?"

"No, she went to the store. She'll be sorry she missed you."

"Well, actually, you could probably help me. Do you have your airline tickets handy?"

"Yep. I've been carryin' 'em around in my purse so I wouldn't lose 'em."

"What are the numbers of your flights here and back?"

"Hang on," she said. He heard the receiver clatter on the table as Sissy went off to retrieve her bag. She was back shortly.

"Gosh, Dad, there are bunches of numbers here."

"Look at the seat-assignment card attached to the ticket. It'll say 'flight,' and there will be a number there."

"Yeah, here it is. "I'm flying east on Fifteen seventy-one and back on, let's see here, Fifteen ninety-two. Why?"

"That's United, right?"

"Yeah. Why do you need to know?"

He lied. "To check your arrival time so I don't leave you stranded at Dulles."

"That'd be bogus."

"Be what?"

"Bogus. Bogue. You know, bad."

"Oh, right. I knew that."

She giggled. They spent a few more minutes chatting until a call-waiting alert diverted Sissy's attention. Pace dialed a United Air Lines 800 reservations number. He asked the agent if he would check the two flights to see what kind of equipment was being used.

"Boeing Seven sixty-seven both ways," the agent replied.

With a sigh of relief, Pace thanked him.

His next call was to Kathy. It was seven-thirty, so he tried her at home first. To his surprise, he found her there. "Early day at the office?" he teased.

"Well, as you pointed out, the Senate's not in session," she said. "I got away at six-thirty. By the way, if I'm still invited, Hugh was delighted to give me next Monday off."

"Great!" Pace responded. "I was going to ask you to go out tonight, but Avery asked Mike McGill and me to have dinner with him, so it'll have to wait for tomorrow, if you're free."

"Tomorrow's fine," she said.

"How are you feeling?"

"I'm hanging in. I hope I don't put a damper on the picnic Monday."

"You won't," he assured her. "It'll be good for you. Did you talk to Boston today?"

"Yes. Dad's fine, and Betsy's better. She's going back to Chicago tomorrow, but she's not going to do her TV show for another week or so . . . you know, give herself some time to come back. Then, if she feels up to it, work will probably be a good catharsis."

He was going to fill her in on his day, but he saw Schaeffer shrug into his suit jacket, ready to leave.

"Gotta go, Kath," he said. "I'll talk to you tomorrow."

The Sexton 811 carrying the registration N464TA was freshly washed and polished; it gleamed in the last rays of afternoon sunlight filtering through the perpetual haze over Jamaica Bay. TransAmerican Captain Everett Kinsley turned the nose of Flight 994 to the centerline of Runway 31L at John F. Kennedy International Airport, next up for takeoff after a forty-seven-minute delay for traffic. The exasperation of inching along a taxiway behind several dozen other aircraft would be offset by the thrill of seeing Manhattan at sunset as the 811 climbed out and headed west for Chicago's O'Hare Airport. Passengers on the right-hand side would be able to share the thrill, while those on the left would have to be satisfied with Brooklyn and Queens. The Statue of Liberty would pass under the 811's nose.

N464TA was passing through three thousand feet when the skyline rose into view like hundreds of symmetrical stalagmites in a gigantic cave. Everything was bathed in the orange glow of the sun setting through smog, and Kinsley heard First Officer Evan Gibson's sharp intake of breath.

"No matter how many times I see it, it gives me a kick," Kinsley said sympathetically.

"What amazes me is that the whole island doesn't sink under all that weight," said Second Officer Bruce Patrick.

Kinsley scanned the skies as the 811 continued to climb. He saw a number of other aircraft, all identified in radio transmissions and flying predictable patterns. He squinted out to the southwest. Even the polarizing lenses in his dark glasses didn't make it easy to spot something flying out of that sun. He saw nothing and reached for the cabin mike to alert passengers to the breathtaking sight about to come up on the right.

He'd just keyed the mike to speak when TCASII, the on-board collision-avoidance display, commanded him to climb.

Kinsley slammed the microphone back in place and hit the triple throttles, jamming them to the wall even as he pulled back on the yoke to pitch up the aircraft's nose. The 811 was already in a steep climb when a controller's urgent voice filled the cockpit crew's headsets.

"TransAm niner-niner-four, climb now!" the controller ordered. "Climb and turn right to zero-three-zero. Unidentified traffic at your nine-o'clock position, one mile, indicating same altitude, closing rapidly. Climb and turn right to zero-three-zero! Acknowledge!"

"TransAm niner-niner-four, roger," Kinsley replied calmly. "Climbing and turning to zero-three-zero."

The captain strained to see past the sun's glare, but nothing came into focus. He felt the ship tremble slightly under his hands and eased forward marginally on the yoke, leveling her by several degrees so she wouldn't stall, yet maintaining a steep rate of climb.

Then it was there. A blue-and-white Learjet flashed out of

the sun and under the 811, the two aircraft missing by less than three hundred vertical feet. Gibson glanced outside and down over his right shoulder as the Lear emerged from beneath them and continued streaking east.

"Damned fool," he muttered. "What's he think this is, a life-size pinball game?"

The radio crackled to life again. "TransAm niner-niner-four, you're clear of the traffic. Turn left to two-niner-zero. You're clear to climb and maintain flight level two-three-zero. Did you see him?"

"Niner-niner-four, roger," Kinsley said calmly. "We saw him. Blue-over-white Lear. Couldn't get an N-number."

"We've got a good transponder track on him," the controller said. "We'll get him. This one'll have to go into the book."

"Niner-niner-four, roger. We'll file a full report when we reach O-R-D. It looked like less than three hundred feet vertical. Thanks for your help today."

"Have a good one."

The rest of the trip to Chicago O'Hare went without incident.

But the strain of emergency maneuvers over Upper New York Bay stretched the longer of the turbine-disk cracks in Number 1 engine to within 3.7 inches of the disk's edge. The next flight operation would push the crack through the rim and unbalance the disk by a tiny fraction. It would be enough, however, to produce a microscopic wobble and a slight increase in vibrations that would compound themselves until the disk shattered.

Schaeffer, Pace, and McGill started their meal with two rounds of drinks and an appetizer of something amazing with smoked salmon that the chef did especially for Schaeffer.

They followed with veal, each choosing a different preparation, but all compatible with Schaeffer's choice of a 1985 Volnay.

McGill begged off after one glass of wine, pleading the

need to arrive with some degree of sobriety back at the Dulles Marriott. So Pace and Schaeffer split the rest, and neither was feeling any pain when the mousse, cognac, and coffee arrived.

During the meal, no one spoke of the Dulles accident or any facet of the investigation and the turmoil surrounding it. They talked of the new baseball season and the inability of Washington to get a pro franchise despite the presence of a great stadium, of the chances the Green Bay Packers would ever again have a championship team, of politics and Presidents, of Watergate and other old political scandals.

When McGill checked his watch, it was after nine-thirty.

"This has been outstanding," he said. "I needed it. I'd like to leave some money with you and get on my way. It's a long trip back to Dulles, and I've got an early start tomorrow."

"You don't have to buy your way out," Schaeffer said. "This is on us. We owe you."

"Why don't we part even-up?" McGill suggested. "I accept dinner in return for the help on your stories, and tomorrow we go in as equal partners. No debts owed or collectible."

"Sounds like a fair deal, Mike," Schaeffer said, extending his hand. "How are you getting back to Dulles?"

"I've got my rental in town," he said. "I followed Steve in this afternoon. Thanks again for dinner. It was a great break." He turned to Pace. "Is there a drugstore near here? I ran out of shaving cream this morning, and I hate getting ripped off at hotel newsstands."

"Same side of the street, two, three doors down on your right as you leave," Pace said.

McGill collected his leather jacket from the comely redhead at the checkroom, dropping a dollar bill on the brown plastic tray sitting on the lower half of the closet's Dutch door. He shrugged into the coat, returning a smile from the young lady that suggested she wouldn't mind getting to know him without his coat and other selected items of clothing. Too bad, he thought. There's never time when I need it.

Outside, McGill spotted the drugstore at the same moment the passenger sitting across the street in a blue Ford van glimpsed him leaving Maison Rouge. Without taking his eyes off the pilot, Wade Stock reached over and tapped Sylvester Bonaro and jerked his head in McGill's direction. They saw that McGill wasn't heading for the garage where he'd parked his car. They exchanged a few words and left the van, walking quickly across the street at mid-block. When McGill went into the drugstore, they spoke again, briefly, and then followed.

Inside the store, they spotted the pilot immediately. He had a can of shave cream in his hand and was walking the aisles, apparently looking for something else. Stock unzipped the front of his windbreaker and walked to the prescription counter. Bonaro remained near the door, crouching down as if to look at a bottom rack of magazines but, in fact, concealing his face from other customers. He saw his partner talking to the pharmacist behind the high counter and noticed with satisfaction the look of fear that crossed the pharmacist's face. Although he couldn't see it, he knew Stock had drawn his gun and was demanding a bag filled with amphetamines. The pharmacist started shaking his head when an elderly woman screamed.

"He's got a gun!"

Stock turned on the couple, then turned back to the pharmacist, who was moving to his left, probably toward an alarm button.

"Don't do it!" Stock yelled, and an instant later, he fired. The pharmacist crashed backward into the shelves that held rows of drug jars, spilling several onto the floor. A bright-crimson stain started spreading across his white coat at the right shoulder, and he sagged as the elderly woman began screaming hysterically.

Behind him, Bonaro could hear other customers in the store running for the front doors, a few screaming themselves. Bonaro glanced at McGill, whose concentration was riveted on the prescription counter. As Stock turned toward the elderly couple, turning his back to the pilot, McGill began advancing.

"Don't hurt us, please!" the elderly man implored. "We didn't see anything. Please!" His wife continued to scream. "Shut up, Florence. Don't look at him. Please don't hurt us."

"Both of you shut up," Stock said. McGill was twenty feet from him, still advancing. The woman continued to scream, and the gunman fired a single shot directly into her open mouth. Bonaro, who was still crouched, saw the bullet blow off the back of the old woman's head, blood and brain matter mingling with her blue-white hair as she hurtled backward and out of sight behind a display of foot-care products. Her husband looked down in abject horror, and as he stared, the gunman said quietly, "You can join her, old man," and fired into the man's chest.

McGill came up directly behind Stock. In a single motion, he grabbed the gunman's arm at the wrist, twisted it up and behind his back and exerted strong downward pressure on the thumb. Stock screamed and dropped his gun. Without letting Stock go, McGill kicked the pistol out of reach beyond the prescription counter.

"Now we'll wait for the police, you fucking piece of shit," McGill spat as he pushed Stock face-first over the prescription counter and held him down. Bonaro had a clear shot. He withdrew a chrome-plated .357 Magnum with a six-inch barrel from his waistband, pointed it at McGill and fired once, the report so loud it reverberated through the store like a cannon shot.

McGill was blown backward off his feet. It felt to him as if he'd been hit in the chest with a baseball bat, but there was no pain. He realized he was on the floor, although he had no notion how he got there. The man with the big silver gun was standing over him, and McGill was looking up the barrel into the blackness of his own future.

"A setup," he said, the harsh whisper gurgling up past the blood flooding his throat from a shattered lung.

He heard the man standing over him say, "You'll never

know," and saw a spit of flame from the gun's muzzle. McGill thought it strange that he heard no sound. He felt his body convulse, and then he felt nothing, for the second shot had plunged through his chest, nicking his heart and severing his spinal cord. Instead of pain, McGill felt a blanket of icy cold envelop him. He was sucked into a long, long tunnel, and he fell, spiraling down into total darkness.

Pace and Schaeffer watched McGill walk through the archway and into the foyer leading to the street in front of Maison Rouge.

"He's a hell of a guy, Steve," Schaeffer said. "How'd you meet him?"

Pace repeated the story as they waited for the waiter to return with Schaeffer's credit card and the bill. The restaurant was busy, and the process took nearly fifteen minutes. That business accounted for, they got up to leave and heard the first distant shriek of sirens.

It was a common sound along that stretch of Pennsylvania Avenue, a main corridor to the George Washington University Hospital. But these sirens weren't going to the hospital. They sounded as though they were stopping right outside the restaurant. Pace felt his heart rate click up.

He muscled ahead of Schaeffer and out the front door of Maison Rouge. People were milling about in the street, awash in the eerie flash of police and ambulance lights. Everyone's attention was directed off to Pace's right, toward the entrance to the drugstore. With Schaeffer behind him, he jogged the hundred and twenty feet or so to the facade that proclaimed he had arrived at "Price-Less Drugs: Items for your home and hygiene, priced less." Pace felt a hand on his arm.

"This is a crime scene, friend. You'll have to move back."

Pace turned and saw a D.C. police officer, a young black man with a hard-set face.

"What happened?" Pace demanded, extracting *Chronicle* identification from his wallet.

"Lieutenant over there's in charge, sir," the officer said.

"Official comments from him only. But generally, it looks like it was a drug stickup gone bad. Some dude went in thinking he could muscle the pharmacist outta some speed. Pharmacist sounded an alarm, and the dude panicked. Some innocent bystanders got blasted."

Pace's breath was coming in short pumps. "Who?" he demanded. He grabbed the cop at the bicep hard enough the rookie thought for a moment he had a problem on his hands.

"I don't know," he said. "I honestly don't. An old couple, I heard, a pharmacist, and some other customer. I don't know names."

"Dead?" Pace asked.

"Some of 'em, yeah."

"No," Pace breathed. "Goddamn it, this *can't* be happening."

He felt a hand on his shoulder. It was Schaeffer. "Let's go see, Steve. There's no sense standing outside speculating."

They approached the lieutenant, whose nameplate identified him as Barnes.

"Lieutenant Barnes, I'm Avery Schaeffer, editor of the *Chronicle,* and this is Steve Pace, one of our reporters. We have reason to believe we know one of the people, uh, involved in there. Is there any way we can check on him?"

The lieutenant was sympathetic. "I recognized you when you walked up, Mr. Schaeffer," he said. "I've seen you on TV a bunch of times. But we've got a multiple homicide under investigation, and I don't have authority to let you in until the medical examiner's people are finished."

"Even if I can identify one of the victims?"

"Well . . ." Barnes hesitated. "Maybe if their personal effects have been collected, I can check out an ID for you, off the record. Who am I looking for?"

"Michael McGill," Pace said. "He's from Memphis. You should find a driver's license and an air-transport pilot's license."

The lieutenant nodded. "Wait here," he ordered.

He was back about two minutes later, looking solemn.

"When was the last time you saw your friend?" he asked Pace.

"Twenty minutes ago."

"Can you describe what he was wearing?"

Pace did, down to the boots and the leather jacket.

"I'm sorry," Barnes said. "He's in there. But it's just as well you not see him. The gunman took particular care to make sure he was dead. Some crazy motherfuckers we got on these streets."

Pace was only half-listening. He was staring beyond Barnes, into the brightly lighted drugstore, but he couldn't see anything. He was breathing hard, feeling the light-headedness of early stages of hyperventilation.

"Mike was murdered," he insisted.

"Yes, sir, they were all murdered, Mr. Pace. Three of 'em. When we catch whoever did this, the charge will be murder one."

"Not that way, goddamn it! I don't mean murdered that way. He was set up."

If Pace had possessed any less self-control, he would have pushed by Barnes and gone right through everybody who tried to stop him from entering the store. Every muscle in him bunched and strained to hold him back, some logical portion of his brain managing to overcome the momentum of his fury.

"Those other poor people, they were window-dressing to make it look like a robbery," he said with force, his words passing jaws set so tight they ached. "It wasn't a robbery, damn it, it was an assassination!"

Barnes regarded Pace thoughtfully, and a crowd began to gather around them. Schaeffer put a hand on his reporter's shoulder again.

"Let's get out of here, Steve. I'll take you home and get you a drink."

Pace shook loose. "I'm not leaving," he insisted.

"The medical examiner will need at least an hour in there, and he's not here yet," Barnes said.

"I'll wait," Pace replied emphatically. "I'm not leaving."

A huge man wearing gray slacks and a herringbone jacket with a gold shield hanging from the breast pocket approached them. He was built like a pro football lineman who'd gone slightly to seed but still could take care of himself.

"Mr. Schaeffer, I'm Detective Lieutenant Martin Lanier." He didn't offer a hand. Schaeffer introduced Pace.

"I understand from Lieutenant Barnes here that the two of you knew one of the victims," Lanier continued. "Then I couldn't help but overhear that Mr. Pace apparently believes there was more than a robbery motive for this."

"You're goddamned right there was," Pace insisted again.

"Listen to me, Pace," Lanier snapped, dropping the Mr. "It's not going to help your friend to go mouthing off at me. And it could get you in a lot of trouble. I'm sorry for your loss, but things like this happen when guns and drugs take over a city. All of a sudden, some junkie who can't afford to buy what he needs walks into a store—"

Pace fairly jumped at Lanier. "This was no junkie, damn it!" He was shouting at Lanier. "It was a setup, and I'm not going to let you write it off as a simple homicide!"

Lanier stood perfectly still and spoke softly. "I'll tell you what you're going to let me do, Pace. You're going to let me do my job. You're going to let me tell you to keep your voice down. And you're going to let me order you away from here. Otherwise, you might find yourself letting me toss you in jail on a disorderly conduct charge until you cool down."

"Let's go, Steve," Schaeffer said. "We'll go back to the office and get a reporter down here right away. Let's give the police some room on this."

Pace whirled on Schaeffer, glaring into his eyes and finding compassion where there should have been outrage. "I'm the one the police need," he insisted. "I'm the one who can tell them who the suspects are."

"Steve, listen. I don't see how this could have been set up to kill Mike. Nobody knew he was coming here. Mike didn't know himself until a few minutes before he was killed."

Pace pushed himself out of the editor's grip. He was trembling with fury. Did Schaeffer actually believe what he was saying?

He staggered away from the drugstore and the horror inside. He wasn't walking anywhere in particular; he wasn't even aware of his direction. He was only aware of his rage.

He took several long, ragged breaths, trying to calm himself. He was at the curb in front of the *Chronicle* building, standing at a lamp post with a trash receptacle chained to it. He kicked the trash bin as hard as he could, hearing it clang against the metal light post and seeing it rock against its restraints. Several passersby stared and moved away.

"Goddamn it," Pace shouted. "Goddamn it to hell!"

He leaned over the receptacle and was sick for a long time.

It was after ten when Schaeffer got Pace up to the tenth floor and into the men's restroom.

Their entrance startled a copy boy named Rudy, who was washing his hands.

"Rudy, do me a favor and ask Paul Wister to come in here right away," Schaeffer said.

"Yes, sir," Rudy replied. "Is there anything I can do to help?" He was looking with wide eyes from the slightly rumpled editor to the enraged reporter and back again.

"No, Rudy, get Paul."

Rudy must have conveyed the idea there was an emergency, because Paul Wister banged through the double outer doors within sixty seconds.

His mouth dropped. "My God, what happened?"

Schaeffer helped Pace off with his sport coat and hung it on an empty stall door. The reporter leaned against the cool wall tiles while a sink filled with water.

"Wash your face, Steve," Schaeffer said, ignoring Wister for the moment. When Pace didn't move, Schaeffer spoke again, harshly. "Clean yourself up! We have work to do!"

Suddenly Pace lost all semblance of control. "What do you mean, *we* have work to do?" He jumped right into

Schaeffer's face, defying the editor's unyielding restraint. "*You* don't have anything to do, because *you* don't believe what happened down there. *You* want to call this another senseless crime in the city. Well, *fuck* that!"

"Watch your mouth, Pace," Wister ordered. "I won't tolerate insubordination."

Schaeffer held up a hand, a signal for Wister to back off. He turned to the national editor. "Two things, Paul. I want you to order the first edition held up, and I want a reporter—I don't care if it's metro, suburban or national—get somebody down to the Price-Less drugstore down the street. There's been a multiple homicide, and we need a story on it tomorrow. Then come back, and I'll fill you in."

Wister, bewildered, looked at Pace again. "We know about the shooting, Avery," he said. "It came over the scanner. Metro has a reporter and a photographer there. The first edition's already gone, but I can pull it back."

"Do it," Schaeffer ordered. "Then think about making two holes on the front page for a spot report on the shooting and a longer piece Steve will write when he gets a grip on himself."

"That sounds like a long delay," Wister suggested warily. "It'll bump all the editions back and cost us a fortune in composing-room overtime."

"I know," Schaeffer snapped. "Just do it!"

"I'll be right back," Wister said. He left to follow orders he didn't understand.

Pace glared at Schaeffer. "I've got a grip on myself, and I've got a pretty good grasp of reality, too," the reporter said.

Schaeffer refused to allow himself to rise to Pace's bait. "Then you know you've got a job to do," he said. "Clean yourself up and get to your desk."

Fifteen minutes later, with Pace working on Schaeffer's story, the editor took Wister into his office and told him about the evening's events and what Pace suspected about McGill's death. As the story went into its graphic details, Wister paled progressively.

"Sweet Jesus, no wonder Steve's out of control," he said. "That's unbelievable. Mike was sitting right here just a few hours ago." Then he straightened. "Is Steve writing that two NTSB investigators were killed in a conspiracy to preserve a cover-up?"

"Of course not," Schaeffer said impatiently. "We don't have that story. He's writing about the coincidence of the deaths within four days of two key members of the NTSB team. I think if we had a mathematician, he'd say the odds of that happening were a million to one against. There will be no accusations, not even a hint we think it's more than coincidence. I'm not convinced it isn't coincidence, but it's still one hell of a story."

"You're sending a message to someone," Wister said. It was a conclusion, not a question.

"Precisely. If there is a cover-up, and if homicide is being used as a convenience to preserve that cover-up, I want the devils behind the scheme to know we're watching."

"At the risk of repeating myself, I think you should consider whether this is a game too dangerous for us to be playing."

"The way I look at it, Paul, the stakes are too high for us not to deal ourselves in."

Pace made it through the eighteen-inch story. It raised fascinating questions and coincidences. Three times during the writing, he forced himself to go back and tone down the copy. In his devastated, furious state of mind, he was writing accusations he couldn't substantiate, or that he wasn't yet ready to make public.

His hands shook, and several times, trying to bring the trembling under control, he grabbed the edge of his desk and squeezed until they cramped.

When he finished writing, he read over the words he'd fed to the computer but barely remembered.

Two key members of the National Transportation Safety Board team investigating last week's fatal crash of a Sexton 811 at Dulles International Airport have themselves been killed violently in the last four days, although police say at this time there is no reason to suspect a link between the deaths.

Mark Antravanian, 48, an engineer studying whether the Sexton's Converse engines played any role in the crash, died in a one-car accident in Fairfax County in the early hours of Sunday morning.

Michael McGill, 52, the chief pilot for TransAmerican Airlines and chief of the systems group within the NTSB's Sexton team, was shot to death Tuesday evening in a Pennsylvania Avenue drugstore, where he apparently walked in on an attempted robbery.

Police in Virginia and the District of Columbia. . . .

Pace broke off reading and closed his eyes. It was like a book-length nightmare, with a new death in each new chapter.

"Steve, drop the story in my basket," Wister called urgently. "We've got to move."

Pace nodded and keyed the story off his screen and into electronic storage, where the national editor could pick it up.

He considered calling Kathy, but thought better of tormenting her with the story tonight. She didn't need that on top of her own grief.

"Do you want me to take you home?" Schaeffer asked. He'd come up behind Pace.

"No, thanks, Avery. I've got my car."

"You'll be all right?"

"I'm not all right, but I can make it home."

"You did a good job tonight. I know how hard it was for you. I'm sorry about Mike, Steve. I am. I liked him a great deal myself. If you need to, you can take tomorrow off. Let us know where to reach you in case something breaks."

Pace was shaking his head. "I don't want the day off. I don't want to sit around thinking about this. I need to move ahead, finish what we started together."

"Do what you think best," Schaeffer said. "But don't

think of yourself as being alone. I'm right here with you, and Paul's behind us. I don't know if your suspicions are correct, but we're going to find out."

Late that night, Pace sat in his living room. It was darkened, except for one light that let him see when his drink was getting low. He consumed half a fifth of Black Jack and remembered Mike McGill.

He'd been trying to get drunk, without success, he thought. He was considering giving up and going to bed when a random image jolted him from his chair. *Of course! It had to be!*

He'd assumed Mike was killed in the aftermath of his confrontation with Vernon Lund over Mark Antravanian's death. But Lund wouldn't have known where to find McGill. Only one person knew that. Only one person knew that to find Pace was to find McGill.

"Goddamn you, you sonofabitch," Pace whispered.

You almost had me believing in you. We probably weren't out of the building before you were on the phone issuing a contract on Mike's life. You bastard! Damn you to hell!

Pace picked up his sport coat and located his small address book in the deep pocket sewn into the lining. Through booze-glazed eyes, he found what he was looking for, nodded as he confirmed the address he remembered and tossed the little book on the coffee table. He strode out of the apartment, slamming the door behind him. Moments later he was back in his car, wheeling onto 22nd Street, west into Georgetown.

Pace was sufficiently drunk that he had to close one eye to keep a focused view of where he was going, but he drove slowly and deliberately to the elegant home on R Street where he had attended two receptions. He knew it would be fruitless to try to find a parking spot on the oversubscribed and narrow Georgetown street, so he double-parked, blocking two cars against the curb. Their owners wouldn't be going anywhere at this hour. And what he was about to do wouldn't take long. Who the fuck cared, anyway?

Pace leaped up the nine front steps and leaned on the doorbell. Nothing. He slapped the brass knocker against the door's metal sounding cap. Still nothing. He was about to press the bell again when the lights went on inside the house and on the front porch, and the door opened. Ken Sachs stood there, blinking in the brightness of his vestibule. He was wrapped in a satiny-looking red and black robe, his hair was tousled, and a heavy beard shaded his face.

"What the hell . . ." he started, and then he recognized his visitor. "Steve? What the hell do you want at this hour? I've got a plane to catch at Andrews at six."

"I don't care what the fuck you have to do," Pace snarled. "I came to tell you your little assassination squad did a real good job tonight."

"What do you mean? Have you been drinking?"

"Goddamned right. So would you if a good friend of yours was murdered, along with some innocent people who did nothing but be in the wrong place at the wrong time."

"What are you talking about?" Sachs demanded. He was fully awake now, his eyes blazing. "Who was murdered? Where?"

"It was real smooth, too, you bastard. Even the cops and my editors think it was a drug stickup. But you and I know better, don't we? You couldn't let someone with Mike's credibility stay alive with his suspicions. So you—"

"Mike? Mike McGill? What—"

"—planned a little scene in the drugstore to make it look like he was killed in a bungled drug robbery. I wanted to let you know I don't buy it. And I'm not going to let it lie, either. You got rid of one problem, but you've still got me."

"Steve, I don't know anything about any of this." There was an edge of anger in Sachs's voice. "But I want you off my property right now. I'll call the police if I have to. I won't have you standing out here cursing me in the middle of the night and waking up the neighborhood."

"I'm going," the reporter sneered. "Have a nice trip to Illinois. Give my regards to Michigan Avenue."

Pace turned from the door, intending to make a dramatic

departure, but the alcohol in his system conspired against him. He lost his balance and slammed into the wrought-iron handrail, the only thing that kept him from pitching head-first down the brick steps. He continued with as much dignity as his condition allowed. He heard Sachs close the door behind him, and the porch light went out, leaving him to find the way to his car in darkness.

Pace let himself back into his apartment a few minutes later. He closed the door and sagged back against it, feeling triumph in the certainty he had found and confronted the mastermind behind the ConPac conspiracy and the murders of Mark Antravanian and Mike McGill.

He spotted his glass on the kitchen counter next to the bottle of Jack Daniels and decided to have a small victory drink. He dropped in ice cubes to the rim and added enough sour mash to cover the ice. He raised the glass in a salute to himself and walked back into the living room.

What had Avery said? We'll push and push until someone pushes back. Well, the shoving match had started, and it would gain momentum when the *Chronicle* hit the streets the next morning. Most people reading Pace's story would find it mildly interesting and possibly a little disquieting. But those readers weren't the audience Pace was after.

Ken Sachs and a small number of others would be able to read between the lines. They would know the two deaths had nothing to do with coincidence, but more importantly, they would know Steve Pace knew it, too.

He went to the window that looked out across the city.

"You bastards," he whispered. "Sleep well tonight, because I'm coming for you in the morning."

BOOK TWO

Book Two

15

There is something very special about Washington, D.C. in the spring.

Life blossoms in a frenzy of dazzling color, a gigantic, delicate floral celebration of the wonder of rebirth and renewal. It is a fragile, transitory thing, a sharp counterpoint to the permanence of the stone, granite, and marble housing the heart and history of the Republic.

Spring begins with the blooming of the very old Japanese cherry trees ringing the Tidal Basin of the Potomac River at the center of the city's monuments area. So welcome is the event the community created in its honor a festival that, regardless of its date, is never quite coordinated with the trees. An extra week or two of winter can keep the blossoms in bud, just as the early arrival of warm weather can coax them forth before they're due. So fragile are the pale pink flowers that any blustery, early spring day will destroy them, and even in the best of years, they survive all too briefly. This year the warm weather arrived several weeks early, and the cherry blossoms were a memory by festival weekend.

As the cherry blossoms succumb, tulip magnolias, jonquils, daffodils, and redbud throw yellow, white, pink and purple hues over the Capital City, soon joined by the dogwood and acres of multihued tulips, lilac, flowering crab, weeping cherry, apple trees, and an array of azaleas.

From the organized gardens of the federal district, the eruption of color and fragrance snakes its way through the residential sections of the city and out the asphalt arteries into the most distant suburbs. On Massachusetts Avenue—known everywhere as Embassy Row—where the word "spring" is different in every tongue, it is the same in every garden, from that which graces the stunning modern architecture of the Brazilian Embassy to those that surround the staid old stone of the British and Vatican official residences. It washes through the postage-stamp yards of Georgetown and reaches onto the more spacious lawns of the quiet neighborhoods straddling Reno Road, where old azalea bushes are cared for with as much love as the old homes. They respond by blooming into a patchwork of red, yellow, coral, orange, lavender, purple, pink and white, drawing thousands of locals who come to admire this tutti-frutti treat for the eyes.

On this day, nearly everywhere in the city and its suburbs, redbud and the graceful, tiered branches of both wild and cultivated dogwood trees reached their peaks, making every patch of natural woodland seem a carefully tended Japanese garden.

Even in parts of northeast Washington and Anacostia, the city's poorest neighborhoods, azaleas sprouted under crumbling brick and flowered amid the garbage. On streets frayed by age and apathy, for a short, post-equinox period in the spring, there was beauty.

It was a time when the pace slowed, when the populace abandoned good restaurants for brown bags and noontime places in the sun, when the city's parks filled with softball games, Frisbees, footballs, soccer balls and lacrosse sticks, when carefully creased pant legs were rolled to the knees and bare feet dipped into the Reflecting Pool, when yearning started for the days the Washington Senators played at old Griffith Stadium, when the air was filled with the rich fragrance of the new-mown grass, when every once in a while, if the wind was right, one could smell the salt water surging up the Potomac River from a random high tide in Chesapeake Bay.

It was a time to marvel at the splendor and savor it, for it would not soon come again.

Chapman Davis had no time to consider the beauty as he bypassed a crowded escalator and leaped steps two at a time from the subway stop deep beneath Capitol Hill. Davis had counted the steps once, ten years earlier, when he'd considered making them part of his daily workout. He gave up the idea when he realized his colleagues wouldn't tolerate spending the day with someone who'd worked up a good sweat without benefit of a post-workout shower.

This day there was no time for such accommodation. Davis felt like the little Dutch boy plugging holes in the dike. You don't worry about a shower with an ocean coming in on you.

The day had started routinely. Davis got out of bed at his Silver Spring, Maryland, townhouse at five-thirty, dressed, stretched, and went out to run his daily five miles. He was four blocks away, hitting his 6.5-minute-a-mile stride, when the morning edition of the *Washington Chronicle* hit his front porch. When he returned, the trouble rose off the front page to assault him like a bad odor.

On the end table in his living room, the red light was blinking impatiently on the telephone-answering machine. The message was from Harold Marshall. It was terse: "Read Pace's story on the front page of the *Chronicle* and meet me at my office as soon as you can get here." "Here," was the operative word. Apparently, Pace's story had jolted Marshall to his office before seven, a full two hours earlier than his usual show-up. Davis showered, dressed, and found his subway train by rote, thinking of little but how to handle the senator from Ohio. There was too much going down to risk an intemperate reaction to a story that was merely a montage of coincidence and supposition. That it hit close to the mark was annoying, but not disastrous—unless somebody overreacted.

Davis could hear the tightness in Marshall's voice on the answering machine. A small snit was not in the senator's repertoire. Marshall was about to cloud up and storm, and his aide's most visceral fear was that the squall would be directed at the *Chronicle*. Davis didn't even want to think about the results. To rage at the newspaper would only deepen its conviction and harden its resolve. If Davis didn't get a lid on it, the volatile politician could blow everything.

The receptionist in the front room of Marshall's suite cocked her head toward his private office when Davis arrived at eight-thirty.

"He's waiting for you," she said. "He's probably paced a new rut in the carpet by now."

Actually, Marshall was standing still before the window behind his desk. When Davis let himself through the eight-foot doorway, the senator turned, picked up a copy of the *Chronicle* and tossed it across his desk, Pace's story face up.

"How the hell did this happen?" he demanded, his voice barely controlled.

"I don't know," Davis replied, scarcely glancing at the report he'd read twice already. "I don't know where they're going with this, but I think it would be a mistake to get involved."

"Damn it to hell, man, we don't need this!" Marshall exploded. "We're almost there. We don't need some crusading reporter turning over rocks just to keep a damned story alive."

"What's the difference?" Davis tried to toss the subject aside. "The NTSB is satisfied with its findings, and I don't think this—this coincidence—is going to change anybody's mind."

Marshall leaned over his desk, his weight resting on his closed fists. Above his half glasses, his blue eyes were cold and hard.

"You get with Lund today and make certain it doesn't," he ordered.

"What can Lund do?" Davis asked in genuine surprise. "This is way outta his realm."

"He can reel it in," Marshall insisted. "He can call a press briefing and question out loud whether the *Chronicle* is trying to throw a red herring into the investigation. Then he can reaffirm the NTSB's confidence that it has found the reason for the accident. Furthermore, he can render the judgment that the deaths of two investigators, tragic though they are, are strictly coincidental."

"Assuming he would do that, it could be viewed as protesting too much."

"He doesn't have to beat it to death. One briefing to throw cold water on this." He pounded the folded newspaper. "They never come out and say *conspiracy,* but that's the implication."

Davis shook his head. "I don't know," he said. "Pace's story is about a coincidence, not necessarily a conspiracy. It doesn't follow—"

"Newspapers don't write about coincidences on page one!"

"Sure they do. Even if you're right, going to Lund might be a bad idea. He didn't take too well to George's visit. Why should he respond better to mine?"

"Because you know what George Ridley doesn't, how to use finesse, how to be discreet and diplomatic. Ridley's a fat-ass blundering idiot. He's got no subtlety in him, no sense of . . . of rhythm." Davis started at the phrase. He looked closely at Marshall's face, trying to determine whether it had been a deliberate racial slur, and decided the senator wasn't sensitive enough to know the difference. Marshall continued his tirade. "He doesn't know how to chat somebody up, how to gain somebody's confidence, how to make a proposal so when hands are shaken later, the other guy thinks the agreement was his idea. You know." Marshall looked pointedly at his aide. "It's the sort of stuff you picked up learning your way around the mean streets."

Davis chose to ignore the reference. "And if Lund throws me out of his office?"

"He won't if you handle him right." Marshall leaned over the desk again. His voice was menacing. "There can't be any turning back, Chappy. Our course is set. We're either going to sail home scot-free, or we're going to be dashed to death on the rocks in trying. All of us. Each and every one. Do I make myself clear?"

Springtime in Washington spread below Kathy McGovern's window at the front of the second floor of the Russell Building. The early lunch crowd already was choosing the best seats in the sun on the lawns of the Capitol. The sky was a brilliant blue, the grass a new, moist green, and there was flowering color wherever one chose to look.

She was sitting in her chair at the window, her back turned on a desk full of work, her eyes focused on the outside but not seeing it. A barrier of grief, now reinforced by fear, had sprung up in her mind, blocking the beauty of the day from her brain, blocking everything but the memories of her brother's death the previous week and the newspaper headline branded in her mind three hours earlier. The headline played over and over, like a closed loop of tape:

Two investigators on Dulles crash
die mysteriously in separate incidents

And the drop-head:

Virginia car crash, District drugstore shooting
come within four days; police uncertain of link

Kathy awakened at eight-fifteen, an hour later than normal, because she hadn't set the alarm and overslept. She rose reluctantly, feeling unrested. She put on coffee and showered, moving through the morning more by rote than by motivation to get to work. It wasn't until she picked up the *Chronicle* that she was able to focus on anything. Then the focus was sudden and sharp.

The headlines leaped at her. The first paragraphs, under Steve's byline, chilled her.

She scanned quickly, trying to grasp the salient points. When she finished, she gulped air, realizing she'd been holding her breath. In numb disbelief, she put the paper on the sofa and poured a cup of coffee, skipping the usual doctoring of cream and Equal. She returned to the living room to read the story again.

She wanted to run to the phone and call Steve, to go to him and hold him and cry with joy that he was alive and share what must have been his overwhelming sorrow for Mike. She picked up the receiver beside her chair—and dropped it back in its cradle. Her gut said a call from her would add to his burden. He had his own heartache now; he didn't need to be reminded of hers.

When Kathy arrived at her office in Hugh Green's suite, there was no message from Steve, and he hadn't called since. She tried to work, but it was wasted effort. So she stared out the window at nothing in particular while her imagination directed something like an old Movietone newsreel showing Mike McGill dying in a drugstore shoot-out while Lowell Thomas's voice gravely intoned the *Chronicle* headlines. Over and over.

She heard a soft knock and whirled in her chair, hoping to see Steve. Instead, she locked eyes with the elegant junior United States senator from Massachusetts.

"Oh, Hugh," she said, sagging back. "I . . . I'm sorry. You're here for those reports on the summer interns, aren't you? I'll have them ready by three, I promise."

Green was shaking his head, his razor-cut brown hair staying perfectly in place, a little long over the ears, graying ever so slightly at the temples. It was a casual, boyish style at odds with his Senate uniform; a medium-weight charcoal-gray wool suit with subtle chalk striping.

"No reports," he said. "I came to talk. If you want to." He pushed himself away from the doorjamb and took a step into the office. He was carrying a double-folded copy of the *Chronicle*'s front section and held it up to leave no doubt about the topic he had in mind.

Without warning, Kathy began to cry, something she was doing often lately, although it was out of character for her under normal circumstances. She could be brought to her emotional knees by tragic movies, sentimental songs, and warm, fuzzy television commercials; real life was something she generally faced with endless stoic reserve. It was a trait inherited from her father, who had an amazing capacity to roll with life's blind-siders. She'd asked him once about that ability, and he'd told her he learned it in law school when he realized that, unlike his well-connected classmates, he would not be invited to join any of Boston's prestigious law firms.

Instead, Joseph McGovern had opened his own office and done well enough as a trial attorney to make a home for his family in an upper-middle-class neighborhood in Wellesley. But he wanted more and saw his opportunity when his brother John asked for legal and financial help to open a restaurant called Milano, near Quincy Market. Joseph backed it himself in return for a one-third share. He never thought he was risking his two hundred twenty-five thousand dollars; he said he knew the restaurant would succeed. In fact, with John hovering over the operation day and night, Milano thrived, and within five years, Joseph's initial investment was worth more than a million.

Using the gambler's rule about riding a winning streak, Joseph McGovern borrowed against his equity in Milano to back other enterprises, which he chose well. His law practice evolved into a highly successful venture-capital operation, and he became a billionaire at the age of forty-one after realizing a tenfold profit on an investment in an old downtown office building. But instead of celebrating by popping Champagne corks in a cushy Boston nightspot, Joseph had a quiet dinner with his wife, Anne, and their four children, Joseph Jr., fourteen, Kelly Anne, eleven, Jonathan, eight, and Kathleen, three. Later that night, Joseph and Anne made love, and he whispered to her, "We made a lot of money today." "Did we make it honestly?" she asked. "Always," he replied.

Three weeks later they bought one of the magnificent old brownstone homes on River Street in the Back Bay area, half a block from Beacon Street and the Boston Common. It was the only home Kathy remembered, and the only public acknowledgment Joseph McGovern ever made of his wealth. If his money made him happy, Kathy never could tell. If occasional setbacks cracked his self-confidence, she could not tell that, either. Not even during the two worst setbacks of his life.

The first had come when Kathy was seven. She had a vivid memory of two policemen knocking on the front door, rattling the antique etched-glass panels, and her mother collapsing a few minutes later. The officers brought word that Joey, then eighteen and a freshman at Harvard, had been killed by a hit-and-run driver while walking to his dorm with some friends after a late movie.

The loss of her older son left Anne McGovern helpless for a year. But Kathy remembered her father's strength. They mourned Joey and buried him, and when it was over, Joseph put his wife to bed and gathered his remaining children around him. He told them something Kathy never forgot: "You have lost a brother, and your mother and I have lost a son. We all loved Joey very much. None of us will ever forget him, nor should we. But his life is over. Ours are not. There is a time to stop and grieve, and there is a time to live and move on. I believe our time has come to move on."

The second tragedy struck eight years later, when Joseph and Anne were sailing with friends off Race Point on Cape Cod and were caught in a thunderstorm. Although they were all expert sailors aboard a craft that could easily weather such squalls, lightning struck the mainmast, breaking off a two-and-a-half-foot section that struck Anne McGovern in the back of the neck. She lived for three days in a coma before losing the battle for her life. Again there was a period of mourning, and again Kathy watched her father pick up the pieces of a shattered life and move on.

With Kelly going to graduate school at the University of Virginia and Jonathan about to become a junior at Harvard, Kathy's goal that summer had been to convince her father she could run the household and steer her life. It devastated her when he told her in mid-August she must enroll at St. Martin's Academy for Girls, in Stockbridge.

When she challenged him, Joseph assured her he wasn't acting out of a lack of confidence, but because of enormous confidence that she could handle the separation. His business affairs were thriving in Europe and the Middle East, necessitating his being out of the country for long periods. He said he had no qualms about leaving her on her own for a few days, but weeks and months at a time was a different matter. The family housekeeper could look after her material needs, but her emotional and spiritual needs demanded professional oversight.

When she started to cry, her father told her to take control, to exact maximum benefit from her environment, to grow, to learn, to gain perspective and insight, to set firm goals and pursue them with single-minded purpose.

With gentle counseling from the nuns, who had been warned of the situation, Kathy got through the first year, unhappy but with grudging acceptance. Her father called at least once a week, no matter where he was in the world, and she always projected the strong stoicism she knew he expected. In spring, Joseph took her back to the Boston house, and they shared a wonderful summer. He made arrangements to stay in the city most of the time, and on those occasions when he had to leave for a few days, he underscored his faith in Kathy by leaving her in charge of herself, while the housekeeper kept track of the more mundane things, like groceries. By the end of August, when the time came to return to Stockbridge, Kathy had developed a taste for independence, and the discipline endemic to a Catholic girls' school was anathema to her.

She would always remember her three years at St. Martin's as the most patronizing of her life and, in a way, the most valuable. She'd entered the school already possessing self-reliance. Three years in the smothering bosom of the Church taught her patience and diplomacy, the skills she prized most highly as she became committed to politics.

That had happened while Kathy was at Boston College and had become immersed in the first Senate campaign of thirty-four-year-old Hugh Green. She joined his staff in mid-July, and a month later showed such promise as an organizer that she was put in charge of the Green Machine, the young people willing to do anything to elect their man, even taking on such unappreciated jobs as door-to-door canvassing and election-day transportation to the polls for the elderly. Green was an easy winner in November, and after the victory party on election night, the senator-elect invited her to seek him out in Washington when she graduated.

She took him up on it, and he needed her. She had a knack for constituent service, and the staff Green put together to do that vital work was in disarray. She took the job with relish and had remarkably quick success. Six years later, when she was a legislative assistant, she took an unpaid leave from Green's Washington office to serve as deputy chairman of his successful reelection campaign. A year later she became his administrative assistant, the number-one staff assignment. She chaired his next reelection effort, and he gained a larger plurality than he'd had in the first two races. That he was headed for the White House in six years—earlier if President Cordell Hollander's current administration didn't shape up—appeared inevitable. That Kathy McGovern would help put him there, and gain an office and a stature of her own, appeared inevitable as well.

Joseph McGovern, now seventy-three, still lived in the same house on River Street. At sixty-five, he met and married Jennifer Wheaton, the widow of a Boston investment counselor. Joseph still kept up an incredible business and social pace. He said he had no intention of retiring or dying until he'd amassed a fortune vast enough to ensure the future of at least a dozen grandchildren, preferably two dozen. Although he surely had done that years before, he repeated the vow each time his own children suggested he think about slowing down.

Kelly had married an English import-export broker. They maintained homes in London and New York, and Joseph saw his two grandsons by that marriage several times a year. At forty-two, it was unlikely that Kelly was thinking about bearing more children. Jonathan was—had been—the chief economist for the Chicago brokerage firm of Lane, Ross & McReedy. His wife Betsy was the hostess of a local television talk show. They had one daughter, with another child on the way, and they had assured Joseph constantly that they wanted a big family. Had Jonny lived, they might have kept that promise. Although he was forty, Betsy was thirty-three and could have had three or four more children had she wanted to. Now, of course, there would be no more.

Kathy had never married, and at the age of thirty-seven in Washington, D.C., a city where it was said single women outnumber single men six to one, her chances were not getting better. She'd had several relationships, one of which was especially promising. The end of that affair three years earlier left her in emotional shambles, but even her closest friends saw only glimpses of her pain. Within a week, Kathy had pulled herself together and refocused on the future. The thought of never marrying occurred to her occasionally. It bothered her only when she imagined being alone during old age, and then it bothered her a lot. But no one knew.

In truth, she'd been happy over the years with the status quo. She had a great career with an unlimited future. Her father's formula worked for her.

Until Steven Pace changed all the equations.

He divided her loyalties, diverted her attention. He became more compelling for her than her work, more important than her professional future. She always had been able to do as her father taught her, but the formula failed when she and Steve became involved. Without realizing it, she had pushed the relationship aside. Now she was having new doubts as her feelings for Steve grew again. And she was far from over Jonathan's death. Her emotions were a jumble. She felt she was losing her focus, and she was not handling well that loss of singular purpose.

It was for that loss and her inability to deal with it that Kathy cried.

Green closed the door and sat in one of the two chairs facing Kathy's desk, after first clearing away a stack of Armed Services Committee hearing transcripts. He did not offer words of comfort or his handkerchief. He had the correct instinct that words would have done little good and a handkerchief, while chivalrous, was rendered unnecessary by the box of Kleenex on her desk. He'd learned in almost thirty years of marriage to his wife Gretchen, who also did not cry easily, the best thing to do was to wait out the storm and be there when the clouds cleared. It proved a short wait.

Kathy plucked a tissue from its box and blew her nose and laughed in the self-conscious way people do when they're embarrassed.

"All I'm doing is apologizing to you this morning, Hugh, but I'm sorry again," she said. "This isn't like me."

"No apologies necessary," Green said sincerely. "You've been on a pretty rocky ride. It wouldn't be normal if you didn't feel overwhelmed. Did my waving the newspaper trigger this?"

She nodded. "I don't think I could exaggerate how much Mike McGill meant to Steve. I feel miserable about it, and coming on top of Jonathan—"

"You and Steve together again, huh?" Green guessed.

"That's an overstatement. But he's been there for me through all this, and a lot of old emotions are coming to the surface."

"When did you find out about this?" he asked, holding up the newspaper again.

"This morning, when I read it."

"Steve didn't call you last night when it happened?"

Kathy shook her head. "The last I heard from him was sometime after seven when he called to say he was going to dinner with Mike and Avery Schaeffer. He said he wanted to see me, but it would have to wait until tonight, if that was okay . . ." Her voice trailed off.

"His story is intriguing as hell," Green said. "It's like he's trying to say something without actually saying it. Do you know any more about it, if I may be so bold as to ask?"

Because she trusted Green implicitly, she told him of her conversations with Pace about the accident. They had been brief, but Steve had mentioned once that he was troubled by

Harold Marshall's actions—had Steve called it interference?—relating to the NTSB investigation. Steve hadn't gone into any details, and she had been too emotionally distracted to ask for any.

Green listened intently, his expression disclosing nothing about his thoughts. As Kathy had seen him do many times during intense Armed Services Committee testimony, he sat with his elbows on the arms of the chair, his fingers steepled in front of his chin. When something struck him as especially important or interesting, six of the steepled fingers went down, leaving only raised forefingers that he ran up and down in the gutter of flesh between his nose and his upper lip.

When Kathy finished, Green pushed himself more erect in the chair.

"I'm happy you and Steve are seeing each other again," he said. "Gretchen and I both like him. Fact is, when you broke it off, I had to stop Gretchen from coming down here and acting like a yenta." He cleared his throat. "On another level, the comment about Harold Marshall fascinates me. On the basest of all possible levels, I'd like to know what Cobra's role is in this." He used the nickname Democrats favored for the senior Ohio Republican but never dared use to his face.

"Nothing if not partisan, are we, Hugh?" Kathy asked, smiling for the first time that day.

"We are partisan, indeed, but it isn't politics that turns me off Marshall. He's such a disagreeable sort."

"Well, I don't know anything else, and to be honest, I think it would be an unfair imposition for me to ask Steve any more about it."

"And I wouldn't ask you to," Green added hastily. "But I think you should get out of here and go find him."

"What for? He's probably at work."

"Then be there when he comes home. He's been there for you. He's probably going through his own kind of hell. Losing a friend is never easy. Losing one this way is crushing."

"If Steve has a place in my life, Hugh, it's not during working hours," Kathy protested. "Those hours belong to you. Besides, I'm already taking Monday off."

"Ah, yes," he said. "The philosophy of life according to dear old Dad."

He saw the glint of anger in her eyes before she opened her mouth, and he held up his hand to fend off the attack.

"I love old Joe, Kathy, you know that," he said. "And you're his daughter. A large part of what made him successful and what's making you successful is your ability to set your sights, plot your course, and never deviate 'til you've planted your flag on a new beachhead. Distractions be damned, full speed ahead. Never waste perfectly good energy on emotions. Right? But unless you have some flexibility, you go through life with blinders on. Then you miss all the beauty on either side of you. And you miss a lot of the pain that makes the beauty look so good by contrast."

"So you want me to look for pain?" Kathy was incredulous.

"No," Green said softly. "I want you to look for Steve. Then take it an hour at a time."

She looked dubious, but she nodded.

"And if he shares any dirt with you about the Cobra, I goddamn well better be the first to hear it." He grinned. "If I can be of any help on it, give Steve my private number."

The tears welled again in Kathy's eyes.

Green walked around the desk, pulled Kathy up into his arms and let her cry.

16

Thursday, April 24th, 11:30 A.M.
Steve Pace tried to ignore the telephone, tried to will away
the intrusion into his uneasy sleep. On the seventh ring he
relented and fumbled above his head for the instrument
screaming at him from the top of his bookcase headboard.

"Yeah?"

"This is Schaeffer. Where the hell were you? In Pittsburgh?"

Pace realized there was a sharp, sickening sort of pain
embedded in his right temple. He rolled onto his back, and
the pain bubbled into his forehead.

"What time is it?"

"It's nearly noon. Get out of bed and get your ass in here.
You are in a shitload of trouble." The last sentence was
pronounced slowly and deliberately, leaving no room for
misunderstanding.

Pace let the receiver fall on the pillow beside his head. He
knew he should be concerned, but his mind was so flooded
with shards of memories from the night before there wasn't
room for another emotional thought. He couldn't immediately recall why he was in trouble, and he chose not to think
about it hard. He decided he didn't care.

With some discomfort, he sat up. He'd pretty much
ripped up the bed during the night, but that didn't concern
him, either. He was drained. Blasted. Empty. He rubbed his
hands over his heavily bearded face and through his hair,
tempted to fall back and drift off to sleep again. Instead, he
pushed himself to his feet, unsure why he made the effort.

He threw on a terry-cloth robe and stumbled into the living room. He opened the front door and picked up the newspaper. Without looking at it, he tossed it on the sofa and went to the kitchen to start a pot of coffee. His eyes fell on the Jack Daniels bottle near the sink. The glass beside it, smudged with fingerprints, was empty but for a half inch of light amber water in the bottom, the remnants of leftover ice and a few drops of unconsumed sour mash. He picked up the bottle and stared at it. It was nearly empty. He recalled buying it on his way home the night before. He remembered why he wanted to get drunk. Obviously, he'd been successful.

It was Pace's intention to shower while the coffee dripped, but the copy of the *Chronicle* caught his eye as he padded past the sofa. It was folded with the top of page one faceup. All Pace could see of his story was the headline. He sat beside the paper and picked it up as though it would burn his fingers. He let the inner sections slide away to the floor as he unfolded the front page. He leaned forward with his elbows on his knees and read what he had written. His hands began shaking. He could feel bile rising in his throat and anger pounding in his head. The inked words blurred, and he clapped his hands together, crumpling the newspaper lengthwise between them.

Pace heard himself shout *"No!"* as he hurled the paper away. With little mass or weight, it barely cleared the coffee table, but as he watched it fall, his eye was caught by the address book lying on the table where he'd left it the night before. He picked it up, noticing it was open to the list of names starting with S. Many of the addresses and phone numbers were scratched out, with new ones squeezed into whatever space was available. Sawyer, Severson, Scanlon, Sanchez, Simpson, Shohenney, Sachs. The last name on the page stopped him.

And then he remembered everything.

By the time Pace walked through the front doors of the *Chronicle* building, he'd figured out what had aroused Scha-

effer's fury. Somehow, word of the reporter's call on Ken
Sachs in the early hours of the morning had gotten back to
the editor. Pace supposed he'd been a little hard on Sachs,
essentially accusing him of complicity in a murder, with
nothing but circumstantial evidence to support that belief.
But even in the harsh light of day and under the cold eye of
sobriety, Pace continued to believe it. Mike McGill had bet
his life on the integrity of the NTSB chairman, and he'd lost.

Pace didn't check for phone messages or remove his coat
before going to Schaeffer's office. There was no sense delay-
ing the confrontation. He had no intention of backing down
from the conviction that a conspiracy shrouded the crash of
ConPac Flight 1117, a conspiracy that continued to take a
toll in human lives. Schaeffer could rage all he liked, even
fire him; Pace made up his mind to push the issue, regardless
of the cost. The ConPac story had become personal. He
owed it to Mike to solve the mystery. And he had made the
promise to Kathy.

He found Schaeffer alone. "You wanted to see me,
Avery?"

The editor looked up, and his face reddened. He jabbed
the index finger of his right hand toward a point over Pace's
left shoulder. "In the Glory Room," he ordered. His voice
rumbled like the distant thunder of a developing storm.

Pace turned toward the editorial conference room, a
dozen steps from Schaeffer's office. He pushed open the oak
door and left it open behind him. Schaeffer entered and
closed it. Pace walked to the big window overlooking the
heart of the nation's capital and found himself wondering
how many deals were being cut at this very moment in those
buildings, and over what, and how many conspiracies were
being hatched, and how many covered up. He sighed deeply
and turned around, his face as blank and neutral as he could
manage.

Schaeffer was watching him closely, his lips drawn tight,
his face reddened from above the slightly lanterned jaw to
the top of the furrowed forehead. He was a man on a barely
controlled burn. Without taking his eyes from Pace's, he

held out his hands toward the clusters of coveted prizes hanging against the rice-papered walls and sitting atop the polished-cherry credenzas.

"You see these?" he started, his voice trembling with anger. "These are awards for past efforts at responsible journalism. *Responsible* journalism!" The thunderstorm broke. "You stand in this room, amid these awards, and appear to feel nothing. You once won the most revered honor of all, yet you stand here now, the perpetrator of one of the most *irresponsible* journalistic acts I have ever had the misfortune to be associated with." Schaeffer's words echoed off the walls and crackled in Pace's ears. The reporter felt himself flush. He hadn't anticipated an attack based on idealism. "I am associated with it," the editor continued, "because, ultimately, I am the one who approved hiring you. I am the one, ultimately, who gave you the aviation beat. I am the one, ultimately, who turned you loose on the ConPac story. And I am the one, ultimately, who will have to withstand the aftershocks of what you've done."

"Just what is it I've done, Avery?" Pace interrupted, slipping his hands inside his coat and pushing them deep into the pockets of his trousers. He meant there to be an edge of challenge in his voice, but as he listened to himself, he wasn't sure he heard it.

"What have you *done?* Are you *that* insensitive?" Pace knew then why Schaeffer had wanted this meeting in the conference room. The place was soundproofed, and Schaeffer was testing the outer limits of the envelope of that technology.

"I'm not insensitive at all," Pace replied. "I assume this is about my visit to Ken Sachs last night. I don't apologize for it. Sachs was the last one outside this newsroom and the restaurant to see Mike McGill and me together. He *had* to be the one who issued the order to kill Mike."

"Oh, really? Let's assume for the moment the shooting was, as you suggest, an effort to make McGill's death look like an accident. I'm not convinced of it, but we'll assume for the moment it's true. Did it ever occur to you someone simply followed McGill all day, looking for an opportunity? Did it ever occur to you when your pilot friend left us at the restaurant, the goons saw their opportunity, formulated their plan, followed him into the drugstore and carried it out?"

"No. Mike would have noticed if someone followed him all day. I would have noticed."

"Why should he? Why should you? Were you trained by the FBI?"

Pace felt a twinge of doubt creep to the edge of his self-confidence. He repelled it defiantly.

"Even if everything you believe is true," Schaeffer continued, still wound tight in anger, "your visit to Sachs last night destroyed all the subtlety we agreed on. The idea was to let your story do the talking. Now you've blown that. You've blown it all. If Sachs is guilty, he's going to send everyone else to ground. If he isn't guilty, you've lost one of the most valuable inside sources you could have." He paused and peered at Pace. "Does any of this make sense to you?"

"I believe what I believe, Avery," the reporter said, but he could feel the doubt returning, gobbling up his self-confidence like an old Pac-Man game, and there wasn't enough defiance left for a counterattack.

"I'll tell you this: If you don't straighten up—and that includes drying out—you're history on this story, and maybe history on this newspaper," Schaeffer warned savagely. He was so worked up that when he pronounced "newspaper," drops of spittle sprayed the carpet. "Too many people spent too many years making the *Chronicle* into one of the most respected newspapers in the country. What this paper is is our identity, our greatest achievement, our lives. And your Pulitzer notwithstanding, I'll see you gone and disgraced before I'll let you bring this paper down."

Schaeffer's reference to drying out hit Pace like a slap in the face. He *was* drinking a lot. He had a clear mental image of a nearly empty Jack Daniels bottle on the kitchen counter.

"How did you find out?" Pace asked curiously.

"What? About your outing last night?"

Pace nodded.

"Ken Sachs was waiting for me when I got in this morning. If you think *I'm* angry, you should see *him*. He feels horribly violated, and I don't blame him."

"I thought he was supposed to leave at dawn on a political trip for the President."

"He was. He said he canceled it on the pretext of an emergency. That's pretty impressive, don't you think? Would a guilty man come in here to confront me in front of most of my staff?"

"Maybe, if he thought he could get the kind of response from you I'm hearing."

Schaeffer shook his head slowly, frustrated. "I've given you my ultimatum, Steve," he said flatly. "You heed it and get your head straight, or you start looking for another job."

Pace felt dazed. He'd walked into the *Chronicle* building confident in what he believed, but like it or not, Schaeffer had shaken his confidence. And there were, Pace had to admit, blurs in his brain, blank spots in his memory, chinks of doubt in his personal wall of fury, all of which, maybe, were signs that Schaeffer's reference to booze was on target.

He was disappointed when he found no messages in his mailbox or on his desk. Calls would have given him something to do, somewhere to make progress out of the mess he was in.

"Hey, aren't you going to welcome me home?" The question came from the desk next to his. Jack Tarshis was back at his post.

"Sorry, I didn't see you, Jack. My mind was somewhere else." Pace shrugged out of his coat. "Where have you been, anyway? You've been gone a month."

"Only ten days," Tarshis replied. "I was in Jackson Hole,

Wyoming. A seminar on preserving the wilderness environment. Good stuff."

Jackson Hole, Wyoming. The memories flooded back. *A place where time doesn't count, only the size of the trout at the end of your line. The little stream, the one winding like a snake through the National Elk Refuge—Flat Creek. No trees to hide me from the fish. Had to crawl through the high grass up to the bank on my knees, with the sun in my face so my shadow wouldn't fall over the water and spook the devils. They can smell a fly rod at a hundred yards. Two great days on the Snake River on the prowl for cutthroat trout. Smartest fish ever created. Bastards can spit out an artificial lure faster than the hand of man can set the hook. Yellowstone National Park. So much to do; so little time. Stalking the rare grayling in the Firehole River, and when hunger calls, going for the big trout in Yellowstone Lake.*

And then another memory. *LeHardy Rapids. Five A.M., on an early June morning. The tourists weren't even thinking about getting up yet. Parked the car off the side of the road and walked down a grassy hillside to the Yellowstone River, then waded a hundred feet upstream and nearly froze my legs off. Found a flat rock where I sat and listened to the birds exalt in the new day. A muskrat was swimming easily, half submerged in the fast-moving water, the beginning of the end of spring runoff. It was chilly. Got down below freezing overnight, but as soon as the sun hit, felt like midsummer. The air's so thin; the sun so intense.*

I saw movement on the other bank. A grizzly sow, thin after a winter's hibernation, but huge. Unmistakable hump above the shoulder blades. Tremendous muscle mass. And two cubs, cubs of the year, for sure. Born in the den while the mother slept. Born no bigger than kittens. Had to work their way up the sow's body to find the nursing stations. She couldn't help. If they missed, they died. But they lived. They grew. They were playing, wrestling on the opposite bank while the sow drank and kept an eye on a shallow backwater, alert for an unwary trout that would make breakfast. I shifted my legs. The sow's head came up. She knew I was there. She saw me, or smelled me, or sensed me, I don't know which, but she knew. She watched. I whispered, "I'm not going to hurt your babies." And she lowered her head to the water again. The Yellowstone River, wide at LeHardy Rapids, separated us. I was no threat to her or to her cubs. She was no threat to me. Her decision to stay at the riverbank was a gift to me, and I will be forever in her debt. When she and her cubs disappeared into the forest, I looked at my watch. It was seven forty-three. I had shared more than two hours with one of the rarest and most magnificent of creatures.

Wading back to the clearing, preparing to climb the bank to my car, I found two tourists standing at water's edge wailing that the bears walked away just as they got ready to take pictures. Did you see him? one asked. Yes, I replied, but it was a her, with two cubs of the year. Of the what? the other asked. Of the year, I explained. This year. Oh, the first one said. Did you get pictures? I smiled. I didn't need pictures. The bears would be with me forever.

The memories flashed through Pace's mind in seconds. The serene look in his eyes was completely opposite what Tarshis had seen moments earlier.

"Steve, you okay?" he asked tentatively.

Hearing his name brought Pace back. He felt a wave of jealousy for Tarshis's freedom.

"You have it made, you know that, Jack?" he said. "You flit around the beautiful places, and you come back and write serious stories like the point guard for some kind of environmental brigade. You spend your whole life on an expenses-paid vacation while the rest of us work our asses off around here and get castrated for our trouble."

Tarshis went white. "Hey, I also go to places like Love Canal and Three-Mile Island."

Pace dropped into his chair.

"Life's a bitch," he said.

Tarshis muttered something about a late lunch and disappeared, leaving Pace alone to deal with his anger. He attempted to read the newspapers, but he couldn't concentrate. He straightened up his desk. He tried to make a list of angles to pursue on the Sexton story, but he couldn't focus on that, either. He scanned the newsroom, hoping to find Glenn Brennan. He could talk to Brennan once he got past the Irish bullshit. But Brennan was out, apparently at the Pentagon. Pace recalled with a wince that he'd made plans for that night with Kathy. He wouldn't be very good company. He called her anyway because he needed someone to talk to, and because he felt guilty about leaving her alone with her own pain.

The receptionist in Green's office said Ms. McGovern was gone for the day, and that alarmed him. She wasn't the type to leave work early. Concerned that she was distraught, or even ill, he called her home. She answered on the first ring.

"Where are you, Steve? I've been worried—"

"I'm at the office. Why are you home?"

"I've been worried—"

"I know."

"No, I, uh, mean about you. I've been worried sick since I saw the paper. I'm so sorry about Mike. I can't believe this is happening. It's like a nightmare, and I can't wake up."

"A good way to describe it," he said. "You're not sick, are you?"

"Oh, no. Hugh ordered me out of the office to be with you. He thinks we can lean on each other. I wish you'd called me last night. I can't even imagine what it was like for you."

"Godawful," he said softly, truthfully. "I came unhinged, unglued—"

"I can imagine—"

"—and I went home and got drunk and did some things I probably shouldn't have. I don't know . . . maybe I was wrong, maybe I was right. I can't sort it all out right now."

She didn't press him for details. "Tonight?" she asked instead. "Maybe we could talk."

"I'd like that. But I don't feel like going out."

"Then I'll come to you. Your place. I'll cook."

"Yeah, right. I'm sure that's just what you feel like doing."

"I'll keep it simple."

He considered it. "I think I'd like that," he said.

"Me, too. Call me here when you're ready to leave the office. I'll meet you."

"You should have a key to my apartment," he said with a slight laugh. It was a throwaway line, and her reaction surprised him.

"Maybe we'll talk about that, too," she said.

Paul Wister approached Pace at midafternoon, fully aware of the hiding the reporter had taken from Schaeffer and the reason behind it. Schaeffer had filled him in.

"Give him a chance to unwind and then wring some kind of follow-up story from him," Schaeffer said. "We can't drop the kind of bomb we did this morning and not have something in the paper tomorrow."

"Metro and suburban are probably working on follows," Wister noted.

"I'm not talking about police-blotter bullshit," Schaeffer thundered. He'd not worked out all his fury on Pace. "I want to know if there's been progress tying these two murders together or proving they're not connected."

Wister watched Pace for the next hour with a mixture of contempt and pity. He'd seen other reporters unravel under pressure, and he thought he saw signs of it in Pace now. He believed journalists should be tougher than ordinary people, and he had little use for those who couldn't be. It was one thing for Pace to rage over the murder of a friend the night before; it was quite another to jeopardize his story, his job, and his newspaper in a fit of drunken frustration later. Wister felt almost smug in his confidence that he wouldn't have reacted the same way. Yet he couldn't help but feel a twinge of sorrow as he watched Pace now, spinning his emotional wheels on his own personal ice patch, trying to deal with the results of his self-indulgence.

He stood before Pace's desk. "The editorial meeting's in

an hour, Steve. What have you got for tomorrow?"

The reporter's head jerked up. His eyes were dazed, his forehead furrowed in question.

"You can't leave the story hanging," Wister said. "We've got to have more tomorrow. Metro and suburban aren't touching it. Everybody figures, after last night, this is your baby."

Pace glanced at his computer terminal as if it were a mortal enemy. He shook his head. "I-I hadn't even thought about it, Paul. This hasn't exactly been my best day."

"It isn't going to get any better, either, unless you start producing," Wister said.

"Produce what?"

"That's your problem. Call your cop sources. See if they've found any links between the two deaths. I don't care what you do, but do *something*. And do it damned fast."

Reluctantly, Pace spun his Rolodex to Clay Helm's card and dialed the number. He identified himself to the desk sergeant.

"He's on 'nother line," the sergeant said, dropping syllables that took up too much of a busy cop's time. "There a message or you wanna hold?"

"I'll hold for a few minutes," Pace replied.

"Your nickel, but if the lines jam up, I'll hafta cutcha loose."

"I assume you'll come back and take a message first?"

"Yeah, probly, if I got time," the sergeant replied. The line went on silent hold.

Pace smiled. What was it about cops and reporters? Even when they didn't know each other, never had a single dealing good or bad, they were instant adversaries.

"If you're trying to get yourself killed, too, your story this morning is a pretty good start," Helm said without preliminaries when he punched up Pace's call.

"What?"

"Jesus, Steve, you've as much as told the killers you're onto what they're doing and why."

"That's the idea," Pace said. "I push until I hit a sore spot and somebody pushes back. When I see who it is, I know who I'm looking for."

"Great plan, except when these people push back, somebody winds up dead."

"Reporters never get killed, except in war."

"I remember somebody in Arizona back in the seventies," Helm said.

"He's the exception."

"There's always a chance."

"Don't be depressing," Pace said. "You had any luck connecting the two murders?"

"That's confidential police business," Helm said formally.

"I thought we agreed we were going to cooperate on this."

"We did, and we can. But not to the point of impropriety on my part. I can't open my files for you. Ask me specific questions and I'll give you specific answers, unless you get into an area that's confidential."

A flood of deja vu hit Pace. Mike McGill had said almost exactly the same thing at lunch, when was it? It seemed a year ago.

"What *can* you tell me?" he asked in exasperation. "Are you working with the District police? Are you making any progress?"

"Yes to the last two questions," Helm replied.

"Who are you working with downtown?"

"Detective Lieutenant Martin Lanier. I understand the two of you met last night. He didn't like you very much."

"Figures. You have any leads?"

"Yes."

"Like what?"

"You've got enough for a story now. I can't tell you any more."

"What story? You haven't told me shit!" Exasperation was nearing despair. "Can I say Fairfax and D.C. cops have leads linking the two murders?"

"No. Say we're exploring leads that *might* link the two deaths," Helm corrected. "We still don't have proof the first one was murder. Or the second one was anything more than it appeared to be. Lanier has serious doubts the drugstore was a setup to get McGill. But there is eyewitness testimony that could provide a link. And I stress *could*. Nothing is conclusive."

Pace sat up in his chair, his interest suddenly renewed. "What eyewitness testimony? There was an eyewitness to the Antravanian accident?"

"No."

"Goddamn it, quit talking in circles!"

"Look, Steve, there is something I'd like to tell you, but as a friend, not as a reporter. If it appeared in the newspaper, we could lose potential suspects."

"Then why tell me at all?"

"For your own protection," Helm said softly. "So when you look in your rearview mirror, you'll know what you're looking for."

"So tell me."

"I have to have your word. Everything I say from here on is absolutely off the record."

Pace scowled and rocked back in his chair. He hated decisions like this. Once he agreed to go off the record, he could never use the information, whatever it was, unless Helm released him from the promise. "Go ahead," he said reluctantly. "You have my word."

"We're looking for a late-model, light-blue Ford van with a bashed-in right front side. The police and firemen at the Antravanian accident recall seeing it at the scene with two guys, one of them shooting video tape. Witnesses outside the drugstore last night say the two gunmen escaped in a late-model Ford van, either blue or green, with a bashed-in right front side. In both cases, the witnesses said they saw streaks of another color paint in the area of the van's damage, either yellow or white. Mark Antravanian's rental car was yellow. That good enough?"

Pace whistled softly.

"You see why it can't appear in the paper?" Helm continued. "The truck would be too easy to get rid of or repair. We can't let these guys know we made their transportation."

"I have a vague recollection of seeing that truck on Georgetown Pike, too," Pace said.

"You do?"

"Mike and I were there, yeah. When our source didn't show that night and we saw the cops scream by, we followed them."

"What do you remember about the van?"

"Not a hell of a lot. Mike and I were standing on the shoulder of the road on the side where the car went off. The van was behind us on the other side of the road. I think I only turned around once or twice."

"Then the left side of the truck was facing you?"

Pace thought for a second. "Yeah, the driver's side. The truck was on the shoulder beside the north-bound lane."

"That jibes with our reports. Our guys saw the damage when the van made a U-turn and headed south after the excitement was over. Can you describe the two men?"

"No," Pace said. "I don't even have a general impression of what they looked like. I think I remember seeing the camera, though. I probably figured them for TV people."

"So did the men at the scene," Helm said. "But no local TV stations have footage of the accident. I checked."

"What do you make of that?"

"Still off the record, right?"

"Right," Pace confirmed.

"It's only speculation, but if it was a contract kill, they might have been shooting proof for whoever hired them. That would be consistent with the theory we developed at dinner in Reston."

Pace let his chair fall forward with a bang. The implications were incredible. "Where do you go from here?" he asked.

"Every investigation is like a child learning to walk," the police captain said. "We take it one step at a time and hope we get someplace useful before we fall on our asses. Keep in touch, Steve. And be careful."

17

Chapman Davis paused for a moment before the closed door of the office in the main Dulles terminal. The hand-lettered paper sign taped at its four corners to the door read, "NTSB. No admittence." He wondered who the lousy speller was.

He knocked softly and let himself in. Vernon Lund had agreed to see him, but Davis wasn't looking forward to the meeting. Lund's previous session with an emissary from Harold Marshall had gone badly—Davis learned how badly a few hours earlier—and he suspected another meeting was the last thing Lund wanted.

Davis had sought out George Ridley at noon, inviting him to lunch in the cramped little dining room on the Senate side of the Capitol. With Congress out for the Easter recess and the tourists at a minimum, there were plenty of tables where the two could sit, eat some of the Senate kitchen's famous bean soup, and talk. Davis had gone right to the point.

"Marshall asked me to see Lund this afternoon. You told me it didn't go well when you were out there. How bad is bad?"

"How do you work for the bastard?" Ridley asked, side-stepping the question. "He's the biggest asshole on the Hill."

"How do you put up with Helmutsen?" Davis asked. "We got our choice of an asshole or a dumb shit. The voters sent 'em to us. Our job descriptions say for better or worse, we gotta put up with 'em. You don't like it, bro', but that's the way it's always been and will forever be."

"I know. I'm fine with most of the minority members. Marshall's pond scum."

"You feel that strongly, why didn't you tell him? The chairman would have protected you."

Ridley responded with a contemptuous noise deep in his throat and shook his head. "The chairman can't protect himself," he said. He put his finger in the bowl of his spoon and rocked the utensil, watching the indentations the end of the handle made as it hit the padded white tablecloth. "When you've been up here as long as me, you get set in the system. And it's a caste system, Chappy, you believe that. As much as we try to resist, we begin to believe they *are* somehow superior. I'm too old to try to change the system, or myself."

"You should have told Marshall you'd see Lund if he got approval from Helmutsen."

"Helmutsen's scared to death of Marshall. He wouldn't have said no if Marshall wanted permission to feed me to piranhas in the Amazon River."

A waiter arrived with two steaming bowls of pinkish bean soup, thick enough to hold up a spoon and swimming with navy beans and pieces of diced ham. He placed one in front of each man and put a ham-and-cheese-on-rye to the right of Ridley's cutlery. He poured fresh coffee for both.

Davis looked at the meal in front of his companion and shook his head. "There's enough cholesterol there to plug every artery in your body, George," he said. "You ever think about diet and exercise?"

"I think about 'em," Ridley replied.

Davis smiled. He tasted his soup, reached for the pepper shaker and asked again about the meeting with Lund as he watched the black specks collect on the surface of the soup.

"There's not much to tell," Ridley said. "I told Lund Marshall was concerned about the findings of the investigation because Converse is an important constituent. I asked how the investigation was going. He told me what everybody already knew: The engines were the center of attention. I told him Marshall wanted to be kept informed of the progress of the investigation, and the senator was very concerned the engines be given the benefit of the doubt." He paused. "No, I said it stronger. I told him Marshall wanted Converse protected to the maximum extent possible."

Davis was using his spoon to fold the pepper into the soup but was paying no attention to the process. His eyes were fixed on Ridley. "So how'd he react?"

Ridley had his arms on the table, encircling his food as though to protect it from theft. He snagged half of his sandwich in his left hand, spooning soup into his mouth with his right, eating at the two alternately, barely taking time to chew and swallow. His mouth was half full when he began to speak, and Davis had to look away.

"He said no conclusion had been reached, and Senator Marshall should be satisfied that the investigation would be thorough and proper," Ridley replied around the food. "I told him the senator wanted total access, and he said he was aware of the senator's position and would be as cooperative as he could be." Ridley took another spoonful of soup, pushing the remnants of the half-sandwich into his mouth after it. "I asked him if he thought it would be possible to blame the accident on something other than a failure of a Converse engine"—the expression on Davis's face changed suddenly from one of intense interest to one of abject horror, and Ridley shrugged—"Hey, I was only carrying the message Marshall gave me."

"Christ, how'd he take *that*?"

"He asked me what I meant. I told him Senator Marshall was concerned about the future of Converse, and it could be detrimental to the company to be blamed for the accident."

"Jesus, of all the goddamned stupid things to say, George." Davis let his spoon fall with a cushioned thud to the table. "It sounds like you were asking him to fix the investigation."

"I carried the fucking message the way I got it, Chappy. If your goddamned senator didn't want to sound like he was askin' any special favors, he shudda rephrased the message. Besides, what did I say that wasn't true? Marshall *is* concerned about Converse, and a finding against the engine *could* be detrimental to the company."

"You could have been a little more diplomatic."

"Diplomacy's for the fuckin' State Department," Ridley snapped, grabbing the other half-sandwich and leaping to his feet. "I ain't his damned goodwill ambassador. That pilgrimage to Lund wasn't my idea, and if you don't like the way I handled things, you and Harold Marshall can damned well go to hell!" He stomped off with the rest of his lunch in his hand, leaving Davis to wonder how he was going to set things right with Lund.

He was still chewing on the problem three hours later when he walked into Lund's temporary headquarters at Dulles.

Pace finished writing and sent his story to Paul Wister. As a courtesy, he filled in Suzy O'Connor and Metro Editor Winston Henry. It kept turf-conscious noses from bending out of shape at the odor of a national-desk reporter farting around in somebody else's territory. Suze winked and gave him a thumbs-up sign. Henry was solicitous. "We figured this was your story," he said. "Let me know if there's anything we can do to help." It was obvious to Pace that both of them knew of his trouble with Schaeffer and were glad to see him working his way out of it.

Pace was exhausted, though he'd been up fewer than six hours. It was a combination of tension and sleep the night before that more resembled a drunken coma than useful rest. He hung around until Wister had a chance to see his copy.

The national editor scanned the story and sent it to Schaeffer. It was second-guessing time, Pace figured. But ten minutes later Schaeffer came out and nodded. He made no effort to make eye contact with Pace, but he didn't hassle him again, either. Wister walked up to Pace's desk.

"Every comeback starts with one step," he said to the

reporter. "Your first wasn't bad."

Pace nodded and averted his eyes. "Thanks," he said.

He suddenly felt so weak and disoriented he didn't think he could stand. He put his head down on his folded arms and tried to make sense of the past week. *Had it been only a week?* Images dashed around behind his closed eyelids like flies around carrion. The dead Sexton jetliner. Kathy in total despair. His lunch with Mike. Kathy again, always and everywhere. George Ridley. The mess in the main Dulles terminal. The flashing red-and-blue police lights bouncing incessantly off his retinas on Georgetown Pike. The body bags. And faces. The stern cop on the Beltway. Kathy again. Avery, smiling. Paul. Avery, furious. Mike on the last night of his life. Ken Sachs. Kathy, leaning into him, holding him tightly, pulling his face down to hers. Kathy . . .

The hand on his shoulder was rough. He shrugged it off. It came back again.

"Hey, laddy . . . Steve, boy . . . Talk to me, Steve, boy."

Oh, shit. That goddamned Irish brogue. Go away.

"Boyo, wake up. Yer snorin' is not doin' a bloomin' thing to help concentration around here. Come on, me friend. This is yer old South Boston buddy offerin' to buy ya a wee beer if you'll jest lift yer head off yer arms and open yer beady little eyes."

Pace lifted his head reluctantly and blinked against the bright fluorescent lighting. Had he fallen asleep? He looked at his watch. It was five-forty. If he had dozed, it was for just a few minutes. He stifled a yawn and smiled sheepishly at Brennan, who responded by tugging at his arm.

"Let's go over to The Grapevine, and I'll buy you a beer to celebrate the end of this day." Brennan laughed. "Then I'll pour you in your car and send you home to bed—or to sleep, whichever you prefer."

"One beer," Pace said. "No more. I have plans tonight."

"It's a promise."

Pace called Kathy and told her he'd be home in about an hour. She said she'd meet him.

The Grapevine, as always at that hour, was jammed and

noisy, filled with off-duty reporters and press groupies, including some reasonably high-ranking government officials. Each had something to say about the current state of world and national affairs, and everyone tried to say it at the same time. The establishment was laid out in a shotgun design, far longer than wide. The east wall was given to a bar. Every stool under the bar's padded wine-leather rim had at least one butt on it, and each space between the stools held at least two more. Four bartenders moved back and forth in perpetual motion, passing each other and then doubling back in a ritual dance to alcohol.

The west wall was lined with wine-leather banquettes, each stuffed to overflowing with more bodies, and in the aisle between the banquettes and the bar—supposed to be kept open for safety reasons—people stood elbow-to-elbow. Waitresses trying to serve the banquettes would turn from the bar, disappear into the crowd and appear again, as if by magic, on the other side to replace stale drinks with fresh, and overflowing ashtrays with clean.

Brennan reached an arm over Pace's right shoulder and pointed to the far end of the bar, where there appeared to be enough room for two more bodies, if the bodies didn't mind intimacy. Pace nodded and turned sideways, slicing his way into small openings between people and pressing his body forward to create openings where none was readily apparent.

"This place is a zoo," he said when he established an elbow hold on a few inches of bar.

"Same every night," Brennan replied, waving past Pace to attract a bartender. "What'll you have? I'm buying."

"Oh, joy and wonderment," Pace smiled. "Anchor Steam."

"You're an expensive date. Remind me never to bring you here again." Brennan caught a barkeep's eye. "An Anchor and a Boodles martini, very dry, twist," he shouted.

The server turned to fill the order when somebody bumped into Pace's back. It was to be expected in this crowd, so Pace didn't turn to see the tall, heavily muscled man shrink-wrapped in tight blue jeans and a turtleneck sweater strained by a size eighteen neck, thick biceps and a massive chest. Pace wouldn't have recognized him, anyway, but the large man knew Pace well. His name was Sylvester Bonaro. His occupation was muscling people. His recent activities involved driving a nineteen-ninety light-blue Ford van with newly acquired damage to the right front side.

Bonaro wasn't in the bar to drink, although he ordered a Budweiser to avoid looking conspicuous, if it was possible for a man his size to look otherwise. When the beer arrived, he poured half into a glass and then left both bottle and glass sitting on the bar as he turned his full attention to overhearing whatever he could of the conversation between Pace and Brennan.

"Rumor has it you had a rough day," Brennan said, tilting his martini to Pace in the manner of a toast.

"I've had better and hope never to have worse," Pace replied, ignoring the glass that came with his beer and sipping the Anchor Steam from the sweating bottle. "Avery landed on me hard. Where did you hear about it?"

"From several people, but they only had it secondhand. Something to do with a visit you made to Ken Sachs a wee bit late for the chairman's taste?"

Pace nodded. "Sometime well after midnight. I was pretty drunk. Woke him up. Accused him of murder. Nothing special."

"Sounds harmless to me." Brennan took a sip of his drink. "You sure about Sachs?"

"I was then."

"Now?"

"I don't know."

At that moment, part of the group standing in the bar's center aisle began to disperse, clearing Pace's line of sight to the wall behind the banquettes. Hung there were rows of caricatures of famous government officials whose comic, profound or otherwise noteworthy utterances were immortalized below their often-unflattering portrayals. He felt his chest tighten as he found the portrait of Henry Kissinger, famed as "the senior official on the President's airplane."

"The whole world knows it. The Russians, the Chinese, the Israelis, the Tierra del Fuegans. I think Kissinger probably told them himself: 'Watch for me. I'm the one who'll be identified as the senior official on the President's airplane.' "

Pace's breath caught as images of the lunch at the Dulles Marriott slammed back at him. God, he missed Mike.

"If you want to call to knock around some ideas, I'll try not to let you go to press with erroneous information. If you call me and tell me you've heard A and you've heard B, I'd be willing to tell you to lay off of A. If you wish to infer that B is the right course, I can live with it, because I won't have violated my trust here. Am I making any sense to you?"

It had made sense then. Nothing made sense now.

The noise in the bar began to fade. Pace's attention was focused on the Kissinger caricature and the painful remembrance of a friend across a dining table, on a roadside washed with the emergency flashers of police and fire vehicles, sharing a bottle of Black Jack in a motel room, talking about an upcoming meeting with the chairman of the NTSB. The doubt and the certainty rang in Pace's head as clearly as if they were being voiced at that moment.

"We're making a terrible mistake if you're wrong about Sachs."

"I'd stake our lives on Ken Sachs being clean."

Stake our lives . . . stake our lives . . . stake our lives . . . stake our . . .

The words echoed in Pace's head, louder and louder, until they became unbearable, and he felt anger roaring in his ears.

"Steve?" He heard the voice close to him, and was unsure if it was real or imagined. "Steve, what are you staring at?"

He turned and saw Glenn's face nearly pressed against his own, and the cacophony in the bar flooded in over the memories, burying them in a tide of human small talk. Pace glanced back to the opposite wall, but the Kissinger picture was obliterated again by the crowds in the bar's center aisle.

He took a long pull at the Anchor Steam, finishing a third of it.

"I think we'd better get out of here," Brennan said, downing the last of his martini and throwing a ten-dollar bill on the bar. "You're white to the eyes."

"They murdered Mike," Pace said, staring at the bottle in his hand. "They murdered Mike, and they murdered Mark Antravanian to cover up something about the Sexton." He looked up to Brennan. "They're not going to get away with it, Glenn." He set the bottle on the bar and shouldered his way past the Irishman, through the wall of humanity, to the front door.

Two pairs of eyes watched him go. Brennan was simply bewildered. Beside him, Bonaro was frowning deeply, and he acted quickly. He pulled three one-dollar bills from his pocket and threw them on the bar beside his untouched Bud. With his shoulders hunched like a football lineman's, he bulled his way past the boisterous crowd and followed Pace through the door and into the cover of growing darkness.

18

Thursday, April 24th, 6:25 P.M.
Bonaro burst out the door of The Grapevine, nearly knocking down two men and a woman about to enter. Without bothering to acknowledge their incredulous expressions, he strode to the curb and looked up and down H Street searching for a sign of Pace.

There he was, about to enter an alley that cut through to Pennsylvania Avenue. Bonaro suspected Pace was headed for his car and toyed briefly with letting his charge go and reporting in. But he thought it better to see the reporter home, to be certain, and then make his call.

Bonaro's instincts were correct. Pace drove directly to his New Hampshire Avenue apartment building, entered its underground garage and disappeared.

Bonaro headed up New Hampshire to Dupont Circle and a public phone. At Dulles, Elliott Parkhall answered on the second ring.

"We got a problem," Bonaro said. "The subject knows. I overheard him tell a friend."

"How much does he know?" Parkhall asked.

"That the engineer's accident was no accident. And the pilot was a charade. He believes the same people did both killings, and he suspects they're tied to the crash."

"Goddamn it!" Parkhall exploded. "I was afraid of that after his story this morning. Where is he now?"

"I put him to bed. I think he's down for the night."

"Where can I find you later?"

"My answering machine. Like always."

"Where the hell is that machine? Where do you stay?"

"That's my business. If you need me, you'll reach me."

Bonaro slammed the receiver back, his contempt for the man on the other end growing with every contact. If the job didn't pay so well, he would have dumped it, just to be rid of the jerk.

Normally he didn't care where his fee came from, but he had some curiosity about the people who ran Parkhall. He wondered if they knew how squirrelly the little shit was. Bonaro never told clients where to find him; he surely wouldn't tell a squirrel. The phone line to his recorder wasn't in his name, and the recording said simply, "Leave a message." There was nothing to tie him to this operation but Parkhall's word, and Parkhall didn't even know his full name. If things went wrong, he would drive back to Baltimore with his partner and disappear into the camouflage of the waterfront, and Parkhall could take the fall. The shit deserved it.

But Bonaro didn't want things to go wrong. His sense was there was too much cash yet to be made. If Parkhall screwed this up, Bonaro vowed, his last act before heading north would be to off the sucker. If Parkhall let somebody chop down the money tree before the harvest was in, he'd by God pay for it. Bonaro started toward his van, then detoured into the Dupont Circle Hotel. The place had a nice bar, and he owed himself a drink.

Elliott Parkhall stared at the dead telephone receiver for several seconds before replacing it in its cradle. What the hell had he said to make the guy mad? He'd simply asked him where he lived, for Chrissake. Screw him, anyway. Who did he think he was? Hell, muscle was easy to find. If the guy got out of line again, he would demand new help. That nigger, Davis, must know all kinds of people in the ghetto with guns and an urge to make some easy money. That was another thing Parkhall resented. He didn't like working for blacks. He never met one he trusted. It was a nigger who'd stolen his promotion at Warner Woolcott and left him to dicker with the NTSB.

The thought of the agency brought Parkhall back to the present and the problem at hand. If Pace was onto the murders, how long until he identified the cover-up? The engineer's heart began to race, and he felt dampness on his palms and through the hairs at the back of his neck. He tried to remember how he'd gotten himself mixed up in this scheme anyway, but the chain of events was muddled in the quagmire of his confused mind. At the moment, the most important thing was to reach Davis and tell him about Pace. Parkhall hoped there wouldn't be another killing. Already he was in way over his head and drowning fast in his own terror.

He let Davis's phone at the Senate Transportation Committee ring eight times before giving up and trying his home. Davis answered in mid-ring.

Parkhall relayed the report from the muscleman who called himself Sly. As he talked, he realized with some alarm he didn't know the big man's last name. If the operation blew up, he wouldn't know who to finger for the killings. Nobody would believe he was taking orders from a high-ranking Senate aide, the way the executives at Warner Woolcott didn't believe him when he warned they wouldn't be able to depend on the nigger who stole the job that should have been his.

"Calm down, Elliott. There's nothing for you to worry about." Davis's deep voice was smooth and reassuring.

"Whadda you mean?" Parkhall fretted. "The goddamn newspaper people know the two murders are connected and tied to the Sexton somehow."

"They don't know anything. They only suspect," Davis said. "That was evident this morning, if you read Pace's story carefully. Suspecting and proving are two different things, and they aren't anywhere close to proving. They're not going to get close, either, unless somebody loses his cool. Understand?"

"What if you're wrong?"

"Then we'll handle it. We'll handle Pace. I'll make some calls. But it's not your affair. You've reported. Your responsibility is covered. Your most important job is in Hangar Three. Keep at it, and you'll be fine. I've got it covered, okay?"

"Yeah, okay," Parkhall said. But he didn't believe it.

Davis hung up gingerly, as though to do otherwise could upset the delicate balance of Parkhall's psyche. Pace *was* getting to be a pain in the ass, there was no question about it. But Davis didn't want to deal with the problem this night. He was still trying to dope out the results of his afternoon meeting with Vernon Lund. It definitely didn't start well. Lund made it clear he resented the implications of George Ridley's visit the previous week. Davis made excuses for it, saying Ridley and Marshall didn't get along, and Ridley could have been trying to make the Ohio senator look bad. Or maybe George didn't understand the message the senator wanted to convey.

There had been no intention, at least not on the senator's part, to imply that the investigation should be skewed in any way. Harold Marshall would be the last man to suggest the probe stop short of the real cause of the accident. But Lund could understand, couldn't he, that Senator Marshall was deeply concerned about Converse? The nation should be very concerned, too. After all, the aviation industry was one of the few in which the United States still led the world, and the future of all components of that industry was vitally important to the country. So if there was any doubt at all about the cause of the crash, it would be terrible to finger Converse simply to have a scapegoat. Lund could understand that, couldn't he?

Lund appeared skeptical, but if doubts about Marshall remained in his mind, they didn't come through in his words.

"Tell the senator we understand his concern," Lund had said. "Tell him we will not point a finger unless there is absolute certainty. The NTSB has never done otherwise, you know."

Tentatively, Davis broached the idea of a final press briefing to nail down the bird strike as the cause of the accident and put to rest fulminating theories about imaginary conspiracies.

He was amazed when Lund responded positively to the idea. "I hate what the *Chronicle* is trying to do," Lund said. "Let me think about it."

The Dulles situation, like Elliott Parkhall's psyche, was in delicate balance. Davis knew he couldn't afford a mistake. He couldn't afford to be distracted by Pace's bar talk. And that's pretty much what it was, he decided, just bar talk. He believed what he'd told Parkhall. Suspecting and proving are two different things.

He would worry about Steven Pace later.

19

While Chapman Davis spent the evening wrestling with the specter of Vernon Lund, Steve Pace wrestled with the specter of himself.

He entered his apartment angry and confused, frustrated as much by his own behavior as by the mystery of Flight 1117. It wasn't like him to lose control, even over a shock like Mike McGill's death. People died senselessly every day. Pace's own parents and younger brother had died while flying home with a friend in the friend's private airplane from an Indiana University basketball game. The accident was as senseless as they come. The pilot had a commercial license, an instrument rating, more than two thousand hours of experience, and a normally level head. But he'd allowed himself a drink or two after the game. For that reason, or for others perhaps, he became disoriented while trying to land at the little airport outside Pace's hometown. Instead of flying his Beechcraft onto the three-thousand-foot airstrip, he'd flown it into the side of a barn.

Pace had been devastated by the accident, but it hadn't thrown him the way Mike's death had. He'd managed to face his life then; he was making a muck of it now. Compared with the strength Kathy was showing in the face of the loss of her brother, he was making an ass of himself.

Maybe it's guilt. Maybe I'm tearing myself apart because I know I'm the one who pulled Mike into this.

He pushed the thought aside and let himself into his apartment.

Kathy arrived a few minutes later, carrying a sack of groceries. She set them on the kitchen counter. When she turned back toward the living room, he was standing in front of her.

"Hi," he said.

She smiled a little. "Hi, yourself."

"You doing okay?"

"As well as can be expected," she said, dropping her eyes to the floor. "It comes back at me at the strangest times, and I start to cry for no reason."

He put his hand under her chin and lifted her face. "Nobody cries for no reason," he said. "I think you have a pretty good reason."

"So do you. Did I tell you how sorry I am about Mike?"

"Uh-huh."

"I remember you talked about him so often. I wish I'd had a chance to meet him."

"So do I," he said, and then laughed. "On the other hand, he probably would have swept you off your feet and taken you away from me."

"I thought you let me go."

He nodded seriously. "I did, once," he acknowledged. "If I ever have the chance to make the decision again, it won't be the same."

Suddenly they were in each others' arms, their bodies pressed tightly. Their kiss started gently, sensually, and built quickly to passionate urgency. Their tongues embraced. He held her head in his hands and caressed her hair. She put her hands on his buttocks and drew him to her.

He pulled away and looked down at her face. "Do you want me to carry you to bed?" he asked.

She laughed. "No," she said. "That would only slow us down."

They made love twice in an hour—something he hadn't done since college—moving quickly the first time, luxuriously the second. It was never more right than it was this evening. For the hour they lay together, neither Mike McGill nor the *Washington Chronicle* entered Pace's mind.

Later, after she had showered and started a light dinner, after he had allowed himself to remember the last twenty-four hours, she asked how he was. He began talking to her. It came slowly.

She neither pushed him for details nor volunteered advice. She offered to mix him a drink, which he declined, so she settled into the couch, content to listen.

Although he hadn't intended to, Pace told her everything, in excruciating detail, about the afternoon and the evening of Mike's death, of the visit to Ken Sachs, the showdown with Avery, his concerns that he was losing control. He said he'd consumed a gallon of alcohol in a week and yet, with the exception of the night before, he'd been able to function on a satisfactory level.

"I don't make sense to myself anymore, Kath," he said. "At a time in my life when I should be settled and happy and secure, I seem bent on self-destruction. And I'm not only taking myself, I'm taking the people around me I love and respect."

He talked for nearly two hours. During his monologue, they picked at dinner, neither much in the mood to eat. They cleaned up the kitchen and moved back to the living room. When he finished, he shrugged.

"From now on, you'll know better than to ask," he said.

"I'm glad I asked," she said. "You're a mess."

"Thanks for noticing."

She snuggled up in the corner of the sofa, tucking her feet under her as she often did when discussions grew serious.

"You've told me two striking things," she said. "First, you feel some responsibility for Mike's death and aren't bearing that very well. Second, you're worried about your drinking, and some people you work with are beginning to worry, too. Is that about it?"

"How come it took me two hours to say that?"

"That's what editors are for," she replied. "Mike's death isn't your responsibility. No matter how much you feel you pushed him, there's no way he wouldn't have followed up on the note and the phone call, even if you didn't exist.

Unless he was less than the man you've described, he wouldn't shrink from controversy. He wasn't following the trail to get a story for you. He was following it to get to the bottom of . . . the accident." Kathy's voice cracked at the reference to the ConPac crash. "He was doing for his profession exactly what you're doing for yours. The fact that you were working along parallel lines doesn't mean you were responsible for him, any more than he was responsible for you."

Pace nodded. "My head knows, Kath. It's my heart I can't convince."

"Your heart will catch up," she replied. "Your head only has to comprehend what happened. That's easy. Your heart has to mend. That takes longer. Take it from me. I know."

He moved over next to her on the sofa and put his arm around her shoulders. "I know you know," he said. "I don't feel very good about bringing my problems to you, considering what you've been going through."

"It occurs to me we're going through almost the same thing," she said. "Maybe shared pain is halved."

"Or doubled," he suggested.

"No," she protested, "not doubled. It's always easier when there's someone to talk to who understands."

He leaned over and kissed her lightly on the forehead, and then abruptly, he stood. "Which brings us to the subject of my new-found alcoholism," he said.

"If you have a problem, you've recognized it," she said. "I'm no psychologist, but I've always heard that recognizing and acknowledging a problem are the first steps toward resolving it."

"It can't be that easy, or everyone with a drinking problem could solve it. I don't know if I have a real problem, or if it's an excess of the moment."

"Even if it's a problem of the moment, it needs resolution," she said. "From what you told me, it almost cost you your job today."

He nodded. "I was well out of control last night. Even if

I was right about Ken Sachs, I should have handled it differently."

"Your symptoms don't strike me as classic alcoholism," Kathy said.

"Why not?"

"This conversation has been tough on you. I've watched you struggle with it. There's no question some things would have been easier to say with a drink in your hand. But earlier, when I offered to fix you something, you turned it down."

"So I'm not an alcoholic. All that means is I don't have any excuse for what I did."

"That's right. And that's the hardest thing to accept—responsibility for your own actions. You only get into trouble when those actions turn self-destructive."

"What does that mean?" he asked.

"You said you and Mike got drunk together on the night of Mark Antravanian's death, but that wasn't a destructive kind of drunk, except maybe to your heads and stomachs. It sounds like last night you were destructively drunk."

"Why the difference, do you think?"

"I think Mike's presence in your life was the difference the first time. His absence was the difference last night." She shifted to a more comfortable position on the sofa. "Look, the high point in your career was winning the Pulitzer, right?" He nodded. "Of course. And who was it who helped guide you through the investigation of the Chicago accident? Mike. Who was it who suggested the series that won the prize? Mike. Who was always there when you needed consultation on other investigations? Mike. And who was there for you this time, helping you expose what could be the biggest and most diabolical cover-up imaginable? Mike again. Then last night, all of a sudden and totally unexpected, Mike was gone. Not unavailable. Gone. Forever. That would be tough for anybody to handle."

Pace's brow knotted in a look of challenge. "Are you saying I can't function as a professional without Mike

McGill? That I can't . . . can't continue working this story on my own?"

"No, Steve, not at all. I'm saying maybe that's what *you* think."

"What!"

Kathy offered no elaboration, letting words already spoken stand on their own. She could see Steve turning them over, rejecting and accepting, weighing and assessing the implications.

"In other words, you're suggesting my self-confidence about this story was inexorably tied to Mike's availability to help me? That even when he wasn't there, I knew he was available? And when I had to face his never being there again, I came apart?"

"What do you think?"

Pace shook his head. "That would make me the most selfish human being alive. It can't be. I don't miss Mike for the professional help I've lost . . . well, I do, of course. It's ridiculous not to acknowledge that." He got up and went to the big living-room window. "But that's not all of it. Mike was special. He was my friend. It's . . . a hard thing to describe."

Kathy got up and joined him at the window. She put her arm lightly around his waist. "Let me put it this way," she suggested. "If Mike had been alive at midnight last night and you'd come up with the Ken Sachs theory for some other reason than Mike's death, would you have gone and confronted Sachs?"

Pace thought about it for a minute and then shook his head. "No," he said. "I probably would have called Mike."

She nodded. "That's what I mean. He was a sounding board, a test track, a trial run. And he was a friend. The pain of losing a friend is always acute. And if that friend is also your partner, your confidant, your pain is compounded by frustration. It's obvious to me that most people would have lost control under similar circumstances."

He turned and looked at her seriously. "You didn't . . . when Jonny died."

She hooked her arm through his and laid her head against his shoulder. "On the same day I lost Jonny, I found you again. And you've been for me what Mike was for you." She paused, debating briefly whether to say more. She was talking again before she knew she'd made up her mind. "And even though I've had you this last week, I still lost control in my own way."

"When?"

"Today, in the office, in front of Hugh."

"What happened?"

"I began to cry. I couldn't stop. That's not like me. I was out of control."

"Over Jonny?"

"No. Well, partly," she said. "But not just Jonny."

"Then what?"

"It's complicated. Too complicated to go through now. I'm not even sure I understand it. What it boils down to, I guess, is maybe I'm too rigid. That's what Hugh said. That I work never to let myself feel too much pain, so I have no yardstick by which to measure joy."

"That's pretty heavy."

"But it's true, I think. I try to be too much like my dad, and I consider myself a failure at times like these, when I can't be that strong."

"Hmm. Or maybe you're trying to be too much like you *think* your dad is."

Now it was her turn to be confounded. "A riddle?" she asked.

"No," he said. "You've always described your father as totally focused, a man who had little time to stray from the path he laid for himself. I saw some of that toughness the night I met him at your house."

"True," she said.

"Even that night, he didn't grieve, and then he wouldn't hear of you hanging around Boston to grieve after Jonny's funeral."

"Or when Joey died. Or Mom."

"That's what you saw . . . what he wanted you to see.

How do you know what it was like for him when he was alone?"

She looked up at him, astonished. "I *don't* know," she conceded. "I don't have any reason to think he was any different when he was alone."

"But you don't *know.*" It was a statement, not a question.

"Well, no, I don't. I . . . I certainly can't ask him."

"No need to," he said. "But a man as caring and loving and devoted as your father doesn't lose a family member without pain. Consider the possibility that he chose to hide it from you—maybe as a way of easing your own anguish. He probably lets himself go when the children aren't around to see it. I don't believe he'd think any less of you for feeling the pain once in a while, too."

"I feel like I've been psychoanalyzed," she said.

"Me, too," he replied. "And I feel better for it."

"So do I," she acknowledged. "Maybe we should do this for each other more often."

He took the chance. "It would be easier if you lived here," he suggested. "Sister Mary Margaret be damned."

"Yes," she said. "It would."

The TransAmerica technicians had been all over the Sexton 811 carrying the registration number N464TA. It was the aircraft's first major inspection since she went into service, and everything appeared nominal. Neither the crews that flew her nor the mechanics who serviced her reported anything out of the ordinary. But given the nature of the questions being asked about the Converse engines, the technicians were paying particular attention.

"Man, I never get over the size of these things," said an apprentice named Jason Mack as he handed a diagnostic tool to his partner, whose upper body disappeared to the waist inside the port engine, where several cowling plates had been removed. The mechanic, whose name was Alan Gleason, was eyeballing engine components under the glare of a high-intensity light he held in his left hand. When he needed an instrument, he shouted his order back to Mack and held his right hand out behind him so Mack could slap the article into his palm. Mack had a full complement of tools and diagnostic equipment in a cherry picker nuzzled up to the huge power plant.

"Watcha lookin' for? Anything in particular?" Mack asked Gleason.

Gleason eased himself out of the engine compartment and turned to the younger man, who was trying to learn the trade. It irritated him that Mack wasn't grasping concepts.

"You know what happened to the Sexton at Dulles?" he asked.

"Sure," Mack replied defensively. "She crashed."

"You remember why?"

Mack's brow furrowed. "She took in a bird, I think."

"And one of the turbine disks fractured."

"Yeah."

"That shuddn'tuv happened."

"Why?"

"Because," Gleason explained, "these babies are designed to take that kinda lickin' and keep on tickin'."

Mack shrugged.

"You read anything about the Sexton out in Seattle?" Gleason asked. "She was ours."

"Inna newspapers, or in company paperwork?"

"Both."

"No."

Gleason closed his eyes and shook his head. "Jesus," he said. "You ever think about goin' into auto mechanics?"

"Nope."

"Too bad. Coupla months ago, we had a turbine-disk fracture on one of ours. Nothin' bad came of it, but what do the combination of those things tell us?"

"Maybe," Mack said hopefully, "these babies should be grounded 'til somebody finds the problem."

Gleason laughed, reluctantly acknowledging his assistant had a point. "But until that happens," he said, "we need to check the disks every time these planes come in for inspection. Understand?"

"Gotcha," Mack said. "You find anything wrong with these?"

"Not yet," Gleason replied, gingerly diving back into the Number 1 pod.

What he was looking for was there, but the only visible manifestation of the spreading fracture was on the side of the disk Gleason couldn't see.

Five hours later, N464TA would be sent back into service with a clean bill of health.

20

Friday, April 25th, 10:10 A.M.

Steve Pace made the long drive out to Dulles Airport for what he hoped would be the last time on this story. Mitch Gabriel called before 7:00 A.M. to say Vernon Lund would hold one final press briefing at ten. Pace couldn't fathom what more Lund had to say, and Gabriel professed not to know.

The trip took fifty minutes, time he spent thinking about his evening with Kathy. The night that began in a misery of soul-searching concluded with the realization that they were something special and they owed it to themselves to be together. They promised each other they wouldn't let their schedules come between them again. They even toyed with the notion of throwing over both their careers and heading south to Islamorada in the Florida Keys to run a bed-and-breakfast and a charter fishing service. "Our Hemingway thing," Kathy called it. "He lived in Key West," Pace reminded her. "Picky, picky," she said.

When she left for her townhouse before midnight, she

promised to return the next evening with enough personal belongings to move in at least for a trial period, long enough to be certain that what brought them together again was more than temporary mutual need. She would be a resident when Melissa arrived for spring break on Sunday.

They discussed the impact on Sissy of finding the two of them living together, but Pace insisted nothing be kept from her. It would be a deception for Kathy to wait to move in until Sissy returned to the West Coast. They wanted to be together. Why play games about it?

Ordinarily, Gabriel's 6:45 A.M. call would have awakened Pace. This day, however, he was up at five-thirty and busy making room in the bathroom and in the bedroom closet for Kathy's belongings when the phone rang. Although he'd had fewer than six hours' sleep, it was sound, sober sleep, and Pace felt more rested than he had in a week.

He parked his Honda in the hourly lot in front of the main terminal and was in the briefing room ten minutes early.

Vernon Lund appeared exactly on time.

"Ladies and gentlemen, I'll make this brief," Lund said. "The overwhelming evidence at this time points to a bird strike in the right engine as the probable cause of the crash of ConPac Flight Eleven-seventeen at Dulles on Thursday, seventeen April, this year. At this time, we have not identified the species. Although a good deal of the evidence was burned during the post-crash fire, identification as a bird is positive. We have also identified secondary damage within the pod that we believe occurred when said engine dislodged from its pylon and impacted with the concrete runway. Our investigation, of course, is continuing, and full public hearings will be held on completion of the investigatory process."

Lund stopped and was deluged by questions. His eyes darted from one reporter to another, unsure whose question to take, settling on no one. Finally one reporter's persistence and decibel level prevailed, and his colleagues ceded the floor to CNN's Tom Petterhoff.

"Can you provide some elaboration on the damage done to the engine when the bird strike occurred and give us a sequence of events during the takeoff roll?" Petterhoff asked.

"I can do neither with any assurance of complete accuracy at this time," Lund replied. "Data taken from the flight data recorder are still being analyzed. It isn't clear yet what sequence of events led to the destruction of the aircraft. As far as damage to the engine, we have a number of broken fan blades, which is consistent with a large bird strike and runway impact. There is additional damage within the turbine compartments that we suspect is due to the runway impact. It is possible some broken blades were ingested, although we aren't certain why that might have occurred. Earlier-generation power plants tended to suffer this type of damage, but the Converse Fan is designed to divert virtually *all* ingested debris—fan blades, birds, rocks—around the turbine compartments into the air bypass and out the rear of the pod. These are questions we still have to answer, if we can. It is possible we'll never be able to say we're positive of anything."

"But you are certain at this point that a bird was the primary cause of the disaster, and not any sort of flaw in the Converse Fan?" The question was from Russell Ethrich of *The Washington Post*.

"That is correct," Lund replied.

"What steps will ya'all take if you find broken fan blades *were* sucked into the turbine compartments?" asked Justin Smith of the *Times*.

"I can't answer that question until we determine that such a thing happened, and if it did happen, why," Lund said. "I already told you that."

Smith had a follow-up question, based on his own exclusive. "You able to confirm that durin' the final moments of the takeoff roll, after the failure of Number Three engine, the crew attempted to take off on the remainin' two engines?"

"Not at this time," Lund replied.

It was Steve Pace who got to the heart of the matter. "Mr. Lund," he asked, out-shouting a local television reporter for the floor, "do you think the Eight-eleven fleet should be grounded until this investigation is completed, in case any sort of redesign is necessary for the C-Fan?"

"Absolutely *not*," Lund thundered, animated for the first time that morning. "So far as I'm aware, there is no way to design an engine to protect it fully against a bird strike. Converse never gave a hundred-percent guarantee the engine would afford such protection. The company claimed only that the C-Fan design would improve the chances of the engine's survival. Furthermore—"

"I wasn't talking about protection against a bird strike," Pace broke in. "You said the engine is designed so *any* debris would be blown out the back of the pod, going around the turbine compartments without breaching them. If, in fact, one or more compartments were breached—"

"I'm well aware what you're asking, and my answer is the same." Lund continued. "I don't know a way to design an engine to fully protect it from ingestion of any foreign matter. Metal fan-blade debris would be even more difficult to deflect than a bird. I'm also well aware your paper has been trying for days to make some sinister mystery out of this tragic accident. I'm not going to help you do that, Mr. Pace. There is *nothing* sinister about the circumstances surrounding the crash of Flight Eleven-seventeen, and there is no reason the traveling public should have any concern whatsoever about flying the Sexton Eight-eleven. I can't say it clearer than that."

"No, sir," Pace replied. The other reporters ceased trying to interrupt, knowing the exchange between Pace and Lund would make good copy. "And I'm not trying to make anything sinister of this tragedy. But if you recall, TransAmerican had a turbine disk shatter in Seattle some months ago, and in that case, no ingested debris was involved."

"What's your point?" Lund snapped.

"That perhaps there's something about this engine we don't know. That it might be prudent to put them on the ground until we find out."

"I don't agree," Lund said. "In any event, that's not the NTSB's decision. It's the FAA's."

"The NTSB can make the recommendation."

"Not this board member," Lund said with a tone of finality.

Lund started to look away, but the insistent tone of Pace's voice drew him back. "One last question," the *Chronicle* reporter said. "What's the purpose of this press conference?"

Lund looked startled. He glared at Pace. "To announce our tentative findings," he said. "You've been demanding to know for more than a week. Now you know."

"We knew before," Pace said. "You wouldn't come right out and say 'bird.' But you said it was something with feathers, so it didn't take a brain surgeon to eliminate cows." Pace's colleagues laughed tentatively. They didn't know where his questions were leading, either.

"Once again I ask, what's your point, Mr. Pace?" Lund demanded.

"Well, the tone of your remarks tends to deflect culpability from Converse," the reporter replied, trying to keep accusatory nuance from his voice. "Your purpose seems less to enlighten the public than to lighten the burden of the engine manufacturer."

Pace's colleagues were stunned by the statement, but no less so than Lund. Russell Ethrich was sitting closest to Lund and thought he saw small beads of perspiration pop on the board member's upper lip. Justin Smith looked from Lund to Pace and back again, sensing there was something very important behind the question, but not immediately able to discern what it was.

"I won't dignify that with a response," Lund snapped. "Are there any other . . . pertinent questions?"

At the forty-minute mark, Lund called it quits, and most members of the media left grumbling about learning virtually nothing new.

Smith hung back to walk out with Pace. "You hittin'

below the belt there, boy, or you know somethin' the rest of us don't?" he asked playfully.

"Fishing, Justin," Pace replied. "Just fishing."

"Yeah? And my Aunty Eloise can grow bullfrogs outta cornmeal." The older reporter stopped, and reflexively Pace stopped, too. Smith rubbed his chin. "You remember me tellin' you some of the people around me are talkin' about you as my replacement when I retire?"

"Sure, and I'm flattered, Justin," he said, "but I don't know why I'd want to jump from the *Chronicle* to the *Times*."

"Money, sonny. They say it talks."

"Maybe," Pace said, nodding, "but I've never pictured myself as a *Times*man. I don't own enough gray suits."

Smith snorted. "An old saw," he said. "I look like that stereotype to you?"

"No," Pace acknowledged with a laugh, "but everybody else in the bureau does."

"Can get used to anythin'," Smith replied. "Even gray suits."

"I'd have to give it a lot of thought, old friend."

"Ain't offerin' you the job, Steve. Ain't mine to offer. Just puttin' you on notice. You got some scoop tucked in your britches you're plannin' to embarrass me with, I could steer *Times* talk away from you pretty quick."

Pace wasn't quite certain how to take that. "Is that a threat?"

Smith smiled warmly. "Nah, just jerkin' your chain." He put a hand on Pace's shoulder and squeezed lightly. "Want to see you do good," he said. "Wouldn't make me unhappy at all to see you followin' these old shoes. You got somethin' good up your sleeve, I wish you luck with it."

"A hunch," Pace said honestly. "It's probably about the wildest goose I ever chased."

"Hope you bag it, boy. See ya 'round."

Smith left—sauntered off would be a better description. Pace felt genuine affection for the man. Their competition had never detracted from their friendship, although the friendship never became as personal as it was professional. Pace found himself wishing it were otherwise.

He followed Smith out of the terminal moments later, reflecting on how touchy Lund had been about the possibility of grounding the 811 fleet. Pace intended nothing malevolent by his question, nor were precautionary groundings out of the ordinary. Yet Lund jumped at the question as though he'd been stung.

So Lund's a defender of the Converse Corporation. Big fucking surprise. How much they pay you, Vern?

That thought would force Pace to make a phone call he dreaded more than anything.

Three hours out of Seattle, on a direct run to Boston, Trans-Am Captain Phillip Jeffries laid his middle finger lightly on the throttle of the Number 1 engine of his Sexton 811, the ship bearing the registration N464TA. The first officer, Graham Washington, looked at Jeffries quizzically.

Jeffries glanced at his copilot. "Feel that," he said.

Washington laid his palm against the white-plastic knob. He lowered his head for a moment, as if listening for something, then glanced at the digital-engine readouts. "What are you getting?" he asked the captain.

"I thought I felt vibration—more than usual," Jeffries said. He put his hand back on the throttle. Then he shook his head. "It's not there now."

"Readouts are nominal," Washington said.

"Probably my imagination," Jeffries said.

"She just got out of overhaul, Skipper," Washington recalled.

"Maybe I ought to go in for one," the captain joked, and they both laughed.

From his seat in a leather armchair in his Capitol Hill office, Senator Harold Marshall reached across a polished-mahogany table and killed the power on his small color-television set, tuning out a commentator's summation of the NTSB press conference. He'd heard enough, and there was a broad smile on his face. He turned to the aide sitting beside him.

"We did it, Chappy," Marshall said. "There were hours when I doubted we could pull this off, but we did it." He reached his right hand toward Chapman Davis, who took it with a nod.

"Yes, sir, I think it sounded all right," Davis said.

"Better than all right." Although it was only a bit past noon, Marshall rose and went to a sideboard, where he opened his bar, dug some whitish-looking ice cubes from a small freezer, and poured generous portions of bourbon for himself and for his aide. Davis preferred vodka, but he said nothing and accepted the glass. "I don't know what brand of soft-soap you used to rub down old Lund, but I don't think he could have made a stronger defense if I'd written it myself."

"Don't get me wrong, Senator, I'm not displeased," Davis said after a sip of his strong drink. "But I'm going to feel a lot better in a few weeks when people have gone back to worrying about who's got the nukes in Russia, or when some huge asteroid will hit the earth and wipe out all life as we know it—anything but airplanes."

Marshall eased himself back into his chair, stretching his long legs out in front of him. "Well, you can worry this thing for a few more weeks if it will make you feel better," he said, "but I, for one, am going to sleep very soundly tonight."

"Tell him it's Steve Pace from the *Chronicle,* and I badly need to talk to him," he said to Ken Sachs's secretary on the other end of the telephone connection. "Sylvia, something unfortunate happened between us, and Ken won't want to talk to me, but it's important."

"I heard you two had a spot of a problem," Sylvia Levinson replied. "I didn't get all the gory details, but I know he was one enraged puppy when he had to cancel that trip to Chicago. I gather the President wasn't thrilled, either."

"I bet not. The whole incident was my fault. I was out of

line, and I'd like to apologize."

"He's at a luncheon meeting, but I'll give him the message when he returns. Meanwhile, if you have anything else to do, I'd suggest you go ahead and do it."

"In other words, don't waste time hanging around waiting for him to call back?"

"Well, it's not my place to say that, but that's what I'm saying."

"Do the best you can for me, will you please?"

"The best I can. Yes."

Attempting optimism, Pace ignored Sylvia's caution and ate lunch at his desk while he tried to make sense of the story. He made three lists: what he knew, what he suspected, and questions remaining without answers. There probably was a story in the unanswered questions.

When the phone at his left hand rang at two forty-three, he was so deeply involved in the sorting process that he resented the interruption and cursed softly.

"Pace," he snapped.

"I don't have much time, and I don't have much inclination to consume it with you, but Sylvia made an eloquent case on your behalf, so I'm returning your call."

Pace felt himself squeeze the receiver when he recognized Sachs's voice.

"Ken, I called for two reasons. I want to apologize sincerely for the intrusion the other night. I was drunk, as I think you suggested at the time. I was upset about the shooting. You were the last one outside people at my office and in the restaurant to see Mike and me together. At the time, in my condition, it was clear to me you must have had something to do with his murder."

"I told you then, and I repeat now, that is absolutely ludicrous," Sachs said. "I have no motive to order a murder and no means to carry one out. Moreover, it isn't clear to me at all, as I gather it isn't clear to the police, that Mike was anything but an innocent bystander."

"My stories the last two days should make you think otherwise."

"I saw your stories, and it's still supposition."

"Well, regardless of what I thought at the time or think now, I didn't have any right to barge in on you, and I *am* sorry. I hope you'll convey my regrets to your wife."

Sachs didn't acknowledge the apology. "What was your other reason for calling?"

"The press conference today," Pace said. "Vernon said there still isn't an explanation of why debris got sucked into the engine instead—"

"I know," Sachs interrupted impatiently. "I saw the press conference on television, and I was fully briefed beforehand."

"Fine," Pace said. "Then you heard me ask if it would be a good idea to recommend grounding the Eight-elevens as a precaution?"

"Yes."

"And you heard Vernon take my head off. He said the paper was trying to make . . . I think he called it a sinister mystery of the accident. We never said anything like that, Ken. What gives?"

"I think your recent stories are saying something close . . . if not explicitly, then implicitly."

"A sinister mystery? Isn't that a little strong? I wrote about a tragic coincidence."

"If you say so."

"Then what was Vernon talking about?"

Sachs paused for a few seconds. "I don't know," he said slowly. "He knows about the little problem we had the other night, and maybe he jumped on you out of loyalty to me."

"I guess that's understandable. Let me ask you the same question I asked him. If there's a mysterious—no, check that. If there's no explanation for why the engine didn't act as it was supposed to, as it was designed to, isn't there cause to recommend that the FAA ground the Sextons until the questions are answered?"

"Vernon seems to think not."

"You're the chairman. What do you think?"

"He's the supervising member of the board. It's his call at this point."

"Damn it, I don't get your reasoning."

"You don't have to. It's not for you to understand. It's our responsibility, and if you media people will leave us alone, we'll take care of it."

"Oh, *come on,* Ken. That bureaucratic bullshit's beneath you."

"Let me put it this way, then. We have proof positive of a bird strike. We are calling that the primary cause of the accident. There are still additional matters under investigation. Period."

"You mean it's possible the aircraft could have survived the bird strike, but something else went wrong?"

"Pace, I didn't say that, goddamn it!"

"What *are* you saying? We were going to work this together, remember?"

"I remember the agreement, but that was before the other night. At this time, I have no outstanding obligation to you. Your action abrogated everything."

"Even getting at the truth?"

Pace winced as the line went dead.

21

Saturday, April 26th, 10:00 A.M.

Harold Marshall slept Friday night every bit as well as he expected.

But he woke up Saturday morning with a severe headache, and that would be the best part of his day.

"Everybody's calling the case closed except the *Chronicle,* and they keep sniffing around the body like dogs on a bitch in heat."

Harold Marshall snarled into the telephone and paced behind his desk as an anxious lion might pace the back of its cage at feeding time. That he had to come to work on the weekend only added to his anxiety. He was supposed to be with Evelyn Bracken today, and she was not taking his absence well.

The extra-long cord spiraling from the telephone flipped snakelike on the floor, coiling and uncoiling as the tension changed, extending first to one side and then the other as Marshall walked and talked. He frequently paced during important conversations. He claimed he thought better on his feet. But the pressure on the carpeting was evident in the rut of threadbare nap marking his habitual course. After his last election, Evelyn pestered him to have the carpeting replaced, arguing the nation's taxpayers could afford to spruce up the office of a three-term United States senator. He brushed her off the way he was now brushing off the calming words from the Converse CEO, George Thomas Greenwood.

Marshall was infuriated and frustrated by Greenwood's inexplicable lack of concern in the face of his company's profound predicament. Although Vernon Lund had come through with a resounding defense of the C-Fan, the media persisted in keeping lingering doubts alive. Yesterday Marshall would have bet a month's salary the issue had been laid to rest. Hadn't he been the one to reassure Chappy Davis? And now he was the one being reassured, and he didn't believe it from Greenwood today any more than Davis had believed it from him yesterday.

Damn the *Chronicle,* anyway. Why did it even have to bring up unanswered questions? The basic question, the only *important* question, was answered: No defect in the Converse Fan was responsible for the nation's worst air disaster.

End of story.

But it wasn't.

"The public criticizes the media all the time, but they *believe* what they read, George," Marshall continued. "This constant pick, pick, pick is going to erode public confidence eventually. Believe me, I know."

"I'm not saying you're wrong, Harold, I'm saying don't overreact," Greenwood replied. "I caught the NBC and CBS news shows last night, and both of them keyed in on the fact that a bird was blamed for the accident. You tell me the *Times* and the *Post* did the same thing this morning, so I don't see it's any kind of big deal for one newspaper to get cranky."

"It isn't that simple, my friend. The *Chronicle* is more than cranky. Listen to the way the story starts: 'Acknowledging still-unanswered questions about the performance of the Converse engines on the Sexton Eight-eleven that crashed last week at Dulles International Airport, the National Transportation Safety Board nonetheless blames the accident on a bird sucked into the plane's right engine.' The reporter—this Pace—gives the official NTSB statement four paragraphs and then goes on for eleven or so about these so-called unanswered questions. And even though the *Post* and the *Times* didn't mention questions in their leads, they dealt with them at length farther down."

"I know. You told me already."

"But it's getting picked up, George! AP is carrying it. CNN showed tape of Lund's press conference. It's bad stuff, and we don't need it. Pace doesn't show any sign of letting up. God knows where he's going with this double-murder bullshit. He's got to be stopped."

"What do you propose we do, shoot him? Then they'd have three murders to write about." Greenwood's tone was derisive. "Be reasonable, Harold. If Lund doesn't waver, and I'm told he won't, the *Chronicle* will go away eventually. And the others will follow."

"What makes you think Lund's solid?"

"I have my sources. They tell me Lund is personally convinced a bird strike caused the crash, and all other issues are peripheral with him. He also knows which way the wind blows. He's a Republican. I'm a Republican. You're a Republican. If we don't chase Cordell Hollander out of the White House next election, we'll get it back four years later, and Lund will be starting with two powerful allies in his bid for the top spot at the FAA."

"Wait. Hold on a second. I haven't committed for Lund."

"But you will."

Greenwood's tone was so matter-of-fact that Marshall was momentarily nonplussed. Had he become such a pawn of Converse that Greenwood could be that certain of his cooperation? Possibly so, he had to admit, especially in light of the chances he'd taken and the deeds he'd done for the company over the years, and particularly in the past week. Nevertheless, the thought chilled him.

"Six years is a long time from now," he said.

"Not in politics," Greenwood reminded him. "People play for a lot bigger stakes far more distant than that."

"Does Lund believe all this?"

"He knows about playing ball, just like you do."

Marshall bristled. "No one has the authority to speak for me about something like that," he snapped. Greenwood's smug assurance was infuriating. But, he acknowledged to himself with great regret, to defy someone was to recognize that his authority existed.

"No one *has* spoken for you, Harold," Greenwood said coldly. "But certain insinuations have been made to Lund on our behalf, and if he believes suggestions about our support extend to you, well, that suits our purpose at the moment. Besides, Lund's qualified."

"Goddamn it, I don't give a shit about who's going to head the FAA six years from now. If doubts about your engine aren't put to rest, there might not be a Converse to support Lund, or me, by that time. Your stock's still sliding, or hadn't you noticed?"

"It'll come back. Major investors still have confidence in this company. I look for institutional buyers to see the bargain and snatch us up damn soon."

"I sold out the day after the accident," Marshall said. "Everything. Every share."

"So I've been told," Greenwood replied. "I'm certain you reinvested the money wisely."

"You know where most of it went."

"Yes, I *do* know. Take care, Harold."

Marshall replaced the receiver and picked up his copy of the morning *Chronicle,* rereading the top of Pace's story, and it angered him all over again. Regardless of what Greenwood wanted, this witch hunter had to be stopped. Marshall's acute sense of things told him the situation was not nearly as positive as the Converse CEO believed.

And he knew with sudden certainty it was going to get worse.

Greenwood replaced the telephone receiver and reached for the humidor on his desk. He extracted one of the illegal Havanas for which he'd acquired a taste no other cigar could fill. The ersatz American and South American products always were trash and always would be. Damn Castro, anyway. If he'd follow the rest of the old Communist axis, his cigars would flood the market—and be a hell of a lot cheaper.

He drew the tobacco under his nose, an unnecessary habit given the unvarying quality of the Cuban product, but he found the aroma soothing. He turned the butt in his mouth, snipped the tip, held the cigar away and thumbed his desk lighter, carefully holding the flame off the tobacco. He watched it light evenly, without scorching.

If someone asked him how he lit a cigar, Greenwood would have had to stop and think about the ritual, but he performed it flawlessly, appearing to pay rapt attention while his mind was ten miles away on something else entirely. At this moment, his mind was more like four hundred miles away on a flamboyant United States senator he was trying to keep under control, and on a series of media reports that bothered him more than he acknowledged.

Greenwood leaned forward into a cloud of aromatic

smoke and punched the intercom button on his telephone. "Lucy?"

"Yes, Mr. Greenwood."

"Is Cullen Ferguson in the building today?"

"I believe he is. Would you like me to get him for you?"

"Yes. Ask him to come up right away. And, oh, once you reach him, you can go on home. I appreciate you coming in this morning to handle the faxes from Washington. Given my illiteracy with technology, I never could have managed it."

Greenwood leaned back in his chair, absently watching the smoke curl about his hand, and considered what it was he wanted Ferguson to do. He settled on a plan well before the vice-president for public affairs knocked on his door and opened it. Visitors to the inner sanctum always were announced. But executives and junior executives in the company were not required to be passed by secretaries. If they knew they were expected, they had only to knock and walk in. Subordinates did it with superiors, superiors with subordinates. There was more dignity in such a system than in keeping a vice-president cooling his heels.

"Even before you ask, G.T., I've been monitoring all the networks and getting the East and West Coast press stories by fax," Ferguson said. "I'm not happy with them. That NTSB briefing should have quieted all the doubts, but they're still seeping up through the cracks."

"I know. I've been briefed on the Washington stories," Greenwood said. "What can we do about it?"

"We're going to be living with it at least through next week. I called an old colleague of mine at *U.S. News* and asked him what we should expect next Monday, and basically, it will be more of the same. I don't anticipate any better treatment from *Time* or *Newsweek*. The fact is, the NTSB conclusion leaves questions open. The media smell blood. It would have affected me the same way during my reporter days. On this side of the fence, though, it's a pain in the ass."

"So what do we do?"

"I got nasty with a couple of reporters after the crash. They pressed me for information I couldn't provide because of the gag order. What I'd like to do now, if the insurance carrier approves, is take a soft approach, see if I can't convince them to accept the NTSB finding and wait for the public hearings to get answers to the open questions. I could approach it on the simple tenet that they owe it out of fairness. I don't know how successful it would be, but I think persuasion, not evasion, is the way to go."

"I agree. And I think you should do it in person. Book yourself into New York and Washington—Washington first—and lay it on. Damn the expense. You've got carte blanche. But we want some mind-sets changed, and fast."

"What about the insurance carrier?"

"It's my decision, and I'll take responsibility," Greenwood said.

Ferguson nodded. "I'm out of here today."

"What do you think she'd like to have for dinner her first night here? I could do the marketing, straighten up the apartment, and get her room ready while you're working today. And don't forget to double-check taking Monday off."

Melissa Pace was arriving the next day, and Kathy had the whole of Saturday to prepare.

"We can go out tomorrow night," Pace suggested as he knotted his tie. "It doesn't need to be anything fancy. With a teenager, the less planning, the better. The only thing I want to take special care to get right is the picnic trip to the Blue Ridge on Monday. Sissy has all the water she needs in San Diego. She comes here to go to the mountains. I already checked with Paul about taking the day off. He said it's fine. I've got so much overtime coming, I think they're glad to see me ask for any of it in comp time."

"Great," said Kathy. "Maybe Sissy and I could fix the picnic together."

Pace smiled. "Hugh hasn't changed his mind about letting you off?"

Kathy shrugged. "It's part of the new me, the me that stops to smell the carnations."

"Roses."

"Whatever."

It delighted Pace to think of the three of them on an outing. He was more confident than Kathy that Melissa would accept the new woman in her father's life. After all these years, he found it hard to believe his daughter still harbored hopes of a reconciliation between her parents.

He took Kathy in his arms and hugged her. "God, it's so good to have you here."

"Almost as good as it is to be here," she said. "Having you around has helped me . . . well, you know."

He pushed her to arms' length and held her there, looking directly into her eyes. "Helped you cope with losing Jonathan? If that's what you mean, maybe you should say it out loud. Dancing around the words won't change anything."

Tears filled her eyes. "I know," she said. "It's so hard."

He held her again and stroked her hair. "It'll come," he said. "It'll come."

"Find out what happened, Steve. Please."

"You don't believe it was a bird?"

She pulled away from him gently. "And you don't, either," she said.

"I have doubts."

"I know. I'm counting on you to reconcile them."

He finished dressing and started to leave the bedroom. She called him back. "Steve, what's this?" she asked.

He saw her holding the scratched metal ball he'd picked up on the field at Dulles.

"I don't know," he said honestly.

"Is it something you want to keep?"

He reached out, and she dropped it in his hand. He turned it between his thumb and forefinger and hoped for an inspiration that would identify it.

"I picked this up in the grass at Dulles when Mike was showing me some of the wreckage," Pace said. "There were a couple more like it scattered around. I didn't mean to carry it off, but we left in a hurry, and I forgot I'd put it in my pocket. I don't think it's anything important, but I can't bring myself to toss it."

"Then I'll leave it where I found it," she said, taking it back and replacing it in the ashtray.

Twenty minutes later, as he sat down at his desk, his phone rang.

"Pace."

"This is Detective Lieutenant Martin Lanier, District Police, returning your call from Wednesday afternoon. Sorry it took me so long to get back. What can I do for you?"

It took Pace a second to remember that he'd called Lanier after he talked to Clay Helm about the progress of the accident investigation.

"I had some information from the Fairfax County Police that they were working with you to determine if there was any connection between the Antravanian and McGill deaths," Pace said, a little surprised he was able to refer to Mike's murder so casually only three days after the fact. Mike's funeral was today in Memphis, but Pace hadn't been able to leave Washington to attend. He shook the recollection from his head before it knocked him off balance.

"I know," Lanier said. "I saw your story yesterday. It was correct, as far as it went."

"As far as it went?" Pace's anticipation rose.

Lanier didn't respond right away. Pace was tempted to prompt him, but he resorted to an old interview technique. When he got an answer that was incomplete or slightly evasive, he waited. Since conversation abhors a vacuum, the subject would become uncomfortable with the silence and start talking again, elaborating on a previous answer. Those afterthoughts often produced the best quotes and most pertinent information of an interview.

The technique worked again.

"I sort of owe you an apology for being so rough on you Tuesday night," Lanier said. "When I got to thinking later about what you said about your friend being a target, good police work dictated I get back in touch. I jumped to a conclusion about motive, and I shouldn't have."

"You mean you're convinced now it was a setup?" Pace asked tentatively.

"Convinced of it, no," Lanier said. "But considering it. Some evidence suggests I should."

Pace wanted to say he knew about the light-blue Ford van, but he had given his word to Clay Helm, and he wouldn't break it.

"Can you tell me what the evidence is?" he asked instead.

"No. But I will tell you word on the street is that nobody's heard about two white junkies working drugstores together."

"Uh-huh." Pace acknowledged the information, and then fell silent again.

"I'd be willing to be quoted as saying we are investigating the possibility that Captain McGill was a target and the other victims were killed to mislead investigators."

"That's what happened," Pace said.

"That's your opinion again," Lanier said. "We're investigating other possibilities, too, among them that the shootings are exactly what they appeared to be in the first place, or the shooters are new in town, or are embarking on a new career."

"What about a possible link between the shooting and the accident in Virginia?"

"We haven't made the connection yet," Lanier said. "But we haven't ruled it out, either. At this point, that facet of the investigation is being conducted principally by the Fairfax Police. Since the Antravanian death appears to be an accident, the Virginia cops will have to come up with some evidence of homicide to keep that line of investigation open. If they have anything, I haven't heard about it."

"I should check with Captain Helm again today, anyhow," Pace said. "Thanks for returning my call, Lieutenant."

"Not at all."

Pace punched in Clay Helm's number and waited for

someone to pick up the phone.

"I was headed out the door," Helm said. "What's up?"

Pace related his conversation with Lanier.

"So, the old hard-ass softened up a little, huh? I don't see he had any choice."

"What about you?" Pace asked. "Any progress?"

"Nothing I can talk about for publication, Steve, but you can say the investigation remains open and active."

"That doesn't advance things much, does it?"

"There's nothing more solid to give you."

"Leads?"

"Ideas more than leads. Procedures we know we need to pursue."

"Can you say any more than that?"

"I can't, no."

Pace reviewed his notes. He could take the murder-investigation story a giant step beyond where it was two days earlier. He told Paul Wister about his conversations with Lanier and Helm, and got enthusiastic approval to write the story.

He stared at his blank computer screen and felt a queasiness rise in his stomach, the sort of feeling one gets when a car takes a small rise in the road too fast, or when a roller-coaster crests at the highest point of the track and starts the long plunge to the bottom.

Pace thought that appropriate. The whole bloody mess had been one long roller-coaster ride, with the highest highs followed by the deepest lows, one after another, after another.

"Hold on with both hands," he muttered to himself. "Here we go again."

TransAm Flight 687 roared out of Logan Airport into the blustery spring sky and turned west-southwest on a course for San Diego. It would be an uneventful trip for the aircraft designated N464TA.

But it would be the last stress load the fracturing turbine disk in Number 1 engine would be able to take.

Drawn to his office on Saturday by a nagging conviction that something was wrong with the world of aviation, Ken Sachs sat behind his desk and read again the newspaper stories on Vernon Lund's final press conference. In the background, CNN droned through special Saturday-morning programming on entertainment, travel, and fashion, but a regular news show would be up soon.

He'd brushed off Steve Pace's question the day before about the need to ground the Sexton fleet, just as Lund had brushed off the reporter. But in reality, he wasn't certain Pace didn't have a valid point. There was a good deal about the performance of the Converse-Fan engine still in doubt. And he still didn't know what had caused the problem with the TransAm C-Fan in Seattle. Were the turbine disks defective? Were the two incidents connected?

He didn't want to undercut Lund, and it was Lund's considered opinion there was no cause to ground the 811 fleet. But, damn it, if safety was the ultimate goal, didn't common sense dictate that all the C-Fan engines be inspected?

The decision made itself.

He thumbed through his Rolodex and found the home phone number for Lane Simmons, administrator of the FAA. It would be Lane's call. Sachs could only recommend. But he was confident about the recommendation.

The 811 fleet had to come down until the reliability of its engines was assured.

"Are you out of your mind? During the heaviest travel season of the year?" Simmons exploded through the telephone into Sachs's ear. "You've got college kids all over the country trying to get home or to the beach for the spring break. The City Council of Fort Lauderdale would have us lynched!"

"I'm not talking about the whole damned industry, Lane," Sachs snapped. "I'm talking about a couple-dozen aircraft. The airlines can haul out other equipment to take up the load."

"Not on this short notice! Spring break began today!"

"We're talking about basic safety here."

"We're talking about revenue here, too," Simmons said. "These newgeneration aircraft cost a bloody fortune. How are the airlines supposed to pay for them? They don't generate revenue when they aren't flying."

"And what do they generate when they crash?" Sachs demanded.

"That's a low blow, Ken. If I was convinced there was a safety factor, I'd order 'em down regardless of cost."

"Then *do* it."

"What's the safety factor? Your own man said yesterday there is absolutely no reason to ground the Eight-elevens."

"I know. I've come to believe he's wrong."

"Shouldn't the whole board make that decision?"

"The whole board isn't here today."

"Your fellow members might think you a little high-handed making the recommendation without consulting them. Vernon Lund might be downright pissed. I would be, in his place."

"That's my problem. I'll deal with it."

"You won't have to deal with it if I don't go along. Nobody will ever know."

"Please reconsider, Lane. I'm begging you."

"No," Simmons said. "The Eight-elevens fly."

22

Sunday, April 27th, 7:00 A.M., Pacific Daylight Time
"Oh, man, this is bogus!" The teenager stood with her mother before the passenger agent at the United Air Lines gate at San Diego International-Lindbergh Field.

"What alternatives are there?" the mother asked.

"There are several," the agent said, smiling at Melissa Pace. "You'll get to Washington today. I promise."

"I hate it when things like this happen," Melissa said.

"Well, if the plane's going to break, it's better to have it break on the ground than after you're in the air," Joan Pace told her daughter.

"Better to not have it break at all," Sissy replied with a teenager's impatience.

The United agent pointed across the aisle. "If you'll step over to our customer-service counter, an agent there will get you on another flight at no change in price," he said. "Then we'll transfer your luggage."

He handed the tickets from the canceled United flight back to Sissy and pointed again at the customer-service desk. Already there were nine people lined up before the four agents waiting for transfers to different flights or different airlines.

"If you want to get to Dulles right about on the schedule, there's an American flight leaving in twenty minutes, but we can't guarantee your luggage will make that flight," the customer-service representative told Sissy when she got to the front of the line. "We can put your bags on the first flight after that, and they'll be delivered to you anywhere in the Washington metropolitan area."

"What's available if I want my bags to get there with me?" Sissy asked.

"How about a TransAm flight leaving in, oh, just over an hour?" the agent suggested. "There's no chance your bags will miss that plane."

Melissa turned to her mother. "I want to fly on the same plane with my luggage," she said.

Her mother nodded. "I'll call your father after you take off and give him your new arrival time," she said.

"It shouldn't be a problem," the agent said. "It looks like you're scheduled to arrive in Washington only about fifteen minutes later than you would have on the United flight."

"How can that be?" Sissy asked. "It's leaving more than an hour later."

"It's a fast airplane," the agent said. "A lot faster than the older planes."

When they reached the TransAm gate, Sissy's plane was parked there, and was being serviced by fuel trucks, baggage handlers, and caterers for the long trip East.

"Wow, that's def," the girl said, smiling as she noticed the blue-and-silver hull gleam under the morning sun.

"It is pretty," Joan Pace agreed. "I think you made a good choice."

Neither noticed that the big Sexton 811, about to leave San Diego for Washington Dulles as Flight 957, carried the registration number: N464TA.

"The NTSB wants *what?*" George Greenwood was stretched out on a lounge chair beside his pool in the warm spring sunshine, reading the Sunday *Youngstown Vindicator*. It was after 11:00 A.M., Eastern Daylight Time. Sissy Pace's flight East had just been handed off to San Diego Departure Control when the call to Greenwood's home came from Harry Birkenkopf, Converse Corporation's chief of contracting.

"I got the call from Ken Sachs himself," Birkenkopf was saying. "He wants the Seattle report, and he wants it faxed to him today. Now."

"Do we have it?" Greenwood asked.

"We have a preliminary we got from the subcontractor a few weeks ago," Birkenkopf replied. "The final isn't due for, I dunno, maybe a week or two."

"How much different will the final be?"

"Not much, I don't think."

Greenwood paused. "Why does Sachs want it today? It's Sunday, for chrissake."

"He was adamant, Mr. Greenwood."

"Tell me again what the report says."

"It suggests the turbine disk in Seattle was subjected to some unusual vibrations."

"How?" Greenwood demanded. "What kind of vibrations? From what source?"

"Unknown," Birkenkopf replied. "We hope the final report will tell us."

"Is it possible a flaw was manufactured into the disk?"

"You know how those things are inspected. I doubt a flaw could have gotten by."

"Is it possible the engine was vibrating excessively?"

"Also unknown. After the disk was replaced, the engine was bench-tested. Vibrations were nominal. There's been no repeat of the incident since the engine went back on line."

Greenwood took a deep breath and blew it out. "So that still doesn't get us to what the NTSB wants with this report on a Sunday."

"No, sir."

"Did you ask?"

"I only said I'd have to call you."

"Call Sachs and tell the asshole to call me," Greenwood said. "I'll decide what we do."

Greenwood's phone rang again in fewer than five minutes.

"Why you workin' on Sunday, Ken?" the CEO asked jovially. "Tryin' to show me my tax dollars hard at work?"

Sachs was in no mood to joke. "The FAA's making a decision on what to do about the Eight-eleven fleet, and I want your report on the Seattle incident to provide some perspective," he said.

Greenwood felt himself go tense. "What decision?" he asked.

"Whether to ground them for engine inspections."

Greenwood came off the lounge chair. "Why in the hell would they do that?" he thundered. "There's nothing wrong with the C-Fan. Your own top investigator said so."

"Ours is an advisory role, as you know, George. The FAA makes the decision."

"Then why didn't the FAA call for the Seattle report?"

"Because depending on what it says, it will be a part of our recommendation. I want it now, George. Your man has my fax number. Today."

"Well, I lean toward waiting for the final report," Greenwood said smugly.

"Fine, then I'll tell the FAA you've refused to disclose what happened in the Seattle case, and I consider that alone to be grounds for suspicion about the C-Fan's durability."

"Simmons won't buy that," Greenwood said.

"Are you willing to take the chance?"

He was not. "I'll have it faxed within the hour," he promised. He called Birkenkopf and told him to send the report to Sachs.

"It'll take me a little bit to get to the office and get it sent off," Birkenkopf said.

"I told him an hour," Greenwood replied. "If you stretch that hour, I won't care at all."

Then Greenwood began trying to reach Lane Simmons.

While Greenwood talked to Sachs, Steve Pace got a call from his ex-wife.

"What happened to the United flight?" he asked when she told him of Melissa's schedule change.

"It broke down, that's all I know," Joan replied.

"What's the new flight?"

"TransAm Nine fifty-seven. It's due to arrive at four-fifty, your time."

Pace felt a hot sting of anxiety. "What's the equipment?" he asked urgently.

"What?"

"What kind of equipment is it, Joan? What kind of plane?"

"I don't know," she snapped in response to the tension she heard in his voice. "You know I don't understand that stuff."

"Describe it," he ordered.

"It was blue and silver. It had two wings and a tail and big wheels underneath."

"Joan!"

"I don't know, Steve. It was a new airplane, I guess. The

agent told Sissy it was so fast she'd get to Washington only fifteen minutes later than her original flight."

"Damn, it's an Eight-eleven."

"Steve, you're frightening me."

"I'm sorry," he said sincerely. "I don't like the idea of her being on an Eight-eleven when we still don't know what's wrong with them."

"There haven't been any problems since the crash."

"No, but there was an incident before Dulles."

"I didn't know that. You should have told me."

"I called a few days ago to ask about Sissy's flights. When I found out she was on Seven-sixty-sevens, that was the end of it. Who can predict a flight will be canceled?"

"Well, I don't think there's any need to worry," Joan concluded. "The flight got off fine, and the weather's good all the way to Washington."

"I'm sure you're right," Pace said.

Kathy McGovern listened to the Washington end of the conversation from the living-room sofa. When Steve hung up, she joined him in the kitchen. "Anything wrong?" she asked.

"Sissy's going to be a little late getting here," he said. "Her flight was canceled, and she took a later one."

"Is that all?" Kathy asked.

"Uh, no," he said, shoving his hands deep into the pockets of his denim shorts. "Joan let her switch to a TransAm flight. It's an Eight-eleven."

Kathy's hand flew to her mouth, and she swallowed hard. Then she shook her head, as if dismissing a thought. "They've been flying safely for more than a week since the accident, Steve," she said. "I don't think . . ." She let the thought slide.

Pace put an arm around her shoulders. "I promise not to become a basket case in the next four hours if you won't," he teased.

"Okay," Kathy said. And her mouth smiled.

Her eyes didn't.

George Greenwood wasn't having luck reaching Lane Simmons because Simmons was driving from Kensington, Maryland, into Washington, D.C. to meet with the board of the NTSB. Simmons had resisted the meeting. He made up his mind the day before there was no need to take the drastic step of grounding the 811 fleet. But earlier that morning, Ken Sachs had called him at home. During the previous evening, Sachs said, he contacted all the members of the NTSB board, and they were assembling in Sachs' office to discuss his recommendation. Simmons thought he had no choice but to join them. He also thought he was being sandbagged.

By the time Simmons arrived at the NTSB's headquarters, the board members were there.

Sachs met him. "I appreciate you coming down, Lane," he said. "You know everybody?"

Simmons called each of the board members by name as he shook hands around the conference table. He paused longer when he got to Vernon Lund.

"Good to see you, Vernon," he said. "It's a shame you have to come in on Sunday when what you probably need more than anything is some rest. You did a nice job on the ConPac thing."

"Thank you," Lund replied dourly. "It was a terrible tragedy."

Simmons sat down and rocked back in his chair. "So why have you called us here, Ken?" he asked.

Sachs pointed to a photocopy of the report faxed from Youngstown minutes earlier. Each place at the table had a copy. Simmons could see that some board members had read and marked theirs already.

"Take a minute with that," Sachs said.

"Don't we have this on file?" Simmons asked.

"We didn't," Sachs said. "We should have, I think, but we didn't. I doubt your people have it, either. From the way George Greenwood talked, he didn't intend for any of us to see it until after the final comes in."

"Personally, I'd prefer it that way," Simmons said.

"In ordinary circumstances, I wouldn't disagree with you," Sachs pressed. "I don't consider this an ordinary circumstance."

With a sigh of resolution, Simmons picked up the short sheaf of papers and read. Some members of the board re-read with him. Lund sat still, staring straight ahead. Sachs guessed he objected to having his personal conclusion about the C-Fan engine challenged. He'd get over it.

Six minutes later, Simmons threw the papers back on the table. "So what?" he challenged.

"Vibrations, Lane," Sachs said. "Unidentified excessive vibrations. I don't have to lecture you on the damage excessive vibrations can do to an aircraft engine."

"No, you don't," Simmons agreed testily. "But you do have to explain to me how this . . . this very preliminary statement could possibly justify grounding a fleet of airplanes."

"Amen," Lund said.

Martha Halleck, the junior member of the five-member safety board, leaned over the table. "Maybe excessive vibrations weakened the C-Fan at Dulles, so when the bird was ingested, the disk was too weak to withstand the additional stress," she suggested.

"Pure speculation," Simmons replied.

Sachs banged a fist onto the table. "Lane, this board voted four to one before you arrived to recommend grounding," he said. "Are you prepared to dismiss that without consideration?"

"I have considered it," Simmons insisted.

"Maybe not long enough."

"What's that supposed to mean?"

"You should consider how it will play to the public that the FAA turned down a nearly unanimous recommendation by the NTSB on such a serious matter," Sachs suggested.

"You'd leak it to the press?" Simmons asked. "That's the most underhanded blackmail—"

"Not blackmail, Lane. Merely the certainty that somebody on the staff wouldn't be able to resist letting it out. This is a formal board meeting. The minutes are available to the staff. If something unfortunate should happen to another Eight-eleven, they'll fry you. And it's my guess the President wouldn't stand for the embarrassment."

"I'd have your job for a leak like that," Simmons threatened.

Sachs raised his hands in concession. "You haven't got the authority. But maybe you have the clout. So you can have the job now, if you want it. Issue the order first. Ground those planes."

Simmons looked around the table. "You all feel strongly about it?" Everyone nodded but Lund, who shook his head emphatically. Simmons' gaze stopped at his old friend. "Looks like we're outmanned, outgunned and outmaneuvered, Vern." Then he turned to Sachs. "You've got your grounding, effective immediately. But only for engine diagnostics, nothing more."

"That's all we asked for, Lane."

Sachs stood and extended his hand.

Simmons ignored it, turned on his heel and left the room.

Captain Conrad Dixon thought he didn't like the feel of the Number 1 engine of his Sexton 811. The vibration he sensed through the throttle was pronounced.

"Throttle back in increments; see if we can get rid of it," Dixon told First Officer Patricia Singleton.

The copilot pulled the throttle lever back a fraction of an inch and shook her head. "It's still there," she said. "But the readouts are nominal."

"Try a little more—" Dixon began. He was interrupted by a call from a regional ground controller monitoring Flight 957.

"TransAm niner-five-seven, call your company on the St. Louis frequency and report when you come back," the controller said. Dixon and Singleton exchanged glances. Calling TransAm operations as they approached their destination was standard procedure, but to be asked to call in mid-flight was most unusual.

"TransAm niner-five-seven, roger," he replied. Dixon was about to change frequencies when he heard the ground controller talk to another flight. "TransAm eleven-six-seven, call your company on the Memphis frequency and report when you come back," he said.

"What's going on?" Singleton asked.

"Let's find out," said Dixon. He set the TransAm frequency in St. Louis into one of his radios and made contact.

"The FAA has just ordered the entire Sexton Eight-eleven fleet grounded for emergency engine diagnostics," an operations official told Dixon. "You have the option of continuing to your destination or setting down now."

"That sounds serious," Dixon said.

"That's what we have to find out," the official replied.

"Stand by," Dixon said. "We'll advise."

He looked across the throttles at Singleton, then lowered his hand to the throttle of Number 1 engine. It was vibrating, if anything, he thought, more severely than a few minutes earlier.

"We're going to take her into St. Louis," he said.

Singleton nodded her concurrence, and Dixon informed his operations chief.

"Any reason you don't want to drive it to Dulles?" the operations chief asked.

"We're already having some problems with Number One engine," Dixon said. "I don't want to take chances."

"Roger, understood. It's your call," the ops man replied. "We'll inform airport operations and start trying to rebook passengers."

"Niner-five-seven, roger."

Dixon reported his intention back to regional air traffic control.

"Are you declaring an emergency, niner-five-seven?" one controller asked.

"TransAm niner-five-seven, negative," he said. "But we are experiencing some engine difficulty and would appreciate some expediting."

By now, news of the grounding of the 811 fleet was spreading quickly through the aviation industry, and emergency or no emergency, regional controllers and approach controllers at Lambert-St. Louis International Airport acted to get the TransAm 811 down as quickly as possible. As Flight 957 changed course, First Officer Singleton reported the unscheduled landing to the passengers.

"We are experiencing some minor engine difficulty, and the captain has chosen to land at St. Louis as a purely precautionary measure," she announced over the public address system. "There is absolutely nothing for you to be concerned about. We'll be on the ground in a few minutes. Our ticket agents are working now to find all of you seats on other flights into the Washington area. We are sorry for the inconvenience, but the captain believes caution and your safety are paramount. Thank you for your patience."

In seat 29A, Melissa Pace heaved a huge sigh. Everything was conspiring against her.

Flight 957 was on downwind to Runway 12R, with two turns yet to make to final approach, when the deteriorating turbine disk in Number 1 engine disintegrated. In the cabin of the aircraft, it sounded like an explosion.

"Oh, my God, we're going to be killed!" said the middle-aged man in the seat next to Melissa Pace. There were muffled cries and sobs from elsewhere in the cabin. Melissa looked out at the engine hanging under the port-side wing. It was her sense that the explosion had come from there. The leading edge of the wing was slightly behind her seat, and she twisted her head down, trying for a better view. She thought she could see a ripple in the metal of the engine cowling, but her view wasn't good enough to be certain. There didn't appear to be a fire, and she found that comforting.

"We're okay," she said to the man in the next seat. "We're going to be fine."

"How the hell would you know?" he asked savagely. "You're a kid."

"I know all about airplanes. My dad's the aviation reporter for the *Washington Chronicle*."

"Oh, joy," the man said and let his head loll back on the seat.

On the flight deck, the crew hadn't heard anything, but everyone felt a definite lurch. The readouts on Number 1 engine went crazy.

"Shut it down," Dixon ordered as he and Singleton watched the automatic electronics to reconfigure the aircraft controls to fly on the two remaining engines. The captain turned to the flight engineer, Peter Savich. "Pete, make a quick damage inspection in the cabin," he ordered.

Savich burst through the cockpit door and scanned the passenger area, struggling to keep his face and manners composed. "We're fine," he told several distressed customers. "We'll be on the ground momentarily." He satisfied himself that whatever had happened to Number 1 engine had not damaged the cabin and returned to the flight deck.

"No problem except the passengers are scared shitless," he reported. "They think they heard an explosion."

Singleton scanned her control panels. "No fire or smoke alarms anywhere," she said.

Dixon had reported the engine failure to the approach controllers, and they gave him clearance to come straight in. The Sexton touched down seven minutes later, rolling nearly to a full stop on the runway before Dixon gingerly advanced power to taxi the crippled jetliner to a gate.

Half an hour later, with everyone safely inside the terminal, the flight-deck crew and Hal Carleton, chief of Trans-Am operations in St. Louis, inspected the engine from the ground.

"My, God, will you look at that!" Singleton whispered. She was looking at the surface of Number 1 engine facing the aircraft cabin. There was a fourteen-inch gash in the cowling, ripped by the jagged piece of metal that protruded through the tear.

Singleton pointed it out to Dixon. "If it had come through and breached the fuselage . . ." she said, unable to speak the words to finish the thought.

Dixon shook his head. "We are too fucking lucky to live," he said.

Steve Pace waited nervously in front of the passenger-arrival doors in Dulles' main terminal. They were the ports at which the people-movers deposited passengers from the mid-field terminal, including those just in on TWA Flight 742, the one Melissa boarded after the unexpected stop in St. Louis.

He was still at home when the desk called to tell him the FAA had issued a press release about the grounding of the 811 fleet.

"What prompted it?" he asked the weekend editor, Julia Hershowitz.

"The release doesn't say anything except the move is—quote—a precautionary measure designed to allow complete inspection of all Converse Fan engines—unquote," Hershowitz said. "I know you're off today, Steve, and it's well deserved, but—"

"Glenn can handle it, Julia. I'm on my way to Dulles to pick up my daughter. In fact, she's on an Eight-eleven. Have they been ordered out of the air?"

"The release doesn't say. Let me check the wires," Hershowitz said. "Hmm, well, the last AP story says the crews of three Eight-elevens in flight chose to divert to the nearest airport, while others continued to their original destinations. It doesn't say which flights diverted."

"I'll call the airline," Pace said. "Meanwhile, switch me to Glenn. I'll give him some numbers to call. And I'll call you from the airport to see if there's anything I can do from there."

"I appreciate it, Steve. Hang on, I'll transfer you . . . hey, wait a second. We got an 'Urgent' from AP on an Eight-eleven en route to Washington from San Diego. Is that your girl's flight?"

A surge of adrenaline hit Pace in the chest. "It must be," he said. "What happened?"

"Hold on, let me find the story." During the pause, Pace's

left hand began to cramp. He realized he was holding the telephone receiver in a death grip. "Here it is," Hershowitz said after a wait that seemed an eternity. "Let's see. Let me read it to you:

"The left engine of a TransAmerica 811 was seriously damaged in what some passengers described as an explosion as the aircraft attempted to make an unscheduled landing at Lambert-St.Louis International Airport Sunday.

"The incident, in which no one was injured, occurred an hour after the Federal Aviation Administration ordered the nation's fleet of Sexton 811 aircraft grounded for engine inspections. The captain of TransAm flight 957 . . ."

"That's Sissy's," Pace interrupted.

". . . decided to divert to St. Louis after experiencing engine problems en route from San Diego to Washington's Dulles International Airport, scene of the nation's worst air disaster 10 days ago. That accident, which killed 334 people, involved a Sexton 811 owned by Consolidated Pacific Airlines. The National Transportation Safety Board has concluded tentatively the Dulles accident was triggered when a bird was sucked into one of the aircraft's engines.

"In Sunday's incident, the captain of flight 957 was told of the FAA order grounding the 811 fleet and was given the option to go on to Dulles or abort the flight. Because of the trouble his aircraft was experiencing, he elected to divert to St. Louis, according to airline officials. The damage to the left engine, the cause of which is still under investigation, occurred minutes before touchdown, the officials said . . ."

"That's enough," Pace said. "No injuries, right?"
"Right, the story says it again farther down," Hershowitz assured him. "The plane taxied safely to a gate and passengers were able to debark—what the hell kind of word is

that?—in normal fashion. Nobody hurt. Just some pretty shaky folks."

"I better get off the phone. Sissy might be trying to call. Tell Glenn to check my Rolodex for the numbers he needs. There are a lot of home numbers there. I'll check with you later."

He hadn't hung up ten seconds when the phone rang again.

"Daddy?"

"Sissy! I heard you decided to go to St. Louis," Pace joked. He hoped that hearing no worry from him would calm her.

She giggled. "Oh, I didn't decide, Daddy. The pilot did. It was kind of exciting. Do you know what happened?"

"A little bit. You okay?"

"Oh, sure. Fine. But now I'm on a TWA flight, and it's leaving like right now. I wanted to give you the time and flight number."

He jotted them down. "I'll be there—unless you decide to take any more side trips," he assured her.

"Well, you better have some fun in store for me, cause it sure has been a hassle getting there," she said. "Gotta go. See ya."

Marveling at his daughter's resilience, he called Joan to reassure her that Sissy was well.

"You were right about the Eight-elevens," she said.

"You couldn't have known," he replied, and she was grateful he wasn't angry.

With some time to spare, Pace tuned in CNN. His phone rang again. He was surprised to hear Cullen Ferguson's voice.

"Where are you?" Pace asked.

"At the Capital Hilton," Ferguson said, "and none too soon, from what I hear."

"You have anything to say about the groundings?"

"I'm stunned," the Converse vice-president said. "I hadn't heard this was coming. From what Vernon Lund said Friday, I assumed a grounding wasn't even a remote possibility."

"Is that for quotation?"

"Sure. I don't have anything from the higher-ups yet, but I'll call you when I do."

"I'm off today, Cullen, and I'll be leaving for Dulles to pick up my daughter in a little while. Glenn Brennan's working the story for us. You know him?"

"I don't think so."

"He's a good man. I'll call and give him this quote, and he'll call you for more later. What's your room number?"

Ferguson gave it to him.

"What brought you to town?" Pace asked.

"I came to deal with some of the public-relations flotsam still bobbing around the crash."

"You're a little late," Pace told him.

"I know," Ferguson acknowledged. "We didn't handle this very well, Steve, and I'd like an opportunity to talk to you about it. Can you make dinner tonight or tomorrow?"

"Ah, no. We're going to the mountains tomorrow."

"Tuesday then," Ferguson persisted with a laugh. "I'm not leaving town until we get a chance to talk."

"Call me at the office Tuesday morning," Pace said. "Maybe I can make lunch."

Pace wanted to tell him to go to hell, but he and Ferguson needed each other in some strange, symbiotic way. So he made a note to himself about lunch on Tuesday with Ferguson and put it on the table by the front door, where he left things he wanted to take to the office.

Waiting at Dulles, Pace realized he was nervous, less about Sissy's escape over St. Louis than about his daughter's reaction at finding her father living with a woman who wasn't her mother. He and Kathy debated whether she should go to the airport, or whether it would be better if he met Melissa alone. Kathy was all for going, but they decided it would be easier on Steve—never mind Melissa—to have the opportunity of the long ride back to Washington to talk.

"We might even go around to Great Falls on the Maryland side," Pace said. "Sissy loves that spot, especially when the water is raging. That would be a good place to talk."

"What are you going to say to her?" Kathy asked.

"I'm going to tell her the truth, that I'm deeply in love with you and there's no chance her mother and I will be together again, although we will always remain good friends," Steve said. "I've never lied to Sissy. The trouble with lying is you have to remember what you said so you don't contradict yourself later, and kids pick up those things."

"Be gentle with her. That's a big disappointment for a fourteen-year-old with dreams of seeing her family united again."

Pace was so deep in thought he almost missed seeing Melissa when she left the people-mover and entered the terminal. For one thing, he barely recognized her. She was half a head taller than the last time, her hair was several inches longer, and she was wearing makeup. *Makeup! Dear, sweet Jesus, she's just a baby. What on earth can her mother be thinking?*

"Daddy!" She recognized him before his mind came to terms with the sight of her. She broke into a grin and ran toward him, her arms open, a funky denim purse trailing off her right shoulder and a large paper shopping bag—one of those with the twisted paper handles that usually tear out from the roots—dangling from her left hand, probably filled with gifts from La La Land.

Steve bent to embrace her and had to stand upright again, so much had she grown.

"Baby, hi," he said. "It's so good to have you here. Gosh, let me look at you." He held her at arms' length. "You look absolutely beautiful. What's that stuff all over your eyes?"

She colored slightly and bent her head. "You don't mind, do you? All the kids my age do it, and Mom said it was okay as long as I didn't overdo it."

"All the kids?"

"Yep."

"Even the boys?"

She burst into giggles. "Oh, Daddy!" She giggled again. "Well, actually, now that you mention it—"

"I don't want to hear about it," he said, feigning horror. "I want to hear about you. You look great, or did I say that already?"

"You said that already. So do you. You don't mind, do you? About the makeup, I mean."

He put an arm around her shoulder and squeezed. "I don't mind," he said. "Let's get your luggage and get out of this rat trap, whadda ya say? You've spent enough time in airports today."

"That's for sure."

"Want me to carry the bag?"

"No, that's okay, I got it." She stopped in her tracks. "Dad, when we were landing, I think I saw the place where that plane crashed. It was all black and ugly."

"I'm sorry," he said. "In retrospect, for a lot of reasons, I wish now I'd had you come into National Airport downtown. But you would've had to change planes in Chicago, and that's a bear." He laughed. "So instead, you changed planes in St. Louis."

She shook her head vigorously. "Oh, no. I'm glad it happened the way it did. First the engine explodes on my plane, then I see where another plane crashed. That's *excellent!* When the kids back home hear about it, they'll think it's *awesome.*"

It's awesome, all right, he thought, *but not in the way the kids back home might think.* To them—to Melissa—seeing a crash scene was no more or no less than looking at a fire-gutted home or a three-car pileup on the freeway. Awesome, but not real, not in the context of any of their personal experiences. How could a fourteen-year-old relate, after all, to the death of more than three hundred people? There was no basis for comparison. Having an engine self-destruct in mid-flight, the sight of the crash scene—none of it had been trauma for Melissa at all. It stuck in her mind as something to dazzle her friends with when she took the memories home. *Totally awesome. Far out, Dude. Boss.*

As they walked through the terminal toward the escalators down to the baggage pickup area, Steve took the moments to drink her in. Her brown hair was so dark it looked almost black. Her darkish complexion—an inheritance from her mother—had been deepened by the Southern California sun. She must be five-feet-five already, maybe a shade more, and she was only fourteen.

She'll probably wind up about five-ten. She has her mother's long legs, and she's beginning to fill out just right.

Am I supposed to be thinking about my own daughter this way?

I guess I'd better. If I'm noticing, what's going through the heads of the hormone monsters she's encountering at school? I've got to send her mother some money for baseball bats. Maybe a bodyguard.

"You dating any?" he asked without meaning to.

She looked up at him and smiled tentatively. "Oh, a little, after school. If I go to a dance or a movie with a guy, Mom always insists on driving us. It's dumb sometimes, you know? There's this one guy, Cody, he's sixteen, and he's got his driver's license, and he's real responsible, you know? And I like him a lot, and he likes me. But Mom won't let us go out alone at night in his car. It's a hummer-bummer, lemme tell you. She won't let me go out with him unless she drives us or his dad does. It makes Cody feel like a little kid, and I'm afraid he's not gonna keep asking me out if Mom insists on acting like she doesn't trust us. I mean, we're not gonna get into trouble. Cody hasn't had an accident or even gotten one single ticket, and he's been driving for five whole months."

"That long, huh? An Indy candidate if ever there was one."

"Yeah!" she exclaimed, apparently thinking he was on her side.

"Well, we'll talk about it," he said, stepping off the escalator and guiding her around to the proper baggage carousel.

It's okay, Dad. She looks eighteen, but she still thinks like a kid. Be grateful for small favors.

Their conversations covered school and boys, her mother and boys, her future and boys, and had started into what she would like to do on her vacation when Pace swung his car onto the Beltway and headed around toward Maryland from Virginia. Melissa caught it right away.

"Where're we going?" she asked. "Did you move?"

"No, but since you're in blue jeans and sneaks anyhow, and it's a beautiful afternoon, I thought you'd like to swing out by Great Falls."

"Now?"

"Why not?"

"It's getting kinda late, isn't it?"

"It's just five-thirty. There's plenty of daylight left."

Melissa frowned slightly. She turned to her window and stared at the passing traffic.

Conversation ceased.

They walked along the old C&O Railroad tracks and the C&O Canal and over the woodsy trail to the overlook above the Great Falls of the Potomac River, a waterfall that long ago crumbled into a mile-long, grade-six rapid. Rapids didn't come any wilder. This one didn't burble over rocks and riffle over pebbles. It roared past house-sized boulders, pounding with furious force, breaking a wide, tranquil river into mountains of white froth, deadly eddies of hyperactive water plunging down inclines and climbing back over itself, and whirlpools that trapped everything floating by, spinning it in a mad vortex and either swallowing it or dashing it to bits. No kayaker of sound mind would consider tackling Great Falls in the spring; it was dangerous enough at low water in the fall. But even as Steve and Melissa watched, two boys who lived life believing in teen immortality climbed to the top of the largest of the rocks in the center of the rapids. Pace had no idea how they got there alive, no notion of how they would get back.

He and Sissy settled on two adjacent flat rocks, where the water spray couldn't quite reach them unless it was borne on a breeze, and they watched the river's tumult in silence for several minutes. Steve was about to say something profound when Melissa got right to the point.

"You want to talk to me about Kathy, don't you?"

"How did you know?"

She shrugged. "Mom told me, I guess," she said after a few seconds.

"Your mom?" Pace was incredulous. "What does your mom know? We haven't talked about it."

"From your answering machine," Melissa said. "The voice says Kathy McGovern and Steve Pace aren't home right now. Mom heard it yesterday when she called you to reconfirm my flight time. She told me so I wouldn't be surprised when I found you living together."

Pace had forgotten about the machine. Well, at least it relieved him of the chore of breaking the news. He put his elbows on his knees and stared at the ground between his shoes.

"Sissy, I'm in love with Kathy," he started hesitantly.

"Are you going to get married?"

"I . . . I don't know. We haven't talked about it."

"Mom's got a boyfriend now. His name's Larry. He stays over sometimes." Melissa dropped the news as casually as if she were asking for a glass of water.

For an instant, for a very guilty instant, Steve felt a wave of jealousy. "What's Larry like?"

"Oh, he's okay." Melissa said with another shrug, in the manner of a teenager asked about the status of her homework.

"What does he do?"

Melissa looked at him quizzically. "You mean his job?" Steve nodded.

"He's a lawyer. He's rich, too. He's got a big sailboat that has a motor in case there's no wind, and eight people can sleep on it. It has a kitchen and a bathroom right on board. Larry lets me steer sometimes, and he's teaching me to sail."

"You like him, don't you?"

"I told you, he's okay."

"Is he nice to you and your mom?"

"Oh, yeah. He's always fixing things around the house and helping me with algebra. I hate algebra, and I didn't understand it until Larry explained it to me. I still don't know why I have to take it. Who cares if x equals y squared? I'm not ever gonna hafta know that stuff."

"You might be surprised. Sometimes it comes in handy."

"Yeah? When?"

He was on the spot. Ten seconds later, he hadn't come up with an answer, and they started laughing. He held out his hand to her, and she reached over and took it.

"Sissy, I know you've been hoping your mom and I would get back together," he said gently. "There were times when I thought maybe we could. But we live so far apart, and she has her life, and I have mine. We still love each other, and more than anything, we love you. That has always been true, and it will be true forever. But," he paused and sighed, "I don't believe we'll ever get married again to each other."

"Yeah, I know," she replied. "I kinda doped that out."

Again, Pace was astonished. "You did?"

"Yeah, Dad. I'm not a kid, you know."

He squeezed her hand. "No, I guess you're not."

"But one thing bothers me."

"What's that?"

Melissa looked at him with a wickedly mischievous gleam in her deep blue eyes.

"How come," she said, "it's okay for you and Kathy to live together when you're not married, and for Mom and Larry to stay together sometimes when they're not married, but I can't go out with Cody in his car?"

23

Kathy cleared her throat and rapped her knuckles on the table, demanding attention.

"Okay, listen up. We could sit here all morning and talk over dirty breakfast dishes, but that won't get the picnic done. I repeat, we have baked ham and turkey, Swiss cheese and cheddar, rye and cracked-wheat bread, veggies, fruit, seltzers, Cokes, beer, and lemonade. I'm taking orders on what you all want for lunch."

"I think I'd like roast beef on a Kaiser roll," Pace said.

"Da-a-a-a-d," Melissa scolded, sounding like a bleating sheep.

"Okay, out!" Kathy ordered, waving him from the kitchen. "Out! Out! Out! Melissa and I will pack what we want."

Pace listened to the giggles behind him. He settled in the living room with the morning paper and left the kitchen things to the women. *Like we were a family . . . Stop it! That's not the way it is and not the way it will ever be. You can't change it. Be grateful for what you have.*

But he couldn't let it be. He wallowed in the pleasure of it. The paper lay ignored on his lap while he watched Kathy and Melissa do the breakfast dishes, rubbing maple syrup from the plates and milk scum from the glasses before the dishes were stowed in the dishwasher. Pancake crumbs slid off the no-stick griddle with a swipe of a damp paper towel, but Kathy hand-washed it with soapy water anyhow and rinsed it, and Melissa dried.

Kathy was still in anguish over her brother's death, but she was making a determined effort not to let her grief bubble to the surface in front of Melissa and dampen the teenager's fun. Sissy knew about Jonathan's death; Pace told her on the way into town from Great Falls. And Sissy said the right things when she first saw Kathy at the apartment. After that, they set the subject aside.

Pace glanced at the front page in his lap, at Glenn Brennan's lead story. Brennan had reached Cullen Ferguson at his hotel and Whitney Warner in Los Angeles. Ferguson professed outrage at the groundings, particularly, he noted, since the NTSB board member overseeing the investigation of the ConPac crash concluded such a move wasn't necessary. Whitney was her normal, calm self. Sexton wished the FAA hadn't deemed the action necessary, but in view of what happened to TransAm Flight 957, the precaution was in order. She threw Converse a bone, saying Sexton was confident the C-Fan would pass the inspections without difficulty.

Brennan also reached TransAm officials and the president of Wentworth Fabricating Company, the manufacturer of turbine disks for Converse. TransAm had no statement of any significance. Seymour Wentworth's statement was self-serving claptrap about using only the best technical equipment and having state-of-the-art inspection practices.

There were quotes from Lane Simmons and Ken Sachs; Pace winced when he saw Glenn had been able to get a statement from Sachs. Vernon Lund refused comment. There was nothing from Harold Marshall, which Pace thought strange. The previous evening, Brennan said he'd called the Ohio senator and was confident Marshall would call back. Apparently it didn't happen.

Brennan did a good job with the story, and Pace felt a twinge of guilt taking such a momentous day off. But when he dropped the paper and refocused on the kitchen, guilt faded in a wash of pleasure at seeing Kathy and Melissa enjoying each other.

As soon as the kitchen was spotless, they started messing it up again, wrapping sandwich meat and cheeses in foil and then sealing the packages in ZipLoc bags so melting ice in the cooler couldn't seep in. They cleaned and wrapped vegetables: lettuce for the sandwiches, celery, carrots (washed but not scraped, because then you lost a lot of the vitamins, Kathy said), radishes, red and yellow bell peppers, and light-green florets of something called broccoflower. Next the fruit, wedges of melons mostly, and grapes, and finally, on top of everything, two full loaves of bread.

We must be meeting the Third Army at Front Royal, he thought. *Hey, belly up to the cooler and build yourself a club sandwich. Have a beer on Steve Pace. It's the least I can do for our boys (and girls) in khaki. Now get back out there and defend Skyline Drive. The invaders will be here any day. You'll know them, because all the men will be in pink-plaid Bermuda shorts, oxford shoes, and black, knee-high socks. They'll have cheap cameras hanging around their necks. All the women will be dressed in short shorts that show off their cellulite and poochy stomachs to best advantage. If they try to escape in their cars, you'll know 'em by their out-of-state license plates and because they all drive too slowly and pass on curves and pull off at every scenic overlook. We want these tourons out of our mountains. All of you have been briefed on the touron—half tourist and half moron. Now let's get moving. And hey . . . let's be careful out there.*

"If you two don't quit horsing around in there, we'll get to Skyline Drive in time to turn around and come home before dark," Pace called into the kitchen. "And quit cleaning vegetables. There's only three of us."

"Are you all ready to go?" Kathy asked him.

"The camera and the binocs are right by the car keys," he replied. "Ready when you are."

"Well, we'll be another fifteen minutes, that's all," she said. "Why don't you stuff your nose back in the paper, and we'll holler."

But there was nothing in the paper he wanted to read, nothing new on the ConPac accident.

"I've got a better idea," he said. "I'll go get the car gassed up and meet you back here."

"Why don't you double-park and wait for us in front?" Kathy suggested. "We can bring the cooler, two tough old broads like us. That way, you won't have to put the car back in the garage."

"You sure you can wrestle that thing down? You've got half a Safeway store in there."

"Oh, Da-a-a-a-d," Melissa bleated at him again. "Women are as strong as men and not nearly as likely to get hernias."

Pace and Kathy exchanged amused glances.

"Where'd you learn about hernias?" he asked his daughter.

"In school, in hygiene class," she said as though he should have known. "You shudda seen the boys blush when the teacher talked about sperm cords. It was too cool." She broke down in a spasm of giggles.

"Right. Ho-kay." He couldn't think of anything else to say.

"We'll meet you downstairs," Kathy said, rescuing him. Then she lowered her voice. "You'd better get out of here while you can."

He slung the camera over one shoulder, the binoculars over the other. "Don't forget to lock up," he called back inside and closed the door.

He was whistling for sheer joy when the elevator stopped in the garage beneath his building. The shaft occupied an area as large as three parking spaces. The doors opened facing the west wall, which was lined by a row of end-in parking spaces that sloped upward and around to the right to upper-level parking and then around again to the garage door. The east wall was the same, except for the three spaces lost to the elevator shaft. Pace thought he lucked out when it came to parking assignments. His space was the first one next to the concrete wall of the shaft, a perfect spot, particularly when he had a large load of groceries to carry.

He noticed the lights over his space were out—as were

those on the opposite wall—throwing the area into a darkness in which his car was little more than a silhouette. The building-maintenance people were thorough and would have the lights replaced in a few hours.

He used his back to block the elevator door open for a few seconds, using the light to find the keys to the car's door lock and the ignition. He walked behind the vehicle and came up on the driver's side.

It could have been a shadow, or a hint of movement, or the slightest sound—he had no idea what—that made the back of his neck crawl as surely as if a garden spider were picking its way through his hair. He stopped by the driver's door, his eyes probing the shadows that had gone from harmless to ominous in the space of a few seconds. He saw nothing and was chiding himself about fear of the dark when a powerful pair of arms grabbed him from behind. The right arm encircled his neck, threatening to strangle him; the left dragged his left arm behind him and twisted it upward toward his shoulder blades. Pace thought surely a bone would snap. The car keys fell to the concrete floor and skittered away, sounding eerily like a half dozen rats frightened by a sudden light.

Pace was about to yell when a huge figure rose up in front of his car's grille, advanced on him in two steps and drove a fist into his gut, just below the point where the two sides of his rib cage turned up and joined at the bottom of the sternum. The blow drove every cubic inch of usable air from his lungs, and he felt certain the breakfast in his stomach would soon follow. His knees buckled. He would have fallen but for the assailant holding him up.

"You feel like you're gonna die, and you are, but not right this second." The voice rasped from behind his left ear. He could feel the hot breath on the side of his face, and he would have detected its slightly sour smell had he been able to inhale at that moment.

This can't be happening! Not here. Not today.

"Where's your wallet, asshole?" the voice behind him rasped again, and this time Pace got a whiff of rotting teeth.

He didn't answer the question—he wasn't certain he could talk yet—and his captor jerked his left arm a little higher. This time he felt muscle tear in his shoulder, and he found enough breath to groan.

"I asked you a question, asshole. You hear okay?"

Pace nodded.

"Then you gonna give me an answer?"

"T-To what?" His voice was barely a whisper.

"Whatsa matter, you don't hear so good after all? Or maybe you don't understand? Maybe we gotta help you understand."

The man in front smashed the left side of Pace's face, snapping the reporter's head into the shoulder of the arm still wrapped around his throat. The ring on the assailant's hand cut Pace's cheek to the bone. Blood coursed into his mouth, down his neck onto his shirt, and he thought he would black out. He wished he had when a fist smashed into the place below his sternum again, driving out what little air he had been able to restore to his tortured lungs. Again his legs buckled. The man behind him released Pace's neck and used his free hand to pin Pace's right arm. His captor changed position only to give his partner a shot at the right side of Pace's head. It came as another backhand blow, although this time Pace saw it coming and slipped it, avoiding a broken jaw. Nonetheless, the blow packed enough power that the world in front of his eyes misted over in red, then went out of focus.

Let it be over.

Pace felt his arms released, and he felt them fall dead at his side as he started to sag. But the man in front grabbed his shoulders and held him upright. The man behind drove both his fists into Pace's kidneys. This time he knew he groaned; he heard himself clearly. His shoulders were released, and he pitched forward. The big man in front did nothing to break his fall. He sidestepped Pace's body easily, letting him crash into the driver's door and slam onto the cement floor. The jolt of the fall started lightning bolts of agony dancing through his nervous system.

Pace felt one of his tormentors dip into the left hip pocket of his blue jeans and slide out the folding canvas sport wallet there, while the other pulled the Seiko chronometer from Pace's left wrist and twisted the gold and black-sapphire ring from his right ring finger.

"Another victim of senseless violence in our crime-ridden capital," one of them said.

Pace was turned over on his back, and he saw a form standing above him with something in its hand. There was a click as a long blade snapped into place. He tried to squirm away, but the second man pushed his booted foot into Pace's torn shoulder, holding him down.

"Finish it, and let's get out of here," the man said to his partner.

The one with the knife dropped to one knee beside Pace, and at the same moment, the reporter heard a new voice.

"Hey, what's goin' on over there? Ya'all get 'way from him!"

It was Howard, the day maintenance chief. Pace recognized his Southern drawl.

The one kneeling beside Pace jumped to his feet. "Let's go," he whispered to his partner. "Hit the guy and knock him down."

Pace heard the two sprint away, and then he heard Howard yell. He heard a body fall, accompanied by the sound of splintering glass.

Gingerly, fighting off nausea, Pace crabbed around to see what was happening. Howard was struggling to his feet, being careful not to cut himself on the shards of neon tubes lying shattered over the garage floor.

"Doncha worry, Mista Pace," Howard was saying. "I'm goin' fuh help."

Pace looked up the sloping floor in the direction the two assailants were running. He saw them jump into a light-blue van backed into a space near the top of the incline. He couldn't see their faces—the world was coming at him in too many waves of sickening blur—but when the truck pulled out onto the ramp, he saw clearly that its right front quarter was crumpled, and he saw what appeared to be slashes of a lighter-colored paint ground into the original blue. He squinted to see the license plate, but all he got were dark letters and numbers on a light field. Maybe Maryland. Maybe anywhere.

He gently lowered his head to the cool cement floor, taking care to keep the side with the deeply lacerated cheek turned up, and watched the back of the van climb and circle around to the right, out of sight. He realized they'd intended to make him victim number three hundred thirty-seven in the Sexton tragedy, and but for Howard's timely arrival, they would have succeeded.

You bastards. You goddamned bastards!

And then the world winked out.

Chappy Davis hunched over the morning papers spread across a small table at the end of the living room where a four-lamp chandelier, with bulbs designed to look like candle flames, dropped from the ceiling, denoting the space as the dining area of the Maryland townhouse. Under orders, he'd taken the morning off to deal with the men who'd been sent to kill Steve Pace. His eyes played back and forth over the lines of the *Times,* but the connection to his brain was severed by anxiety, and nothing his eyes saw registered with him.

Davis believed they were going too far this time. He believed it the night before, when he received the instructions and argued his position to no avail. He continued to believe it, fervently and fearfully. Pace had to be discouraged from further pursuit of the Sexton case, but you don't kill a reporter without raising your risks exponentially. The woman and the girl were complicating factors. What if Pace couldn't be taken alone? The order was to kill Pace on Monday and make the murder look like a mugging. Neither Pace's girlfriend nor his daughter were to be hurt. But who knew those two psychotics from Baltimore? Was there any restraint in them? They weren't above kicking in Pace's apartment door and shooting everybody unlucky enough to be inside.

He hadn't wanted to be part of this. It made him sick.

He pushed his chair back and went to the refrigerator, pulling out a bottle of orange juice and swigging down three fast gulps. Too much vodka the night before, drunk to blunt the impact of the assassination he'd ordered, had left a thick, thirsty taste in his mouth that only orange juice would cut.

Outside his kitchen window he saw seven little kids too young to be in school playing on the swings in the common area. Their laughs and shrieks of delight reached him, reminding him of the long-ago innocent years of his own life, when the only conspiracy that touched him was his older brother's to watch a pubescent girl next door undress for bed each night.

He smiled at the memory and slipped the bottle of orange juice back into the refrigerator as the telephone rang.

"Yes?"

"We got the mugging part done, but we got interrupted before we could kill him," the voice said. "We had to get out before we could be identified." There was no anxiety or regret in the voice at the other end of the line. The tone was as matter-of-fact as if it had been ordering a pizza. Davis, however, felt immensely relieved. He'd had enough death for a while.

"How bad is he hurt?" the Senate aide asked.

"He'll live. But for a coupla days he'll regret it. We can try again later."

Davis had an inspiration. "Maybe you won't have to," he said. "There might be another way. I'll let you know."

"So maybe you got what you needed after all," said the voice. "Now we get what's due us, right? In full."

"Today?"

"Man, we don't work on credit."

They made arrangements for Davis to deliver fifteen thousand dollars in cash an hour later to a man in a light-blue Ford van that would be parked in front of the south entrance to Woodward & Lothrop's downtown store. Davis counted out the money from the stash in the false bottom of the fourth drawer of his bedroom wardrobe. He slipped a hundred fifty hundred-dollar bills into a shoulder pouch lying on top of his dresser. Then he peeled off his clothes. He wasn't dirty, but he stepped into his shower to try to soap away the general feeling that he was unclean.

It wouldn't wash off. It was a feeling that long ago had penetrated his skin and soiled his soul.

24

Sometime and Nowhere

It was hard to see across the riffling water because each little disturbance on the surface caught the brilliant morning sunshine and beamed it back, a thousand tiny lasers knifing through his vision. He squinted and tried to make out the huge form on the opposite shore. But for some reason, it was dark on the other side, and he couldn't distinguish details of the thing over there. Why was he the only one concerned about it? Mike, Kathy, and Sissy were sitting on the big stadium blanket spread out over the table rock above the high-water line, eating sandwiches and fruit. Every time he tried to get their attention, either they didn't hear him or they laughed and ignored his concern. He saw himself imploring them to put the food back in the picnic hamper and hurry away with him; the thing across the water was coming for them. And it wouldn't take long for it to get there. After all, the water was ... what? A stream, a lake, a river? He wasn't certain. It looked wide, but he could see all the way across. Why wouldn't they listen?

He heard the sound of a large object hitting water, and he spun, straining to see what it was. But there was nothing his eyes could make out through the curtain of dancing lasers except the darkness on the distant shore. Or was it on the distant shore? It was moving toward them, a murky blackness creeping across the water in their direction, overtaking and snuffing out the lasers as it progressed, swallowing the beautiful daylight, hiding something hideous and deadly in its shroud. It was coming for them. Hurry, he pleaded with them. Please, get up and let's get out of here. Leave the food. Get up and run.

Run!

He looked over his shoulder and saw that half the width of the riffling water had been consumed by the darkness and the monster within. But when he turned back, Mike and Kathy and Sissy were pouring lemonade and laughing, and someone new had joined them. Avery was there. It's all right, Steve, he was saying. There's nothing out there that's going to hurt you. We're all safe on this shore. Relax. Nothing can touch us here. Nothing.

No!

He knew they weren't safe. He could feel the thing out there touch his mind with its ghastly intent and raise the hairs on the back of his neck in a salute to terror.

Run!

Now the blackness was nearing their shore, and without even turning to look into the face of his fear, he could feel it smothering the warmth of the sun and reaching out toward them.

And then Mike was gone. Vanished. He thought he heard a distant scream, the bloodcurdling cry of a wounded animal brought to ground, shrieking with pain and the knowledge of certain death. The dread crawled up his spine and squeezed his heart. He reached out for Kathy and Sissy, determined to drag them to safety, but the blackness overtook him a moment before his hands could grasp theirs, walling him away. He felt a hot breath on his back and whirled to confront whatever it was, his arms thrown over his face. At first he could see nothing, but as his eyes became accustomed to the dark, he saw that his enemy was a man, a mere man. It had a man's face, the face of someone he knew.

Then, as he watched, the nose and mouth lengthened into a fearsome snout, the lips drawn back to reveal long razor teeth with traces of the bloody flesh of the beast's last kill packed against the gums. The face was covered in fur, and yet it was familiar.

It was the eyes, the eyes he knew! The creature had cold, glacial-blue eyes.

Beneath those eyes, beneath the gory mouth, caked in the creature's fur, were more of the bloody remains of its last kill. They ran down the neck to the body, which was furred with the silver-tipped brown hair of the great grizzly and appeared to grow before him, until it loomed over him at a height of perhaps ten feet.

As he strained to identify the face, a great paw lashed out, its three-inch claws ripping his face. The other paw swiped and dug in, holding him fast, its claws embedded in his lower back. And the head came down, the head that now had human eyes and a bear snout. Its enormous mouth was open, its teeth bared. He could not avoid the fangs, and they sank into the tender place where his neck joined his shoulder. Severed arteries hosed his blood over the bear's head and onto its shimmering fur. He was dragged upward, into the chest of the beast, and crushed by its enormous arms. He could hear the snap of his ribs, feel the breath squeezed from his lungs, see his own body collapsing as the great man-bear killed him. And then came another scream . . . so much like the agonized howl he'd heard moments earlier.

Only this time the dying animal was Steven Pace.

25

The first sensation of anything real was the pain of each breath.

Steve Pace was coming from someplace very dark to someplace bathed in light, vaguely aware that each step forward carried him farther and farther from the comfort of the dark, the comfort of oblivion. He could not stop his progress. He was driven to move up, toward the light, toward the pain, no matter how much he wished it otherwise. And he *did* wish it otherwise. Every breath was agony. His head ached frightfully. The pain in his back was sickening. Each step of the journey brought his suffering into sharper focus.

And then he was back.

He was all the way back.

And he dared not move.

He squeezed his eyes to resist the reflexive act of opening them. He didn't want to see where he was so much as he wanted first to feel it.

He was on his back, and he was warm. That was good. His arms were extended down the sides of his body, his palms resting next to the roughness of institutional sheets. There was something in his nose. He could feel it feeding cool, dry air to his lungs, and he could feel the rawness the dry air created in his nasal passages and his throat. He could feel the plastic tube running from his nose, over his cheek, and on to wherever plastic tubes go. There was tightness accompanying the pain on the left side of his face, and a dull ache over the right side of his jaw.

Tentatively, he tried to move, and his left shoulder screamed a plea to stop.

He opened his eyes.

He had no trouble recognizing his location as a hospital room, and no problem recalling what had put him there. But he had no sensation of time, no idea how long he'd been unconscious, no recollection how he'd made the trip from the cold, dirty floor of his basement garage.

He was alone. Gingerly, he turned his head to see if a nursing call button was hanging where he could reach it to summon someone who could tell him how badly he was hurt. He found it at the same moment the door to his room swung open under the hand of a middle-aged doctor who walked with the confidence of a man who knew exactly what he was about. When the doctor saw that his patient was conscious, he grinned from his wide friendly mouth to his warm brown eyes and fairly bounced across the twelve feet from the door to the bed.

"Hey there, guy, how yew all are?" he asked jovially in an accent Pace couldn't quite place. "Nice-a yew to drop by dis party. Ah am Kevin Christian Boudreaux—Casey to mah frens. Ahm a Loo-zee-anna Cajun an' mo' proud-a it than I cud told yew. Imma ver' good doctor, all-so, and I gonna be yo' tour guide for dis cruise. We hope yo' 'commodations is o-kay anna food pal-a-ta-ble enuf it don' make you gettin' sick all on the clean sheets. Lifeboat drill's at three a.m. in de mornin', jes when youze sleepin' bes', and if yew miss 'nother one, we gonna re-voke your bathin'-room priv-leges. Now, yew got some queshuns?"

Pace laughed softly and then grimaced as the response tugged at stitches and shook up places strained and bruised.

"Does every room come with a floor show?" he asked, surprised that he could barely get his voice above a hoarse whisper.

Casey Boudreaux was shining a penlight in Pace's eyes, testing pupil reflex. "Only the private rooms," he said, his accent miraculously gone. "We figure we need to give you something extra to justify the cost." He pulled back and looked at the patient, apparently satisfied with what he was seeing. "How do you feel?"

"Never better," Pace replied.

It was Boudreaux's turn to laugh. "Aren't you going to ask me where you are and what happened?"

"I know what happened, and I'd be very surprised if I'm not in a hospital."

"Doggone it, all the fun's gone out of being a doctor," Boudreaux lamented, falling into a bedside chair. "Nobody ever asks the good old questions anymore."

"Would you settle for, what happened to your accent?"

Boudreaux shrugged. "Mah axcen? Dat ol' ting? It's jes somethin' I trew on. Sholy yew got a better queshun dan dat."

"Well, let's try, How bad am I hurt? Will that do?"

Boudreaux shrugged again. "I guess, if it's the best you've got. For starters, I'd say you're in some considerable pain."

"No wonder you're a doctor," Pace said.

"If you want the gory details, let's start from the head and work our way down. You've got a cut over your left cheek that took eleven stitches to close. It will heal with a slight scar a plastic surgeon could fix, although your girlfriend, or your wife, or both, might think you look sexier with it. Underneath the stitches, your cheekbone is broken, although the break is reasonably minor and should heal without any assistance from me, more's the pity. I've got two kids in college and could use the surgical fee. You've got a knot on your right jawbone a sailor would be proud of, and it's a wonder your jaw isn't broken. Your left trapezius muscle—the one that keeps your head from flying off your shoulder—is slightly torn, as is the muscle layer over your abdomen. The oxygen is to make breathing easier. You have unbelievable-looking bruises over each kidney, and those organs have been battered to the point that you'll curse the person who did this to you every time you piss for the next week or so. There might be a little blood in the urine, and if there is, we'll have to keep a close eye on you.

Eventually you'll be good as new, and I think it's safe to say you *will* play the accordion again."

"I never played it before."

"I told you, I'm a great doctor."

Boudreaux did his best imitation of a rim shot.

"Now," the doctor continued, "it's time you saw to your guests. They've been waiting hours to pay their respects."

"Who?" Pace asked. "How long have I been here?"

"Oh, good," said Boudreaux. "That's close to the good old question, 'How long have I been out, Doc?' I appreciate your indulgence. To answer, it's Monday night, about eleven-twenty or so. You've been here close to twelve hours, but you've been lousy company."

"Where's here?"

"George Washington University Hospital."

"Who's waiting to see me?"

"A wide assortment of cops, two lovely, worried ladies named Kathy and Melissa, and some guy named Schaeffer, who's paying for your private accommodations. Most people's insurance only pays for semiprivate."

"Can you send them all in at once, so I only have to go through the story one time?"

"Only if they're all out in thirty minutes," Boudreaux said. "I'm leaving orders with Alice the Wonder Dog, the head night nurse on this floor, to give you my special knock-out elixir in precisely half an hour so you can get some rest. The more you sleep, the faster you'll heal and the less you'll feel how bad you hurt. I'll be around to see you again tomorrow."

"Maybe tomorrow you can teach me to cook Cajun," Pace suggested.

"Sure," Boudreaux said, "but only if you teach me to play the accordion."

The ensuing reunion went as Pace imagined it would. Kathy and Melissa were loving and hugely concerned, Avery Schaeffer tried to be a comfort, telling his reporter he should concentrate on mending and not worry about his work.

Glenn Brennan had been assigned to pick up the Sexton story until Pace could get back. Also, all doctor and hospital bills were paid; what the *Chronicle*'s insurance didn't pick up, the paper would.

The assortment of cops included Detective Lieutenant Martin Lanier from the District of Columbia Police and Clay Helm from the Fairfax County Police—although Helm hung back and said nothing until the others departed—and a regular D.C. detective named Willard Brown, who would take Pace's statement.

The police officers who responded to Howard the custodian's frantic call to 911 found Pace unconscious beside his car. They assumed then, as Lanier and Brown assumed now, that Pace had been mugged, given the missing wallet, watch, and ring.

"It wasn't a mugging," Pace insisted. "These were the same guys who killed Mark Antravanian and Mike McGill. They took my watch and wallet to make it look like a mugging."

He started to say something about the blue van. But since Clay Helm told him about it off the record, he must pretend he didn't know of the vehicle's special significance. He would mention it in the course of giving his statement. He wished they would get to that.

"Avery, would you see that Kathy and Melissa get home all right?" he asked. He tried to convey through his expression that it was more than a casual request, and he saw Schaeffer catch the inflection, if not the reason for it.

"I'll be happy to," the editor replied. "In fact, we probably ought to be going now. Your doctor made it obvious he didn't want anyone staying longer than necessary."

The women kissed and hugged him, and he tried not to let it show that the attention was painful. They promised to return in the morning.

When they were gone, Pace turned to Brown. "Are you ready to hear what happened?"

"Ready," Brown said, opening his notebook.

Pace told the story, finishing with the details of his assailants' escape in a light-blue van with a damaged right front.

Standing behind the other cops, Clay Helm pursed his lips and shook his head slightly. Lanier looked startled. "You sure about the van?" he asked.

Pace opened his mouth, but Helm pushed himself away from where he'd been leaning against the door frame and spoke first. "He's sure," he said.

"How do you know?" Lanier asked.

"Because I told him about it earlier," the police captain said. Before Lanier could protest, Helm added, "It was off the record. I told him because I wanted him to know what to look out for, for his own safety. I thought he was in danger. Obviously, I was right."

Lanier grunted and turned back to the bed. "So what's the whole story, Pace?"

"I told you. They were going to kill me," the reporter said. "They wanted it to look like a mugging so you wouldn't suspect my murder was tied to the other two. One of them was kneeling beside me with a switchblade when Howard showed up. His timely arrival prevented my untimely departure. The two men knocked Howard down, got into their van and took off. I was still conscious, and I saw them drive away. I recognized the vehicle from Clay's description. It had the damage to the right front and scrapes of a lighter-colored paint around the damaged area."

"What was the second color?" Lanier asked.

"Light. I don't know exactly."

"What was the make and model?"

Pace bristled. "How the hell should I know?" he snapped, raising his head and shoulders from the pillow, then quickly falling back as pain slapped him down. "I'm sorry," he said when he caught his breath. "I wasn't seeing anything very well. I couldn't read the nameplate on the truck."

"Did you get a color on the plate?" Brown asked.

"I got an impression. Dark letters and numbers on a white field. Maryland plates."

"What makes you think so?"

"There was an emblem, a crest, in the center of the plate.

I don't remember a lot of details, but Maryland plates have the state crest on them."

"There was a commemorative Virginia plate a few years ago that had an emblem in the middle, too," Brown said.

"No," Pace replied firmly. "Those colors aren't right. And that emblem was circular. This one was more square."

"A lot of states put some sort of emblems on their plates. It didn't have to be Maryland."

"No. This one was from Maryland."

"You sure?"

"Hell, I'm not absolutely sure of anything, Detective, except the blue van."

"Is there anything you left out?" Lanier asked.

Pace rolled his head on the pillow.

"Well, if you think of anything, I'm leaving my card on the table beside your bed," Brown said. "If something comes up, give me a call. I'll be in touch again as soon as I have any news."

The two District of Columbia police officers departed, leaving Pace alone with Clay Helm.

"Why'd you tell 'em you told me about the van?" Pace asked.

"I didn't see any reason not to," Helm replied, moving to the chair beside Pace's bed. "We're all on the same side." He paused before he asked, *"Are* you sure about the van?"

"Positive," Pace said. "Absolutely positive. It was the light-blue van, damaged on the right side, and I saw streaks of a light paint, like yellow, or maybe white, in the area of the damage."

Pace saw Helm study him closely.

"Why do I sense you don't believe me?" he asked.

"I don't have any reason to doubt you," Helm said. "What I was thinking is that none of your testimony would hold up in court."

"Why not?" Pace asked incredulously.

"The nature of your injuries, especially since you were hit a couple of times in the head. You said yourself your vision was fuzzy. Who's to say it wasn't a green van that looked blue to you? Under oath, you'd have to give up the fact you'd been warned by the police to watch out for a damaged light-blue Ford van. You'd also have to admit you knew Mark Antravanian's rental car was yellow. That would give the defense a chance to make a pretty good case that you saw what you wanted, or expected, to see. And even if your identification is correct, how the hell many light-blue vans are there in the metropolitan area? Since you can't say positively it was a Ford or a Chevy, or for that matter, a Toyota, I'd say the field of choice is pretty big. And given our traffic, the chances are pretty good more than one light-blue van would have damage on the right side."

"Shit!" Pace objected.

Helm shrugged. "Did you actually see light-colored paint streaks, or only silvery metal showing through where the factory paint job was scraped off? And if there were lighter paint streaks, who knows where they came from? Any given blue van could pick up paint streaks in any number of places."

"But it would shorten the odds by a good bit."

"Some, yes. How much? Who knows. Again, probably not enough to dispel the timeworn, juror-tested notion of reasonable doubt."

Pace let his head fall back on the pillow again. "This is a nightmare," he said, "and I'm sick of it."

Helm pushed himself up out of the chair and put a hand on Pace's uninjured shoulder. "For the time being, I suggest you follow your editor's orders and concentrate on getting well."

"What about the case?"

"You let Marty Lanier and me worry about that. That's what you pay us for."

Pace nodded miserably. He was about to say something when a nurse came in with a tray.

"Oh, I'm sorry," she said when she saw Helm. "I thought everybody had gone but the patient. Dr. Boudreaux left orders for medication."

"I was just leaving," Helm told her. He turned to the

reporter. "I know this sounds stupid, but try not to worry about things you can't help. Get some sleep, hotshot."

A moment later, when Helm was gone, the words came back and hit Pace so hard he choked on his medication. *"Get some sleep, hotshot."*

That's what Mike had called him.

The nurse doused the light and eased out the door, and Steve Pace lay in the dark, anger and frustration washing over him like waves on a beach. Despite the sleeping pills, he would not doze off for hours.

26

Wednesday, April 30th, 9:00 A.M.
Casey Boudreaux discharged Pace two days later, acknowledging cheerfully that most recovering patients fare better at home.

Boudreaux pushed Pace's wheelchair to the hospital door personally, carrying on nonstop in suspect Cajun dialect about how the reporter should take care of himself.

"Now yew hain't got but a single wel-come in this hos-pi-tel, unnerstan'? I don' wanna be hearin' yewv been puttin' yer batter' ol' body here in fron'a no more persons who wanna be beatin' the bejezzes outta yew, cuz I don' do no doctorin' on the same beaten-up persons no more dan once. If yew come sa-shayin' through here all beat up agin, ya jus' gonna hafta fine yerself diffren' medicine-type personnel what can do your doctorin', cuz ole Casey here, he don't have much truck for people with no more sense than to let there be a second time around. Man, a crawfish got more sense dan dat, and a crawfish hain't hardly got no sense a-tall. Now yew gonna be lookin' some better when ya haul yer car-cass back here on Friday for yer checking-up, or I gonna be some kinda aaaan-gry, an' if ya never befo' done seen no angry Cajun, I can only say yewd be advised to keep it that way."

Kathy and Melissa walked beside the wheelchair, hearing Boudreaux's routine for the first time. Under other circumstances, both would be laughing, but neither was tempted this day, nor was Pace, despite going home. He was angry in general, and they were angry with him.

The swelling in his face was down, the blood that appeared briefly in his urine had disappeared, and his torn muscles were healing. He was ambulatory, if gingerly so. Both Casey Boudreaux and Avery Schaeffer ordered him to stay home and stay quiet; Schaeffer assured him the crash story was under control.

"We're keeping close tabs on the NTSB investigation, the FAA investigation, and the police investigations. If there's more to find, they'll find it, and we'll report it," he said. "So far, there hasn't been anything new out of Dulles, and inspections of the Eight-elevens haven't turned up any more suspect turbine disks. I think we had a couple of fluke problems in Seattle and St. Louis."

Pace had spent most of the night awake again. Only the pain of movement stopped him from tossing and turning. His mind created one scenario after another in an attempt to find a logical reason for the crash and all that followed it. He couldn't make it play. The pieces wouldn't fit.

And he acknowledged candidly to himself that he was troubled by Clay Helm's assessment that his description of the van in which his assailants fled could be demolished in court; his expectations had been raised by Helm's own admonition to keep watch for such a vehicle.

When they had come to pick him up that morning, Pace told Kathy and Melissa for the first time the full story of what happened in his parking garage.

"I think I'm a rational person, at least when I'm not railing at Ken Sachs in a drunken rage," he'd said. "I can tell the difference between reality and hallucination. For one thing, the longer you're awake after even the most vivid dream, the fainter the memory becomes. The memory of what happened to me in the garage, what I saw and what I heard, isn't fading a bit."

"I don't doubt your story. Nobody does," Kathy said. There was an edge in her voice that matched the deeply troubled look on her face. It had been there since he'd revealed his belief that the two men who assaulted him were probably the same team that killed Mike McGill and Mark Antravanian.

"In retrospect, it's unfortunate Clay Helm told you about the van, but he was only trying to help," Kathy had concluded.

"I don't doubt you, either, Dad," Melissa added with a bright smile. "You wouldn't lie about what you saw."

"Thank you, ladies. Your confidence and support are appreciated."

A look of worry set itself on the teenager's face. She watched Kathy pack away the few personal items they'd brought to the hospital for Steve and bit her lower lip. "Are you gonna do any more reporting on the story?" she asked.

"Well, I guess not for a while. Mr. Schaeffer has ordered me to stay home for the rest of the week."

"What about next week?"

"We'll have to see what next week brings, honey. If there's still a story to be reported, I'll be the one to do it."

"Steve!" Kathy had looked up from her packing with horror on her face. "How can you say that in the same minute you told us the men who did *this*—" she held out her hand toward him as though she were conducting a tour of his battered body "—are the same ones who committed two murders? How can you be so . . . so cavalier about it?"

"I'm not being cavalier about anything," Pace had insisted, his voice rising in frustration. "But I am *not* going to let those bastards run me into a corner with my thumb stuck up my ass, hiding for the rest of my life." He raised his hands before Kathy could say anything about his language.

"Sorry. But I mean it."

"Nobody's asking you to hide," Kathy snapped. She was highly agitated. "That's ridiculous. That was never even on the table. We're merely suggesting maybe it's time you grew up and quit playing cowboys and Indians, it's—"

Steve had sat straight up in the hospital bed, driven by outrage so intense it masked his pain. *"Cowboys and Indians?"* He heard his voice rise, and he knew he shouldn't let that happen. But it wasn't something he could easily stop. "This is not a game. I can't believe—"

"Not a *game,* no. Nobody seriously meant to imply it's a game. But murder investigations aren't what the *Chronicle* pays you to do. Chasing bad guys is a police function, not a reporting function. And despite the fact that reporters and cops sometimes collaborate, cops don't try to write newspaper stories. And reporters shouldn't try to hunt down criminals."

"Kathy, ever since the accident, you've been begging me to find out what happened, what killed Jonathan. And now you're telling me you want me to stop?"

She looked as though he had slapped her in the face. Tears glistened in her eyes. "That's not fair," she said angrily. "I never asked you to get yourself killed for me, or for Jonathan."

"Hell, I didn't say you did," he'd snapped. "But how am I supposed to find out what happened to the Eight-eleven if I don't go after the story? How—"

Her sob broke him off in mid-sentence. "I've already lost one man I loved," she said. "I couldn't bear it if—"

"Oh, for chrissake, cut out the hysterics." His voice was thick with angry sarcasm. "It doesn't become you. What would dear old Dad think?"

She'd glared at him, her eyes narrow and dancing with fury. "You bastard," she hissed. "You son of a bitch. You don't get it at all, do you?"

"No, I guess I don't."

Pace caught sight of Melissa, backing away from them, her forehead deeply furrowed in concern, and he realized that he and Kathy had been shouting at each other. He sagged back onto the pillows in misery. Weariness and dull pain combined to drain the last of his strength.

"I'm sorry," he said softly. "Let's not hammer this out here, okay?"

So it was when Casey Boudreaux had arrived minutes later with the wheelchair, Pace was willing to accept the ride to the hospital's front door, a destination far too distant for his legs and spirit to carry him. Boudreaux's Cajun lecture failed to lighten anyone's mood.

The ride from the hospital to Pace's New Hampshire Avenue apartment building was short and very quiet. Despite his resolve to try to relax, Pace could not keep his eyes from darting back and forth across the path of Kathy's red BMW convertible, keeping watch for a slightly wrecked, light-blue Ford van lurking in an alley or a side street.

If it was there, Pace didn't spot it.

Mostly he saw the usual assortment of homeless and those who were happier panhandling than working. Directly across 23rd Street from the hospital's main entrance, one man caught Pace's attention. He sat cross-legged on the sidewalk, his back against the chain-link fence of a hospital-staff parking lot, an empty KFC bucket beside him. In his lap he held a sign: I'M HUNGRY. There was something primal in the simple plea, but Kathy was past the man before Pace could suggest pausing to give him a few dollars. A gauntlet of Washington Circle beggars waved plastic cups at passing cars in hope that those in their Mercedes or BMers or Jags would lower the windows of their fifty-thousand-dollar automobiles and drop a few coins for the wretched who hadn't the price of a hot meal. But it was spring, and the wet, wintry bluster that seeds lucrative guilt wilted under the warming sun. The only windows lowered were to let in soft, fresh air. At that hour of the day, the windows of opportunity for the needy were closed.

Pace shoved the scene from his mind and debated what to do about Kathy and Sissy. He felt sick when he thought of what the scene might have been had the two of them accompanied him to the basement garage. Would all three have been killed? He knew if—no, *when* he went back to the Converse story, he would be at risk, and their proximity to him could endanger them as well. He told Kathy the day before he was thinking about sending Sissy home early, and asked if she wouldn't feel safer back in Georgetown for a while. She dismissed the suggestion out-of-hand.

"I don't think Melissa would understand anymore than I would understand," Kathy said.

"It's not a matter of rejecting either of you," Pace explained. "It's for your own safety."

"Well, you and Melissa's mother have to decide what to do about her safety, but I decide what to do about mine, and I'm staying," Kathy insisted.

Brave lady. Strange attitude. She was willing to put herself at risk, but rejected his risking himself. Pace didn't understand. He wondered how much he'd damaged their relationship with the scene in the hospital room.

Kathy's BMW swung off Washington Circle and headed north on New Hampshire Avenue. Pace let his mind drift.

I've never felt threatened here. Crime was something that happened to other people. I live in a good neighborhood, a good building with a coded garage door, security in the lobby twenty-four hours a day, good lighting, good locks on the doors. Mugging is the last thing I feared. Did I create a scenario to cover a crime I thought would never reach me? Did I transmute two street punks into something more sinister?

Bullshit. I know what I know. I know what I saw.

"I know what I saw," Pace muttered as Kathy's car slipped into a two-hour parking spot about twenty-five paces from the entrance to his building.

"Nobody's questioning that, Steve," Kathy responded. "Nobody's suggesting you're telling anything but the truth."

He dismissed her support with a wave of his hand.

The telephone message-recorder in Pace's bedroom was flashing—urgently, he thought. When there was trouble, the red light seemed to blink faster and brighter than for social calls. He knew before he replayed the messages that several would be from Joan. He refused Kathy's offer to retrieve the messages. That he would do himself. He was not an invalid.

"Would you at least write down any that are for me?" she asked in something of a huff. "I live here, too, you know. And then would you please get into bed?"

Pace nodded agreement on both counts, and when the bedroom door closed, he switched the recorder to the playback setting. He heard the tape respool for nearly two minutes. That meant there were plenty of messages. They began to replay.

"Hi, Steve, this is Sally. Just wanted to let you know I'm thinking about you. Clay said he saw you in the hospital and you looked awful. Call me when you feel up to it, and we'll talk about the Antravanian accident. No hurry. There's nothing new at this end. Get well. *Beep.* Steve, this is Joan. Will you call me as soon as you can, please? I'm a little concerned about Sissy. Oh, you, too, of course. *Beep.* Hi. It's Joan again. I was checking to see if you were home yet. *Beep.* Click. *Beep.* Steve, old boy! Glenn here. I've got a coupla six-packs of Guinness ready for sharin' when you feel up to it. Call me when you want to talk about the Sexton story. The urgency is obvious. But don't call 'til you're feelin' better." *Beep.*

"Steve, this is Hugh Green. I was troubled to hear about your, well, your accident. I'd like to talk to you about it when you're back on your feet. I'd like to help where I can—if I can. Meanwhile, tell Kathy to take as much time as you two need together. If I had a Jewish mother, she would say Kathy should stay home and fix you a nice bowl of chicken soup. If you need anything, let me know. Meanwhile, when Kathy has a free minute, would you ask her to call? It's not urgent. Maybe she should try me at home tonight. Between seven and eight, if that's convenient. After eight, Gretchen and I will be on our way to a reception at the French Embassy. Eat your heart out, kid. *Beep.* Click. *Beep.* It's Joan again, Steve. I know I must sound like a pest, but please call me as soon as you can. *Beep.* Click. *Beep.* Welcome home, Mr. Pace. You got lucky this time. Don't press your luck." *Beep. Beep. Beep. Beep. Beep.*

The five tones signaled the end of the tape, but Pace didn't hear them. He was staring in disbelief at the mechanical message-taker, stunned by the audacity of the last message. But it was his proof he hadn't dreamed or invented the blue van. The attack on him was deliberate and premeditated, and his attackers knew exactly who their target was. He listened anxiously as the recorder rewound, a mechanical device that knew nothing of the content or impact of the messages it relayed. It couldn't hear, couldn't think, couldn't decipher the difference between life and death, joy and terror. It responded only to the electronic commands programmed into it, spit the short audio bites back on request, and then sat quietly, awaiting its next unanswered telephone.

When the friendly green playback light gave way to the red ready-light, and one long tone indicated the machine was reset, Pace hit the play button impatiently, demanding the messages be given again. But the machine only spooled up and back, the green light winking flirtatiously, as though seeking business. But no calls came, and gabby green gave way again to ready red.

"Kathy!" He almost hit the play button again, but he was desperately concerned that he hadn't done what was necessary to preserve the messages. "Kathy!" She was the mechanical one. She would know. *Dear God, let it not have been erased.*

The bedroom door opened and Kathy rushed in, obviously concerned about the urgency in his voice. He didn't even look up.

"The messages. I played them through, and the tape rewound. How do I get them to play again?"

Kathy started to ask why, but his anxiety made her push aside her curiosity and turn her attention to the machine. "Did you get five beeps?"

"Yes," he said, nodding furiously. "And then it re-spooled. And I hit the play button, but the messages didn't play back again."

Kathy sighed. "Then they're gone. If you want to save them, you have to hit the stop button as soon as you get the five beeps. Rewinding is the erase mode."

When Glenn Brennan showed up at the front door with two six-packs of Guinness and a broad Irish smile, Pace was ready for the relief. He'd spent the day alternately sleeping, reading, brooding, and talking on the phone to friends and associates who called to wish him well.

Only Glenn showed up with a drink in his hand.

Kathy and Melissa went out after dinner to do some shopping. They left Pace lying on the couch, propped up with pillows so he could sift through two local newscasts, three network news reports, and the MacNeill/Lehrer Report on WETA. He urged them to go, sick to death of Melissa's fawning and chilled by Kathy's sincere, if distant, concern.

After coming to terms with the fact that he would never retrieve the telephone messages on his machine, he returned Joan's calls. Yes, he assured her when she answered on the first ring, Sissy was fine. No, he said, she was not in any immediate danger. Yes, he agreed, if he thought there could be any problems for their daughter, he would put her on the first plane back to San Diego. No, thank you, he did not need her to fly East to take care of him.

Care wasn't what he lacked. What he needed, *damn it,* was for somebody to *listen* to him.

27

Thursday, May 1st, 8:00 A.M.

Chapman Davis pulled into the driveway at Harold Marshall's Chevy Chase, Maryland, home precisely on time. He and Marshall were scheduled to inspect the remains of the wrecked Sexton 811 and get a personal briefing from Vernon Lund at nine-thirty. The last thing Marshall told Davis before leaving the office the evening before was to pick him up early, because the normal morning rush around Washington would make the drive to Dulles a test of endurance. The trip took an hour from Chevy Chase in off-peak hours. It would take ninety minutes in the early morning, even going against the heaviest traffic most of the way.

So Davis left his townhouse shortly after seven-thirty, unsettled at the prospect of driving from his racially mixed Silver Spring neighborhood to predominantly white Chevy Chase, an old, wealthy community on the Maryland side of the northern District of Columbia border. To say minorities weren't welcome was an overstatement; there were high-ranking, dark-skinned diplomats from Asia, Africa, Central and South America. They lent an international flavor to the neighborhood. African-Americans who wanted to live in Chevy Chase, assuming they could afford it, were consigned primarily to those quarter-million-dollar homes of less than fifteen hundred square feet tucked back on narrow side streets off the main roads. In Youngstown, Ohio, a quarter-million dollars bought a mansion. In Chevy Chase, it bought a tiny plot and three bedrooms in an affluent ghetto.

Early in his manhood, Davis abandoned the doctrine of

the liberal conscience. When he returned to school after his brush with the law, he chose a political-science major and an economics minor, deliberately donning the cloak of conservatism, not so much out of moral certitude as personal conviction that the Republican Party was where the money lived. He believed the truism that one becomes more conservative as one acquires more to conserve. It's righteously easy to sanction expensive, tax-paid human-services programs when you're the servee and pay no taxes; it's much harder when it means cutting back on country-club extravagances. At least that was the simplistic way it looked to a basketball-player-turned-killer-turned-student, whose father and older brother still tried to make a living as steelworkers in a town abandoned by big steel years earlier. Grubbing from job to job, barely staying off welfare and above the poverty line was no way to live.

That perception had driven Davis into the arms of the game-fixers at Ohio State. They paid him handsome sums to take bad shots, to miss key plays down the stretch, not actually losing games, but keeping the scores under the spread at which Ohio State was favored by the bookies to win. Once he was discovered and banished from the team, the same perception drove him to the streets. He left the life only because Harold Marshall's formula for success was less dangerous. Marshall's financial largesse generated no special loyalty in Davis, no feeling of kinship, or even of friendship. Davis's decision to live life Marshall's way was a dollars-and-cents matter. Nothing more or less.

Marshall got his money's worth. Davis lied for him and intimidated people on his behalf. He solicited and accepted campaign contributions from those with whom Marshall wouldn't want to be associated publicly, gave the donors false identities for the Federal Election Commission's records, and saw to the fulfillment of political promises that generated those contributions.

Marshall's "dark-side" demands were few, but when they came, their audacity more than compensated for their infrequency. This mess with Converse went well beyond the audacious.

Davis turned off Connecticut Avenue onto East-West Highway, prime real estate territory directly opposite the pricey and exclusive Columbia Country Club. He might have imagined it, but his black face seemed to draw attention from passing drivers. His new Ford Thunderbird seemed inadequate among the fancier domestic models and imports indigenous to the neighborhood, and he somehow felt the need to apologize for threatening local property values by driving a mere twenty-six-thousand-dollar car onto these streets.

"Don't ya'all fret none. Ize here to pick up Massa," Davis whispered to wind blowing past his open window. He turned into the driveway of Marshall's five-bedroom home, hoping the senator didn't expect him to jump out of the car and hold open the passenger door. He was grateful he had a two-door car, certain if he'd brought a four-door model, Marshall would have gotten in the back, turning Davis into a chauffeur. As it was, Marshall slid into the front beside Davis. If he expected his aide to jump out and hold the door for him, he did nothing to indicate it.

"Morning, Chappy," he said. "How's traffic? The radio said the Cabin John Bridge is a mess."

Davis groaned. The bridge over the Potomac River linking Maryland and Virginia was in a perpetual state of construction. It was built originally with fewer lanes than the Capital Beltway that feeds it from both directions. Each time the bridge was widened, the Beltway was widened, too, creating a permanent bottleneck of cars and trucks during both morning and evening rush hours.

Still, he would rather face a jam on the highway than spend another half hour visiting suburban Maryland's emerald corridor. He wondered what the neighborhood would think if this black boy showed up with a two-million-dollar cash down payment and bought a house smack in the middle of all this arrogance. He supposed the men in their thousand dollar suits and the women planning social strategies beside their private pools and on their private tennis courts would overlook his skin color when they saw the color of his money. He smiled at the prospect.

That was, after all, what this was all about.

The traffic at Cabin John was bad, but not as bad as it could have been, backing up only to the River Road area. Once they got into Virginia and onto the Dulles access road, there were only a few private cars and a dozen or so steel-gray Washington Flyer cabs to weave through. Davis rolled to a stop in front of the chain-link gate by Hangar 3 a full ten minutes before they were scheduled to meet Lund. He identified himself and his passenger to the airport police officer with the clipboard and gave the reason for their visit. The officer scanned down the top sheet of paper and flipped to a second. He scowled and repeated the process, shaking his head more emphatically the nearer he got to the end of his list.

"I'm sorry, Mr. Davis, but I don't see your name on the roster," he said. "You sure you got the right day?"

"Of course I'm—" Davis started, but Marshall cut him off.

"I'm United States Senator Harold Marshall, and I know what today is, and I know Vernon Lund, a member of the National Transportation Safety Board, is expecting us. I won't be delayed." He waved in the general direction of Hangar 3. "Go call whoever you have to, but get us in there!"

"Senator, I'm not trying to be difficult. I simply don't find your names," the officer said. "I'll go check. Please, both of you stay in the car, and Mr. Davis, sir, please turn off your engine."

The officer walked toward the gate, then turned back when he continued to hear the car engine running. He caught Davis's eye and pointed to the car. Then he tucked the clipboard under his left arm and crossed his hands at the wrists, an aviation signal to stop.

Davis swore as he moved to comply. "What the hell does

he think I'm going to do, ram the damn gate? How am I supposed to run the damn air conditioning?"

He and Marshall sat glumly without further words. The police officer was back in about three minutes, nodding. He stuck his head down beside Davis.

"I'm sorry, Senator," he said directly to Marshall. "There was a mix-up on the roster sheet. Mr. Lund is expecting you. A car is on the way out to lead you in. It will have a sign on the back that says, 'Follow Me.' Be just a minute, sir."

Marshall nodded curtly. "How quaint," he whispered.

Lund was effusive in greeting Marshall, less so in acknowledging Davis. The aide guessed their earlier meeting, and perhaps his disastrous encounter with George Ridley, were still eating at him. Lund apologized profusely to Marshall for the mix-up at the gate. Marshall wouldn't let it go.

"If you can't make an appointment with a United States senator without screwing up, how are you supposed to keep something as large and complex as the Sexton investigation on track?" he demanded.

Davis stopped listening and turned his attention to activity in the hangar.

The place was enormous, but every available square foot of floor space was in use to reconstruct the crushed jetliner. Jagged, blackened pieces had been set down in approximately the positions they'd occupied when the Sexton was whole. But sections, and sections of sections, were missing, either vaporized in the flames or sent off to a laboratory for closer inspection. The impression was of a skeleton from which some bones had been vandalized, lying spread-eagled, unable to muster the substance to live again.

Around the floor, men and women, singly and in small groups, bent over pieces of the debris, examining them, jotting notes, sometimes carrying a small something off to be observed under magnification. Davis marveled that out of the mess of the accident, so much of the jetliner had been found and identified.

The exception, he noticed suddenly, was the Number Three engine. The left engine was there, detached from the wing, but resting on the concrete floor. The disfigured tail engine and what was left of the vertical stabilizer lay on the floor. But the right engine, the one that had wrenched itself from its mount, was gone.

"Excuse me," he interrupted as Lund was finishing his final defense of his own competence. "Where's Number Three engine?"

"In the back," Lund said quickly, openly grateful to have the subject changed. "We're in the final stages of examination."

"I'd like to see it," Davis said, then remembered this was Marshall's tour. "Ah, Senator, I assume you want to take a look."

Marshall nodded. "That's my primary mission here."

"This way, Senator," Lund said with a nod to Davis indicating he was invited, too. "Be careful not to touch anything. We don't want to alter the evidence, but beyond that, some of this metal is very sharp, and we wouldn't want you hurt in the line of duty."

Davis saw Marshall roll his eyes. This guy Lund was a real dork.

"When will you be shipping the engine back to Converse?" Marshall asked as they walked down special pedestrian lanes marked with bright yellow tape.

"As soon as we're finished examining it here. Unless lawyers start filing liability suits and get the hangar sealed before we get the engine out."

Even mangled, the C-Fan was awesome in size. It towered over the the three men, intake gaping like the open maw of a giant whale. Most of the fan blades were missing, their stumps looking like jagged, broken teeth. Beyond them, Davis could see some of the engine's turbine machinery still in place, although the front compartment had been removed. He suspected the littered bench behind the engine held most of the missing pieces.

"It's hard to tell exactly," Lund was saying to Marshall as they inspected an area of missing fan blades. "Some undoubtedly were broken by the bird strike. The others broke on impact with the runway. We found pieces of blades all over the place."

"And what's this?" Marshall had moved to the side of the engine. He raised his hand above his head and ran his fingers along a rupture in the sheet metal.

"Be careful, that's very sharp," Lund warned. "The ingested debris smashed a turbine disk. A section of the disk breached the pod. That's it right over there."

Marshall looked pointedly at Lund. "Did a problem with the disk cause this accident?"

Lund nodded. "I know what you're asking me, Senator, and I don't know the answer."

"Converse deserves an answer," Marshall said. His voice was cold. "A whole fleet of airplanes with this engine has been grounded, causing Converse a great deal of embarrassment, and very possibly some financial loss. The company deserves to know, once and for all, that there are no peripheral issues here, that a bird strike was the sole cause of the damage to the engine, and that there is no pattern of turbine disk problems."

"I think the NTSB has come as close as it can to saying that."

"You haven't said absolutely this disk did not break due to a manufacturing defect."

"We still don't know. We suspect, but we don't know for certain. That probably is a determination that won't be made for some time, particularly because we have to factor in the disk that cracked in Seattle and that godawful thing over St. Louis."

Exasperation was written all over Marshall's face. "Let me put it another way," he suggested. "If the broken pieces of blade hadn't penetrated the turbine compartment, could this aircraft have survived the bird strike?"

Lund shrugged. "That would be pure speculation, Senator," he said. "But surely there is reason to think that with damage limited to the loss of a few blades, the crew should have been able to stop the airliner without serious damage."

"Jesus," Marshall whispered. He stared up at the ragged breach in the pod's skin for a full minute. "The Converse people aren't happy about this at all."

"I'm sure," Lund replied.

28

Friday, May 2, 9:20 P.M.

They had it out after dinner.

With little to do for the last forty-eight hours but brood, Pace had given considerable thought to what lay ahead for him. He would return to work on Monday and resume stewardship of the Sexton story, such as it was. And despite all the advice to the contrary, he would pick up the thread of the conspiracy theory, give it a yank and see what unraveled.

Not that he knew where to begin. He was convinced he hadn't dreamed his assailants' blue van, any more than he dreamed the greeting on his answering machine. There were two murders, and they *were* murders. Two men from the same go-team don't go down violently under suspicious circumstances within days of each other. It doesn't happen. He refused to let it go. Part of his tenacity was for Kathy, part of it was for Mike. And part of it was his certainty of the existence of a crime somebody was trying to cover up.

There was no question it would be a dangerous undertaking. He was confident he could disregard the threats to himself, but he couldn't ignore the proximate danger to Kathy and Sissy. They were innocent bystanders. They had to go. That's what he had to tell them tonight.

He brought it up when the dishes were done, and Melissa

was reaching for the TV remote. "Sissy, don't turn that on right now," he said. "I've got something the three of us have to talk about."

"Sure, Dad. I was just going to run the dial."

"What's up?" Kathy asked. Her mood sounded upbeat, but Pace knew she still smarted from the confrontation in his hospital room.

"It's about next week," he said. "I'm going back to work. I'm going to pick up the Sexton story, and I've decided I'm going to pick up the investigation, too."

Melissa expelled a sigh of concern. Or was it exasperation? Pace couldn't be certain. Kathy watched him without expression He guessed she knew what was coming.

"Sissy, I changed your reservation. I'm going to send you back to California tomorrow."

"Aw, Dad, why? You're not even going back to work 'til Monday."

"It's only one day's difference. We'll make it up another time."

Melissa, her face screwed into a deep frown of disagreement, turned her head to the side and down, the way teenagers do when they want to let a parent or a teacher know they disapprove but don't dare speak that disapproval. Kathy continued to watch him without any expression at all. Their eyes met and held for several seconds.

"What about me?" she asked finally.

"I think you should go back to Georgetown," he said softly, so it was less an order than a suggestion open for discussion. He could see, however, that Kathy knew he had made up his mind.

"What if I don't think I should go?"

"I'm not going to throw you into the street. But I don't want to have to worry about you every minute, either."

"Don't be a chauvinist; it doesn't become you. I can worry about myself," she insisted.

"I'm sure you can. But that won't stop me from worrying."

Now she was making no effort to hide the aggravation.

"Why would you worry less if I'm in Georgetown? That's crazy, you know. If they want to find me, they can reach me there as easily as here."

"But you won't get hurt just because you're by my side. That's the whole point."

Kathy stood and walked over to him. "What you're really suggesting is that I go back to Georgetown so I won't keep telling you you're doing things you shouldn't be doing and getting into things that are none of your business."

"No, that's not it."

"You're playing this out like Gary Cooper in *High Noon*. Send the schoolmarm home 'til the shooting's over, and if the hero survives, he'll come back and carry her to the altar. Well, *damn it, Steve,* I'm not some helpless schoolmarm to be sent away like that. And if you insist on doing it, I might not be there when you come back for me. *If* you come back for me."

Her eyes were glistening, and Pace thought he couldn't possibly love her more. He stood and gathered her in his arms, both of them oblivious to Melissa's presence. They stood like that, saying nothing, for several minutes.

"At the risk of starting the argument again, part of this is for you, Kathy," he said.

"None of this is for me," she snapped. "It started out to be for me, but now it's for you, for some macho image you have that you're the only one who can make the paybacks for Jonny and Mike. Well, nobody asked you for that. Jonny wouldn't have wanted it. I can't believe Mike would have asked. And I *damned well* didn't want it."

She rested her head against his shoulder. "You won't change your mind, will you?"

Pace shook his head. "No. But we don't have to end it like this. Stay the night."

This time Kathy shook her head. "No. I think I'd better not. I'll come by sometime next week while you're at work and collect my things. Fortunately, I left a lot of stuff in Georgetown."

"Why don't you leave your things here?" he asked.

"You'll be coming back."

She shook her head again. "I don't know. A relationship cuts both ways. I know you think this is in my best interest, but I think you're being overly protective, like I thought my father used to be after Mom died. I have a lot to think about. I don't want a relationship with my father."

She pulled back slowly, letting his hands trail down her arms. She turned and picked up her briefcase from where she always left it by the front door.

Without looking back, she let herself out.

Standing by the sofa, unable to move, Pace felt his insides coil into a knot and shrink into a cold spot right at the center of his gut.

Sissy sat on the sofa and read for the rest of the evening. A moody silence shrouded the hours until she went to bed shortly after eleven. Pace tried to start a conversation with her, to gauge the depth of her displeasure and to try to dispel some of her concerns. She responded only once.

"You know," she said, "you throw away all the good things that ever happen to you."

"I haven't thrown you away," he said.

She was silent.

"Sissy, talk to me."

More silence.

"You must know I love you. I'm not doing this because I don't love you."

His daughter picked up her book and disappeared into her bedroom, closing the door softly but firmly behind her.

Half an hour after Sissy turned in, Pace doused the living-room lights and went into his bedroom, where all the scents and sights were reminders of Kathy. He tried not to see her clothes when he hung his in the closet, tried not to notice her lotions and perfumes on the vanity in the bathroom. He tried. But it didn't work.

He walked to his bureau and leaned against it, facing it, his arms outstretched, his hands gripping the edge of the oak top. He did a few gentle pushbacks, trying gingerly to relieve the tension in his shoulders without aggravating his injuries. But that didn't work, either.

Absently, he picked the scarred metal ball he'd found at Dulles from its place in the amber ashtray and turned it slowly between his thumb and forefinger. He looked at it without seeing it. His chest felt tight; he thought he could almost feel his blood pressure rising. He took several deep breaths.

"Damn it!" he swore. "Damn it to hell!"

With fury and the sick feeling of being alone once again in that bedroom, he hurled the ball at the wall behind the bed. He watched it career through the air and hit the white-painted Sheetrock with a dull thud. It appeared to stick there for a moment, and then it dropped away, leaving a crater in the soft wallboard. Pace heard the ball hit the bare wooden floor beside the wall and roll away. He hadn't the slightest idea where it went, nor did he care to find it.

29

Monday, May 5th, 9:10 A.M.
To outward appearances, Steve Pace looked healthy and chipper when he walked into the *Chronicle* newsroom on his first day back at work. He timed it to arrive earlier than most of the national staff because he didn't want to make a grand entrance. He didn't want anyone making a big deal of his return. He didn't want to talk to anyone about anything. The appearance of good health belied the turmoil he felt. The last three days had been wrenching.

He put Melissa on an airplane home on Saturday after

spending a sleepless Friday night in his newly empty bed. His daughter spoke barely six sentences to him, but in those few words, she managed to express her conviction that he was wrong to return to the Sexton investigation, he was stupid to treat Kathy like a child, and she didn't think much of his sending her away, either.

When he kissed her at the gate and said he would see her during the summer, she replied, "Yeah, well, maybe." Then she disappeared into the crowd on the airway to her plane.

Back at home, dirty dishes were piled in the kitchen and his bed was unmade. He'd busied himself cleaning the place, trying again not to notice Kathy's things in his closet and bathroom. By early afternoon, he came face-to-face with the reality that there was no more housework to do.

In the guest bedroom, where he had a small office setup, he saw that Sissy had stripped her bed, made it up again with clean sheets, and folded and piled the soiled bed linen and towels on the old metal trunk at the foot of the bed. Kathy would have done something thoughtful like that, too. That image twisted the cold knot in his gut.

He'd thumbed to the C listings in his telephone file and found Eddie Conklin's number. Unlike his first attempts, which seemed like months ago, he reached the technician on the first try.

"Hey, I read about your run-in with the bad guys," Conklin said sheepishly. "I kept meaning to call you, but—"

"No sweat, Eddie," Pace said quickly. "I wasn't in much of a mood to talk to anybody. I'm back in business now, but it occurs to me I haven't seen any stories recently about the flight data recorder. Is there anything new?"

"I'm not working the Sexton case anymore, Steve," Conklin said. "Since the bird-strike finding, we've pulled back to a small crew. The metallurgists are the only ones still fully geared up, and they're about to give way to the Converse people."

Pace frowned. "What do you mean?"

"About what?"

"Giving way to the Converse people."

"Oh, well, you know, the engine will be sent back to Converse, and their people will tear it down and try to find out if anything could have been done differently, better," Conklin said. "Same old same old. You let the guys who built the thing figure out how to fix it."

"That's crazy!" Pace insisted.

"Why? It's SOP."

"What if there's something there the NTSB hasn't found yet?"

"Like what?"

"Hell, I don't know, Eddie. Anything."

"Is there something you know that I don't?"

Pace took a deep breath. "No," he acknowledged. "But none of this feels right."

"Why, I ask again?"

"Because if there's something wrong with that engine, instead of or in addition to the notorious bird strike, you're putting the evidence right into the hands of the people with the biggest stake in covering it up."

"That's paranoid," Conklin said.

"That's right," Pace admitted. "It is. I give you that. I subscribe to that, in fact. But I stand by my concerns."

"The only way the NTSB could hold onto the engine is if a court ordered it impounded in response to a lawsuit."

"What sort of lawsuit?"

"An injured survivor, in some cases. In this case, the family of one of the victims."

"And there aren't any suits yet?"

"Not that I've heard of. At least none that asked the court to keep the engine under government control."

"What's the timetable for shipping it back to Ohio?"

"Don't know. I'll see if I can run it down for you."

"Thanks, man. I owe you one."

"I'll collect, too," Conklin replied.

Pace had to force himself not to pick up the phone again right then to ask Kathy if she and her father, or maybe Betsy, would be willing parties to a suit that would keep the C-Fan in government hands. It would be completely improper and unprofessional for him to get involved. Even if he could justify it, Kathy wouldn't do it, not for herself, not for Jonathan.

And certainly not for him.

More colleagues than he would have liked stopped by Pace's desk to chat about his ordeal and to ask how he was feeling. Others waved and called greetings across the newsroom. Paul Wister said it was good to see him and they would talk later, after Pace had a chance to go through his mail and telephone messages. Avery Schaeffer stopped by, too, and sat down at the always-vacant seat assigned to Jack Tarshis, the peripatetic environmental writer.

Schaeffer clapped his hands to his thighs. "So, how you doing?"

"Well, thanks," Pace replied. "Except for a few black-and-blue marks, I'm doing well."

Schaeffer bent closer and lifted his head so he could look out of the bottom of his bifocals. "There's still some swelling on the cheek, I see. You're going to have a nice scar. Hurt much?"

"No, not much."

Schaeffer leaned back in the chair again. "The women taking pretty good care of you?"

"Pretty good," Pace said. He didn't want to get into that. "A little overbearing sometimes."

"How long's Melissa going to be here?"

Pace sighed. It looked as though he was going to get into it, like it or not. "I put her on a plane back home Saturday morning, Avery. We felt it was time."

"Oh?" Schaeffer looked surprised. "I thought she said she was staying two weeks."

"She was supposed to, but it didn't work out." Pace was growing impatient. He wanted to get on with work.

"I hope it wasn't a problem between Melissa and Kathy," Schaeffer said, prying without meaning to. "They seemed to be good together."

"No," Pace said. "That wasn't it."

Schaeffer regarded him for a moment longer. "You okay?"

"Yes," Pace said, trying to sound reassuring. "I've got a stack of stuff piled up here, and I've got to talk to Paul and Glenn about the Sexton investigation."

"We're worrying that one to death. You think it's still worth it?"

"Don't you?"

"I don't see a whole lot of movement by the NTSB," Schaeffer said. "They've pretty much closed the book on the investigation."

"There are still the two murders . . . and one mugging I'm particularly interested in."

"If there was no cover-up, doesn't that kill the theory that the violence was intended to preserve a conspiracy?"

"I'm not certain there was no cover-up," Pace insisted. "Because we haven't found it doesn't mean it isn't there. And if it is there, the violence theory stands."

Schaeffer pursed his lips and nodded. "Okay," he said. "Take it where it leads, within reason. But don't obsess on it." He got up and started to leave, then turned back. "And be careful," he added.

As Schaeffer walked away, Pace concluded the talk was the editor's way of putting him on notice that his time on the Sexton story was limited, unless there were developments.

"Well, lookie here," Glenn Brennan said, pulling up to Pace's desk. "We have a bona fidey, garunteed, right-on newspaper reporter back at his desk after a narrow brush with the Grim Reaper, praise the Lord. Makes me proud to be an American. How the hell are you, good buddy?"

"You as a good ol' boy could put me back in the hospital," Pace said, accepting Brennan's extended right hand.

"How're you feeling?" Brennan asked.

"Physically, I'm fine," Pace said. "Affairs of the heart are a little shaky."

"Oh?" Now Brennan occupied Tarshis's seat.

"I sent Sissy back to her mother a week early, and when I suggested to Kathy that she put some temporary distance between us, she walked out without even saying thanks for the memories," Pace explained. "Said she'd be back for her things later. My source in the NTSB lab says the investigation is practically closed and they're getting ready to ship the engine back to Converse, along with any dirty little secrets it holds. And it's supposed to rain. So how's by you?"

Brennan put his feet up on Tarshis's desk and tried to light a cigarette without being noticed. He failed. But he took three deep pulls at it before Ginny St. George, a general-assignment reporter who specialized in national-security stories, brought him a triple-folded piece of aluminum foil she ripped from a sandwich carried in for lunch.

"Why don't you go outside like all the other smokers and accept the fact that your ambient smoke isn't welcome in here?" St. George demanded.

"Ambient smoke?" Brennan asked in mock confusion. "Doesn't ambient mean friendly?"

"No, and you know it doesn't," she replied. "Now put it out before I have you nuked."

She hustled back to her desk, and Brennan tugged at the cigarette once more in defiance before stubbing it out in the makeshift ashtray.

"You're beautiful when you're polluted, you know?" he called after her.

St. George shook her head in exasperation, and Brennan turned back to Pace.

"Well, Steven, my man, I have to tell you that after hanging around this story while you were inconvenienced, I began to get whiffs of the foul smell of decay. The leads have dried up, and so, I'm afraid to say, has the interest of yon supervisors. They're ready to move on."

"Anything about this story strike you as not quite right?" Pace asked.

"Everything's not right," Brennan replied with a shrug and a shake of his head. "We just had the worst airplane accident in U.S. history. Nothin' right about that."

Pace wouldn't be put off. "Did you get a chance to talk

to the lead investigators? Lund, Padgett? Elliott Parkhall, the guy in charge of the power-plants group?" he asked.

"I called Lund once, after the FAA put the Eight-elevens back in service. He wasn't interested in talking. He was feeling pretty smug, since he said all along there was no reason to ground them."

Pace nodded. "You didn't get any kind of rapport with him?"

"How do you develop rapport with a toad?"

"I'll take that for a no."

"He didn't give me a chance. I asked for comment about the FAA not finding any problems with the C-Fan, and he said what you saw in the newspaper: 'I told you so.' That was it."

Pace sighed. Time passed in silence until Brennan asked, "What're you thinking?"

"The unthinkable," Pace replied.

"Cryptic, aren't we?"

Pace smiled. "What I'm thinking, you wouldn't want to be associated with."

"Try me," Brennan insisted.

Pace shrugged. "Suppose, for purposes of discussion, there was no bird strike and the whole pile of evidence was manufactured—"

"Say *what?*"

"—to lead investigators away from the real cause of the crash."

"My unlimited capacity for blarney has been exceeded," Brennan said. "You've got a crash, and immediately you've got ten thousand people all over the scene. Nobody could go around inventing—or hiding or changing—the evidence."

"Somebody might have been able to get to the starboard engine," Pace said.

"You're losing me, boy."

"The focus of attention on the day of the accident was the fuselage and all the bodies. Nobody was paying a lot of attention to the engine. By the next morning, everybody was all over it, including the reps from Sexton and Converse. The question is, who had a chance to see the engine between the crash and, say, dawn on Friday? A list of those people would give us a list of those with opportunity. Then we narrow it down to those who also had motive."

"It won't wash," Brennan said. "First off, nobody knew the plane was going to crash. Once it went down, your theory supposes somebody realized there was something to cover up, came up with a plan on how to do it, fabricated the phony evidence, drew the whole power-plants team into the conspiracy, and planted the fabricated evidence. That's not possible!"

Pace shook his head. "Not necessarily. What if our villain was a member of the go-team?"

"Jesus, that's a stretch," Brennan said.

"This was supposed to be a blue-sky exercise."

"It was that, for sure," Brennan said. "So where do you go from here?"

"I think it's past time Elliott Parkhall and I had a face-to-face chat."

30

Monday, May 5th, 1:40 P.M.

Pace didn't get around to Parkhall until after lunch.

While rummaging through his mail, he took several phone calls from friends on the staff welcoming him back and wishing him well. Suzanne O'Connor stopped by to give him a hard time, and Sally Incaveria called.

"So how're you doing?" she asked brightly.

"I'm okay," he said.

"Good. What's the status of the Antravanian accident?"

"I should ask you. I haven't talked to Clay recently. Anything happen while I was away?"

"Personally, or professionally?" she asked.

"Oh? How about both?"

"Personally, I'd say I'm very happy you invited me to dinner at Reston. Professionally, I think I mentioned the case to Clay maybe twice. He didn't have anything new. All the police will say officially is they're still investigating."

"I'm pleased for you on the first count," Pace said. "On the second, I'd appreciate it if you'd keep the case active in Clay's head so he doesn't forget it's still important to me."

After lunch, he called Mitch Gabriel, chief of public affairs at the NTSB.

"Hey, man, I heard you had a run-in with some guys who didn't like the way you dress," Gabriel joked without bothering to say hello.

"Didn't like the way I look, either," Pace said. "They redid some body parts for me."

"No important parts, I hope."

"None of any consequence. Just my face."

"Oh, good. I'm glad it wasn't serious. What's up?"

"This is going to sound like a strange question, Mitch, but do you consider the Sexton investigation over?"

"Over? As in completed?"

"Yeah."

"Not officially. We have probable cause. But there's still technical work to do. The metallurgists are running tests on the turbine disks. There'll be the public-hearing phase to present evidence and findings, and the board will issue a final report. That's when it's over officially."

"But for all intents and purposes—"

"It's pretty much over now, yes."

"You don't expect the team to find anything else?"

"I don't think the team expects to find anything else."

Pace was quiet, and Gabriel picked up on the silence.

"Why? What's bugging you? You still on your murder/conspiracy kick?"

"You don't think it's a huge coincidence that two members of the team met violent deaths during the early stages of the investigation? Doesn't that bother you at all?"

"Sure it does," Gabriel said quickly. "I knew both men well, and I liked them, especially Mike. But coincidences do happen, even if there's only a million-to-one chance. A million-to-one chance is a chance nonetheless."

"And how about the beating I took? I was the only reporter in town who connected the two deaths and was writing about them. How does that factor into your odds?"

"I don't know," Gabriel admitted. He sounded uncomfortable.

"And add this: Why did it take Vernon Lund twenty-four hours to report evidence of a bird strike? His first word on it was at his press briefing Friday evening, more than a day after the accident. The evidence should have been obvious from the get-go. Why didn't he mention it Thursday?"

"Even if that's true, I'm not sure I follow the implications," Gabriel said.

"Seems to me the bird gore should have been spotted sometime right after the accident."

"Maybe it was."

"But nobody said anything to the media until Friday? Come on, Mitch."

"That doesn't knock me out of my chair, actually," Gabriel said. "The first hours of an investigation are incredibly busy and confusing. Most of the attention was focused on stabilizing the fuselage. Maybe the engine team didn't mention it to Lund until Friday, or maybe the team told Lund and he decided not to make it public right away."

Pace felt the cold chill of logic in Gabriel's proposition. "Is there some way you could find out for me?"

"I could try. What you want to know is when Lund first learned about the bird remains. Anything else?"

"Not at the moment."

"I'll get back to you."

Pace pulled up to the gated entrance to the Dulles field shortly before three o'clock. An airport police officer approached his car.

"Yes, sir?" the officer said.

Pace flashed his press credentials and asked if there was a way to get a message to someone inside Hangar 3.

"I can send a message in," the officer said, "but I can't let you through."

"I don't want to go in," Pace replied. "I want somebody to come out."

The reporter sent word to Elliott Parkhall that he was outside with some very important information. While he waited for an answer, he got out of his car and leaned against the hood. He expected Parkhall to tell him to go to hell. Pace's message was a huge bluff.

But it worked.

"Look, I don't have to talk to you guys. That's not my job," Parkhall said as he came through the gate and approached the reporter.

"I know it isn't, Mr. Parkhall, and I won't take up any more of your time than I have to, but there are a few important things we need to talk about."

"I don't have anything to say. Mr. Lund spoke for the go-team."

"The official press briefings are over, but I still have some questions."

"What makes you think I can answer them? Or would if I could?"

"Let's get in the car. I'll turn on the air and we can relax."

"I told you to talk to the press officer," Parkhall insisted. "I don't do interviews."

"Do you do drinks?" Pace asked.

There was a pause. "Not unless I know why."

"Let's say, no ulterior motives. Just a talk."

"Not until I know why."

"You remember Watergate?" Pace asked.

"Oh, fer . . . what is this, a pop quiz?" Parkhall sounded and looked flustered. He stood opposite Pace with his feet spread and his arms folded.

"The eighteen-and-a-half-minute gap," Pace said quickly, pressing his advantage. "A critical meeting in the Oval Office during a major crisis over a political conspiracy, and the President's secretary admits she accidentally erased eighteen and a half minutes of a tape recording of that meeting. It's the tape that could have proved the President of the United States was a felon. You must have heard about it. It was in all the papers."

"What the hell has it got to do with me?" Parkhall demanded.

"Yours is the not-so-famous eighteen-and-a-half-hour gap, the time between your first examination of the Converse engine out there and your first report of seeing sliced and diced bird in it. It's been bothering me that Vernon Lund didn't mention anything about a bird at his press briefing the evening of the crash. He didn't mention it until the next day. So I asked the NTSB this morning to find out why. Seems Lund wasn't told about it until the next day. By you. Is there some reason you didn't tell him sooner?"

Pace was getting nasty. But he was on a roll. "And then we could talk about the forty-eight-hour gap, the time between Mark Antravanian's disappearance and the time his body was identified. A key member of your team disappears without explanation, but you never mention it to anybody. We got more gaps here than the Green Mountains. Now, do you want to have that drink?"

"No," Parkhall said vehemently, backing away from Pace, "and don't bother me again."

Pace considered the confrontation during the drive back to Washington. He'd given the tree of conspiracy a strong shake. Now it remained to see what fell out.

Pace slammed his fist into the top of the dashboard. *"Damn it,* what a *stupid—"* He pulled off on the side of the Dulles access road and reached to the passenger seat for his folder of investigation documents. When he put his hands on the one he wanted, he began thumbing the pages as quickly as he could.

"Air frame, ATC, come on, come on," he urged, flipping to the last pages. "Power plants!" he said triumphantly. He read the names aloud: Parkhall, Antravanian, Comchech, Teller. The four assigned members of the power-plants group. And he hadn't even tried talking to two of them. Perhaps they would answer the key questions: When had they first seen the engine? When did they realize a colleague was missing?

He would wait until that evening and call Comchech and Teller at the Dulles Marriott from his apartment. Caught alone in their rooms, they might be more inclined to talk to him . . . if they weren't part of the conspiracy, too.

That evening, as he walked home from work with the go-team list in his pocket, Pace spotted the blue Ford van.

It was following him across town on M Street. He looked at it carefully, trying to find new details to describe it, any partial piece of the license plate, even a definite make on the state of registry. But the driver realized he'd been seen and reacted quickly. The truck turned south onto 19th Street and disappeared into the last of the rush-hour traffic. Pace raced across M Street, oblivious to the honking motorists who barely missed him. He pushed off the front of a red Cougar and careened past the bumper of a Yellow Cab. He barely skirted the left fender of a Toyota Tercel and actually ran across the big front bumper of a delivery van that pulled up behind a Lexus so close he couldn't get between them. Then he raced down 19th, hoping the van would be delayed by the traffic long enough for him to overtake it. But after running two blocks and finding nothing, he stopped, his chest heaving from the exertion and the adrenaline that propelled him. It was gone; where, he had no idea.

Pace didn't get much of a look at the driver, but he got a good view of the bashed-up right front quarter. There were, among the dents and scrapes, streaks that definitely were yellow paint. When he headed back toward his apartment building, it was with the firm and smug satisfaction of having flushed Elliott Parkhall from the slime pond. Parkhall must have sent the van, perhaps with instructions to let the reporter spot it. A ploy to scare him off, maybe.

He let himself into his apartment, went straight to the refrigerator for one of the Guinness Stouts Glenn left behind, and sat back on the sofa with a thud.

Then, remembering what had happened the last time he'd sicced the dogs on himself, he got up and double-locked his front door. That would keep a mugger out, he figured, if the mugger happened to be eight years old and new to the profession.

He took a long pull at the Guinness and heaved a deep sigh of thanks. As much as he missed them, at least Kathy and Sissy were safely out of it.

"We told you before, Pace, don't press your luck. You think we're stupid, right? Believe me, we ain't. No more warnings. Or maybe you'd like us to mess up your girlfriend, or your daughter, next time. Don't make any difference to us. We know where they both are. We can get them any time."

Pace found the message when he went into the bedroom to undress for a shower and saw the red light blinking on his recorder. He put the machine on playback, hoping the message was from Kathy. It never crossed his mind that it could be something he should preserve, so he was in the bathroom when the message began. The voice was not the same as on the first warning, the one he found when he came home from the hospital. When he realized what the caller was saying, he ran for the machine to stop it from respooling. He didn't make it in time.

Damn! Damn! Damn!

Frantically, Pace dialed Kathy's number on O Street, more concerned for her safety than for the evidence he'd lost. Just when he was sure she was safely away from him . . . there was no getting away from him. He let the phone ring seven times. There was no answer.

He called Hugh Green's office. Again no answer.

Furiously, he thumbed through his address book for the number of D.C. Detective Martin Lanier. He'd left for the day.

"Please," Pace urged the desk sergeant, "call him at home or in his car and tell him it's an emergency. Tell him it's Steven Pace from the *Chronicle,* and I need to talk to him right away."

The sergeant, in a flat tone that said he took desperate calls all the time, promised to try.

When the phone finally rang, it jarred Pace out of a troubled half sleep on his living-room sofa. He snatched up the receiver.

"Pace, that you? This is Lanier. I got your message a few minutes ago. What's going down?"

Pace told him.

"I'm on my way," Lanier said.

He answered the call Code Two, lights flashing, no siren. Other drivers still gave way, and he didn't make citizens angry by waking them up without cause. And Martin Lanier was fairly certain this run was without cause.

In his years on the force, he had seen his share of obsessed people: crack-heads crazy to smoke a pipe of crystal cocaine, paranoids absolutely convinced they were being stalked by werewolves or space aliens, a man in Southwest who spent six weeks hunting down the thug who slashed his wife and finally blew the junkie's head off with a shotgun while the street cops, Lanier was convinced, looked the other way. He knew how to deal with those. They were textbook. But the manual didn't give guidance on how to handle nutball journalists. That razor-cut, computerized Fairfax County cop, Helm, he believed Pace. But not Lanier. The pieces didn't add up for him.

The detective pulled up in front of Pace's apartment and double-parked. He glanced at the clock in the dash. It was already Tuesday morning. He'd been at work more than fourteen hours.

"You better have something more than fantasy for me, Pace," he whispered into the empty car. "I've had about all of you I can stand."

31

Lanier found Pace's story unconvincing.

He figured the next step was up to Pace's supervisors. Never having been much for channels, Lanier called Avery Schaeffer to set up a private meeting. He had an afternoon call to make in northwest Washington and asked the editor to meet him at the National Cathedral.

"You know the Bishop's Garden?"

"Of course," Schaeffer replied.

"Okay, twelve-thirty," Lanier said.

Schaeffer drove north on Massachusetts Avenue, up the grade to the top of what was called Mount St. Alban in the late nineteenth and early twentieth centuries, when the high ground overlooking the federal city was a fashionable retreat for wealthy residents seeking relief from Washington's oppressive summer heat.

President Grover Cleveland had actually established a summer White House up here in—Schaeffer frowned, trying to retrieve that bit of trivia from his memory—eighteen eighty-six maybe. That old building was gone now, but the President left his mark on the area. It was called Cleveland Park and became one of the best residential areas of the District of Columbia. Many of the houses were built in the nineteen-twenties and were much favored by wealthy lawyers and high-level government officials, who spent lavish amounts of money restoring and upgrading the old residences. Schaeffer thought President Cleveland would con-

clude Americans had gone mad if he returned today and
learned how many millions of dollars those homes were
worth.

Schaeffer found a place to park on Newark Street and
walked three blocks south to the National Cathedral
grounds. The cathedral was an awesome gothic building,
and standing atop Mount St. Alban, it was visible from
almost anywhere in the District of Columbia and from some
areas of suburban Maryland and Virginia. Its foundation
stone was laid in nineteen-seven. It's official name was the
Cathedral Church of St. Peter and St. Paul. But no one
called it that.

Schaeffer followed the stone walkways to the Bishop's
Garden. Lanier was waiting. "Mr. Schaeffer, thanks for
coming. I'm sorry to be so mysterious."

Seeing Lanier brought back difficult memories. "We
never meet under very pleasant circumstances," Schaeffer
said.

"Lot of people feel that way about cops. Some days we
feel that way about ourselves."

Schaeffer realized they hadn't shaken hands. He thought
about rectifying that, but dropped the idea as awkward. "So
what's on your mind?" he asked instead.

"Steve Pace," Lanier replied directly. He repeated the
story of the night before and with it, his conviction that
Pace was not telling the truth about what was happening to
him. If Pace persisted in disrupting police business with this
obsession of his, there would be charges.

Schaeffer listened to the story without interruption. The
diffident way he asked the first of his two questions belied
the tension he felt.

"Had he been drinking?"

"You mean, was he drunk? No, not that I could tell. I
don't know if he'd maybe had a beer or two, but he was in
complete control."

"Are you certain Pace's statement is false?"

"I've asked myself that question a hundred times, Mr.
Schaeffer," the detective said. "I'm as certain as I can be.

There's no evidence there were any threatening messages on his answering machine. He admits he doesn't have a witness who heard either of them. There's no evidence at all that this blasted blue van even exists."

"Oh, yes there is," Schaeffer corrected. "Several rescue workers at the scene of the automobile accident in Virginia reported seeing it there. As I recall, it was also seen around the drugstore where Mike McGill was killed."

"Correct, but in both cases, eyewitnesses reported seeing a blue van with a dented right front. No details. No license number. Not even a vague idea which state's plates it carried. In short, nothing to corroborate that it was the same vehicle. And to repeat the question my superiors keep asking me: You have any idea how many beat-up blue vans exist in the greater Washington area?"

"I know," Schaeffer agreed. "But it's the thread of consistency that gives Pace's story some credibility."

"I think it's the thread Pace grabbed and embellished for the sake of his credibility. He added it to the story of his beating, and now he's seeing it everywhere. But only when he's alone." Lanier took a deep breath and let it out slowly between ballooned checks. "I think the bottom line here is: Your boy needs professional help of a sort neither of us is qualified to give. I think when someone pulls hard on that thread running through his story, the entire fabric will unravel, and he could unravel with it."

Steve Pace sat at his desk and drummed his fingers against the side of the telephone. He held the receiver to his left ear, on hold, waiting for Howard Comchech to pick up on the other end. Since he hadn't had the chance to contact either Comchech or Teller the night before, Pace called them at Hangar 3. He wondered if either would meet him in person if he drove to Dulles.

His nerves were rubbed raw. He'd had the sense the night before that Martin Lanier not only doubted his story about the telephone messages and the blue Ford van, but was beginning to doubt his sanity as well. When the cop left his apartment, he tried again to reach Kathy, but even at 1:00 A.M., there was no answer. He slept fitfully and awoke unrested. Before he even started coffee, he called her. And again there was no answer.

He finally reached her at the office at ten-thirty. She said she spent the night at the Greens'. She was cool, distant. Nonetheless, he told her about the new message on his answering machine.

"What am I supposed to do about it?" she asked.

"Maybe it wouldn't be a bad idea for you to stay with Hugh and Gretchen a while longer."

"Oh, really? You think that would stop someone trying to reach me? They do know where I work. I could be shot on the street, run down by a car—"

"Stop it!" he demanded through clenched teeth. "This isn't funny."

"And I'm not making a joke of it," she said. "It doesn't matter where I am, whether I'm with you, or at home, or with the Greens. If they want me, they can get to me. That's what I was trying to tell you the other night. You didn't understand then, and you don't understand now."

Pace played the conversation back in his mind. She was right, of course. And he didn't know how to deal with that.

"This is Howard Comchech."

The voice brought Pace back. "Mr. Comchech, thanks for coming to the phone. I'd like to talk to you. If I drive out to Dulles this afternoon, would you have a few minutes?"

"About what?" the investigator asked. "I'm not authorized to say anything about the crash."

"Yes, sir, I know," Pace said. "I wanted to talk about Mark Antravanian."

"Mark? Tragedy. Just a tragedy. I simply don't understand what he was doing out at that hour of the night."

"That's what I'm trying to find out," Pace said.

"Well, then, Mr. Pace, there isn't anything I can help you with. I don't know the answer."

"When did you first hear he was missing?" Pace thought he'd better get what interview he could by phone.

"I didn't know he was missing at all," Comchech said. "When we got together, uh, now I don't recall what day it was exactly, but it turned out to be the day Mark was killed, I mean, it was the morning . . . I mean, he died, as I understand it, sometime after midnight, and this would be daybreak of that same day . . ."

"Sunday, April twentieth," Pace suggested.

"Ah, yes, it was a Sunday, because one of my colleagues, William Teller, was going to church before he joined us, to early service so he wouldn't put us to any trouble by being late to get to the task at hand. At any rate, when Bill arrived, we noticed Mark wasn't there. Bill asked Elliott about him, and Elliott said he thought Mark was ill. When we found out later that he had been killed in a car accident, Bill suggested maybe Mark had been trying to get to a doctor or a hospital in the middle of the night. I don't know any more about it."

"Did Elliott Parkhall ever say anything more to you about Mark?"

"Not really, except after his body was identified, Elliott said what all of us felt—that it was a terrible tragedy and a horrible waste. Mark was a very decent man."

"Mr. Comchech, when was the first time you looked at the starboard engine of the Sexton?" Pace asked.

"Well, let me recollect," the investigator said. "It was early in the morning on the day after the crash."

"Had any of you looked at the engine the day before, the actual day of the crash?"

"Well, of course, you know, it wasn't precisely a crash, because the aircraft apparently never got off the ground—"

"The day of the accident, then?"

"No, not that I know of," Comchech said. "Bill and I didn't get there until very late Thursday night. We didn't think we'd be of much use at that hour, so we turned in so we could be ready and alert the next day."

"How about Elliott and Mark?"

"I think they both got to the scene shortly after the accident," Comchech said.

Pace was puzzled. "Mark worked for McDonnell Douglas in California," he recalled. "How could he get to Dulles that fast?"

"He was on the East Coast on business, as I recall," Comchech said. "In Boston or New York, or some such. He hopped a shuttle."

Pace's heart was pounding hard. "So Mark and Elliott both got to Dulles in time to see the engine on Thursday?"

"Oh, yes," Comchech said. "In fact, Bill's right here. Let me put him on the line. I'm certain he can confirm that."

Pace forced himself to be calm, and he quizzed Teller as closely as he'd questioned Comchech. Their stories matched exactly.

Both were able to place Parkhall and Antravanian at Dulles on Thursday. And Pace was more certain than ever: Parkhall had done something that defied imagining. Antravanian found out about it. And Antravanian paid for that knowledge with his life.

But understanding that was a long way from proving it.

32

Wednesday, May 7th, 9:00 A.M.
"There is absolutely no question about it, G.T. That's why I tried to reach you last night. It couldn't have happened any better for us."

Harold Kingsley Marshall was pacing at high speed behind his desk, his excitement too high to contain. On the other end of the private line, in Youngstown, George Thomas Greenwood was trying to calm him down enough to get the story straight.

"You're talking to a brain marinated in fine brandy last night, and you're going to have to humor me. Don't jump around. Tell me, detail by detail, from the beginning."

"Okay," Marshall agreed. "I got a call last night about eight. It was from a seductive young thing whose name you don't need to know. She's one of my legislative assistants, and she's seriously dating a *Chronicle* reporter—or maybe a photographer, I don't know—named, ah, Hogan, I think it is. It doesn't matter."

"Right, Harold," Greenwood said impatiently. "Get on with it."

"This LA is in love with the newsie, but she's very loyal to me. Ever since the accident, she's been feeding me intelligence that crosses her pillow about the *Chronicle*'s plans. I didn't ask her to do that. I don't encourage people to sleep around to gather gossip."

"I understand, Harold. What did she tell you?"

"Steven Pace was busted off his beat. She didn't know why, but he's not only off the Sexton story, he's off the aviation beat, demoted to general assignment."

"Who's been assigned to aviation?"

"I don't know. It's not important. Whoever it is doesn't have any ego invested in the Sexton story and isn't likely to pursue anything that isn't fed to him by the NTSB. That's the way the *Chronicle* brass wants it."

"Is that so?"

"That's so, G.T. That's absolutely so. We are home scot-free."

Steve Pace's new hours were 10:00 A.M. to 7:00 P.M., more or less. Any assignment could roust him earlier or keep him later. But there was nothing special for him early his first day on general assignment, and that was fine, because his insides were tied in knots so tight it was doubtful he could have concentrated on a story.

Pace wasn't so humiliated by the move to general assignment as he was furious it happened when he was getting close to a break in his investigation. He'd tried to argue his way out of the change, but Schaeffer was adamant.

"I told you not to obsess on this, Steve, and you turn around and start calling police to your apartment at all hours with stories about lost phone messages and mysterious blue vans that follow you in the night," Schaeffer said, almost sadly. "I'm sorry."

"I'm not making up this stuff," Pace insisted. "So the cop has his doubts. Frankly, I don't blame him. But I'm not hallucinating or fabricating these things. Those messages *were* on my machine. That van *was* there yesterday. More on point, yesterday I talked to two members of the power-plants team who can place Elliott Parkhall and Mark Antravanian at Dulles within a few hours of the accident. Both could have seen the engine before the bird remains were reported the next morning. What if Antravanian saw Parkhall do something? He might—"

"Enough," Schaeffer said with a raised hand. "If what you're telling me is true, give it to your friend at the Fairfax Police and let him follow it up. If what you suspect is true, the potential danger to you is too great." He shifted uncomfortably in his chair. "And if what Detective Lanier suspects is true, we need to put some distance between you and this story before he has you up on charges of filing a false police report. This is the only solution I see."

"Shouldn't I be the one to decide if the danger to me is too great?" Pace asked. "I don't need anybody making that decision for me."

"Nonetheless, I made it," Schaeffer said. "And my vote's the only one that counts."

Pace sank into a chair in front of the editor's desk. "Avery, what happened to initiative on this story? What happened to the decision to push and push until somebody pushes back? Why are we so timid all of a sudden?"

Schaeffer grabbed a huge sigh. He rocked back in his chair.

"Look at the whole picture," he said. "There is not one single shred of evidence to link your suspicions to any reality I can think of. The NTSB isn't considering anything beyond the bird strike. The other newspapers don't show any sign of sharing your conviction that a conspiracy's afoot. Steve, it's always great to be out front all alone on a big story. And you gave us that for a time. But you only want to be out front for so long. At some point you want the other guys to catch up, to confirm on their own what you've been writing. There are good reporters working for those other papers. Russell Ethrich and Justin Smith are two of many. Are you telling me Justin wouldn't have hold of this thing by the throat if he thought there was something to it? Back off from it. Look at it through a window of objectivity. The story isn't there. You're chasing a red herring. I've got to put some distance between you and this . . . this obsession of yours."

Pace stood. "I understand what you're saying. I think you're wrong. I think there is evidence of a conspiracy, at least enough to warrant more reporting."

"Stay away from it, Steve. That's an order."

It was a far greater blow when he arrived home that evening and discovered Kathy had come during the day and removed the rest of her things. What a waste. He'd shoved her out of his life for nothing. He wasn't even able to keep his promise to find the clear cause of the accident that killed her brother.

All of that was roiling around in Steve Pace's gut the next morning when his phone rang.

"Pace."

"Hearin' a dastardly rumor about you, boy." The drawl and the syntax clearly belonged to Justin Smith.

"I don't know what you've been hearing, but it's probably all true," Pace replied.

"Up to talking about it?"

"Not much to talk about. *Shit!* Why do I start talking like you every time we get into a conversation?"

Smith chuckled. "Economy of words," he said.

"An act," Pace countered. "So what are you hearing about me?"

"That you got yourself busted off aviation because you

wouldn't let go of some daggone, pie-in-the-sky theory about the Dulles accident."

"True."

"Really?" Smith sounded surprised at Pace's easy acknowledgment. "Want to talk?"

"Not here."

"Lunch, then."

"Where?"

"Old Ebbitt?"

"One-thirty?"

"Sounds good, kid. Call and have me paged if something comes up."

"Will do, Justin."

Even at the end of the lunch rush, the Old Ebbitt Bar & Grille on 15th Street was a mob scene. The tables were close and the din could be unnerving. Despite the proximity of the diners, there wasn't a chance in hell that anybody nearby could pick up the threads of a private conversation.

Pace ordered a Beck's; Smith ordered Heineken. They flipped through the menu and settled on burgers. They gave the waiter the order when he returned with the drinks.

"So how're you doing?" Smith asked.

"Well enough, under the circumstances."

"Feel like talking about it?"

"Not much to tell," Pace said. "I was following some leads . . ." He shrugged. "And some leads were following me. My editors didn't like it. I wouldn't quit, so I got busted to GA."

Smith looked into his beer glass for a long moment and then drained it. He set it on the table and leaned over it toward Pace. "You remember that story I beat you on, the one about the ConPac crew trying to fly the Eight-eleven even after the starboard engine failed?"

"In my nightmares."

"Sources on that story—and I got two—say the flight data-recorder readings on the engine aren't consistent with a bird strike."

"What?" Pace gasped.

"Try to steal that story, and I'll be the next one beats you up," Smith warned.

"Justifiably," Pace conceded. "What's the rest?"

"Just violated every rule the *Times* has by tellin' you as much as I did," Smith said. "That's as far as I go."

"Fine," Pace said. "Fine, I understand completely. When are you going to write this, Justin? It's my ticket back onto the story."

"How so?"

"Your ass will be sticking out there, too, and my editors will know I'm not the only one who doesn't accept the NTSB line."

"Rightly enough," Smith said. "Can't tell you when, or even *if* it will run. Still got some checking to do. Supposed to head out to Dulles this afternoon to see Lund."

"Look," Pace said, "I'm not trying to be an asshole or anything. I wouldn't try to steal your story. Hell, I couldn't if I wanted to, not from a GA desk. But those black-box readings, how far are they off the norm?"

"Don't know the answer, and probably wouldn't tell you if I did."

"What more do you need to write?"

"A lot. But it's comin' together. Reason I suggested lunch, thought there might be somethin' you could tell me."

Pace stared at Smith. "You find me lying in a gutter, and you're going to try to pick my pockets before I get washed away by the street cleaners?"

"No," Smith said definitely. "You know me better than that. I feel obligated to make an exchange of information. That's why I told you about the black-box data, a gesture of good faith."

Pace sagged back in his chair. He believed his colleague, but in reconsidering the lines of inquiry he'd been following, he thought his investigation and Smith's didn't overlap. They'd been following parallel courses on entirely different tracks. He said as much.

"You know where to reach me," Smith said.

Pace felt a sudden chill. "Justin," he said, "watch your back."

Justin Smith pulled into Dulles a little before four o'clock. He parked his car in the hourly lot and found his way easily to the conference room and small suite of offices still being used by the go-team. Lund greeted him cautiously.

"I don't much care for reporters who ask to see me but won't say why," Lund said.

"Newsman's natural paranoia," said Smith. He smiled warmly. "Don't want to give you too much time with the questions, or you might come up with the right answers, and then where would my story be?"

Lund appeared to relax marginally. "So what's on your mind?" he asked. "I'll try to come up with the right answers off the top of my head." He motioned Smith to a seat beside his desk in the small, cluttered office.

"I'll get right to the point, Vernon," the reporter said. "You know me, known me for years. I'm not one to rush off on tangents or put much stock in rumors that come over the transom."

"You've always been very cautious and reliable," Lund agreed. "We all appreciate that."

"So trust me when I tell you I have two absolutely solid sources for what I'm about to tell you," said Smith. "They tell me the readings coming out of the flight data recorder show engine-performance deviations inconsistent with a bird strike."

Lund's face remained impassive, but his eyes locked on Smith's and stayed there. It took nearly a minute for him to respond.

"That's news to me," he said flatly.

"It's true, though," Smith insisted. "At least, it's the interpretation of two good engineers."

"I don't doubt what you say. But I haven't heard it before."

"How can that be? You keep in contact with your lab, don't you?"

"Of course!"

"Then you must have heard the same thing."

Lund shook his head. "I can't help you, Justin." Then he lowered his head and looked at the *Times*man over his half glasses. "You're beginning to sound like your young friend at the *Chronicle,* all bent out of shape over bad rumors and sour speculation. You watch yourself, or you could find yourself busted back just like him."

"Your feelings about Steve Pace aren't my concern," Smith said. "Only came out here to discuss engine-performance parameters."

"Then you're talking to the wrong man," Lund said.

"That's it? You're not going to check downtown?"

"Nope, probably not. And certainly not with you sitting here."

"If I call you later, would you talk to me more about it—after you've had a chance to make some checks privately?"

"Not a chance in hell," Lund said, and the conversation terminated.

Lund waited for ten minutes, until he was certain Smith was out of the building, before he summoned Jim Padgett and Elliott Parkhall to his office. He was in no mood to mince words.

"I've had a reporter in my office—Justin Smith. I'm certain you both know him, or know who he is. He said he has reliable information on findings from the flight data recorder. I want to know if either of you has been talking to him."

"No," Padgett said definitely.

Lund's eyes fell on Parkhall, whose upper lip had grown damp. He was fidgeting. "No, Vernon," Parkhall said. "I don't think I'd know Justin Smith if he walked in here right now. What . . . uh . . . what did he say he found out?"

Lund didn't answer the question. "Either of you been talking to the lab downtown about the flight data recorder?"

Both men nodded. "Last I heard, though, there was nothing very helpful coming out of it," Padgett said.

"Same here," said Parkhall.

"Smith thought there was something helpful," said Lund.

"What?" asked Padgett. "We need to know, if that's true."

Lund chewed on his lower lip as he contemplated the two men standing there. His natural bent was not to trust anybody, but he could think of no reasonable excuse to evade the question.

"Smith said the recorder's data show that the performance of Number Three engine wasn't consistent with a bird strike," he said.

"Nonsense!" Parkhall exploded. "That's perfect nonsense!"

"It seems to me if the lab had something like that, somebody would have called me—or you, Vernon," Padgett suggested. "Have you heard anything like that?"

"No," Lund said flatly.

"Then I wouldn't put much stock in it," the IIC said.

"Justin Smith is a good reporter," said Lund.

"That doesn't mean he's perfect."

Lund thought about that for a moment. Then he picked up his direct line to the NTSB downtown and dialed an extension. He talked to someone in tones so hushed that even in the small office neither Padgett nor Parkhall could make out exactly what he was saying, and both tried. The conversation lasted just short of four minutes. When Lund hung up, he swung his chair back to his two subordinates.

"Well," he said, "I guess it all depends on the spin you put on it."

Now Parkhall's face was sweating noticeably. "What do you mean?" he asked.

Lund frowned at him, wondering why his engineer was so nervous. Had he been a snitch for Smith after all? "It means some data could be interpreted as inconsistent with the ingestion of a bird, or any other debris, for that matter. But I'm told it's far from conclusive enough to warrant changing the course of the investigation."

"That's not very conclusive then," Padgett said. "That's good enough for me."

"Why can't they leave this alone?" Parkhall wondered aloud.

"Who?" asked Lund.

"The damned press," Parkhall said vehemently. "They keep trying to make trouble."

Padgett turned to his companion. "They're trying to do their job, Elliott," he said.

"This *isn't* their job," Parkhall insisted. "This isn't even close to their job." He looked at Lund. "Did you get the impression Smith was going to keep whipping this dead horse?"

"I don't think he's finished with it, no," Lund replied. "Although Lord knows I didn't give him any reason to carry on. I doubt if that will sway him."

Parkhall shoved his hands deep into his pockets. "They keep butting their noses in where they don't belong," he said. "They keep needling and nudging and pushing and shoving, trying to make the facts fit their own preconceptions. They're all trash, and we ought to wipe them out every time we catch them at it."

"In what way?" Padgett asked. "You want to repeal the First Amendment?"

"I wouldn't mind," Parkhall replied. "It would serve the sons of bitches right."

So high was Parkhall's level of outrage that something snapped. It happened between the time he got into his car outside the Dulles terminal and the time he reentered the gate to the field and Hangar 3. He wasn't going to let this situation get as volatile and dangerous as it had been with Steve Pace. It would stop now, today, before anything actually got into the *Times*. He couldn't risk another newspaper casting more doubt on the tentative conclusion of the NTSB investigation. One newspaper's thinly veiled allegations could be dismissed as vindictive. Two newspapers in bed together could be trouble.

In his makeshift office behind Hangar 3, Elliott Parkhall dialed the phone number at the infernal answering machine. No human being ever was there to answer. He wondered again where it was. In a closet somewhere? In a warehouse? Damn Sly anyway.

"Leave a message," the taped voice said curtly.

Parkhall did. The message was detailed. The order said the deed must be done this day.

"And this time," Parkhall concluded, "no rough stuff. I don't care how you do it, but make sure it looks like natural causes. That's the only way you get paid."

33

Wednesday, May 7th, 8:38 P.M.

Justin Smith stifled a yawn as he stepped out of the Woodley Park-National Zoo station of Washington's Metrorail subway system. It had been a long, nerve-racking day, the sort that let him feel all the weight of his forty-one years spent in the grinding competition of the newspaper business. He wasn't exaggerating it to Steve Pace; he was tired and ready to retire, preferably to a place where he would never have to deal with subway schedules and taxicabs again.

He grimaced when he recalled the cost of taking cabs to and from Dulles Airport earlier in the day—nearly a hundred dollars round trip, including tips, and the journey yielded virtually no new data on the ConPac crash.

Smith and his wife Margaret had lived in the Woodley Park area since moving to Washington from New York City

nineteen years earlier. They owned no car when they lived
in New York. There was no need, and no place to park,
anyway. They owned a two-bedroom condominium on the
upper East Side. He took the subway to his job at the *Times*
each day. She did her shopping in the grocery store half a
block from their condo building. Dry-cleaning pickup was
available in an ante room off the lobby. There were a dozen
good restaurants within a two-block radius. Subways and
cabs were readily available for evenings out farther from
home.

When they moved to Washington and sold their condo,
they bought a neo-Georgian brick townhouse built on 28th
Street in nineteen twenty-one. They also bought one car,
which Margaret Smith drove. Justin Smith used the nearby
Connecticut Avenue bus line to get to and from work each
day until the subway went by their neighborhood and cut
twenty-five minutes off the trip to the *Times*' downtown
office.

Over the years, they'd refurbished their home to totally
modern standards. The improvements and the proximity of
the house to the Metrorail Red Line, coupled with the
wildly volatile real estate market in the nation's capital over
the previous two decades, guaranteed the Smiths would
clear more than three-hundred-thousand dollars when he
retired and sold the property, more than enough to buy the
home of their dreams wherever they chose to go. Although
Smith could easily have paid for a second car for commut-
ing, his house had no garage, and street parking in the
neighborhood was so oversubscribed it took a miracle to
find one space, let alone two.

It was getting dark when Smith turned west off Connecticut Avenue onto Woodley. The mass of Wardman Tower,
the residential wing of the sprawling Washington Sheraton
Hotel, loomed to his left. This was a wonderfully rolling
landscape, well above the altitude of the working part of the
city. The air was fresher and cooler than downtown, and
people moved about the streets with energy. Occasionally,
Smith doubted he would leave when retirement time came.

Perhaps, he thought, he and Margaret could stay in their 28th Street home, and he could enjoy the neighborhood with the shops and restaurants he would like to know more intimately.

Smith was about to dart across Woodley and turn north onto 28th when he felt a hand on his arm. Even in this low-crime area, Smith tensed as he turned to look at the person on his right. The man was huge, tall and powerfully muscled, but he was smiling.

"Mr. Smith, sorry to startle you, but your friends at the NTSB sent me," the man said.

That sounded plausible, since the man knew the reporter by name and mentioned the agency that was preoccupying Smith's time. Still, this was a highly unusual way to make contact.

"Who specifically sent you?" he asked.

"Mr. Parkhall," the big man said. "Don't be alarmed. We can talk over here, privately."

He gestured to a darkened, brushy area about twenty feet off the sidewalk.

Smith shook his head. "I don't walk into bushes with people I don't know. Not under any circumstances," he said. "We can talk right here."

"As you wish," the man said. He glanced around, appearing to Smith to be checking for passersby who might overhear their conversation. And, in fact, Sylvester Bonaro was looking for potential witnesses, albeit not for the reason Smith surmised.

More quickly than Smith could possibly have ducked it, Bonaro's right fist snapped up and caught the reporter square on the chin, a sure knockout blow. No one on the street saw it. Bonaro blocked it from view with his massive body.

Quickly, with his left arm, he caught the sagging reporter, who was teetering on the edge of consciousness, and guided him into the darkness of the high bushes Smith had not wanted to approach. When they disappeared from street view, Bonaro let Smith's body slip to the ground. They were joined by another.

"Give me the kit," Bonaro whispered to his partner.

Wade Stock pulled a small black box from his jacket pocket and handed it over. By this time, Bonaro had Smith's right arm out of the sport coat and was unbuttoning the right shirt cuff. He took the box from Stock and set it on the ground beside Smith's lolling head. Then he shoved Smith's shirt-sleeve above the elbow.

"Give me some light here," Bonaro hissed.

Stock held a small, battery-powered flashlight close to Smith's arm and turned on the soft light. Bonaro took a rubber strap from the black box and lashed it tightly around the reporter's arm, about four inches above the elbow. He went back into the box and came out with a syringe and a small vial. In the dim light, he inserted the needle into the vial and withdrew fifty units of insulin. He put the vial back in the black box, gripped Smith's arm tightly at the elbow, and injected the insulin into a protruding vein.

He let the arm drop into the grass and untied the rubber strap. He put the syringe and the strap back into the box, which he snapped shut and returned to Stock. Then he pulled down Smith's sleeve and rebuttoned the cuff.

"Help me with the jacket," he told Stock.

The two wrestled Smith back into his sport coat, laid him back in the grass and waited. Within minutes, Smith went into a seizure, violent and brief. When his body relaxed, he was dead.

"Leave him right here," Bonaro said. "Make sure we aren't leaving anything behind, and check the grass."

By the light of the small flash, the two ruffled the grass where their shoes and knees had made impressions and backed away from the bushes. Stock hurried off down Woodley Avenue, disappearing among the happy strollers along Connecticut Avenue. Bonaro crossed Woodley and headed up 28th Street to the spot where he'd parked the blue Ford van with the damaged right side.

The irony was cruel. In a neighborhood where the shortage of street parking had limited Justin and Margaret Smith to one car, Bonaro had found a spot directly in front of their home.

Margaret Smith reported to District of Columbia police shortly after midnight that her husband was missing. She became frantic after calling the *Times* bureau about ten-thirty and talking to a late-working reporter who said her husband left about seven-thirty, give or take fifteen minutes.

It was too early for the police to express great concern. Many men were late getting home for many reasons. They would not count Justin Smith among the missing at least until the next morning. A detective took Margaret Smith's statement over the telephone, assured her that her husband probably would show up shortly, and ended the conversation.

Justin Smith was found at five-seventeen the next morning, when a jogger running through the Washington Sheraton grounds spotted his body in the bushes along Woodley Avenue. The runner thought he'd found a drunk sleeping it off and didn't stop to take a closer look. When he jogged by the hotel doorman, he shouted that a man was passed out up in the bushes and probably needed help.

The doorman called paramedics, who discovered the truth.

Smith carried plenty of identification, and police were ringing Margaret Smith's front door before six-thirty. Carl Remington, the *Times'* Washington editor, was awakened by Bethesda, Maryland, police half an hour later with the news. Remington immediately notified the *Times'* management in New York.

Meanwhile, after Margaret Smith identified her husband's body, it was transported to the D.C. morgue, where an autopsy was scheduled for that afternoon.

The autopsy would say exactly what Elliott Parkhall wanted it to say.

34

Steve Pace found out when he walked into the newsroom a
few hours after Margaret Smith positively identified her
husband's body. Glenn Brennan was sitting at Pace's desk.

"It isn't enough you've taken my beat, now you want my
desk, too?" Pace asked sourly.

Brennan moved to Jack Tarshis's chair. "Justin Smith
died last night," he said bluntly.

Pace could feel the blood drain from his face. He stared
at Brennan, certain his friend was telling the truth, yet desperate to believe it was another of Glenn's lousy jokes.

"We had lunch yesterday," Pace said, his voice barely
above a whisper.

"Greg Hayward called me about half an hour ago," Brennan said. Hayward was one of the *Times'* best congressional
reporters. He wouldn't be wrong about a thing like that.
"And it moved on the AP wire a few minutes ago," Brennan
added.

Pace sank into his chair. "How?" he asked.

Brennan shook his head. "Won't know until after the
autopsy this afternoon."

"What happened?" Pace pressed. He felt a chill, although
the newsroom's air conditioning wasn't running very high,
and a tingling sensation began among the hairs on the back
of his neck.

"The speculation is he had a heart attack or a stroke
walking home from the Woodley Park Metro stop," Brennan said. "A jogger found his body in some bushes about

twenty-five feet from the street. There's no sign of foul play. The cops are guessing he staggered into the bushes from the sidewalk and died there. The jogger thought he was a drunk and told the doorman at the Sheraton. EMTs found him after the doorman called it in."

"I don't believe this," Pace said. "It's too much of a coincidence."

Brennan did a double take. "What is?" he asked.

"Glenn, if I tell you something, will you promise not to go mouthing off to everybody in the newsroom?" Pace saw Brennan smile mischievously. "I mean it, damn it!" Pace insisted.

"Okay." Brennan nodded.

Pace glared at him. "Never mind," he said. "Forget it."

"Hey, I said okay," Brennan protested. "What's with you? I didn't know you and Justin were all that close."

"It's not like we were lifelong buddies," Pace acknowledged. "But we were friends. He told me the other day he was about to retire and that *Times* editors were talking about me."

"You'd leave here for the *Times*?" Brennan asked in disbelief.

Pace waved him off. "I haven't given it any thought," he said. "I haven't been offered anything, and under the current circumstances, I doubt I will be. But I appreciated him telling me. He also told me about an angle he was following on the Dulles accident."

Brennan closed his eyes and let his head fall back limply. "Oh, Jesus, not that again."

"That again," Pace confirmed. "That's why we had lunch. He wanted to tell me about it."

"He gave you his story?" Brennan asked incredulously. "Give me a break."

"No, he didn't give me his story," Pace snapped. "He was trying to tell me I wasn't the only one suspicious of the findings. He had some good tips involving material retrieved from the flight data recorder."

"And now the story belongs to you."

"No. I don't know who Justin's sources were. But the fact that he was poking around makes me wonder if he really died of natural causes."

"Oh, come on—" Brennan started to say, but Pace cut him off.

"When Justin left me at the Old Ebbitt yesterday, he was headed to Dulles to talk about his tip with Vernon Lund," Pace said. "Then all of a sudden he turns up dead. I don't buy it."

"I don't suppose you have any witnesses this time, to the fact that you and Justin had lunch together yesterday?" Brennan asked.

"Why would I need witnesses?"

"If you're going to Avery or Paul with this story, it will help to have somebody who can corroborate at least part of it. Otherwise it's gonna be like your answering-machine messages—your word against a total lack of evidence."

Pace shrugged. "I guess the restaurant can confirm Justin had reservations for two yesterday," he suggested.

"So what? That doesn't put you there."

"Our waiter might remember."

"And if he doesn't? That's a busy place."

"Well, Justin had an appointment with Vernon Lund."

"And you think Lund would confirm that, if Lund was involved in killing him?"

"All right, maybe not, but somebody at the *Times* bureau would know where Justin was yesterday afternoon."

"Maybe. If he told anybody."

Pace ran a hand through his hair. "Oh, man, I don't believe this," he said.

"It ain't fair," Brennan agreed, "but right now, it's so. If you're going to take this to Avery or Paul, you're going to have to bring evidence to back it up."

Brennan wandered off, and Pace reached for the telephone book. He would call the Old Ebbitt and see if he could find anyone who remembered him. It was too early for them to be busy. Somebody would have time to check yesterday's reservations and run down their waiter.

But when the phone book fell open to the blue pages of the District of Columbia's government listings, Pace got another idea.

"This is Steven Pace at the *Chronicle*. Could I have the medical examiner's office, please?"

The city operator who answered the call was singularly impertinent. "You can dial that number direct," she said.

"If I had the direct number, I would dial it," Pace replied. "Perhaps, if you'll connect me, the medical examiner will give me his number."

The city operator cut him off.

"Damn it!" Pace swore as he redialed. This time he got through.

"Can you tell me what your call is in reference to?" one of the ME's secretaries asked.

"It's about an autopsy today on a man named Justin Smith," Pace said.

"Oh, yes, we've had other calls about that," the secretary said. "I'm afraid Dr. Jackson isn't answering questions. You'll have to go through the regular public-information channels."

"I'm not asking for information," Pace said. "I'm calling to give Dr. Jackson some information pertinent to his investigation."

"You're not calling in reference to the results of the autopsy?"

"No. I think I already said that."

"Your name?"

The reporter left his name and phone number. The secretary said she would see that Dr. Jackson got the message.

And Pace sat back to wait.

The last three weeks had been the most bizarre in his life, he thought, from the highest highs to some pretty deep lows. People already were noticing his byline on stories that had nothing to do with airplanes and Glenn Brennan's name on Sexton stories, even though the two had switched assignments only two days earlier.

Kathy had called him at home the previous evening. She

sounded upset for him, and he tried to be philosophical. They talked all around what was on Steve's mind, and when he finally asked whether she was coming back, he didn't think he handled it as well as he wanted.

"Kath, I screwed this up," he told her. "The one thing I've been able to hold onto for the last few days is the hope we can put what we had back together again. It knocked me down hard when I came home and found you'd been there to get your things."

She didn't say anything for what seemed an eternity. When she finally gave him an answer, it was less than he'd hoped for, but more than he'd feared.

"I don't know that we have a future, Steve," she said. "I'm still trying to sort that out, to sort out how I feel."

"I didn't think you had any doubts," he said.

"There was a time when I didn't. But when you sent Sissy and me away . . . well, Sissy I could understand. You can't leave a kid alone in a situation like that, and her mother was panicky. But me? Why me? That was demeaning. To me, it read like a message that you think you have to take care of me. You don't. I've been making my own decisions for a long time, and making them rather well, and I resent you ordering me around."

"I didn't intend to order you to do anything, although looking back on it, I can see how you'd interpret it that way at the time. I didn't give you much opportunity for discussion. Would it help to say I'm deeply and abidingly sorry?"

"Sure, it helps, but it doesn't solve anything. I'm afraid chivalry is a part of your character, and while it's very romantic and decent of you, it's misguided when I'm involved. You can say you're sorry. You can promise it won't happen again. But if it's part of your thirty-nine-year-old nature, you might be beyond changing. Besides, I have no right to try to change you. You are who you are, a good and special person. I don't have a right to tell you to be a different person for me."

"Would it help if I try to change—not because you want me to, but because I want to? And if I was trying because

I wanted to, you could kick my butt any time you noticed backsliding."

She laughed lightly; the sound thrilled him. Too soon she was serious again. "Do you think you could keep that promise?"

"I'm willing to try."

She asked for more time, and he gave it to her willingly. To refuse would be to lose her, and any alternative was better than that.

He was thinking about all that when Clay Helm called, a few minutes before Pace had to leave the office to cover a press conference at the Republican National Committee. He told the Virginia cop he was in a hurry.

"What I have will be worth your time," Helm said. "I've got *news*. You interested?"

"Yeah, I guess," Pace said.

"Okay. We've got this forensic technologist in our lab, a real bulldog when it comes to staying with a case as long as there's hope for a solution. We told her to let the Antravanian thing be, that the file was open but it wasn't a front-burner kind of thing, you know?"

"Yeah."

"She was so intrigued by the case that she started putting in her own time—lunch hours, a little time after work, that sort of thing. She went over that hulk inch by inch, and yesterday she found a paint sample from the driver's side of the car that didn't match the paint samples taken from other areas on the body. There were similar elements, but they weren't the same."

"What are you getting at, Clay?"

"The inconsistent sample is a possible match for a Ford blue."

Pace felt his pulse jump. "A Ford blue applied to late-model vans, by any chance?"

"Among other models, yes."

"And this leaves us where?"

"Well, our tech says she could make a definite match if she had a paint sample from the van in question."

"We don't have the van in question."

"No, we don't. But if you should see the van again, I'd suggest getting paint from the damaged area."

"Can I bring you the moon and the stars while I'm at it?"

"No, I wouldn't have any place to keep them."

Pace had just put the phone down when it rang again. It was Dr. Emil Jackson, the District of Columbia medical examiner.

"This is highly unusual," the doctor said.

"It's a highly unusual situation," Pace replied. "Have you performed the autopsy on Justin Smith yet?"

"No, I'm about to begin."

"Doctor, would you check carefully for signs of violence? I think—"

"Now see here, young man," Jackson interrupted. "The District of Columbia police don't suspect anything but natural causes, and I take my lead from them."

"I know what the police suspect," Pace insisted. "And I know why they suspect it, but they don't have some of the information I do. Mr. Smith was a reporter for *The New York Times*. He was working on a dangerous story. I think somebody killed him."

"And you haven't told this to the police?" Jackson sounded incredulous.

"I just found out Justin's dead," Pace replied. "I plan to go to the police today."

"There isn't any outward sign of violence," Jackson said.

"But you and I both know there are ways of killing people to make it look natural."

"Mr. Pace, you've been reading too many detective thrillers."

"You could be right, Doctor," the reporter said. "But please keep an open mind."

Jackson didn't promise anything. But an hour later, with Justin Smith's body lying on the cold metal autopsy table, the medical examiner took special care to preserve a generous blood sample . . . just in case.

The next shocker of the day was waiting for Pace when he returned from the press conference at the Republican National Committee. It was a message from Sexton's vice-president for public affairs, Whitney Warner. He returned the call.

"Steve, God, it's good to hear from you," she said.

"It's—"

"No, hey, let me finish my little spiel here before you say anything. First of all, it was absolutely horrible of me not to call as soon as I heard you were in the hospital. Things were going fits around here, but that's not any excuse. I feel terrible about it, and I'm deeply sorry. I'm also devastated to hear you're not going to be covering aviation anymore. I want to hear every last detail of what happened. First of all, how are you?"

Pace deliberately hesitated for a second. "Uh, oh, me? You want me to talk now?"

"Yes, smarty, it's your turn."

He smiled. "I'm fine. All the cuts are healing and the bruises are in that final, ugly yellow stage. Most of the damage left isn't visible to the naked eye."

"Is there a lot of that kind of damage?"

"Some. It will go away, too. In time."

"Can you tell me everything that happened?"

"I don't think you want to hear it all."

"I do. Oh, maybe not all the lurid details of the beating, but everything else. Especially why those boneheads you work for took you off the beat."

Pace told her most of it, concentrating on his conviction that a conspiracy was in play that cost the lives of Mark Antravanian and Mike McGill, and maybe now Justin Smith. He assured her he never suspected that her company had any role in the plot.

"So that's why I'm not on the beat anymore," he concluded. "I kept running around accusing people of murder and assorted cover-ups without evidence, just hunches. That's frowned on in the civilized world, and in the newspaper business, too."

"Lord, what an awful period for you," Warner replied. "I don't know how you managed to keep your sanity."

"There are those who think I didn't."

"Oh, you did. You sound like you're doing fine sanity-wise. You know there's something that, well . . . oh, never mind."

"What?" Pace chuckled. Warner was not one to be at a loss for words.

"This is almost too weird."

"Whitney, you and I have never had secrets."

"Sure we have," she said, her tone lightening. "But they were so secret, you never knew about them."

"I'll phrase it another way. Is something on your mind?"

"Yes, maybe. It's something that didn't mean anything to me. I mean, it meant more to Dave Terrell than it did to me. I only cared because David did. I didn't think it was very important, to be honest. Oh, I don't think he thought it was important, either. It just bothered him."

"What the hell are you babbling about?"

"Wait, let me get out my calendar here. I don't want to be wrong about dates."

Pace waited. He heard the sound of papers shuffling and pages turning. The Sexton vice-president was searching her ever-cluttered desk for something.

"Here it is," she said finally. "Okay, here it is. It isn't much, I don't think, but in context with your suspicions, it's damned scary."

"What, Whit? Will you get on with it!"

"The crash happened April seventeenth just before eleven A.M., local time, right?"

"Right."

"That's eight A.M. here."

"Yeah, right. Where are you going with this?"

"Bear with me, Steve. I've got to take this a step at a time because I'm thinking on my feet here. So it's eight A.M. here. We hurry, hurry, hurry and put our own team together to get to the crash site. We need Dave Terrell because he was one of the chief engineers on the Eight-eleven project. Ah, you know him, don't you?"

"Sure. We met when I did the stories on the Eight-eleven, before it went on the line. And I talked to Dave at Dulles once or twice after the accident. He didn't have much to say."

"I don't think he knew anything," Warner said. "Anyhow, at the time of the crash, thank God, Dave and some of the other key engineers were already in Washington for a congressional hearing, so they shot right out to Dulles. I think they were credentialed and on the field by three p.m."

"That sounds reasonable."

"Well, there wasn't much they could do in those first hours," Warner explained. "I mean, they watched the fire and rescue people do their thing, and chatted up some of the NTSB and FAA people on the scene, letting everybody know they were there and eager to help. But there wasn't any real investigative work to do. So when the starboard engine and what was left of the starboard wing were secured, Dave walked out to have a look at them and to do what he could to help identify bits and pieces lying around."

"What are you trying to tell me?"

"Well, there was a lot going on. Dave didn't know exactly what he was looking for, and everything was burned, so it could have been hard to spot. He might have missed it."

"Missed what?" Warner didn't usually circle tough subjects; she'd home in and attack head-on. So Pace found her hesitation maddening.

"Feathers, blood, some sign of a bird strike."

All of a sudden, Pace felt a hollow sensation in his chest, the sort of reaction one gets when the heart goes on holiday in the throat without warning.

"I'm not sure I'm following your implications, Whit," he said, trying to keep the astonishment out of his voice.

"Well, talking about it afterward, Dave was more embarrassed than anything else. He said he thought he must be getting old. I figured it was the confusion, but now I think maybe it was something else. Steve, Dave said he didn't see any signs of a bird strike. No blood, no gore, no bones, no feathers, no nothing. The question is, if it wasn't there on Thursday afternoon, how come it was there on Friday morning?"

35

Friday, May 9, 9:30 A.M.

"Steve, this is the *Chronicle* switchboard," a woman's voice said. "I have a call for you from a gentleman who identified himself as Emil Jackson. Do you want me to patch him through?"

Pace, who was walking out his front door when the phone rang, felt his heart leap. "Yes!" he said emphatically. "By all means."

There was a click. "Mr. Pace?"

"This is Steven Pace, yes."

"Doctor Jackson, medical examiner's office."

"Yes, sir?"

"I'm sorry to bother you so early," the doctor said. "I called you at the office, but they said you weren't in yet, and I'm headed into a long series of meetings. They wouldn't give me your home phone number."

"That's company policy," Pace said. "You're not bothering me at all."

"I would have called back yesterday, but I wanted to run some tests on Mr. Smith's remains, and the results didn't reach my desk until this morning. I'm afraid the findings don't fit your suspicions. We scanned for a good number of poisons, and all the tests came up negative."

"Then what killed him?"

"It's hard to say. There were no obvious abnormalities of the brain, no obstructions of coronary arteries. Mr. Smith was in fine physical condition as far as we could determine. The best bet is an arrhythmia resulting in a heart attack, in layman's terms."

"Why can't you be certain?"

"These things are not always easy. There was nothing about the condition of his heart that would lead one to expect an episode of arrhythmia. Yet these things do sometimes happen. We will be signing this off as natural causes."

"I still don't buy that, Doctor, especially in light of Justin's condition," Pace said. "What if something other than poison was used?"

"I can't test for every known substance in the world," Jackson said defensively.

"Even if you suspect murder?"

"I don't suspect murder. You do."

"Damn," Pace said softly.

"Um, there is one thing, Mr. Pace," Jackson said. "Do you know if Mr. Smith had given blood lately?"

"I have no idea. Why?"

"Well, I can have the police check with his widow."

"Why?" Pace asked again.

"It isn't anything conclusive, or even very meaningful, but I did find what I believe is a needle mark in front of the elbow of his right arm."

Pace walked into the *Chronicle* newsroom twenty minutes later, sat down at his desk and reached for the telephone to call Ken Sachs. It rang in the same moment.

"Pace."

"Steve?"

"Yes."

"This is Sylvia Levinson, Ken Sachs's secretary. Could you hold for the chairman, please?"

Involuntarily, Pace pulled the receiver down and stared at it in utter disbelief, then put it back to his ear.

"Uh, sure, Sylvia. Sure."

"Thank you." There was a small laugh in her tone.

"Steve, this is Ken Sachs."

"Funny thing. I was about to call you."

"Yes, well, I'm not surprised. Thought I'd hear from **you** earlier, as a matter of fact."

"Indeed?"

"I got a phone call at home last night—I get a lot of distractions at home where you're concerned. It was from a friend of yours, I believe. Whitney Warner, a vice-president of Sexton."

"Whit called you? Why?"

"Same reason you were going to call. She told me about your conversation yesterday. At least she told me what Dave Terrell told her. She said that after talking to you, it seemed a lot more important, especially in the context of new information you have from the police about Mark Antravanian's death. I'm up to speed on Dave Terrell's story. Suppose you bring me up to speed on the Antravanian matter."

God bless you, Whit.

Pace was especially careful not to embellish anything and to make it perfectly clear there was no positive ID on the paint sample as a Ford blue, nor would it be clear, even if the sample turned out to be a Ford blue, that it came from the suspicious van.

"Hum, yes," Sachs said noncommittally when Pace finished. "I suppose you have an idea of what you'd like to do next."

"I'd like to look at the engine. I'm not putting myself forward as somebody who could find evidence that trained aviation investigators couldn't see, but they weren't looking for the same thing I'm looking for."

"What exactly is it you're looking for?"

"Something inconsistent with the notion that a bird flew into the engine and began a chain reaction that tore the thing apart."

"You know I'm not happy with this," Sachs said. "NTSB investigations are inviolate. We don't let outsiders in because we don't want the purity of the investigative process tainted in any way. Yet I'm calling you because of Whitney Warner, the consummate outsider in a case like this, an outsider with a vested interest. And you! Christ, you're so far outside you're not on the same planet. Letting you anywhere near the engine goes against everything I know, everything I believe, against all my instincts."

"But you're going to do it anyway?" Pace asked hopefully.

"Yes, damn it, I'm going to do it anyway, because this is outside the realm of anything I know, everything I believe, and my instincts tell me I have no choice. Lund and Padgett will scream their bloody heads off, and I'll have to find a way to deal with that."

"I appreciate it," Pace said sincerely. "When can I get access to the hangar?"

"I'm going with you, and I can do it this afternoon if you can."

"I'll be there. Where should I meet you?"

"In the lobby of the Dulles Marriott at two. We'll leave your car in the lot and take mine so it won't be a hassle getting past the gate. You know I hate this, don't you Pace? I hate it because of what it signifies and because it's you."

"I can understand on both counts."

Pace was surprised at how easily he got a few hours' leave. It was a slow day for general-assignment work, and Wister agreed to let him take some of his amassed overtime in comp time. But, true to form, the national editor got in a lick for procedures. "Next time," he told Pace, "remember to ask for comp time in writing at least forty-eight hours before you want to take it." Pace left the office before Wister could change his mind and was twenty minutes early getting to Dulles.

The nondescript white sedan with the U.S. Government license plates pulled into the parking lot fifteen minutes later. Pace recognized Sachs at the wheel, alone in the car. Pace got out of his own car and walked up to the sedan before Sachs had time to park and get out. He knocked on the passenger-side window. Sachs leaned over and opened the door.

"Get in," the chairman ordered. He didn't offer his hand. Then, "There are terms," he said.

"What?"

"I don't think they'll give you a problem. If there's a story here, it's yours. I'll see to that. I'd owe you that much. You'll have it alone. In return, however, I call all the shots. If we find anything, I alone decide what action to take, when it will be taken, and when it's time to go public with it. I won't put this car into gear unless you agree. You can get out and walk away, and I'll proceed with this thing alone. Or you stay and, in essence, take orders from me."

"All right. I'll do it your way."

"I thought you would," Sachs said smugly. He keyed the ignition and pulled away toward the Dulles terminal. "Avery Schaeffer made the same decision."

Pace whipped around to face Sachs. "What are you talking about?" he demanded.

"I called him after we talked this morning," the NTSB chairman said in a tone that indicated it was no big deal.

"Avery knows where I am?"

"And what you're doing."

They entered the hangar a few minutes later, and Pace was struck by the sheer size of the place, more still by the enormity of the task facing the NTSB. As vast as the hangar was, the remnants of the huge jetliner consumed most of the floor space.

"They take up a lot more room when they're still in one piece and standing on all three legs," Sachs commented.

"Yeah, I guess so," Pace responded lamely.

"Let's get started," Sachs said. "Although I have to tell you, I hope there's nothing new here to find."

Pace shoved his hands deep into his pockets. His eyes dropped.

"What's wrong?" Sachs asked. He got no answer. "Steve?"

"The night Mike asked me to go with him to meet his anonymous caller, he said something like that, about how we might have hopes for different outcomes. I was looking for a big story. What he wanted was for it to turn out to be nothing, for the integrity of the system to stand up."

"You and he were close, weren't you?"

"Yes," Pace said. "For a lot of years."

"Mike and Mark were good men, and that's a nice epitaph when you think about it."

Picking through the debris, they started toward the back of the hangar, where the Number 3 engine was waiting.

"Are any of the investigators still around?" Pace asked.

Sachs shook his head. "The power-plants team left yesterday. Lund's back downtown. Jim Padgett's still around, but I don't know if he's actually on the field. I left a message that we were coming, so he'll show up."

They stood shoulder-to-shoulder in front of the maw that had been the intake end of the huge Converse Fan. There were shards of metal and dangling wires and hoses everywhere.

"How does anybody make anything of this?" Pace marveled. "I saw you guys do it in Sioux City, and I still don't believe it."

"We're looking for inconsistencies," said Sachs. "Anything that doesn't look right."

"None of it looks right."

"You know what I mean."

And so they looked. A half hour turned into an hour and then into ninety minutes, and they found nothing that didn't have a reasonable explanation. They talked about possibilities. The conversations were increasingly technical, and eventually beyond Pace's knowledge of jet-engineering technology. If there was anything there, it was little wonder the experts didn't spot it.

And it wasn't pleasant work. Some of the remains of the bird had been removed for identification that ultimately showed the unfortunate creature to have been a hawk. But most of the bits and pieces of feather, flesh and bone—many of them burned—still adhered on flat surfaces and in crevasses beyond reach. Dried blood was sprayed widely.

Pace stepped back from the engine to stretch neck and shoulder muscles cramped by the odd angles at which he'd been twisted as he looked over as much of the inside of the engine carcass as he could reach. The intake looked like the mouth of an old man with most of his teeth missing. Many of the fan blades had been shattered by the impacts, first with the hawk, then with the ground. Of the surviving blades, seven were smeared or dotted with blood. The bird probably died on initial impact, a millisecond before its body was chopped to bits. It never knew what hit it.

Sachs stepped back to join him, also rubbing cramped muscles.

"You see anything at all?" Pace asked with some hope but no expectations.

"Not really," Sachs said. "But I've got to tell you, something doesn't feel right."

"What?"

"I don't know. I can't put my finger on it. I expected to find inconsistencies. If I believed this bird strike was real, as our investigators did, nothing would look out of the ordinary. But looking at this mess with doubts in my mind . . . oh, hell, I don't know. Something is reinforcing those doubts, but I don't know what it is."

"I'll be damned if I see it, either," Pace admitted. He turned his back on the engine. "I keep thinking, what should Dave Terrell have seen that night if this was a bird strike? I look at the blood on those blades up there, and I think, shouldn't he have seen that? But maybe the dried, burned blood looked like dried mud. Who could tell? And now, after the investigators have been all through the engine and cleaned it up some, who knows how much bird gore there was to see? A hawk is a big bird, but its pieces could get lost pretty easily in an engine this size. Maybe Terrell didn't see anything because the evidence wasn't all that obvious."

"Maybe," Sachs agreed. He moved back to the engine, beckoning Pace to follow him. He continued his thought. "But look here, around the stumps of the broken blades. There's more blood. Out here, in the front of the engine, where the bird hit. It looks obvious to me."

"When you know what you're looking at, it's obvious. To a casual observer—"

"I don't think under any circumstance you would describe Terrell as a casual observer."

Ken Sachs continued to stare at the engine's front rim. Pace started to say something, but Sachs waved him quiet. So, for the next twenty seconds or so, Pace watched Sachs watching the engine. Finally, the NTSB chairman turned around slowly.

"I know what's bothering me," he said. "You helped me define it."

Pace gave him a questioning shrug. "What?"

"This plane is doing a hundred sixty knots or more and here comes the hawk." Sachs began pacing back and forth in front of the intake, his hands doing graphics for his speech. "Splat. Hawk meets spinning fan blades. End of hawk."

"So?"

"A lot of the mass of the bird should have been dissipated by the initial impact, shouldn't it? I mean, suppose you've got a twelve-pound bird to begin with. After the impact and the blade action, the pieces sucked in shouldn't weigh anything more than a few ounces at most, and those should have been easily diverted around the turbine housing and out the back of the engine pod."

Pace tried to anticipate where Sachs was going. "That's been the question, whether the Converse diversion design works," he said. "All of it, including the fan blades, should have been diverted—"

"No, no, no," Sachs interrupted. "You're not following me. The ingestion of the fan blades is something else. You're talking about huge pieces of alloy. I'm talking about tiny pieces of bird. The dynamics of the fan blades would be on the opposite end of the scale from the dynamics of little pieces of flesh and bone and feathers."

"And?" Pace waited.

"Most of the remains of the bird should have blown around the turbine housings, right?"

"I guess so," Pace replied. "Yes."

"Then why is there so much fucking bird gore in this engine?" Sachs asked. "Where in hell did it all come from?"

Pace stared at Sachs in silence for a moment. They were on the same track, at last. "Playing devil's advocate," he said, "what if the bird was somehow impaled on a broken blade, so it got sucked into the turbine area more or less whole, and then got shredded by a rotating disk?"

"Then why is there so much blood on the front of the intake?" Sachs asked, shaking his head. "The impact and the ingestion would have happened too fast for the bird to have bled all over everything like this."

Pace looked back at the maw of the engine, at the unbroken fan blades hanging from their mountings. "Ken, where are the blades that broke away?"

Now it was Sachs's turn not to understand. "I don't know. They were recovered. They've got to be around here somewhere. Why?"

Pace moved off quickly, his head turning left and right. "Just help me find them."

It was the easiest task of the afternoon. The splintered, shredded fan blades were stacked in a corner of the hangar, stored there without apparent purpose. Eventually they would be shipped back to Converse, where engineers would assess their failure and try to improve the blades' design and, perhaps, their tolerance for bird strikes.

"Can I touch these things?" Pace asked excitedly.

"Tell me why?" Sachs ordered.

"Blood. I'm looking for blood. There's blood all over the goddamned place, all over the guts of the engine, all over the surviving fan blades, all over the rim of the intake. There should be blood on these things, too, shouldn't there? Somewhere in here are the blades the bird hit. Shouldn't there be some trace of blood here?"

Sachs nodded, seeing exactly where Pace was leading. "Let's look together," he said. "They're heavy as hell, and the edges are sharp as razors."

The job took more than an hour, largely because of a dramatic interruption.

Pace and Sachs had examined about a third of the broken fan blades when Jim Padgett walked into the hangar. Sachs introduced him to Pace.

"I know who he is," Padgett said coolly. "He has a phone call."

"Here?" Pace asked.

"Right here," said Padgett. "It's your office."

Pace took the call at an extension in the hangar. "I didn't think you'd want to wait for this one," Glenn Brennan said at the other end. "Dr. Jackson called for you. I was sitting at your desk when the call came. The good doctor is very agitated. He wants you to call him right away."

"How'd you find me?" Pace asked.

"Paul knew where you could be reached."

Pace smiled. And it was Paul, he thought, who'd given him all the crap about asking for comp time forty-eight hours in advance. He must have loved that little charade.

Pace took the number from Brennan and called the medical examiner. Jackson came to the phone immediately. "You still haven't called the police," he said.

"I haven't had a chance," Pace replied honestly. "From what you told me, there didn't sound like much reason to hurry."

"There is now," Jackson said. "It tweaked me a little when you pointed out I'd only tested for poisons and not for anything that could make death look natural. So I sat down and thought about ways you could kill someone without being detected. There aren't many, you know."

Pace was listening intently. "And you found something?"

"I tested a few theories and, yes, I found something. You

remember the Von Bulow case?"

"Vaguely," Pace said.

"Oh, well, that's not important. But it's what prompted me to test for insulin."

"Insulin?" Pace asked. "That's for diabetes. Justin didn't have diabetes, did he?"

"No," Jackson said. "But his bloodstream was loaded with insulin "

"Paint me a layman's picture, Doctor," Pace said.

"In its natural form, insulin is produced by the pancreas and regulates blood-sugar levels. If your pancreas doesn't produce insulin—or doesn't produce enough—blood sugar goes up, sometimes way up, and the result after a period of time can be heart attacks, stroke, blindness, gangrene, any one of a number of pretty horrible side effects. That's why diabetics take insulin, either orally or subcutaneously, so they get what they need that their bodies aren't providing."

"And?"

"If I were going to check your blood sugar, I would tell you not to eat or drink anything after dinner, and to come in for the blood test about eight or nine the next morning. That's called a fasting blood-sugar. I would expect, under normal circumstances, to find anywhere from six to twenty-six micro-units of insulin in your blood. Justin Smith's stomach was empty, suggesting he hadn't eaten in six or seven hours. His natural insulin level should have been down near the fasting level. But when I checked, his reading was ninety micro-units per cc. That's off the scale. Coupled with the needle mark on his arm, I would say he was injected with fifty to fifty-five units of insulin intravenously."

"And that would—"

"You're not supposed to take insulin intravenously," Jackson continued. "That would make an overdose even worse. Fifty to fifty-five units would have dropped his blood sugar too low for the body to survive it. Within minutes of the injection, he would have gone into seizure and died."

"You think that's what happened?" Pace asked.

"With a reading of ninety micro-units on an empty stomach? Yes, I think that's what happened. I'm certain enough that I would testify in a court of law."

Pace whistled softly. "Why didn't you find this during the original autopsy?" he asked, more curious than accusatory.

"It's not among the things we normally test for," Jackson said. "I wouldn't have spotted the needle mark, at least I wouldn't have had second thoughts about it, if you hadn't asked me to watch for anything suspicious. And I wouldn't have tested for insulin if you hadn't goaded me."

So there it was, all laid out in a nicely corroborated package. Justin Smith becomes suspicious of the bird-strike theory. He takes his suspicions to Vernon Lund. And the same night he winds up dead of an injected overdose of insulin, administered to make death look natural.

Grimly, Pace told Sachs and Padgett of the medical examiner's findings.

"What are these people trying to hide?" a stunned Ken Sachs demanded. "Who are they?"

"Well, Justin did come out here that day to see Vernon Lund," Pace said.

"No," Padgett responded. "With all due respect, Ken, Vernon Lund isn't capable of ordering dinner without help, let alone somebody's murder. And he wasn't the only one who knew Justin was here and what he wanted."

"Oh?"

"Sometime after Justin left, Vernon called me in to discuss the *Times*' allegations. Elliott Parkhall was there, too."

"Parkhall's the one who strikes me as a little wimp," Sachs said.

"The whole time we're talking to Mr. Lund, Elliott is sweating and getting real jumpy," Padgett said. "Then he starts raving about the press sticking its nose in where it doesn't belong. He was quite agitated. Near as I can recall, he said something like, 'They're all trash, and we ought to wipe 'em out every time we catch 'em at it.' "

"Jesus," Sachs said. "You don't suppose he took himself literally?"

"I wouldn't bet against it," Pace said.

Padgett was eager to get involved, so Sachs explained their theory about the amount of bird in the engine.

"That's the most unbelievable thing I ever heard," the IIC responded. "The power-plants team would have noticed."

"Not necessarily," Sachs said. "Not if they were accepting at face value what was given to them. There's bird all over the engine, therefore there must have been a bird strike. How much bird there is becomes irrelevant. It's there. You accept that as a given and go on."

Padgett nodded his understanding. "So what are you looking for in this pile of blades?"

"More blood," Sachs said. "As my able colleague pointed out, if there was a bird strike, somewhere in here are the blades the bird actually hit. They should have blood on them. And other blades should be as splattered with blood as those still attached to the fan."

"Sounds reasonable," Padgett acknowledged.

And so the three of them looked. They looked carefully, at everything. A few times they thought they'd found something, but the smears turned out to be caked mud or dried muddy water. At the end of an hour, they'd been through the entire pile, and there wasn't a trace of blood anywhere in it.

Padgett got up from his crouch. "I don't even want to begin to believe this," he said.

Sachs stood up beside him. "Neither do I. But I don't think I have any choice. I think it's likely that whoever sprayed the bird gore in the engine missed these blades because they were still scattered all to hell-and-gone around the airport property. Our conspirators couldn't find them."

Padgett and Pace both nodded.

"Jim, I want these blades moved downtown to the lab right away in a locked and guarded vehicle," Sachs ordered. "I want every surface, every edge, gone over by every scientific means at our disposal. I don't want there to be even a single, remote, one-in-a-million chance that some evidence of the hawk is overlooked. And you don't have to explain to anyone why we're looking. Tell them I authorized the examination and if anybody has any questions, they can call me. When you get the blades out, I want this hangar sealed until further notice. Armed guards around the perimeter. Nobody gets in or out without your authorization and mine. They have to have both, okay?"

Padgett nodded.

Sachs watched the IIC depart and folded his arms, as though he felt a chill. "Well, the investigation was never closed, so I guess it wouldn't be right to say it's been re-opened," he said. "But it's certainly gone off on a new tangent."

"Not to be parochial about this, Ken, but when can I write the story? Once word gets out that Justin Smith was murdered, everybody's going to be turning over rocks."

Sachs gave him a rueful smile. "You can be parochial all you want. That's your job. You can write the story as soon as the lab finishes examination of the blades. I'll call you personally, and I promise you at least a full twenty-four hours alone with the story. If the lab doesn't find any more than we found, it will be conclusive in my eyes that we've got a problem here. Fair enough?"

"Fair enough, if it doesn't leak before you call me."

"It won't leak. You, Jim and I are the only ones who know, and Jim and I aren't going to talk to anybody. It won't leak from the lab, because nobody at the lab will know why they're checking the blades. You're safe."

"Sounds like it," Pace agreed.

"I wish I could say the same for the traveling public."

"What do you mean?"

Sachs looked positively grim. "Maybe it didn't occur to you," he said. "In addition to having a conspiracy on our hands, we're back to square one in this hangar. If there was no bird strike, we don't know what caused this crash, and we don't know it won't happen again."

BOOK THREE

36

Wednesday, May 14th, 11:13 A.M.

The floor of the United States Senate chamber was placid. Clerks and pages stood in place because the Senate was in session, though only in an official sense. The junior senator from Florida sat in the presiding officer's chair, a duty he assumed because it was a trivial job at this hour, and when the job was trivial, those lowest in seniority were expected to assume it. Presiding over the Senate during the period called Morning Business involved recognizing members who wished to have the floor, and helping rule on questions of parliamentary procedure. The questions of parliamentary procedure arising during Morning Business were never of any consequence. A high-school student-body president could have handled it.

In the rear corners of the chamber and at the doors to the cloakrooms, Senate aides with the heady prerogative to be on the Senate floor clustered to bask in the reflected glow of each other's power and privilege. They might have been discussing matters as important as appropriations bills, but more likely it was one of the three S subjects: sports, scandals, or sex. Sharp eyes could pick out seven senators, each awaiting his or her turn to read into the official Senate record a speech carefully crafted to stroke the sensibilities of the folks back home. Since no specific issue was before the Senate at the moment, there were no constraints on the subject matter the senators chose to address. A visitor could come away with the impression the Senate heard nothing but occasional lectures on the value of farm subsidies, or the dangers of nuclear space garbage, or the progress of trans-Arctic dogsled treks, or the virtues of Billy Bob Keckaman, who had been selling electric widgets from exactly the same electric widget stand in Thumbsucker, Alabama, for sixty-four years without a dissatisfied customer.

If there was any substance at all, a speech might draw a reporter from a home-state newspaper. If the home-state newspapers didn't have Washington correspondents, the duty to chronicle the oratory fell to a junior wire-service reporter, as the job of presiding over these speeches fell to a junior senator.

The Senate chamber occupies the second floor of the Capitol. Above it, on the third level, are balconies, called galleries, reserved for the media, visitors, and senators' families. There was a time when a senator could see if he or she was being chronicled by glancing up at the press gallery and counting noses, but that was no longer the case. Many reporters preferred to sit in the comfortable third-floor press room behind the gallery and monitor the floor action via closed-circuit television, called C-Span II. And since C-Span was on cable television, reporters without other business at the Capitol could sit in their offices, or even at home, and report on the day in Congress.

But this day was one of the rarities. On this morning, the media and visitors' galleries were filled. None of the business on the Senate floor appeared unusual, but Senator Harold Marshall had asked for five minutes during Morning Business. His appearance was gleefully anticipated. He was well known as the product of and the able spokesman for the Converse Corporation. After the long story in the morning's *Chronicle,* it was almost inevitable that Marshall would have something to say and that his legendary temper would be on high burn.

Marshall had not yet taken the floor, and in the media galleries, reporters were studying copies of the *Chronicle,* trying to digest every nuance of Steve Pace's story. It was bannered across the top of page one and was as astounding as some of the old Watergate stories.

NTSB Reopens Dulles Probe Amid New Suspicions

Bird-strike theory
now in doubt as new
evidence uncovered

The story disclosed the NTSB's laboratory found no
trace of flesh, feathers, or blood on any of the fan blades
broken in the accident and recovered away from the main
body of the engine. Nonetheless, the engine was filled with
bird remains. Investigators speculated that the evidence was
planted. The story quoted one investigator, who was not
named, as telling the NTSB he looked at the engine on the
afternoon of the crash and saw no evidence of a bird strike.
The story also disclosed that the leaders of the investigation
were not informed until the day after the accident of a
substance, believed to be the remains of a large bird, found
inside the engine. That information was made public the
same afternoon. The sudden new interest in the accident
was another in a series of strange occurrences surrounding
the crash.

In a sidebar, Pace retold the story of the deaths of Mark
Antravanian and Mike McGill, bringing up to date the
police investigation of both cases. He also wrote of Justin
Smith's death, reported as a murder earlier in the week by
all the Washington media. But for the first time, the killing
was linked directly to Smith's suspicions that a cover-up
clouded the investigation of the ConPac crash.

Officially, the NTSB, the Sexton Aircraft Corporation,
and the Converse Corporation were declining comment. It
was, all in all, a compelling read.

Steve Pace was not in the press gallery to cover Harold
Marshall's speech. He could have appropriated the story,
but he and Paul Wister agreed he could accomplish more by
staying in touch with the NTSB and the police. Jillian
Hughes was in the gallery for the *Chronicle*. She was fielding
all sorts of questions from her dumbfounded colleagues, but
she was able to add nothing to what her newspaper printed,

because she knew nothing more. She had no idea where Pace's information came from or where he was going with it. Other reporters told her the NTSB was declining all comment on the *Chronicle* story. They were frustrated, and she understood. But she could offer no help, and would not have done so in any event.

A murmur of "There he is" rolled along the gallery desks as Marshall strode onto the floor from the Republican cloakroom. Hughes knew Glenn Brennan, probably along with a few dozen other reporters, was stationed in the cloakroom to catch the Ohio senator both before and after his speech. She wondered if they got anything but bluster.

No one had the floor, so Marshall marched to his desk amid the other mismatched desks. With one exception, that of the senior senator from Delaware, all the desks were the originals that had come to the Senate chamber as each new state was admitted to the Union. Marshall's dated back to the early nineteenth century. The old furniture was non-utilitarian at best, but that didn't matter. Senators spent very little time at them and did no work there. Marshall clipped a small microphone to the breast pocket of his suit coat and asked to be recognized. The junior senator from Florida acknowledged the request and recognized Marshall for the standard five minutes. Had the Ohioan chanced to glance up, he would have seen that this was to be the best-covered piece of Morning Business of this Congress. But Marshall had no use for the media, not on this day.

"Thank you, Madam President. I rise this morning in a sense of outrage at the scurrilous accusations made in a newspaper I refuse to name. It deserves no publicity for its mendacious conduct in ignoring all relevant facts in order to score a cheap exclusive that bears no resemblance to the truth as we know it." Marshall's face was pinched in the same fury reflected in his voice.

A Utah reporter whom Hughes knew only slightly leaned toward her and whispered, "When you don't like the message, you blame the messenger, right?" She waved him quiet.

Marshall continued. "There is no mystery about the tragic crash of ConPac Flight Eleven-seventeen at Dulles Airport last month. I do not believe there is anyone here among us who would not take whatever action he could, at whatever cost, to go back in time and reverse history. But we cannot bring back the dead. That is not within the power of even this august body. It will not do anyone any good at all for the media to persist in sniping at the ghosts of some imagined conspiracy. It serves only to perpetuate the pain of those left behind by the victims of Flight Eleven-seventeen. And it impugns the integrity of one of the finest, most forthright industries in this great nation.

"The Converse Corporation has been one of the strongest vertebrae in the backbone of this country's aerospace industry. It has been pivotal in the jet aircraft industry, which, I would like to point out, is one of the few endeavors in the world in which the United States still has technical dominance. Riding on Converse engines, the American aircraft industry has continued to swim upstream against the outflow of U.S. dollars and growing balance-of-trade deficits. To question the integrity of the industry or any of its components borders on the un-American. These new accusations are a travesty of justice. They represent all that is wrong with the media in this country. They do not wish to help the United States regain the economic health that once made us the most powerful nation on earth. They wish only to tear down the country for today's black headline, to castigate honest men and women for some personal thrill, to drag a vital component of a vital industry through the mud just to sell newspapers. It's enough to make me question the validity of the First Amendment to our precious Constitution.

"I know that is a startling and unpopular thing to say, but someone, somehow, has got to stop these people, to bring them to ground, to make them accountable for their indiscretions and baseless accusations. It is time—no, it is past time—to let the media of this country know we are watching closely, and we don't like what we see and read. These are despicable, groundless, wicked lies, and they must be stopped. One way or another, I shall see that done. Meanwhile, on the chance someone missed my definition of these character assassinations, I repeat: They are lies, lies, *lies, lies, lies, lies, lies!*"

Marshall's face grew red, and he hammered his fist through the air at each repetition of the word "lies." He was out of breath. He slammed his microphone onto his desk and strode off the floor, forgetting to yield the balance of his time back to the chair. Senators were not above putting on floor shows in the Senate, but Marshall's explosion was no show.

"I hope to heaven your paper is right," the Utah reporter said to Hughes as he got up from his chair. "Because if you're wrong—"

Hughes was furious. It was irritating enough to listen to Marshall take the Senate floor and vilify her newspaper, but it was one of the prices you paid to work for a high-profile publication in the nation's capital. It was quite something else for a colleague to pile it on. She knew what was at stake in the *Chronicle*'s reporting; more important, the editors of the paper knew, and they were confident of Steve Pace's facts. But there were some in the press corps so jealous of others' success they felt compelled to snipe at good stories they missed. Hughes thought their pretense of cynicism both phony and insulting. If they didn't consider a public scandal worth their time, they should find something else to cover and keep their own counsel. Better yet, they should find another profession. At the very least, she thought, they should find a seat in the press gallery somewhere else than beside her.

Hughes clomped down three flights of Capitol steps, trying to pound down her irritation. She found herself standing outside the Capitol's East Front, what most people thought of as the business side of the building because that's where they came and went. Actually, it was the back, facing the Supreme Court and the Library of Congress over an expanse of lawn and trees. The ceremonial side was the West Front. From the steps there, one could look over the Mall, a vast, green open space extending all the way across town to the Washington Monument, the Reflecting Pool and the Lincoln Memorial. It was a magnificent view, one too few visitors or residents ever saw. But today was not the day for seeing it. Hughes was freezing.

A late-spring bluster was passing through the area, bringing a surge of cold Canadian air and a chill wind highly unusual for Washington this late in the spring. The temperature dipped into the high thirties in outlying suburban areas the night before, and forecasters said it wouldn't get above the mid-sixties in the nation's capital on this day. Hughes was certain it was still below sixty, and wind made the damp cold feel even more frigid. It cut to the bone.

She had made a tentative appointment to see Senator Garrison Helmutsen, chairman of the Senate Transportation Committee, after Marshall's speech. Now she faced a long two-block walk in the biting wind to get to his office in the Hart Senate Office Building. She stuffed her notebook in her purse, shoved her hands into the pockets of her wool skirt, and set off at a brisk pace.

She was cursing the slow traffic signal at First and Constitution when her eyes fell on a blue van parked in the block of First Street between the Russell and Dirksen buildings. She could see only part of the back and the driver's side, but she was certain there was a Ford insignia on the right rear door. She laughed at herself for thinking this could be the van of Steve Pace's nightmares. Nonetheless, instead of cutting up Constitution to the Hart Building, she detoured down First, alongside the Dirksen Building. About fifty feet from the van, she stopped in her tracks, feeling a constriction in her throat. A man walking behind her, as briskly as she, bumped into her.

"There's no stop sign on this sidewalk, lady," he said sarcastically as he detoured around her without apology. "If you want to stand out in the wind, that's your business, but get out of the way of those who don't share your enthusiasm."

Hughes nodded and stepped toward the curb. There was no one else on the block. The wind blew straight up the street from the north, and nobody else was enthusiastic about challenging it. She approached the van, her eyes glued to the sight that had stopped her short in the first place. Glenn told her the previous week that a van like this one could be pivotal in proving Steve Pace was telling the truth. Glenn said the right front was wrecked and mentioned that there might be some yellow paint scraped from a car with which the van collided.

It was there, just as Glenn described it. Hughes suddenly felt colder than the wind chill. She jotted down the license number. It was a Maryland plate. Then, on a whim, she pulled two tissues from a travel pack of Kleenex in her purse. Using a long fingernail, she carefully scraped a little of the yellow paint into one tissue. She tried three times before she got enough; the wind kept blowing the flakes away. She stashed the first folded tissue in her pocket, then looked for a place to take a sample of the blue paint. That was easier and quicker. Some large, loose flakes came off in her hand. She backed away from the vehicle. A woman walking past eyed her suspiciously.

"I had an accident," Hughes explained. The other woman nodded, ducked her head deeper into her coat, and walked on.

Hughes hurried around to the back of the Dirksen Building and darted inside through the "Press and Visitors" entrance. She put her purse on the X-ray machine used for security and walked through the metal detector. She grabbed her purse and ducked around the corner, where the Capitol Police at the door couldn't see her. She leaned up against a wall and shivered. It was a deep spasm that wouldn't end. A young man, probably somebody's legislative assistant, saw her distress and stopped.

"Anything wrong?" he asked.

Hughes shook her head. "Just cold."

"You shouldn't be out today without a coat."

"I know," she agreed. "I didn't think about it this morning."

He nodded slowly. "Well, I hope you don't get sick."

"Me, too," Hughes replied and shivered again. "I'll get some coffee, and I'll be fine."

The man moved on. Hughes knew she hadn't been shivering from the cold.

The chill she felt was fear.

"What the hell do you mean, you don't know? What happened to that little slut you keep on your payroll to report these things? She only get laid on weekends?" G.T. Greenwood was in high dudgeon, and Harold Marshall was the target.

People in Washington didn't speak that way to Marshall; he went to great lengths to cultivate an image precluding it. But Greenwood was CEO of Converse, his best constituent and most lucrative fund-raiser, so he reined in his natural instinct for indignation.

When he arrived at his office this morning, Marshall found a message from Greenwood. He ignored it as he polished his tirade for the Senate floor. Greenwood called again, and Marshall told his secretary to say he wasn't there. There were two more messages when Marshall returned from the floor. He wished in retrospect he'd gone right out for a long lunch somewhere. But he knew he'd have to face Greenwood sooner or later, so better it be sooner and get it over with. Once done with Greenwood, he could give serious consideration to going home.

Marshall felt dizzy and vaguely nauseous. He'd been experiencing the dizziness with some regularity of late, and it was particularly bad when he left the Senate floor. He walked to his office across the Capitol grounds rather than take the underground subway, hoping the cold, fresh air would clear his head. But the dizziness affected his balance, and once he thought he nearly fell. At the moment, he tried to focus on defending himself against the abuse from the Converse CEO.

"George, she's not a slut, given all I know, and I don't keep her on the payroll to spy on the *Chronicle*. I don't know if she had any notice of this. I assume if she learned anything, she would have told me. She always has. I'm not going to order her to sleep with the photographer to get information for you. That would be unconscionable."

"What the *Chronicle* is printing is unconscionable, Harold," Greenwood spat back at him. "We can't tolerate it. We had this mess in hand, under control. The fire was out. Now somebody's rekindled it, and I want to know why, and on what evidence."

"I can't answer your question. I'll talk to her. But I'm not going to prostitute her."

"Why not? You've already done much worse. We're dealing here with something that could bring this company down. I won't let that happen, Senator, and I don't care who I have to sacrifice to prevent it, is that clear?"

"I've already done everything I can. And I've gone way over the bounds of propriety and law in doing it. If the Ethics Committee ever got hold of this, it would finish my career. I don't see how I have the means to discredit the *Chronicle* stories."

"Do you have the means to find out what they're based on?"

"No. What do you want me to do? I've lied for you. I've cheated for you. I've used Davis to do things that shouldn't have been done. My neck is out as far as I can stick it. What more exactly, is it you think I can do?"

"Surely you can do something more than take the Senate floor and threaten to overturn the First Amendment! Christ, what were you thinking of? We want to appease the media, not wave a bloody rag under their noses."

"So, fine. Suggest something."

"Cast some doubt about the motives of the people behind this. I'll fax you some material you can use."

"Like what?"

"Sachs did consulting work for MacPhearson-Paige before he went to the NTSB."

"So?"

"Do I have to paint you a picture? M-P is one of our chief competitors. Maybe you should suggest he's taking money under the table to discredit us."

"How, exactly, do you plan to prove that?"

"We don't have to prove it, Harold." The exasperation in Greenwood's voice was growing. "All we have to do is suggest a motive for deceit, put the kibosh on this thing quick."

"But that's Sachs. I don't know that he's behind this."

"Oh, shit. He's the goddamn chairman of the NTSB."

"Maybe the impetus for this came from within the go-team," Marshall suggested.

"Harold, for chrissake, we're not trying to be accurate here; we're trying to discredit the new suspicions. Since Sachs worked for one of our competitors, hang it on him. Let the public think the NTSB chairman can influence a go-team. And so what if he can't? None of the poor unwashed out there knows that. Why don't you suggest the guy had an ax to grind, a future to consider? Hell, Cordell Hollander isn't going to be President forever. When he's out of office, Sachs is going to be looking for a job. Maybe he's trying to build that future on our dead bodies? At least let's plant the seed of that idea."

"You know it's bullshit."

"I don't know it. And I don't care. I want you to convince the American public it could be so. Go back out on the floor and talk about his association with Mac-Paige. Or call a press conference. Or leak it to the *Post* or the *Times*. Hell, I don't care how you do it; just do it! Make it a conflict-of-interest thing. Hang this sucker around his neck so heavy he won't be able to raise his head to kiss his wife hello."

In his office in the suite occupied by the Senate Transportation Committee staff, Chapman Davis was having his own problems. Sylvester Bonaro showed up unbidden, demanding to know if his deal was about to come apart.

"I can't believe you had the balls to waltz in here," Davis railed. He whisked Bonaro out of the offices, where there was absolutely no privacy, and into the committee's empty hearing room. There they sat huddled in a corner, talking in stage whispers.

"That damned reporter is getting too close," Bonaro said. "You and your boss don't pay me enough to hang around and take the fall for this. I can disappear back into the Baltimore waterfront in an hour, and nobody will find me. Now, what's the plan?"

"There isn't one I know of," Davis answered honestly. "This just hit us this morning. We didn't have any warning." He cupped his hands and wiped them down over his face. The stress was beginning to wear on him. This definitely wasn't the political career he'd envisioned. "I don't think it would do us much good to take Pace or his girlfriend out now, would it?"

"Yeah, right," Bonaro sneered. "The guy writes a story about how somebody's fucked up the Dulles job, and he and his girlfriend turn up dead. What more proof would anybody need?"

"I suppose," Davis agreed. "What I suggest you do is get yourself off the streets and wait until you hear from me." He looked at Bonaro sharply. "How'd you get here this morning?"

"What? I drove."

"The van?"

"Yeah. It's my wheels."

"Did you get it fixed?"

"Hell, who's had time?"

Davis jumped to his feet and glowered down at the bewildered Bonaro. "Jesus, get it the hell off the streets! Ditch it. Burn it. Crush it. I don't care what the hell you do with it, but get it away from here. I mean it, Sly. There's always a chance somebody spotted it in Virginia or at the drugstore. Hell, Pace could have seen it in the garage. Somebody could have made the license. Destroy the damned thing—"

Bonaro rose in protest.

"I mean it, man. I'll pay for a new one. My word. But that van's got to get gone, now and forever."

"So what am I supposed to do for wheels in the meantime?"

"Take a fucking taxi!"

"To a hit? That's a swell idea."

"There aren't going to be any more hits. This has already gone too far." But Davis relented. "Okay, garage it, someplace where you can get to it in an emergency, but someplace nobody will see it. Take cabs or buses or Metro. Buy a new one, I don't care. Send me the bill. So now you got a new truck and an expense account out of this. See how easy I am if you go along?"

"Yeah," Bonaro agreed. "You people are fucking nuts, you know?"

37

Wednesday, May 14th, 2:35 P.M.

Steve Pace scooted into the editorial conference room five minutes after his meeting was to have begun with Avery Schaeffer, Paul Wister, Clayton Helm, and Martin Lanier. There was an undefined disorder to the session, given that no one had called it; it simply came to be. Clay Helm was one of the first on the telephone to Pace after the NTSB story broke. He got the reporter at home during his first cup of coffee. Lanier tried Avery Schaeffer at home, only to find at seven A.M. that the editor was already on his way downtown. He reached him at seven-thirty. Then Helm and Lanier reached each other. Lanier called Schaeffer to ask for a face-to-face, but Schaeffer wasn't available. So the D.C. detective lodged the request with Wister. Schaeffer wasn't available because he was talking to Pace, who had gone to his office to say Clay Helm would like to come in for a chat.

So it was at two-thirty they were all there, each looking to the others to open the discussion. Schaeffer suggested they delay until Pace could join them.

"He's on the phone with a radio station in Cleveland, I think, doing a live interview on the story this morning," Schaeffer explained. "He'll be along shortly. Anyone need coffee?"

Everyone accepted, so Schaeffer ordered several carafes, plus cream and sugar, from the executive dining room. Now they were waiting in curious silence for Pace and for coffee.

The reporter apologized for being late. "I couldn't get them off the phone," he explained.

"No problem," Schaeffer said with a smile. "We're wondering why we're here."

Lanier wasn't at all reticent about explaining his presence, although he looked embarrassed. "Well, obviously, we, ah . . ." He paused and cleared his throat. "In light of the paper's story this morning, we are, how should I say, in a position to reopen the investigation of Captain McGill's death. If there was a conspiracy to cover up the reason for the ConPac crash, that lends some credence to Mr. Pace's belief that Captain McGill was killed to protect the deception."

Pace smiled. *It's Mr. Pace now. No more Rodney Dangerfield in the respect department.*

Clay Helm followed up. "The Fairfax County Police take the same position," he said. "What I am here for is to gather anything that will move along my investigation."

"Right," Lanier agreed.

"I don't know if information of that nature exists," Schaeffer replied. "And I would very strongly oppose any request for reporters' notes."

"I know that's off limits," Helm said. "I guess I just want to talk it all through."

"I don't know if we can add much," Schaeffer said.

"Ah, Avery, I think maybe there is something, although I don't know how you want to handle it," Pace said. "Just before the call from Cleveland, I got a call from Jill Hughes." He turned to Lanier and Helm. "She covers the Senate for us. On her way to Senator Helmutsen's office this morning, she spotted a blue Ford van parked on First Street, next to the Dirksen Building." Now everyone leaned forward perceptibly, concentrating on what Pace was saying. "She told me she didn't know why it struck her. Lord knows there are millions of blue Ford vans around, as some of you gentlemen have been telling me for weeks. But she walked over to look at it. It had a bashed-in right front—" his gaze shifted to Helm "—and it had streaks of yellow paint in the torn metal."

"License plate?" Helm asked tensely, seeming to hold his breath.

"Maryland. She wrote it down."

"Al-l-l right!" Schaeffer erupted, his right hand slapping the cherry table. "The pendulum has swung back to the good guys."

"There's more," Pace said, shifting in his chair. "She got paint samples."

"What!" Helm's mouth dropped open. "How?"

"Said she scraped 'em off with her fingernail, and she said I owe her for polish. She got some of the yellow and some of the blue wrapped in separate tissues, and she's on her way in here now. She would have called sooner, but she's been cooling her heels in Helmutsen's office for a couple of hours and didn't want to risk using a phone there."

"Good decision," Helm said.

"I think somebody'd better bring me up to date on this paint thing," Schaeffer said.

Pace realized Schaeffer didn't know of the results from the police lab and filled him in.

When Jill arrived, Schaeffer introduced her around, offered her a cup of coffee, which she accepted gratefully and used as a hand warmer. She repeated what they had heard from Pace, with a few additional details.

"All the while I was scraping the little shavings off the van, I kept expecting somebody to come up behind me and grab me, the way they do it in horror films," she said a little sheepishly. "I guess in real life, you don't get caught that way."

"Not necessarily," Helm said. "What you did was invaluable, but it *was* dangerous. As much as I appreciate the evidence, we don't need two reporters to worry about. In the future, call us and we'll take the samples." Then he smiled at her.

Hughes laughed, embarrassed. "Actually," she confessed, "I wanted to stay and stake it out, the van I mean. But it was so damned cold, and I didn't have a coat, and there wasn't any inside office overlooking the street right there. I guess I'm not as tough as Spenser."

"Spenser?" Wister asked.

"You don't know Spenser?" Hughes' eyes were wide. "Don't you read detective stories?"

"Oh, is that it?" Wister said derisively. "I don't read fiction."

Hughes sighed. "Actually," she said, "I guess I knew that."

Ken Sachs called shortly after three-thirty.

"This is still on a sources' basis, right?" he asked.

Pace promised any information he used would be attributed to "sources who asked not to be identified."

"It's to your advantage, Steve. We've decided not to say anything publicly until Monday morning, at the very earliest. So you've got the big exclusive alone for a couple more days. I don't want it that way, but there are too many unanswered questions for a news briefing."

"So I'm out on the limb alone for the whole weekend?"

"Unless your competitors have sources we haven't muzzled, that's the way it is. Hey, I promised you a day. I didn't think you'd bitch about five."

"Ken, there are some stories you don't want to be alone

with too long. People begin to think maybe you got it wrong."

"You don't have it wrong. You were the only one who had it right. Let me tell you quickly what's going on, because I've got a meeting coming up. We sent two technicians we know we can trust into the engine this afternoon. They're charting every single place where the bird remains can be found and estimating to within as close as they can come the volume and weight of the material in each spot. Obviously, some volume and weight were lost because the flesh and feathers were torched somehow, and more has been lost since due to evaporation and removal for identification, but—"

"Where is this leading?"

"We're coming up with a series of computer simulations showing what would happen to a red-tailed hawk that flew into a Converse Fan operating within the parameters this one was. We got that data from the FDR."

"The flight data recorder can't tell you how an engine would spray bird gore around."

"No, but a computer can. The FDR tells us how the engine was operating—rpms, vibrations, that sort of thing. We feed the data into the computers, then factor in a bird strike, and the simulations should give us a pretty good picture. If we're right, we'll see if the remains in the engine are in the quantities and locations the computer projects. If they aren't, we'll be able to make a pretty fair case that something ain't kosher."

"That's kind of tough, isn't it?" Pace asked. "Wouldn't it depend on whether the bird flew in headfirst or was sucked in sideways or backwards, or obliquely, or whatever?"

"There are a lot of variables, yes, including the weight of the bird. Males weigh more than females, older birds more than young," Sachs confirmed. "All that could affect the simulations, but that's the reason to do multiple runs. We'll look at all the variables we can think of."

"What kind of time frame are you looking at? It sounds like a huge job."

"It is a huge job, and it would be utterly impossible without computers. Even with computers, we'll be working in teams, twenty-four hours a day. I don't know how long it'll take, but we're in for the duration."

"Oh, man. Good luck," Pace said.

"By the way, you'll be interested to know we pulled Parkhall in. The son of a bitch is as jumpy as a May fly in heat, but that could be nothing more than just the way he is. I guess I'd be jumpy, too, if somebody suggested I covered up the cause of a major aviation disaster."

Pace felt his face flush. "I think somebody did accuse you of that recently," he said. "If drunken recollection is correct, you didn't get jumpy at all. You got mean."

"Yeah, well, that's behind us," Sachs said. There was a pause. "I didn't think I'd ever hear myself tell you this," he continued. "But looking back, under the circumstances, if I'd been you, I would have suspected the same thing. Drunk and devastated by the death of a friend, I might even have made the visit you made."

"That's a decent thing to say."

"Having said it, I have to ask you a question."

"What?"

"Do you still think I had something to do with Mike's murder?"

"Did you?"

"No."

"Do you still believe I'm some sort of paranoid making up stories that somebody murdered Mike and Mark to abet a cover-up?"

"No, not anymore."

"I guess we're square then," Pace suggested.

"Not quite," Sachs said. "There are still scores to settle."

"I'm in," Pace said. "Whatever needs to be done."

"I know you are," Sachs replied. "You're a relentless bastard. Anybody ever tell you?"

"Yeah. As a matter of fact, Mike McGill told me just before he died."

At 4:00 P.M., the Federal Aviation Administration announced that the nation's fleet of Sexton 811 aircraft had been grounded again as a precautionary measure until it could be determined what caused the ConPac crash at Dulles Airport.

Given the day's myriad developments, it was after eight o'clock when Pace finished his Thursday story. Although he and his editors were supremely confident of the story's accuracy, Pace hated the attribution. Once again the best information was attributed to "sources who asked not to be quoted by name," or to "sources who asked not to be identified." Some readers inevitably believed unnamed sources were figments of the reporter's imagination, that disclosures attributed to unnamed sources were highly suspect. He hoped fervently the NTSB could go public with its suspicions early the following week and confirm that he had been writing about real people making legitimate statements about real problems.

His phone rang.

"Pace."

"Did I catch you at a busy time?" He recognized Kathy's voice, and his heart leaped.

"There is no bad time for you to call," he assured her.

"I think I owe you an apology."

"Good. You can get in line. I've been hearing it from everybody today. No, actually, you can go to the head of the line. You're the most important one. In fact, you don't have to apologize for anything at all. Just come home."

"You haven't heard what I was going to say."

"I don't have to. Hearing from you is enough."

She laughed softly. "No, I called to tell you something." He said nothing, a silent consent for her to go on. "When I saw your story this morning, I realized I didn't have any right to make some of the judgments I made," she said, "especially, well, given the thing about Justin Smith. That's awful. I get sick when I think it could have been you . . . still could be you. But I don't know your business, except for what I've soaked up from you, and I didn't have any right to suggest the course you should take. My misjudgments were made only out of concern for you. I hope you believe that."

"I do," he answered gratefully. "Now tell me you're coming back."

"Actually, what I called to tell you is that I'm going away—"

The gut-clutching pain returned. "What? Why?"

"Oh, not for long, only a week. I'm going back to Boston to see Dad and to think over some things. I know how I feel about you, and I'm pretty sure I know how you feel about me. But I'm not sure our strong wills won't clash again. I expect they will. I want our relationship, if it continues, to be smooth, and free from potholes like the one we fell into this time. I want to figure out if I can make that happen. I haven't had any vacation in a long time, and Hugh suggested I take some now. I think it's a good idea. Besides, I love Boston in the spring. All the good things I remember about growing up there happened in the spring. I need to go back and clear my head."

"Sweetheart, there hasn't been a couple in the history of mankind who didn't get bounced around by life's bumps and potholes. Don't plan our future on some idealized notion that there will never be problems. If you do, we have no future."

"My head knows that," she said. "Now I have to convince my heart."

"I love you," he said.

"And I love you."

The line went dead, and he felt empty again.

38

When the phone rang at his apartment early that afternoon, Steve Pace was certain he knew who it was.

"Can you meet me?" Ken Sachs asked.

"Sure. Where?"

"The hangar. In an hour."

"I can't get in."

"Oh, yeah. Right. Sorry. I'm already thinking of you as a member of the staff. I guess those aren't liberties I'm supposed to take."

"No. Avery wouldn't like it. And I'm kind of fond of my job. At the moment."

"Okay, at the Marriott. Same place we met before, in the parking lot."

"What's up?"

"We've got the results from the first computer runs."

"And?"

"The results are pretty conclusive. I don't think they're going to change."

"Are you going to tell me, or should I schedule a nervous breakdown on the Beltway?"

"I'm going to show you. And I'm going to give you a story that will shake this town like an earthquake."

Pace appeared in the newsroom a little after four o'clock, a sheaf of large papers rolled under his arm. Paul Wister could tell he was carrying a big story by the way he walked.

"So, yeah, what?" the national editor asked as the reporter approached him.

"Can we go in the Glory Room, where we can spread some papers out?"

"Sure. I'll get Avery and meet you."

"Avery's working on Sunday?"

"You think he'd miss being in on this?"

Pace's smile served as an answer.

When Wister and Schaeffer entered, Pace had several large sheets of computer graphics spread out across the table. Three were in black and white. The fourth was in color.

The two editors flanked their reporter.

"What are these?" Schaeffer asked.

Pace explained them in the order he laid them out. "This first one represents the computer's best estimate of where the remains of an average-sized red-tail hawk would wind up if it flew headfirst into a Converse Fan operating at takeoff thrust." He pointed to several blackened areas around the perimeter of the engine. "These ink smears represent pieces, uh, well, material that probably would have been channeled into the open space between the guts of the engine and the skin. That material would have continued through and out the back without doing any damage or touching any working parts except the fan blades. These jagged outlines represent pieces of fan blades broken by the impact. Most of them go around the engine, too, although the computer projected that a big enough piece could conceivably be ingested, and it's represented by this outline here. But the black smudges are what's important for now. That's where the bird would have gone."

He looked to see if his editors were following him, and both were nodding. He moved on to the second sheet.

"This is what might have happened if the bird was sucked in backwards. As you can see, there's not too much difference. Ken explained to me that in the computer projections, the mass of the bird is the mass of the bird, no matter what direction it's flying. The principal difference is that if the bird was flying in the same direction as the plane was moving, its own forward speed would detract marginally from the velocity of the impact. If it flew into the engine head-on, then its forward speed would increase the impact marginally. Again, what's important is where the remains go, and as you can see, the smudges are in pretty much the same place either way."

He moved to the third sheet. "Now this is where the NTSB team actually found the bird remains."

"It's not even close," Schaeffer said.

"Nope. Ken figures when they spritzed the stuff around in there, they didn't make any effort to duplicate scientific reality. Heck, they probably didn't know what that reality was."

"Well, this is pretty solid evidence, but there's still nobody to pin it on," Wister said.

"What's this last sheet?" Schaeffer asked.

"This is a color overlay showing where the computer projections say bird remains should have been and where they actually were found. Where they should have been is in blue, and where they were is in red."

"At the risk of repeating myself, they're not even close," the editor said, repeating himself.

"Not even close. And these comparative figures down here—" Pace pointed to the bottom of the page "—are estimates of the actual volume of bird in the engine versus what the computer says should have been there. If you add them up, you'll see there are four times more red volume than blue volume. In other words, there's four times more bird inside the engine than the computer says there should be."

"And that's because the computers say in a real bird strike, three-fourths of the bird's volume would have gone around the engine and out the back of the pod?" Schaeffer asked.

"At least."

"Paul, get the art department to reproduce this last graphic for tomorrow. And let's do a companion chart on the volume figures. We're going to let this story run." He turned to Pace.

"This is damned fine work, Steve. Vindication must taste pretty sweet."

Pace shook his head. "Not yet. Not until we nail down who did this."

When Wister left, Schaeffer asked Pace to sit down. "We have a problem," he said. "How well do you know Tim Hogan?"

"The Hulk? Our photographer?"

Schaeffer nodded.

Pace shrugged. "Reasonably well. We've worked a lot of assignments together, including this ConPac crash. He's a pretty good guy. Why?"

"You see him socially?"

"We don't hang out together, if that's what you mean. He's a good deal younger, and he has more stamina for the singles-bar scene than I do. I see him at company parties, and we were softball teammates last year."

"Did you ever meet his girlfriend?"

Pace laughed. "Which one? From what I've heard, Hulk's personal crusade is to bed every unmarried woman in Washington before he's thirty-five."

"Apparently there's one woman who's been a regular for a couple of months. She's a legislative assistant on Harold Marshall's staff. She knew every move this paper was making on the ConPac story—at least she knew as much as Tim knew, and that was most of it."

"How do we know this?" Pace asked. "A tip?"

"No, the woman confessed to Hogan, and Tim came straight to us. As you can imagine, he's sick about it."

"He'd be sicker if I had my way," Wister said as he reentered the room. "He'd be on the street. He's put us in a hell of a fix."

"Not necessarily, Paul," Schaeffer demurred. "But what we *do* have—" and here he turned to Pace "—is some good reason to reconsider your suspicions about Marshall. *Was* he trying to sway the NTSB investigation? Then maybe he's behind the phony bird strike."

"Could be," Pace agreed.

"You have sources, right?" Wister asked.

"Sort of," Pace said.

"Use them," Schaeffer ordered.

"They're political," Pace pointed out. "They've got Democratic axes to grind against Marshall's Republican skull."

"All sources are political," Schaeffer said. "All of them have axes to grind, or they wouldn't be talking to us. It isn't our job to make judgments about their motives. But we keep their biases very much in mind and remember that we have to be able to prove what they tell us. We don't take their information at face value."

"Right," Pace agreed, and Schaeffer smiled.

"So go find us another story."

George Ridley returned Pace's call shortly before ten o'clock that evening, one home phone to another.

"I wanted to tell you what we're letting loose in the morning," Pace lied.

"I figured there was another shoe to drop," Ridley replied. "What size is it?"

"Eighteen triple-E."

"That's Republican size. Big."

"Real big."

"Would you care to give me a clue as to the style and color?"

"Incontrovertible proof that the bird evidence was planted."

"Well, I probably could muster enough interest to read about that. Everything you've written lately has been mildly interesting. But," Ridley paused, "this is the first time you've been kind enough to call me the night before with a preview of coming attractions."

Pace confessed, "I have another reason for calling."

"Why did I know that?"

"You remember the conversation we had at Dulles the morning after the accident?"

"Right after I left Lund? Sure."

"You remember we talked about a certain senator who might be overstepping himself?"

"Yep. You wanted me to keep an eye on him for you."

"Well, not quite. I suggested if you saw anything suspicious, I'd like to know."

"I remember. I haven't seen anything. On the other hand, I haven't been looking."

"There's reason to look now."

"What?"

Pace could hear the sudden interest in Ridley's voice, so without naming names, he told him the story of Tim Hogan's girlfriend. He was shocked when Ridley named the names for him.

"Hey, everybody knows she's bedding Hogan, and everybody knows she's squeezing him for info," Ridley said. "It's not unusual, man. Every time somebody on the Hill gets involved with a fucking journalist, it's expected that tales will be told. It's part of the scenery up here. Makes for damned juicy gossip."

"No question," Pace agreed. "But in this case, it wasn't gossip she was looking for."

"I see where you're going with this. She finds out stuff the senator doesn't know, stuff the senator's very important constituent wants to know before it hits the papers. Senator has a mole in the chicken coop who can make him look like he's wired to good sources, so he uses her boyfriend's pillow talk to bolster his own stock with the homies. What a grungy thing to do."

"Who knows what other excesses a man like that might be capable of?" Pace suggested.

"It's worth further examination," Ridley concurred.

"Discreetly, of course."

"I'm always discreet," Ridley replied.

And Pace broke up, laughing so hard he didn't hear the Senate aide slam down the phone.

39

Monday, May 19th, 7:00 A.M.

"Good morning. I'm Frank Greshhold, and this is AP Network News. Could someone fake the cause of a major aviation disaster? That is the astounding report this morning in the *Washington Chronicle*. The story discloses there are serious doubts about the conclusion by the National Transportation Safety Board that a bird strike caused the April seventeenth crash of a ConPac Eight-eleven jetliner at Dulles International Airport outside Washington, D.C. That crash killed three hundred thirty-four people, making it the worse aviation disaster in U.S. history. The *Chronicle* reports that NTSB computer simulations of a hawk flying into a Converse Fan engine conclude most of the remains of the bird should have gone around the engine and harmlessly out the back. However, technicians calibrating the amount of material found inside the engine say there probably is enough to account for the whole bird. NTSB sources quoted by the *Chronicle* say while the evidence is circumstantial, it is a virtual statistical impossibility for the accident to have occurred as originally believed. They told the newspaper they are working under the assumption there could have been tampering with the engine after the accident to make it appear bird ingestion caused the crash when, in fact, the real cause could be much more sinister. An incredible story unfolding in Washington, and we'll stay on top of it for you all day. More, after this . . ."

Steve Pace reached over and turned off the alarm, remembering as he did so the last time the ConPac crash had been the lead story on the AP radio news. That was the ghastly day Justin Smith scored heavily on him. Well, friends, score this one for Steve Pace, unassisted. He thought Justin would have been proud.

He rolled onto his back, and his right arm flopped across the empty expanse of the other half of his bed. It hit cool sheets instead of the warm Kathy-body he wished for. She was in Boston, consulting with dear old Dad. There was no way Joe McGovern would tell her to give up an open-ended career in politics to set up housekeeping with a newspaper reporter, for chrissake. "Keep your eye on the ball and swing through nice and smooth," old Joe would tell her. "Never lose sight of the objective. Don't let anything distract you."

Pace felt a blue mood bumping up against his professional jubilation, and he made an almost physical effort to force it aside. He concentrated on what he had to do today, and that consisted mostly of keeping in touch with Ken Sachs and staying on George Ridley's ass.

He tossed the covers aside and was about to get up when the phone rang.

"Steve, it's Clay Helm. I hope I didn't wake you."

"You didn't. What's up?"

"Your stock, for one thing. We got a match."

"The paint?" Pace's stomach muscles tightened, and he pulled himself into a sitting position, feeling a new adrenaline rush.

"The very same. The blue matched the spectrograph of the sample our tech found on Antravanian's car, and the yellow flakes your reporter chipped off the truck matched the base color of the burned car."

"Does that prove intent?"

"Not in and of itself. But since the same blue van was at the scene of the accident later, with its occupants videotaping the recovery of the body, and it was nearby when Mike McGill was killed, and again when you were beaten, the commonwealth attorney has more than enough to take to a grand jury. You and Jill will have to be witnesses."

"That's a problem," Pace said with a frown. "You'll have to take it up with Avery. I know I can't volunteer to appear. I think you'll probably have to subpoena us and be ready to fight off the paper's attorneys."

"Understood. We'll do what it takes. I thought if you happened to be fishing for a story, the paint match might give you something to write." Pace could hear the smile in Helm's voice.

"Oh, I think I'll be able to put it to some use," he replied. "Have you talked to Lieutenant Lanier about it yet?"

"Yeah, last night. He says the U.S. attorney in the District wants a grand jury, too. That would mean two grand juries gnawing at the same bone. And, ah, I shouldn't be telling you this, so I didn't. Understand?"

"Sure."

"You should check with the Justice Department. If these murders were committed to abet a conspiracy to cover up the cause of a commercial plane crash, they're going to be coming in with the heavy hitters."

"Justice knows what you've got?"

"Yes. And what the NTSB has."

"FBI?"

"You got it."

"Can you narrow it down any further? Like a name?"

"I'd start with the U.S. attorney for the District of Columbia."

"Stan Travis."

"The very same."

"The very same Stanley Eastman Travis III, who once said the public should never have any access to any information about federal criminal investigations?"

"That's the man."

"Gee, Clay, thanks a lot."

"My pleasure."

Pace was in the office before Schaeffer and Wister came in, so he walked down the stairs to see if Suzy O'Connor was around. She was. Pace wondered if she ever went home.

She was scanning a variety of morning papers. Pace plopped down in the lone chair beside her desk. Without an audience of her own staffers nearby, she skipped her usual theatrics and smiled at him.

"I'd ask you how you're doing, but it's fairly clear from your front-page run you're doing fine," O'Connor said.

"Yeah, things are looking up," Pace replied.

"So what brings you to Ms. O'Connor's neighborhood?"

"Have you heard from Sally lately?"

"Incaveria?" Pace nodded. "I heard from her yesterday," O'Connor responded. "We talked about a story she's been hammering."

"Did she say anything about the fatal on One-ninety-three?"

"No. Is there something new to say?"

Pace gave her a quick synopsis of his conversation with Clay Helm that morning, and the suburban editor whistled.

"That's something. God, what a story! Are you going with that tomorrow?"

"I hope so."

"What do the D.C. cops say?"

"I haven't called them yet."

"So what can I do?"

"If I write the story, I'm going to ask for a double byline. Sally should share the credit."

O'Connor smiled and shook her head. "That's nice of you, Steve, but you'll have to send flowers or candy. I can't let her anywhere near that story."

"Why not? You were hot for her to have a piece of it a couple weeks ago."

"Things change. This week she happens to be engaged to that Fairfax Police captain, which would make any involvement in this story a conflict of interest. Our policy is clear."

"Engaged?" Pace was dumbfounded. "She's only known the guy three weeks."

"I guess he swept her off her feet."

"Or vice versa. She could do that to a man."

"So she could."

"It's strange Clay didn't mention it this morning. After all, I'm the one responsible for their chance to get acquainted socially."

"Well, it's usually up to the lady to announce an engagement, isn't it?"

"How the hell would I know, Suze?"

She thumped a finger in his chest. "Maybe you should find out. Information like that could come in handy some day."

Pace stared at her for a moment. "From your mouth to God's ear, Ms. O'Connor."

"Oh?" The editor looked interested. "Somebody I know?"

"No," Pace said, subdued. "Sometimes I'm not even sure I know her."

He got up and walked away, humming the refrain from Doc Watson's "Life Gets Tee-jus, Don't It?"

Yeah, Doc, it do.

Wister was just sitting down when Pace popped back into the newsroom.

"Well, you're certainly feeling your oats this morning, running up the stairs," Wister joked. "A man of your age should think about getting into exercise slowly. Or is this what a banner headline out front will do to your spirit?"

"It helps," Pace laughed. "Listen, if you think today was good—"

They were interrupted by Wister's telephone. Wister motioned Pace to wait.

"Really?" Wister said after listening to the caller for about half a minute. "No kidding? What do you make of it?" He gestured to Pace to sit down in the chair next to his desk. "He's right here. We were chatting when you called . . . I don't know, but I'll ask him to wait until you get in . . . okay, Avery."

When Wister hung up, he was shaking his head. "Incredible," he said. "Absolutely incredible." He turned to Pace. "Avery got a call early this morning from Harold Marshall, who was bent totally out of shape, almost incoherent. He was ranting about your story, and then he tried to hype Avery on the idea Ken Sachs opened the new investigation because he has a personal interest in seeing Converse bankrupted."

"Like what?" Pace asked.

"According to Marshall, Sachs did some lucrative consulting for MacPhearson-Paige."

Pace nodded. "I think he did do some work for M-P after he left United, but M-P was only one of his clients. He had a very nice business as a rep for clients who had dealings with U.S. Government agencies and overseas."

"He did work overseas?"

"For his consulting business, yes."

"Was he registered as a foreign agent?"

"Oh, yeah. That was the first thing I checked when his appointment was announced. His filings were never even late. He did everything by the book, and as far as anybody knows, including a friend of mine at the Justice Department, there's never been a hint he abused or misused the regulations."

"Squeaky clean, huh?"

"To the extent anybody is ever totally clean, I'd say yes. Hell, when Mike and I were debating whether we could trust anybody at the NTSB, Mike said the one guy he'd stake his life on was Sachs."

"But after Mike was killed, your first instinct was that Sachs was responsible."

"I was wrong."

"So now you're convinced Sachs is okay?"

"It took some pretty convincing proof to get him to reconsider the bird-strike theory. If he wanted to do something to hurt Converse, he'd have done it long before."

Wister pursed his lips. "I hope you're right. You're riding a very fast horse here, Steve. I'd like to see it out front at the finish."

Schaeffer, Wister, and Pace talked well into the morning, going over facts, probabilities, and suspicions. It was like trying to put together a jigsaw-puzzle picture of a blue sky. All the pieces looked the same, with only slight gradations in shade.

"Sum it up, Steve," Schaeffer said at last. "What have we got?"

"We have three distinct story lines: the rigged investigation, the three murders, and the mystery of where Harold Marshall fits into it, if anywhere. It still could turn out he's only trying to come to the aid of a beleaguered constituent."

"I agree," said Wister. "And I think we'll stay out of trouble here if we don't strain to connect the dots. Let each story play itself out. We've got the sources wired. Except for what the NTSB, the Justice Department, or the police choose to confirm officially, I don't see how we can be bested on this one."

"Are you satisfied about Ken Sachs and the MacPhearson-Paige thing?" Schaeffer asked his national editor.

Wister nodded. "I think Steve is right on that score. Unless somebody can show us concrete proof Sachs acted inappropriately on behalf of his client, it stinks like an old fish. I think Marshall laid it out there as a smoke screen."

"I want us absolutely certain of that," Schaeffer said. "I don't want to determine it isn't true simply because we don't want it to be true."

"I'll go back over it," Pace said. "I think I covered all that ground, but you never know. I could have missed something."

"For one thing," Wister suggested, "you should call Marshall and ask him what prompted his call to Avery this morning. That would do two things. It would show Marshall we're not working only one side of the street, we're interested in the whole story. It could also give you a feeling for whether he's got something or he's bluffing."

"I think we should do all that, but—"

Schaeffer was interrupted by a knock on his doorjamb. It was Alec Stenofsky, the managing editor. "Sorry to interrupt, folks, but I thought you'd like to see this."

He handed Schaeffer two sheets of computer paper that

appeared to carry the printout of a wire story. "Thanks, John," said Schaeffer, glancing at it. "Good Lord."

Wister and Pace waited expectantly. Schaeffer finished reading and handed the pages to Wister and offered a synopsis to Pace.

"Converse is making Marshall's allegations public and official," he said. "They issued a statement in Youngstown suggesting the NTSB fabricated the evidence against a bird strike to damage Converse and seed the fortunes of Ken Sachs, former consultant to MacPhearson-Paige."

"That's libel," Pace said.

"Could be," Schaeffer agreed. "They're demanding Sachs step aside immediately, and they're asking the President to fire him if he refuses. They've also asked for an immediate congressional investigation, and they quote Marshall as saying he will personally lead the inquiry by the Senate Transportation Committee."

"Can he do that, as a minority member of the committee?" Wister asked, not glancing up from the story he was reading.

"I don't know," Schaeffer said. "He's ranking minority member—"

"And Garrison Helmutsen isn't the strongest man in the world," Pace offered.

"—and, that's right, he could probably browbeat Helmutsen into doing it out of a, quote-unquote, sense of justice."

Wister looked up at Pace. "Where are Sachs's political loyalties?"

"He's a Democrat," Pace said.

"So there you are," said Schaeffer. "If the majority on the Transportation Committee doesn't go along, it looks like they're protecting one of their own." He paused and drummed the desktop with his fingers for a moment, then added, "I think we're stretching you too thin, Steve. Let's bring Jill Hughes in. God knows, her quick action on the van broke open the murder cases. She deserves a shot at part of the story. With all you have to cover at the NTSB, the D.C. and Virginia cops, and the Justice Department, you're already running at top speed. Do you mind?"

"No. That's fine," Pace replied. "But I want to hang onto the other threads myself."

"I don't see any problem, unless you get overloaded," Schaeffer said. "How about if we have Glenn pitch in, too? You two get on well, and this is a story he'd take any piece of he could get. You're still the point man. This is your baby, and you've been through hell for it. But I want news stories, not heroes, and I'd like Glenn in for support, even if he only does leg work."

"I think I can handle it alone." By the tone of his voice, Pace meant to make it plain his objection was not a strong one. He certainly didn't object to Glenn. If he had to take help, he'd just as soon take it from Glenn as anyone.

"Trust me on this," Schaeffer said. "When this one starts cracking open, it's going to break in places we haven't even dreamed of. You'll be working seven days a week. You're going to need some relief."

"You're the boss," Pace replied with a shrug that said he would accept the order gracefully.

"You bet your ass," Schaeffer boomed. "And I'm damned glad somebody around here finally noticed."

40

Monday, May 19th, 1:30 P.M.
To say the hastily called press conference was tumultuous would have been gross understatement. Most of the major news organizations in the Western world had at least one reporter crammed into the auditorium. Photographers

fought with television cameramen for elbow room, and radio reporters struggled to find open space on the podium where they could clamp microphones. The wooden structure, with the NTSB logo on the front, looked like an electronic forest.

They were drawn there by Mitch Gabriel's notice that the NTSB chairman would respond to a multitude of questions.

An NTSB aide had taped single sheets of paper to two rows of chairs at the front of the room, scrawling on each sheet the name of a news organization that regularly covered aviation matters. All of the major newspapers, wire services, and networks had reserved spots, as did the trade press. Pace noticed with satisfaction that he was front row, center aisle. Since the television cameras were consigned to the back of the room, Pace had an unobstructed view of the dais and, presumably, a clear shot at being recognized with a question for Sachs.

He expected a sort of grudging coolness from his colleagues, and that's pretty much what he got, except from Jeffrey Hines, the veteran aviation writer for the *Los Angeles Times*. Hines was assigned the seat to Pace's right. He slumped into it, made eye contact with Pace, and grinned.

"You don't look too bad for a man come back from the dead," he commented.

"Was that the word around?"

"The gospel, I heard."

"I got a few lucky bounces."

The commotion in the room pitched up a notch, and Pace saw Ken Sachs walk in, followed by Vernon Lund, Jim Padgett, and Mitch Gabriel.

"They're bringing out all the guns," Hines noted, echoing Pace's thought.

"They'll need 'em," Pace said. "Did you see the rocket out of Converse this morning?"

Hines nodded. "The sonic boom broke a couple of windows in the newsroom. You think that's why they called this?"

"I'm sure somebody will ask."

Ken Sachs took the podium, and the room quieted expectantly.

"Ladies and gentlemen, I'll get right to the point," he began. "There have been very serious allegations made in the last few days to the effect that the apparent cause of the crash of ConPac Flight Eleven-seventeen on April seventeenth was somehow faked. As incredible as it sounds, there is evidence to suggest that the allegations are true."

Sachs paused as an audible murmur swept across the room. Then he continued. "We planned to meet with you today to bring everyone up to speed on the nature of our renewed investigation. Now the need is doubly important. I understand the Converse Corporation has issued a statement alleging that for reasons of my past brief association with another major engine manufacturer, I have impugned the ConPac evidence. Before you ask, I am here to say the charge is absurd. Mac-Paige was a client of my consulting firm for a short period seven years ago, and on one specific project involving the sale of aviation equipment to China. Because some of the equipment was included on a list of items that could not be sold abroad to Communist countries, Mac-Paige retained my firm to attain a one-time exemption. We were partially successful. The sale was approved with the exception of one computer component, which, I might add, was not essential to the completion of the deal. That was my only relationship with the company."

Sachs paused to be certain everyone was following him, then continued.

"Since I put my interest in the consulting firm into a blind trust during my tenure at the NTSB, I am not aware of the identities of new clients taken on in my absence. In an effort to abide by the rules of the blind trust, but at the same time to fulfill what I believe is my obligation to full disclosure, I asked the solicitor general's office this afternoon to contact one or more of the present officers of the firm to determine whether there has been, in my absence, further dealings with MacPhearson-Paige. The answer is no. I have copies of the solicitor general's hand-delivered letter to me stating as much. I hereby issue a public challenge to Converse to produce evidence to the contrary, and until the company does so, I consider the matter closed. I am not going to step aside. And the President assures me he has no intention of asking for my resignation or firing me."

"Mr. Sachs, can you tell us—" A reporter in the back of the room began a question, but Sachs cut him off with a wave of his hand.

"When we are concluded here, I will take a limited number of questions, but not now," he said sternly. He turned to his left. "Mitch, you want to handle this?"

Gabriel stepped up, the cluster of microphones taped, clipped, and piggybacked to the podium almost obscuring his face from Pace's view.

"As most of you know," Gabriel began, "it's the policy of the National Transportation Safety Board in cases of serious aviation accidents to withhold from the public for at least sixty days the transcripts of dialogue on the thirty-minute tape loop in the cockpit voice recorder. There are good reasons for this practice, none of which we need to reiterate now. Today we're taking the extraordinary step of releasing the transcript early—" again a murmur ran through the room "—because the reaction of the ConPac crew as the Number Three engine began to break up was one of the strongest pieces of evidence we had to support the notion of a bird strike, and we want you to hear—"

"You trying to justify your mistake, Mitch?" The voice came from behind Pace. He recognized it as a television network reporter's.

Gabriel nodded his head reluctantly. "I guess you could say that, Pete. The bird-strike theory was a mistake, an incredible, unbelievable mistake, created by an equally incredible and unbelievable conspiracy to mislead us. Unintentionally, the crew of Flight Eleven-seventeen compounded the error, and we're here today to give you all an opportunity to hear how it happened."

"Were there shortcomings in the investigatory procedures, Mitch?" Jeff Hines asked.

Gabriel turned to Sachs with a look that asked the chairman if he wanted to handle it. Sachs stepped back to the cluster of microphones.

Sachs didn't pull his punches, although the wounds were self-inflicted. "That's something we're looking at very hard, Mr. Hines. The idea that someone would—or could—divert an investigation of this nature by planting phony evidence never occurred to us. And that's one of the reasons it almost worked."

"And now you believe it?" Jeff Hines doggedly slipped in one last question. Gabriel started to intervene, but before he could, Sachs gave Hines a stunning one-word answer:

"Yes."

Clerks from the public-information office came into the room carrying huge stacks of stapled transcripts. They walked to the center aisle, one by the first row on the right, the other by the first row on the left. Each counted the number of people in the row, counted off an identical number of transcripts and handed a small pile to the nearest reporter, who took one and passed the rest along.

Gabriel watched until the process was half-finished. "Ladies and gentlemen," he said, "you know what this is about, and I suggest we get on with it without further delay. Each of you has, or soon will have, a copy of the transcript of the last minutes of ConPac Flight Eleven-seventeen, scheduled for a nonstop flight from Dulles to LAX on Thursday, April seventeenth. The cockpit voice recorder contains a thirty-minute tape loop, so at any given instant, the last thirty minutes of what went on on the flight deck can be recreated. Most of the tape from the Sexton is taken up with ground-to-ground communications—the cockpit crew talking to ground controllers, copying clearances, and so on. We had a sterile cockpit. The CVR picked up no extraneous conversation. The preflight checklist was followed in every detail. In short, in the light of what we know today, there is nothing about what you will hear that points to a deficiency by the crew. I have a copy of the actual voice tape here—"

He nodded toward a tape player set up on a low table to his right. It was wired to two speakers at the back of the podium.

"—and those of you who want actualities are hooked in, I understand. We'll begin."

The room was deathly quiet. Each journalist had a pen in hand, ready to make margin notes, but even their collective breathing was inaudible. There was the feeling they had gathered to witness an execution.

Gabriel switched on the player, and the room was filled with the voices of men who did not know they were about to die.

The early portion of the tape was routine. The crew got takeoff clearance, and the big ship began to roll. First Officer Jeremy Dodds called off the Sexton's rising ground speed as it raced down Runway 19R toward the velocity that would permit the transition—the rotation—from earthbound bus to flying machine.

"One hundred knots." Dodds' voice was flat, unemotional. "One-ten . . . one-twenty . . . one-forty . . . v-one!"

Suddenly the mood changed from the monotony of routine takeoff to uncertainty and apprehension. Pace followed the transcript:

DODDS: EPR's nominal.
PECK: It's Number Three. Rejecting!
PECK: Dulles tower, this is ConPac heavy—
DODDS: No! Captain, I've already called v-one. We're past v-one! There's not enough runway left!
PECK (to Dulles tower): Stand by, we've got a problem.
PECK: Shutting down Number Three. Full power to One and Two!
PECK: What was that?
DODDS: No clue.
PECK: Go-Go-Go!
DODDS: It's shaking us apart! Breaking up! Must a sucked in something. A bird.
PECK: Haul it up. Get her nose up! Get it up!

DODDS: It's gone!

(Unintelligible.)

UNIDENTIFIABLE VOICE: Gonna need help.

DODDS: More than help. My God, she's going over!

PECK: No! Dammit, NO!

DODDS: Right wing—cracking. We're killing—

UNIDENTIFIABLE VOICE: We're dead!

DODDS: —everyone.

PECK: Who the hell is that? Move it, man. Get it outta there!

CARSON: *Oh, shit!*

UNIDENTIFIABLE VOICE: Good-bye, honey.

There was an unearthly roar, and then there was silence.

Mitch Gabriel reached over and clicked off the tape deck. Except for someone's soft sobbing, it was the only sound in the room. For a full minute, no one spoke, no papers rattled, no pens scratched. Except for a few who were openly emotional, no one even moved.

Then, from somewhere in the middle of the room, a man's voice spoke an epitaph: "God rest their souls."

"Amen," said Gabriel, his voice quavering. "Ladies and gentlemen, we'll take your questions now."

41

Monday, May 19th, 3:30 P.M.

"And they bought it?"

George Thomas Greenwood, CEO of the Converse Corporation, sounded at once amazed and angry. "I don't believe they bought it like that," he said.

"It sure looked that way to me, G.T.," Chapman Davis

replied, his voice sounding as though it were coming from a deep well. He was on a speakerphone in Harold Marshall's office, with Marshall. If he could outlaw one thing in the world, beside the free press, Greenwood thought it would be speakerphones. Davis was elaborating. "Sachs's denial was believable. And the damned tape had them all so shook up they didn't have the energy to go for his jugular."

Davis had invited himself to the NTSB news conference and stood behind some cameramen in the back of the room so he wouldn't be noticed. He slipped out as soon as Mitch Gabriel cut off questions and was long gone before any journalists left. He came back and briefed Marshall, who placed the call to Greenwood.

"Is that *Chronicle* reporter behind the new investigation?" Greenwood asked.

"I don't know," Davis said. "His first story came out of the blue."

"I saw it," Greenwood said.

"I didn't get any feeling from it, or from what followed, what started all this up again."

"Nor did I, G.T.," Marshall added.

"Didn't anybody ask at the press conference?"

Davis nodded at the blind phone. "Yes, as a matter of fact, somebody did ask what prompted the computer runs—" he began flipping through some pages of his notebook "—and, uh . . . oh, here it is . . . Sachs said it was, uh, he said—quote—in the process of analyzing the performance of the engine, it came to our attention there was something irregular in the quantity and dispersal of the bird remains throughout the engine—unquote."

They heard Greenwood exhale heavily at the other end of the line. No one said anything for a long moment, and then Marshall asked the question that was on Davis's mind, too.

"G.T., I went out on a pretty slim limb when I called those newspaper editors this morning and accused Sachs of a conflict of interest. When you asked me to do it, I took you at your word that you had evidence to support the charge. But now, with the media buying Sachs's denial, I feel like somebody sawed off the limb behind me."

"Your damned limb isn't going to give way, Harold. Do you take me for a complete idiot?"

"Can you tell me what your information is?" Marshall persisted.

"I can, if I have to, produce testimony that MacPhearson-Paige promised Sachs a large retainer and a good deal of lucrative business after he left the NTSB if he looked out for the company's interests while he was in Washington. Good enough?"

"Good enough, yes," Marshall said, obvious relief showing on his face and in his voice.

"Thank you," Greenwood said sarcastically. "I've got some other business to attend to."

The line went dead.

In Youngstown, Greenwood set his phone down and glanced across his desk at Cullen Ferguson, just back from a relatively unsuccessful fence-mending trek to the nation's capital.

"I swear to God, these Washington types would never make it in the corporate world," Greenwood said derisively. "They're all a bunch of fucking pansies." He nodded toward the phone. "Did you see those two while you were there?"

"I saw Marshall several times. Davis just once, as I recall. The senator fidgets a lot, and he's been having some attacks of dizziness, I don't know what that's about, maybe stress. Davis struck me as pretty solid. What were they asking about this time?"

"They want to know what evidence I have to support the allegations against Sachs."

Ferguson cleared his throat and pushed himself straighter in his chair. "Frankly, G.T., I intended to ask you the same thing. The press release we put out this morning has my name on it, and I'm getting a lot of calls from reporters who want more information."

"What are you telling them?"

"We're not prepared to elaborate at this time. What else can I say? I don't know any more."

"Tell them this: During your final weeks with the news magazine, you were researching an article on the aerospace industry. In the course of the interviews, you were told by sources at M-P that they were counting on Sachs to look out for them in Washington and, in return, they were prepared to make him a wealthy man when he went back to his consulting firm."

Ferguson's eyes went wide, and his mouth dropped. Then his lips started moving, but no sound emerged.

"What is it?" Greenwood asked, laughing. "You look like a guppy trying to swallow something too big for its gullet."

"That . . . that's not true," Ferguson managed to stammer.

"What's not? That you swallowed something too big for your gullet?"

"No! I never had any information like that! Where'd you get that idea?"

"It came to me in a flash of inspiration."

"What?" Ferguson rose, somewhat unsteadily, to his feet. "You made it up? God, I . . . Jesus. *Why?"* He put his hands on the edge of Greenwood's desk to steady himself and leaned slightly toward the CEO. "Why would you do a thing like that?" Abruptly he turned from the desk and started pacing. "What if this goes to court? What if I'm called to testify? I can't get up on the witness stand and say what you just said. It would be a lie!" He turned back to Greenwood. "Perjury, George. It would be perjury. They could send me to prison, for God's sake."

Greenwood rose slowly and moved around his desk toward his private bar. Ferguson's eyes followed his every step.

"Sit down, Cullen," he ordered sharply. "Have a drink. Think this over. If this went to court—and the odds are long against it, because I don't think Sachs has the stomach for a court fight—the only thing you could go to jail for would be contempt, and then only if the judge ordered you to disclose your sources and you refused. Most judges won't get into that kind of hassle. It makes them look bad when reporters—or former reporters—sit in jail cells for heroically protecting whistle-blowers. The most you'd get is a fine, and the company would take care of it."

He handed Ferguson a generous Cutty on the rocks, which the vice-president took, although what he wanted was to toss it in the CEO's face, like they used to do in movies.

Ferguson sank heavily back into his chair and took a long pull at the drink. "I feel sick," he said weakly.

"You'll get over it," Greenwood assured him. "There will be a nice little something in your next paycheck to help calm your nerves."

Ferguson peered at Greenwood over the rim of the crystal glass. "What if I refuse to do it?"

"Then you're on the streets, with no way to pay your alimony and child support," Greenwood said quickly in a matter-of-fact tone, as though he were ordering oysters for lunch. "But why would you refuse? You don't have anything to lose." Greenwood could see the disbelief in Ferguson's eyes. "Okay," he conceded, "let's do a worst-case scenario. You have to tell this little story, we later wind up in court for whatever reason, and you have to perjure yourself. The judge insists you disclose your sources, you refuse, and you go to jail. There's some legal limitation about how long a judge can keep a person locked up on a contempt citation, like a year or something, and after that, you're back here and on the job like nothing ever happened. And while you're away, the company is paying your alimony and child support, your rent and utility bills, and we're banking your salary and bonuses for you while you're boarding at state or federal expense. When you get out, you've got a nice little nest egg and a clean slate. That almost makes it worthwhile to go up for a few months, doesn't it?" Greenwood laughed heartily.

Ferguson didn't. "You think everything that goes wrong

can be fixed with money?" he asked.

"Fixed with money? No," said Greenwood. "But money buys the *means* to make the fix. You just have to be quick on your feet."

And he laughed again.

Later in the afternoon, Greenwood called Washington again. This time he wanted to talk only to Chappy Davis.

"How is Marshall holding together, do you think?" he asked.

"He's nervous, and why shouldn't he be? I'm scared to death myself."

"Are you going to crack on me?"

"Have I ever?"

"No. But you've never had your balls exposed this way before."

"Mine are no more exposed than yours."

"What's that supposed to mean?"

"If this ship sinks, all the rats will drown together."

"Is that a threat?"

"No. An honest assessment."

"Is there a weak link? What about the two from Baltimore?"

"I paid 'em off, and they're history."

"Their van?"

"Scrapped. They took it to a junkyard and had it crushed. It's gone."

"What if somebody made the plates?"

"What if they did? Bonaro registered it in some name he took off a tombstone. Phony address, too. With their payoff, they were going to buy a new truck and see how business is in Chicago. But I paid 'em enough that if business is slow in Chicago, they won't feel a need to come back here for a good long time. I'll be sending you the bill today. It's heavy."

"I told you that didn't matter. You'll get your money. You got any other concerns?"

"Only one. Parkhall."

"How do you figure him?"

"Terrified. Sachs already had him in on the carpet once. He tells me he took the line there was a bird in the engine the first time he looked at it, the night of the accident, and he never had any reason to doubt its authenticity. He says they bought it. Since he's free, I guess they did, at least for the time being. The reporter went out to see him, too. That didn't help."

"Ultimately, you know, Parkhall's the dumb fuck who blew this for us. Doesn't he have any notion at all how a jet engine works? Jesus, how'd he ever get a job in this business? Why didn't he put more of the stuff in the flow-through areas? Why didn't he look for broken fan blades?"

"I asked him. He said he didn't think of it, he wanted to get the job done and get lost."

"Well, he's lost, all right." Greenwood paused. "If he should disappear, does that cut off the trail to the rest of us?"

Davis closed his eyes in despair. He knew what was coming next. He'd hoped it wouldn't come to this, but he knew it had to.

"Besides Bonaro and Stock, he's the only link to the rest of us."

"Then he's gotta go."

"Oh, man," Davis moaned. "With Bonaro and Stock gone, who's gonna do it?" He knew the answer before he asked.

"A man's got to do what a man's got to do," Greenwood said.

"Mr. Greenwood, when I started working for you and Senator Marshall, murder wasn't part of the contract."

"The only contract we ever had was if you did what we told you to do, nobody would find out about the dead bodies or the drugs or the point shaving in your past—"

"That was years ago. Nobody's gonna give a damn today."

"Is there a statute of limitations on murder one? Even if you're not charged, what will the allegations do to your bright future in politics? Think about it."

Davis had thought about it, even as dread of this very phone call weighted him down all day. He knew he wouldn't say no. Why did he bother to struggle?

"Do it, Chappy," Greenwood said calmly. "Just do it. Nothing showy. We're not sending any messages this time. We want Mr. Parkhall to disappear."

"I'll take care of it."

"Today."

"I . . . I'll try."

"Call me when it's over."

"Yes, sir."

That night Davis picked up Parkhall at his Virginia apartment on the pretext of going for a drive to talk about how to handle the new direction of the NTSB investigation. Earlier, the Senate aide had gone deep into northeast Washington, to a place where an old friend sold whatever was needed on the streets, and bought a hot .38-caliber snub-nose that he tucked into the back of his waistband. His jacket hid it well.

He and Parkhall drove south, in what apparently was a random direction, for Davis went to great lengths to pretend he wasn't paying attention to where they were going. At one point, Parkhall asked why they were going so far, and Davis acted startled, saying he wasn't even sure where they were. But he knew. They were in the upper Tidewater area, a place of bogs and swamps and poverty. Davis pulled onto a dirt road and stopped.

"I think we're going to have to double back to get home," he said. "But I've got to take a leak. How about you?"

"Not really," Parkhall said.

"Well, do me a favor and try, okay? I don't want to have to stop again on the way back. It's getting late."

"Okay," Parkhall agreed.

They groped their way to neighboring trees, and while Parkhall had his pants open, concentrating on not splashing himself, Davis walked up behind him and put two bullets in

his head. He pulled a small flashlight out of his jacket
pocket and hoisted the dead body under the armpits. He
cursed himself for not remembering he would be walking
backward at this point, but by twisting his upper body
around and holding the flashlight so it shone behind him, he
was able to reach one of the mud bogs his mother always
warned him not to get close to when he was a kid growing
up around here. The bogs were graves for hapless animals,
and probably for a few people, too, who fell into them
accidentally and couldn't get out before they were sucked
into oblivion. He watched until Parkhall's body disappeared completely, then threw the hot .38 in after him and
started walking slowly back to his car.

He stopped halfway, at the same tree where Parkhall peed
and died, to be sick.

42

Tuesday, May 20th, 10:32 A.M.
Pace would always remember this morning because it was
the day everything hit the fan and sprayed in all directions.
It was as Avery Schaeffer had predicted. When the story
broke, it cracked in places he hadn't imagined. Everyone
wanted an investigation. There were inquiries at the NTSB,
of course, but also at the Justice Department and within one
federal and one state grand jury. The Transportation Committees in both the House and the Senate were making
noises about hearings, and there were calls from Hill Democrats for a Senate Ethics Committee examination of the
involvement of Harold Marshall. In addition, the Securities
and Exchange Commission announced it was looking at the

trading of Converse shares on the New York Stock Exchange. A lot of reporters were getting bits of the story, but Pace still had the hottest piece.

Television news and every major newspaper in the country led with the amazing disclosure that the NTSB was now treating the bird-strike theory as a botched attempt to cover up the real reason for the ConPac crash. Wister decided the night before that Pace's two big stories should be separate, and they made one beautiful package. The page-one headline was a rare two-line banner:

>   NTSB suspects cover-up in ConPac accident;
>   Grand juries probe deaths of investigators, reporter

The press-conference story ran down the right side of the page; the grand-jury story down the left. Both carried Pace's byline. He stashed a dozen extra copies of the front section in his desk to add to his clip file. He didn't have many days this good.

If the grand-jury story staggered *Chronicle* competitors, it also staggered Stanley Eastman Travis III, United States attorney for the District of Columbia. He had stormed into the newsroom half an hour earlier, and Pace could see him engaged in heated discussion with Avery Schaeffer in Schaeffer's office, with the door closed. Travis was steamed about the *Chronicle* story on the grand juries. When Pace called him the night before, he adamantly refused to discuss anything—not even to confirm or deny that an investigation was in progress.

When Travis left a few minutes later, he looked as indomitable as when he came in. Schaeffer didn't come out to report on the meeting, so Pace supposed it wasn't of consequence to him, although he was powerfully curious.

Given Travis's attitude, Martin Lanier wasn't likely to give up much information connected with the federal investigation, and Pace suspected Helm would say nothing about the Virginia grand jury.

He called Maryland DMV about the license-plate number Jill Hughes had taken from the blue van on Capitol Hill. The vehicle was registered to Eugene Tolliver of Baltimore. When a reporter from the Baltimore bureau checked the address, he found it was a vacant lot. He also could find no living Eugene Tollivers in Baltimore. One in Lanham was too poor to own a Ford van, another in Chaptico had moved there only a week earlier from West Virginia and drove a Toyota Tercel, and one in Frederick owned a van, a brown Plymouth Voyager, and his neighbors said they'd never seen him with a blue Ford of any body type. Hours of work produced only the certain knowledge that the two men seen in the blue Ford van were professional muscle who didn't use their real names.

On the Hill, fully seven committees of the House and Senate were considering different angles of pursuit. Jill Hughes and Glenn Brennan were juggling those. Someone had to check the annual financial-disclosure records all members of the Congress and their top aides must file each May. If Marshall had a personal stake in Converse, financial statements at the Secretary of the Senate's office were the public documents in which that interest would show up. Pace called the Senate Press Gallery to tell Jill and Glenn he would check the records that afternoon. When they didn't answer his page, he left a message.

It was some time before Jill Hughes got Pace's message because she was staked out in a hallway of the Hart Building, outside the closed doors of the Senate Select Committee on Ethics, waiting for word on whether there would be an investigation into the bizarre behavior of Ohio's senior senator, Harold Marshall.

At the same time, Marshall and Senator Garrison Helmutsen were meeting in the Minnesota Democrat's office in the Russell Building to hash over Marshall's demand for an investigation of Ken Sachs' links to MacPhearson-Paige. Glenn Brennan had that one covered. He was stationed across the hall from Helmutsen's office, at a point where he could watch all the exits—in case Marshall tried to get away without confronting the army of journalists waiting to intercept him. Two hours into the watch, the senator emerged.

"I have no comment on anything," he said, trying to push his way through the crowd.

"Senator, will the committee hold a hearing?" someone asked.

"I suspect the committee eventually will hold a hearing on something," Marshall snapped. "Most committees do."

"Will there be an investigation of Ken Sachs?" another pressed.

"I'm not the chairman anymore. You'll have to ask him."

"Are you and the chairman at odds over this?" Brennan asked, pressing his way to Marshall's side as the senator tried to move up the hallway, surrounded by journalists as tightly as a shell encases a walnut.

Marshall looked sharply at his questioner. "Over what could we possibly be at odds?"

"Over Ken Sachs's handling of the ConPac investigation," Brennan clarified.

Marshall stopped and looked down to the point on Brennan's chest where his press IDs hung from a chain around his neck. Marshall frowned and squinted at the ID, then pressed the bridge of his nose between his thumb and first finger. Brennan thought he saw him sway.

"You're from the *Chronicle*?" Marshall asked.

"Yes, sir. Glenn Brennan."

Marshall's hand dropped from his face. "Get out of my way," he snarled. "I have nothing to say to you or to anyone else from that scandal sheet." He looked away and then turned back. "Did you people ever think about selling your product at supermarket checkout stands? That's where it belongs."

"Regardless of how you feel about the *Chronicle,* we're all here for an answer to the same question, sir. Will there be an investigation of Ken Sachs?" Brennan was trying hard to be polite and not let Marshall's insults provoke him. They stood toe to toe.

"Get out of my way," Marshall hissed. "Get out of this hallway. *Now!*"

"Senator, with all due respect, this is a public hallway, and I have every right to be here."

Marshall's face went scarlet, and the rest of the journalists grew silent. They sensed that Marshall was about to lose it, unless he got himself under control and backed away from the confrontation he'd created. But backing away was not the style for which he was infamous. Around him, Brennan could hear the whirring of motor drives. He was certain the TV video cameras were rolling, too, but he didn't want to break eye contact with Marshall long enough to look for them. He was willing to choke back his contempt for the man he faced, but his Irish temperament wouldn't let him blink first.

In a low voice filled with rage, Marshall asked, "Do you want me to call the Capitol Police and have you forcibly ejected?"

"No, I don't, Senator," Brennan replied evenly. "Even if you called them, I don't think they'd have grounds to throw me out. I'm not creating a nuisance or a hazard."

"Well, what in hell do you call this?" Marshall thundered. Without taking his eyes off Brennan, he waved his right hand out expansively, meaning to underscore the huge crowd around them. But he miscalculated how closely the others had moved in, and his hand hit a camera and the side of the head of the Reuters photographer using it. The blow carried enough force to knock the camera to the floor and the photographer back into colleagues, who reached out to support him.

Someone picked up the camera and handed it back to the Reuters man. The front element of the lens was shattered, and there could have been other damage that ruined his film. Enraged at the prospect, the photographer turned on Marshall.

"Who the hell do you think you are, for chrissake?" he screamed at the senator. "You just bought yourself a lawsuit, you sonofabitch!"

That snapped Marshall's last ligament of reason. He grabbed the battered camera from the photographer's hand and began using it as a weapon to clear his way out of the crowd. Holding it by the shattered lens, he began swinging it back and forth in front of him, as though he were using a machete to clear a jungle path. When his eyes fell on Brennan, they filled with new anger, and he lunged at the *Chronicle* reporter, smashing the camera into his face. Brennan felt his nose break and warm blood flow into his mouth. The taste of iron was powerful. He reeled backward into a wall and fell over, conscious but stunned. Marshall hurled the camera at Brennan's falling body, hitting him square in the neck and opening a deep cut. With attention turned elsewhere, Marshall hurried off, shouldering his way past four police officers running up the corridor toward the commotion. They recognized Marshall and made no effort to stop him. Not until a few seconds later did any of the journalists think to pursue him.

But by the time they reached the end of the corridor, he was nowhere in sight.

"He did *what*?"

If there was anyone in the *Chronicle* newsroom who didn't hear Schaeffer's bellow, it was a wonder. It fairly shook the glass of his office wall. Paul Wister's head snapped up, as did Alec Stenofsky's. Only Steve Pace didn't appear shocked. He was on the telephone with Willis Worsely, an old friend from the *Chronicle* newsroom, now a highly paid reporter for WRC-TV. Worsely had witnessed Marshall's assault on Brennan and called Pace as soon as he filed an initial report with his own station.

"I think Avery just heard," Pace said.

Worsely laughed. "I could hear him from here."

"So how bad is Glenn hurt?"

"I don't think it's as bad as all the blood made it look," Worsely said. "I'm sure his nose is broken, but they'll pack it and he'll talk funny for a few days."

"He's talked funny most of his life," Pace said.

"Ta-da-ch-h-h," said Worsely, giving Pace a vocal rim shot. "There's a cut on his neck, too, but it's not close to anything important. I'm not sure which hospital they carted him off to, but I think he needs some emergency-room types to throw some stitches into his neck and cotton wadding into his nose and he'll be on his way back to you."

"You saw the whole thing, huh?"

"Sure did. I'll be a witness for him if he wants to sue the bastard."

"Glenn didn't provoke it?"

"Don't you trust him?"

"He's got an Irish temper, remember? Didn't you ever hear about getting your Irish up?"

"When we say that in the ghet-to," Worsely pronounced it as two words, "we mean a guy's ready to get laid. Never could figure why we all called our dicks 'Irish.' "

Pace was convulsed. Worsely, educated at prep school, Yale, and George Washington University, loved to pretend he'd been raised in a slum. He did great comedy with that premise.

"Hey, man," Worsely said, "it's not nice to be laughin' that hard when one of your bes' friends got his ass carted off to a hospital on account of stories you been writin'."

Pace got himself under control. "I wasn't laughing at Glenn. I was laughing at you."

Now Worsely chuckled. "I did the street-dude act for my sister once and didn't know my dad was listening. He ordered me never to do it again in his house. He made me feel like a dork for making fun of street kids. But, hey, the way I look at it, it's a part of black culture. It's the way it is today, like slavery is the way it was a hundred fifty years ago."

"It was more like a hundred thirty years ago, Will."

"Well, history never was my best subject."

"What was?"

"Calculus."

"Shithead. You *are* a dork. Thanks for the call."

"No sweat. Tell Glenn I said hey."

When Pace hung up, he found Avery Schaeffer standing by his desk. "You heard?" Schaeffer asked.

"Yeah, just now. How is he?"

"He's at Sibley. His nose is broken, but not badly. They stitched up his neck, gave him some pain medication and antibiotics and released him. A D.C. cop is taking him home. They're going to take his statement."

Pace's eyes were drawn to a point behind Schaeffer. "Did you say they're taking him home?"

"Yes, wh— Oh, no." Schaeffer wheeled around and saw Brennan walking toward him, flanked by the police. "What are you doing here?" the editor asked. "You're supposed to be resting, you damned fool. And while I'm on the subject of foolishness, when did it get to be SOP around here for my reporters to lead with their faces instead of their pens?"

"Aye din start it," Brennan said, the wadding in his nose making him sound like he had a championship cold.

Pace got up and examined Brennan's face. "I've think you've done it, Champ," he said. "You look worse than I did."

"Uck you," is what it sounded like Brennan said, and everyone, even the cops, broke up.

"Go home," Schaeffer said. "We can cover for you."

"Will not," Brennan objected. "I'mb fine."

"Well, I'mb the boss, and I say you're not fine."

That afternoon Avery Schaeffer issued a statement on behalf of the paper: "It is tragic when a reporter, lawfully and quietly engaged in the pursuit of his profession, is brutalized by a man holding one of the highest public offices in the land."

As Schaeffer's statement was distributed, Steve Pace worked in the Senate's public-records office, tracking the financial dealings of the senior senator from Ohio. The results were tantalizing and frustrating at once.

Harold Marshall had precious few investments, but he had one that made up for the dearth of others—in the Converse Corporation. He owned stock in the company, and he had income from that stock. How much in either category was only a guess.

In the "Assets" category, Marshall listed the common stock. The declaration of the stock's value was a multiple choice of ranges, each succeeding range higher than the last. Marshall indicated that the value of his stock fell into the highest category: more than two hundred fifty thousand dollars. It was meaningless. The value could have been two hundred fifty thousand and one, or a thousand times that. The rules of the Senate didn't require Marshall to be more specific.

Under "Income," it was the same thing. Marshall declared his annual income from the Converse stock at more than a hundred thousand dollars, the highest choice in that category. Again, it could have been a thousand times a hundred thousand, but Marshall didn't have to say so.

The information wasn't new. Ohio papers had written for years that Marshall had sizable holdings in Converse when he took office and during the period when he'd negotiated for the company's move to Ohio. But no one knew when the stock was purchased, or at what price.

There was nothing in the latest disclosures that carried the story one inch farther along.

Damn! Pace thought. *You aren't going to help me, are you, you sonofabitch?*

43

The news hit Pace like a balled fist in the stomach. It almost knocked the wind from him. "Maybe he's gone into hiding," he suggested.

"Where's he going to hide?" Clay Helm asked. "And why would he leave without clothes, shaving gear, toiletries . . . anything?"

"Wasn't somebody guarding him?"

Helm hesitated. "No. But somebody should have been. He was a material witness."

"You think he was the link, for sure?"

"Had to be. We back-checked everybody's schedule. He was the first member of the power-plants group on the scene. Antravanian got there a few hours later."

There it was: confirmation of what Pace had learned from Comchech and Teller. Parkhall and Antravanian were the first from the power-plants group to reach the Converse engine. Antravanian was dead. Now Parkhall was missing.

Pace's heart was racing. "You have any problem with me writing this?"

Helm hesitated again. Pace could imagine what was going through his mind. "I don't think I want you to do that," the police captain said. "There's too much that would track back to me. Normally I wouldn't give a shit, but this is grand-jury business, okay? There's a difference. A very big difference. I was just trying to keep you updated."

"You know the rules better than that, Captain," Pace scolded. "You can't tell me something and then put it off the record later, after you find out I want to put it in black and white."

"Could you let it slide this once?"

"Clay, I can't let the disappearance of a material witness slide by."

"So what do you suggest?"

"How about 'sources close to the grand jury'?"

"That's me. They'd finger me in a minute."

"Okay, who else knows all this?"

Helm hesitated. "Well, of course, members of the grand jury. The Justice Department knows. I think maybe the NTSB knows."

"That's a lot of people, Clay. Why would it come back to you?"

"People around here know I talk to you."

Pace relented. "Okay, how about this? I'll confirm it with somebody else; then I can say that 'several sources familiar with the investigation confirmed . . .' Will that do?"

"I don't know. Call me before you write anything. Let's talk about it again."

"Fine. But you don't want Steve Pace leaving telephone messages for you, do you?"

"Right. I'll get back with you this afternoon."

Pace called Ken Sachs. He wasn't in, but Sylvia Levinson knew where to reach him and said she would have him call.

He did, ten minutes later.

"Where are you, Ken?"

"At the hangar."

"Can you talk freely?"

"Freely enough, yes. What's up?"

"You know your number-one material witness has disappeared?"

There was silence on the line. "Where'd you get that information?" Sachs asked finally.

"I can't tell you. You know I can't. I just wanted to make sure you knew."

"What you wanted," Sachs said icily, "was for me to tell you I already knew it so you could use my statement to confirm your information. Am I right?"

"Right."

"The answer is, yes, I found out this morning, but I don't want you to quote me."

"My word on it," Pace said.

After clearing the sourcing for the next day's story with Clay Helm, Pace drove to Parkhall's apartment to have a look around. If nothing else, it would provide some color for his piece on the man's disappearance.

He parked in a visitors' spot in front of the tall tower on Shirley Highway and walked in the front door. There was no such thing as a doorman, but there was a desk clerk in the lobby.

"Help you?" the young man asked impatiently, never lifting his head from the stack of papers he was sorting.

"I'm looking for Mr. Parkhall's apartment," Pace replied. "Mr. Elliott Parkhall."

His lobbyship squinted, appearing to size up the man standing on the other side of his counter. "You from the police?"

"No. Why? Should I be?"

"Only police allowed up there," the young man said, dismissing the stranger.

"What if I lived on the same floor?"

"Then I'd know you. And I don't."

"Then allow me to introduce myself. I'm Steven Pace, from the *Washington Chronicle.*"

The young man's eyes widened momentarily, then became icy again. "Police didn't say anything about letting any newspaper people up there. 'Sides, there's a cop outside the door. Wouldn't let you in."

"Suppose I ask him."

"It's a she, and it wouldn't make no difference."

"I see. Are you the police, too?"

"Nope."

"Then you can't stop me from going up. What's the apartment number?"

"Sorry."

"I could get into the elevator and check every floor."

"It's your time. But it wouldn't be worth the trouble."

Pace relented. "Okay, suppose I ask you a question."

"You already did."

Good line, Pace thought. This guy had to be an Al Pacino fan.

"Another question."

"No law against that."

"Were you on duty here Monday, probably evening?"

"Yep."

"Did you see Mr. Parkhall come in or go out?"

"You gonna quote me in the newspaper?"

"Depends on whether you have anything to say."

"I don't wanna be in the newspaper."

"Okay, then I won't quote you. Can you answer the question?"

"Yep."

"*Will* you answer the question?"

The man shrugged.

Pace reached in his pocket and pulled out a twenty-dollar bill. He'd never paid for information before, but then, he'd never conducted an interview in a gangster movie before. He held up the bill.

"Would this make a difference?"

"Probly."

"Good. Did you see Mr. Parkhall come or go Monday evening?"

"Yep. Both." The young man reached across for the money. Pace pulled it away.

"That's no answer. When did he come, and when did he go?"

The young man let his hand fall and pursed his lips in frustration. "That's two more questions."

"It's my money."

The desk man shrugged. "Can't say exactly. He came, maybe about six-thirty or seven, usual time after work. Left again about nine."

"P.M.?"

"I don't work A.M."

"After he left at nine, did you see him come back?"

"Nope. But I'm off at midnight. Mighta come in late."

"Did you see if he left with anyone?"

"Couldn't see who it was. But I noticed the car. Nice car."

Pace's eyebrows arched. "Really. What was it?"

"Thunderbird. New one. Silver-gray. Just like the one I want."

"That's a pretty expensive car."

"Tell me about it."

"Did you see who was driving?"

"Told you no already. It was dark. And I wasn't paying attention to the driver. Just the car. Nice car."

"So you said. You didn't happen to notice the license plate, did you?"

"Nope. Just the car."

"And Mr. Parkhall got into the car?"

"Yep."

"And drove off?"

"Well, he didn't drive. He got in the passenger side. Somebody else was driving. But I didn't see who it was. I was looking at the car."

"Ah, yes," Pace said. "You liked the car."

"Loved it."

"And you didn't see Mr. Parkhall return before you went off at midnight?"

"Nope. Told you that already."

"Did you tell all this to the police?"

"Two, three times. You gonna give me the money?"

Pace handed over the bill. "You've been a big help, ah, what did you say your name is?"

"Didn't. Don't wanna be quoted in the newspaper."

44

Chapman Davis stood in the driveway of his townhouse and stared with loathing at the silver Thunderbird he had loved only hours before. The *Washington Chronicle* had made it the most conspicuous automobile in the greater metropolitan area.

He cursed his stupidity for not having rented a car for the job, but who could have imagined he would be spotted? Maybe he could have it repainted. Black would be a good color with the maroon interior. No one would doubt that black had been the car's original color. Except too many people knew the car came off the assembly line a silver gray. God knows, he'd showed it to enough colleagues. He'd bragged about it, even brought a Polaroid snapshot to the office. Repainting it, if he were found out, would point the finger of guilt right at his nose.

No, he would have to tough it out and find an alibi for that night. So far as he knew, the license plate wasn't made. And the person quoted in the paper hadn't seen the driver. *If that was the truth.* Goddamn it, anyway. He'd been so careful about everything else, why hadn't he thought about the car?

He got in and thumbed the ignition, then triggered his garage-door opener. He slid the car into hiding and determined he wouldn't drive it again until this whole thing blew over.

If it blew over.

Pace had blown the lid off, and he reveled in the feeling a reporter gets when he's so far out ahead on a story nobody has a prayer of catching up.

He'd had two exclusive stories this morning, one on the disappearance of the chief material witness in the ConPac crash investigation, and a second, smaller story about the financial ties of Harold Marshall to the Converse Corporation.

Although Marshall's holdings in Converse weren't news in and of themselves, they made interesting reading when paired with reports that the senator intervened for the company with the NTSB during the original ConPac investigation. The story told how Marshall had sent an aide, who was not named, to talk to Vernon Lund on Converse's behalf. That original investigation, the story pointed out, exonerated the engine on the strength of evidence now discredited.

Yesterday had been, in Paul Wister's words, a career performance.

Pace had just finished shaving when the phone rang. It was the call he least expected.

"I'm back," Kathy said. "Am I still welcome?"

"Kath!" The excitement in Pace's voice was clear. "When did you get in? I thought you said you'd be gone a week."

"Late last night. There wasn't any reason to stay in Boston any longer."

"Why? Was something wrong?"

She laughed lightly. "Sort of. Dad was kind of pissed off at me."

"About what?"

"You."

Pace was stunned. "Me? Why?"

"Well, let me see if I can quote him. It went something like 'You've found a wonderful man who cares a great deal about you. If he offended your feminist sensibilities by going a little bit overboard in looking out for your well-being, you should realize he was doing so out of the best of motivations and not on some selfish whim.' That's close, anyhow."

"Your father said that?"

"Uh-huh. And I agree with him. I should have been more understanding about the pressure you were under."

"Well, maybe you could develop that understanding if you practiced."

"I can't practice from my house in Georgetown."

Pace's heart leaped. "You could move closer."

"How much closer do you think I'd have to come?"

"It depends on how proficient you want to get. If you want to become an expert on me, I guess you'd have to live here."

"Would I be welcome?"

"How fast can you get here?"

"Tomorrow night."

"I'll come by and help you with your things."

"No, I'll just show up. Maybe about dinner time. How's that sound?"

"Could we have dinner right now?"

She laughed again. The sound thrilled him. "It's too early. Besides, I've got a great idea for dessert."

"When I was a kid, if I was real good all day, my mom sometimes would let me have dessert before we ate."

"I don't believe that for a minute. But tomorrow night we could make an exception."

"Then again after we ate."

"Possibly."

"Hurry."

Pace's phone was ringing urgently when he reached his desk at the office.

"You don't know the half of it," George Ridley said without preliminaries. "Why the hell didn't you tell me you were writing about the Cobra? I could have helped."

"I don't have a Harold Marshall quota," Pace replied. "I can write about him as many times as I have something to say."

"I appreciate you not mentioning my name in the story, by the way, but you need to know I'm not the only one he sent to the NTSB."

"Who else?"

"Chappy Davis, at least once. Chappy debriefed me before he saw Lund."

"Did he say why he was going to Lund?"

"Yeah, sure. He said he was going to try to help Converse some more. It was right after Chappy went out there that Lund held the extra briefing where he said there wasn't any reason to ground the Eight-elevens."

Pace whistled softly. "Did Chappy ask for that?"

"Dunno. But I don't believe in coincidence."

"I guess I'll just call Mr. Lund and Mr. Davis and see what they have to say about all this."

"I got something else for you, too."

"You're a bundle of information today, aren't you, George?"

"I'm adorable, too. You been by the SEC?"

"Why would I be?"

"To check on Marshall's holdings in Converse."

"That's not public information, beyond what Marshall discloses in his Senate forms."

"Yes, it is, you dumb shit, if he owns more than five percent of the outstanding shares of the company."

"I never considered that. Where would a simple lawyer get—"

"Ask if the man's ever filed a Schedule Thirteen-D. And, Pace?"

"Yeah?"

"Have fun."

Behind the locked door of an office in the Russell Building, the three Democratic members of the Senate Ethics Committee met privately to discuss the matter of Senator Harold Marshall. They couldn't make a decision for the whole committee, but they hammered out their own feelings so they could present a united front. Seats on the panel were divided equally between Republicans and Democrats so that whichever party ruled the Senate could not use the committee for partisan politics. To have given the majority party more seats than the minority—as was the case with most other congressional committees—would have put in the majority's hands a tool too tempting should anyone want to attack a disliked member of the minority on flimsy or outright bogus charges. Hugh Green, in whose office the committee members met, favored the even split. It meant committee investigations were the result of bipartisan decisions, much more palatable to the public than political decisions.

"We don't want to leave ourselves open to charges we railroaded him," Green was saying.

"You're jumping to the conclusion we're going to find him guilty of something, Hugh," said Virginia Senator Stephen Hay Adams, considered among the more level heads in the Senate despite a confused genealogy. He was descended from the second and sixth presidents of the United States, John Adams and John Quincy Adams, both federalists, and from John Hay, who was Republican President William McKinley's third and last secretary of state. That he called Virginia home was traceable to the Hay side of the family, which had originated in the District of Columbia. His generally liberal voting record was hard for many Virginians to swallow, but the senator, in his mid-fifties, was in his third term. He won initially by the narrowest of margins, with the liberal voters in northern Virginia and the blacks of Richmond and Norfolk slightly edging the conservative voters from the southern and western parts of the state. Adams proved adept at constituent service and won his second term with a six-percent plurality, his third term with an eight-percent margin. It seemed he could stay in the Senate for as long as he liked, or for as long as he tended dutifully to the myriad interests of the home folk.

"You're right, Stephen," Green said. "I've got an attitude problem when it comes to Marshall. Perhaps I should disqualify myself from these deliberations."

"I don't think that's necessary," Adams said. "It doesn't matter what you say among friends. You'll have to be careful in the hearings. Marshall is likely to come equipped with considerable legal help, and they'll jump on any hint of personal prejudice. So, I could add, will our friends on the other side of the aisle."

Harley Stinson cleared his throat. It was loud enough to gain him the floor. Stinson was a rotund Senate fixture from West Virginia. He was among the most conservative of Democrats and came to the meeting with a natural bent against an investigation of another member of the club, regardless of the member's political affiliation. He was shaking his head, and if the meeting hadn't been on such a serious subject, the sight of his head going one way and his four chins flapping the other, then vice versa, would have been comical.

"Ah truly believe we are lettin' partisanship cloud our vision here," Stinson said with more of a hill drawl than came naturally to him. He often reverted to the old West Virginia twang when he was thinking as he spoke. The slowness of speech gave him time to think.

"What do you mean, Harley?" Green asked.

"What has our colleague from Ohio done to warrant an ethics investigation? There is no evidence, no evidence a-tawl, he has done anythin' for his own personal gain. He has gone to the limit to defend a constituent, I will admit, but ah do not believe his confrontation with that reporter in the halls of this very buildin' is an ethics matter. He was tryin' to leave a meetin', and the media people would not leave him be. They blocked his way and refused to allow him to pass"—which came out as "pay-iss." "Are we to judge him for forcin' his way through a mob?"

"He didn't force his way through; he assaulted a man without justifiable cause," said Adams. "And we can't ascribe his actions on behalf of Converse to mere constituent service, Harley. He owns a fortune in Converse stock, and he sent a tax-paid aide to the NTSB to plead the company's interests. That would be dead wrong even if he didn't own the stock. Constituent or no constituent, it's improper to attempt to influence a federal investigation."

"You gonna base an Ethics Committee investigation on an uncorroborated newspaper article?" Stinson asked. "And on the other, about him hittin' the reporter, if there was a wrong done, then it's up to the victim to press charges. It's not up to this committee to sit in judgment."

"I strongly disagree, Harley," said Green. "His actions are the epitome of conduct unbecoming a member of the Senate, and that's our mandate."

"It seems to me we hold the hearings and let the matter find its own course," said Adams. "The hearings will be behind closed doors, no press coverage. What's the harm?"

"The harm," Stinson objected, "is ever'body will know the hearin's are goin' on. There will be inevitable leaks of information, and we could be tarrin' a man who doesn't deserve it. That's the harm."

"It's obvious the vote in here is two to one to hold the hearings," said Adams. "Hugh, you have any idea where our counterparts stand on this?"

"I gather they're unanimous against, but Frank Hopper is on the line. I don't think he'd raise strong objections. He hasn't much use for Marshall, either."

"Can we bring him over?" Adams asked.

"Converting Frank Hopper isn't on the floor at the moment," said Green. "Our position on the question of investigating Harold Marshall is our only business right now. Do we vote?"

"Do we have to?" asked Adams.

"I don't want anybody saying I forced him into this," Green answered.

"But you did, didn't you?" Stinson said with a nasty edge in his voice.

"*No!* I did not," Green objected. "You had your say, Harley. And I offered to stand aside. I don't know how it could get any cleaner. We agreed in the beginning the Democrats would stand united in whatever decision we made and the majority opinion would rule. What the hell is stuck in your mountain craw?"

"You wanna know, I'll tell you," Stinson said, using his elbows to heft his considerable bulk more upright in his chair. "Ah think you're doin' this outta personal loyalty."

"To whom?" Green demanded.

"To that purty little gal that's your AA," said Stinson. "Ah hear she's sleepin' real serious with the *Chronicle* reporter who's been breakin' all these stories."

Green shook his head as if to rid it of cobwebs. Then he came out of his chair and around his desk toward Stinson, a vengeance in his eyes that caused Adams to rise to restrain him.

"You goddamned hillbilly sonofabitch, I ought to kick your ass," Green snarled. "I've never done anything official for personal reasons in my life, and you know it. My AA will have no role in these hearings. For you to suggest I would do otherwise is below contempt."

"You want to hit me, Hugh?" Stinson asked calmly, not moving from his chair. "You mad enough to take a swing at me?"

"You're damned straight I am."

"So how do you suppose Harold Marshall felt when he was subjected to even greater provocation from a herd of goddamned media, with cameras rollin' and flashes poppin'?"

Green went suddenly slack. He looked at Stinson for a long minute. Then he returned to his desk.

"Point taken, Harley," he said, sitting down heavily. "Point well taken. The assault is off this committee's agenda."

The clerk in the public-records room at the Securities and Exchange Commission was very helpful, a particular comfort to Steve Pace because he felt out of his element amid the jargon, acronyms, and esoteric concepts of the securities world.

"Yes, sir," she said. "We do have a filing for a Harold Marshall."

Pace sat down beside her at the microfiche machine and stared at the pictures of the document. "Tell me what I'm looking at," he asked. "This is a brave new world for me."

She smiled in an accommodating way. "This is called a Schedule Thirteen-D. You have to file it if you acquire more than five percent of the outstanding shares of a publicly traded company."

"I'm with you that far," Pace said. "What do these numbers mean?"

"Harold Marshall bought fifty thousand shares on this date, and at the time of purchase they amounted to five-point-three percent of the outstanding shares in the company. Then he shows here that this was a block purchase—I mean he bought it all at once; the holdings didn't build up over years. And here where it asks his intention in making the purchase, he says it was an investment."

"That's a strange question."

"In theory, if you buy a big percentage of a company's stock because you intend to take over the company, you're supposed to report it. Obviously, that could have an impact, good or bad, on other investors' interest in the company."

"Is there a way to find out if Marshall still owns the stock?"

"If there's a change in status, he's supposed to amend this statement to show that, but there's no amendment on file here."

"Then as far as you can tell, he bought fifty thousand shares on this date, and he still holds exactly fifty thousand shares."

"Right, unless he filed an amendment very recently and the paperwork isn't here yet."

"Is there a way to check?" Pace smiled at her sweetly.

"I could make some calls."

"I'd appreciate it. Should I wait?"

"It won't take long."

It didn't. The clerk returned in twelve minutes. "There is an amendment," she said. "It's a good thing for you we checked."

"How significant is the change?"

"Pretty significant. He sold all of the stock last month."

Pace sat bolt upright. "All of it?"

"Every last share, on April seventeenth."

Pace felt his heart slam into his ribs. "The same day as the crash," he said, his voice barely more than a whisper.

"A copy of the amendment is being sent down," the clerk said. "I assumed you'd want to have it."

"Indeed I do. And a copy of the original filing, too," he said.

The clerk leaned over and pressed a button on the microfiche. A copy slipped out the bottom of the machine. The clerk smiled at him.

"I never was mechanical," Pace explained.

"There you are, Pace! I hoped I'd find you." The voice came from behind the clerk, but Pace recognized it.

"George, hi. What brings you here?"

"Looking for you. Find anything interesting?"

The clerk excused herself. "I'll bring you that copy as soon as it gets here," she said.

"Thank you," Pace replied. Then he told Ridley what he'd found.

"I shudda been a reporter," Ridley said. "I got all the right instincts."

He opened his thin briefcase and pulled out a dog-eared copy of *The Wall Street Journal,* open to an inside page, and a yellow pad with a lot of numbers and notes on it. "I also read this rag cover to cover," he said. "I had more than a hunch what you'd find here."

"Don't keep me in suspense," Pace said.

"Look here," said Ridley. "This is a story on April eighteenth, the day after the ConPac accident, about the impact on Converse stock. It says all the shit you'd expect about the stock taking a beating. But here, look at this one paragraph: 'NYSE officials say a single investor sold fifty thousand shares of common stock just before noon. They attributed the subsequent precipitous slide in the stock's value in part to the uncertainty created by that sale.' "

Ridley pointed at the fifty-thousand figure in the story and then at the fifty-thousand figure on the paper in Pace's hand. "He bought in when the price was good, but when the accident happened, it was 'Fuck you, Charlie.' "

"Let's talk this through. Since Marshall dumped the stock, what motive would he have left to carry water for Converse? He didn't have to stick his neck out with the NTSB. He was out of it, and probably richer for it."

"He still had a constituent to protect. And he had the opportunity to make another killing. After he sold, the stock's price went right into the toilet, right?" Pace nodded. "Say he buys back in again at bargain-basement rates, all the while he's scheming to get the C-Fan exonerated from blame in the accident. If he's successful, the stock goes right back up. It's ingenious."

"Can we figure what he made on the sale?"

"We can take a run at it," Ridley said.

They found that on the day Marshall filed Schedule 13D with the SEC, Converse stock closed at fifty-nine dollars a share after hovering right around that figure for the entire week, a pretty reliable barometer that the price Marshall paid was in that ballpark. The purchase price would have been $2.95 million. On April seventeenth, it opened at seventy-nine and a quarter. If all fifty thousand shares sold for two and a quarter points under the opening, at seventy-seven dollars, Marshall would have reaped $3.85 million—a nine-hundred-thousand-dollar profit.

"Less broker commissions on the buy and sell," Ridley cautioned.

"It was still a handsome profit, George," Pace said. "And he'd been collecting dividends all those years, probably more than enough to offset broker charges."

What Pace didn't add was the thought that $3.85 million would finance a dandy cover-up.

45

In his office, alone by his own order, Harold Marshall
rubbed his temples. The dizziness returned in waves.

He knew the Democratic members of the Ethics Committee had voted to hold formal hearings on his conduct and
thought they could get at least one Republican to go along.
If that weren't the case last night, it surely would be this
morning after everyone in Washington read the *Chronicle*
story detailing the enormity of his holdings in Converse and
his profits from the stock sale on the day of the ConPac
accident. How Steve Pace had pieced together the details
was beyond him. Although the reporter's figures weren't
exactly correct; they erred on the conservative side.

Well, fuck Pace. Fuck 'em all. They didn't know what he
used the money for, and they'd never find out.

If only the dizzy spells would go away, and he could
concentrate . . .

In the *Chronicle* newsroom, Pace was accepting congratula-
tions.

"Yowser. I'd probably kill a few people for somebody
who handed me nearly four million dollars," Glenn Brennan said. "Far be it from me to suggest how a superstar
should pursue this story, but I wonder where a hick lawyer
like Marshall got the millions it cost him to invest in Converse in the first place. He inherit money?"

"I don't think so," Pace said with a frown. "That's a
pivotal question."

Brennan leaned in close to Pace in a conspiratorial way. "What if Converse paid him off for arranging those tax concessions on the move to Ohio? They lay a cool three mil in his hands. He is overcome with gratitude and turns around and invests the whole wad in the company."

Pace picked up the thread of the thought. "And when the company needed somebody to finance a cover-up, he cashed in the stock and had nearly four mil at his disposal." Brennan was nodding. "Actually, that occurred to me yesterday," Pace said. "Suspecting it and proving it are vastly different things."

"I'd give a week's pay to be a fly on the wall in Hugh Green's private office today," Brennan said. "I bet he's got some interesting ideas where to take this. And speaking of Green, here comes Jill. What's the poop from the ethics front, kiddo?"

"I haven't talked to anybody yet," Hughes said. "Uh, Steve, you suppose you could give me a little help with this thing?"

"Sure, if I can. What do you need?"

"There's a report around, unsubstantiated, that committee Democrats met yesterday and voted to proceed with the Marshall investigation, assuming, of course, they can get a Republican to go along. Given today's story, I think they've probably got a shot. Could you, uh, you know, call Hugh Green and ask him about it?" Hughes continued. "He'd talk to you. You've got kind of a special relationship."

Pace was annoyed that Hughes would ask. "Hugh and I don't have a special relationship," he said, keeping his voice unemotional. "Hugh's administrative assistant and I have a special relationship. That's different. And I won't trade on it."

"Don't you think he'd understand, given the circumstances and all?"

"He might understand it, but I'm not sure Kathy would. Aren't there any other options?"

"I've got calls in to the other Democrats, but they're not returning them."

"How about the Republicans? They'll know if an investigation's in the works. Green's probably talked to them by now."

"I know. I'll try. I thought Hugh Green would be a shortcut."

"Maybe, but the cost would be too high," Pace said. "I can't risk it. Besides, I'm not sure about the ethics of it."

"Okay, I understand. I'll keep after it the old-fashioned way."

"Thanks for understanding, Jill."

"I'm sorry I asked."

"No reason to be. I'm sorry I can't help."

"So am I. This could be a problem for us down the road."

"I hope not," Pace said. And he meant it.

Pace intended to talk to Kathy about the incident with Jill Hughes. He wanted her to know it happened and how he reacted. He wanted her to believe that he wouldn't let a big story—he wouldn't let anything ever again—jeopardize their relationship.

But he didn't quite get around to mentioning it.

When Kathy knocked on the apartment door shortly after seven, he had been waiting and on edge for nearly an hour. When he heard her, his heart skipped.

"Why didn't you use your key?" was all he could think to ask her. It was a dopey question from a man who felt dopey and dizzy and very much in love.

"I didn't think it would be appropriate, at least not this time," she answered.

"You look wonderful," he said, feeling like a schoolboy seeing his first prom date.

"So do you," she replied. "It feels like it's been a long time."

"It has."

"Are you going to ask me in?"

"Is begging okay?"

"Begging is good."

They embraced as though they wanted to meld their bodies, which, if the truth be known, was exactly what they intended to do. But they progressed as tentatively as two kids on a first date. He asked her about her family. She asked him about his job. It was stiff. But halfway through the first glass of wine, they made eye contact and began to laugh.

"Why don't we have dessert?" Pace suggested.

"Just what I'm hungry for," Kathy agreed.

Had they been younger, they might have ripped each other's clothes off there in the quiet familiarity of his bedroom. But as adults, they relished the preparations. She took off her blouse. He helped her take off her bra and bent to caress her breasts with his mouth. She nuzzled his neck and undid his belt and his pants. She slid her hands beneath his briefs and teased him there, and he lifted her skirt and did the same for her.

"Oh, God, Steve, let's go to bed," she said.

The first time, it was quick for both of them. The second time, they made a project of it, exploring each other's bodies with their hands and their mouths, relishing the renewal of desire. The second time, it was long, and it was loving, and when it was over, Pace laughed.

"What's so funny?" she asked.

He caught his breath. "When I won the Pulitzer Prize, I remember I told somebody it was better than an orgasm. But now I think I overstated it."

"You haven't won a Pulitzer in ten years," she reminded him. "Maybe you've forgotten how good it is."

He put his mouth over the nipple of her right breast and caressed it with his tongue. He thrilled when he felt the little mound of flesh dimple and harden in response. "The Pulitzer never did that for me," he said.

At Evelyn Bracken's insistence, Harold Marshall called his doctor at home after dinner to report the dizzy spells. The doctor came over and examined Marshall but found nothing wrong. He ordered him to the hospital for a series of tests first thing the next morning.

Ultimately, the tests told the doctors nothing. There was nothing apparent in the pictures from the CAT scan to explain the spells Marshall described. In the absence of proof of a problem, the doctors were left to their diagnostic instincts. Since they read newspapers and knew who they were treating, they believed their best clue lay in Marshall's high blood-pressure readings. The problem had to be related to stress and should be treated as such. They prescribed medication and weekly checkups. They knew of nothing else to do.

Their error in diagnosis would be obvious soon enough, although in the aftermath of the next episode, they would examine the CAT scan again and agree the problem was too small to detect at the time. Doctors protecting other doctors? Perhaps. But the aneurysm that had formed in the wall of a blood vessel at the base of Harold Marshall's brain—in the balance center—was tiny, indeed. The bouts of dizziness he experienced were caused by the aneurysm's pressure against a major posterior communicating artery in a network of arteries known as the Circle of Willis.

Had the CAT scan been done two days later, the aneurysm would have been apparent to anyone trained to read the pictures. But it wasn't apparent on this day.

And later, it would be too late.

46

Monday morning it was still raining.

It was the fourth straight day of the deluge, and the radio news people talked about flooding in the low-lying areas, especially along the George Washington parkway. The traffic jams were enormous, and everyone shared the gray mood that rivaled the color of the sky. But Steve Pace showed up for work looking renewed.

He and Kathy spent the weekend doing anything that struck them of a moment. They took long walks in the warm rain. They rented a bunch of classic old movies and watched them on the VCR. They cooked exotic meals and drank great wines. They watched a thunderstorm from the roof of the apartment building, risking being struck by lightning to see the light-and-water show.

"Do you think if we drove out to the country, you could put on a light, airy dress and run through a field of wild flowers in slow motion?" Pace asked her as they stood on the roof.

"In slow motion?" she asked.

"Yeah," he said. "Pretty girls do it all the time in perfume commercials on television."

"Those are tampon commercials," she corrected.

"Then forget it," he said. "Please, God, don't let tampons interfere with this weekend."

Kathy laughed in the breezy way Pace loved. "Don't worry," she assured him.

They even talked of marriage, and neither shrank from

the thought. It was a breakthrough for Pace, as he thought it must be for Kathy. Hell, having an honest and open relationship was a breakthrough for him.

It was the greatest feeling in the world.

And he would have some time to enjoy it before his euphoria was shattered.

Avery Schaeffer came ambling by Pace's desk. "You weren't in the paper all weekend, you know," he reminded the reporter. "I figure you didn't work the requisite eighty hours last week."

The words were harsh. But the light in Schaeffer's eye gave him away.

"Yeah, I think I quit at sixty-seven or sixty-eight," Pace replied.

Schaeffer slid into Jack Tarshis's ever-vacant chair. "What do you have in mind for the week now that your extended vacation is over?"

"Extended vacation?"

"You took the whole weekend off?"

"I made some phone calls on Saturday and Sunday."

"Produce anything?"

"No. Nobody called me back."

"Then they don't count for much."

"And I was going to put in for overtime."

"Forget it. You'll be lucky if you get paid at all."

"Then I guess I'd better get to work." Pace got serious. "The major question is, where is Elliott Parkhall? I checked in with that crazy desk man at his building. The police are still standing guard over his apartment, and Parkhall hasn't showed. If I had to guess, I'd say he's left the country, or more likely, he's dead."

"There's still the very critical question of what caused the ConPac crash," Schaeffer said.

"Absolutely," Pace agreed. "Ken Sachs is first on my call list this morning."

"They going to resume daily briefings?"

"No. I talked to Mitch Gabriel on Friday. He said since

there's a criminal matter involved, the agency more than likely won't say anything more about its investigation. Whatever they find will go straight to the Justice Department."

"What about the other members of the original team on the engine? Would they have anything to say?"

"Comchech and Teller? I tried them a couple of times. Their offices refer me to the Justice Department. Both had their home numbers changed, and the new numbers are unlisted."

"How about the Sexton engineer, the one who saw the engine a few hours after the crash?"

"Dave Terrell, right," Pace said. "Same thing. I begged Whitney Warner to get me an interview with him, but he's been put under wraps by DOJ, too. I've got his home phone, but when I call, the only people who ever answer are his wife or a teenage kid, and when they find out who wants to talk to him, they inform me very politely he has nothing to say."

"They've closed off most of your avenues, haven't they?" Schaeffer said glumly.

"I guess that's what grand-jury investigations do," said Pace. "But I'm going to keep—" He was interrupted by his phone. If he let it ring, it would kick back to a clerk who would take a message. Pace didn't know whether Schaeffer wanted him to ignore it or not.

"Take it," the editor said. "It could be a lot more important than this conversation."

"National desk. Steve Pace."

"I have some information."

The look of surprise on Pace's face alerted Schaeffer.

"Who is this?" the reporter asked.

"You don't care. All you need to know is what I know."

Pace started taking notes, trying to get both sides of the conversation. He knew the voice, but he asked anyway. "If I don't know who you are, how can I evaluate your reliability?"

"Just listen. You can check it out."

"Go ahead," Pace urged.

"You know Chapman Davis?"

"Sure."

"He drives a silver-gray Thunderbird. Brand new."

Pace went cold. "So do a lot of people."

"True. But it's an interesting coincidence, isn't it?"

"Is he the one who picked up Elliott Parkhall last Monday night?"

"No idea. That's what investigative reporters are for, isn't it, to find out those things?"

"I suppose so. Thanks."

"I could surprise you and call again. There's something even bigger in the works."

"Anything you can tell me?"

"Not now."

"You have my home phone?"

"Yeah. Don't worry. I'll find you if I need you."

The line went dead. Pace expelled a long, low whistle as he finished his notes, and Schaeffer waited impatiently to learn what the conversation had been about. Pace didn't waste words getting to the point.

"The head of the minority staff of the Senate Transportation Committee, a Marshall appointee, drives a brand-new, silver-gray Thunderbird."

"Holy shit!"

The two men stared at each other for a long moment.

"Who was that?" Schaeffer asked, nodding toward the phone.

"He wouldn't say, but I recognized the voice. George Ridley."

For a second, the name didn't mean anything to Schaeffer; then he pointed his finger at Pace in a gesture of realization. "He's the one who told you Marshall was pressuring the NTSB."

"Right," said Pace. "He's the majority chief of staff on the same committee."

"Do I gather they don't like each other?" Schaeffer asked.

"Not necessarily," said Pace. "Oh, they're totally different types. Ridley's white, solidly middle-class, blustering, profanc, and out of shape. The only exercise he gets is flapping his lips, bending his elbow, and chewing. Chappy's almost the exact opposite: black, from a blue-collar family, an ex-college basketball player who still runs every day. I like him, a lot more than I like George Ridley, as a matter of fact."

"A black Republican?"

Pace shrugged. "It happens."

"Did Ridley, or whoever that was, know if it was Davis who picked up Elliott Parkhall?"

"He said he didn't, which kind of leaves me up a creek, with an interesting clue but no smoking gun."

Schaeffer laughed. "That's a maimed metaphor if I ever heard one."

Pace laughed, too. "Nobody's perfect."

"Where'd you hear that?" Clay Helm asked without surprise. Pace expected surprise. It's not every day a reporter gives a cop a tip that could break open a case of multiple homicide.

"I can't tell you where I heard it," Pace said.

"What if I told you I had to know?"

"I still couldn't tell you. I couldn't tell you if you swore me in and put me on the witness stand. The caller wouldn't give his name."

Pace could almost hear Helm thinking it over. "You recognized the voice, though, didn't you?" Helm asked.

"What makes you think so?"

"You're taking it as serious information without checking it out. That's not like you. If you didn't have a fair idea who your tipster was, you'd have checked it out and then called me."

"I do think I recognized the voice," Pace conceded. "But I'm not absolutely certain, and if I were, I still couldn't tell you. You know that. Did you already know about Davis?"

"No, I didn't," Helm said. "And I'm sure Marty Lanier doesn't know either, or he'd have called me. Did you tell him?"

"He doesn't return my calls."

"Smart man. The less he says to the media, the less chance he'll get his butt kicked by the redoubtable Stanley Eastman Travis."

"The third."

"The third. I wonder what the first two were like."

"One of them was the real Darth Vader."

Helm laughed. "He does sound a little like that, doesn't he? George Lucas should sue. So anyhow, what are you going to do with the T-bird info?"

"I don't know, to be honest," Pace said. "It's not something I can write."

"If it were me, I'd get a court order and search the car for evidence. Obviously, you can't do that. You could try asking."

"Oh, right, the direct approach," Pace scoffed. " 'Chappy, how'd you like to implicate yourself in a felony murder?' "

"You're off base right away," Helm chided. "We don't know there's been a commission of a felony, or even a misdemeanor, for that matter. Elliott Parkhall simply can't be found at the moment. Maybe he felt the need to get away for a while. He wasn't under orders not to leave town. Even if I got my court order and found Parkhall's fingerprints in Davis's car, that would only prove that at some time or other, Parkhall was in the car. Not that he was driven to his death in the car, or even that he was in the car on the night of his disappearance."

"Are you going to look at the car?"

"You bet. I'm going to get that subpoena as soon as I get you off the telephone."

"But you said that wouldn't prove anything."

"Not on the face of it, but if we find evidence Parkhall was ever in Davis's car, we'll sweat the hell out of Davis and break him."

"Break him on the basis of evidence you yourself called circumstantial?"

"I might have a little something more up my sleeve."

"Want to share? I just gave you something good," Pace said.

"Not for publication."

"I won't quote you."

"I don't mean not for attribution. I mean not for publication. At all. Ever."

"What?"

"Well, maybe sometime. But not until I say specifically it's all right. We don't have many ways left to go with this, Steve. Off the record, I think Parkhall's probably dead, and I think his death likely came at the hand of whoever drove him away from his apartment last Monday night. But if you report that, or if you report we've got a lead on the suspect, the suspect will go to ground, and his car probably will, too."

"You mean he'd hide the car," Pace said.

"No," said Helm. "I mean he'd destroy the car. We think that's what happened to your blue Ford van."

Pace hadn't thought of the van in days. "You lost me," he said.

"Look, your reporter, what's her name, the one who spotted the van on the Hill—"

"Jill Hughes."

"Jill, right. She found the van parked outside the same building where Chappy Davis's office is. We tell Davis of that. Then we tell him an FBI informant says a late-model blue Ford van matching the description of the one Hughes saw, damage and all, was driven into a junkyard outside Baltimore. It was brought in by two men who fit the vague descriptions you gave us of the two who assaulted you. The driver, who was the owner, paid to have the van destroyed, compacted in one of those hydraulic contraptions that turns a two-ton vehicle into a two-ton block of steel. The junkyard owner remembered the case because the van was in good condition overall and he wanted to buy it for parts. But the owner wouldn't hear of it. The FBI's trying to find that block of steel now. We could still reconstruct some evidence if we could pull the mess apart. But it's not in the junkyard anymore."

"And you don't want the same thing happening to the T-Bird," Pace concluded.

"That's it. Do you know where this Chapman Davis lives?"

"Uh, Maryland, I think, but I'm not sure. Maybe I can find him in the Congressional Staff Directory. Let me look."

Pace thumbed through the thick volume. "Here it is," he said and gave Helm an address in Silver Spring. "What if you don't find Parkhall's prints?"

"A lot would depend on the circumstances. If it appears the car's been wiped, then that's suspicious in itself. If there are a lot of prints all over the place, and none of them is Parkhall's, we go off to look for another silver Thunderbird."

Helm paused for a moment. "I've given you enough information to keep you in exclusive stories for a week. But your gain could be our loss forever, if you get my drift."

"I've never gone back on my word in my life."

"I'll let you have it all as soon as I can."

47

Tuesday, May 27th, 11:30 A.M.
The wheels of justice were spinning fast. Clay Helm got his search warrant, coordinated with Silver Spring police, and planned to move on Chappy Davis before work this morning.

Pace was tempted to stake out Davis's house and watch the police proceedings, but Paul Wister advised him not to. So he spent the morning trying to concentrate on last Sunday's *New York Times* crossword puzzle.

Twenty-four across: former slave. Easy. That was "esne." A perfect crossword-puzzle word. Novices wouldn't know it; veteran puzzle addicts knew it well. And it contained four letters that would fit easily into intersecting words. Like twenty-four down: formerly. Easy again. "Erst." Pace wondered idly if American slaves, once freed, thought of themselves as "erst esnes."

He'd completed most of the puzzle—except for the top right and the middle left—when his phone rang. He attached no particular significance to the ring, since he'd been on and off the phone all morning. So he was still racking his brain for the name of a city in western Algeria as he fumbled for the receiver.

"National desk. Steve Pace."

"This is your friend with subpoena power. Thanks for no story this morning. We executed the search warrant in the company of the Silver Spring police at six this morning," Helm said. "Davis absolutely freaked. We hadn't even told him what we'd come to search for, but his eyes immediately went to the garage. That's when I knew we had him."

"That's conjecture, Counselor."

"So the CID team dusted the car and came up with Elliott Parkhall's prints all over it in areas where you'd expect a passenger to leave prints. There were other prints on the passenger side, too, including Harold Marshall's. Davis's were the only prints on the driver's side. And there was no evidence the car had been wiped clean at any point."

"What did Davis say?"

"Very little, actually. He said he wouldn't talk to us without a lawyer present, which was a very good decision on his part. Except for one thing." Helm paused.

"What, for God's sake? I could have a heart attack here any moment and die without knowing what you're talking about."

"He admitted he's the one who picked up Parkhall on the night of his disappearance."

"Bingo."

"He claims, however, that he merely drove around with Parkhall and talked about the new investigation of the Con-Pac accident, specifically its relevance to the Converse engine. He said he did it because Harold Marshall asked him to find out what he could. He said Parkhall was reluctant to talk about it, since the engine was still the subject of an NTSB investigation. After finding out very little of any use, Davis said he dropped Parkhall back at his apartment shortly after 1 a.m. He swears Parkhall went back into the building and that was the last he saw of the man. Claims not to know anything about where Parkhall is today."

"I thought you said he wouldn't talk without an attorney present."

"I did. And that's what he said. But he talked anyhow."

"Do you believe him?"

"Not for a minute. Oh, I believe he picked up Parkhall, and I believe they probably talked about the crash investigation. I even believe he's been operating under orders from Senator Marshall. After all, he's Marshall's man. What I don't believe is that he returned Parkhall to his apartment building or, for that matter, that Parkhall ever will return."

"How can you prove it?"

"Tough. But we have ways. We're holding Davis as a material witness, and we've got his wallet, with all his credit cards. If he drove around from nine p.m. until one a.m., or even close to it, he might have needed to stop for gas someplace. He's got three oil-company cards in his wallet. We've asked the companies to check for charges to his account on Monday, the nineteenth, or early on Tuesday, the twentieth."

"What if he charged gas, but the station hasn't submitted the bill yet?"

"Possible, but most stations operate on such close margins the owners don't waste any time. I'm trying to think positively."

"Have you brought him back to Virginia?"

"Can't. Have to extradite him, unless he waives it."

"So how much of this can I use?"

"Almost any of it," said Helm, "as long as I'm not a part of the story and the Fairfax Police aren't mentioned except as a party to the search of the premises around Davis's home."

Pace rolled a chair up to Paul Wister's desk and told him what he'd learned. Wister nodded his head a couple of times, but otherwise did nothing to break the narrative.

"This is treacherous, Steve," he said when Pace finished. "When we wrote about police looking for a silver, late-model Thunderbird, we were safe. There are so many of them around we couldn't be accused of pointing a finger at anybody in particular. Now we're dealing with an individual whose reputation will be sullied, even if he's innocent."

"I don't see how we avoid it unless we withhold the story. You're not suggesting that?"

"No, we have to write the story. But it never hurts to discuss the implications for fairness. And there's another issue. How do you protect your source?"

"I don't name him."

"You need to do more than that. The information you've got is too closely held, and too many people know you and Helm are thick."

"What do you suggest?"

"Call every cop who has anything to do with the Parkhall investigation—D.C., Maryland, Virginia, FBI, everybody, even the NTSB—and try to get a second source to confirm what Helm told you. Let everybody know you're calling everybody else. You'll cover Helm's tracks."

"I should have thought of that."

"No, you did what you're paid to do; you got the story. I'm paid to look for problems and solve them. So we've both earned our salaries today."

Pace pushed the chair back. "I'm on it," he said.

"What are you calling me here for, for chrissake?"

"Why shouldn't I call you at your office, George? It's where you work. You sound like a man who feels guilty

about something. You been makin' anonymous phone calls
about silver T-birds again?"

"Funny," Ridley said. "You're real funny. So what is it?"

"I'm looking for Chappy. Have you seen him around
today?" Pace tried to sound nonchalant. He suspected he
didn't fool Ridley.

"You know he isn't in today," the Senate aide replied.

"I thought as much. You know where I could find him?"

"You also know that."

"No, I don't, George."

"I heard the Montgomery County Jail. But that's hear-
say."

"Now whatever would he be doing there?"

"Time."

Pace made the rest of his phone calls.

The FBI, as usual, had no comment on anything. A reporter in the *Chronicle*'s Montgomery county bureau was
able to confirm, by looking at the police blotter, that a man
named Chapman Davis was in custody. No charges were
specified, and the police would say only that charges were
pending. Pace was fairly certain the "charges pending" status wouldn't last long. The police would have to charge
Davis or let him go.

He was surprised when Marty Lanier took his call. But he
wasn't surprised that he came away from the encounter with
no information. "I appreciate the job you're doing, but I
couldn't discuss this with you if I wanted to," Lanier said.
"Travis would be upside me like a horny hound on a leg."

It would have been funny if it weren't so believable. "I
know how Travis can be," Pace said. "I had a run-in with
him myself. He thinks I'm tapping his grand jury."

"Are you?"

"No comment."

"Right." Lanier chuckled. "I shouldn't have asked."

As soon as Pace hung up, the intercom on his phone
buzzed. "Come on in here," Schaeffer said. "Let's talk
about this story."

Paul Wister was in Schaeffer's office when Pace arrived.

"Paul filled me in on the Davis situation," said the editor. "Is there any more you can add?"

"Montgomery county police acknowledge they're holding Davis, but they say charges are pending and won't go into any details. George Ridley confirmed Davis didn't show up for work."

"Where is Marshall now?" Schaeffer asked.

"On the Hill, I guess."

"Find him. See if you can get him to comment on this, including the fact that he once sent Davis to make Converse's case with the NTSB. Then write the hell out of it."

"And if he won't comment?"

"Write the hell out of it anyway. We're obligated to give him the opportunity. We're not obligated to hold the story if he declines to take it."

Pace got up to leave, but Schaeffer called him back. "I want you to hit the Marshall angles of this story high and hard," he said. "He's the big fish we've got on the hook, and I want to land him."

48

Wednesday, May 28th, 7:10 A.M.

Harold Marshall sat alone in his bedroom, propped up by pillows in his expansive bed, the morning papers spread before him. He dreaded the idea that the phone would ring within minutes and that George Greenwood would be on the other end, undoubtedly with a sheaf of fax paper in his hand, the latest-breaking news from the *Washington Chronicle*. Greenwood calls were coming in at an average of three a day. Most of the time he railed at what he called "leaks, lies, and innuendo." He seemed to think Marshall could snap his fingers and make them go away.

But the strong current of events had gone well beyond the point where a single senator, and one under considerable stress and suspicion, could do anything to redirect attention.

Marshall reread the latest in the *Chronicle* and shook his head angrily. His staff had told him the day before of Chappy Davis's detention; apparently someone recognized his car and reported it to the police. That flashy damned car. Why on earth had Davis used it to pick up Parkhall? Of all the stupid, damned decisions. Marshall hoped Chappy would hold together. He didn't need his aide cutting any deals.

Pace had tried during the previous afternoon and evening to reach the senator, calling his office, his home, and even Evelyn Bracken's home. Marshall refused to take or return the calls. Thus the story ran without his comment, and he knew that made him look worse, but at this point, there wasn't anything he could have said to make things better. He could have denied everything, which would have been a lie, and everyone would have recognized it for what it was. Marshall rolled his head against his pillow. He didn't have the answers. He wasn't even certain he knew all the questions. But he knew the newspaper scared him half to death.

He had reached the point where he greeted each new morning with apprehension. He took the first of his three daily doses of blood-pressure medication even before he picked up the papers at his front door. Generally, he found he was justified in doing so. Barely a day passed without another assault on him. God, if they ever got the whole story . . . he banished the thought as he felt perspiration seep from the pores of his forehead.

He finished with the *Chronicle* and laid it aside. Now he fingered the front page of *The New York Times.* His name was nowhere on page one because the *Times,* if it knew of Chappy's arrest, did not know enough to attach any significance to it. But Marshall knew he'd be on the front page of the *Youngstown Vindicator* and countless other Ohio rags, if not today, then tomorrow, for his hometown and home-state newspapers surely would pick up whatever The Associated Press carried of the *Chronicle* stories. The *Vindicator*'s chief political writer had been trying to reach Marshall all week, but he was dodging those calls, too.

Evelyn had come over to fix his dinner the night before and spent most of the evening pressuring him to file some sort of lawsuit to stop the *Chronicle*'s reports. It proved useless to try to convince her there was nothing to be done. The United States Supreme Court years earlier struck down the concept of prior restraint when the U.S. government tried to stop *The New York Times* from publishing the Pentagon Papers. That decision provided newspapers ample protection against prepublication suppression. He couldn't sue for libel. He was too much a public figure, and there was no apparent malice in the *Chronicle*'s reporting. He couldn't argue reckless disregard of the truth because, unfortunately for him, everything the paper printed was accurate.

Evelyn understood none of it. She kept keening, "Well, think of *something*!"

He contemplated going to the Senate Ethics Committee and telling everything, but he was honest enough with himself to recognize he wouldn't be willing to tell every last little bit of the story, and withholding anything would finish him. He knew the committee had his stock records. He knew questions would be asked about the money: where he got it, what he did with it. He'd never thought he'd have to face those questions, and he knew he wasn't prepared to answer them. No amount of pressure would make him answer. When the committee called him, he would go, and he would answer truthfully every question asked, except questions about his money.

God, he'd made mistakes in his life, major, major mistakes. But how had it come to this? He didn't believe he was an immoral man, but he most certainly had sold his soul for Converse. Over the years—and over the last few weeks—

he'd done things he once would have considered unthinkable. Now there were demands that he pay the price. He
wouldn't let the Senate ship him off in disgrace. He would
go, if it came to that, fighting to the end and with his head
high. But there would be no capitulation. He firmly believed
what he'd done was for a higher good. It was a conviction
that no amount of public pressure would vitiate. No, he
wouldn't tell them about the money. Never. That would
enrage his colleagues, but he didn't care. Maybe, just
maybe, he could weather the storm.

But he doubted it.

When he threw back the covers and stood up, his head
began to spin again.

49

Thursday, May 29th, 3:24 P.M.

In the confines of his holding cell at the Montgomery
County Jail, Chapman Davis snapped shut the book he'd
been trying to read. He'd gotten through just five pages in
the last hour, and he couldn't recall a thing about any of
them. After nearly three days of incarceration, the waiting
and the uncertainty were taking their toll.

His lawyer was trying everything to win his release. But
attorneys from the Justice Department argued he was a bad
risk. Given his resources and the severity of the crimes of
which he likely had some knowledge, he probably would
flee, they argued, and the courts kept buying that argument.
So here he sat, his muscles going to mush, his conditioning
going down the toilet.

In the privacy of his own mind, he acknowledged if he got

loose, he probably would run. He was in a no-win situation. No one ever would be able to prove he'd killed Parkhall, since there was no proof Parkhall was dead, nor could anyone prove he carried the cash that paid for the phony bird evidence. But there was a good chance the Ethics Committee would take Marshall down, and a slimmer but real chance Converse would collapse with him. It would be too easy for too many people to plea-bargain their way to one of the federal golf-club prisons at the price of the skin of their "black boy." And he had no doubt they would do it.

He threw the book against the cell wall and cursed the stupidity that brought him to this. Then he lay back on his bunk and listened to the shouts and the laughter of children at afterschool play somewhere nearby.

Children were playing outdoors after school everywhere, taking advantage of the warming weather and the lengthening days. As they were playing in Montgomery County, Maryland, so they were playing down in the Tidewater lowlands of Virginia. A few were even playing in places their parents had warned them time and again not to go, areas pocked by mud-filled sinkholes capable of sucking a body into oblivion as fast as a rock would sink to the bottom of a pond.

When something went down in a Tidewater sinkhole, usually it stayed down. Occasionally, however, as flesh decayed and gas built up in body cavities, a carcass would return to the surface, if ever so briefly. The turkey vultures indigenous to the area made the sinkhole region a regular stop on their scavenging tours because more days than not, the remains of some hapless animal would be available for lunch. If there was a little mud with the meat, no matter. The birds' physiologies could tell the difference, keeping what their bodies needed and excreting the rest.

On this sunny afternoon, two youngsters, age seven and nine, roamed farther from home than they realized, so engrossed were they in their game of cowboy and Indian.

Suddenly the younger one, whose name was Isaac, realized where they were.

"Pauly, we're not supposed to be here," he shouted at his friend. "This is where the stinkholds are."

"Yeah," agreed Pauly, his eyes wide with wonder. "There's a big one right over there. Let's go look."

"No-o-o!" Isaac objected. "My mama would whup me. We gotta go home."

"Oh, come on, or are you a scaredy-cat? There's a buzzard over there eatin' on somethin'. Let's see what it is. We won't get close, or are you afraid I'll push you in?"

"Oh, Pauly. I don't wanna go."

"Then I'm gonna go alone, and I'll tell ever'body Isaac's an old scaredy-cat."

Little Isaac made rocking motions, like he wanted to go forward with his friend but he didn't want to, either. He watched in terror as Pauly got closer.

"Be careful, Pauly," he shouted.

The vulture in Pauly's view looked up with its blood-red eyes, then lowered its red head again, correctly assessing the boy as no threat.

Pauly could hear a kind of ripping, slopping sound as the big bird tore at its meal, and his eyes widened in a horror so great it would consume his sleep for months to come.

"Isaac! *Isaac!* C-c-co-ome here! *Quick!*"

There was little visible above the surface of the mud, only a head and one grotesquely curled hand. The bird was standing on the head. The eyes were gone, and the holes were filled with mud. The nose was a bloody stump; the vulture had finished off most of it as an appetizer since it was the most prominent feature. The flesh of one cheek was gone, too, and the bird had gone to work on the other, ducking its head to tear away meat and exposing the skull, which gleamed white against the rusty brown of the muddy, untouched places.

"Isa-a-a-ac!" Pauly was about to wet himself, and he grabbed at his crotch to try to stop it. *"Isaac! Isa-a-a-ac!"*

"Wassa matter with you, Pauly?" his friend asked, so

unexpectedly close behind him that the larger boy started in fright. "It's just a dummy." The little boy began to chant: "Pauly's a-scared of a du-u-ummy. Pauly's a-scared of a du-u-ummy."

"It's *not* a dummy, Isaac," Pauly insisted in a fear-choked voice so low that Isaac had to strain to hear. "Dummies don't bleed."

Isaac looked at his friend, and then he looked closer at the spectacle in the sinkhole. As they watched, the great vulture spread its wings to their full six-foot extension and seemed to levitate from the ripped head before it glided directly at the two young spectators.

The boys looked at each other with identical wide-eyed, terror-filled expressions, then turned and ran like hell for home.

50

Friday, May 30th, 6:00 A.M.

"If I woke you, I don't apologize. This is Harold Marshall."

Pace had been in an REM sleep cycle, deep in a dream interrupted by the jarring jangle of his telephone. He fumbled for the instrument, fighting not to lose the thread of his fantasy, and thought he mumbled hello. When he heard the identity of his caller, the dream was lost instantly.

"Yes, Senator, I've been trying to reach you."

"I didn't wish to be reached."

"Then why did you call?"

"To tell you I plan to ask the Senate Ethics Committee for an opportunity to appear before it to answer all questions I deem fit at the earliest possible date. I will request the hearing be public. Then I will leave my fate to Providence."

"Why would you volunteer to appear?"

"I know a lot of people detest me, Mr. Pace. I am blunt, sometimes condescending, occasionally obnoxious. I have a very short fuse, as your colleague, Mr. Brennan, can attest. But I am an honest man, and I am loyal. Perhaps in these past weeks, my loyalty has strained propriety, but I don't apologize. I did what I believed I had to do."

"When will you make your request to appear?" Pace asked. He was scribbling notes as fast as he could write on a pad he kept on his nightstand.

"Today, although I don't know when, or if, the committee will deem such an appearance appropriate. I plan no announcement. I wanted to tell you myself before you found it out from one of the back-stabbers with whom you run."

"I don't run with back-stabbers, Senator. I deal with forthright, honest people, who feel wrongs have been done."

"They're back-stabbers from my point of view."

"I'm sorry you feel that way, but I understand."

"No, you don't. You don't understand anything, Mr. Pace. Nothing at all."

And the line went dead.

Pace replaced the receiver and reached over to turn off his alarm. He wouldn't need it; there would be no more sleep this morning.

"That was certainly something." Kathy's husky voice stated the obvious.

"It sure was."

"What did he say, or is it privileged?"

Pace smiled at her and stroked the side of her face. "Not privileged. In fact, your boss is about to hear from him. He wants a hearing before the Ethics Committee. And he wants it public."

"No kidding?" Kathy propped herself up on her left elbow, and the sheet dropped away from her, exposing part of her right breast.

"No kidding," Pace said as he reached over to cup the exposed flesh. "And, thanks to him, we have an extra hour to ourselves this morning." He bent to kiss her.

"Oh, no," she said, pulling back. "This isn't the movies, dear boy. There will be no kissing before mouthwash."

He fell back on his pillow. "Hey, kid, wanna share the same glass?"

"You are *so* naughty." She giggled, and left their bed for the bathroom.

At the office several hours later, Pace got an urgent phone call from Clay Helm. "Sometimes we're too lucky to live," the police captain said. "The courts were about to kick Davis free for lack of charges, but the fates were on our side."

"What are you talking about?"

"You ever hear of a little town in the Tidewater area named Deltaville?"

"No, I don't think so. The name sort of fits the area, though."

"Yeah, doesn't it? Last evening I got a call at home from the Middlesex County sheriff's department. They found Elliott Parkhall."

Pace's pulse jumped. "No fooling. Are they holding him?"

"In a manner of speaking. He's dead."

"Oh, no," Pace groaned. "I don't suppose it was natural causes."

"Not unless it's natural to die of a heart attack caused by two bullets in the head."

"I guess that wouldn't qualify, no."

"It was pure luck. Whoever snuffed him dumped his body in a mud bog—they call them sinkholes down there. The mud is thick, but Parkhall's decomposition created enough gas in his abdominal and chest cavities that he popped to the surface and became buzzard bait."

"Spare me the gory details," Pace pleaded.

"They're gory all right. Some kids happened upon the

rather grisly scene. They were so scared one wet his pants. There wasn't much left of the man's face, but the medical examiner was able to pull a good set of prints. After that, the ID was easy."

"How does that implicate Chappy Davis?"

"Remember I told you we were checking gasoline credit-card purchases on Davis's accounts for late on the night of the nineteenth or early morning on the twentieth?"

"Sure. And something came up, right?"

"Right. Davis stopped for gas in Tappahannock about one A.M. on the twentieth. That's right on the way to or from Deltaville. In this case, probably from. We found the attendant who made out the charge. He remembered Davis's car clearly, and he remembered Davis because—these are the attendant's words—'he looked kinda sick.' He also recalled that Davis was alone. All this is going to be announced at a press conference at three this afternoon in the commonwealth attorney's office here. Davis is being held officially for extradition to Virginia on charges of first-degree murder."

"Oh, man, it's all coming unstuck, isn't it?"

"These things have a way of doing that."

Paul Wister sent Glenn Brennan to cover the Virginia press conference, leaving Pace free to pursue the ramifications of his early morning conversation with Harold Marshall. Pace agreed grudgingly to the plan.

"You hate to let any piece get out of your hands, don't you?" Wister asked with a grin.

"You think that's selfish?"

"No, I think it's both admirable and understandable. But there's too much happening on too many fronts to heap it all on your shoulders."

"I guess so," Pace acknowledged.

Wister plucked notes from his desk. "Let me tell you what we're up to for tomorrow," he said. "I hope to hell nothing major happens anywhere else in the world, because we've got a very full agenda for A-section just covering the Marshall story. The plan now, and this could change, is to give you and Glenn the top of the page. Your story will be on your interview with Marshall and any reaction you can get from members of the Ethics Committee. Yours will be the lead story. Glenn's piece on the press conference will be the off-lead. Jill Hughes is working on profiles of both Marshall and Davis. One or both will start on One-A, depending on available space, but we might also open up some inside pages if we're snowed under with copy.

"Suzy O'Connor assigned a reporter, and I'm not sure who it is, to go down to Deltaville and interview the two kids who found Parkhall's body. Eddie Balsiero is going along to take photos of the kids and of the bog where the body popped up. He's also going to try to get a photo of the attendant who IDed Davis at the Tappahannock gas station. We've got a Maryland police reporter working on the Davis extradition. Since the discovery of Parkhall's body and the extradition won't be announced publicly until three, I think we've got a leg-up on all the Deltaville and Tappahannock material, maybe even on the Maryland angle. We owe Clay Helm a big favor for giving us the advance notice."

"For a lot of other things, too," Pace said.

"I know, although I don't imagine he'd want them publicized."

"I'm sure he wouldn't."

Wister tossed his notes back on his desk. "What's your best guess about the way this all came down?" he asked. "Given all you know, who are the bad guys here?"

Pace perched on a corner of Wister's desk. "The most likely scenario is this: When Converse was out on the West Coast, it was a company with a lot of promise and very little cash. Its expenses were enormous. It had a lot of great ideas and superior engineering capability, but it lacked the resources to get those ideas out of the drafting stage."

"Do you know all this to be true, or are you conjecturing?"

"I know it's true. I have a huge file on Converse."

"Okay, go ahead."

"Well, along comes Harold Marshall, who arranges major financial incentives, including huge tax abatements, if Converse will relocate to Youngstown, Ohio. The company makes the move. All that is a matter of public record. Marshall's a civil lawyer, without great personal income or family money. My theory—and this *is* theory—is Converse slipped him enough money to buy the fifty thousand shares of stock. It was his payoff for his help. I assume that sort of thing's illegal."

"Wouldn't the IRS notice something like that?" Wister interrupted.

"Then? Maybe, maybe not," Pace said with a shrug. "But I bet they've noticed now. Anyhow, after the ConPac crash, Marshall recognized if the Converse engine were to blame, his stock, and perhaps Converse itself, could go down the tubes. The company has most of its immediate future tied up in that engine. So he unloaded his stock and wound up using part of the proceeds to pay for the cover-up."

"There's no way he could have acquired the stock on his own, bought it with his own money?" Wister asked.

"Not with his limited resources."

"That's the way it looks to me, too." Wister paused. "Could he have had income from a source not obvious to us?"

"I guess, but I don't know what it could be. He came into the Senate already owning the Converse stock; it's on his first financial disclosure. There is no other major source of income listed for that or any year since. If it existed, it ended when he was elected, and we couldn't find out what it was without his tax records."

Wister shook his head. "My caution light is blinking," he said, "and I haven't the faintest notion why."

"Because the scenario that makes the most sense, that seems the most logical, is almost too pat," Pace said.

"Do you doubt that scenario?" Wister asked.

Pace ran a hand through his hair. "I don't know, Paul," he said. "I honestly don't know."

Pace transcribed the quotes from Marshall that he'd scribbled hastily in his bedside notebook. Then he placed calls to the members of the Ethics Committee. He'd finished the last call when his phone rang.

"National desk. Pace."

"What's goin' on?"

"Mornin', George."

"I've developed a problem," Ridley said. "I need a news fix a couple times a day. I don't seem to be able to wait for the next morning's paper lately."

Pace smiled. "What's your point?"

"I figure you owe me lunch, and I could pick your brains about what's happening behind the scenes. Strictly off the record, of course. I just like to keep up."

"I guess I do owe you lunch by now," Pace acknowledged. "There's a great Japanese sushi place on Twentieth, between L and K. Wanna try it?"

"I like my sushi fried."

Pace smiled. "Why did I figure that? How about Mr. K's?"

"Your nickel? That's a little pricey for me."

"The paper's nickel."

"One o'clock."

"See you there."

They were seated off the main room of the huge, ornate Chinese restaurant at 21st and K streets. It was unlike any Chinese restaurant Pace had ever been to. The kitchen took traditional dishes and turned them into gourmet dining experiences and charged appropriately high prices. This was no wonton-and-fortune-cookie joint. This was strictly uptown.

Pace and Ridley each ordered a beer, and the reporter began scanning the multipage menu. Ridley's lay unopened on his serving plate.

"You're not eating?" Pace asked, joking.

"You know better," said Ridley. "I'm having pressed duck."

Pace glanced down the list of fowl entrees. "I don't see it here."

"It's never on the menu. You have to know to ask for it."

When the waiter showed up, Ridley asked.

"Yes, sir," the waiter said. "It is twenty-four ninety-five."

Pace almost choked on his beer. "You ain't no cheap date," he said.

"And you wouldn't love me if I were," Ridley replied.

"I suppose you want all the courses, too?" Pace asked.

"Of course. I would wish this to be a culinary highpoint in my year."

"I thought PBJ on Wonder Bread was your thing."

"I've had worse."

While they waited for their food, Pace extracted an oath of silence from the Senate aide and filled him in on developments in the Parkhall disappearance. When he reached the part about the kids finding the body, Ridley demurred.

"Spare me while I'm eating."

They made small talk and traded theories about Marshall and the fake-bird evidence in the C-Fan. Generally, Pace learned nothing new.

But lunch was great, even though the bill came to nearly seventy-five dollars.

Before the tip.

They emerged into the bright afternoon sun, and Pace said he would walk back to his office. It was too nice a day for a taxi.

"Why'nt you come up to the Hill with me?" Ridley asked.

"I've got work to do, George. Maybe another time."

"It'd be worth your while, I think."

"Why?"

"Gary wants to see you."

"Gary?"

"Helmutsen, the chairman. Remember him?"

"Oh, I don't think of him as Gary. What does he want with me?"

"Dunno. But he said it was important."

"Is he in?" Ridley asked as he walked past the senator's secretary.

She nodded. "He's been waiting for you."

Pace and Ridley pushed through the high door into Garrison Helmutsen's inner sanctum, a dark, walnut-paneled office overburdened with huge mounted fish, pictures of famous people catching fish, fishing trophies, fishing magazines, cutsie fish sayings carved into rough-hewn slabs of wood, and two large, framed posters of Minnesota lakes with bass breaking water.

"You do much fishing, Senator?" Pace asked as the two shook hands.

Helmutsen smiled. "When I can," he replied. "Had more time for it when the Republicans were running the Senate. Almost too bad we took it back. Don't repeat that. I'll deny I said it."

"Your secret's safe with me, sir," Pace replied as he sat down in an overstuffed leather chair indicated by Helmutsen. "George said you wanted to see me."

Helmutsen nodded, and his blond hair swayed on his head. Nobody would mistake him for anything but Scandinavian, even one who didn't know his name. He had a reputation as a hayseed; he both looked and acted the part. He tended to be quiet and not very forceful.

"As you can imagine, I've been reading your stories with a great deal of interest, particularly your stories about my esteemed colleague from Ohio," Helmutsen said.

"I understand you and he are great friends," Pace said with a straight face.

It was Helmutsen who chuckled. "What we have is great," he said. "I would not describe it as friendship."

"And what can I do for you?"

"You're doing very well. It's what I can do for you." He paused, as if considering something very weighty. "Mr. Pace, I know I am reputed to be one of the Senate's lesser lights. I don't pretend to be a great statesman; I don't even aspire to it. But I am not stupid. And I can only be pushed so far. Harold Marshall has exceeded even my great capacity for tolerance.

"As you probably know, I attended the University of Minnesota. During four very happy years there, I became close friends with another student, named Archer Smith. We were fraternity brothers, classmates, roommates, and nearly inseparable. I introduced him to the woman who became his wife. He told me he owed me a huge favor for that, and I should stash it away until the day came when I really needed something only he could provide. Then I went off to law school and he enrolled in graduate school and got a master's degree in criminal justice. He's now a special agent with the FBI."

"What does that have to do with me?" Pace asked.

Helmutsen hefted a thin sheaf of papers, encased in a black-plastic cover. "A couple of days ago when Harold Marshall was putting enormous pressure on me to investigate Ken Sachs—for no good reason apparent to me, I might add—I began wondering about my colleague's motives. Then when I read your story on his Converse stock transactions, I began wondering what he'd done with all that money. I went to Arch and called in that favor."

"After all these years?" Pace asked, incredulous.

Helmutsen nodded. He tossed the papers on his desk and they slid across to the edge, where Pace could reach them. The reporter left them untouched for the moment.

"I gather this isn't something Senator Marshall would want made public?" he asked.

"I don't think so, no," Helmutsen replied.

"Why don't you give it to the Ethics Committee?"

"Because I'm not at all certain the Ethics Committee has the balls to stand up to Marshall. If it doesn't, this story will never get out, and I want it out."

Pace cleared his throat. "I'm intrigued as hell, Senator, but I'm a little uneasy about acting as the vehicle for your vengeance."

"I'm offering you what I think is a legitimate news story," Helmutsen said, showing no anger at Pace's challenge. "If you don't think so, I can still offer this to the Ethics Committee. The choice is yours, really."

Pace reached out and picked up the packet as though he thought it would burn his fingers. It was a confidential FBI report, with a covering letter from Archer Smith.

"I want the letter back," Helmutsen said. "I don't want any evidence of Arch's involvement to leave this office. But I included it for you to read so you could verify the authenticity of the document."

Pace nodded. The letter was perfunctory, but it did allude to the attached results of an investigation of Harold Marshall's April nineteenth transaction in Converse common stock. When Pace finished reading the letter, he handed it back to Helmutsen.

The report contained a breakdown of both the purchase and the sale of the Converse stock. The figures given were much more precise than those Pace had had to work with, although he was cheered to see his imprecise calculations hadn't been far off the mark.

It got a little complicated from there. It noted that most people who buy and sell stock regularly have accounts with brokerage firms. Stock purchases are paid for out of those accounts, and profits are returned to them. Generally, the report said, it would take ten days to two weeks for the proceeds from a sale to show up in the owner's account, and the owner would have to wait that long to get his hands on his cash.

But in the case of Marshall's sale of fifty thousand Converse shares, the proceeds were wired by his broker on the same day to Marshall's checking account in Washington at the Riggs National Bank, across the street from the Treasury Department.

"Nearly four million dollars to a checking account?" Pace asked aloud of no one in particular.

"Read on. The best part lies ahead," Helmutsen said.

Minutes before the bank closed, according to the report, Marshall went in and withdrew one million dollars in cash.

Bank officials told the FBI he put ten thousand one-hundred-dollar bills in a briefcase and walked out of the bank with it. No security guards, no qualms, no nothing. He left as though he'd cashed a fifty-dollar check.

On the date the FBI report was written—the previous day, Pace recalled from the covering letter—the balance of the funds remained in the checking account.

Pace looked at Helmutsen in disbelief. He could feel his mouth open. "Ten thousand hundred-dollar bills?" he asked. "I wouldn't have thought banks kept that many."

"They don't as a rule," Helmutsen said. "I got some clarification. Marshall called ahead to let Riggs know what he wanted. They had to scramble, but they put it together for him."

Pace continued to read.

Acting on an FBI request, the federal banking officials conducted a search and found a new account opened in the name of Ernest Peters in an Alexandria, Virginia, savings bank early the next morning in the amount of seven hundred fifty thousand dollars. Peters brought in cash. By comparing handwriting and through a description of Peters given by bank officials, the FBI was able to conclude that Ernest Peters was, in fact, Elliott Parkhall, the man in charge of the investigation of the C-Fan at Dulles.

"So Parkhall was paid off to fake the bird strike?" Pace asked.

"Supposition," Ridley said.

"What happened to the other quarter-million?"

"No word, and the FBI won't speculate," Helmutsen replied. "I don't mind, though. Maybe Marshall held it back to cover future expenses. Or maybe he gave the whole million to Parkhall, and Parkhall kept two hundred fifty thousand for immediate payoffs. Find Parkhall, find out."

"Parkhall's dead," Pace said matter-of-factly. "His body's been recovered."

Helmutsen heaved a huge sigh and shook his head. "What a fucked-up mess," he said.

"It was good of you to see me, Hugh. I know you didn't have to."

"I had no reason to refuse."

Harold Marshall and Hugh Green faced each other across the big old mahogany desk in Green's Senate office. It was late. The office staff was gone for the day. Marshall asked expressly for the privacy. He refused to walk the halls of Capitol Hill, absorbing the looks of anger or pity or contempt from those who recognized him. And for a person who read the papers these days, with his photograph appearing everywhere, recognition would come easily.

He dressed casually for the meeting: slacks and loafers, a sport shirt, and one of those old-style cardigan V-neck sweaters Perry Como popularized. The sweaters were functional and comfortable, and Marshall took care to preserve his collection.

"I want to testify at the earliest possible date, and I want the hearing to be public—press, radio, television, C-Span—the works," Marshall said.

"I don't know if there's going to be a hearing, Harold," Green said. "The committee is split right along partisan lines. Unless one of us or one of them relents, we're deadlocked."

"And if you get a Republican to vote with you?"

"Then we'll have a hearing, and we will gladly hear you, although I imagine the plans would call for your testimony to be taken behind closed doors."

"There's no need for that. I have nothing to hide." Marshall's clear blue eyes never wavered. Green wondered if he thought he was telling the truth.

"Harold, the big stock sale the *Chronicle* wrote about—was the story accurate?"

"More or less," Marshall conceded. "I don't see what's wrong with that. Isn't it reasonable to assume, given the initial reports of the events surrounding the accident, that any prudent Converse stockholder would have sold out?"

"Perhaps so, yes," said Green. "Then what did you do with all the cash?"

"I'm not prepared to say."

"And where did a civil lawyer from Ohio, with modest family means, get the funds to acquire all that stock in the first place?"

"I'm also not prepared to answer that."

"Now, or ever?"

"Ever."

Green ducked his head in frustration. "Harold, for God's sake, you know that answer won't wash."

"It will have to suffice."

"They'll crucify you."

Marshall shrugged. "I'm willing to take the chance. And if I'm willing to risk it, why aren't you willing to allow me to assume the risk? Surely you aren't going to claim you're looking out for my best interests." Marshall's voice oozed sarcasm.

Green sighed deeply. "No, you've always been very capable of looking out for yourself. But I don't want the hearing turned into a sideshow. I won't have it used as a soapbox for you."

"Then you don't want me to have my say?"

"Of course you can have your say. But I don't even know if there'll be a hearing."

"And if there is a hearing, you'll put forth my request to appear at a public session?"

"Yes."

"Without objection?"

"Yes."

"Thank you."

After Marshall left—neither man had offered to shake the other's hand—Green sank back into his chair.

"You've got something up your sleeve, you crafty old bastard," he said to the empty office. "But I'm damned if I can figure what it is."

51

The ConPac accident investigation was now well into its
seventh week, and Steve Pace felt as though it must be the
seventh year. He'd been running nonstop on adrenaline,
and his body's ability to manufacture a new supply was
ebbing. Or maybe it was his increasingly wonderful relationship with Kathy that was causing the problem. He cherished
every moment they had together, and with days off tenuous
at best, he tried to cram everything he could into the hours
that circumstance and deadlines gave them. Maybe he
wasn't burning out on the story so much as he wasn't giving
his body the time it needed to recharge during his rare
off-hours.

The end of the previous week cost him an enormous
amount of emotional energy.

When Pace returned to the office on Friday afternoon
with the FBI report supplied by Garrison Helmutsen, his
editors were stunned. Avery Schaeffer actually called Helmutsen to hear for himself the circumstance under which
the senator had come into possession of the document. He
didn't mistrust his reporter; he simply wanted to hear it
firsthand.

When he was satisfied, he and Wister, in consultation
with Pace, decided to hold the story for Sunday. There were
a lot of people to call for comment, not the least of whom
was Marshall himself, and great care had to be taken in
writing the story lest it accuse Marshall of more than the
somewhat odd financial transaction detailed in the report.

Unanimously, they hated the idea of wasting the story on a Saturday, when most people were thinking more about getting away for recreation than about reading newspapers.

Pace reached Marshall late Friday night. The Ohio Republican sucked in a sharp breath when told what the FBI report said. He did not deny it, but he was anxious about whether the FBI also knew what he did with the million dollars in cash. Pace told him about Elliott Parkhall's sudden fortune, and Marshall laughed.

"Think what you will," he said. "I have no further comment."

Pace wasn't able to reach any Riggs officials who would comment, but one of the *Chronicle*'s business writers had a source at the Riggs office where Marshall banked. The source added some nice details about the transaction that spiced up the story.

Hugh Green was scheduled to meet this day with the entire six-member Ethics Committee, and he was expected to get a majority to approve an investigation of Marshall's dealings with Converse.

This also was a day to check in with Ken Sachs on the progress of the NTSB investigation, with Clay Helm for developments on the Parkhall murder, and to catch up with the grand juries.

He struck news on his first call.

"I thought you'd lost interest in me," Ken Sachs said. "I know it's a lot more exciting chasing falling stars on Capitol Hill than dealing with technical data developed by an obscure little federal agency."

"Feeling inferior, are we?" Pace replied.

"Actually," Sachs said, "I've been relieved not hearing from you. Then I didn't have to tell you things you have no right to know at this stage."

"Like what?"

"Oh, so suddenly you need me?"

Pace laughed. "Maybe I should go home and get drunk tonight and come over to see you about one a.m. At least you're used to dealing with me at that hour in that condition."

"Spare me," Sachs pleaded. "I capitulate. I'll tell you everything I know."

"Which is?"

"Well, it's good new evidence, but not anything that's going to knock your socks off."

"Let my socks be the judge."

"Same rules? No attribution."

"You think we're fooling anybody?"

"Probably not, but at least it gives me leeway to deny I'm the source."

"Same rules. Give me all you've got, and no post-midnight visit."

"Fair enough. Metallurgy tests show the initial impact on the engine's fan blades originated from inside the engine itself."

"Translation?"

"Some of the blades were broken when the engine smashed into the runway and bounced along in the infield. But a number of them, and we don't yet know exactly how many, although I'd guess it was in the nature of a dozen, were broken during the initial engine failure, while the engine and wing segment were still attached to the aircraft. The metallurgy examination shows they were bent outward by some catastrophic event from within the engine, as opposed to being bent inward as they would have been in a bird strike."

"So it wasn't a bird strike. That's not new."

"We had circumstantial evidence," Sachs said. "This is concrete, infallible proof. Stuff that will stand the test in court if we ever have to go."

"You and I saw the result of the turbine disk fracture," Pace said. "But the wedge of disk blew out the side of the pod."

"But when it broke loose, it tore up a lot of stuff inside the engine. There was a lot of ricocheting shrapnel flying around in there."

Mentally, Pace scratched his head. "Then you're still on the first rung of the ladder? Still not a clue to why this particular engine self-destructed?"

"Not a clue."

At the same time Pace and Sachs were bantering their way to the reporter's next page-one story, Hugh Green was meeting in a locked and guarded Capitol hideaway with the full Ethics Committee. He would take a vote on proceeding with an investigation and, if that carried, present Harold Marshall's request for a public hearing at the earliest possible date.

It was a difficult and strident session. Green told himself it would break along straight party lines, and he was right, with one notable exception. Frank Hopper, a first-term Republican from Iowa, was impassioned and eloquent about aviation safety and public confidence. The other two Republicans expressed varying degrees of doubt about the committee conducting an investigation based on newspaper allegations.

"That is total bullshit," Hopper exploded. "Marshall concedes what's been printed in the *Chronicle* is accurate. The implications here are so clear it hurts to look at them. The man bought and paid for a cover-up that almost worked, and if it had worked, we'd be flying Eight-elevens all over the country with impunity, without a second thought, each one a time bomb. How many more people would have died before we came around to thinking maybe we hadn't found out everything about the Dulles accident? I'm sorry, but I have very little sympathy for Harold Marshall's vulnerability here. He created it himself."

The others regarded him silently for some time, unable to assess the exact cause of his distress. Eleanor Justica, the ranking Republican and a neighbor from Indiana, finally asked him.

"What's your problem, Frank? We're trying to decide if there's enough evidence for an investigation, and you seem ready to convict and sentence."

Hopper, who stood five-nine and was often described as looking like a junior-middleweight boxer in top form, cupped his left fist inside his right hand and pressed the assembly against his neatly cleft chin. A lick of straw-blond hair tumbled onto his forehead, and he looked every bit the Midwest country boy he was. When he attempted, after a few moments, to answer the question, his voice was soft and quaking with emotion.

"I'm a hometown boy, you know," he began slowly. "Before I was elected to the House, not to mention the Senate, I managed the family farm. We had a lot of debt on equipment, and what equity we had in our land we used each year to borrow the money to buy the seed to plant the corn, and we prayed for enough rain to give us a crop that would pay the debt and our living costs through another year. Most years, it worked. But three bad drought years in a row drove us to the financial brink, and before we went entirely over the edge, my dad sold out the land and bought one of the grain elevators outside town. We were still subject to the whims of the weather, but not so bad as if we'd stayed with farming. We saw our friends losing their land to the banks. I almost felt guilty that we'd escaped the same financial ruin. I wanted to help. That's why I got into politics. To think I'd get elected to Congress on my first-ever try was pretty naive, but the people were looking for an alternative, and I guess they saw it in me.

"One of the things I swore was I'd never forget my roots. And one of the things I did to keep that promise, in a small way, was to stay a member of the EMT squad I worked with since high school. I paid a lot of my way through college working the ambulance squads during the summers and pulling vacation relief over holidays. So even after my first election, whenever I'd get back home, I'd make certain to pull some EMT relief shifts.

"Back during nineteen eighty-nine, I was home for some meetings, trying to convince folks George Bush really did have a farm policy, when the United Air Lines DC-ten crashed at our airport. It was amazing the crew even got the plane to the ground. The tail engine came apart during flight and tore up all three hydraulic systems, so the pilots had hardly any flight controls at all. Most of the people on board survived the crash, and they got most of the attention in the press. And that was okay, because the crew had done a heroic, incredible thing getting enough control that anybody lived. But I saw the other side of the story.

"I got a call that my old EMT squad needed every available hand. I got to the airport just before the crash and saw it happen. We went out in the cornfields to find anybody left alive. At first, I didn't see anything but dead, broken-up bodies. Then I found this unit of three seats from the coach compartment torn out of the airplane intact. Three seats, three people sitting there, still strapped in, in a cornfield a hundred yards from the crash. The seats were in perfect condition, but the people weren't. A man in one end seat was decapitated. In the other outside seat, a body had been cut clean in half. There was a woman in the middle seat, so torn up she should have been dead. She was missing an arm and the lower part of one leg, and there was a piece of metal embedded in her skull, but she was alive, and—God knows how—she was conscious. I was trying to get her out of her seatbelt, and she kept repeating, 'Why? Why? Why?' She died in my arms. To this day, I still see the question in her eyes and hear the disbelief in her voice.

"Seems to me when we build these huge airplanes, we ought to be able to forecast anything that could go wrong with them. I'm willing to stipulate that the aerospace industry in general tries to do that. But sometimes they make design mistakes and learn about them the hard way. The idea that people, including our colleague from Ohio, would risk countless more lives to cover up a problem is wholly unacceptable to me. I suppose my two colleagues here feel I'm being disloyal in taking this position so strongly, but I won't have any more Iowa cornfields on my conscience."

For nearly two minutes, nobody in the room said anything. Frank Hopper sat with his fists pressed against his chin, staring at the table before him, seeing nothing actually there but, instead, ghosts and bad dreams from a bad day. His two Republican colleagues studied him, trying to set aside the emotions he'd evoked. Jack Alogato, a hard-nose from Long Island, was more successful than Eleanor Justica of Indiana. She found herself deeply moved by Hopper's story, and her views abruptly changed on the Marshall investigation. Hopper had convinced her it must go forward.

Green and Adams exchanged a glance. They knew they had one GOP member on their side. It was of their own colleague they were unsure. While they agreed initially to stay united, it wouldn't break any law for Harley to back away; he sat staring into space, nodding slightly.

Green seized the moment. "We vote," he said. "The question before us is whether to convene an investigation of the dealings between Senator Harold Marshall and the Converse Corporation, and if we so decide, whether to hear, at the earliest possible date, the testimony of Senator Harold Marshall of Ohio at his request. I think a show of hands will be sufficient on the question. All those in favor—"

Green glanced to his Democratic colleagues first and was happily surprised to see Stinson joining Adams in voting aye. Then he glanced to his left and was stunned. Both Frank Hopper and Eleanor Justica had their hands raised.

"Those opposed—"

Jack Alogato raised his hand.

"The chair records that Senators Stinson, Adams, Justica, and Hopper vote aye; Senator Alogato votes nay. The chair votes aye. The vote is five to one in favor. The chair proposes that committee staff undertake an immediate investigation and that the committee itself hear from Senator Marshall on Friday, June sixth, at ten a.m. Is there objection?"

He looked to both sides and saw no movement.

52

The Hart Building hearing room could seat a hundred sixty people comfortably if they were all small children. The staff of the Senate Ethics Committee crammed in two hundred thirty-six chairs to accommodate the enormous demand for seats.

John Ingersoll, the Ethics Committee's chief of staff, had to scrounge up a place in which to hold this session, because the committee had no hearing room of its own. Usually its work was done behind closed doors in a small library/conference room, or in the private office of a member senator. It was not the best of situations, but it was an improvement over the old years, after the committee was created by the Ninety-fifth Congress in nineteen seventy-seven, when the staff was housed in what was euphemistically called the Senate Annex. In its previous incarnation, the annex was the old Carroll Arms Hotel, a genteel, slightly seedy place during its heyday. It became less genteel and more seedy when it closed as a hotel and opened as spillover offices for Senate staff who couldn't be shoehorned into the two existing Senate office buildings. When the new Hart Building was completed during the eighties, the Ethics Committee staff and the other poor cousins from the Carroll Arms found themselves back in the mainstream of congressional business.

Ingersoll preferred the old quarters, when the staff worked in what had been the Carroll Arms bar. "It was the perfect symbolic place," Ingersoll said. "Take any Senator who's ever gotten himself into trouble, trace it back far enough, and you'll find it started in a bar someplace."

The general public would have access to one back row of seats. Each shift of public spectators would sit in for twenty minutes, then new spectators would take their places. It was time enough to get the flavor of the day's events. Senate staff had two rows. Every other seat in the room was reserved for newspaper, magazine, television, and radio reporters. Still, demand for media seats far exceeded supply. Reporters could cover the hearing from their offices or from the Senate Press Gallery by way of C-Span II, but there was a compulsion to be in the room, to watch the reactions of the principals, which the television cameras couldn't always pick up.

Steve Pace didn't have to worry about getting a seat. The *Washington Chronicle* had a reserved spot at a press table, although the chairs were packed so closely that no one had much elbow room.

Television crews were set up in a balcony above the outside edges of the press seats and at each end of the bench at which the committee members would sit. The arrangement gave each network the opportunity to show senators asking questions and Marshall answering them. Most of the still photographers were assigned sitting positions on the floor below the committee bench, facing the witness table. They would sit there through the hearing with their lenses trained on Marshall, waiting for the gesture or the facial expression that would give them their shot of the day. The hearing would be punctuated by the click of shutters and the whir of motor drives.

Steve Pace was in the room fifteen minutes early, but it was so jammed he had to pick his way through human limbs to reach his press table. Once there, he found that another reporter had put a huge briefcase right behind his chair, leaving him no room to pull out the chair so he could sit down.

"You mind moving that?" he asked.

"And where do you propose I put it?" the other reporter asked indignantly.

"I have a suggestion, but I wouldn't make it in polite company," Pace growled. "I don't give a damn where you stow it, just get it away from this chair so I can sit down."

The other reporter muttered an obscenity loud enough for Pace to hear as he wrestled the case to a spot between his feet. The fellow looked uncomfortable sitting that way, but it wasn't Pace's problem. The man should have known better than to bring the case into the hearing room.

"Star reporter gets prime seat but has to wrestle for it," said a voice to Pace's right. He turned his head to see the grinning face of Jeff Hines of the *L.A. Times*.

"Hey, Jeff," Pace said. "I didn't expect to see you here."

"I've been behind you on this story every day," said Hines. "My editors thought I should continue to hold down that position."

Now Pace laughed. As the *Chronicle* reporter turned to his left to look at the committee bench, Hines would, indeed, be at his back.

"If you can't see, let me know and I'll remove my head," Pace joked.

"Taking it off yourself is better than having it handed to you, which is what you've been doing to me the last couple of weeks," Hines said. "I don't know where you've got your sources buried, but when all this is over, you ought to dig 'em up and treat 'em to a grand dinner."

"I don't think anybody's going to want to be seen with me for a while. Some people don't even like me calling anymore."

"I don't doubt it. If Stan Travis ever finds out who you're talking to, he'll lock 'em up and toss the key in the Tidal Basin."

"Or one of those Tidewater sinkholes," said the reporter across the table. Pace didn't recognize him, although the piece of white paper taped to the table surface in front of him said he worked for *The New York Times*. Pace extended his hand and introduced himself.

"Greg Hayward," said the *Times* correspondent, grasping Pace's hand. Pace had seen the byline on major congressional and political stories.

"It's nice to meet you," Pace said. "You covering this as a political story?"

"Not really. It doesn't fit into a nice category. It's the best story of the day, and I'm happy to get it. Justin Smith would have drawn it in other circumstances."

Pace felt the sadness overtake him. "I miss him," he said.

"So do we all," Hayward replied. "If nobody from the *Times* has had the grace to thank you, a lot of us who loved Justin appreciate what you did. If you hadn't talked to the medical examiner, we wouldn't know how Justin died. I don't think he would have rested very well."

"I knew Justin was too ornery to keel over."

"Believe it," Hayward said. "I don't think we have anybody to replace him yet."

"You'll find someone. A spot in the *Times* Washington bureau shouldn't be hard to fill."

"They're talking about keeping the job in New York."

Pace was surprised. "Why? All the regulatory apparatus is here."

Hayward shrugged. "They've been doing a lot of things that defy understanding. I try to keep a low profile and hope they'll leave me alone."

Pace twisted around, trying to spot Jill Hughes among the throng of reporters. She was assigned to do a color piece on the hearing, to capture the mood of it. He located her where he imagined she'd be: front row, center. They made eye contact and Pace gave her a warm smile.

A door behind the bench opened, and the six committee members filed in, followed by Ingersoll and a lawyer named Brent Hammond, retained as special counsel for this investigation. Following them came Harold Marshall and a man whom Pace didn't recognize.

"Well, well, well," Greg Hayward said. "Only the best for the Cobra."

"Who is he?" asked Pace.

"Woodrow Wilson Vredenberg," said Hayward.

"Good Republican name."

"Vredenberg?"

Pace smiled. "What can you tell me about him?"

"He's a high-priced, high-power trial attorney from New York," the *Times* reporter explained. "Knows his way around Wall Street, too. He could tie this hearing in knots if Green doesn't do something to control him. He'll whereas and whyfor us to death."

"Why should he do that?" Hines asked. "His client asked for this session."

"I'm only telling you what he could do."

Pace flipped open his notebook and jotted down the name of the lawyer. Greg Hayward spelled it for him.

"Hey, Pace, here's your prime source." The voice belonged to Joe Howard, a veteran Senate reporter for the AP. Howard cocked his head toward the bench. Kathy had come in to talk to Hugh Green and was bent over next to him.

"Wrong," Pace said. "Not that lady. Regardless of her personal feelings toward me, her professional loyalty is to Green."

"That's your story," Howard said nastily.

"Yeah, that's my story. You got a problem with it?"

"Give it a rest, Joe," Hayward said quickly. "You got a big mouth."

"And maybe you wanna do something about it?"

"No, I want *you* to do something about it," Hayward replied angrily. "Shut it!"

Howard snorted and turned back to his notes. Pace continued to stare at him in anger and disbelief. He felt Jeff Hines lean into his shoulder.

"Let it alone, Steve," Hines said, loud enough for Howard to hear. "He's not worth it."

Pace broke off the stare, but the knot in his gut wouldn't loosen. He let himself look back in Green's direction, but Kathy was gone. He turned to Hines. "She isn't a source," he said. "It would be too obvious, and it would end her career."

"I believe you," the *L.A. Times* reporter said. "And if I

didn't, what difference would it make? It's nobody's business but yours."

"Thanks."

"De nada."

The cast of players was in place, and Hugh Green rapped his gavel.

"This is a very unusual proceeding this morning," he said. "This committee is accustomed to conducting its proceedings in executive session, not to keep truth from the public, but to protect the lives and careers of those under scrutiny. We act very much like a grand jury, hearing evidence from many sources, occasionally engaging in fishing expeditions and speculation. To have such evidence made public could do irreparable harm. Moreover, unlike the regular committees of the Senate, there is no majority here; the seats are divided evenly between the majority and minority parties. Although the subject of the committee's investigation asked for this hearing, and asked that it be public, the request would not have been honored but for a bipartisan vote to make it so. I have no other opening statement, but I will offer each of my colleagues five minutes for initial remarks." He turned to his left. "Senator Justica?"

"I could have missed this part," Jeff Hines whispered to Pace.

"How can you say that?" Pace challenged. "They've all got shiny new soapboxes."

Hines pointed a pen at Pace's nose. "My point, exactly. You're *so* perceptive."

Eleanor Justica was, by any estimation, an elegant-looking woman. That her presence came naturally made her all the more appealing. The Republican Party counted itself fortunate to have her. The Democrats would have given anything to steal her away. That wasn't likely. Indiana isn't a Democratic stronghold, and as the daughter of a wealthy corporate executive and the wife of a successful and highly regarded thoracic surgeon, she wasn't inclined to be stolen. This day she was dressed in a striking plum-colored suit and had her light brown, shoulder-length hair pulled back over her ears and held with decorative combs. When she let her hair fall naturally, she had a tendency to keep pushing it back over her ears like a schoolgirl. She didn't want to be seen on television constantly fiddling with it.

"Thank you, Mr. Chairman," she said. "I don't plan to use my entire five minutes. This hearing was scheduled at the behest of my friend and colleague, the honorable senator from Ohio, and I don't want to infringe on his time. I will state for the record that I was one of those who voted to go forward with this unusual session, not in order to bring Harold Marshall before the nation to humiliate or denigrate him, because I don't believe that will be the result of this hearing. I firmly believe the senator from Ohio is a capable, honest, and forthright man, who acted in the best interests of a constituent and did nothing whatsoever wrong by any standard this committee or the general public can use to judge him. I fully expect he will answer the questions of this committee completely and openly and at the end of the day's proceedings, we will be able to terminate any further inquiry into his actions. I yield back the remainder of my time."

Green's voice was resonant. "Senator Stinson."

The West Virginia Democrat made a clearing sound in his throat, almost a cliché of an Southern orator preparing to speak. It prompted Hugh Green to remind him, "Five minutes, Senator." That brought laughter from the Senate staff members and reporters who knew Stinson's tendencies all too well.

"Thank you, suh. Ah ahm aware of the rules of these proceedin's." Stinson cleared his throat again, almost in defiance. "Ah ahm reminded here today of the awesome duality of the responsibility we all take upon our shoulders when we assume a seat in the United States Senate." Stinson began in the leisurely drawl that was his trademark and became more pronounced when television cameras were watching. "On the one hand, we are told we have been elected to represent our constituencies to the best of our abilities, and that means lookin' out for what's good for our people and our commerce and our states. But we are also told we must uphold the Constitution of the United States of America, and that means there must be some balancin' of interests between what's best for our constituencies and what's best for our country. That is a verrah delicate balance. Ah don't know that my colleague from my neighbor state of Ohio has done a thing wrong in that regard. But the allegations that have been buildin' up against him are formidable, indeed."

Stinson removed his glasses and wiped his eyes and his face with a handkerchief retrieved from a hip pocket. It was the right gesture, although no one who saw it could have pinpointed exactly why it was right. It used up nearly a minute of his allotted time.

"It pains me, ladies and gentlemen," he continued. "It pains me considerably. Ah do not believe this man is capable of serious ethical misconduct. Ah have known him too well for too long to believe that. We have been on different sides of too many issues and on the same side of some. Ah have worked with him and against him for years without seein' a single ethical misstep on his part. So it is difficult for me to believe now that he has made the grievous breaches of conduct of which he appears to stand accused, mostly by the media. In the earliest stages of this committee's work, it was not my feelin' that anythin' would be gained by puttin' the honorable senator from Ohio through an inquisition. But ah, too, voted for this hearin' because ah came to believe the allegations against Senator Marshall were so serious he should be given the earliest and most public method of exoneratin' himself. It is mah fervent hope he can do that verrah thing. Ah hope he will answer all the questions put to him with the same honesty and candor ah have come to expect from him over our many years of workin' together, and ah hope he comes through this ordeal unscathed." Stinson drew a deep breath. Many in the committee room hoped it was a signal he was finished. In fact, he was getting wound up.

"The world is a-changin'. Ah wish ah would have the privilege of livin' long enough to see the results of those changes. But ah suppose, by the time we see the results of the current changes, the'll be new changes. Things are changin' all over the place, faster than most of us can keep up with 'em. We've got historic things goin' on in Europe, or Eastern Europe." He waved his hand. "Ah guess it's all one Europe now, or gettin' that way fast—faster than this old World War II veteran can keep up. We got changes in Central and South America, changes in Africa, changes right here at home. Maybe for folks like Harold Marshall and me, the changes are comin' too fast."

He paused again, appearing lost in thought, and then resumed. "Mah point is, Harold Marshall came to this United States Senate when we were operatin' under a set of rules slightly different from the set of rules we have today. The old rules led to abuses, there's no question about that, and the new rules, well, we don't know how they're gonna work out, but at least we're tryin'. And that's the message ah think ah wanted to get across this mornin'. We're surely tryin'. And if some of us don't quite hit it right the first time, well, ah'd hope there'd be some understandin' about that. Ah'd hope—" The Stinson drawl had used up more time than his mere words would have, had they been read without the slow-motion theatrics.

"The senator's time has expired," Green said.

"Ah ahm sorry, Mr. Chairman," Stinson said. "Ah had not expected to exceed mah time. Ah would like the full text of my remarks to be printed in the record of this hearin'."

"Without objection, so ordered," Green said. "Senator Alogato."

The New Yorker pulled himself erect in his chair and coldly surveyed the audience he could see arrayed before him. How many more were looking in on television, he couldn't know, but he knew those in his presence were hostile, and he played to that.

"I don't mind stating for the record that I believe this committee is here today playing out a charade choreographed by the liberal media of this country, who, throughout modern history, have made it their personal crusade to pillory fine, upstanding, patriotic Americans who don't happen to share their liberal political philosophy." Alogato saw Harold Marshall bow his head and mistook the gesture for one of thanks. In fact, Marshall had been afraid this was exactly the sort of defense he would get from the conservative New Yorker, and it was exactly the kind of defense Marshall knew would not play well with his constituents, who were, after all, no fools.

"I voted against this hearing," Alogato continued. "It's premature. In his rush to defend his good name, I believe my friend from Ohio has not permitted himself time enough to review the evidence and mount the sterling defense of which I am certain he is capable." He nodded toward Vredenberg. "No offense, Counselor."

"No offense taken," Vredenberg replied.

Alogato concluded, "Mr. Chairman, I am on record as opposing this hearing, and I have nothing further to say at this time. I would like to reserve the remainder of my time until such point as I can put it to better use."

"These are opening statements, Senator," Green replied. "You basically have your say, and if you don't use your allotted time, it's time lost. Do you want to reconsider your decision to relinquish the floor at this point? If you choose to do so, our conversation will not be deducted from the time you have remaining."

Alogato glared at Green, who was making him look as though he didn't know the rules. Rather than risk further damage, he backed out gracefully. "You are correct, of course, Mr. Chairman," he said. "But like the gentlelady on my right, Mrs. Justica, I do not wish to detract time from what I am sure will be an able self-defense by Senator Marshall."

Pace swallowed the laughter, but all around him he heard snickers from reporters more attuned to feminist sore spots than Jack Alogato. To refer to Eleanor Justica as the "gentlelady" was, in the arcane decorum of the United States

Senate, perfectly proper and unobjectionable. But to refer
to her in the second reference as "Mrs." rather than as
"Senator" was inexcusably sexist, and Jack Alogato would
pay for the slip somewhere in the newspapers the next day,
not to mention the next time he wanted anything from the
feisty female senator from Indiana.

Hugh Green suppressed his own smile and plunged
ahead. "Senator Adams."

"Mr. Chairman, I deplore the fact that the tenuous evidence being explored by this committee is, at the same time,
playing out before the public," Adams said. "I think it is
because of media attention to this story Senator Marshall
felt compelled to come here today to defend himself. I am
sorry he felt that was necessary. But I intend to hear him out
with my mind wide open. He has a commendable record in
this body. He is an honored colleague and a noble foe, and
I wish him well. I yield back the remainder of my time."

"Senator Hopper."

"I have no statement to make at this time, Mr. Chairman," the Iowa Republican said in a voice so soft the audience had to strain to hear it, despite the loudspeaker system.
"I relinquish my time for opening remarks while stipulating
that I wish to retain my time for direct questions to Senator
Marshall."

"No problem," Hugh Green promised. Then he leaned
forward in his chair. "Senator Marshall, I would like to
formally introduce you to our special counsel for this proceeding, Mr. Brent Hammond."

Sitting alone at the bench to the left of the senators,
Hammond looked up from his notes and nodded toward the
witness chair, although he had twice talked to Marshall
during the previous week. The introduction, although unnecessary, was standard procedure.

"Senator Marshall, would you introduce the committee
to the gentleman seated with you at the witness table?"
Green continued.

Marshall cleared his throat. "Senator Green, members of
the committee, Mr. Hammond. The gentleman on my left is

Woodrow W. Vredenberg, my attorney."

Green jumped right in. "Mr. Vredenberg, we're glad to have you here today," he said. "But I must tell you, sir, that you have no official standing. You may consult with your client at any time, but I will not tolerate you injecting yourself into these proceedings at any point, under any circumstances—"

"Senator Green, I must object—" Vredenberg tried to interrupt, but he'd miscalculated the will of his adversary.

"No, sir, you may not object," Green said. "You may not say anything at all, except very quietly and very privately to your client. You were neither called nor accepted as a witness, and therefore you may say nothing to this committee. Is that understood?"

Vredenberg glared at Green and said nothing.

"Mr. Vredenberg," Green continued, "so far as this committee is concerned, you are a potted plant in this room today, and we will hear no more from you than we would hear from any other ficus in our presence. There will be no debate on that point." As the observers in the room rocked with laughter and Woody Vredenberg turned purple, Green turned to Marshall.

"Senator Marshall, please stand and be sworn."

Marshall took the oath to tell the truth, which left him open to a perjury charge should he fail to keep the sworn promise. But the oath required only that he tell the truth regarding those things about which he chose to testify. Keeping some secrets did not equate to perjury.

Green continued. "Senator, since you requested this hearing, I presume you have something you would like to say. So if you wish to make an opening statement, the floor is yours for as long as you choose to keep it."

Marshall was rubbing a spot on his lower forehead, above the bridge of the nose. He felt slightly dizzy, fighting off the same spells he'd been living with for weeks. He pulled a pair of glasses from the breast pocket of his suit jacket and began reading from a sheaf of papers. As he did so, clerks handed out copies of the statement to the media.

"Mr. Chairman, members of this distinguished committee, I want first to thank you for agreeing to this unusual public session." He thought his voice sounded weak and unsteady. He tried to project more authority. "For weeks now, the reputation I spent so many years building has been reduced to dust by constant pounding, hammering, and pummeling in the press. The stories have been filled with innuendo, half-truths, and some outright lies. I could have waited the weeks and months it would have taken you— given the complexities of this case and the myriad other tasks that face you—to finish your investigation before speaking out. But by that time there would have been nothing left of me to salvage, nothing at all worth keeping, because I don't believe the ongoing public assault of Harold Marshall will abate until I am exonerated of wrongdoing beyond all reasonable doubt, or driven from this town in disgrace."

Marshall rubbed his forehead again and motioned to Vredenberg to pour him a glass of water from the icy pitcher between them. He took two sips and pressed on, speaking slowly.

"Let me give you a little history I think you will find useful. It is no economic secret that the American steel industry has been decimated as the Japanese undercut American steel prices on world markets, including right here in our own country. As our steel dominance, then our automotive dominance, slipped away across the wide Pacific, that belt of great cities that gird the Great Lakes saw jobs disappear, factories and foundries close, homes abandoned and repossessed by lending institutions that could not recoup their losses because there were no buyers. It is no accident that those cities—Milwaukee, Chicago, Detroit, Cleveland, Pittsburgh, Buffalo—became known to the world as the Rust Belt.

"I would ask you, have any of you ever seen a once-mighty factory that has been shut down for five years, with no maintenance, no refurbishing, no life? It rots and turns to rust, figuratively and factually. And rust is not a static thing. It spreads slowly throughout a community, eroding everything in its path. It erodes commerce. It erodes the quality of life. It erodes public confidence. The major cities of the Rust Belt are not the only ones to feel the spread of this rot. Satellite communities like Youngstown and Warren, Ohio, Flint and Pontiac, Michigan, Gary, Indiana, and so many more, are quickly diminished by the spread of the same economic plague that affected the larger cities. Many of the smaller communities don't have the economic diversity to survive the death of their prime industry. Milwaukee can always sell beer. Chicago can always sell beef and tourism and commodities futures. But what is Youngstown, Ohio, going to sell after its steel markets are gone? The answer is—or was: nothing."

Marshall paused and took another sip of water. Green, who was watching him closely, thought he was growing pale, but he brushed aside the concern. It probably was the television lights. Marshall cleared his throat and resumed.

"Several years ago, this was the condition to which my city, my Youngstown, had fallen. There were other serious economic problems statewide. As the eighth largest defense-contracting state in the Union, Ohio was feeling the economic pinch of the reduced number and decreased size of defense contracts as the Soviet threat diminished. The companies feeling the pinch were high-tech companies, and with state and federal aid, many of them were able to retool and retrain and reconfigure to meet the demands of new markets. But what do you do with eight hundred acres full of old, dirty buildings that the world and modern technology have passed by? And what do you do when you don't have one eight-hundred-acre site, but dozens? I pledged to northeastern Ohio I would do everything in my power to turn the Mahoning Valley around.

"I knew the Converse Corporation was not happy in southern California. The company's financial problems, coupled with the high cost of labor and the high cost of living, threatened the firm's very survival, despite the fact that it had a most promising line of new jet aircraft engines.

So I went to the governor of Ohio, I went to the Legislature, I went to the mayor of Youngstown, I went to the City Council, I came to the Congress and the U.S. Commerce Department, and I put together a package of incentives that prompted Converse to close up shop in California and move to Ohio. Setting up the new shop was a long, tedious process. But it got done. And when Converse opened its new doors, the impact cut unemployment in half, created dozens of ancillary businesses that in turn created spin-offs of their own and gave Youngstown back its pride and dignity. So why do you question, why do you doubt, that I would do anything, *anything,* in my power to save the company that saved northeastern Ohio?"

Marshall's voice had risen in a crescendo, his emotion giving him strength. His was a spellbinding presentation. Steve Pace noted the Ohioan had the undivided attention of every member of the committee. No one fidgeted, and there were none of the hushed conversations among committee members that often take place during presentations of prepared testimony. Eleanor Justica even waved off a staff member who came to give her a message.

Marshall drank more water and stretched his shoulders in the manner of someone trying to loosen tight neck muscles.

"Would you like to take a break, Senator?" Green asked.

"Hell, no," said Marshall. "I'm just getting wound up."

Green smiled, and saw many others in the committee room smile, too. Old, weird Harold was captivating his audience.

But a delay in the proceedings was inevitable. Bells rang and lights lit up around the perimeter of the hearing-room clock, signaling a Senate floor vote. With apologies for the delay, the committee members left to say yea or nay to the Presidential nomination of a controversial conservationist to a key position in the Interior Department. The nomination had become a battle between those who would preserve the pristine qualities of large tracts of undeveloped land and those who saw the land as a source of commodities: oil, gas, coal, timber, gold, silver, uranium. The vote would be close, and party leaders expected every senator to be present.

Committee members began returning forty minutes later. Even if word had not preceded them that the nominee was confirmed, the reporters could have predicted it from the look on their faces. The environmentalists were smiling; their opponents, if not grim, certainly looked businesslike. Marshall appeared several minutes later and resumed his place at the witness table. He spoke a few words with his attorney and then turned to face Hugh Green.

"Senator Marshall, I apologize for the interruption, but you know the importance of that vote as well as any of us."

"I was aware of the importance of it, Senator Green," Marshall said. "I must say, however, I had hoped for a different outcome."

"That was clear from your vote, Senator. Are you ready to continue?"

"Ready and eager," Marshall said and picked up where he had left off.

"Ladies and gentlemen, there seems to be a great deal of concern that on two occasions, I sent members of the staff of the Senate Transportation Committee to Dulles Airport to confer with a high official of the National Transportation Safety Board on what level of blame would be placed upon the Converse Fan engine for that horrible, tragic accident in April. Were my inquiries construed by the NTSB as pressure to take it easy on Converse? I don't think so. I hope not. I surely don't want any repetition of that awful day, and I would do nothing to prevent the NTSB from carrying out its mandate."

Marshall let his voice drop so low those in the room could barely hear him, although those watching on television could hear him quite well. He began with his head bowed and slowly raised it until his eyes looked directly toward the cluster of television-camera lenses trained on him.

"Three hundred and thirty-four lives. Three hundred and thirty-four sets of hopes and dreams. All gone. Could anyone contemplate the enormity of the tragedy and not want the reason for it discovered? Could anyone look at the television, the magazines, the newspaper pictures of the loss of innocent life and not want to do everything, *every little thing,* to prevent a repetition of the carnage? The members of this committee have known me for years. Is there any one of you who could say with certain conviction that I am a man who would see innocent people killed and do nothing to prevent it happening again? Do those of you who dislike me think me such an ogre that I would knowingly, willfully, stand in the way of a thorough investigation? Or in any way attempt to influence the judgments of the men and women dedicated to finding that flaw, or that one mistake, that, if corrected, would ensure there is never a repetition of the tragedy? Do you think me that kind of man? Frankly, I can't believe that you do.

"In my years in the Senate, I have been consistent in my votes to aid the oppressed, the downtrodden, the homeless, the hungry, the sick and the dying and the poor and the dispossessed. I have, on occasion, voted against the will of my party's leadership because of my conviction that we must look out for each other or humanity surely will perish. Some critics have suggested I'm in the wrong party. I don't think so. Humanitarianism is not indigenous only to Democrats. It has been my history, my life—" he raised his eyes to the cameras again "—my record, that people's welfare comes first. That is why I fought to bring Converse to Youngstown. There were people who needed jobs, people who needed paychecks, people who needed their dignity restored. Would I have risked myself to help the company that saved my hometown? Yes. Of course. Without a second thought. But would I have risked the lives of thousands of innocent people who board airliners every day as an act of faith? No, ladies and gentlemen." He began to shake his head. "No. No. No. Never."

Suddenly Marshall looked pained, not physically, but emotionally. His voice cracked. "I have too much regard for human life—and for what is lost when a human life is snuffed out before its time—to ever, *ever,* do anything to risk that happening to anyone."

He opened his hands to the committee in a gesture of supplication. "Judge me. And if you must, judge me harshly. But tell me one thing. My conscience is clear, and I am at peace with what I have done. How many among you can make that statement?"

There was a pause of nearly ten seconds before Hugh Green drew in a deep breath of recognition that Marshall was finished.

"That was an eloquent statement, Senator Marshall," Green said. "You are an eloquent man. Our chief counsel, Mr. Brent Hammond, is scheduled to handle the first round of questions for you but—" he glanced up at the wall clock "—I see it is nearly twelve-thirty, and I think this would be an appropriate place to break for lunch. Without objection, we are in recess until two o'clock."

As committee members, reporters, Senate staff, and public spectators filed out, Marshall remained at the witness table, reflecting on his impact.

"You were good, very, very good," Woody Vredenberg told him.

Harold Marshall cast his attorney a withering look of disdain. "Screw that," he said and began to gather up his papers. "I was brilliant. I was totally fucking brilliant."

Green gaveled the afternoon session to order at six minutes past two o'clock.

"Senator Marshall," he said, his deep voice commanding quiet in the room, "I anticipate being able to complete our questioning by five o'clock, at which time you will be permitted to make a closing statement, should you so choose. Is that satisfactory?"

"Completely," Marshall agreed. "Although I am here for as long as you need me."

"We appreciate it, Senator. All right. Mr. Hammond, who has taken charge of our staff investigation, will open the questioning. Mr. Hammond will have an hour, after which each of the six members of the committee will have twenty minutes apiece. I think that should bring us to five o'clock and give everyone a chance to be heard. Mr. Hammond."

Brent Hammond was an enormously serious lawyer, in his mid-thirties, with longish blond hair falling to his collar, perhaps to make up for what he was losing above his forehead.

As the six members of the committee made their opening statements, Hammond remained intent on the substantial pile of documents before him. But when Marshall made his opening statement, Hammond stopped reading and focused on the Ohio Republican, his eyes never leaving Marshall's face. If Marshall noticed, he didn't react outwardly. But Steve Pace noticed and concluded Hammond's hard gaze would have unnerved him.

"Senator Marshall, I'd like us to begin at the beginning," Hammond said. And he did. He took Marshall through a dozen questions about the relocation of Converse, about the company's relationship to the Mahoning Valley, and to the senator himself. He asked preliminary questions about the Dulles accident, about how Marshall first heard of it, and what he had done during the next hours.

"I returned to my office," Marshall said.

"To do what?"

"I beg your pardon?"

"Why did you return to your office?"

Pace saw the senator frown deeply, as though trying to recall what he was thinking at the time.

"I don't recall exactly," Marshall said. "I think it seemed the thing to do, the place to be."

Hammond fixed Marshall with that stare again, a look that said "I don't believe you," but he made no comment.

"Do you remember what you did when you returned to the office?" the counsel asked.

Marshall clasped his hands and let them slide between his knees under the witness table, so his elbows were resting on his thighs and his shoulders were lowered almost to the tabletop. It was impossible to tell if he was trying to recall old memories or hunkering down for a fight.

"As I recall, Mr. Hammond, there was a call waiting for me from Mr. George Thomas Greenwood, chief executive officer of the Converse Corporation. He wished to speak to me about what I knew of the accident."

"Why would that be, Senator?"

"Because, as you know, and everyone in this room knows, Converse makes the engines for the Sexton Eight-eleven, and they're made in my state."

"And what were you able to tell Mr. Greenwood at that time?"

"What time?"

"At the time you found a call from him waiting for you."

"Nothing. I found myself asking him for information. He'd been watching television and had seen the first news reports. I hadn't seen anything."

"What else did you discuss?"

Marshall shrugged. "Nothing."

"Did you agree to call him back later?"

"Not that I recall."

"Did he say he'd call you?"

"He might have. I don't remember exactly what we said. It was a pretty hectic time."

"I see." Hammond shuffled a few pages of notes. "It was at approximately this time, then, Senator Marshall, that you began to consider whether to sell your considerable stock holdings in the Converse Corporation?"

"It was," Marshall confirmed without hesitation.

"Can you tell this committee what your thinking was?"

Marshall pushed himself erect in his chair and drew a deep breath.

"Yes, Mr. Hammond, I think I can tell you exactly. The bulk of my net worth was tied up in that stock . . . I never made any attempt to hide that. It is on the financial-disclosure forms I file every year with the Secretary of the Senate. I was concerned about—how shall I put it?—keeping all my eggs in one basket. I had great faith in Converse, great faith in its future, great faith in its future in Youngstown. I also felt a very keen sense of personal loyalty to the company. It had, after all, taken an enormous financial risk in relocating to Ohio. I felt back then the stock purchase was justified. But even before the ConPac accident, I was considering diversification. The accident only prompted the inevitable. I—"

"Excuse me for interrupting, Senator." Hammond was looking at his notes, but his voice was directed strongly at Marshall. "Going back a minute, you said Converse had taken an enormous financial risk in relocating to Ohio?"

"Yes."

"Really? Was the risk that great? After all, the city of Youngstown, Mahoning County, the state of Ohio, the federal government, all created substantial incentives for Converse to make the move, didn't they, in the form of tax abatements and write-offs? It looks to me as though there was far greater risk to Converse in staying in southern California, given the high taxes, high cost of living, high wages, and so on." Now Hammond looked directly at Marshall. "Isn't it true, instead, that you and Mr. Greenwood were able to calculate to the dollar how much improved company profits and earnings would be if you could get a very specific set of financial concessions from local, state, and federal authorities? And isn't it further true that you personally lobbied said authorities, from the President of the United States down, to grant those concessions? And finally, isn't it true that you bought the stock in the first place because you were impressed with the value of the economic concessions granted to Converse?"

Marshall paused before answering, returning Hammond's gaze with an unflinching glare of his own. Woodrow Vredenberg leaned over to advise the senator, but Marshall waved him off.

"Are you asking me about my purchase of the stock, or my sale of it?"

"Both. You said you sold the stock the day of the ConPac accident because of your concern that all your eggs, as you described them, were in one basket. So the question arises as to why you invested so heavily in Converse in the first place. When I asked you about that, you testified it was a gesture of faith in the company. I'm asking if your faith wasn't so much in the company as in the value of the package of economic incentives the company received from taxpayers."

"I think that is a rather slanted way to put it, Mr. Hammond, but your facts are essentially correct," he replied in measured tones.

"So on one hand, we have a stock purchase based on gratitude and faith in a company, given a valuable set of economic incentives. On the other hand, we have a stock sale, executed after a single aircraft accident, when you were suddenly overwhelmed with concern that your investment portfolio wasn't sufficiently diversified. What I don't understand is, what was there about this one accident, terrible though it was, that made you lose your gratitude and your faith?"

"I told you earlier, Mr. Hammond. I was uncomfortable at having all of my investments tied up in the one company."

"Right. Then I asked you why you let that happen in the first place, and we started going in circles. To avoid doing so again, I will ask you simply, why didn't you sell a portion of your Converse stock last January, before the accident? And why did you sell all of it?"

"It was a decision of the moment."

Brent Hammond cocked his head and raised an eyebrow. "Are you in the habit of making four-million-dollar decisions of the moment?"

"No," Marshall replied simply.

"Was it a decision of the moment to buy the stock?"

"As I told you, it was a decision based on my faith in the company and its management, coupled with my conviction that Converse would do exceptionally well in Ohio's economic climate."

"Ah, yes, I recall that." Hammond went back to his notes. "Senator, was your faith in Converse so tenuous, was the financial health of the company so tenuous, that this one accident was sufficient to shake the faith that prompted you to buy the stock in the first place?"

"Of course not. It simply served to bring back to mind the fact that I wanted some diversity."

"Of course. And what other stocks have you bought with the proceeds of this sale?"

"None yet, Mr. Hammond. I've not had the opportunity to investigate any new investment opportunities. I've been busy."

"All right. Now, Senator, isn't it a fact when you're buying and selling stock out of a money-market account, it takes a week or more for the proceeds of a sale to show up as a credit on your cash balance?"

"I don't know."

"I'm told that's the case. In any event, it's highly irregular that the proceeds of this sale were credited to your money-market account and transferred to your checking account in the same business day."

"Is that a question?"

"No, it's a statement of fact. The question is this: Did you order that transfer?"

"I did."

"Why?"

"Why what?"

"Why did you transfer all of that money out of a money-market account paying nearly eight-percent interest into a checking account paying nothing?"

Marshall protested. "I don't think this line of questioning is at all relevant here."

"We do, Senator. Would you answer the question, please? Why did you transfer nearly four-million dollars to your checking account?"

"Because I wanted to."

"That's not responsive."

"It's the only answer you're going to get."

"And was it simply because you wanted to that you showed up at the Riggs office on Pennsylvania Avenue shortly before two o'clock on the same day, April seventeenth, and withdrew one million dollars of the deposit *in cash?* Specifically, in the form of ten thousand hundred-dollar bills?"

"Yes."

"Yes, what?"

"Yes, I did it because I wanted to."

The room came alive with half-whispered expressions of disbelief from reporters and other spectators. The buzzing was accompanied by some derisive laughter. It threatened to get out of hand, and Hugh Green gaveled it down.

"I will have order," he said gravely, and the room quieted.

Hammond continued. "Did the bank happen to have ten thousand hundred-dollar bills on hand, Senator?"

"I don't know," Marshall said as cooly as if he'd been asked for the temperature outside. "I called ahead to tell management what I wanted, so it was ready when I got there."

"What did you do with the money?"

"I took it home."

Even the implacable Hammond was stunned by the answer. "Home?" he asked.

"Home," Marshall confirmed.

"Why would you take that amount of cash to your home?"

"And yet again, Mr. Hammond, I did it because I wanted to."

Hammond was losing patience. "What did you do, Senator, unwrap all those bills, throw them in the middle of your bed and bounce in them?"

Woody Vredenberg, red with anger from his shirt collar to his forehead, slammed a fist on the witness table in a gesture of disgust and protest. Hugh Green smiled.

"I believe we have a protest from the potted plant to your somewhat satirical question, Mr. Hammond," Green said, bringing down the house. "I will ask that you withdraw it."

"Withdrawn," said Hammond, still serious.

Green said, "Continue."

"Is the cash still in your home?" asked Hammond.

"No, though I wouldn't tell you if it were," Marshall replied. "That would invite burglary."

"Where is the money now?"

"I don't know specifically."

"Senator, I have to remind you that you are testifying under oath."

"I haven't forgotten, Mr. Hammond. The answer is truthful. I do not know specifically where the money is now."

"But it's no longer in your possession?"

"No."

"Who did you give it to?"

Marshall leaned back in his chair and expelled a long sigh. Then he leaned forward and crossed his arms on the witness table in front of him, leaning close into his microphone. "I believe we have reached the point in this inquiry where I must decline to answer your question," he said.

"I'll bet we have," Hammond said disparagingly, and Vredenberg's fist slammed down on the witness table again. "Withdrawn," Hammond said quickly, and the room laughed once again. The committee counsel fixed his gaze on the witness.

"Senator Marshall, this committee is investigating the possibility of a willful, organized attempt to conceal the true cause of the crash of Flight Eleven-Seventeen at Dulles International Airport on April seventeenth. The committee has reason to believe there was scheming, conspiracy, and payoffs intended to protect the Converse Fan engine. Now here you are, admitting that on the day of the crash, you—with an acknowledged interest in the well-being of the Converse Corporation—took possession of a great deal of cash that cannot be traced. And you will not tell this committee what you did with it. If you were sitting up here, sir, don't you think you'd find that somewhat suspicious?"

"Possibly. But that's speculative. I don't know."

Hugh Green leaned across his Democratic colleagues and whispered for Hammond's attention. The counsel turned, automatically swinging his microphone away so his conversation would not be overheard. While most eyes in the room were on the two of them, Vredenberg took the opportunity to talk with his client, clapping his left hand over Marshall's microphone so their talk, too, would remain confidential. Marshall sat with his head bowed, the thumb and forefinger of his right hand squeezing the bridge of his nose.

Green again rapped for order, and Hammond resumed his questioning.

"Senator, changing the subject for the moment, tell the committee a little about yourself, if you would . . . your background, and so on."

"It's not a very interesting story, I'm afraid," Marshall said. "I attended Ohio State and the University of Michigan Law School. I practiced law in Youngstown for more than twenty years, staying active in a number of civic affairs. When I decided to run for the Senate, I ran on issues many voters cared deeply about, and I was elected. I've been here ever since."

"What type of law did you practice in Youngstown for those twenty-some odd years, Senator?"

"Civil law."

"Specifically?"

"I had no specialty as such. I did estates, divorces, adoptions, a little real estate."

"It must have been a very lucrative practice."

"No, Mr. Hammond, civil lawyers have steady work, but it doesn't make them rich."

"Did you inherit a lot of money?"

"No. My father was a civil lawyer before me. I actually took over his practice."

"So you didn't inherit a lot of money, and you didn't earn a lot of money?"

"That is correct."

"Then where did you get the three million dollars you used to buy the Converse stock?"

Marshall saw the question coming, and he was ready for it. "From my bank account," he said.

Hammond leaned forward and bored in. "That's not an answer, Senator. Where did the money come from?"

"Again, I do not believe it is in any way relevant to this hearing."

Hammond glanced back down at his notes. "It's expensive to run a statewide election campaign in Ohio, is it not, Senator?"

"It is."

"How did you finance it?"

"I had a lot of financial backers."

"Was Converse among them?"

"It was, but only through its political-action committee and by virtue of contributions from some of its executives."

"In point of fact, Senator," Hammond was still looking at his notes, "every single top executive of Converse contributed to your campaign to the maximum extent allowed by law, as did Converse Employees for Better Government, the company's PAC, is that not correct?"

"I don't recall. It could be."

Now Hammond looked up. "What possible interest could a California company have in the first-ever campaign of a long-shot candidate for the U.S. Senate from Ohio?"

"Like the PAC name indicates, Mr. Hammond, better government."

"Come on, Senator, you can do better than that."

"During the time of my Senate campaign, I was also working to get Converse the incentives it needed to move to Ohio. I imagine company executives and workers were grateful for that."

"Uh-huh," the counsel said and glanced down again. "I see you also made a substantial contribution of your own money, in the nature of something over a million dollars."

"That's not illegal."

"No, it's not." Hammond looked again at Marshall, his eyes hard. "But it is very strange that a simple civil attorney, with no apparent means to such wealth, would have that kind of money to pour into a campaign, as it's strange that the same simple civil attorney would later turn up with three million more to buy heavily into the stock of one of his biggest campaign benefactors. Again, sir, the situation demands some kind of an explanation from you."

"Then we have once again reached an impasse, Mr. Hammond, because I do not believe such information is in any way relevant to this inquiry."

Marshall was frowning deeply. It appeared to those looking at him that he was angry, but in fact, the dizziness was escalating rapidly. He desperately didn't want to ask for a recess; he wanted to get this ordeal over. Hammond began hammering at him again.

"It is not only relevant to this inquiry, these matters go to the very heart of the inquiry," Hammond was saying. "I believe answers are—"

But Marshall had ceased listening. At the base of his brain, the small artery weakened by age and stress had burst, flooding the surrounding brain tissue with blood.

Hugh Green's first thought when he saw Marshall rise from his chair was that the senator had become so angry he was physically going after Hammond.

Woody Vredenberg had the same thought and put his hand on his client's sleeve.

Hammond didn't understand what was happening.

Steve Pace thought Marshall was ill and was about to run from the room.

Eleanor Justica thought her Republican colleague was rising to make some sort of impassioned statement that would shed the controversy, and Brent Hammond, from his back.

Stephen Hay Adams thought Marshall was standing to make a grandstand play.

Harley Stinson was making notes on questions he planned to ask and wasn't watching, but the sudden silence in the room made him look up as Marshall began to fall over.

Only the young senator/paramedic from Iowa, Frank Hopper, realized immediately what was happening. "Heart attack or stroke," Hopper whispered to himself as Marshall collapsed across the witness table and slid away. Hopper vaulted the committee bench before anyone else could react and was at Marshall's side in five strides.

But he was too late.

The senator from Ohio was dead before he hit the floor.

BOOK
FOUR

53

Steve Pace felt a lack of closure, a sense that he'd somehow been cheated of the opportunity to see the best story of his life through to a logical conclusion.

As often as he told himself it was indecent to think of a man's death that way, he couldn't get past the fact that the public might never know how Harold Marshall nearly pulled off what surely would have been one of the biggest corporate cover-ups in the history of the modern world.

Pace spent the weekend in an emotional dumpster. Kathy worked at talking him out of his funk, but her heart was only half in it since she was feeling some of the same thing. Hugh Green was storming around in a smoking bad mood.

"This is the ultimate pail of bovine crap from a renowned bullshit artist," Green said.

Marshall's body was returned to Ohio on a private aircraft— "What ever' sombitch could afford if he managed his portfolio wisely," Harley Stinson is reported to have remarked nastily in the Senate cloakroom.

A family friend announced that funeral services would be private, and indeed they were. Nobody could even find out which funeral home was handling the arrangements, or exactly where Marshall would be buried. Even Republican senators who wanted to attend were assured their concerns were appreciated but their presence was not required.

Harold Marshall disappeared from the face of the earth, "which, I suppose, is what death is all about," said Avery Schaeffer. He appeared totally unmoved by Marshall's passing. He argued that the story was still very much alive, that Converse was still suspect, and lest the newspaper's aviation writer forget, there still was no explanation for the ConPac accident.

Pace understood all that. But he was having a hard time maintaining enthusiasm about it because the personification of the story was gone, and his absence diminished the telling of it somehow.

Steve and Kathy were thumbing aimlessly through the Monday-morning papers when the phone rang. It was Paul Wister.

"What are you doing at the office so early?" Pace asked.

"I'm not at the office, I'm still at home," Wister said. "I just got a call from the early wire desk. The United States attorney for the northern district of Ohio has called a press conference for one o'clock this afternoon. Reports are that one, and possibly several, Converse Corporation executives have been indicted in connection with embezzlement of company funds."

"Federal charges? I didn't think embezzlement was a federal crime," Pace said.

"It isn't normally, but it's alleged this money crossed state lines for criminal purposes, i.e., the abetting of the disruption of a federal investigation."

All of the self-pity and ennui drained away, and Steve Pace went to full alert. "Who's involved? What's the disruption? What funds?"

"Easy, boy!" Wister said. "Get on an airplane and fly your fanny to Youngstown, where you undoubtedly will find the answers to all those questions. I've ordered the wire copy sent to your apartment by messenger, so it should be there within the half-hour. Then you'll know everything the rest of the world knows. Avery is hot for this."

Pace smiled. He had no problem at all believing that. If there were indictments and convictions of Converse officials based on a federal investigation prompted by *Chronicle* stories, Schaeffer would be making room for another Pulitzer on his Glory Room wall.

Pace clicked on CNN, figuring at that hour he was more likely to get updated reports on the all-news station than from the commercial networks. He repeated Wister's report to Kathy. She was enormously excited.

"Keep me posted," she said. "I'll get you a reservation. Which credit card?"

"Take the American Express card in my wallet . . . and have a ball, kid."

"You want to come back tonight?"

"Leave the return open. I could need some time out there."

"God, you get to go to all the great places."

She was giggling in an unseemly manner when she left the room.

Kathy got him on a nine-thirty-five flight to Youngstown by way of Pittsburgh and reserved a rental car for him there. He tried to read the wire-service stories as he shaved and only succeeded in nicking himself under the chin. He tore the corner off a tissue and stuck it over the tiny puncture, hoping he remembered to remove it before he got to the press conference. How would it look if a nationally acclaimed reporter showed up with a bloody scrap of toilet paper sticking to his neck?

Kathy threw clean shirts, underwear, and socks into a small flight bag while he dressed. "You want extra ties? An extra pair of pants?" she asked.

"Yes and yes," he said. "I hope I'll be back tonight, but don't count on it."

"How about an extra blazer?"

"Shouldn't need it. I'm wearing the blue blazer and the gray slacks, and I got the medium-blue slacks back from the cleaners. Throw those in, and that should hold me."

"You sure? I can throw the chinos in, too. There's plenty of room in the bag."

"I won't need 'em. I'm going to report a story, not to live there."

"Where's your laptop?"

"On the closet floor. Would you check it for me and make sure there are extra batteries."

Kathy dragged the black, hard-sided case from behind Pace's shoes and popped the lid. "You've got an unopened pack of double-As."

"Fine."

She was shaking her head. "When's the paper going to dump these old Tandys and get something that belongs in the late twentieth century?"

"Get rid of my Trash Two-hundred? Do you know how long I've had that thing? It's family."

"Yeah, your grandfather."

He sucked down the rest of his coffee, grabbed the flight bag and the computer case and leaned down to kiss Kathy, who was sitting on the edge of their bed.

"This is the first time I've felt good about the story in three days," Pace said.

"I know. Hugh's going to be in a lot better mood today, too."

"Getting off the dime helps. At least *something* is happening."

"So go forth and score one for the guys in the white hats."

He held his arms out, a piece of luggage dangling from each hand. "How do I look? Good enough for Youngstown?"

"You'd look better without the yellow toilet paper on your Adam's apple. It clashes with the red in your tie."

"Oh, shit," he said.

Pace read and reread the wire copy the messenger delivered to his door. He read it in the taxi, he read it in the waiting area before his plane began to board, and he read it twice during the flight to Youngstown. He began to fantasize about the press conference:

Someone inside Converse had embezzled funds used to pay for the cover-up of the cause of the ConPac accident. Harold Marshall had been on the take from Converse since the company began negotiations to move to Youngstown.

That's how he'd amassed the fortune to buy all the Converse stock he'd acquired. Marshall directed the cover-up and paid the bills; Chappy Davis was his agent. It was a wonderful fantasy, and it lasted until someplace over central Pennsylvania.

Then the inconsistencies began to gnaw at Pace: Why did anybody have to embezzle company funds to pay for the cover-up if Harold Marshall already had those funds in stock and cash?

Well, maybe the cover-up cost more than Marshall had.

Except Marshall hadn't spent the whole four million. There was three million still in his checking account.

Maybe Converse officials embezzled funds to reimburse Marshall for his expenses in bankrolling the cover-up.

That angle had possibilities.

Maybe the embezzlement happened years earlier, when somebody at Converse originally misappropriated the funds Marshall used to buy the stock.

If so, why did it take so long for auditors to uncover the fraud?

Little of it added up, and the arithmetic was giving Pace a headache.

The Boeing 737 touched down at the Youngstown airport more or less on time, and Pace was on the road in twenty minutes. He found the federal building with only one wrong turn, and pulled into a parking lot with more than an hour to spare. He locked his overnight bag in the trunk, taking only a pen and a notebook with him, and began walking through the city's streets, not so much to get the flavor of the town as to try to break down the questions badgering his mind.

U.S. Attorney Allison Giavanova was a serious, no-nonsense prosecutor in both appearance and demeanor. It was a presence she cultivated to get past the fact that her family, two generations earlier, was prominent in running the gambling and prostitution vices for organized-crime syndicates in Cleveland, Youngstown, and Warren. She had an uncle in Lorain who was said to remain active in prostitution and drugs in the ethnic neighborhoods west of Cleveland. Giavanova, as an assistant U.S. attorney, once indicted her uncle, although he escaped conviction on a technicality. She never stopped trying to indict him again until she was promoted and moved to her current assignment. There was growing statewide interest in a Giavanova candidacy for governor, but she showed no inclination to run, preferring to devote her energies to razing what some of the more disreputable members of her family and their cronies had built over the years.

When she strode to the dais before an overflow crowd of reporters and photographers, the room grew silent in anticipation. Giavanova was dressed in a slim-fitting gray suit with a red-silk blouse, and red, low-heeled shoes that did little to raise her physical stature beyond her natural height of five-feet-four. Her dark-brown hair was pulled straight back from her face. She wore little makeup, rounding out the what-you-see-is-what-you-get image, and Pace liked her immediately.

"Ladies and gentlemen, thank you for coming. Late yesterday afternoon, a federal grand jury handed up indictments of a major local corporation, one of its chief officers, a high-level United States Senate aide, and two residents of Baltimore, Maryland, based on evidence of public corruption. A second officer of the corporation was named as an unindicted coconspirator. I regret I was unable to give you the opportunity to see the indictments before we began this press conference, but the task of making enough copies for all of you and getting them collated and stapled proved somewhat more arduous than my staff anticipated. The copies are coming now, and you will have them in ample time to ask questions."

A quick reading showed that those indicted, in addition to the Converse Corporation itself, were George Thomas Greenwood, the company's chief executive officer, and Chapman Davis. The two Baltimore men charged were identified as Sylvester Bonaro and Wade Stock. The unindicted coconspirator was Cullen Ferguson, vice-president of Converse for corporate relations. With growing apprehension, Pace scanned the papers again. He could find no mention of Harold Marshall's name. *Damn!*

Giavanova continued. "It is the government's contention that on April seventeenth of this year, George Greenwood, chief executive officer of the Converse Corporation, withdrew the sum of one million, one hundred thousand dollars from a discretionary company account he alone controlled and transferred the sum to Mr. Chapman Davis, the minority chief of staff of the Senate Committee on Transportation. In addition to the funds, Mr. Greenwood transmitted to Mr. Davis by facsimile machine a damaging personnel file on Elliott Parkhall. Mr. Parkhall had been named by the National Transportation Safety Board to head the team investigating the role played by Converse engines in the crash of Consolidated Pacific Flight Eleven-seventeen at Dulles Airport in Chantilly, Virginia, earlier the same day. Mr. Greenwood intended, and Mr. Davis understood, the funds were to be used for the purchase of an operation to intentionally falsify the cause of the crash in order to direct the blame for the accident away from the Converse Fan engines.

"On the same afternoon, April seventeenth, Mr. Davis, then in possession of the funds and the personnel material faxed to him by Mr. Greenwood, met with Mr. Parkhall on Theodore Roosevelt Island and transferred to Mr. Parkhall eight hundred fifty thousand dollars of the Converse funds. Mr. Davis also gave to Mr. Parkhall in a sealed container the remains of a red-tailed hawk, origins unknown, for dispersal throughout the severely damaged starboard engine of the Sexton aircraft. At the time, the engine was lying well away from the rest of the aircraft wreckage and was readily accessible to investigators from the National Transportation Safety Board, especially to those who, like Mr. Parkhall, were conducting the power-plants portion of the probe.

"It is further alleged that Mr. Parkhall, abetted by Sylvester Bonaro and Wade Stock, used a portable compressor to distribute the manufactured evidence into the demolished engine sometime during the evening of April seventeenth, and further used a device, probably a portable acetylene torch, to burn some of the remains in order to simulate the post-crash fire. For their services, Mr. Parkhall paid Mr. Bonaro and Mr. Stock one hundred thousand dollars, retaining seven hundred fifty thousand dollars for himself, which he placed in a new account at the First Savings Bank of Alexandria, Virginia, under the alias of Ernest Peters. On another occasion, Mr. Davis paid Messrs. Bonaro and Stock directly for services rendered. The cash for that transaction came from the two hundred fifty thousand dollars that Mr. Davis had kept from the funds transferred by Mr. Greenwood. The funds were cached in Mr. Davis's home in the false bottom of a bureau drawer.

"Included in further services to be rendered by Messrs. Bonaro and Stock was the ongoing security of the aforesaid operation. We have reason to believe that among the security services rendered was the murder of Mark Antravanian, another member of the National Transportation Safety Board investigative team. This occurred after Mr. Parkhall learned that Mr. Antravanian arrived at the crash site a number of hours earlier than expected and had witnessed the distribution of the bird remains in the Converse engine. Since murder is not a federal crime, this evidence has been turned over to the proper authorities in the Commonwealth of Virginia. We further believe that Messrs. Bonaro and Stock were responsible for the subsequent deaths of Captain Michael McGill, also a member of the NTSB team, after learning Captain McGill had been contacted by Mr. Antravanian and told of the conspiracy to divert the federal investigation, and of Justin Smith, a reporter in the Washington bureau of *The New York Times*. And finally, we believe they were the individuals who severely beat Steven Pace, a reporter for the *Washington Chronicle,* in an incident intended to result in his death. The evidence in those three cases has been turned over to the proper authorities in the District of Columbia."

It felt strange to Pace to hear his name in that context. Giavanova continued.

"Cullen Ferguson has been named an unindicted coconspirator because he had good and sufficient cause to believe, but did not report to authorities, that the Converse Corporation in general, and Mr. Greenwood in particular, were attempting to circumvent the mandate of the National Transportation Safety Board and were prepared to manufacture evidence and testimony if it became necessary to protect the financial interests of the company. Mr. Ferguson, however, cooperated with our investigation of this matter and we, in turn, agreed not to seek a conspiracy indictment against him. That about covers the facts of this case—"

Fully sixteen reporters jumped to their feet, shouting questions.

"—and I will attempt to answer questions, but I will not tolerate being shouted at. Remain in your seats, raise your hands, and I will recognize you as equitably as possible."

Like chastised schoolchildren, the reporters sat down again, and two dozen hands went up.

Giavanova, like most public figures, felt most comfortable dealing with reporters she knew, so she recognized the *Youngstown Vindicator* representative first.

"Yes, Bill."

"How did Mr. Greenwood happen to have a personnel file on Elliott Parkhall, and what was its purpose?"

"We have examined a number of Mr. Greenwood's personal computer files and have determined that he kept very detailed personnel records on scores of aviation experts, including members and staff of the National Transportation Safety Board," Giavanova said. "The files dwell on what could be considered points of vulnerability among the subjects, matters by which they might be blackmailed or manipulated. The files are very much on the order of those kept on political figures by J. Edgar Hoover when he directed the FBI, and we have reason to believe that's where Mr. Greenwood came up with the idea for building his own library. How Mr. Greenwood came into possession of such information, and whether, or how, it has been used before, are unknown at this time."

"A follow-up?" the *Vindicator* reporter asked.

Giavanova nodded.

"Where are those files now?"

"In the possession of the Justice Department."

"One more follow-up?"

Again Giavanova nodded.

"Was Mr. Parkhall being blackmailed?"

"I think manipulated is the better word, but I'm not prepared to go any further into that at the moment." She looked to the other side of the room and recognized a local television reporter.

"What was Harold Marshall's role in all of this?" the reporter asked.

"The fact that the senator has passed away makes moot any possible indictment of him," Giavanova replied. "We can't prosecute a dead man. However, I will say that during the course of the investigation, insofar as we have examined Senator Marshall's role in this matter, we found possible instances of improper behavior, but nothing of a federal criminal nature."

"Can you be specific about the nature of this, uh, improper behavior?" the reporter asked.

Giavanova sighed and appeared ambivalent. "That's not proper subject matter for this forum," she said hesitantly, "but I will tell you Senator Marshall appears to have had few scruples about how he used his Senate aides."

"Meaning?" the reporter pressed.

"Well, it appears to be true that he used both Mr. Davis and another aide to pressure a leader of the NTSB investigative team to help Converse. There was nothing illegal about it. No threats were made. No money or favors passed hands. It's not a matter for criminal investigation so much as a matter for review by the Senate Ethics Committee, which, of course, has ended its investigation. It also appears Senator Marshall occasionally gave Mr. Greenwood the use of Mr. Davis for whatever purposes suited the Converse CEO. It certainly would be a violation of Senate rules of conduct for an aide on the Senate payroll to be working concurrently for a private company, but again, that's out of our jurisdiction."

"Why did Chapman Davis permit that, and what sorts of things did he do for Converse?"

"Again, that's not my jurisdiction, but from what I understand, there are some criminal matters in Mr. Davis's background that were being held over his head."

"Held by whom?"

"By both Senator Marshall and Mr. Greenwood."

"What types of criminal matters?"

"That's not relevant, and I don't want to go into it." Giavanova started to recognize someone else, but the television reporter got in one last series of questions.

"So Greenwood and Marshall were blackmailing Davis into running this cover-up?"

"We're charging that Mr. Greenwood did, yes."

"Not Senator Marshall?"

"We don't know what the senator's role was."

"Did he have *any* role in the cover-up?" the reporter asked. "What about his money?"

"I have no answer for you on that, Bob," Giavanova said, frustrated and eager to go on to another line of questioning. "We were pursuing that as the last phase of this grand-jury proceeding, but when the senator died, further investigation on our part was deemed unwarranted, and we went with what we had to that point." She looked to her left, toward another section of television reporters. "Yes, Ginny."

A pleasant-looking blond woman in her late twenties rose to her feet. "Are you saying that Senator Marshall has been cleared of wrongdoing, or that you stopped looking before you found anything?"

Giavanova shook her head once and smiled. "That's a

loaded question," she said. "A grand jury does not clear or convict. A grand jury looks for evidence of criminal behavior. To the extent that we looked at Senator Marshall's behavior, we found nothing criminal."

Ginny pressed on. "Are you saying that if you'd continued to look, you might have found something?"

"You're asking me to speculate on what might have been."

"No, I'm not," Ginny insisted. "I guess what I'm asking is, is it true that you didn't go as far with your investigation of Senator Marshall as you would have if he hadn't died?"

"I would say yes, that's true."

Now three reporters shouted for recognition, forgetting the ground rules in their eagerness to be heard. Giavanova raised a forefinger to her lips, and then recognized one of them.

"I don't understand why you stopped investigating Senator Marshall's activities because he died," the reporter said. "If you'd gone ahead, isn't it possible you would have found evidence that some of those named in the indictment—or even others not named—were guilty of additional crimes?"

"Again, you're asking for speculation," Giavanova said. "If we had reason to believe further investigation of Senator Marshall would have led to additional criminal charges against these defendants or others, we would have continued." She looked around again and recognized another local television reporter. "Yes, Nathaniel."

"So what you're saying is, the investigation, so far as it went, turned up no evidence of criminal behavior by Senator Marshall?"

"I think I've said that at least twice already."

"But you can't account for his source of capital to buy the Converse stock or for what he did with the proceeds of the sale of that stock?"

"No, we cannot. But those facts were not the point of our investigation."

Nathaniel wasn't satisfied yet. "So whose idea was it to

stop the investigation without looking any farther?" he asked.

Now Giavanova was clearly uncomfortable, and she chose her words carefully. "I would say the decision was a joint one, made by me in consultation with officials at the highest levels of the Justice Department."

"The attorney general?" someone asked.

"I don't want to be that specific," Giavanova replied.

"Why not?" the anonymous voice asked.

"I am here to discuss the details of this indictment," she said. "I won't go beyond that."

The briefing droned on, but little new came of it. There was no question but that the indictment, coupled with Giavanova's statements about possible improprieties in Harold Marshall's conduct, did nothing to clean the senator's sullied reputation.

But deep in his heart, in the hidden place where each man has to be honest with himself, Pace acknowledged the nagging doubt that Harold Marshall masterminded this conspiracy, or even was a serious part of it.

54

Wednesday, June 11th, 11:15 A.M.
Pace's conviction slipped again, harder this time, when he got the call from Eddie Conklin.

It had been two days since the press conference in Ohio. Although the coverage of the event by the media emphasized that the grand-jury investigation terminated before the degree of Harold Marshall's culpability could be determined, there was a general recognition that the extent of the late senator's guilt was uncertain at best. Avery Schaeffer and Paul Wister strongly endorsed the notion that Marshall, dead or alive, could not be given the benefit of the doubt until unanswered questions about his mysterious wealth and his use of the profits from his stock sale had reasonable explanations. Publicly, Pace agreed. Privately, he worried.

That was why the call from Eddie Conklin jolted him to the marrow.

"I can't talk very long, but I felt like I owed you this call after dodging you so thoroughly right after the crash," the NTSB technician said.

"What's up?" Pace asked.

"Maybe you've already heard this. You have sources a lot better than me. Did anybody tell you about the metallurgical report on the turbine disk of Flight Eleven-seventeen?"

Pace sat up straighter. "No," he said. "I got a preliminary report that there was some difficulty finding the flaw in it."

"It's final now. The report came in late yesterday. Since we found out the bird strike was phony, everybody assumed we'd turn up some sort of flaw in the disk that would tie it to the problems in Seattle and St. Louis. It took a long time to do the testing because the disk off the ConPac plane was so badly broken up. The engineers had to sort out which fractures and cracks were caused by the stresses and the pounding associated with the accident and which existed prior to the crash."

"And?"

"They concluded that all the damage to the disk was caused by the violent vibrations that shook the engine loose from its pylon or by multiple impacts with the runway. They said they couldn't find any preexisting flaws at all."

Pace felt sick. "That doesn't make any sense, Eddie," he said. "Something went the hell wrong with that engine. What caused the vibrations in the first place?"

"We're back to the drawing board."

"Shit!"

"My sentiment exactly."

Looking back on it later, Pace never could pinpoint what prompted him to call Ken Sachs at that moment. He wanted to know the cause of the crash; so did everybody else. But he didn't expect Sachs to have it. So why did he ask: "Can we look at that engine again? Together? And maybe take Bill Teller or Howard Comchech along?"

"You're kidding," Sachs responded. "Why?"

"No better reason than it was the scene of our first big breakthrough, and from what I've heard about the final metallurgy report, we could use another breakthrough."

"We?"

"I've taken a proprietary interest."

"So I see. And I guess I can't blame you."

"Can we go?"

"Right now?"

"Why not? You got something more important on your plate?"

"Good point. I'll meet you in the Marriott parking lot in ninety minutes."

Shortly after one-thirty, Pace slid into the passenger seat of Sachs's government-issue sedan.

"Bill Teller's waiting for us at the hangar," Sachs said. "Howard Comchech can't make it. He's—I guess I'm not supposed to be telling you this—but he's testifying this afternoon before the Virginia grand jury."

Pace nodded.

"What's eating you?" Sachs asked.

Pace shrugged. "I can't put it into precise terms because I don't know exactly," he said. "I feel like I'm living in a world filled with smoke and mirrors."

"I can give it better definition than that," Sachs offered. He pulled up beside the hangar, put the car in park, and turned to face the reporter. "You figured you had Harold Marshall pegged as the instigator and bankroller of a cover-up, and then Marshall got away from you, first literally, and then legally. Somewhere in the back of your mind it's nagging you that the stroke that killed him might have been brought on, or at least hurried along, by the pressure you and your newspaper put on him. Am I anywhere near close yet?"

Pace regarded Sachs. "Too close," he admitted.

"And even though the net you cast caught a bunch of bad guys, it was almost by chance, something out of your control."

Pace nodded.

"The package isn't nice and neat."

"Not at all," Pace said. "And I admit to a certain amount of anxiety about that. I don't want any more surprises."

"I don't blame you," Sachs agreed. "But what do you hope to find out here?"

"Answers."

"Read: salvation?"

"Maybe."

"We got lucky the first time. It's naive to think it could happen again."

"Probably."

"So," Sachs said as he opened the car door, "let's go see what there is to see. The naive aren't always wrong, you know."

Bill Teller and Jim Padgett were waiting for Sachs and Pace inside the hangar, neither investigator certain why he was there and both uneasy about Pace, who seemed to be able to go where no reporter had gone before.

Pace himself was beginning to feel uneasy. Why in hell had he wanted to come out here again? There was no reason to think he'd find vindication deep in the wreckage of Flight Eleven-seventeen.

Sachs, Padgett, and Teller were watching him in anticipation. He shrugged. "Do you all feel certain it was the splintering of the broken turbine disk that triggered the destruction of Number Three engine?" he asked.

All three nodded, and Padgett spoke for the group. "No question about it now," the IIC said. "That was the first link in the chain of events."

"Or the second," Pace said. "The first was whatever caused the disk to break up."

"Right," Padgett agreed. "That's the mystery."

"Could I look at what's left of the disk inside the engine?" Pace asked.

"There's nothing left of it in the engine," said Teller. "All the fragments were shipped off for metallurgical inspection. I can show you where the disk was, for whatever good that will do."

"I don't know what good it will do, either," Pace admitted. "I truly don't. I'm not going to find something the experts have overlooked."

"You did the last time," Sachs said.

"No, *you* did the last time," Pace pointed out. "You were the one who got the sense there was more bird in the engine than there should be."

"But I was out here looking because of you."

"Well, look some more," Pace suggested. "Maybe you'll come up with another insight."

Only two people at a time could squeeze through the opening cut in the engine pod. Pace and Sachs went in first, then Pace came out and Padgett went in with Sachs. Eventually, over the next hour, the teams shifted until everyone had a chance to look at the engine with everyone else. Pace and Teller were the last team. As they crouched amid the wreck of the C-Fan, Pace asked Teller to describe for him what the destruction scenario had been.

"What do you mean, exactly?" Teller asked.

"Tell me what was doing what as the plane began its takeoff roll," Pace explained.

"Well, you know how a jet engine works, don't you?"

"In theory."

"You know that compressors, like that one up there, raise the air pressure, and the combustors, here, raise the air temperature with burning kerosene. As all that hot, pressurized air rushes toward the exhaust, down there, it passes through the turbines that drive the compressors and the fan."

"Yeah, that's pretty basic," Pace said.

"It is, but jet engines aren't all that complicated."

"And the disk that failed was where?"

"In the turbine that was up there," Teller said, pointing toward the front of the engine.

"Can I take a look at it?"

"I don't see why not. You've seen everything else."

The turbine was on the floor in the shadow of the big engine. Part of it had been cut away so its stationary blades and rotating disks were visible. Each rotating disk was in its own slot. One slot was empty. Pace asked for a flashlight and directed the beam into that compartment.

"What am I looking at?" he asked.

"That's where the broken disk was," Teller said. "It rotated in there on bearing balls."

"I don't see any bearing balls," Pace said, dousing the light and turning toward Teller.

"All we could find were removed for examination. They're over here on this workbench."

They were there, several dozen of them, in an open metal container. The sight of them caused Pace a pang of guilt.

"May I?" he asked, reaching for one.

Teller shrugged.

Pace picked up several and rolled them in his hand. "They're in pretty bad shape," he said.

Padgett stepped forward and looked at the metal balls Pace was holding.

"They're all like that," the IIC said. "They were subjected to intense punishment when the engine burned and flailed around on the ground."

Pace frowned and stared hard at the objects in his hand, as though they were crystal balls and would answer all his questions. And maybe they could. He looked to Padgett.

"You say the damage to these was done *after* the engine separated from the wing?"

"Yes, we think so," Padgett replied.

"What would the implications be if this damage occurred earlier?"

"Significant," Padgett said. "But there's no way to prove it."

Pace dropped the metal balls in his hand back into their container. "Are all the bearing balls from that disk compartment accounted for here?" he asked.

Padgett looked at Teller.

"All but seven, I think," Teller said.

"Seven?" Pace asked.

"Seven, yes, I think so," Teller replied.

"Sonofabitch," Pace said in a voice so low he might not have been heard had the other three not been paying close attention. "What if," he said, "what if I told you I know where some of those seven are, and I can prove the damage they sustained happened *before* the engine crashed into the runway and burned?"

"I'd say you'll have gone a long way toward solving our mystery," Sachs said, his voice filled with anticipation. "Where are they?"

"Some of them, four as I recall, are in the grass near the runway." Pace cleared his throat and looked abashed.

"And one is under my bed."

It took no persuasion, after he told his companions the story of his trip to the field with Mike McGill, to convince them to drive to the same site. Sachs sought and was granted permission to drive down a section of Runway 19R, and air traffic was held briefly as the government car negotiated the broad ribbon of concrete.

Pace put them as close as he could to the spot where Mike had parked, and Sachs turned the car into the grass.

"Not too far," Pace suggested. "You don't want to wind up on top of those things."

"I can't leave the car on an active runway," Sachs replied.

"According to Mike, when the engine passed here, it was still airborne," Pace said. "The scar on the runway up there is where the engine first hit the ground."

They all looked to Padgett.

"That's right," the IIC confirmed.

"So if we find some of the missing bearing balls here," Pace proposed, "we can safely conclude that they fell from the engine before it was damaged by ground impact or fire."

"Oh, it was on fire at this point," Padgett corrected. "But the fire wouldn't have messed up the balls as bad as you saw them back at the hangar."

"So let's start looking," Sachs said.

The four of them advanced, shoulder to shoulder, into the grass, scuffing along as they went. They found nothing. Pace suggested they try a little farther north, and again they found nothing. After another pass even farther north and one farther south, Sachs called a halt.

"There've been all kinds of heavy equipment crisscrossing this area," he said. "Those balls could be buried in the dirt by now. Let's get a metal detector out here and be a little more scientific about this."

It was 5:43 P.M. when the first metal ball was discovered and dug up, not far from where the group halted its first pass through the grass earlier in the afternoon. Minutes later, a second was found, and then a third.

"I saw five, all told," said Pace. "Counting the one back in my apartment, there should be at least one more out here."

But it wasn't to be found. Finally, at six-thirty, Sachs called a halt to the search. Scraping with his thumb at the dirt clinging tenaciously to one of the balls in his hand, he said, "Let's get these to the lab for a hard look," he said. "We should know something tomorrow."

"Can you conclude anything about their condition?" Pace asked.

"They look pretty bad, but I'm not an expert," Sachs said. "I'll take these downtown along with the collection back in the hangar. We'll compare them and get some answers."

They loaded the bearing balls from the hangar into Sachs's trunk, and he put the three found that day in his pocket, ensuring they wouldn't be mixed up. Then he drove Pace back to the Marriott parking lot.

"Once again you've given us what we needed," Sachs said to the reporter as he pulled up beside Pace's Honda.

"I guess we'll have to see," Pace replied as he cracked open the passenger door.

"Oh, by the way," Sachs said, "I'd appreciate it if you'd search your apartment tonight and turn in that little souvenir you took."

Pace sighed. "I told you it was by accident," he said. "It wasn't marked as evidence. I still wouldn't have taken it, but Mike had a sudden emergency, and we scrambled to get out of there. I dropped the thing in my pocket without thinking."

"I believe you," Sachs assured him. "I didn't mean to sound accusatory. But it's evidence now—critical evidence."

"I know."

"Actually, I'm sort of glad you did pick it up."

"Why?"

"Think about it," Sachs said. "If you hadn't seen that metal ball staring at you from the ashtray on your bureau for days on end, you might not have recognized the importance of the bearing balls you saw today in the hangar. Then where would we be?"

Pace shook his head. "You were right," he said. "Even the naive get lucky."

55

Steve Pace was impatient as hell when Ken Sachs called.

"Sorry it took so long," Sachs said, "but our techs compared every bearing ball we had from the engine with the three we found in the grass and the one you turned in yesterday."

"And they found . . ."

"Bingo," Sachs said.

"Now there's a scientific term for you."

"Don't be a smartass just because you solved the mystery for us."

"Solved it?" Pace thought that a lot more credit than he deserved.

"You certainly led us to the solution."

"Enlighten me, Ken."

"The balls we found in the grass exactly matched the general scarring patterns as the balls that remained in the engine, pretty conclusive proof the bearing burned out," Sachs said.

"Wait a second," Pace said. "Walk me through this."

"Sure. When I say the bearing burned out, I don't mean it melted in the fire; I mean it was subjected to extreme and excessive friction."

"By what?"

"I'm coming to that," Sachs said. "You asked me to walk you through this, so be patient. The bearing is the apparatus that keeps a turbine disk rotating smoothly on a single plane. The disk rests on the balls within the bearing. When the bearing balls were damaged, the turbine disk lost support. In other words, it began to wobble. The wobbling generated enormous vibration, and finally the disk shattered. One wedge burst through the side of the pod, and a lot of smaller pieces ricocheted around inside, tearing up the guts of the engine. Eventually the vibrations tore the engine loose."

"Where does all that get us?" Pace asked.

"It gets us to what caused the crash," Sachs said.

Pace fairly snapped to attention in his chair. "You're toying with me, Ken," he said.

"Not deliberately. Bearing failure is something you'd normally attribute to age, but this engine had only three hundred forty-eight hours on it. It was a baby, in aviation terms."

"And?"

"And so we had to go looking for another reason."

"And you found it?"

"We found it. And it's one of the most astonishing things I've ever heard. I'm going out of town for the weekend, and I'm not taking calls from reporters for the rest of the day, so you'll have this story alone until we hold a press conference Monday morning. There are very few other people who know the details, and I'm fairly certain none of them will talk to reporters."

"So what is it?"

"The bearing burned out because it wasn't being properly lubricated."

"Well, I wouldn't go back to *that* gas station," Pace said. "You can't get anything checked right at those self-service places."

"Not funny, Steve," said Sachs. "It wasn't that nobody checked the oil, it was that somebody put contaminated oil in the engine."

"*What?*"

Sachs continued. "Let me explain how the Converse Fan operates pertinent to this discussion. It isn't lubricated like a car engine, where the oil sloshes around and eventually coats everything. In the turbine disk bearing, the oil is sprayed directly onto the bearing balls through a nozzle. Generally, it's more efficient."

"Generally?"

"It ceases to be efficient when the nozzle gets clogged."

"With sludge? That engine was practically new."

"Not sludge. A peanut shell."

"Oh, come *on!*"

"I'm not kidding," Sachs insisted. "It floored us, too, so we went back and interviewed everybody who touched the engine at Dulles. The service crew had been interviewed several times by the go-team, but when we went back, we knew the right question to ask. We wanted to know if every drop of oil that went into the engine was from cans freshly opened during the service work. It's standard procedure to throw away partially used cans. It might sound wasteful, but the reason we do it is precisely to avoid what we have here. Procedure wasn't followed in this case. One can of oil was opened, as best we can figure, about eleven hours before the ConPac service work. Only a few ounces were used from the can, and the service tech couldn't bear to waste the rest, so he put it aside. Incredibly, while the can was standing open with the filler tube stuck in it, somebody nearby was shelling and snacking on peanuts. A piece of shell drifted into the filler tube. When the oil was poured into the Con-Pac engine, it washed the shell in, too. If the shell had been smaller, it would have blown right through the lubricating nozzle harmlessly. But, tragically, it was too big and it stuck, blocking the flow of oil to the bearing."

Pace felt weak. In the last incredible two months, this was the most incredible thing of all. "For the lack of a nail, the war was lost," he mumbled.

"Exactly," Sachs agreed. "A fucking piece of peanut shell."

"Then there was nothing wrong with the Converse engine itself?" Pace asked.

"Nothing at all."

"It *can't* be nothing!" Pace insisted. "How do you explain

Seattle and St. Louis? They weren't *nothing*."

"No, they both were something, but not the same something, and not even close to what happened to Dulles," Sachs said. "Here's the short course; you can catch up with the full report later. There was a microscopic crack in the disk involved in the Seattle incident. It occurred during the manufacturing process at Wentworth Fabricating and got past inspectors there, as well as at Converse. It shouldn't have happened, but it's not a crime. Engine vibrations exacerbated it, and eventually it manifested itself in a way the Seattle flight crew could discern. The problem with the St. Louis disk was damage during shipment from Wentworth to Converse. A section of the wood crating material was smashed, and something, maybe a nail, hit the disk and chipped it slightly. When the disk arrived at Converse, the damage to the crating was recorded and photographed, but nobody passed the word to anybody up the line that the disk should be inspected for damage. Unfortunately, it was installed with the chip undetected, the chip spread into a major crack, and you better than most know the rest of the story."

"How did you find out about the chip?"

"Modern metallurgical testing can find things you can't begin to imagine."

There was silence between them for several moments.

"So that's it?" Pace asked, finally.

"That's it," Sachs said softly.

Pace remembered something then, a question that lingered in his mind without an answer. It was a tidbit from his disjointed conversation with air traffic controller Barry Raiford on the afternoon Flight Eleven-seventeen was destroyed. It had stuck in his mind, a factoid that refused to go away.

"Ken, back an eternity ago, on the day of the accident, an eyewitness told me he saw some smoke come from Number Three engine while the ConPac flight was still at the gate. You have any idea what that could have been?"

"Yeah, I remember from your story," Sachs said. "I recall thinking at the time it was probably a compressor stall. I don't have any reason to think differently now. All the information we have, from the black boxes to eyewitness accounts, indicates that the engine was performing flawlessly. There's no reason to think it would have done anything but continue to perform flawlessly for the rest of its life. The Converse Fan is a good engine. There isn't a thing in the world wrong with it."

Pace sat in silence for a span of seconds, deep emotions stirring and shoving aside any excitement he felt for the story.

"Then all of this," he said slowly, "the crash, the cover-up, the murders, the payoffs . . . they were all for *nothing*?"

"Sadly, yes. The crimes committed to protect the reputation of the Converse Fan engine needn't have happened at all."

56

Wednesday, July 9th, 7:00 P.M.

Summer had come in earnest to Washington, D.C.

Outside the *Chronicle* Building, early evening temperatures were in the upper eighties, and the humidity was stuck in the oppressive seventy-five-percent range. It was, all in all, very much like a sauna.

Ordinarily, Pace would have been grateful for the excuse to stay indoors, but this evening he would have preferred the sauna. He and Schaeffer were staying late for a meeting set up hours before by special request.

It had started with an afternoon call to Schaeffer from a woman named Sharon Marshall. She said she was the daughter of the late Ohio senator and wanted to talk to Schaeffer and Pace. Just the two of them. Nobody else. She wanted to come in after most of the staff was gone so as few questions as possible would be asked about who she was and what she wanted. Schaeffer, wary of such encounters, said he wanted one of the paper's attorneys present. She refused, protesting there was no need. She said she was not coming to make threats. Schaeffer and Pace had been on edge ever since.

It didn't take much to put Schaeffer on edge. As Pace counted, the editor's frustration with the lack of progress on the Marshall angle of the Converse conspiracy had lasted, unbroken, for a month. No one mentioned Harold Marshall's name in connection with the scandal anymore; it seemed he had taken the secrets of his profound financial success to the grave with him. Schaeffer could not let loose of that, although other developments in the case should have raised his spirits.

Pace was first with the story of how the cover-up conspiracy came unraveled after Converse's vice-president for corporate relations, Cullen Ferguson, had rebelled against the company's chief executive officer, George Thomas Greenwood. Greenwood demanded Ferguson sign a sworn affidavit to the effect that he, Ferguson, while still a reporter, uncovered damning evidence about Ken Sachs's professional relationship with MacPhearson-Paige, a relationship that would support the accusation that Sachs had a conflict of interest when it came to the Converse investigation.

After a nasty argument, Ferguson had appealed to Alan Hirschman, chairman and president of the company. Ferguson complained that Greenwood was acting in an unprofessional, and possibly illegal, manner and was at least partially responsible for the diversion of the NTSB investigation. Ferguson implicated Harold Marshall, too, but that part of his story was ignored by Hirschman and, subsequently, by the federal grand jury. Hirschman began his own internal investigation, and a company auditor uncovered Greenwood's embezzlement. The chairman toyed with the idea of firing Greenwood and quietly letting the matter drop, but company attorneys advised him if Greenwood's illegal activities ever came to the government's attention, hiding them could prompt legal action against Converse and bring more adverse publicity. So Hirschman went to the FBI.

The FBI went to Ferguson, who set them onto Chapman Davis. Davis held out briefly against the pressure, but with Greenwood no longer around to support him, he had nowhere to fall back. He told the agents everything. That included the story of how he was first recruited by Marshall and later used for dirty political assignments by both the senator and Greenwood. Davis also gave up Sylvester Bonaro and Wade Stock and fully explained Elliott Parkhall's role in the Converse cover-up. The Ohio grand jury took it from there.

A week earlier, Ferguson had been deleted as an unindicted coconspirator on grounds that by reporting the crime to a higher company authority, he'd stepped out of the conspiracy. It was a fine point that didn't take into account the weeks Ferguson spent at Greenwood's elbow, watching him concoct and direct the cover-up, but Pace could live with it. Nobody asked him, actually.

The D.C. grand jury indicted Greenwood, Davis, Bonaro, and Stock on federal civil rights charges in connection with Mike McGill's murder. The Virginia grand jury returned indictments for murder against the same four in the Antravanian killing, and against Davis and Greenwood in Parkhall's death. Neither Bonaro nor Stock had been found. Both made the FBI's most-wanted list.

There was general agreement within the profession that Pace was the hands-down favorite for a Pulitzer Prize in national or local reporting, but even that consensus failed to assuage Avery Schaeffer's anger over the lack of progress on the Marshall angle.

Pace guessed that anger was at the root of the editor's unease over the upcoming meeting with Marshall's daughter.

The reporter saw the event was at hand when a dark-haired woman, who appeared to be about forty, showed up in the newsroom at eight twenty-five. She stopped at the receptionist's desk, and Pace saw the receptionist pick up her telephone. He saw Schaeffer do the same a few seconds later. The receptionist pointed the way, and the woman walked toward Schaeffer's office. She was painfully timid. Every time she approached an occupied desk, she moved to the far side of the aisle, as if afraid something would reach out and grab her. She kept her eyes lowered in the way a person does when she hopes that if she doesn't see you, you won't be able to see her. Pace felt sorry for her.

He saw Schaeffer rise politely when she walked into his office and point her to one of the chairs in front of his desk. They chatted for a moment, and then the editor reached for his phone. Pace put a hand on the receiver of his, expecting the buzz that came a second later.

"I guess my blind date's here," he said without preface.

"Steve, could you come in?" said Schaeffer, not responding to Pace's lame humor.

"Sharon Marshall, this is Steven Pace," Schaeffer said. The woman stood quickly and extended her hand. Pace accepted it. Her grasp was weak and moist. "Why don't we all sit down?" Schaeffer suggested, and they did. There were a few seconds of awkward silence.

"Miss Marshall . . . it is Miss Marshall, isn't it?" Schaeffer asked, and she nodded. "Miss Marshall, you requested this meeting, and we were glad to oblige you. But the hour is late, and we would all like to get home, so could we come right to the point?"

There was the old, blunt Avery, Pace thought.

"Yes, of course," she said, reddening and obviously flustered. "I'm very sorry I kept you, but the opportunity to talk to the two of you is very important to me. It's one of the most important things I'll do this year."

And I'll bet she's enumerated them, Pace thought. *Burying your father is number one, probably followed by food and shelter, and closely after that, talking to two journalists.*

Pace assessed the woman. She did, indeed, look to be in her forties, although that would have made Marshall a very young father. He decided she must be younger than she looked. Her eyes darted constantly, a disconcerting habit, as was the constant wringing motion she made with her hands as they lay in the lap of her dark paisley shirtwaist dress. Her shoes were plain pumps, medium heeled and in a green color that came close to matching one of the minor colors in the dress. She wore pearl studs in her pierced ears and a single eighteen-inch strand of pearls around her neck. Simple, effective, and somehow old-fashioned, Pace thought.

"I guess what I came for is to tell you about my family," she began. Pace found it hard to imagine Harold Marshall as a family man. "There aren't many people who know United States Senator Harold Marshall had a family," she continued, "but he did, and I'm one-fourth of it. He had a wife and two children. I'm the older of the children. My younger brother's name is James."

"How old are you?" Pace hadn't meant to interrupt to ask that question.

"I'm thirty-one, and Jimmy's twenty-six," she said.

Pace's face must have exposed his surprise, and he saw her recognize it.

"I know," she said, lowering her eyes. "Everybody tells me I look older. When I was a kid, I loved it. Now it's beginning to sound horrible." She laughed a little embarrassed laugh.

"Anyhow, my brother is what this is all about," she said. "He has serious health problems. We first started seeing them when he was four. He developed a physical tic, like a muscle spasm he couldn't control. And he would make crazy sounds, like clicks and grunts and barks. By the time he was seven, he'd developed a compulsion to shout words like 'shit' and 'fuck.' " She blushed. "God knows where he picked them up. I don't think he ever heard them at home. Oh, he also became hyperactive. It's all part of a disorder known now as Tourette's Syndrome, but back in the seventies, nobody knew very much about it."

Schaeffer interrupted her. "Miss Marshall, what does any of this have to do with us?"

She sighed. "It has everything to do with you, Mr. Schaeffer," she said more forcefully than Pace expected. "If you'll let me finish, you'll see that."

Schaeffer bowed his head in agreement and waved his hand for her to continue.

She said, "There was so little known about Tourette's back then that Jimmy was eight years old before a doctor got him started on some medication to help him. I think the first one he took was an antipsychotic called Haldol. Except in times of extreme stress, the Haldol controlled the tics and stopped the coprolalia, uh, the compulsion to shout curse words. But the drug depressed Jimmy, so doctors gave him a second medication, called Bensylate, to counteract the worst of the reaction to the Haldol. Jimmy also began to receive psychotherapy to help overcome the emotional problems the Tourette's Syndrome caused." She paused, trying to gather her emotional strength.

"For almost two years, Jimmy led a nearly normal life. He was able to go to school. His classmates stopped making fun of him, and he was happy, except he said he felt 'slow,' and he forgot stuff all the time. The doctors said that was normal. A Tourette's victim is so hyper that when medication slows him to a normal pace, he feels like he's moving through Jell-o. Mom and Dad felt like that was a small price to pay for relief from the symptoms of the disease.

"Jimmy became more willing to take social chances, to be with other people. He began to gain a measure of self-confidence since he didn't have to worry about embarrassing himself, or us, in public. When he was nine, he watched Dad get ready to go on a fall hunting trip, and he wanted to go along. Of course that was impossible. But in the months that followed, going hunting became an obsession with Jimmy. It was all he talked about. Finally, in the spring, Dad began to talk to Jimmy's doctors about the possibility, and they agreed the medication was helping him enough that he could go on the trip and carry a gun. So for his tenth birthday, Daddy got him a twenty-two rifle." She smiled. "I remember Jimmy was so happy and so proud. He practiced with the rifle all summer, shooting at tin cans and paper targets Dad set up for him out in the country.

"When the next fall came, Dad set aside a weekend day when he would take Jimmy out on his first rabbit hunt. The whole family was going to go—you know, to give the kid a lot of support—but I came down with the flu and had to stay home. A couple of days before the trip, Jimmy started agitating to go off his medicine on the day of the hunt so he wouldn't feel slow. Mom and Dad didn't want to permit it, but Jimmy's main doctor said it would be all right if it wasn't for more than the span of one dose. But as it turned out, it wasn't all right at all."

Sharon Marshall stopped and bit her lower lip. Pace and Schaeffer waited patiently for her to continue, and when she didn't, Schaeffer prompted her. "Miss Marshall?"

She looked up, startled. "Oh, I'm sorry," she said. "I've never told this story to strangers, and it's sort of hard. Late on the day of the hunt, Jimmy showed the first signs of the tics returning. Dad noticed, and he tried to take Jimmy's rifle away, but Jimmy wouldn't hear of it. He was a proud little boy. He knew the symptoms were coming back, but he was determined to carry his own gun through the fields and back to the car. Rather than cause him stress, which could have made the symptoms worse, Daddy let him keep the rifle. Ten minutes later—they could see the car from where they were standing, and Jimmy's medication was in the glove compartment—it happened. Jimmy had a bad convulsion, and he accidentally pulled the trigger. The bullet hit my mother in the chest, piercing her heart. She died instantly."

Schaeffer leaned forward in his chair, totally focused on the story now. Pace felt as though he was intruding on a family tragedy he had no business witnessing. Sharon Marshall plunged on, her voice quavering.

"The effect of something like that would be severe for any child, but for Jimmy, it was catastrophic. He shut down. He stopped speaking, but not for organic reasons. The doctors said he was 'electively mute.' He acted functionally retarded, unable to feed or dress himself. Daddy tried to keep him at home and care for him with a nurse around the clock, but when Jimmy became encopretic and enuretic, which means he lost control of his bowels and his bladder, six nurses came and went, and Daddy finally gave in and put Jimmy in a residential treatment center.

"With the institution came institutionalization. Jimmy was surrounded by children who truly were retarded, and he was cared for by adults who treated him as retarded. He received no stimulation, and his withdrawal from the world became more and more complete. When he was fifteen, a new psychologist at the school recognized that he could be helped. It took four years of daily work, but she began to draw him out, to force him to do things for himself and to be more self-reliant. His own expectations for himself began to rise, and that helped increase his sense of self-respect. He began to speak again."

"Where was this treatment center?" Schaeffer asked.

"In Cleveland," she said.

"Okay."

"When he was nineteen, Jimmy got a day-job folding laundry. Just after his twenty-first birthday, he moved to a Boardman, Ohio, halfway house that served as a supervised home for eleven functionally impaired young adults. Jimmy learned to do his grocery shopping, to take care of his money, and to use a checkbook. He got a job at a neighborhood filling station, where he still works. It's a low-pressure job. The customers know him and accept the fact that he's impaired. He has his own apartment, and," she smiled, "a girlfriend. He gets along fine, all things considered.

"The last time Dad saw Jimmy was on Jimmy's thirteenth birthday. I remember Dad ran away in tears. He couldn't bear to be around his son. He couldn't handle the guilt he felt for a whole lot of things: for bringing an afflicted child into the world, for buying Jimmy that rifle, for not taking it away from him at the end of the hunting day, for not being able to keep him at home so he could be with his family, or what was left of it. Even as Jimmy got better, Dad couldn't bring himself to visit. It would have meant explaining where he'd been for the past several years. He was also afraid if Jimmy remembered him, it could bring back the horror of the day his mother died and set Jimmy back emotionally."

Pace put up a hand. "You mean Jimmy forgot his family?" he asked.

Sharon Marshall nodded. "When Jimmy left the treatment center, he had selective amnesia. He could recall recent things very clearly, but he had no memory predating his sixteenth birthday party. He didn't even know me as his sister. He thought of me, and still thinks of me as a friend, somebody who calls every day to say hello and to ask if things are okay, who brings presents on birthdays and holidays, checks his bank account and gives him money when he needs it. Dad always made sure I had enough money for both of us." She laughed ruefully. "We had more than enough, actually. Dad insisted I invest money for my future and Jimmy's. But we could never spend everything he gave us. All the money everybody's fussed over so much, it was Daddy's legitimately. So was all the Converse stock. The million dollars he took out of his bank in cash on the day of the airplane accident . . . well, he sent it to me."

She picked up her purse and fished in it for something. What she pulled out looked to Pace like a bankbook. She opened it and handed it to Schaeffer.

"You'll see I made a deposit of one million dollars to my account the next day," she said.

Schaeffer examined the book and nodded. Pace thought he paled a bit.

"So you did," he said. "How did he get it to you?"

She laughed that embarrassed little laugh again. "By Federal Express," she said. "He took all those bills and put them in two of those cardboard Federal Express envelopes and sent them by overnight delivery. Wouldn't they have died if they'd known what they were shipping?"

"They wouldn't have accepted it, I don't think," Pace said.

"No, probably not," she agreed. "Daddy said the envelope contained personal papers valued at ten dollars, or something like that."

"Why didn't he send you a check?" Schaeffer asked a bit gruffly.

"Because he didn't want there to be any record of the transfer that could lead people to me. He wanted Jimmy and me to have complete privacy always."

Pace was beginning to feel anguish bordering on pain. "Is that why he didn't tell the truth to me, or to the Senate Ethics Committee?" he asked.

She nodded. "He was afraid the media, or the committee, or both, wouldn't accept his story until they'd tracked Jimmy down and confirmed his existence, and his condition. He was afraid that if anybody found Jimmy, they would ask him about his father and that it could trigger a whole new breakdown."

Schaeffer leaned back in his chair. The look on his face was stern. "That's a very touching story, Miss Marshall," he said. "But where did your father come into the money to buy fifty thousand shares of Converse stock in the first place?"

She nodded as though she'd been expecting the question. "It was part of the settlement of a malpractice suit against the doctor who'd agreed that Jimmy could go off his medicine the day of the hunting trip. We settled out of court for seven million dollars, and the settlement was sealed by mutual agreement so nobody would ever know. He bought the stock as a personal gesture of faith in Converse during the company's relocation. He sold the stock right after the accident because he knew its value would fall, and he was paranoid about risking any part of the nest egg he'd created for Jimmy and me." She paused and smiled. "He told the truth to the Ethics Committee, except he left the impression he was worried about his own future. He wasn't. He was worried about his children."

She glanced up at Schaeffer, and then looked to Pace.

"You know," she said, "except for buying his house on East-West Highway, he never spent a penny of the settlement on himself. He kept almost all of it for us. It was probably an overreaction on his part to sell all the Converse stock after the accident, but you have to understand Dad was carrying around such a huge burden of guilt that no amount of money was enough to assuage it, enough to make him feel secure about his children's future. He didn't have anything to feel guilty about, but he never accepted that. He always felt the whole thing was his fault. And he wouldn't tell anybody the story of what happened because he wouldn't jeopardize Jimmy's privacy. He was willing to die to prevent that. And, I guess, he did."

She paused for a second, then went on, tentatively. "I know Dad wasn't the nicest man. A lot of people didn't like him. He could be abrasive and mean-spirited. But he wasn't always like that. He changed after Mom died, and he got worse after he had to send Jimmy away. I don't know why he did the things he did for Mr. Greenwood, or why he used Mr. Davis like some sort of . . . of criminal slave. Maybe he was bent on self-destruction." She shrugged. "I guess we'll never know. But Dad wasn't a bad man. He couldn't have condoned or ordered murder. For God's sake, it was the violent loss of a life he loved that twisted him emotionally in the first place. No, he couldn't have been involved in anybody's murder, and if he'd known murder was planned, he'd have tried to stop it. I know that. I know that, and I knew him better than anybody. He was a good man destroyed by a horrible, terrible set of circumstances. He had an abusive side, a spiteful side. But that wasn't the man. That was the shell he built around himself so nobody could see his pain."

Pace thought Schaeffer looked stricken. There was a heavy silence in the room.

"What do you want from us?" Schaeffer asked quietly.

"Nothing," Sharon Marshall said. "I didn't come here to make threats or cause problems. I wanted you to know the truth. You're the ones who heaped on all the suspicion that Dad was guilty of something horrible. I thought you should know that he wasn't." She tossed a file of papers on Schaeffer's desk. "Here are copies of my brother's medical records, so you know I'm telling the truth."

She paused again, and when no one said anything, she spoke.

"I had a long talk with Dad's doctor after Dad died. He's pretty sure the stress of this Converse scandal led to the stroke. He'd never had high blood pressure before, not even in the worst time after Mother died. He developed it when everybody started writing stories about the bad things they thought he'd done. Maybe at that point he already had the aneurysm. And maybe he would have died from it eventually, anyway. Or maybe not. We'll never know. There's nothing you can do to bring him back, but if you could find a way to help clear his name, I'd appreciate it. If you can't, then let the story die. Carry his innocence in your hearts. You've given me what I asked for, a hearing." She plucked her bankbook from Schaeffer's desk, slipped it back into her purse, and got to her feet. "You'll not see me or hear from me again. I appreciate your time."

Then, without making an effort to shake hands, she walked out into the newsroom and disappeared from sight.

"Jesus," Pace said, watching the door through which she'd left.

He looked at Schaeffer and saw that the editor was as pale as a blank sheet of paper.

"What did we do?" Pace asked quietly.

After a time, Schaeffer replied, "We executed an innocent man."

57

"Clay, I've got to know. I'm sorry I have to ask, and I swear it's not for publication, but I have to know what Chappy Davis told you about Harold Marshall."

Clay Helm thought he'd never heard Steve Pace more agitated. Not even in the hospital after the phony mugging. Clearly, something had rocked him.

"We've had this conversation before," Helm said. "The security of the grand-jury process and all."

"I *know* that," Pace said. "But this is important. Somebody told us Marshall couldn't have been involved in the murders, somebody who seemed credible. Only Davis knows for sure. And I have to know. I think you should be able to understand that."

Helm did. He could hear through the desperation in Pace's voice that the reporter wasn't asking him to justify suspicions of Marshall's complicity; he was asking for the truth.

"Davis says he took those orders directly from Greenwood," Helm said.

There was silence.

Helm knew the impact his words carried. He hadn't wanted to be the one to break that news. He searched desperately for a way to soften the blow. "Steve, there wasn't anything you could have done differently," he said.

"Sure there was," Pace replied glumly.

"Hey, I'm a cop. Criminal investigations are my business. I read your stuff every day. I don't remember once thinking you'd gone farther than the evidence warranted."

"It was the sum total of it. We kept beating up on Marshall day after day after day. We put him under enormous strain, and some people think that's what caused his stroke."

"What people?" Helm insisted.

"I'm not at liberty to say."

"Oh, thanks. I trusted you enough to violate the rules of the grand jury a few minutes ago, but you don't trust me enough to tell me who's accusing you."

Pace sketched the story for Helms, using no names, dates, or places. "And that's all off the record," the reporter concluded.

"Sad business," Helm agreed. "How do you know it's true?"

"The source left copies of medical records. They check out. There was also a bankbook that backed up the story. It was the McCoy, too."

"No wonder you're bummed."

"It goes a little beyond bummed," Pace said.

"If it does, you're being way too hard on yourself," Helm replied. "Good Christ, what if Marshall wasn't involved in murder? The guy was the shithole of the year. He lied for Converse, he cheated for Converse, he tried to pervert a federal investigation for Converse. He pulled Chapman Davis out of a slum and turned him into a well-educated political aide so he could turn around and blackmail a basically vulnerable man into doing all sorts of unspeakable things. And then, when the time was right, and conveniently forgetting the Thirteenth Amendment to the Constitution, Marshall gave or sold Davis to Greenwood so his good friend could use the guy, too. Oh, Marshall didn't give the orders to kill, but he knew. He couldn't have *not* known. He set this thing up as surely as if he'd bought the guns."

"But what if he didn't know?" Pace asked.

"What on earth could possibly lead you to even consider that?"

"My source says that as much of a jerk as he became after

his wife died and his son went off the deep end, he wasn't bad enough to take a life or to order someone killed."

"And you believe that?"

"Why shouldn't I?"

"How would your source know?"

"This source knows, believe me."

Helm heard Pace sigh deeply.

"Steve, this is going to be with you for a long, long time. You're going to have to learn to live with it. You can live with it while you're wallowing in a lot of self-pity and doubt, or you can live with it and carry on and grow. I'd suggest the latter."

They said nothing for five full minutes, each averting his eyes from the other, staring instead into the depths of intimate regret and trying ineffectively to come to terms with it.

Schaeffer sat quietly at his desk, his hands in his lap.

Pace was hunched forward, his elbows on his knees, his eyes fixed at an unseen place on the carpet between his feet, while the memory camera behind his eyes played a highlight film of the past thirteen weeks. Over and over, the question ran through his mind: *Where did I go wrong?*

He didn't realize he'd asked it out loud. He was startled out of his trance by the sound of Avery Schaeffer's big fist hitting the top of his desk.

"Goddamn it, Steve, *you* didn't go wrong!" Schaeffer said with vehemence. "That young woman came here to make us accept the guilt for her father's death, and it's tempting to do that. But the guilt is his own, not ours."

Pace frowned. A few minutes earlier Schaeffer appeared deeply burdened by the weighty cloak of remorse Sharon Marshall fitted for them; now he rejected any responsibility at all. Pace saw that his lack of understanding exasperated the editor.

"Sharon Marshall would have us believe that our stories—our harassment, if you accept her interpretation of it—put such pressure on her father that he busted an artery and died. Although it's tempting, and I admit I considered it, I won't accept that kind of responsibility. We didn't force him to lie. We didn't force him to cover up truths that would have exonerated him from criminal culpability. He took on that role for himself for whatever misguided reasons. If it was emotional tension and pressure that killed him, it was of his own making, not ours."

Pace didn't want to defend Harold Marshall, but he heard himself doing so. "He was protecting a vulnerable child, Avery!" he argued. "Wouldn't any parent?"

Schaeffer exhaled a deep breath. He fished in his pants pocket for something and came out with a ring of keys. Selecting a small one, he swiveled around to the credenza behind his desk and unlocked the bottom cabinet compartment. When he opened one of the doors, Pace saw there a fully equipped bar, even containing a small ice-maker. Schaeffer filled an insulated bucket with tiny cubes, hauled out two glasses and a quart of Jack Daniels.

"This your brand?" he asked the reporter.

"It'll do, if you don't have any good stuff," Pace joked, wondering how it escaped office gossip that Schaeffer had a bar there.

The editor grabbed the ice bucket and the bottle and told Pace to get the glasses. "If you want water in yours, you'll have to get it from one of the fountains in the newsroom," he said as he got up from the desk. "Let's go sit in the Glory Room, where nobody can watch us get drunk."

The first drink Schaeffer poured was modest enough. They would get bigger later.

"You know," he said, putting coasters under the two glasses, "this is only the second time I've used that bar. The first time was the night Henry Kissinger came by after hours to talk about our editorial reaction to the opening of relations with China. When was that? God, decades ago." He dismissed the passage of time with a wave of his hand and went on to other things. "I don't like having a bar there. I don't think booze has any place in a newspaper office, old traditions of a bottle in the bottom drawer of every desk notwithstanding. Hell, I'm beginning to wonder if booze has any reasonable place in human life. Cornelia says it never did a damn thing good for anybody, and when I'm into my first wonderful martini of the night, I tend to ignore her. But she's probably got a point." He laughed. "It certainly didn't help your relations with Ken Sachs."

"That's healed," Pace said, quickly enough that he sounded defensive.

Schaeffer nodded. "Obviously," he said. "I didn't mean that as a criticism. It was the first example that came to mind. And speaking of Cornelia, I guess I'd better let her know not to hold dinner for me. I'll be here a while."

"You don't have to stay on my account, Avery."

"I'm not. I'm staying on mine. I want to talk this through. I'm going to call home, and you should do the same, so the ladies don't worry."

Both telephone conversations were brief.

"My initial reaction to the meeting was abject remorse," Schaeffer said later. "That makes me angry. I'm not guilty of anything. Neither are you."

Pace ran a hand through his hair. "I don't want to be argumentative, Avery," he said. "It's probably true that if Marshall had been open about his source of personal funds, if he'd told the world about the son he was trying to protect, the stories about him would have been different. The pressure on him would have been much less. But his effort to protect his son would have been destroyed."

"Why are you so sure?"

"Because Jimmy would have been common knowledge, and that would have ended his privacy."

"Why is that necessarily so?" Schaeffer persisted. "What makes you think the world would beat a path to Boardman, Ohio, to buy gas from a kid with Tourette's Syndrome?"

Pace shook his head. "I didn't mean that. But the Washington stories would have been picked up by the wire services, and the wire stories would be in the local Ohio papers. Somebody out there would try to interview Jimmy. And even if they didn't, the kid can read. If Sharon Marshall's telling the truth, newspaper stories could have brought back all the lousy shit Jimmy Marshall's forgotten. And the memories could set him back a dozen years or more. That's what his father understood. That's the truth he died to protect."

Schaeffer looked at his reporter in disbelief. "Jesus, you wanna give Marshall a medal of honor? You're making him sound like a fucking hero."

"I didn't mean to," Pace said. "I was thinking of him more as a father so desperate to protect a child he was willing to risk his career to carry it off."

"We're not talking about an innocent here, you know," Schaeffer said.

"That was Clay's point, too. But nobody's ever gonna prove it."

Schaeffer shrugged. "I think it will come out when Davis and Greenwood go to trial."

"They'll probably plead out."

Schaeffer shrugged again. "So?" he said. "What does it matter? It's moot now. I only mentioned it to keep in front of your guilt-ridden eyes the fact that the dedicated daddy you're defending wasn't exactly the Albert Schweitzer of the political jungle."

Pace nodded. "I know all that intellectually," he said. "What I can't escape is that we smeared the reputation of a man who, it turns out, was only trying to protect a developmentally disabled child. And the pressure our stories exerted could have, *could have,* contributed to his premature death." Pace looked Schaeffer straight in the eye, and his voice developed a hard edge. "I don't understand why that doesn't bother you a little bit."

Schaeffer broke the eye contact first. "It bothers me, Steve," he said softly. "It bothers the hell out of me."

He scooped more ice into each of their glasses and lifted the bottle of Black Jack again. Pace capped his glass with his hand palm down, a signal he'd had enough.

"Please," Schaeffer said quietly.

Pace withdrew his hand, and the editor poured. The combination of old ice, new ice, old melt and new sour mash filled the glass to the brim.

Schaeffer did the same for himself, then sat back heavily in his chair. He slouched, so his back was at an angle to the seat and the chair back. His legs were extended straight out in front of him, crossed at the ankles. He had his hands folded in his lap, and his face was slack. Pace could see him thinking, collecting thoughts he wanted to put into words.

"I stand by what I said before. I don't feel guilty, I refuse to feel guilty," Schaeffer said glumly. "More than anything, I hate Harold Marshall right at this moment. It isn't that I hate him for what he did. I hate him for what he made me do. By refusing to answer the questions that desperately needed answers, he forced my hand. He forced me to accept things that weren't true. He backed me into a corner."

Pace considered that for a moment and nodded. "Could you—or I—have responded differently?" he asked.

Schaeffer shook his head slowly, and he sat there shaking his head for a long time.

"That's what bothers me so much, Steve," he said finally. "I think about what we did, what we wrote, the decisions I made, the instructions I gave, and I can't pinpoint the moment I made the misjudgment, or, in fact, *if* I made a misjudgment at all." He shook his head once more, decisively, and sat up straight, reaching for his glass. "I don't think I'm deceiving myself. I don't think I'm lying to myself. I think, with the little time I've had to consider it, if I were confronted again with the same sets of circumstances that confronted me in April and May and June, I would make the same decisions."

"Do you think they were the wrong decisions?" Pace asked.

Schaeffer nodded. "Some of them, yes, obviously."

"And yet you'd make them again?"

"Probably."

"Even though they were wrong?"

"We had no reason at the time to think they were wrong."

Pace took a long pull at his glass and sighed deeply. "How," he asked, "are we ever supposed to know?"

Schaeffer shrugged. "We have our training, our professional experience, our experienced judgment. They're supposed to guide us."

"And when they guide us wrong? Then what do we do?"

"I don't know," Avery Schaeffer said. "I really don't."

They sat there in the Glory Room and talked until nearly midnight, the conversation getting more theoretical, more esoteric, as the hour got later and the volume of Black Jack consumption grew. Schaeffer finally ordered his reporter to go home—by taxi—and get some sleep. Schaeffer told him not to worry about Sharon Marshall. He would take care of that situation. He didn't know how, exactly, but it was his problem, and he would deal with it.

Schaeffer sat in the Glory Room, alone, for several more hours. He had nothing more to drink. He spent most of the time gazing at the awards surrounding him, caressing them with memories, as he struggled to recall how he'd made the decisions then, on each of those stories, about what to write and how to cast it. He remembered most of it. And in the remembering, he realized some of those earlier decisions had been as difficult and as chancy as those he'd made this time.

Where had the process gone wrong?

The question swam in and out of his consciousness like a poltergeist, inflicting fear and anxiety and misgiving, and then disappearing, leaving behind the certainty that the apprehension was a bad dream. But it came back in waves, like nausea. The question pounded at him, relentlessly, for more hours than he knew were passing. He realized suddenly the sky was growing brighter, dawn was approaching. Another workday was upon him.

And for the first time in Avery Schaeffer's professional career, a newsroom wasn't where he wanted to be.

58

Thursday, July 10th, 6:38 A.M.

The sun was up fully when Schaeffer let himself back into the *Chronicle* Building after scouting up breakfast and coffee. The early security man, who had come on duty since Schaeffer left the building, was obviously surprised to see the editor at that hour.

"You're in early, Mr. S.," he said, his expression quizzical as he noticed the unshaven face and the rumpled suit.

"Actually, this is the end of a late night, Pete," Schaeffer replied amicably. He walked into a waiting elevator and listened as the doors closed on the security guard's response.

He rode alone to the tenth floor, got off and strode into the newsroom. It was so strange, he thought, to see it empty. It was not the way he would have wanted to remember it.

He let himself into his office and activated the personal computer on the credenza behind his desk. He had gone over and over the words he would write in the signed editorial the following day. The *Chronicle* had never run a signed editorial in its history, as far as he knew. This one would be different. It had to be. His fingers moved across the keyboard, and the words he formed in his mind re-formed on the gray screen before him:

"This is an apology.
"It is a personal apology from me, not an apology for the Washington Chronicle, *nor for anyone else on the staff.*
"It is an apology, overdue but heartfelt, to the late Sen. *Harold Marshall, R-Ohio, and to a young woman I met*

recently. It is possible that terrible wrongs have been done. It is possible that Harold Marshall, for all his infamous hostility, venality, and questionable judgment, might have been innocent of some of the crimes suggested by this newspaper. I know now that Harold Marshall, for all his secrecy about things we badgered him to make public, for all his defiance in the face of accusations about his role in the Converse conspiracy, likely played no role in murder. It is even possible that his so-called crimes were limited to the lack of wisdom he exhibited in sending two aides to plead Converse's case prematurely before investigators with the National Transportation Safety Board. Misjudgment is no crime; indeed, if it were, we would all be in jail.

"The greater misjudgments were mine. I alone made the decisions about how the Converse conspiracy should be covered by this newspaper, about how much pressure should be placed on Marshall for disclosures of his financial dealings with Converse, about how far this great newspaper would go in insinuating a man's guilt absent the presence of hard, indisputable evidence. I thought the circumstantial evidence warranted the coverage we gave to it.

"Sadly, I know now, it did not.

"How I know, and what I know, I will never make public. I have been asked to hold a confidence, a secret Harold Marshall died protecting. I will not violate that confidence.

"I do not apologize for the main body of reportage on the ConPac story. This newspaper's role in exposing a vile conspiracy to hide the cause of the tragedy cannot be overstated. Were it not for Steven Pace's dogged reporting at the risk of his own life, the worst aviation disaster in the history of this country might have passed into memory mistakenly attributed to a bird strike on a jet engine. Deliberate and heinous murders might have been attributed to accident or circumstance. The mistakes made related only to Harold Marshall's role in the conspiracy. And those mistakes were mine alone. I can't put my finger on exactly the moment, exactly the decision, that steered our coverage up the dark road of error. That there was an error would be easier to live with if I thought I could identify it and in doing so, render it impossible for me or for anyone else to make that error

again. Try as I might, I have not been able to do that.
"And that is a burden for the ages."

He thought about adding the words, "I'm sorry," but
that would be gilding the lily. He reread his words, spell-
checked the copy, and sent it to Paul Wister's personal file
with a note explaining what it was. Satisfied, he opened a
new file and wrote a memorandum of explanation to
Creighton Pollock, owner of the *Washington Chronicle*. He
told Pollock, in confidence, a great deal more than he told
Chronicle readers about the Marshall situation. And he told
Pollock that he was going away for a while:

". . . I don't know that my job will be waiting for me when
I get back. I don't know that you'll want me back. If you do
replace me, I hope you will give every consideration to Paul
Wister. He has grown in the last few months, and he is ready.
With sincere thanks for your confidence over the years, and
with sorrow for errors of recent weeks, I remain,"

> Sincerely,
> Avery

He ran off a hard copy, placed it in a sealed envelope, and
put it in the interoffice mailbox. It would find its way to
Creighton Pollock later that morning.

He went back to his office, erased the Pollock file for
security reasons, and was about to turn off the computer
when he had a second thought. He dashed off a memo to
Steve Pace, sent it to Pace's personal file, and then shut his
system down. He glanced at the clock. It was seven-
eighteen. He picked up the phone and dialed his home.
Cornelia answered on the first ring.

"Still in bed, sleepyhead?" he asked.

"No," she said. "I woke up a half-hour ago and found
you already gone, or still gone. Did you ever come home last
night? I was afraid something was wrong at the office. I
turned on the television, but there's no big news story
breaking. Where are you?"

"At work."

"Why? What's wrong?"

"We'll talk about it later."

She was silent for a moment, trying to comprehend. She said she didn't understand.

"I told you I'd explain later," he said seriously. Then he brightened. "Hey, kid, you remember the trip around the British Isles you've been bugging me about for the last seven hundred fifty-one years?"

He could hear her smile when she replied, "It's only been five or six."

"Well, it feels like seven hundred fifty-one. Wanna take it now?"

"Avery, are you serious?"

"Never more so."

"When?"

"Tomorrow. Today. What's wrong with today?"

"But . . . but we can't," she said, obviously stunned. "How could we?"

"You call a travel agent, make reservations all over the place, we go to Dulles, and we leave. That's how."

"Can you get away?"

This time he was the one who paused. He almost said that now, more than ever, he *had* to get away, but he stayed upbeat. "Sure, why not? I'm the boss."

"We can't leave today. That would be impossible."

"Why?"

"What about clothes?"

"Take what you think you'll need for the basic stuff—touring, dining elegantly, walking, and sleeping. If we need anything else, we can buy it over there. Then if we need a steamer trunk to come home, we'll buy a steamer trunk."

"There are still things I need, things you need."

"Okay, so we'll go shopping."

"When?"

"What time do the stores open?"

"Today?"

"Absolutely."

"Ten, I think."

"I'm on my way."

Schaeffer was gone when Paul Wister found the editorial. Stunned, he searched the building for Schaeffer and didn't find him. He called Schaeffer's home, but received no answer. He finally got around to calling Creighton Pollock. It wasn't something he wanted to do, but he needed guidance. Pollock had already read Schaeffer's note to him. He asked Wister to bring the editorial to his office. He read it there, twice, and when he finished, he said tersely, "Run it. Run it signed, as he asked."

"What?" Wister asked in amazement. "We've never done that before."

"Never had to before," Pollock replied, and that was the end of the conversation.

Steve Pace found the personal note from Schaeffer a few minutes later. He read it twice. He felt his breath catch, and he got up to get a cup of coffee, turning his computer screen to black so no one else would see the message while he was gone. When he returned, he drank the full cup of hot liquid before he could bring himself to turn up the screen again.

> *"In the end, Steve, you can only be true to yourself. You try to set certain standards for yourself, which, in the face of all sorts of temptation, you must hold sacred. That, apparently, was my failing. I was tempted. I was too much tempted. Somewhere, somehow, I was convinced to lower my standards. I didn't even realize I was doing it. To this moment, I can't pinpoint exactly when I crossed that line. But this I do understand: The failing was mine, not yours. The responsibility is mine, not yours. You did as you were asked, you did the best you could, and you did well. That's all any editor could ask of a reporter. I'm proud of you.*
>
> *"Now go and have a drink to me, to the good times and the successes. Put this behind you. Get on with your life and your*

career. I'm going to be sitting on your shoulder all the way,
whispering in your ear: Don't be wrong, and don't get beat."

With affection and admiration,
Avery

EPILOGUE

EPILOGUE

Later that year, near the end of October

They sat on the Islamorada beach in the hot, late-afternoon sun, watching the crashing waves driven by the incoming tide. Steve Pace thought he must be the happiest man alive. Kathy McGovern-Pace, his wife of three months, sat at his side. She was holding his hand, as mesmerized by the ocean as he, alive with wonder and expectation. In her belly a new life was growing, confirmed by her doctor only hours earlier. Their child would be born in May.

When she had given her husband the news, he embraced her and cried. He wanted to open a bottle of champagne, but she told him she wouldn't drink, to protect the new life within her. So he settled for a beer for himself that he carried to the beach and had long since finished.

They were married early in August, the week he quit his job at the *Chronicle*. She must have become pregnant soon thereafter; the doctor thought about August twentieth. They followed their dream, buying a small motel and a charter fishing business on Islamorada in the Florida Keys, and they moved there quickly. Her father had insisted that his investment counselor find the right place for them, and once found, he insisted on paying for it as a wedding gift. He wouldn't hear of a loan. All he knew was that the opportunity had come for the arrival of more grandchildren.

When they were settled in the small house next to the motel, Melissa Pace came to visit. She welcomed the reconciliation as much as they. In fact, it was Kathy who invited her, and the teenager jumped at the opportunity. The circle of Steve Pace's life was complete.

He'd left the *Chronicle* without recriminations. Paul Wister assured him a job would be there for him if he ever chose to return. At the time, he thought he would never go back, but he wasn't fool enough to close out the option.

"I forgot to tell you the other news," Kathy said suddenly.

He looked at her expectantly.

"Avery's come home from Europe, and he's back as the editor of the paper," she said.

"Where'd you hear that?"

"From Hugh. He called this afternoon, before my doctor's appointment. He said if you went back, he wanted me to come back, too. He's under a lot of pressure from the party to make a run for the White House, and I think for the first time, he's considering it seriously."

"No fooling? When did Avery come home?"

"I guess about a week ago."

"Is he okay?"

"From what Hugh said, I gather he's in great good spirits, ready to take on the world."

Pace shook his head in wonder. "It took guts to take off like that, not knowing whether he'd have a job to come back to."

"He's always been a gutsy guy."

"If Avery's back as editor, I wonder what's going to happen to Paul. He's been acting editor since Avery left. Will he be satisfied going back to the national desk?"

"Hugh says he's going to become executive editor, or something like that. Maybe you should call up there and find out."

Pace rolled the empty beer bottle around in the sand. "So Hugh offered you your old job back?"

"Uh-huh."

"You want to go back?" he asked.

"I don't know," she said. "Do you?"

"I don't know." He spread his arms, encompassing the expanse of sea. "This is terrific."

"We could lease it and then take it back when we're ready to come down permanently."

"Or we could stay."

"We could do that, too."

He looked at her, trying to gauge her feelings. "What do you want to do?" he asked.

"I think I'd like to stay at least until the baby is born. I'm not insisting on it, but I like Dr. Haviland. I'd like him to do the delivery."

"Then we stay."

"But that's not the only consideration," she said. "What do you want to do?"

He thought about it for a minute, then admitted, "I don't know. I love being a reporter. But if I go back, there will be questions and looks, and I don't know what job they have for me. I might not like it."

"Then you wouldn't have to take it."

"But you've got a terrific opportunity with Hugh. I don't want to screw that up."

"Hugh isn't putting pressure on me for a quick decision. We have time."

He squeezed her hand. "Then let's take it," he suggested.

"I'd drink to that . . . if I were drinking," she said.

They were quiet for a long time.

"If the baby's a boy, I think we should name him Jonathan," he said softly. "It would be a closure of sorts."

"How about Jonathan Michael? That would make the closure complete."

"I'd like that. He was a good friend."

She was staring at the ocean and the setting sun. He was drawing something in the sand. By the time she noticed, he had finished. He'd modeled an airplane there, using a stone to dig the lines of a shape that looked as much like a Sexton 811 as he could create on a beach.

"That's pretty good," she told him. "But it's below the tide line."

"I know. That's where I wanted it. Let's go home."

AUTHOR'S NOTE

John Galipault died today.

Most of you who read this never knew John. And that is your loss.

Suffice it to say that anytime you step aboard an airplane, whether a two-seater or a giant jetliner, your trip will be safer because John once walked this earth.

He was the founder and president of the Aviation Safety Institute, an organization dedicated to precisely what its name suggests. Perhaps you saw one of John's frequent appearances before Congress on national television, pushing for one air safety improvement or another.

He was a test pilot.

He was a flight instructor.

He was a college professor.

He was a writer.

He was a lacrosse coach.

He was a nag.

I remember a morning twenty years ago—when we were just getting to know one another—talking to John on the telephone about an aviation story, the exact nature of which I've long since forgotten. I recall his barely controlled frustration at having to explain to me exactly what it means to say an airplane has stalled. (Hint: It has nothing to do with the engine.)

"Heller," he bellowed down the phone line from his office outside Columbus, Ohio, to mine in Washington, D.C., "if you're going to write about airplanes, at least you could learn to fly so you understand what you're writing about!"

It was a direct order, and I obeyed.

Over two decades our working relationship became a deep friendship.

After reading this story, you will understand what I mean when I say John Galipault was my Mike McGill.

The last conversation we had, in fact, concerned this book. He had been kind enough to read the manuscript for technical accuracy, but he had an additional question on his mind.

"Did you pattern Mike after me?" he asked, sounding at once embarrassed to probe and too curious not to.

"Yes," I told him. "I think I did."

"Neat," he replied with a laugh. "I like that."

It is only fitting, therefore, that I take this opportunity to say goodbye.

John, my friend, you are missed.

Jean Heller
January 3, 1993